KALLE PÄÄTALO

STORM OVER THE LAND

A NOVEL ABOUT WAR

From the Finnish Novel *MYRSKY KOILLISMAASSA*
Translated by Richard A. Impola
Cover Illustration by Carl Gawboy

FINNISH-AMERICAN TRANSLATORS ASSOCIATION
NEW PALTZ, NEW YORK

ISBN 1-880474-06-9

Printed by Braun-Brumfield
Ann Arbor, Michigan

First Printing October 1993

"Who said we lost the war? We're free, aren't we?"

At a family reunion in Siikajoki in the summer of 1986, someone present referred to Finland's having "lost the war." Toivo Impola, who, like the men in this book, had been through the Winter War, the Continuation War, and the campaign in Lapland, was quick to respond. His words are quoted above.

It is to his memory that this translation is dedicated.

Kalle Päätalo is by far Finland's most popular living novelist. With over thirty novels to his credit, a recent count shows his sales approaching the three million mark, an amazing number in a country of some five million people. Readers agree that Päätalo's truth to life and experience keeps them reading his books.

Storm Over the Land (*Myrsky Koillismaassa*), is a novel in the author's *Koillismaa* series. It describes the impact of World War II on the people of a wilderness area in northeastern Finland.

In August of 1939, the Hitler-Stalin non-aggression pact divided northern Europe into spheres of influence, giving Stalin a free hand in the Baltic countries of Finland, Latvia, Estonia, and Lithuania. Under pressure from the Soviets, all but Finland agreed to the presence of Russian troops on their territory, with results that we all know. In November of 1939, four Russian armies attacked Finland. Few believed that Finland could survive the onslaught. Soviet leaders anticipated an easy victory, and planned for a campaign that would last twelve days. (See Engle & Paananen, *THE WINTER WAR*, 2nd ed.,1992.)

The rest is history. When the cease-fire took effect 105 days later, the Soviet armies, according to Krushchev's memoirs, had lost a million men. The Finns lost 25,000 dead and 55,000 wounded. Although the peace terms imposed upon Finland were harsh, she remained a free country.

The Winter War was not the end of Finland's trials. From March of 1940 until June of 1941, an uneasy peace prevailed. During that time, the Finns were under pressure from both the Soviet Union and Germany to side with one against the other in the coming war between the two. Denied the possibility of remaining neutral, she chose to side with Germany as the lesser of two evils, but the Finns insisted that they were *co-belligerents* rather than *allies* of the Germans.

During the *Continuation War*, which lasted from June of 1941 to September of 1944, the Finns recaptured the lands ceded to the Russians after the *Winter War* and penetrated into Soviet territory, but in September of 1944, forced to retreat by the Soviet armies, but exacting a heavy toll as they withdrew, the Finns again made peace with the Soviet Union. The agreement required them to drive out the German troops then in Finland. In the resulting campaign, the Germans adopted a scorched-earth policy, and much of northern Finland was virtually destroyed.

Like Kauko, the protagonist of his novel, Päätalo volunteered for service in the Winter War, but was not in time to see combat in it. He is a veteran of the *Continuation War.* Any reader will sense the background of real experience underlying the thin veil of fiction which Päätalo casts over his action.

Like many Finnish writers, Päätalo is concerned with communicating experience rather than with spinning an interesting yarn or interpreting events. Storm Over the Land tells not only of battles, but of life in training camps and on the home front, of civilian evacuations, of community and personal life disrupted by the war. The author's intent is to give a complete and vivid picture of the times, to have a reader relive its history.

The only book which has a comparable effect on me is Studs Terkel's "The Good War": An Oral History of World War Two. The two books are of course different in form. One is the print version of a series of tape-recorded reminiscences about the war-time experiences of the narrators. Päätalo uses the more conventional form of the novel. The object of Terkel's book is to make the war real to people who might view it as a "story from the past." The same impulse is evident in Storm Over the Land. It matches Terkel's work in its vividness and concrete sense of reality.

The central metaphor of the novel is the storm of war; everything that happens, happens because of the war. It sweeps over the community, disrupting its life, and dispersing its people. It forces Ivar Sääskilampi and Kosti Mäkinen into a renewed confrontation with traumatic events in their past. It sends Auku Sammalsuo off on a disastrous hunting expedition.

Some of the battle scenes are gruesome. The picture of war presented in Storm Over the Land is not the "clean war" of *Desert Storm*, as edited by the Pentagon. Besides its cost in dead and wounded, the war disrupts the normal course of human relationships, those of Elma and Kauko, for example. Readers familiar with these two characters from Our Daily Bread, the first novel in the series, may find their behavior disappointing or shocking.

Päätalo's novels are characterized by a strong social awareness, a sense of community as well as of individual character. By following three families — the Sammalsuos, Malinens, and Sääskilampis — through the period of the wars, he conveys as complete a sense of the times as possible.

I owe very much to Veli and Toini Känninen of Fishkill, New York for their help in the translation of idiomatic and dialect expressions not readily accessible, if at all, in dictionaries. Any errors are purely my own.

The following list of family members is offered for ready reference. Note that the name of the family and the name of the farm are often identical.

SAMMALSUO
- Maija, mother, widowed
- Kauko, son
- Aili, daughter
- Auku, son
- Väinö, son
- Liisu, daughter

SÄÄSKILAMPI
- Ivar, father
- Petti, mother
- Bert, son
- Irja, daughter

MALINEN (OLKIVAARA)
- Nestor, father
- Mari, mother
- Toivo, son
- Elma, daughter
- Svante, son
- Taimi, daughter
- Teuvo, son
- Jaska, son

NAAVALA
- Akseli, father
- Elsa, daughter
- Hilja, daughter

Irja Sääskilampi is married to Kosti Mäkinen, (the *Tampere Boy* of Our Daily Bread). They have two sons, Ilmari and Pentti. Two daughters, Tuulikki and Leila, are born to them during the course of the novel.

Jonas Niemi and Jalo Kieppi are two soldiers who become good friends of Kauko. Simo Mutka is a type figure of the Finnish wilderness soldier of the Winter War.

Most of the place names in the novel are real, as can be seen from the map on the following page. A few are fictitious. The Sammalsuo-Malinen-Naavala home community of *Järvenkylä* (Lake Village) and the Sääskilampi home community of *Vaarakylä* (Hill Village) correspond to *Jokijärvi* and *Tyräjärvi* on the map. *Alasalmi* is the lower part of *Jokijärvi.* The church village often referred to (a kind of administrative center for a parish) is the Taivalkoski church village.

The opening action of the novel finds Kauko Sammalsuo as a volunteer on his way to a training center. His mother and Mari Olkivaara are on their evacuation journey with their younger children. Nestor Olkivaara is going directly to the front to volunteer for combat, and Kosti Mäkinen and Bert Sääskilampi are already in the war.

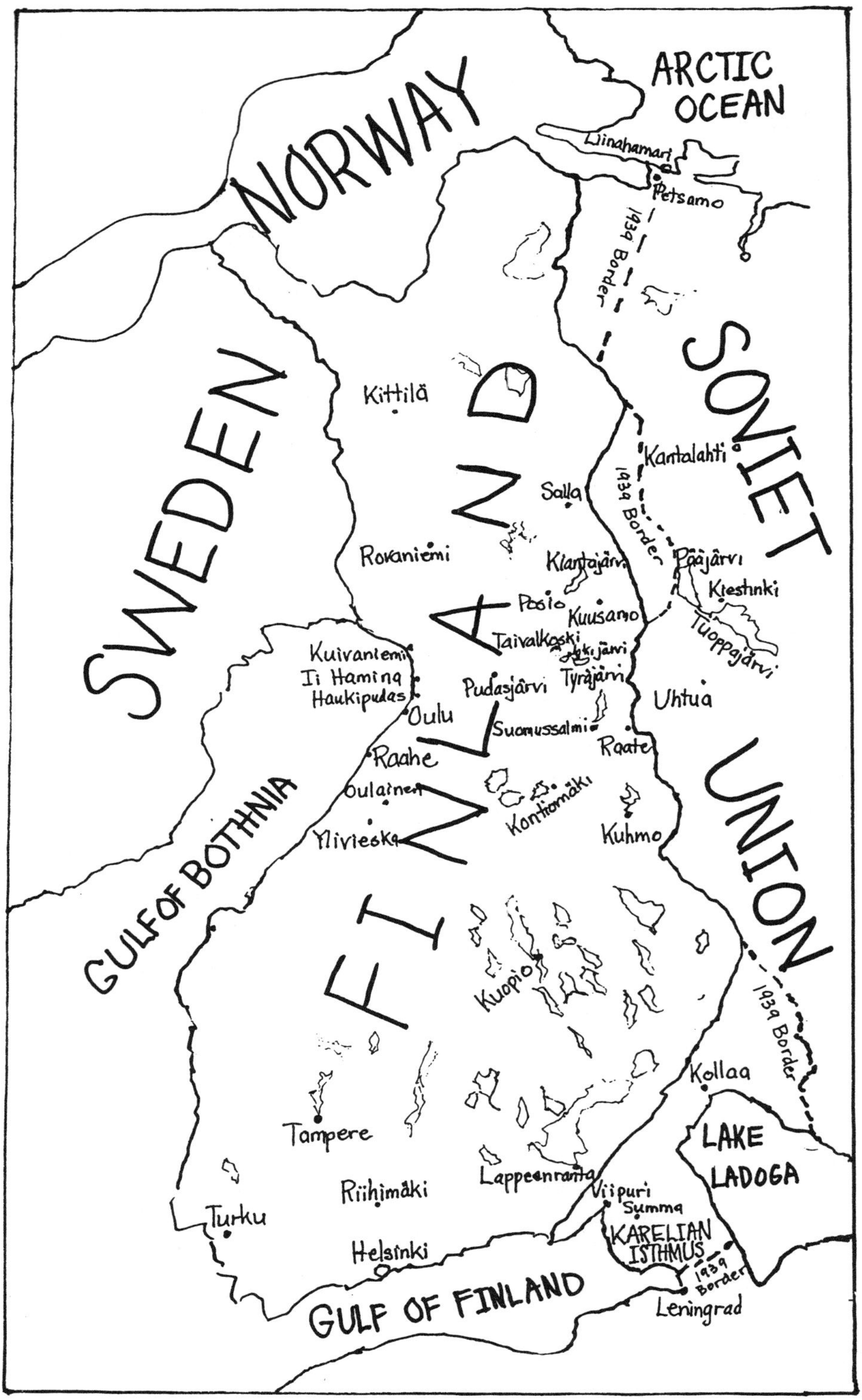

NORWAY
ARCTIC OCEAN
Liinahamari
Petsamo
1939 Border
SWEDEN
FINLAND
SOVIET UNION
Kittilä
Kantalahti
Salla
1939 Border
Rovaniemi
Kiantajärvi
Pääjärvi
Kiestinki
Posio
Kuusamo
Tuoppajärvi
Taivalkoski
Kuivaniemi
Ii Hamina
Haukipudas
Pudasjärvi
Tyräjärvi
Oulu
Uhtua
Suomussalmi
Raate
Raahe
Oulainen
Kontiomäki
Ylivieska
Kuhmo
GULF OF BOTHNIA
Kuopio
1939 Border
Kollaa
LAKE LADOGA
Tampere
Lappeenranta
Riihimäki
Viipuri
Summa
Turku
KARELIAN ISTHMUS
Helsinki
1939 Border
GULF OF FINLAND
Leningrad

CHAPTER I

1

For the first time in his life, Kauko saw the lights of a city. The headlights of the postal bus had already been picking out houses built closer to one another than he had ever seen before. Now the buildings were bigger. They lined the sides of the road the vehicle was traveling. It crossed over a bridge. During a drive of some 300 kilometers, the bus windows had thawed enough so that one could see through them.

"These Oulu types are stingy with their lights."

"Military orders. They have to black out the windows."

"Not many street lights on either."

Although Kauko was straining to see everything around him, he was still able to hear the discussion going on behind him. How many lights had there been before, he wondered. Weren't a huge number of them still lighted? Was that what big-city buildings looked like? How many stories high could that one be? Kauko tried to count the rows of windows on it. By the time he got to four, they had passed the building.

"This is the bus station," said the mail driver.

The vehicle began to empty out. Old men and women, with a sprinkling of young women among them, clambered out. Along the way, the bus had kept picking up young men of Kauko's age, and he got out along with them. A freezing wind stung his face.

As he stood beside the bus, a feeling of isolation crept over him. It had already begun to affect him on the way. Arrival in town had stirred his interest, but now he felt alone.

The older passengers walked away from the bus, some of them toward a low building nearby. It must be the bus-station waiting-room, thought Kauko.

"I guess I'll trudge over to the old digs," said one of the men, hoisting his pack to his shoulders.

"Yeah, I always stay at the same place too."

Kauko's sense of isolation increased when he heard men who had been in the city before making plans. Those with places to stay trudged off in different directions. The broad strap of a leather pack slapped one man's back with each step. A birch-bark carrier held another's goods. One woman had a knotted sheet draped over her shoulders. They all disappeared into lanes formed by the high buildings.

Kauko stood there in his jacket, suitcase in hand. The high collar of a stout homespun woolen shirt shielded his neck. He had to keep shifting his fur hat from one side to the other to keep his ears warm. A half dozen young men stood around looking at one another. A couple of them, who seemed to know each other, were talking. The rest of them, like Kauko, merely stood looking around. Soon the tailpipe of the yellow bus that had brought them from the uplands began to rumble, and the vehicle swung around in the open space.before the station. Kauko's eyes fixed on the side of the bus, then followed its snow-laden rear. When that too disappeared into a chasm between the stone buildings, he felt like crying. The last tie to his home region was now cut. Tomorrow the same bus would make the return trip. In the evening it would pass by their church village.

Where were his mother, his brothers and sisters? A part of the family, Mother, Liisu, and his brother Väinö, had been evacuated to someplace outside Oulu.

"Godalmighty, guys, but that's one strong wind!"

Kauko turned around. A boy about his age who stood behind him took off his cap. His legs astride his suitcase, he turned the cap over in his hands and said:

"I don't care of these city types die laughing, I'm putting my ear flaps down. I've faced winds before, but a helluva wind like this is new to me."

"This must be that sea wind. The old folks call it salty," said Kauko, shifting his hat to cover the other ear. His gloomy face brightened. He looked at the much slighter youngster, who pulled his cap straight down over his ears.

"At least my ears won't freeze," said the young man. "Is our boy from Kijanta joining the army?"

"You mean me?" asked Kauko.

"Yes, you! This wind is going right through my pants."

"I guess I'm joining the army."

"You left Suomussalmi for nothing then. Isn't that where the big ruckus is going on right now? You could have grabbed a gun and started picking off those attackers."

"They don't take you without training, do they? And I'm not

from Suomussalmi."

"But you talk like they do in Kijanta...Even the devil would freeze here. Let's get out of the wind before our mugs freeze."

The young man picked up his suitcase and Kauko did the same.

"I come from near Suomussalmi, but from another parish."

"I change my shirts in Posio. I've faced the winds of Kitka, but they don't bite like this. Shall we go into the waiting room or find a java hut?"

"What's a java hut?"

"A java hut? You don't seem to know much about the world. It's a kind of coffee shop. Some call them tar pumps."

"If it's a place where people go, then let's do it. We'll get something warm to thaw our innards. The others are all leaving..."

The two upland lads walked toward the center of the city. The wind was not as raw in the streets where they were sheltered by buildings.

"Where do you report?" asked Kauko's companion.

"At Oulainen. And you?"

"At Lahti. It's a long way to sit on a train."

"You must know this town pretty well."

"I've been here a few times. I was a water boy on freight carriers. And you? What coffee shop shall we go to?"

"It's all the same to me. This is the my first time here."

"You must be from the sticks. It's a wonder you weren't afraid of the bus, ha, ha. There's a coffee shop on the second floor over there."

The boys stood in front of a building. People walked the streets, most of them in uniform. A man wearing a splendid fur cap and carrying an army overcoat on his arm passed by. With every stride he took, Kauko heard the clink of metal. He gazed after the retreating figure. Then he said:

"What were those things clinking on that man's heels?"

"Aren't they the iron points they dig into horses' ribs?"

"Then they were spurs. Toivo Olkivaara told me about them. He must have been a high-ranking officer. Toivo said—Toivo is a neighbor and he's in the army—Toivo said the higher brass wear them."

"I don't know a thing about the army's organization. But I guess we'll have to snap to attention in a few days when a big

wheel like that comes along. Shall we go in?"
"Let's go. We need something to warm our insides."

2

The railway coach was packed with people. Kauko and the lad from Posio sat huddled side by side. Their coach was directly in back of the engine. Its puffing sounded strange to Kauko's ears. The coach swerved suddenly to one side and then set off in another direction. The people standing in the aisles gripped the seat supports more tightly. Someone fell between the seats and cursed angrily. A woman's voice called on the Lord. Kauko grabbed at the side of the seat.

"Damn, I almost fell! It scared me." The words escaped Kauko.

"It's tossing us around the way the devil tosses a beggar," said the boy from Posio.

A sergeant and another soldier were seated opposite them. The sergeant's lips lengthened into a smile. "Is this your first trip on a train?" he asked.

Kauko looked at his companion, the boy from Kitka, who merely looked back at him. The lad drew back the curtain over the window and looked outside. Kauko sat back, resting his elbows against his thighs, and said:

"I...ah...haven't been in one of these wagons before."

"You were showing your pass to the conductor just now. Are you going into the army?" The sergeant looked inquiringly at Kauko.

"I guess that's what I'm getting into," said Kauko.

"Do you have far to go?" asked the soldier sitting next to the sergeant.

"I go to Oulainen. I looked at the map in the coach vestibule just now. It's just a little way."

The sergeant looked as if he was in a good mood. As soon as he sat down, Kauko had smelled the liquor on his breath. His friend had been drinking too. But neither had had very much. The sergeant tucked a finger under his collar and said:

"Do you know what branch of the service this color stands for?"

"No," said Kauko.

"It's infantry green," said the soldier coming to his aid.

"It just so happens that we're going to the same place. You look strong enough. I'll take you into my squad if we wind up in the same company."

"That would be fine," said Kauko. "This war business is all new to me."

In the hubbub back at the railway station, Kauko had again felt alone and so homesick as to be on the verge of tears. The boy from Posio was not shy, and Kauko had been the next after him in line when their orders were stamped. Together they had scanned the schedule on the station wall, trying to find out what train they were supposed to board. But it was a complicated matter. The backwoods boys had had to ask the station master, who had told them what train to take and had even led them to a coach. Oulu was now behind them, and Kauko was feeling better again, since a real army man, a sergeant to boot, was talking to them.

The boy from Posio drew his head back from under the curtain. He looked sourly at the men opposite.

"I have to sit on these wheels all the way to Lahti."

"You can't get there on these wheels," said the soldier. "You have to change at Riihimäki. I have orders to go to Koria. Just stick with me and we'll get there."

The boy's eyes lighted up and he said, "It's always nicer to travel with someone you know. Not that I couldn't get there on my own. I know how to talk."

"You boys must come from near the eastern border," said the sergeant.

Kauko's companion explained where each of them was from.

"Must have been this big lad's neighbors they brought to my parish as refugees," said the sergeant.

Kauko looked at the speaker. He was forced to swallow.

"They emptied out the place. The weaker ones were all taken to the coast. Where are you from, sergeant?"

"Haukipudas. They brought in a lot of people there who couldn't take the war."

"When did you leave home?" asked the soldier.

Kauko dug his watch out from under his waistband.

"It's not past midnight yet, so it was this morning."

"Was the front still at Suomussalmi?"

"There was heavy fighting at Alasalmi," Kauko replied to the sergeant.

"...why try to stop the Russians? They'll cut Finland in two at Oulu. Then what's to be done? Those north of Oulu will be stuck there. Southern Finland will be hemmed in. The Russians will come into Turku and Helsinki from Estonia. Then you can really sing the *Internationale.*"

"What the hell rubbish is that old man spreading?" said the soldier, turning to look back at a man whose voice had risen above the other sounds in the bus. The sergeant turned too.

"Is it that runty old buck back there who is sounding off?"

"His mouth has been going ever since we left Oulu," said the boy from Posio.

Kauko's mood swung back to gloom. The little-black-bearded man looked to him like some kind of warlock. Would mother and Liisu and Väinö too be left behind enemy lines?

"The bosses are getting men killed for nothing. The Russians were almost to Pudasjärvi last night. With their machines, it's a short hop from there to Oulu. If we stopped making them mad by fighting, nothing bad would happen to the common people. Think of what it was like in the depression. The Russians might lop off a few of the bosses' heads, but we would be better off."

"God protect us!"

The words were shrieked out by a woman sitting nearby. Weeping aloud, the young mother pressed her small boy to her bosom.

"They're nowhere near Pudasjärvi. That's a big lie!"

Kauko heard the words ring out and watched as the woman clutched the child fiercely to her breast. His eyes fell.

"Isn't there anyone here who'll shut that old man's mouth? Who the devil wants to listen to such a liar?"

The sergeant sprang to his feet as he spoke. He walked up the aisle and stood facing the man. His cheeks were a fiery red.

"Who's paying you to tell these lies, buddy?"

"Paying me? All I know is what I've heard, that they've driven us back to Pudasjärvi."

"Your kind would go back without being driven, but real Finns wouldn't. There's a man sitting opposite me who came from near the front today. The line is at Alasalmi."

"Why is that old man lying then?" asked a man's voice.

"Thank God," one of the women sighed.

"Keep that trap of yours shut."

Threats could be heard from different parts of the coach. They silenced the man. After a short time, he took his pack from the rack and began to shove his way toward the rear of the train. The sergeant returned to his seat, dug out a cigarette, and offered one to his seat partner and to those opposite. The boy from Posio took one but Kauko shook his head. When the sergeant reached out a burning match toward Kauko's partner's cigarette, a thick, dirty gauze bandage showed on his wrist.

"What happened to your wrist?" asked Kauko.

"A rifle bullet hit it. That's why I got a short leave. It still oozes a little pus, so they're sending me to a training center."

"Where did you get hit?" asked the boy from Posio.

The sergeant lighted his cigarette. He took a couple of puffs from it and said:

"On the Karelian Isthmus."

3

"Can't you fit any more up there?"

Maija Sammalsuo and Mari Olkivaara were standing in a crush of people. The words came from an outer door. She and Mari had already reached the first step of a stairway inside. From it one could see the mass of people filling the front hallway in back of them. The two wings of the double front doors were wide open. The doorway was choked with people pushing and shoving to get inside. They were the old and the infirm, and mothers with children.

"In God's name, try to push up to the top floor! The poor kids are freezing," shouted a tearful woman's voice from the door.

"Isn't there a bit of room up there?" said Maija. "There are still a lot of people out in the cold."

"They don't seem to be moving up the stairs," said an old man from above them.

"Isn't there anything you can do? We grown-ups won't freeze, but the children are getting numb. We came all the way from Näljänkä in the cab of a truck."

The speaker outside the door was a youngish man. One of his legs was a withered arc. He leaned on a stout, knotty cane to keep his balance as he hopped on his good leg.

Maija Sammalsuo groped to one side. She could feel Väinö's hair with her hand. The throng pressed Liisu into her skirt. At least the children were still close to her. Maija leaned down and whispered:

"Väinö, are you hungry?"

The boy stared wide-eyed at his mother.

"No. There are lots of people here. Where's Liisu?"

"On the other side of mother," said Maija.

"I'm hungry and I can hardly breathe in here."

Maija patted Liisu's cheek. The girl's small hand clung to her wrist.

"Be patient, Liisu," said Maija.

The crush of people moved upward slightly. Maija's foot found a purchase on the next step, but then the mass of people stopped. She was pinned more tightly against the railing and squeezed closer to Mari.

"They're yelling from above that we're going to eat soon," said Mari.

"A stew would taste good. We had only a bite for breakfast and nothing on the bus," said Maija. "I wonder what time it is?"

A fat man next to her dug at his waistband, his toothless mouth fixed in a grimace. At last he found his watch and said:

"It'll be midnight before long. It's a quarter to eleven."

"No wonder the kids are crying," said Mari.

The sound of children crying came from the stairs above and from the hallway below them. Mothers hushed and consoled their little ones. Near Maija and Mari stood a young woman holding a small child in her arms. Maija's eyes kept going back to the woman's face. It was pale. Two small boys at her skirts kept reaching up towards her. Their identical size and looks told Maija they were twins.

"Mummy, mummy, up, up."

"Mummy has no room. Seppo is asleep. If you can just wait a little longer, we can sit down."

"Let me hold the little one. You'll faint soon."

The woman burst into tears as she looked at Maija.

"We sat in a bus all day. It's really hard." She handed the child, who was less than a year old, to Maija, who cradled it in her arms and said:

"You poor little thing. You know nothing about the world's wickedness."

Maija's eyes grew moist as she thought of her own Anni, now dead. The Creator had done wisely in sparing her these trials. What more did they have to face? The first day of evacuation had been so difficult. Anni's strength would never have been equal to it.

Children crying. The soft voices of women. The rumble of men's. Minutes creeping slowly by.

"Try to push ahead. There are children still out in the cold," shouted a man's voice outside the door.

"Let's try to stay together, no matter where they take us."

Maija looked up from the sleeping child and saw the helpless look on Mari's face.

"We'll stick together. Are you feeling nauseous? Your face is all gray."

"I'm getting tired and I feel a little dizzy. If we could only..."

At that moment, a woman's scream of terror pierced through the other sounds. It came from above. Maija saw a bundle of clothing come hurtling down the empty stairwell between the railings. It nearly grazed her face. She heard the scream of a child. Then something smashed into the floor below.

"My baby! Good God! Catch him. He fell!"

The scream of the woman above pierced the hearts of everyone in the crowd. People covered their eyes. There was silence except for the agonized screaming that filled the stairwell. Then a man's voice shouted from above.

"A child fell!"

Maija looked over the railing. On the floor below, a man was bending over a bundle of clothing. Blood and a kind of whitish pulp were spattered on the mosaic tile floor. Maija averted her eyes. She squeezed the stranger's child closer to her breast. Her legs trembled and her heart was pounding. From above came a mindless cry:

"My baby! My baby!"

The cry came nearer. A blond woman rushed down flight after flight, scrambling over people's heads and shoulders.

"Did the poor child fall from up there?" someone whispered.

"From the top floor," said a man standing near Maija and Mari. Then he shouted, "Catch her, catch the mother or she'll fall too."

"Will you give me my child? I can manage her myself now. Thanks for holding her."

Maija handed the child to its mother and pressed Liisu closer to her.

"My child, my child."

Three men were now carrying the blond woman in their arms. Her lips kept repeating the same words over and over. Her eyes stared upwards, unblinking.

"Please don't. Just rest," one of the men said.

"Calm yourself now. God will not desert you in your need." An old man was stroking the woman's hair with his big-knuckled hand. His voice shook as he spoke.

The jam of people began to move up the stairs. The news traveled down to them in whispers.

"They're letting us into the rooms."

✧ ✧ ✧

The bus was cold when it left Oulu. A few kilometers outside the city, a cloud of steam burst out from under the engine hood. The driver steered the bus to the side of the road and stomped down furiously on the brake pedal. A span of cleared space on the windshield fogged up immediately.

"Now this damned heap is boiling over."

Furiously scratching the back of his head, the man plunged out of the door. A cloud of chill vapor poured in when he opened it. From outside came the sound of harsh cursing.

"What happened to the bus now?" asked a woman.

"The engine must have overheated," said an old man.

"He's cursing a blue streak," said another.

"He's tired. He couldn't keep his eyes open while he was driving."

The last speaker, a woman who was sitting in the front seat, looked back over her shoulder and added: "He said he drove a bus load of evacuees from Kuusamo with only one eye open."

A man sitting near the front of the bus rose and went outside. They heard him asking the driver a question in a voice so soft they could not make out his words. But the driver's answer came through clearly enough.

"To get the cows home quicker, goddammit!"

The man returned hastily to his seat. Väinö rose from beside his mother and said:

"I wanna go see what's wrong with the bus too."

"Stay here," said Maija. "You'll just make the driver angry."

Muttering a protest, Väinö sat down again. A few other boys began moving down the aisle. The man who had been outside said:

"Stay in your seats."

"Has the bus broken down completely?" asked a man in the rear seat.

"I don't know. The driver didn't have much to say. He seems to have a pretty short fuse," answered the other.

Liisu was asleep in her mother's lap. Maija wrapped the bottom of her coat around the child. Even though the midday sun sifted through the side window of the bus, it was still so cold she kept curling her toes up inside her shoepacs trying to keep them warm. Her knees were chilled. In almost every seat, people were banging their feet together. Their outer footwear was frozen stiff.

"How can an engine heat up in weather this cold?"

The man who had been outside answered her.

"The driver was just cursing about having covered the radiator too well."

"Are you freezing, Väinö?"

"My feet are—a little," the boy answered.

The driver stepped back into the bus. He blew on his blackened fists and said:

"Goddamn this cold!"

Digging a comb from his pocket, he began to scrape the ice from the windshield with the back of it. The eyes of nearly fifty evacuees stared at the slowly widening darker patch on the glass. The field of vision it opened up was broader for those sitting up front. The sun shone with a dazzling brightness. The bank left by a snowplow cast a broad, dark shadow on the road bed.

"Will this bus still go under its own power?"

For a long time, there was no answer to Maija's question. She was already beginning to regret having opened her mouth. Scowling, the driver kept scraping the frost from the windshield. Then he plumped himself down on the seat and said:

"If it doesn't, there are plenty of people to push it. And if anyone is in a hurry, he can always walk. There's road enough for that — it goes all the way to Petsamo."

Tears rose to Maija's eyes and she dabbed at them with a corner of her head scarf. The driver glanced into the rear view mirror and bowed his head. For a long time he sat rubbing his temples.

"I didn't mean to snap at you," he said. "It's just that I'm so damned tired."

The sound of the idling motor rose nearly to a howl and the bus started off slowly. The sun that had been shining through the side window now shifted to the rear. Maija's spirits rose. We're heading north, she thought. She wrapped the bottom of her coat more tightly around Liisu. Then she looked at Mari, who was sitting across the aisle, and said:

"I wonder where Mrs. Naavala wound up going."

"I don't know. So many people from Järvenkylä disappeared in the crowd at Oulu."

"They said at the school that some of the Järvenkylä evacuees would be taken to parishes south of Oulu," said Taimi Olkivaara, who was sitting next to her mother holding her youngest sister in her lap.

Evacuee...for the first time Maija had a clear idea of the word's meaning. She had heard it before. People had used it repeatedly the last few days, but it had gone in one ear and out the other. Now it stuck in her mind. *Evacuee.*

"How do you think they're getting along at Järvenkylä?" asked Mari.

"Is Kauko in the army yet?" Maija wondered aloud. "And how is Aili doing with the cows? And if only Auku doesn't go and shoot himself."

"Oh, they'll be all right. Elma will go and help Aili. If only they are still at home. They were saying at Oulu that the Russians have pushed past Alasalmi."

"That's just a rumor. We met so many men and so much equipment on our way to Oulu that the Russians will have had a bellyful."

Maija looked at the speaker, an older man sitting in front of Mari, and sighed with relief. His words had dispelled her doubts.

"The land is so flat here," said Taimi, scratching a hole in the ice on the window with her fingernail. She gazed out steadily for awhile and then said:

"We just passed a building that said *Haukipudas Cooperative* on the wall. "

"That doesn't tell me anything," said Mari. "I wonder where Nestor is."

"At Alasalmi," said Maija. "He's sure to have gone there."

"If only he hasn't been shot."

"Why start to cry about something like that, Mother? Father's been in a war before," snapped Taimi, jabbing her mother in the ribs.

"But he was a young man then. Now he's old and slow."

"That's not so. Jeez, didn't he go hopping through a wet swamp that summer, trying to get around a pile of bear shit. He moved fast enough then."

"Kids remember the funniest things," Maija chortled.

Even Mari was forced to smile. The bus was traveling at a good rate of speed. To the children, the trip was exciting, but their elders' eyes were red from the lack of sleep. They'd had almost none the night before.

"If only this trip would end and we could get a decent night's sleep, " said Maija from across the aisle.

✧ ✧ ✧

"We made it," said the driver as he stopped the bus.

"Is this the end of the line?"

"This is it," said the driver. He got up, opened the door of the bus, and added, "You see, we're in the yard of a fine schoolhouse."

The evacuees from the uplands began to clamber out of the bus. Maija shook Liisu to awaken her. The girl stared at her mother for a moment, but her eyes kept closing.

"Liisu. Liisu. We have to get off the bus now."

The girl sat up in her mother's lap and looked around.

"Are we in the Naavala yard now? Are we at home?"

"No, child. But this is as far as we are going."

"Have we been evacuated?"

"Yes, and we have to hurry out now. Did Väinö take his lunch bag with him?"

"He had it in his hand when he got off," said Taimi Olkivaara.

"I dreamed that Kauko came from Naavala to get us. He was

wearing the same kind of clothes as the soldiers," Liisu explained, her eyes still dazed with sleep.

Out in the yard, the old people were stretching their limbs. Some of them kept kicking one shoe against the other to keep their feet warm. A few of the just-awakened children were crying. A number of young women in the uniform of the auxiliary came out into the yard. They smiled and took the shy, staring backwoods children by the hand. Among the greeters was an old man dressed in the Civil Guard uniform. He was tall and strongly built. His stance was erect and he had the look of one accustomed to command.

"Welcome, you upland people," he said. "Hurry now, go in through those open double doors. It's warm inside, and the women have the food ready."

The bus load of people began filing into a number of large classrooms. A wave of warmth greeted them at the schoolhouse door, along with the aroma of pea soup. Adam's apples began to bob up and down, and eyes grew brighter.

"Let's settle down in that classroom, Mari," said Maija.

"It' s warm near the stove," said Taimi.

When the newcomers had stripped some of the clothing from their numb limbs, a uniformed woman came to the door.

"Now for the food. The soup and dishes are in that kitchen. Make yourselves at home. The poor children are freezing."

4

"Well now, upland boy. Grab your gear and get off."

Kauko, who had slept poorly for many nights, awoke with a start. He reached up and took his traveling bag down from the luggage rack. Then he looked wide-eyed at the sergeant, who was putting on his overcoat.

"A-are we there already?"

"No need to panic. I just wanted to wake you up in time."

The sergeant sat back down again. Fully dressed now, he lighted up a cigarette. Kauko sat down too and set his bag between his legs.

"You didn't have far to go," said the boy from Posio.

The train was braking strongly. The sergeant got to his feet and Kauko followed his example. He said to the boy from his neighboring parish:

"I wish we could have gone further together. Stay well. Maybe we'll meet again some day in the same logging camp back home."

"If we finish this big logging job first."

The boy laughed, but the expression on his face remained taut. The slight tipsiness of the sergeant and his friend had passed during the trip. Sighing heavily, the sergeant said to the soldier:

"Say hello if you happen to meet anyone I know."

"You too. Try to cope."

"Come on now, upland boy, follow me," said the sergeant.

Dozens of young men from the coaches of the train were left standing on the station platform. Again Kauko thought of his home and family, but the thought faded as the men gathered into one group. They all clustered around the sergeant and Kauko.

"It just keeps getting colder," said the sergeant looking up at the sky.

Kauko looked up too. A full moon shone and stars twinkled in the sky. Suddenly he thought of Elma. Had only a day passed since he had looked up at the same starry sky and out across the Järvenkylä wilderness from the old windmill? It was probably Elma's turn on watch now. Or his sister Aili's. He hadn't asked. Perhaps it was Hilja Naavala who was now gazing out over the eastern woods.

"What draft group are you boys from?"

The sergeant's question wrenched Kauko's thoughts away from the woods of home. All the young men looked at one another. An answer was slow in coming. Finally one of them said:

"I volunteered."

"So did I," said another.

"Same here. I asked to be shipped out too."

It soon became apparent that almost everyone there had entered service as a volunteer. The wounded sergeant soon became a father to the group. He was all of three years older than those who were gathered about him.

"I wanted to go to the front, but they sent me here first to learn this war business. They made me come, even though I've bagged many a bird in my young days," said a boy, scratching the skull beneath his fur cap.

At that moment, a man in an army overcoat stepped around the corner of the station. When he opened his mouth, it looked wide and black, and big enough to put a fist in.

"Were there any recruits on this train?" he roared.

The frosty, packed snow screaked under uneasily shifting feet. The man's shout had made the new arrivals mute. Some of them looked at one another; others at the sergeant in their midst.

"Are you dumb? Are you all totally deaf?"

"You seem to be on the warpath, Corporal."

The sergeant stepped out from the circle of young men surrounding him. Then he continued:

"Of course, there is a war on now."

"Sergeant sir! I meant the recruits. I'm here to meet them."

"Go to hell with that *sir*. Which way is the school?"

The corporal, who had snapped to attention now shifted to an exaggerated *parade rest*. Then he gestured with one hand.

"That way. It's not far from here."

"What draft group are you?"

"Last September's."

"And you're already through non-com school?"

"Not quite. They cut it short and ordered me to a training center."

"Well, show us the way so we can get in where it's warm."

Everyone with orders to report here follow me," said the corporal, who was standing with his thumbs hooked under his belt.

"Where's my buddy. Ah, here he is. Join the group."

The corporal and the sergeant walked off abreast, with the young men trailing along behind them. The corporal looked back and then sidestepped along as he spoke.

"Try to march in a column of twos. Two men, side by side."

Kauko was walking along behind the sergeant. He saw the corporal look back at them and then take a few dance-like steps, after which the two leaders' steps began to crunch in unison on the snow. This is what they call marching, he thought. He tried to match his steps to the sergeant's by watching the rhythm of the body swaying along before him, but he kept taking steps that were too long. He had to shorten his gait. The effort to keep in step with the sergeant demanded all his attention. Later only a hazy memory of that evening's journey and its surroundings remained in his mind. The buildings looked like those in the church village at home, but probably covered a wider area.

✧ ✧ ✧

A tired-looking clerk corporal sat at a desk in the school's anteroom. There were papers on the desk and lights burned on the ceiling. Kauko was among the first to enter the room.

"Passes and orders here."

The corporal's voice sounded tired too. Scowling, he shifted his feet and leaned his upper body from side to side. Then he growled:

"These desks were made for grade-school kids. My legs are getting stiff. May I have your orders, sergeant?"

"Here they are. Have I come to the right place?"

"No doubt. The non-coms bunk in that teachers' room." The clerk pointed to a door behind him.

"Now for you recruits. You, big-shoulders there. Where are your papers?"

Kauko was looking confusedly around him. He started at the corporal's sharp glance.

"I have my p-pass."

"Then wake up, man. Get over here now."

"Sammalsuo, Kauko Japheth. Ha, ha, now that's a real back-country name."

There was a look of amusement in the corporal's red-rimmed eyes. Kauko was embarrassed. His eyes fell. His hands seemed to be in the way, and he thrust them into his pants pockets. Then he said:

"They call me Kauko."

"Maybe they did before, but now you're recruit Sammalsuo, Kauko Japheth. And take your hands out of your pockets...And you, the skinny one back there. Bring your papers here."

Kauko was reduced to a state of confusion. The sarcastic, half-shouted words had completely dumfounded him.

"Step aside, Japheth, step aside," barked the clerk.

The sergeant sat on a stool near the door. Whenever he raised a cigarette to his lips, the bandage on his wrist came into sight.

Kauko almost leaped to the side of his train companion. The sergeant smiled and said:

"Come and sit down. How do you like this business?"

Kauko's mind grew calmer. It was his good luck to have a real soldier as his traveling companion. Should he start calling him sir?

"Sergeant, sir, it's all so strange and new."

"Don't waste your *sirs* on me. You can use them on your platoon leader tomorrow. I have to laugh when I think of when I joined the army. It was in Kuopio. They had a real barracks there."

Kauko's shyness diminished. Everyone has to put up with this in his turn, he thought. The sergeant's comment on his own days as a recruit gave him confidence. He watched the others step up to the desk one by one. Finally the clerk said:

"There are empty bunks in that classroom. Everybody turn in. There'll be some heavy drilling tomorrow."

"Let's go and check out the bed space," said the sergeant.

"You were supposed to be in with the non-coms," said Kauko.

"I don't feel like stumbling around in there so late at night."

Double-decker bunks had been crowded into the classroom. The corporal who had met them at the station turned on the lights. There was a rustling in some of the bunks, and fearful, sleepy faces peered out from under blankets. From other bunks came the sound of snoring.

"Recruits have been coming in all day," the corporal said to the sergeant.

The sergeant tossed his pack onto an empty bunk and sat down to take off his shoes. As he did so, he said to Kauko:

"I'm going to sack out here. The next bunk is empty. Flop down on it."

Kauko pulled off his Lapland boots but left his trousers and woolen shirt on. There were only a bare mattress and a blanket on the bed. The corporal was already turning off some of the lights. Kauko pulled the blanket over him.

Although a lazy sense of well-being began to flow through his limbs under the warm blanket, a shade of disappointment entered his mind. Why exactly had he come here when he didn't have to? He could have stayed at home to take care of Auku and Aili, perhaps for the whole winter. By then, the war might have ended. Guarding the bridge was an important task too. The way things had started out wasn't like the heroic deeds that had thrilled him when they had read *The Tales of Ensign Stahl* in school. It all began to seem pointless. He had wanted to show what a former ward of the community could do. Could he undo what he had done? Could he tell them tomorrow that he was needed at home? But then what could he say to the people there? He would have to lie. Even the sheriff would get to hear of him as a hero who had left his post.

Kauko's thoughts turned to mother, Liisu, and Väinö. God protect them and everyone. Don't let the front at Alasalmi give way. Let all of Finland be saved.

But before he fell asleep he began to regret his misgivings. The bed he lay on was better than he had often had in logging camps. Boys of his own age lay snoring all around him. He was no worse off than the others. If they could take it, so could he. Mother used to say that a lesser man always *meant to* but a good man *did.*

✧ ✧ ✧

It seemed to Kauko that he had just fallen asleep when a raucous shout awakened him:

"Reveille!"

Kauko leaped up like a cat on hot coals. Sudden movements made the bunks on all sides rustle. Shaking in every limb, Kauko searched for his boots. As he jerked them on, he was close to tears. The boot tops seemed tight and his socks were left bunched up under the soles of his feet.

"No need to hurry on the first day. Tomorrow, if the old signs hold true, you'll be hustling through morning calisthenics."

The sergeant lolled on his bunk as he spoke. Then he sat up and calmly searched out his footwear. Kauko's limbs stopped trembling. Well, it's not quite the end of the world, he thought. Still he knew that he would remember this first reveille till the end of his life. Into the classroom doorway stepped a buck sergeant with a yellow braid on his arm. He shouted:

"Get ready for morning tea! Time five minutes!"

"This is where it begins. I'm off to see the other stripers. Just take it easy. Do as you're told and you'll be OK."

"Everyone has to take his turn as a recruit. It just seems tough because it comes at you so fast," said Kauko.

"I felt the same way once. Then none of this made any sense. But we're in the real thing now. See you."

"See you. I'll come and talk to you if things get really tough."

"That's OK with me."

5

The previous night at Oulu, most of the evacuees had only been able to doze for short periods. When the sun had traced its low arc in the sky and had sunk beyond the broad expanse of the sea, one after another, the elderly lay down to sleep. The worn-out backwoods people slept on platforms, on wood boxes, but most of them lay on the floor. When Maija awoke, it seemed as if she had just closed her eyes. The children were sound asleep. For a moment she was not sure if it was morning or still late afternoon. The lights were on and the wall clock pointed almost to five. Old people accustomed to early rising came and went. Mari sat up too and Maija said to her:

"The poor kids were so tired. Liisu seems to have wet herself. That hasn't happened in years at home."

Electric lights were something new to many of the backwoods people. Their eyes, opening from a sound sleep, lingered on the lights and the schoolroom walls for a time.

"When I woke up just now, I thought I would have to go and milk the cows," said Mari.

"I had to look around for awhile too, before my brain told me there was no barn and no cows," said Maija.

"It just keeps getting colder," said an old man who had been outside.

"And that wind from the sea is poison," said another.

"I wonder how they're doing at the front?" said an old woman. "When the Lord starts to punish people, he doesn't run short of ideas."

"Even old people can't remember cold like this."

✧ ✧ ✧

During the day, a truck arrived, bringing bedding and other belongings that had been hastily snatched up on leaving home.

"Our things don't seem to have come," said someone.

"Nor ours," said another.

"The few things we had seem to be lost too."

Most of the people dug in vain through the heap of goods. Mari Olkivaara and Maija Sammalsuo were among the lucky ones — their few bundles did turn up. Now at least they had their own bedclothes. The truck driver and his assistant became the focus of sharp questions and bickering.

"Don't panic yet. Another truck is coming this afternoon."

This news calmed the people, who were already getting frantic. The promise was fulfilled. The rest of the belongings arrived around noon. The goods from home made them feel less abandoned. They were a link to the backwoods they had left behind.

In the afternoon the people from Järvenkylä began to chat with other evacuees. It turned out that an old man from a nearby building had logged in their area in his younger days. That set the conversation flowing freely. First one man, then another remembered him.

"Weren't we in the same logging gang near Irni that winter?" recalled one of the old backwoodsmen.

"Right, that's where it was," said the visitor.

"Time changes people," said the first.

"No one stays the same when the years pile up," said the other.

A stoutish woman came up to Mari and Maija. There was a friendly smile on her face. She first shook hands with Mari and then said timidly:

"God's greetings."

"God's greetings," replied Mari.

The woman's face lighted up. She extended her hand to Maija.

"My name is Tyyne. We all follow the teachings of Laestadius. God's greetings...since we can't wish you God's peace in these times."

Maija's expression brightened.

"It's good to find witnesses to the same belief here on the coast. It's like a weight off one's shoulders."

The visitor began to question the women from Järvenkylä about their journey. Finally she took Liisu into her arms, stroked her hair, and said:

"Will your mother and brother come to live with us?"

Liisu hung her head and plucked at the woman's buttons.

"Tell your auntie now."

"Liisu is shy. She's always lived in the backwoods," said Maija.

"I really came here to find a family to live with us. How does that strike you? We don't have a big place, but like minds can make room."

Maija looked at Mari and saw the fear in her eyes.

"This Mari is our neighbor. We've shared our sufferings and small joys up to this day, and we've decided to stick together come what may. But I'm very grateful."

"If you can put up with crowded quarters, why don't both of your families come? I'm glad to help out my fellow human beings."

"My goodness, what could be better!" said Maija.

"It will be great for us neighbors," said Mari, overjoyed.

"Then it's settled. I'll send my husband Leevi to get you with a horse. Your goods can come on the same load. My husband is hard of hearing, but if you shout, you can get through to him."

The visitor rose. She took Liisu into her arms once more and said:

"I liked this bright-eyes from the start."

Before leaving, she patted the youngest Olkivaara girl on the head and said:

"You're so big already that I can't lift you up. Welcome to our home."

Mari sat and stared across the classroom. There were tears in her eyes. Instinctively, Maija clasped her hands in prayer over her knees.

CHAPTER II

1

Icicles were forming on his mustache. A pack kept his shoulders warm. Motorized columns roared along the road. Vehicles kept going by him in both directions. Ear flaps pulled down over his ears impaired his hearing. The blast of a truck horn sounded from right in back of him. He scrambled to the side of the road, his skis slithering on its hard surface.

"The devils. They'd run right over you!"

Skiing on a crooked, plowed road was a new experience for Nestor Malinen. His legs were already tired before he reached Vaarakylä, and he was getting otherwise frazzled. He was no longer in top condition. He decided to stop and empty the load from his bladder. It wouldn't look like resting.

Nestor stuck his ski poles into the plowed bank and began digging at the buttons on his fly. His numbed fingers made it a painful task. He had to jerk back his rear end, and the sudden movement sent a twinge of pain through his back.

"Not much left of the old tool but a shell. Damn, now it's running onto my boots."

Two trucks came rumbling toward him.

"Hell, was that women in those trucks? Well, I won't stop now just because of them."

The trucks drove by, their windows thickly coated with frost. Several pairs of booted legs stuck straight out from the platform of the second. Nestor's fingers trembled as he closed the buttons. He was forced to swallow hard.

"Looks like they're hauling logs back from Alasalmi."

He stood there on his skis. The setting sun cast long shadows from trees heavy laden with snow. The upland hills rose in the distance. Wood grouse sat like black dots on the boughs of the trees, which glowed red in the setting sun.

Nestor lifted the flaps from his ears. He could hear the rumble of artillery to the northeast. Pulling his earflaps down again, he announced to himself:

"Heavy fighting going on there."

He turned his eyes back to the plowed road, then raised them once more. Far off stood the summit of the hill that rose from the shore at Järvenkylä.

"I never noticed how clearly you can see Lapinvaara from here."

Beyond Lapinvaara was Olkivaara, his home cottage. This side of it was Sammalsuo, their nearest neighbor. He felt homesick. What if he were to turn his skis around? Men are needed at home too. There was no one there who could pull a man's share of the load. Akseli Naavala was busy in the church village all the time. At home, things were under control, but at Sammalsuo, the care of the animals had been left to the children. Even Kauko was all for getting into the war. And they needed a real man to guard the bridge. If those Russian-trained saboteurs came to wreck it, what could boys do?

"But why all this nonsense? When did I ever back out of anything?"

Nestor began to ski onward resolutely. When he reached the edge of Vaarakylä, he saw that it was getting very dark. He went into the Sääskilampi house for the night.

✧ ✧ ✧

"They say we have to drive our cows away tomorrow," said the maidservant at the house where he was spending the night.

"They've been going by Järvenkylä. Back there I passed Ryti-Veeti's wife driving her livestock along the road."

"Yup, every house has had to be emptied. I was told to issue the order," said a man in Guard uniform who sat on a bench in the room.

Nestor looked askance at the speaker. Pine logs burned on the hearth. Blankets hung over the windows by the maid kept the light from being seen outside. When Nestor said nothing, the Guardsman asked:

"So you're on your way to Alasalmi?"

"That's the way my skis are pointing."

"And you're going as a volunteer?"

"They didn't send me one of those white greeting cards."

The man, who was younger than Nestor, lived over in the church village. He fished out a package of cigarettes, opened it, and held it out to Nestor.

"I don't care for that fancy tobacco. It's too weak for a roll-your-own man," said Nestor, digging out a plug of tobacco from which he rolled a butt.

"Was it last winter that you were a driver on my logging job?"

"I guess so. That's when I had that bad-tempered nag to fight with. It seemed like the end of the world then. Now it wouldn't matter."

"I'm surprised you're getting into this war of your own free will." The words of Nestor's ex-boss ended in a smoker's cough.

"Why should you be surprised? Huh?"

"Well, we all have to pull together now, but there would be enough for a man of your age to do on the home front. Me, I'm organizing these evacuations, for example."

"I've been in a war before. Had full training in the Civil War. Even fired off tons of machine-gun bullets."

The man leaned forward on his elbows and blew smoke through his nostrils. After a long pause, he said:

"I had a completely different picture of you."

"I know. People used to call me the Olkivaara communist. But no one ever said it to my face. I suppose you had the same idea?"

"Something like that. Do you remember how you mouthed off to me that Easter-time in the church village?"

"When and where? I don't remember."

"We were at an encampment. I asked you when you would join the Guard. I didn't like your answer."

"Oh, now I remember. I told you I didn't have time to join a gang of bull-eaters. The things that stick in your mind," Nestor said, laughing.

"You could have said something else."

"Well...I was pretty drunk at the time. A man's likely to say almost anything then. But I wasn't far off the mark. Didn't you eat a lot of beef stew during that encampment? And when the hell would I have had time to fool around with a rifle?"

"Well, it's all in the past now. I just happened to think of it."

"And I didn't mean anything bad by it...it was just a joke."

Nestor glanced at the woman servant sitting nearby. She rose and went into the kitchen. He continued:

"And now we've run into a jam and men are needed."

That ended the discussion between the two. The frost cracked in the corner timbers of the house. The foreman made a short trip outside. When he returned he said:

"The moon is bright out there."

Nestor drew one corner of the blanket away from the window, looked out, and said:

"If I was a little younger, I would start off right now."

"Let's sleep the night first and go on in the morning."

The servant peered out from the kitchen door and said:

"Would you visitors care for some food?"

The three ate in silence. It was odd not to have a single member of the homeowner's family at the table. There was an abundance of food, including reindeer meat and whole milk.

2

"Auku, you can go and get a load of hay from the haybarn."

"I'm not a horse," said Auku to his sister Aili.

"Then drive a cow if you like, but we have to get some feed into the cow barn."

"Oh shit. I have to work day and night." Auku, who had been sprawled out on the bed, sat up yawning. "I spent the night watching out for Russian saboteurs at the bridge, and now I have to go and haul hay. Don't you think, Aili, that things are going to hell?"

Elma Olkivaara was washing dishes at the table and Aili was fussing over the stove. Both of them wore the uniform of the Women's Auxiliary. Sloshing the dishes vigorously in the water, Elma looked over at Auku and said:

"You're the master of the house now. And the boss isn't allowed to complain."

"I was huddled up in that windmill too," said Aili.

"You probably let those broomtails trample the hay," said Auku. "I just hauled two loads into the loft."

"Feed the cows yourself if you think so."

"Phooey! Now I'm supposed to be a dairymaid."

Auku pulled on his woolen shirt, picked up his mittens, and pushed out through the door, pulling on his cap as he went.

"Pitch on a full load and I'll come and pull it with you."

Auku did not answer Elma's remark. The frost-laden door creaked as he disappeared through it.

Elma often stopped in to see Aili and Auku Sammalsuo after her watch was over. Aili was able to milk the cows, but Elma wanted to help the young homemakers. Maija had asked her to do so during the evacuation. She and Aili got along well together, and Auku, in his own way, was a pleasant companion to chat with.

"Do you think Auku is ready with the load yet?" said Elma.

"He just left. There's no hurry. What do you say, Elma, if we bake some bread cheese, since there is so much milk?"

"Do we dare make a fire in the fireplace during the day?" asked Aili. "It *is* prohibited. Brrr, it's so cold here. My teeth are chattering. That stove doesn't throw much heat."

"Really, let's do it. You make some today and I will tomorrow. You send yours to Toivo. You can put the gloves you knit into the same package. You finished them, didn't you?"

"Yes, but they didn't turn out well. I made a mistake in tapering the trigger finger."

Elma did not respond to Aili's words, but stared into the fire now beginning to burn in the fireplace. Soon the birch blocks were blazing brightly. Aili turned and saw Elma's absorbed look.

"Kauko would be happy to get a package from you."

"And Toivo one from you. That's why I suggested this exchange."

"You don't think Hilja will mind?"

"That's silly. Why should she?"

"Because she and Toivo write to each other."

"Nonsense. The boys will be happy to get a package and Hilja won't mind."

Elma rose to her feet, put on her coat and uniform cap, and walked over to the window. The sun had just risen above the trees. It cast a reddish glow on the floral patterns made by the frost on the window panes.

"He writes the nicest letters I've ever read."

"Oh. he can write well enough, but try to get a word out of him when you're talking. Just between the two of us — has he ever kissed you?"

Elma blushed. She turned and looked straight at Kauko's oldest sister, but soon she averted her eyes.

"Why do you want to know?"

"Just because...he's always been such a bumpkin."

"One doesn't tell kids about such things," Elma said with a laugh. "Now I have to go and help Auku. And if it bothers you so much, the answer is no," she said as she closed the door.

✧ ✧ ✧

Auku laid the pitchfork on the broad-runnered reindeer sled, picked up its rope, and started off toward the haybarn at the edge of the woods. Along the path he could see the tracks of rabbits which had come to nibble the tufts of hay fallen from earlier loads. A willow thicket grew near the barn. Its branches were coated with frost.

"I should find time to set out some snares," said Auku to himself. "The wood grouse are having a ball eating the catkins."

Near the barn, Auku had set a number of wire rabbit snares.

"Those long-legged devils won't run all the way into the snares. Here one of them stuck his head into the loop, but then pulled it back. Damn, if I only had a box trap!"

Although artillery roared sporadically in the east, Auku's eyes kept scanning the signs of nature's doings. He forgot where he was, forgot the times they were living through. Even an ermine had been snooping around under the barn.

Briskly, Auku pitched the hay onto the sled. He would need to get two loads, and then he would be free of the task for a week. And who knows...they might be the last ones. If the Russians broke through at Alasalmi, they would soon be here. The soldiers at Naavala said things looked that way. If that happened, they too would have to leave this place in a hurry. With luck they'd have time to take the cows with them. That would be some march, leading the cows all the way to the seacoast, although you wouldn't catch him leading a cow...that was for damn sure.

"You've finished the load already!"

Elma's words jolted Auku from his train of thought. "So you did come," he said.

"I really did. Now you have a round-headed horse to drive. Will the load stay on?" asked Elma, picking up the sled rope.

'You'll never catch me driving a two-legged mare!"

" You're too fussy. What's wrong with me?"

"It just won't work. Come and push from behind. I'll get into the traces."

"Even a good offer gets turned down," said Elma, walking around the sled. "Look where a reindeer and two calves have been trying to get into the barn."

"They can't do any damage. I put enough poles across the door to keep them out."

"Mmph...shall I give you the word to start pulling?"

"You've got a stallion in the traces now that can make a load move."

Auku leaned heavily into the rope while Elma pushed from behind on the handle of a pitchfork stuck into the load. The runners screaked on the snow.

"Hey, Auku!"

The sled stopped. Auku looked back.

"What now?"

"What's that roaring noise? It's coming from the east."

Both turned in the direction from which the rumble of war could be heard continually. The sun was in the southeast. It did not shine directly into their eyes, but it made seeing difficult.

"There. Look, Elma. Just below the sun."

"A plane. And it's quite close."

"It seems to be coming toward us. It must be a Finnish plane."

Elma and Auku moved closer to the load of hay and shielded their eyes from the sunshine. Auku's voice trembled with excitement and his eyes shone.

"It sure is loud. Have you ever seen an airplane?"

"No, but we could hear them flying over the backwoods the time they bombed the church village. Why is it making that noise?"

"It's growling nicely. It's pointing its nose right at us. Soon we'll almost be able to touch it with a pole." Auku's voice was ecstatic.

"Look! Why is the snow spurting up like that?" cried Elma.

A long row of spouts erupted from the snow. The plane seemed to be plunging right at the two of them.

"Elma! It's a Russian plane. It's firing a machine gun. Get behind the load. Quick!" shouted Auku.

The two of them scooted to the other side of the sled. Auku even tried to thrust his head underneath it. Their hearts were pounding. The plane roared over them, the gust of air as it passed rumpling the hay. Then it carved a long arc over the lake. Elma stood up first and Kauko quickly followed suit.

"They'll have to start raising our insurance rates here," he said.

"Now they're shooting at Olkivaara and at Jussi Ylikylä's place. You can hear the machine gun chattering again. I wonder how Vante and Tuomas are doing."

They saw Aili run bareheaded and coatless out to the back of the barn, from where she shouted to them:

"What was all that racket?"

Elma and Auku looked at each other but did not answer.

"Auku, what kind of mischief are you up to now? You broke a window. Were you target practicing with icicles?"

"What window?" snapped Auku, still following the plane with his eyes.

"Why the window of the main room! Come and see. Two panes are all smashed to bits."

Auku pointed toward Ylikylä.

"Look over there. Jussi's windows must be smashed to smithereens."

Aili caught sight of the diminishing aircraft and said:

"Did the plane make all that noise?"

"Did you think it was a hoot owl?" Auku grinned.

Auku's knees were shaky and his whole body was trembling as he pulled the sled to the front of the barn. He followed Aili and Elma into the house. Looking at the splinters of glass on the floor, he said:

"Damned bandits, shooting innocent people. Looks like these days you need a shotgun with you to go take a pee."

Aili and Elma hung a piece of blanket over the broken window. It made the room darker. A feeling of gloom fell over the three of them.

"The walls are full of holes too. Girls, look! One bullet hole after another up close to the ceiling. And the bullets have gone through the logs close to the floor too."

While Auku was investigating the holes in the walls, Elma cried out:

"Where's that water running across the floor coming from?"

Auku and Aili looked where she was pointing. A patch of water was spreading across the floor from underneath the water bucket near the stove. Auku walked over to it.

"Well I'll be damned if there isn't a hole in the side of the bucket. It's pouring out from there like from a bull's throat. It has to be plugged."

Auku stuffed rags into the hole with the tip of his knife. Then he said:

"I'll have to go and see if they killed the cows."

He was soon back from the barn. The girls looked at him questioningly, but he was slow to answer. Finally he spoke:

"The cows are alive and well. And our cat, Oskar Portimo, is sitting on the edge of the stove twitching his tail and licking his chops."

"Now I have to go home to Olkivaara. I wonder how Tuomas and Vante are. Maybe they're both dead."

A lump rose in Auku's throat too. He almost barked at the two girls.

"Why the devil did you have to start sniveling, Aili? And don't you start with the waterworks, Elma. Those things can't hit people. All they can do is shoot up walls and windows."

✧ ✧ ✧

"Were you very scared?" Elma asked her cousin Tuomas.

"I couldn't believe it was going to shoot. All I heard was a roar, and then it was already zooming over Ylikylä."

Elma and the boys circled the wall inside the house and then she went out to look at the barn, but they found no extra holes anywhere. When they returned to the house, Elma asked:

"Have you eaten yet?"

"Well, we've shoved a few dry crumbs under our ribs," said Svante.

"It's not healthy to light a fire during the day," added Tuomas.

"That must be why they shot up the Sammalsuo house," said Elma. "I'm going to sleep now. I'll cook something for you when it starts to get dark."

She walked through the kitchen into her own bedroom. It felt cold. Opening a drawer of the bureau, she dug out an envelope. It was addressed to Miss Elma Malinen and stamped with the words *ARMY POST OFFICE*. She drew out the two folded sheets it contained. They were covered on both sides with small handwriting.

Somewhere out here 12-28-1939

Elma Dear!

Now I'm far away from home. We had to leave very

suddenly. Being here is like a bad dream, but every night I dream that it is summer and I am in Järvenkylä. Now that I am far away, I have the courage to write and say that you are one of the people I see in almost all my dreams. We're often alone together. Then when the duty officer barks out reveille, it's the meanest sound in the world.

Elma read the words over again. Tears in her eyes, she went on.

...I don't even know where mother, Liisu and Väinö were evacuated to. I wonder if anyone has stayed there in Järvenkyla. If you get this letter, answer it. Will you? Send mother's address, if Aili and Auku know it. When you write to your family, send them my regards. I got a letter from Toivo when I first wrote to him. He is in a tough spot. Anyone can see that—he's on the main front at Summa. How is your father doing? I read in the papers that the worst pressure on the Alasalmi front has been withstood. The fighting must be hot and heavy near the Suomussalmi church village.

They say we won't get much training before we are sent to the front. We'll see where I wind up. It's why I came here, but we can't get into this war business without training. We're housed in a school. We're not allowed to say where, but who would go shouting that out anyway.

It must be very cold up in that windmill. It was cold when I stopped there the night before I left. The moon was bright and we were together. I often think of the night we swam together in the moonlight many years ago. Do you still remember when we slept in the hay on that abandoned farm. If I get back from this trip, I'm really going to buy that farm. When I go to bed after evening prayers and close my eyes, I always see a new house there. A main room and a kitchen and two bedrooms in back. And a new cowbarn too. And the nicest part of it is this—I always see you moving around there.

Once this world is straightened out, maybe that will be possible. Or will it, Elma? Auku and Väinö will soon be able to take care of the Sammalsuo place. I'm sure your mother and mine will come to visit us often.

Today is Sunday. It will soon be chow-time. So I'll try to scribble the last of this. Be sure not to show this letter to anyone. It's meant only for YOU. You will write to me, Elma? (I can call you my Elma, can't I?) Look in on Aili and Auku's housekeeping. They're still children. It's just about chow-time now. I'll be waiting for your letter. Let's hope our own dear homes and all of Finland can endure this trial. Being here isn't all I imagined, but I can bear it as well as the next man. Warmest regards to you and yours. From Kauko.

Elma read the letter slowly, rereading passages here and there. She herself had seen the windowless gray walls of the abandoned farmhouse, having just skied by it on her way home. It's no wonder Kauko remembers our being there, she thought. A large flock of wood grouse had flown up from a willow thicket nearby. She must remember to tell Auku to set snares there.

She heard the sound of footsteps crossing the kitchen floor. Quickly she brushed away a tear with the back of her hand and tried to shove the letter into the envelope, but the door opened before she succeeded. Svante stood in the doorway.

"Show me Kauko's letter."

"No way. But he sends you his best regards."

"Do you think I care to read it. You know why I asked." The boy laughed.

"I'm really going to sleep now," said Elma.

"When do you have to be at the windmill?"

"At ten. Wake me up at about six to cook and milk the cows."

"Start snoring then. Tuomas and I will cut some wood."

Svante left the room. Elma slid the letter into its envelope. When she opened the bureau drawer, the strong fragrance of sweetgrass rose to her nostrils. It grew in thickets along the shore, and during the summer she had picked it by the handful. It made clothes stored in bureau drawers over the winter smell good.

She took a few of the dried blades of grass and stowed them

gently in the envelope. It was strange that she hadn't noticed the fragrance when she had opened the drawer to take the letter out. I'll put them into the letter because Kauko likes plants so much, she thought. She pressed the letter to her breast and thought of the time she and Kauko had been swimming at Lapinhieta. She had never before or since that time felt a naked man's body against her own. A warmth flooded her breast as she remembered that night. She glanced at the door. Alone in her room, she could give voice to her longing:

"Kauko..."

Then she put the letter in among the folded garments and closed the drawer.

3

Nestor Malinen remembered Kosti Mäkinen's telling of his arrival in Vaarakylä along this same road. He had been hungry, he said, and it had been very cold. It's cold now too, thought Nestor, but I'm not freezing. It had been different with Kosti in those days. Easy to see why...tramping a trail like this in freezing weather, wearing only a summer suit and patent-leather shoes.

Absorbed in these thoughts, Nestor Malinen skied eastward. He could have gotten a ride if he had waited by the roadside at Sääskilampi, but it was nice to ski straight through the backwoods. He knew this road well, had traveled it many times on his way to logging sites. It had once been a road for horses, and probably a reindeer trail before that. Draft reindeer had perhaps pulled sleds over it for a generation or two. It ran close by the place where Nestor Malinen had been born, then skirted the high hills and went on through to the church village of Suomussalmi.

Occasional human dwellings huddled by the wayside, their windows thickly coated with ice. Twig brooms angled across their doors proclaimed that the owners had been forced to leave. Rabbit tracks led right up to the fir boughs spread before the front steps. The wilderness people who had occupied the houses were now living somewhere on the seacoast.

Although Nestor had left Vaarakylä early in the morning, the sun was already at its height when he reached Pyhäkylä. His belly was beginning to growl with hunger. Before the village came into sight, he turned up his earflaps and stood leaning on his ski poles to listen. He could hear the roar of motors and the thunder of artillery not far away. Had the Finns been forced to withdraw from Alasalmi?

A familiar house came into view. Laukki, his horse, had often stood in its yard with his blanket on, chomping his feed. Unlike many, this house was not abandoned. A sled and driver were in the yard, and people were stirring there as they once had when the house had been the headquarters of a logging operation. A strange chill made Nestor stop at the edge of the woods. What if the Russians had already taken the place? He must ski closer under cover of the cowbarn.

Nestor turned off the road and plowed through the deep snow toward the rear of the barn. There was a good spot behind the manure pile from which to get a good look at the men who were stirring in the yard.

"Stop! Don't move!"

Nestor's jaw dropped and he stood there staring at a man who had leaped out from behind the manure pile. The man wore a top sergeant's stripes on his coat. The barrel of his pistol was pointing at Nestor's face from a ski's length away.

"Get that gun to hell out of here!"

"Don't move a muscle! If you do I'll shoot," yelled the pistol wielder.

Nestor's fear subsided. At least the man looked like a Finn.

"Why the devil are you pointing that thing at me?"

"Shut your mouth. We don't want any spies nosing around here. Don't move!"

"Now you're about to hear what cursing sounds like. Is this any way to treat a man who's come to help you? Put that thing in your pocket. It's shaking like the devil."

"I'm giving the orders here. Hey guys...help! We've got a spy here."

"What kind of stupid idiot are you? Can't you hear that I'm talking perfectly good Finnish? If I was a spy or something, I would have smashed your head in with a ski pole. Trampled you down into that manure pile, that's what I would have done."

Men with rifles came running up. Gun barrels pointed at Nestor. Bolts clicked as rifles were cocked. The sergeant thrust his pistol into the holster hanging at his belt and said:

"We're taking this one alive. Watch that he doesn't touch his pockets."

A withered-faced man in civilian clothes came traipsing up after the soldiers. He stood in back of them and peered from his old man's eyes at Nestor standing there on his skis.

"I don't have time to say hello, Manne, but tell these gunners to stop pointing those things at me. You, at least, know who I am."

"Of course! Point your guns at the sky, boys. This man is no spy. I know him well. He's from the next parish."

"Well then! Is everything straightened out now? Hullo Manne. So you didn't go to the coast with the women?"

The wizened old man stepped up to Nestor, extended a hand, and said:

"Hullo, hullo. How's it going with you now? If I remember right, you got converted. God's greetings!"

Nestor shook his friend's hand. "How's yourself? I got out of this religion thing. You've got a big crowd in that house of yours."

"So you gave up your belief at a time like this. Well, it takes all kinds..."

The soldiers gazed at the man carrying the pack. Icicles hung from Nestor's mustache, and his eyebrows were frosted over. Nestor skied into the yard, came to a stop before the sergeant, and said:

"You look to be about my age. How far into the fifties are you?"

"Halfway through."

"My eye is still pretty sharp. I figured you for that on first sight. I'm dragging through my fifty-fifth. Where do the big bosses hole up?"

"The battalion commander is lodged in the house next door. Our company commander is in this man's house." The sergeant pointed to the man Nestor knew.

"So the high muckamuck is staying next door. You're pretty well up there in rank yourself. Men wearing your stripes used to curse me out twenty years ago. I might have to start calling you sergeant if they take me into this war business. Otherwise I won't. Where do these men come from, the ones who are gawking at me?"

"From Tampere," said the sergeant. "Damn it to hell, it's cold. Let's go inside, men."

By now the group that had come out to see Nestor had grown to dozens of men, and the snow in the yard crunched continually under the feet of new arrivals. Nestor looked around at the men.

"Not a single face I know. Does every man jack of you come from Tampere?"

Each soldier seemed to be waiting for the next man to answer. Some were stamping their feet while others were slapping their crossed arms against their chests.

"Most of us are from Tampere," one of them finally said.

"Well, not all of you are old lummoxes. You look pretty young yourself," said Nestor, addressing the speaker. "You could almost be my son."

The soldiers traded glances. Some of them were beginning to smile.

"I was in Tampere once myself, sighting at smokestacks along a rifle barrel. It was during the civil war. They made me a soldier in that war of liberation."

Some of the men looked at Nestor with interest. Others scowled.

"But hell, my shoulders are getting kind of cold. You say the big boss of this logging job is in that house next door?"

"The top war lord is making his home there," said Nestor's friend.

"Then I'll go and settle this business right now. I'll just hoist my skis against this wall where they'll be out of the way."

"I'll go and show you the way," said Nestor's friend.

Vehicles were standing near the house next door, and men were moving around its yard as Nestor approached. Inside, the main room was packed with soldiers. They were sitting on benches, and sleeping on the floor. A few men's stockinged feet could be seen protruding from on top of the huge brick baking oven. Some of the men were eating.

"Follow me."

Nestor pushed through the room in the wake of his friend, who opened a bedroom door and shoved Nestor through it. Three men were standing at a table. They raised their eyes from a map spread out on it.

"Hullo..."

The youngest man at the table scowled. First he looked inquiringly at the oldest in the group and then he glanced toward Nestor.

"What's on your mind?"

"Well, there's a little something, if you have the time to listen."

The youngest man stepped up to Nestor, sized him up, and said:

"Well at least take your hat off."

"I guess I can. It's warm enough in here without it."

Fumbling, Nestor took his hat into his hand.

"I'm looking for a logging job. They told me out there that this is sort of the bosses' hangout. Is an old man like me good enough for this business?"

"What kind of joke is this? This is not..."

"You can stop that, Vilenius."

"Yes, captain, sir."

Nestor judged the captain, who had taken a step toward him, to be in his thirties or forties. His eyelids were red. He hasn't been getting much sleep, thought Nestor. Loggers' eyes are like that when they have to stay awake long hours on a drive. The captain spoke:

"Judging by your dialect, you're from this area."

"My home cottage is a six-hour ski trip from here."

"I don't know the area and I don't know the dialect. I gather from what you said that you want to get into the service."

"That's what I'm saying. Don't you need men to carry a gun now?"

"We're glad to have them. Have you had any training?"

"Me? Hell yes. Why else would I barge in here?"

Nestor dropped his hat and mittens to the floor and groped inside his blouse with one large fist.

"Where the heck did I put that thing? I remember I stuck it in here when I left. I can't seem to get my fingers on it. Could it be in my other breast pocket? Lemme feel. Of course, here it is. If the captain wants to, he can take a look at it. Here..."

The captain took the crumpled service record and leafed through its pages.

"The brats, I mean my heirs, have been scribbling on it with a pencil, but a man with your young eyes should be able to make it out."

"No problem."

An expression of interest spread over the captain's face. From time to time he looked up at Nestor, then went back to the papers.

"You had machine-gun training in the war of liberation?"

"Yah, that's what they taught me. But they called that lead-spitter a Gatling gun in those days."

"An unusual coincidence that my uncle was your battalion commander."

"Your uncle. Well that is...So Medlund was your uncle?"

The young second lieutenant and the first lieutenant, who were standing at the table, exchanged significant glances. The second lieutenant coughed.

"He really is my uncle," the captain said.

"Medlund must be top brass if he's still alive."

"He's a colonel now."

Nestor stood with the papers in his hand. The captain moved over to the window. He looked up at the sky through the melted patches on the panes.

"Well, how about it. Will I get into this war logging business?"

"As a way of getting replacements, this is a little unusual. But these are unusual circumstances. So that..."

"Nothing is the way it used to be."

"You interrupted me. Are you used to handling horses?"

"Why hell yes. I've hauled logs for ages. They took my own lop-ears into the army. He's a little bad-tempered. But my old Laukki, who was killed by a bear some years ago, now there was a log-hauler's buddy. If the captain could have seen..."

"We have to cut this short. We're in a hurry. You'll be a driver in the supply company. You'll report..."

"Hell no! I didn't come here to drive boneheads. I want to get a gun into my hands and head for the front. Be a driver! No, my good man, I could have done that without a war."

"Doesn't Malkanen know that in the army, it's the superior who gives orders?"

"Oh, you infantrymen—your captain uncle too—you're good at giving orders. But I'm turning down this horseman business. And my name isn't Malkanen, it's Malinen."

The captain was close to laughter. He turned to the table and said:

"Lieutenant Salminen."

"Captain, sir."

"Add Private Malinen to your company roster."

The captain turned to Nestor Malinen again.

"Do you know the wilderness to the east?"

"Well if I don't know it, who does? I come from this corner of the backwoods. I know Alasalmi like I know the palm of my hand. I know it sounds like bragging, but I'm not a man who gets turned around in the woods."

"The matter is settled then."

The captain went back to the table and the lieutenant in turn took his place before Nestor.

"You've just heard that my name is Salminen. You now belong in my company. You will go at once to the next house and report to Sergeant Tulimaa. Show him your records and tell him you've come at my orders. Is this clear?"

"Well, my brain hasn't stopped working up to now."

"Good. We'll see you soon then."

"Is that the same stupid sergeant that was going to shoot me awhile ago? That's a damn dumb trick — not to recognize a man who comes from here. Well, I guess I'll take off now."

The officers looked at one another. Nestor bent over to pick up his cap and mittens. Then he shoved his way out to the door.

"Now there's a reservist for you."

The captain scowled at the second lieutenant.

"He's an old man already, but he might make a good guide on patrols."

"We might have trouble teaching grandpa military courtesy," said the second lieutenant.

"There's no time for that in a war. Let's get on with planning the patrol route. We stopped at the west end of Piispa Lake a while ago," said the captain. The point of his pencil touched down on the end of a line being drawn eastward on a map. "Cross over here after dark."

4

The shore of the lake looked as if the Creator's shovel had left it unfinished. A steep bank rose to a crest about two fathoms from the water's edge. From there it sloped down to a woods further back. One could imagine that the Great Shovel Wielder had neglected to level off the mounds of earth left from digging one side of the lake.

Just in back of the crest, a man lay on a bed of fir boughs. He could lie in his natural shelter in perfect safety as long as he had the patience to keep his head down. As he stared out over the lake, he wondered if the Creator had prepared this ridge just for these times. Off to one side could be heard the cracking of rifles. An occasional artillery shell exploded on the left in the direction of a highway.

Was something moving on the other side of that bay? The man pressed his cheek into the cold stock of his rifle. A small sideways hitch of his shoulders set the bead of the sight directly on the suspicious discoloration. Someone *was* moving out there. Now he was crawling toward a spruce tree that grew on the very edge of the lake.

"Now, buddy, you just made a stupid move."

The man holding the rifle uttered the words without conscious thought. He lined up the bead in the notch of the rear sight. One had to aim a little high. That should be it. He had dropped many a winter-feeding wood grouse at this range. An index finger encased in a woolen glove squeezed the trigger and he felt a jolt against his shoulder. His ears rang. The figure crawling on the opposite shore bounced up onto its knees and toppled over backwards. A gray felt boot was left jutting up from the snow.

"I told you it wasn't healthy to crawl around like that."

Immediately following these words, the man turned swiftly to look over his shoulder. His ears had caught the sound of boot soles on the snow.

"You've found yourself a fine breastwork, Mutka."

Simo Mutka's lips stretched into a fleeting grin as he said to the man who came up to him in a low crouch:

"I'd say it hides my whole body."

"That man on the other shore didn't stay under cover," said

the tall man, lying down next to Mutka on the boughs.

"Did you see me knock him off?"

"I was watching from behind when you killed him. Will you have a cigarette?"

"Thanks a lot. I will."

Simo Mutka turned over on one side. He stuffed the cigarette into a holder with his grubby fingers, took a few deep drags, and said:

"A smoke is the main thing, but it would be nice to have some food now."

"We should be able to eat when it gets dark at the latest. The mess kitchen has been steaming away down in that hollow. The cook doesn't exactly like to move around during the day."

"And in the evening there's a bright moon. Can't they get some fresh men in here soon? It would be easy to fall asleep on these fir boughs and freeze to death."

"We'll get replacements soon," said the man beside him. He wore the bar of a second lieutenant.

"Who are they supposed to replace? There are mighty few cutters out on this logging job."

"That's true enough. A whole regiment is supposed to be coming. But they're taking a long time."

"Why should they hurry out into this cold and these bullet storms? The devil only knows where they are — maybe they stopped in town to do some drinking."

There was a scowl on Simo Mutka's face. Smoke seeped out from his flat nose and his protruding upper lip.

"They're doing their best. I mean, it takes time to move an outfit a long distance and..."

"Is that another devil raising his head like a worm out of the earth?"

Simo Mutka's rifle flew up to his cheek. He steadied it for a second and fired. When he spoke, his face was expressionless.

"Do you believe I can still drop a wood grouse at 200 yards?"

"I don't doubt it. As they say around here, you're a real gunner. That snooper had bad luck."

The broad expanse of the lake gleamed in the midday sun. Shadows from the opposite shore stretched out over its snow cover. Chattering bursts of machine-gun fire could be heard. Artillery shells exploded near a schoolhouse.

A chickadee fluttered from tree to tree and both men's eyes followed its movements. Simo Mutka rolled his cigarette to the other corner of his mouth with his tongue. Staring out over the lake, he said:

"Tell me, Mäkinen, why do such stupid things happen in the world?"

"Do you mean this whole war?"

"I was thinking mostly about shooting those men. One bullet and a man is dead. Doesn't that bolshie's boot sticking up there give you the willies?"

"It does, when I think of total strangers killing one another. I mean, you and that man out there. You never did any harm to each other."

"You know what's odd — you didn't know anything about me before I came into the reserves?"

"Not much," said Lieutenant Mäkinen.

"I was a thorn in the neck of the authorities in my home parish. I did this and that with a rifle that you weren't supposed to. Not so long ago, the sheriff searched my house. He was looking for elk meat."

"Was it Pulkkila who was after you? Did he find any?"

"It was Pulkkila and he didn't find any."

"But there would have been some to find?"

"A little bit. Half an elk carcass in a cave in the snow."

"Shot without a permit?"

"Now why in the devil should there be permits for something like that? Why should anyone have to ask for them?"

"If the sheriff had found it, it would have meant jail for you."

"I know. I would have wound up in a cell. Pulkkila is a good old boy, but even a sheriff can't do anything about the law. Yet just now I blew the life out of two human beings, and I don't think you're aiming to arrest me."

A twinkle appeared in Kosti Mäkinen's weary eyes and the shadow of a smile crossed his lips. He peered out over the snowy crest of the ridge and said:

"The ways of the world aren't always consistent."

"I don't understand those fancy words, but I tell you right now, I'll never take a cross or medal for killing a human being."

The discussion was cut short. The men pricked up their ears as a rumbling began in the wooded hill across the lake. Shells whooshed through the air. Both men huddled down.

"They're landing far behind us," said the lieutenant.

"The supply company must be getting clobbered."

"They're still bursting back there. As long as they don't blow up the kitchen."

"Now they've turned their barrels. They're pasting the school again. I don't like those guns at all. They give me the willies," said Simo Mutka.

"They've got such a damned good location up on Haapo Hill."

"And plenty of pieces to fire with. We have only a few mortars. Why doesn't Aapo answer him back?"

The lieutenant glanced at his watch.

"We're short of rounds. I talked to the major a couple of hours ago. He said we're waiting for more."

"What the devil is that rig starting out across the sound?"

"There's more than one. Here comes a second, and a third. It's pure hell that we can do nothing against them."

"Here they come, like loads of logs. They're lumbering toward that schoolhouse again. And there's a bunch of *Vanyas* waddling along behind them."

"I have to go and see what those machines are up to. And we at least have to throw a scare into those men duck-walking along behind them. Keep your eyes open, in case they try to fan out on this side. Our lines are spread thin."

Kosti Mäkinen ran crouching toward a bridge which marked one end of his platoon's sector of the lines. The tanks were already growling halfway across the sound. Simo Mutka clamped his teeth down on the cigarette holder in the corner of his mouth. From his position, he had a side view of the men plodding after the tanks. He drew back the bolt of his rifle with the crook of his forefinger. There was a click followed by a bang. A man behind one of the tanks tumbled into the snow.

Simo heard the chatter of a machine gun start up on his right. But the iron boxcars kept pressing on toward the shore. Now they had reached the western bank. Hard-eyed, Mutka watched them roll onto the land. The last of the Russians ducking behind them sank to the snow. Would the tanks turn his way? That would start a mean game of tag. No, they weren't coming. They were after the schoolhouse again.

Simo's tension eased. His wife and child came into his mind again. How was Lassi getting along? The poor kid couldn't even walk without help.

"What the hell business did they have to come here?"

Simo Mutka's voice shook. Although he kept a constant watch toward the left, where he could hear the racket of the tanks, he kept glancing around near him as well. He tried to listen too. There was neither sight nor sound of the little bird.

"I knew it. Even a chickadee is scared off by this racket."

✧ ✧ ✧

The lieutenant ran in the shelter of a natural gully. He drew a big Mauser from its holster. The man in the position next to Mutka's was huddled down in his hole.

"Lieutenant, Lieutenant! The tanks have crossed over again. There's nothing we can do. They're awful. They give me the shakes."

"Riekki! Just stay in your position. They won't come here."

The man's eyes were round and staring and the rifle in his hand was shaking.

"What if they circle around and come up behind us?"

"They won't come along the shore. They've done the same thing many times before — yesterday too. They just circle the school and go back."

"But they killed so many men. There's nothing a man can do if..."

"Just stay where you are. They won't come to kill just one man."

Kosti Mäkinen could feel his heart pounding. Rage and a sense of helplessness made him grit his teeth. He left the scared soldier and ran along the shore. Sergeant Bert Sääskilampi's squad sector extended to one end of the bridge ahead. A machine gun opened fire from across the sound, its stream of bullets kicking up founts of snow. Kosti Mäkinen threw himself down. He could hear the bullets pinging through the shore growth. Then the volley moved on. Kosti began running again, and came on a corporal firing toward the bridge from behind the crest of the slope.

"Which way is Bert?"

"He went running toward where the tanks rolled ashore."

During the preceding days, the snow had been trampled into a smooth surface. Mäkinen ran in the direction indicated by the corporal. Broad, thick willow copses grew close along the roadway. It was there he found his wife's brother, crouching in a fold of ground behind the willows, looking toward the bridge. There was a soldier beside him.

"They're back at it again," said Bert.

"How the devil can we fight tanks with our bare hands," raged Janne Latvasuo. "It's such a damned dirty trick. They come here just to taunt us."

"Don't they think the school is enough of a wreck already?"

"They don't seem short of men, anyway," said Bert, looking at the black bundles sprawled on the bridge embankment.

"You might think that some day they'd get the idea that bullets let the air out of men," said Private Latvasuo, a peace-time keeper of reindeer in Järvenkylä.

Their eyes thin slits, Kosti Mäkinen and his men stared toward the hamlet. The tanks ground past his men's positions — were actually in back of them.

"But they don't let the air out of tanks," he said. "I mean, they just play merry-go-round at that school."

"What a fix we're in! Trying to fight a war without weapons."

Bert jerked out the words. He could see men run crouching around the buildings that were still unburned and could hear shouted commands. Two men broke from the shelter of the buildings and ran toward the woods. At almost the same instant, they both pitched headlong into the snow.

"You'll see a lot of them running when they panic," said Bert.

"Last fall I still didn't believe that it would come to this. I didn't believe...Oh hell! Mäkinen, can't even you get us some bigger guns here?" Janne Latvasuo's voice was hoarse.

"They come in a slow trickle....The tanks are leaving now, one after another, like buggies on their way from Easter service."

Janne Latvasuo leaped to his feet.

"I'll see if they're such hard-headed bulls that nothing will work against them."

"Don't be a fool! You can't do a thing with a rifle."

The lieutenant's cry had no effect. The man dashed into the dark mouth of a culvert under the road and disappeared from sight.

"Janne's going crazy," said Bert.

"Watch out. They're shooting in every direction like mad," said Mäkinen.

Their tracks clanking and turrets revolving, the tanks returned the way they had come. Puffs of snow danced up on all sides. Fragments of frozen earth flew through the air. Lieutenant Mäkinen, Sergeant Sääskilampi, and a few soldiers crouched behind a huge boulder. They kept circling it to the side opposite the tanks as the vehicles moved toward the shore.

"Now they're going over the culvert," said Kosti.

At that instant a shell burst against the side of a crag nearby. One of the soldiers cried out and dropped to the snow. The rest huddled closer to each other. The motors pounded. There was a wild shout.

"So there's no way to deal with you, you bastards! Well at least this devil..."

The bursts of machine-gun fire from across the sound were a constant danger to Kosti Mäkinen. He dragged himself over the snow alongside the boulder to where he could see the culvert. He saw a man dart out of its square opening and climb up onto the last tank.

Rage burned in Janne Latvasuo's mind. He felt no fear. He was a man in whom action blotted out the instinct for self-preservation. Once he had even clubbed a bear with a wooden pole. Prodded out of his den in the springtime, the animal had charged out into a group of men. His friends had had to shoot the beast as it hugged him. The same wild feeling gripped him now. He forgot everything around him and suddenly found himself rampaging on the bobbing metal hood of the tank. His feet kept slipping.

"I have to hit it there. If I bend that, it won't be able to shoot. There! There!"

Gritting his teeth, the man hammered with his rifle at the gun barrel protruding from the turret. The turret kept revolving and the gun revolved along with it. The gun barrel quivered with each shot fired from it. The man on top of the tank kept leaping like a log driver on a breaking log-jam. The rifle stock splintered under his blows.

"Goddamn! If I only had an ax."

Janne Latvasuo flailed at the gun with the barrel of his rifle. Then that too slipped from his frozen mittens.

"I'm going to finish this! Goddamned if I'll stop!"

His voice shook with helpless rage. He threw himself at the gun barrel with his bare hands, wrenching it upwards, struggling as if he were prying a heavy log out of the snow. The turret revolved and the gun barrel shook with every shot fired. Janne Latvasuo hung from the revolving turret, shouting and cursing.

Something heavy struck his back and then his shoulders. The light was failing. For a short time, his hands clung to the gun barrel and then everything went black. He slid down in front of the moving tank and one of the tracks passed over his body. Underneath was a sheet of ice. Blood poured from his mouth and nostrils. Janne Latvasuo felt no pain. In a few seconds a crushed bundle of rags came into view from underneath the tank. The road surface at that point was higher in the middle. The men behind the rock saw a red stain spreading toward their side of the road. Kosti Mäkinen drew back behind the rock. He saw Bert cover his face with his hands. He knew that Janne Latvasuo was dead. His Järvenkylä reindeer grazing grounds were left without a herdmaster. Perhaps they too would soon be lost.

"Is this why Janne made them release him from the hospital early?"

said Bert.

By now the tanks were clanking far off. They teetered up the steep bank of the opposite shore. A barrage of mortar and artillery shells began to rain down from Haapo Ridge. The shells battered the remains of the bridge at either end.

"If we don't get help soon, we'll have to leave," said one of the soldiers.

"Over my dead body," said Bert Sääskilampi to the men lying beside him in a shell hole.

Only when the evening moon rose did the barrage let up. Kosti and Bert crawled out closer to the bridge approach.

"You stay here," said Bert. "I'll go and drag in Janne's body."

Bert crawled on his belly to the roadside. He could just reach one of the legs sticking out toward him. He began to pull, but staggered back and rolled down the shoulder of the road. In his hand was a leg that had torn loose at Janne's thigh. For a long time, Bert lay there, pressing his face into his hands. Then he said:

"This has to be a nightmare."

"No, it isn't. Let's try it together," said the lieutenant.

Together they crawled up the bank. The crushed heap of clothing was already frozen to the road, but with great effort the two men worked it loose. Soon two crouching black shadows reached the shelter of the willow copse carrying a frozen mass in their arms. They laid the remains of Janne Latvasuo at the base of a big rock.

"How will the Latvasuos manage now?" said Bert.

Kosti Mäkinen was silent for a long time. Finally he turned and said:

"Things seem to have quieted down. I'll go and see about food for the men."

CHAPTER III

1

For the elder Sääskilampis the days as evacuees passed slowly. Ivar, especially, seemed to be in a torpor, while his wife sat clicking her knitting needles the livelong day. Her heart ached as she watched the woman of the house going about her chores in the kitchen.

The main room of their evacuee home was much smaller than the one at Sääskilampi. The walls were of fiberboard and the ceiling beams were boxed in with veneer paneling. Here there was no smell of drying reindeer hides. Even the wall clock ticked away the hours with a different sound from the one at home.

One day as the adults sat in the main room, there was a sudden thumping out on the porch. The door opened slowly and three young boys stood there.

"Grandpa, grandpa, isn't it true that we have lots of reindeer?" shouted Ilmari.

Their feet thumping the floorboards, Ivar Sääskilampi's grandsons, Ilmari and Pentti, dashed across the room and wedged themselves between their grandfather's knees. The son of their hostess, a boy about their age, remained standing further off. The cheeks of all three were red. Ivar Sääskilampi wrapped his arms around the boys.

"We do have a few. Why do you ask?" he said.

"'Cause Veikko won't believe us. He says only Lapps have reindeer. So there too! Now do you believe it?"

"Is that what you were arguing about?"

"And Veikko says there isn't a war," lisped Pentti, the younger of the two.

Irja Mäkinen came in from the kitchen. She wore a loose dress over her swollen middle. Lately her cheeks had become hollow.

She smiled when she saw her boys.

"There wasn't a war when we left," she said.

"We could hear the war. It was thundering at Suomussalmi," said Pentti, stumbling over the words.

"You mustn't argue about such things, children. May God grant the sounds of war don't reach this far," said Petti

Sääskilampi. She dropped her knitting into her lap and said, "Come here Pentti, and Grandma will take off your coat."

Of the family that owned the house, only the young daughter-in-law and her son lived there, along with the old master of the place, bed-ridden after a stroke. The woman came in from the kitchen and took off her son's outerwear.

"You must get along with each other, children. Ilmari and Pentti's father is at the front like your father. You mustn't argue over nothing."

"But my father has braid on his shoulders," said the son of the house.

"But our father has bright buttons on his collar," said Ilmari.

"Braid is better than buttons, isn't it Mommy. Daddy had many buttons on his coat too. They had a lion's picture on them, didn't they Mommy?"

The mistress of the house too was close to laughing. Looking at Irja, she said: "What should we tell these scamps, Irja?"

"I don't know. The rascals seem to know all the answers."

"Let's play together, children. It's warm in the house. Where are the reindeer I whittled from kindling wood yesterday?" asked Ivar Sääskilampi.

"Yea, let's get those reindeer!" shouted the boy of the house.

Ivar Sääskilampi rose and tapped out the dregs from his pipe on the hearth. It was an action he had performed thousands of times at home, and it brought the main room there to his mind. Sighing heavily, he returned to his chair, refilled his pipe, relighted it and said:

"I wonder if they've been forced to drive the cattle away from Vaarakylä?"

"We don't know," said Irja with a sigh.

"The poor cows will be numb with cold, and their milk bags will freeze," said Petti.

No one said anything for a time. Then, staring at the floor, Sääskilampi spoke:

"It was stupid to leave the work at home to a hired hand."

"You couldn't have done it. Just calm down and rest," said his daughter.

"How can I rest here? I'm always thinking of our home and the countryside."

"We have a good hired hand. He'll take care of the animals

and the house," said his wife.

"I don't know. Can he even hitch up a horse?"

"There must be men around who can do that," said Irja.

"There's no reason to worry," said the young lady of the house, heading for the kitchen. "Why don't you go and talk to grandpa in the bedroom. You two must have something left to talk about."

"Maybe I'll go out and take a little walk."

"Don't go. It's so hard for you to breathe in this cold," said his wife.

"I'll just go and look around. It will make the time pass more quickly."

Ivar Sääskilampi began to dress for the walk. It was slow work getting into his woolen overcoat and it made him pant for breath.

"Remember now, you're not strong enough to walk long distances. Ilmari could go along with you," said his wife.

"I'll be OK. Let the kids play indoors."

✧ ✧ ✧

"This town of Ii Hamina hasn't changed," mused Ivar Sääskilampi as he walked down its winding lanes. "There's the house I've thought about so many times during the past twenty years. Just as it was then — the only change is the wood siding nailed over the logs. We used to go in through that porch door." The erratic heartbeat of the old man quickened. The door to Hilkka's bedroom was on the left side of the porch. From that same bedroom window, one could see the swiftly flowing Ii River. He'd had to slip out of that window the night Hilkka's father had knocked at the door. The old man had been furious, and had threatened to shoot through the door.

The snow crunched under the old man's slow footsteps. There had been a café in the main room of the house where the men who sorted the logs after the drive hung out on Sundays. They had served the whiskey neat there.

"I keep thinking about it."

Startled, Ivar Sääskilampi looked around, but calmed down when he saw there was no one to hear the words that had escaped him. Ear flaps covered his ears. Mittens of dog fur kept his hands warm, although there was little blood left to flow in his veins these days. The pulled-up legs of his Lapland boots kept the cold wind from his legs. Mainly women and children walked the main street of the town. Another old evacuee was out looking at the houses along the winding lane.

Ivar Sääskilampi walked to the lower end of the town. There the houses were sparser. He crossed to the far side of the plowed road, stopped, and gazed at the snow-covered channel of the river that lay below. The Ii was a broad river here toward its mouth. This was where they used to sail in the summer. The sorting area was quite a bit further down. Ivar Sääskilampi turned toward the left. There he could see the smokestack of the old Kestilä sawmill. It was still standing, although the mill was said to have been abandoned.

The same water, which at this point showed a dark, melted patch, flowed past his home village of Vaarakylä. It flowed under the Naavala Bridge on its way west, sucking in many a tributary along its course. Old tar-boat men used to say that it stretched some 300 kilometers in length from Vaarakylä to this place. At Vaarakylä, people rowed boats on this same water, and in the winter, it was crossed by roads with stakes to mark them. Residents rinsed their clothes in it during the summer and young people dunked themselves in it when it was hot. Was it two summers ago that he and that hussy from Viipuri...?

Until now, a kind of numbness had dulled his thoughts, but suddenly he was fiercely homesick. He saw his home area in his mind. On cold days, pillars of smoke rose up from people's homes and the well sweep pointed at the blue sky. Reindeer trotted on the ice and dug at the rye fields. The smoke rising behind the eastern woods was a handsome sight...Here the man's thoughts stopped short and his heart ached. Now there was another kind of smoke over those same hills. It had already been widespread when the evacuees were leaving, like the smoke from forest fires burning across the border in Russia on warm summer days. The homes of the backwoods dwellers were burning, sometimes whole villages. Their own countrymen had set fire to them. They were determined to leave the Russians no place to get warm, so the soldiers coming from Alasalmi had said.

His thoughts came back to the present. It was thirty years ago that he had walked these same paths. He had been light of foot then, not missing a step in even the liveliest of polkas.

"Agh...a man can't stop thinking."

A glance around calmed him down. He went on talking to himself.

"Will I make it a bit further? We used to drown our sorrows in that grove near the Kestilä sawmill. I'll try to walk at least that far."

He kept on walking. Slowly. He was breathing hard.

"There's the church now," he said. He could see the sun tinting its roof and steeple red.

"It's an old building. That's what they said that summer. Russian marauders were supposed to have burned the old church here ages ago. I didn't even think of going inside it when I was young. I wonder what it's like. I once spent a jolly Sunday out in back of that church. The woman was from Oulu. We went back there. The bugs bothered us a lot because we didn't have too much on."

The man paused in his slow progress and looked back.

"I must have been talking to myself. Was it Käyrä's reindeer brand that was open at the left with a notch at the bottom? Has Bert come back yet from skiing after the reindeer? We have to start haying soon."

Everything danced crazily around him. The frozen woods seemed now atilt and now horizontal. That church looks strange...standing on its steeple in the snow. Now the steeple had spun upright again. His dog-fur mittens clutched at his chest.

"How did my mind get so confused? It slipped a cog just now at the card game in the woods. My step keeps getting shorter. I'll keep on going. Easy now, easy."

The old man went on at a stalking gait. His heart had nearly stopped, but nothing could be done about that. The years rolled back, flickering like a sun reflected in the water. The house he had passed shortly after leaving their lodging forced itself into his mind. It was his second summer as a log sorter at the mouth of the Ii river.

✧ ✧ ✧

"Are you getting into the card game?" asked his buddy.

It was Saturday evening. They were shaving on the river bank near the boarding house. Logs floated by them on the Ii River. Their shift at the sorting place didn't come until Monday.

"Maybe I'll look around in Hamina," said Ivar Sääskilampi.

"But shouldn't we go to the sauna now?"

"Let's go, but when you've had enough of the other, come to our usual stamping-grounds," said Mikkos-Vertti with a broad grin.

"When I've had enough of what?"

"Don't try to pull the wool over a buddy's eyes. I think your latest partner's name is Hilkka."

"I get enough of card-playing at home," laughed Ivar.

"They tell me the girls of Ii don't spend much time at the sewing circle when you're in town," said Vertti. "But listen, we've still got over a half of that straw boss's jug in a hole back there."

"Well, if you feel like drinking, start pouring. And even if it hasn't been announced in church, I may show up at your game. Let's go to the sauna now and take a few dips in the river. After all, it's water from home."

✧ ✧ ✧

Ivar Sääskilampi, a thirty-year-old landowner's son from the uplands, went marching along the road from the river mouth to Ii Hamina. Patent leather shoes gleamed on his feet and sharply pressed trousers swung along at a fast clip. The knot in his tie was a slight hindrance to his breathing. It was a summer Saturday evening, drawing on toward fall. The reddish afterglow of the sunset still lingered in the sky. His nose caught the scent of drying hay, and the barley in the fields was turning yellow.

A minor but troubling thought flashed into the mind of the man striding so briskly along. Haying must still be going on at Sääskilampi. The grain harvest would soon be upon them. The farm work suffered in his absence. Well, the old man had money. Let him hire help. The log-sorting job would be over by autumn. Then it would be nice to follow the reindeer back at home. To romp around there the whole winter. Then go back to the coast in the spring.

There stood the cluster of houses at Ii, sometimes known as Hamina. A young couple came toward him, walking arm in arm. The girl couldn't help glancing aside. Her eyes followed him, the upland man, walking by. Ivar's chest swelled. Ahah! Her escort jerked angrily at the girl's elbow. Ivar chuckled. Out of pure deviltry, he should turn back and tell the Hamina man to let go of that girl's arm.

But let him keep his catch. Hilkka was sure to be waiting for him by now. Last Sunday he had been romping with a girl who lived near the station. And on Saturday, a jug had muddled up the night's doings. But it was healthy for girls to watch and wait sometimes. Otherwise they got too conceited. Hilkka too.

The narrow lanes of the village turned the faint twilight into half darkness. He stopped before an outside door. This was where Hilkka would be waiting in the bedroom. As long as he didn't run into the old man on the porch. He could be pretty ugly when he started sounding off. It was good that he and Hilkka had arranged to leave the door unlocked.

The slender upland man glanced around him. No one was in sight. He grasped the door handle. What the hell! For a moment he stood dumfounded, and then he pulled harder. Was she offended at his staying away last Sunday? Maybe she was waiting on the porch. She might be listening to hear if it was the right man coming. He ought to say something so that she would not wait in vain.

"Hilkka!"

After whispering, he moved to the side of the door. From there he could slip in quickly. There was silence, except for the pounding of his heart. What was she waiting for?

"Hilkka! It's Ivo here. Just open the bolt!"

Not a sound. What was this? A cat came creeping around the corner, tail in the air, seeming to walk on tiptoe. It rubbed against his legs and began to purr.

"Get the hell out of here!"

He sent the yowling cat sailing through the air. The noise it made scared him so much that he darted around the corner and stood there waiting for the sound of the door being opened. It did not come. All he heard was the crunching of sand under someone's feet.

Ivar Sääskilampi shrank back against the wall into the shadows as a woman went mincing by. Heart pounding, he stood there waiting for Hilkka to open the door. Something was wrong. Before this, she had waited eagerly for him.

Early that spring, Ivar had succeeded in taking her home from a dance. From then on, they had spent their weekends together. There had been other girls — just to keep his hand in — maybe a half-dozen during the summer. But Hilkka was the best. He had been after only one thing with the others.

Now his heart was pounding with apprehension and disappointment. Had she just gone coolly off to sleep? Hardly — she was quick to take offense. He'd seen that during the summer when he'd met her one Sunday evening with another girl on his arm. He'd had to spend a long time pacifying her over a little thing like that. This must be a fit of petulance. What if he were just to let her sulk? To go after other game? There was Anni, who lived near the station, and Helmi at Yli-Ii.

He turned toward the lanes of the village but his heart was bitter. Good God — couldn't a person wait any longer than that without acting up? She could very well have been standing behind the door grinning at his behavior. No, damn it! I'm not leaving like a scared puppy with its tail between its legs. I'll go around that corner to her window. When she opens it, I'll tell her to kiss off. Might even raise my hat to her. It's a dandified gesture, but I'll show her I can use it too. Hilkka might even come trotting after me, but let her, this time.

He moved along the wall, ducking below the window so as not to show himself. Standing beside the window, he reached over and tapped the pane. There was a rustling on the bed inside. It hadn't taken much to rouse her. She'd probably been lying awake, waiting for him.The window would soon open, the same one he had slipped through when Hilkka's old man had been raising a ruckus at the door.

She was taking a long time. Did she think it was someone else tapping at the window? I'll tap again. Not too hard, just a light rap with my knuckles. Now the bed was creaking. The window would soon open. Was his hat on right? He would check it. Just as it should be — tilted to one side. He would raise it to her, say good morning, and then turn and amble off around the corner with his head held high.

Why was she dawdling?

Inside there was silence. For a third time he tapped on the window pane. What the devil had gotten into her? I have to show her my face, he decided. Young Master Sääskilampi moved over to the window. There was a high stone foundation under this part of the building. His face reached only to the lowest pane.

"Hilkka!"

The room was dark, but from inside she should be able to see him against the lighter background of the sky. Hell...nothing.

Ivar drummed on the glass.

"Hey, Hilkka!" he said.

Someone turned over suddenly in the bed.

"What goddamned fool is making all that noise at this hour of the night? He's got a hat like a scarecrow's and he sounds like a woodpecker on a dry tree. Goddalmighty, where's my belt and knife?"

It was a harsh male voice and he could hear the words clearly.

"Don't go out there with a knife. Let's just keep still."

He could hear Hilkka's panicky whisper through the window. Ivar Sääskilampi crept along the wall. His heart seemed to be splitting in his breast. God help him. Blood roared in his ears. In a rage, he bent down, grasped a piece of stone sticking out of the foundation, and jerked at it, but the stone would not budge. Its sharp edge cut a deep gash in the palm of his hand. He gnashed his teeth. Forget it, there were big enough stones elsewhere.

He scanned the surroundings feverishly, but saw nothing he could throw into the room. Then his brain began to function again. Forget it. Keep your prize, but remember, I was here first. I know that woman through and through. I've done just about everything with her. Go ahead and plow the furrow I opened. Ivar laughed bitterly.

✧ ✧ ✧

Ivar Sääskilampi turned and walked away, like a person in a bad dream. Gritting his teeth, he kicked at a stone the size of two fists and cried out in pain. His big toe felt as if it had been put out of joint. He went straight to the room where he was staying with his friend. Mikkos-Vertti's bed was empty.

"Agh, I'm not going to cry over a whore. Where's that flask?"

Ivar fumbled at the back of a dark closet and felt the cold, flat surface of a metal flask. It was full. He tilted his head back and gulped the liquor down.

"Agh!"

The cork squeaked at intervals as he closed and then opened it again. On a nail hung the leather belt which he wore at work. Ivar Sääskilampi took it down, opened its buckle and released the loop that held his knife and sheath. He shoved them into his pocket. They did not show from underneath his coat. Once more the flask tilted upward toward the ceiling.

"Ugh! That's enough poison for now. Let's go and see what kind of hero is sharing my bed partner."

✧ ✧ ✧

"Hey old man! Didn't you hear the horse coming? It almost climbed up your back."

Ivar Sääskilampi's thoughts had been wandering through times long gone. The angry shout jolted him back to the present. Frightened, he tried to move his legs faster. His single-soled Lapland boots slipped on the icy road and the old man fell to his knees.

"Whoa! Do you insist on being trampled, old man?"

As clumsily as a hibernating bear, Ivar Sääskilampi scrambled to the side of the road on his hands and knees. Snorting steam through its nostrils, the horse came to a stop, its hoofs almost grazing him. He felt a sharp twinge of pain in his chest. Clumsily he struggled to his feet.

"Didn't you hear the sleigh bells? And I yelled too."

"N-no. This fur cap was over my ears."

The horse, which was pulling a load of hay, danced nervously in place. A firm pressure on the check-rein drew the corners of is mouth upward. Its long hair was coated with frost. Only now did Ivar Sääskilampi realize that the person gripping the reins was a woman.

"Easy, Puhuri! Let's go now. I wonder what upland backwoods they dragged that old man from."

The rear of the well-packed load of hay was drawing away from him. The horse seemed eager to go on its own. The sleigh bells jingled and the sled runners slid from one side of the icy, plowed road to the other. The woman looked back, obviously wanting to see what kind of old coot her horse had nearly trampled. Her cheeks glowed red beneath her fur hat.

"Old man..."

The words slipped out from under his frozen mustache. He brushed the snow from his knees and coat with his fur mittens.

"Old man," he repeated aloud, and went on thinking: This is fate's mockery too. Why else had he been dragged to this very place, Ii Hamina, to escape the war? Thirty years turn a man into a sick and aging creature.

He went on walking beside the plowed bank. He had come a

long way. There was the tilled field, beyond which began the groves near the Kestilä sawmill. First a right-angle turn and then straight across the fields to the mill. He should really go back. But he would take a look; the place was familiar, and he was no longer breathing so heavily. The scare had probably been good for him. Now the turn. I know the place. I went by here in the early hours one August morning. Across the field, from that direction. My step was light then — liquor gave it an added lift.

✧ ✧ ✧

Dawn was just rising beyond the woods as the young man half-trotted along the road.

"That's a nice chunk of rock. It'll really smash the pane to pieces when I throw it."

Ivar Sääskilampi picked up the fist-sized stone from the road and dropped it into his pocket. Again he bent over.

"And here's another, in case the first misses. Now on to Hilkka's window and let fly."

He reached the corner of the house. His rapid breathing eased off, and his raging thoughts calmed down. No, it wouldn't do to go throwing rocks around wildly. Hilkka's new stud was bound to come out. He would have a good view of the man from the corner of this storage shed when he slipped out of the door or window. He sat in the shadow of the shed, took the stones from his pocket, and set them on the dewy grass like loon's eggs on a sandy shore. If I hit him in the rib cage with one of these, he thought, it's sure to knock him to his knees. Then I'll...agh...he patted his back pocket under his coat tails and felt the weapon there.

The sun had risen over the woods. It shone straight from the direction of his home parish. He could hear the rush of the Ii River in his ears.

"It was stupid to leave the flask behind."

His rising intoxication began to ebb. The black snake of jealousy burrowed deeper into his heart. Now he's having his farewell piece.

"If I could just get my hands on that boar...!"

Never before had Ivar Sääskilampi suffered such torment over a woman. Or over anything else, for that matter. He went on babbling to himself. It helped. He kept grinding his sound and healthy teeth against each other. From time to time he picked up one of the rocks and turned it over in his hand. If I hold it like this, I'll be damned if I don't catch that stud between the shoulder blades. When I was a kid, I had fun knocking off songbirds with rocks.

"I never would have believed that Hilkka...When I didn't come last Sunday, she must have had such an itch that she had to have a boar."

There was a slight thump in the room. The curtain at Hilkka's window was drawn aside. Ivar rose to his feet and took a couple of crouching steps. Now he was completely hidden by the storage shed and he could see the window through the notched ends of the logs. It was being opened cautiously. A woman's bare arm swung out along with the sash. The window creaked and the woman's hand held it motionless for a long time. The lips of the man watching drew into a sneer. Let it creak so damnably that the old man would hear it. But finally the window was pushed wide open. A thick, somewhat tousled mop of woman's hair came into view. A face turned and gazed for a long time in every direction. Then a male voice mumbled something and the head was drawn back inside. There was the sound of whispering and even a little giggle.

A man's leg was thrust out the window, and then another. Things grew darker before Ivar Sääskilampi's eyes, but he was still able to see that the man was wearing patent leather shoes and black breeches. Now his legs dangled side by side, a good two feet from the ground. His pants were stretched tight across the seat. Now, godalmighty, to lambaste him with a rock. But at that instant the man dropped to the grass and began straightening his coat. Once more he reached back to the window and took Hilkka's face in his hands. Now they were slobbering kisses on each other. By the eternal...!

"I'll come on Saturday," the man said.

"Be sure to come. I'll meet you at the station."

"I always keep my word. It was wonderful."

Turning, the man crept along the wall and came toward the storage shed, where Ivar was peering around the corner. There was a grin on his face, as if he knew of his rival's existence. A sheath knife dangled from the belt under his coat. He turned the corner, passed along the side of the building, and disappeared into the lanes of the town.

The last traces of Ivar Sääskilampi's intoxication disappeared. Though he had seen the dark-haired man's features for only a half-minute, he knew he would never forget them. The man had the looks of a prince in a story. For a long time, Ivar stood leaning against the wall before he turned and began walking toward the river mouth. He could not sleep for the rest of the night, nor for the whole of that day. All of Monday, he worked at the sorting like a sleepwalker. In the evening, he did what had been in his thoughts all that time.

✧ ✧ ✧

"You're putting on your Sunday duds. What's up?"

"I thought I'd go to town."

"You're not your old self," said Mikkos-Vertti as he watched Ivar dress.

Luck was with Ivar as he walked down the familiar main street. He saw Hilkka approaching from a distance. She came toward him with a smile on her face.

"Ivar! I haven't seen you for some time."

Hilkka stopped before him, spread out her arms in a feminine way, and said:

"I won't let you by until you tell me where you've been hiding these past two weekends."

Rage boiled up in him but he covered it by looking down at the ground. He swallowed the words that were already on his tongue.

"I've been working," he heard himself saying.

"And I've been waiting for you. I went to bed early last Saturday, I was so lonely. I thought you'd gone to cut those big barley fields."

"What the hell big barley fields? Who's been talking about that?"

"Now, now. Don't look so angry. You did yourself, remember? When you'd been drinking and I was sulking in my room."

"You believe a drunken man's talk? Where would a rover like me get barley or wheat fields? Would I be working here if I had any?"

"You're not telling the truth, but let's not talk about that. Where are you going, all dressed up on a weekday?"

"I'm looking for girls."

"You won't get anyone to go with you when you look so sour."

"Maybe there are some who are crazy enough...Well, I won't keep you any longer."

With these words, he walked by Hilkka, but his gait was slow and indecisive. She would probably soon panic, and call him to come back. If she didn't, he could still go to her room that night.

"You've gotten to be so high and mighty. I was feeling good because I thought you were coming to my room to talk to me."

Ivar stopped and stood there scraping at the sand with the toe of his shoe.

"I will, if you think I'm good enough for you."

"Why, what a strange thing to say. Besides, father's gone fishing for the whole night."

✧ ✧ ✧

If she didn't recognize me through the curtain the other night, she must have been as hot as a mating wood grouse, thought Ivar, as he lay in bed with Hilkka, looking out at the dark sky. It had been clear then, and his fellow cocksman had even been able to see his hat...A woman like Hilkka could twist and turn like a corkscrew when she wanted to.

"You just keep looking out the window and brooding. Why?"

"I wonder if winter is setting in around Savukoski—I mean, where I come from."

"Is that it? I thought it was something else."

"What could that be?"

"I don't know. Just now when you..."

"When I what...? Don't start crying now."

"Just now when you did it...it was as if you were somewhere else."

"What did I do?"

"You know...you took me so quickly and coldly."

"Say it was rape, and you can feel innocent."

"That's not what I mean. But you always used to hold me close so nicely. You stroked my hair and...This time you wanted it right away."

"So I did a bad job of warming you up. Then it's best that I leave."

"Don't tease me. Come and hold me close."

Spite struggled with a desire for possession within Ivar. He was tickled at the thought of having the first course of the dark man's meal next Saturday. But just one more, and then she could be a beggar's whore for all he cared.

He turned and drew the girl toward him. But his fondling was calculated, and it was dark enough in the room for him to smile openly in scorn.

"Now you're being sweet again. Ivar, if you're a man of your word, you don't have to hold back. You don't have to be careful...But don't, don't do that."

✧ ✧ ✧

The next day, Ivar Sääskilampi collected the wages due him and took a buggy to the station. He did not see Hilkka, nor did he want to. He simply boarded the train for Oulu at the Ii station and chugged along to that city. From there, a long chain of relay stations stretched to the uplands. For many days he rode the jolting freight wagons eastward. His father, Aatovi was pleased to have his son home in time to complete the harvest. On the dark autumn evenings, Hilkka's image kept coming back to his mind, bringing with it a feeling of apprehension and longing. He began to frequent drinking parties in a neighboring parish, sometimes staying over for more than one night. The memory of Hilkka began to fade, and during the winter weekends, another name began to etch itself on his heart. Petti's family owned a herd of reindeer, many milking cows, and broad grain fields, but they did not shun the handsome future master of Sääskilampi. He was tall and handsome, and the house of Sääskilampi had a reputation for affluence. Even Ivar's rather heavy drinking bouts were not regarded as excessively sinful by Petti's pious, fundamentalist parents. A man is only young once...

The young master of Sääskilampi spent most of his winter weekdays following the reindeer. It often happened that after a day of toiling with the animals, evening would find him conveniently close to Petti's parent's land. Reindeer were not bound by parish limits, and the Järvenkylä herds roamed the woods bordering the home of the future mistress of Sääskilampi. Toward spring, Ivar's overnight stays shifted to Petti's bedroom. The master and mistress of the house did not protest then either. A landowner's son would always make amends if things went amiss.

But Ivar's feelings were not focused exclusively on Petti. The girls from the coast kept haunting his mind. The thought of Hilkka, especially, kept recurring. His yearning for her was accompanied by an odd nagging of his conscience. The arrival of spring diluted his longing to a degree. The charm of the wilderness allayed his yearning for other places. Waterfowl returned from the south, and at night the call of mating wood grouse could be heard. The winter silence of the wilderness gave way to new life. Frozen waters thawed and the glow of the sun was reflected in their waves.

The remnants of the snow vanished along with the ice. The shouts of log drivers echoed along the river banks. Capstans creaked on the upper lakes of the Ii River basin as men turned their drums on the rafts of logs. But the enchantment of spring dissipated, and restlessness again swelled in the young man's breast. One day as he was putting the final touches on the spring planting with his father, he halted the horse that was drawing the harrow and said:

"I've made up my mind. I'm leaving again, father."

Aatovi looked up from under his rag of a hat.

"Is it the coast you're itching for again?"

Ivar could hear the disappointment in his father's voice. He could not bear to look at the old man's sad face, but bent down to pluck a handful of the spring's first growth from the field. Crushing it into a green ball, he tossed it from hand to hand as he spoke:

"A man is only young once. You can get yourself a hired hand for the summer."

"Maybe so. Are you thinking of the log sorting again?"

"That's what was on my mind. They pay pretty well too. I'd like to stay the summer again."

"No hired man can fill your boots," said his father. He bit off a chew of pikanell. "But I won't stand in your way. And it would be useless to try."

✧ ✧ ✧

Sitting on a jolting wagon from the uplands to Oulu would have upset a weaker stomach, but Ivar suffered only sore buttocks. After many relay stages, he arrived in Oulu late one sunny afternoon and spent the night at a familiar inn. In the morning he exchanged his Lapland boots for patent leather shoes and put on a suit, then went out to stroll the streets of the town. Loggers, and farmers who had finished their spring planting roamed through the streets.

Around noon, he went up to the ticket window at the railway station.

"A ticket to Ii," he said.

There was plenty of time before the train left and he went out to walk the streets again. A man had to view the rush of life when he had the chance. That's why he had come.

"Well, if it isn't Ivo Sääskilampi!"

He spun around. The words came from a side-street he had just passed.

"And here comes Mikkos-Vertti. How about that!"

"Put her there. How the hell are you?"

"And you? What brings a Kijanta man to town?"

Mikkos-Vertti bared his tobacco-stained teeth in a smile.

"The Ii log sorting, the same as you. Am I right?"

"Almost. I just bought a ticket to Ii."

"Well then, the same train will rattle our bones. I was there already—went day before yesterday and came back last night."

"Why all the coming and going?"

"They don't start work until the day after tomorrow. I got a room in the same house as last year. Say, why the hell did you rush off like that last fall?"

Ivar Sääskilampi looked down at the ground. He saw a small stone there and kicked at it so hard it flew across the street and smacked into the foundation of the building opposite. Then he said:

"Damn it! I almost broke that cellar window."

"That was a near miss. but with your money you could afford to pay for it."

"What are the chances of getting a room? There must be a lot of men there."

"The streets seem to be full of them."

"Did you try for a job with the same boss?"

"The same. Listen Ivo, a little bird told me that time goes slow for you in the backwoods, and here I've got the same room as last year and no one to share it with yet."

"Well, you're a good buddy. Then we're all set to amble on down to Ii Hamina and start working. Let's get a flask to celebrate."

"Good idea. Spoken like a real buddy."

"Let's hunt one up right now."

The two men from the backwoods of East Finland tramped the stone-paved streets of the city. Ivar's patent-leather shoes flashed in the sunshine. Vertti walked beside him, as gingerly as if he were on hot coals. He said with a grimace:

"These Lapland boots are damned well not made for walking the streets. My feet are so sore."

Ivar looked down at Vertti's boots. They were dark from greasing, had curled-up toes, and tops that came up to the knee.

"What's happening in Ii lately?"

"Nothing much. Ouch, dammit, those paving stones are sharp...Oh, there is one thing. I saw a pretty sight. Can you guess what it was," Vertti said with a laugh.

"How am I supposed to guess?"

Ivar looked at Vertti mincing along beside him. There was a grin on his face and the wad of tobacco tucked below his gum line made his lower lip protrude.

"It has a little something to do with you."

Ivar's eyes fastened on his partner. The sweat raised on his shoulders by the heat of the afternoon suddenly turned cold.

"How? What does it have to do with me?"

"I ran into Hilkka — the woman you were running around with — on the main street. She's getting kind of big around the middle, most of it up front..."

Now a cold sweat burst out on Ivar's forehead too. He looked away. They had come to the waterfront. Large warehouses built of notched logs stood there, with people swarming around them.

"Let's go and sit down. There are benches near that warehouse."

"Sounds good to me," said Vertti Mikkonen.

Ivar Sääskilampi's sturdy legs gave way as they reached the bench. The slight apprehension he had felt all winter was now a rampaging fear battering his heart. That was the meaning of those repulsive dreams. It was true, all too true...

"Even at the boarding house, there was talk about it. They were saying that Ivar Sääskilampi had been courting Hilkka. I told them that boy could have as many Hilkkas as he wanted."

"Goddamnit, stop that babbling!"

Vertti Mikkonen's jaw dropped, erasing his grin. He stared

wide-eyed at his partner, who was wiping the sweat from his brow.

"Okay, okay. It's none of my business."

Ivar pulled his knife from its sheath, and Vertti's hand went to his belt as well. But Ivar merely shaved a splinter from the bench, sharpened its point, and began to pick at his teeth with it. His hand was shaking.

"A piece of sugar got stuck in my tooth and it was starting to ache."

Starting out again, they found a dealer to sell them a flask. Ivar paid for it, refusing to accept the money Vertti thrust upon him.

"Let's walk to Hupisaari," he said.

"There are bushes there where we can tip a flask," Vertti agreed.

The place was known to them from earlier visits. The roar of Meri Rapids lulled their ears, but it did not bring peace to Ivar Sääskilampi's mind. Even their increasing intoxication could not do that for him.

"Was she really that way?"

"No doubt about it. So pregnant she was puffing. She must be due any day now."

Drinking brought small relief to Ivar's pangs of conscience. People have strange premonitions, his father, Aatovi Sääski-lampi used to say. Just such forebodings had haunted Ivar all winter long.

The afternoon wore on and the sun sank lower.

"You don't seem to like the booze the way you used to," Vertti Mikkonen said.

"It doesn't seem to have any taste," said Ivar.

"Don't you think we should head back for the station. The train leaves before long."

Ivar looked at the sun in the sky and then at his watch.

"It'll be leaving soon."

"Yeah, let's go or we'll be late."

They walked to the bridge. When they had crossed over to the city side, Ivar stopped and looked at the ground. He turned away from his partner, who had also stopped. After a long pause, Ivar looked directly at Vertti again, and said:

"Listen, they say it's the women who always change their

minds, but for once I'm going to pull that woman's trick."

"You mean you're going home again? When you just got here?"

"I'm heading for the uplands tomorrow. They need me there to work. And then this business...We're buddies, aren't we?"

Ivar looked Vertti squarely in the eye, and Vertti returned his gaze.

"And good buddies," he said.

"You must have guessed that I'm sneaking off. I don't want to show my face to people in Ii...especially to that Hilkka."

"Well, that looks a little like running away. But who can swear on a Bible that her big belly comes from your pants?"

"That's just it. I have a strong suspicion."

Ivar told Vertti what had happened on the Saturday night when the stranger had been in Hilkka's room.

"Now I see why you left so suddenly," said Vertti. "So there was another man there. I don't know if I could have kept from hitting him."

"It wasn't easy to curb my temper."

"Well, you've been a good partner. We could have had some good times, but I understand."

"I'll be glad if you don't talk about where I live. I kept it to myself there at Ii."

"I'm not the kind to talk, especially in a case like this."

Ivar walked to the station with Vertti. The last traces of his intoxication had disappeared.

"If you happen to be in Vaarakylä, drop in to see us."

"I sure will. I'll make it my first stop there."

"This looks like my last summer on the coast."

"You have spent a couple of summers here. If I had a home, I don't think you'd find me mucking around in this place."

The train whistle blew. The cars began slowly to move northward. Vertti hopped on to the steps of one of them and said to Ivar, who was walking alongside the train:

"I won't tell tales. You can bank on it."

✧ ✧ ✧

A couple of years later, Ivar Sääskilampi sat by the open fire reading a newspaper. Abruptly he thrust the paper closer to the burning pine blocks. It began to tremble in his hands. The noise of a block cracking in the fire brought him back to reality.

"Petti, come here," he cried.

A buxom young woman carrying a child on one arm entered the room and stopped before him.

"What did you say?"

"This paper has some terrible news in it. It's a real shocker."

"Is it about that war in Turkey. That's supposed to end soon, isn't it?"

"Well, that too...but there's a story about a man who used to be my partner. He was killed up north."

"My God! Who? Where?"

"His name was Mikkos-Vertti. You didn't know him, though he was born in southern Kijanta. He was a wanderer."

"And now he's dead?" said his wife.

"Another worker stabbed him at Rovaniemi. Right in the heart. One..."

"Ivar, stop it. It's horrible."

"It turns my stomach too. We were good friends then."

His young wife stood beside him gazing into the leaping flames. The child on her arm did so too and pointed at the fire with his little hand. His eyes sparkled and he babbled ecstatically. Ivar Sääskilampi put the paper down and patted his wife gently on the belly.

"How is the girl getting along in there?"

"She must be doing well. I'm not having a bit of trouble."

Ivar reached out and said:

"Let Bert sit in his father's lap. We men can watch the fire burn."

His wife went into the kitchen. The boy babbled away in his father's arms and pawed at the mustache the man was growing.

"Father's boy...Are you going to be a reindeer man?"

At the same moment, he thought of Ii Hamina. What did Hilkka's child look like? Was it a boy too? It would be a full year older than the one on his knee.

These reveries stayed with Ivar Sääskilampi through the years. Often on a trip to Oulu, he thought of going on to Ii, of walking its main street once again, but his nerve always failed him. Not that he was afraid of being recognized there now. Over the years, he had developed from a half-baked young man into a portly, mustachioed hulk. He had kept track of the time: if Hilkka's child were still alive, it would now be in the prime of life. Did the boy — he always thought of it as a boy — look like him? Or did it resemble the dark-haired man?

His restlessness increased as the years went by. The wild days of his youth had been cut short. Only heavy daily labor could dull the ache in his breast, but it could not keep him from thinking. Time after time, his mind went back to the coast. Before his first trip there, he had experienced no joy. Life had been hard work from early morning till late at night. On a few occasions, he had managed to paw the maidservant at home.

His wife put on weight over the years and the children grew up. On some of his trips to Oulu, the master of Sääskilampi, now counted among the true believers, had taken to drinking. Drinking companions led him to the company of women. Soon he got into the habit of stopping to visit a woman named Salli on every trip to Oulu, trips that were quite frequent for a time. No novice herself, she now first experienced the passions of an older man. His longing would build up during the days in the lonely wilderness, and its release was violent. And Ivar Sääskilampi never haggled over its earthly price.

But having to wear the mask of religion exacted a far higher price from the man. It ravaged him internally, cleaving his heart. Day by day he felt himself more isolated. His earlier upright and open nature changed; the burden of conscience made him harsh and crabbed. Often his wife was subjected to violent outbursts at bedtime, had to swallow harsh abuse and even threats of violence. Bitterness dammed up during the day burst out within the walls of their bedroom. His wife's nature grew increasingly cold as their wealth accumulated. The time when their children had been born began to seem like a dream.

Am I the father of Hilkka's child? The thought continued to torment him. From time to time it faded, only to flare up again. For years he was obsessed by the notion that he might speak of the matter in his dreams and he would often doze rather than sleep. His wife would awaken to find him sitting there smoking his pipe. She wondered at his behavior and sometimes she might say:

"Don't you feel like sleeping?"

"No."

"But you woke up at four in the morning and you've been working like a fool all day. You ought to see a doctor."

"Why the hell should it bother you? I'm not keeping you awake. Go back to sleep. Snore till you shake the rafters. This damned..."

"Come to bed now. I'll draw the covers over you. Shall I get you a pair of stockings?"

"Well, I'll just finish this pipeful. Go to sleep. You've had a long day too."

"I can't sleep. It bothers me too when you're so troubled. What is there to worry about? You can tell me."

"Don't worry about it. Life is such a goddamned mess. Even the moss froze last fall. Who knows how many cruddy reindeer we'll have left by next fall. How will those thicket-heads be able to dig out their food from under all that snow?"

His wife knew that concern for the reindeer was not the real cause of his troubles, but she did not dare say so. Although she pretended to sleep, she could hear the agitated gurgling of her husband's pipe.

4

"How far did grandpa go?"

Petti Sääskilampi stared out the window. The centers of the panes were icing over although it was warm enough in the room. Irja walked over to her mother and said:

"He's been gone a long time. I wonder which way he went."

"Grandpa went that way. I saw him through the window."

"Ilmari is pointing that way," said Irja to the lady of the house.

The woman came to stand beside the Sääskilampis at the window and said:

"Grandpa's gone toward the lower end of town then."

"Did you see if your father took his medicine, Irja?"

"He did take it, at least this morning," said Irja to her mother. "Ilmari and I will go after him now."

Pentti dashed over to his mother's skirts. Head tilted back, he looked up at her bright-eyed and said:

"Tan I go too? Gwanpa will fweeze."

"You can't and he won't freeze. Grandpa has lots of clothes on," said Petti Sääskilampi.

"If father got lost...let's get our clothes on, Ilmari."

Irja began putting on her older son's outdoor clothing. Pentti stood by sniffling. His grandmother said to Irja:

"Your father won't lose his way. He spent whole summers here on sorting jobs when he was young. Maybe he got tired along the way."

"Maybe he walked far and it's just taking a long time," said the mistress of the house.

"Father sometimes has dizzy spells. His head just whirls. Push your hand through this sleeve, Ilmari. And you, Pentti, stop sniveling. You're just not coming."

"You needn't bother, Irja. Here comes Grandpa into the yard now."

Petti Sääskilampi's face lighted up. She turned from the window and said:

"Is there any coffee left in the pot? Has it gotten cold?"

"I'll go and see," said Irja, and disappeared into the kitchen.

With tired steps, Ivar Sääskilampi entered the room. The boys ran to meet him and hugged the cold legs of his boots.

"Grandpa, grandpa!"

"Gwanpa, they wouldn't wet me come to get you."

"Let Grandpa sit down," said the boys' grandmother.

Although he was panting heavily, the old man's face broke into a tired smile. He rubbed the boys' hair with his mittens.

"Just let grandpa take off his coat and rest a little."

Earlier, when the day was at its brightest, dressing to go out had gone slowly for Ivar Sääskilampi. Still more slowly now, he shrugged out of his overcoat. Then he sat down heavily and groped for his pipe and tobacco, his eyes staring across the room.

"We were getting ready to go after you," said his wife.

For a long time, the man sought to steady his breathing. Then he said:

"It turned out to be a long walk. I went almost to the old Kestilä sawmill. The place hasn't changed much in all these years."

"I hear this place is familiar to you, that you worked at sorting jobs here when you were young."

Ivar had raised the newly-filled pipe to one corner of his mouth. He patted his trouser pockets in search of matches and heard the box rattle, but did not thrust a hand into the pocket.

"What? Who said that?"

"Why, your wife. She said you'd spent whole summers here on sorting jobs. Lots of men from the uplands came here to do that. Who knows, you might still run into some good friends here. Maybe even an old flame," the lady of the house said with a chuckle.

The pipe beneath the mustache shook and the old man fumbled at it with hands that trembled. He glowered at his wife.

"What nonsense has she been talking?"

"Why, we've been talking about anything and everything, especially when..."

"There's no truth in it. Agh, my chest hurts again."

"That's not good," said his wife. "You're not going to have another attack, are you?"

"Me? Cut out the nonsense. It was the mouth of the Oulu River where I was when I was young. One summer I stopped in here for a day. I didn't get a job because there were too many applicants."

Petti Sääskilampi looked at her husband. Although his face had been pitifully tired when he entered, his eyes were now blazing as they had during his fits of temper in his younger days. That look had always silenced her. She rose from the bench and said:

"I must have remembered wrong. It's getting dark all of a sudden."

"It's all nonsense you've been talking. I did get to know the mouth of the river at Oulu pretty well...the days are none too long even in clear weather. No, they're not...boys, come to your grandpa."

Irja looked in from the kitchen door and said:

"Come for coffee, father. Will you have more, mother?"

"I could stand another cup," said Petti Sääskilampi. She looked at the endless translucent blue of the sky still visible outside the window and added, "I wonder how those poor men can keep from freezing on the battle fronts."

Accompanied by the owner's son the two boys went scooting across the floor like weasels, shrieking as they went. As he walked toward the kitchen, their grandfather said to them:

"Boys, you mustn't make so much noise. You're in a stranger's house."

CHAPTER IV

1

The corporal's stripes were still spotless. He stood exaggeratedly erect with the thumbs of his gloved hands hooked under his belt. Every time his mouth opened, a puff of vapor accompanied his commands.

"Left...left...left."

The group of recruits was marching toward the end of their drill field, on which tramping feet had packed a large, smooth circle of snow. They were already some distance from their leader, who raised his voice to shout:

"Left turn, march!"

The first rank of the group began to curve into something that resembled a fish hook. The corporal's mouth opened again:

"Forward, march!"

The line of recruits retraced its course and soon drew abreast of the corporal.

"Hey you in the rear! What were you in civilian life? A sheepherder? Get in step: left...left...left..."

The last and smallest of the recruits skip-hopped a few times until he was in step with the rest.

"Detail, halt!"

The first man of the squad stopped as if he had run into a brick wall. The rest climbed up on the heels of those ahead of them and then jumped back quickly. A few even hissed out despairing curses.

"Godalmighty! You don't move when you're at attention."

The youngsters stood as if frozen in place. The intervals between them were highly irregular. The corporal's eyebrows nearly met in a scowl. For an unnervingly long time he was silent. Then he bellowed:

"Left face!"

Everyone followed the command, except for the first man in the squad, who spun to the right. He caught himself immediately and whirled around again. He was only a split second late in standing with his back to the corporal, along with the others.

"Godalmighty! Doesn't Recruit Sammalsuo know the difference between right and left?"

Kauko felt as if ice water were running down his back. He wished that the snow-covered field beneath his feet would open up and swallow him.

"Y-yes, I know, corporal, sir."

"Then remember it."

The angry roar of the husky corporal standing behind them intimidated the recruits, who all tried to press the stocks of their rifles into exactly the right spot on their sides, as they had been taught to do. The long silence that followed made every heart beat faster. The knees of the more timid began to quake. Kauko felt as if the corporal's eyes were fixed on the barrel of his rifle alone. He tried to ease his body into a more erect posture and to thrust out his chest. His rifle seemed to be tilted to one side a little. He tried to straighten that out too, slowly.

"Right about... face!"

The initial part of the command was drawn out to a nerve-racking length, but the command itself sounded like a rifle shot. Kauko's left leg whipped up like a spring and the frozen heels of his Lapland boots banged together. Only then did he realize that he was the sole man in the squad with his face toward the corporal. "Turn around, quick!" the thought flashed through his mind, but the mental command only made his upper body twitch. He stood there looking the squad leader straight in the eye. The corporal's cold-pinched cheeks turned the color of violet. The seconds dragged on. A hoarse whisper from somewhere alongside him sounded in Kauko's ringing ears.

"That goddamned clown..."

"That does it!"

"Now we're in the soup because of that lout," hissed another voice.

Kauko's jaw tightened. His glance did not waver from the face of his superior, which had grown even darker. "Come hell or high water, goddamn it," thought Kauko defiantly.

"What do you have to say now, Recruit Sammalsuo?"

"Nothing, corporal, sir."

"Even your name tells us you're good for nothing but plucking moss or hoeing a marsh at best. Do you deny it?"

"It seems that way, corporal, sir."

"That you deny it?"
"No, that I'm good for nothing."
"And on top of everything, you're a liar."
An event from his boyhood years flashed into Kauko's mind. He had been pinned to the ground by an enraged shovel man at a road-building site. Although the man was doing his utmost to strangle him, and Kauko was beginning to lose consciousness, he had not been afraid. Now he suddenly felt the same way.
"I'm not a liar, corporal, sir."
"Shut your mouth when I tell you to! You're lying!"
"How have I lied, corporal, sir?" Kauko roared back.
"Button your lip, recruit!"
"I want to know how I've lied, corporal, sir."
The corporal, a farmer's son from Bothnia, had been brought up to respect integrity. He saw the wild gleam in the husky recruit's eye, the clenched teeth beneath tightly compressed lips, and realized that the tense rookie was on the verge of losing control. This recruit would soon be a soldier, he thought, and would overcome his timidity. The two of them might wind up at the front together, or happen to meet in a dark corner of the training camp. Sammalsuo was not, after all, guilty of any great offense. He was timid and unaccustomed to military commands. The corporal's voice was milder when he spoke again:
"You said awhile ago that you knew your right from your left."
"I made a mistake. I forgot that you never make an about-face to the right."
"Remember it now then. Recruit Sammalsuo: About face!"
Kauko's turn was as smooth as a weasel's. He could see the eyes of those near him in the ranks watching him.
"Detail, right face!"
This time there was little to criticize in the squad's execution. They were now facing the corporal, who walked down their line.
"You two on the end, straighten your rifles. The rest of you can do better too. You, second from the left, pull the stock into your side. The first man is carrying his rifle like a soldier."
Kauko's defiance subsided. He swallowed the lump in his throat, afraid that tears might come to his eyes. The corporal took a couple of steps backward and commanded:
"Order arms!"
The rifle stocks thudded to the packed snow, not precisely

alongside the foot where they should have been, but more or less in the correct position.

"Rest!"

✧ ✧ ✧

"Five volunteers!"

A number of recruits were hanging around the school hallway. Some of them were wrangling, others silent in thought. Some munched on cookies they had stuffed into their pockets at chow time. The shout of the duty corporal interrupted their usual evening activities. There was a silence, and here and there a young man tried to duck out of sight behind another. Some began to creep toward the door.

Kauko had been absorbed in reading a newspaper. One of his squad who was chewing on a cookie ducked down behind the paper he was holding and hissed:

"Keep that paper spread out in front of you."

"We're too old to play hide-and-seek."

Kauko lowered the paper, folded it up, and tossed it onto a nearby table. The corporal looked around. His back was directly toward Kauko and his companion.

"Well no one's going to make me peel potatoes, you can be sure of that."

Kauko's companion slipped quickly to the exit and disappeared into the dark shed. Recruits were now disappearing out of the door in a steady stream.

Kauko rose and walked up to the corporal with the yellow braid. Two other men did the same.

"Stop! You two recruits sneaking out the door. Come here!"

Two young men who had been slow in getting out shuffled back to the duty corporal. Now five men stood before him.

"The kitchen got a shipment of herring. Follow me."

Potatoes were peeled and fish cleaned in a basement laundry room. The floor was of concrete and the temperature only a few degrees above freezing. The room smelled of fish and potato peels. The hands of the men cleaning the fish soon grew numb.

"Of all the rotten luck. He got us just when we were going out the door," said one of the men who had been trying to escape.

"I told you we should lie down on the floor behind the table," said the other. "He wouldn't have thought of snooping there. You see what happened with your idea of sneaking out."

Kauko said nothing, but went on stripping guts from herring. The task reminded him of cleaning roach at home in the spring. In the fall too, his mother got whitefish from the men who had nets. They were cleaned in the same way as herring. Even the size of the whitefish from the lake at home was roughly the same.

"Your hands freeze on these lousy fish," said Recruit Sumala, one of the would-be escapees.

"How the devil do you clean these things? The whole gut broke again. We'll be at this till the evening service."

Kauko watched the reluctant efforts of his companions. He took a herring between his fingers and said:

"There's nothing so mysterious about it. Look, just squeeze here under the throat with your fingers and pull out the guts."

"You'd make a good *kitchen-pig* since you know everything about..."

Sumala took up where his companion had left off:

"That's just what our boy Japheth Sammalsuo is bucking for. He's always volunteering for these fish-cleaning bees and potato games."

"Someone has to do it. I'd rather be sitting here than spending my time up there brown-nosing the brass," said Kauko, pointing overhead, from where they could hear angry shouts followed by the sound of running feet.

Another who had volunteered along with Kauko was a small, dry young man from the far north. His name was Kieppi and he belonged to the same platoon as Kauko, but to a different squad. His fingers nipped the guts from the herring at a rapid pace. The third volunteer was an even more strapping young man than Kauko. He came from near Raahe and his name was Niemi. He was in the same company as Kauko and Kieppi, but in another platoon.

"You seem to like eating the herring and potatoes well enough," said Kieppi.

"But we didn't come here to wring fish-necks. There are enough women from the auxiliary stinking up the kitchens to do it. This is women's work," grumbled Sumala.

Recruit Niemi went on working in silence. The herring had a tendency to break in his stiff and heavy fingers. Niemi's slow and awkward movements often reminded Kauko of the dull-witted Sven Tuuva in *The Tales of Ensign Stahl*, but the man was an avid reader. Only Kauko had noticed the intelligence that he hid from others. Kauko and this young man from a large farm near the coast had become good friends. They both spent what little spare time they had in reading.

"I wouldn't envy Japheth at all if they made him a *kitchen-pig*. Even if he could always be in those women's skirts."

"What the devil are you blathering about? And up to now, my name's been Kauko."

"But I hear your middle name is Japheth," Sumala persisted.

"How's the fish cleaning going, boys?"

A non-com entered the laundry room. He was old enough to be the father of the recruits. A buck sergeant's stripes adorned the sleeve of his *Guard* coat, another sign of status. He no longer exhibited the soldierly demeanor taught at the training school he had attended some twenty years ago.

"Nothing to cheer about, sergeant, sir. Our hands are freezing." The mumbled complaint came from one of the recruits who had been dragooned into the work.

"This room is kind of cold," said Mess Sergeant Käsmä.

He remained standing near the recruits sitting around the water bucket. Recruit Sumala glowered at him and said:

"We came here to fight, not to clean fish."

Sumala laid his knife down on his knees and blew on his reddened fists, which were flecked with gleaming scales and crystals of salt.

"A man will catch his death of cold at this goddamned business," he said.

"Let's try to do without cursing," said the sergeant. "Everybody has to take his turn at this."

Annoyed at the crack about the *kitchen pig*, Kauko said:

"I think they're freezing a lot worse at the front. A lot of the boys there would be glad to change places..."

Kauko cut short his words. What business was it of his? Although his eyes were following the movements of his fingers, he was aware that the mess sergeant was looking at him.

"What did you do as a civilian?"

Kauko looked inquiringly at the sergeant. No one was answering his question. He nodded in Kauko's direction.

"You, I mean."

"I was a cottage farmer. I did a little bit of logging, sergeant, sir."

"Is that so? Watching you clean those fish, I thought you had to be an islander. But just between us, there's no need to call me *sir*. Save it for when the big brass are listening."

"At home sometimes we almost had to live on roach. That's where I learned to clean fish."

"I'm a cottager myself. My boy is already old enough to be in a training center. He's at Koria, in the engineers."

The sergeant began to chat with the boys. Kauko found it pleasant and talked freely and easily. Sergeant Käsmä spoke of his children. He had a large family and worried about their welfare.

"I was still young enough for combat duty, but..."

When his words trailed off, the young men around the bucket turned to look at the sergeant. He had taken out his smoking paraphernalia. When he stuffed tobacco from the plug into the bowl of his pipe, he did it with the ring finger of his right hand instead of his thumb. Recruit Kieppi noticed it:

"You had an accident with your fingers. What cropped them off like that?"

The sergeant lighted his pipe, holding the match box between his ring finger and the stub of a thumb. He struck the match with his left hand. His right thumb was missing to the first joint, along with the entire index and middle fingers. The sergeant also looked at the hand. He was slow to answer.

"I once stuck my hand into a bear's gullet," he said.

"They all sat petrified, staring at the hand.

"Where did it attack you?" Niemi said finally.

Again the answer was slow in coming. The man took a deep breath.

"At the mouth of its den. I went to wake it up one spring. My partners didn't shoot straight. I had to shove my hand down its gullet. Well, I have to check the kitchen again. Your stint here will soon be over."

When the sergeant's legs disappeared up the staircase, Niemi said:

"I used to think there wasn't a man left in Finland who had been maimed by a bear. We don't know much about the backwoods here on the coast."

"I've seen plenty of bear hides," said Kieppi. "It's a rare spring around home when they don't kill a bear."

"I've only seen their tracks," said Kauko.

"It's a wonder you haven't killed one," said Sumala.

"Have you heard me bragging so goddamned much?" said Kauko.

"You had to butt in just now when I told the sergeant my hands were freezing. He might have let us go without finishing."

"You can go for all I care. You're not making our work any easier."

"I wouldn't be so ready to open my mouth if I'd called a major a lieutenant."

A herring slipped back into the bucket from Kauko's grasp. He straightened up on the seat, grasping the scaly, slippery knife in his hand. His eyes were fixed on Sumala's face.

"What have I ever done to you? Spit it out."

Niemi straightened up too. He looked inquiringly at Sumala.

"Let him have one in the puss," said Kieppi. "Show him you come from a place where men shave with an ax."

"Most of us here are volunteers," said Niemi, wiping his mouth on his cuff. "We have to stick together because of something bigger. Now we're fighting each other just over a herring detail. We'll be glad to eat those fish ourselves tomorrow. I'm hungry right now."

Kauko's boiling rage began to subside. He was most angered by the reference to a mistake he had made two days ago. Kieppi laughed:

"A recruit is allowed to make mistakes...and a major has a star too."

"But a bigger one. And you should have known by his age that he was too old to be a lieutenant," Sumala kept harping on the subject.

"I suppose you've never made a mistake," said Kauko.

"The major wasn't even mad. He just laughed it off," said Niemi. "Well, boys, let's finish the job. I've got roast pork and butter in a package from home."

"Will you split with everyone?"

"Share and share alike," said Niemi.

They all crouched over the cleaning bucket. Reddened hands groped for the herring that remained. Kauko was the last to thrust his hand into the water. His eyes were still fixed on his tormentor. Oh well, let it go, since that's what Niemi wants, thought Kauko.

2

"Company, reveille!"

For two weeks the same shout had rung out every morning. Kauko could not get used to it. Even now he leaped up trembling. The recruit from the top bunk slid down his back to the floor, legs spread wide.

Socks and shoes were drying on the radiators. Bare feet pattered on the floor of the classroom in the rush to get to the radiators. Kauko tucked his boots under his arm and grabbed for his socks. Then he stood staring at the radiator top and at the next one as well.

"What the hell!" he burst out.

The tops of the radiators were empty. Even the slowest men were hurrying back to their bunks. A solitary pair of torn black machine-knit socks hung from one of the radiators.

"Who the hell took my socks?"

Even while her husband was still alive, Maija Sammalsuo had been in the habit of knitting striped cuffs on socks. They were on every pair Kauko had brought with him. All the upland men wore those heavy gray homespun socks. In the logging camps, it was an important morning chore to decide what socks belonged to what men. To help her husband recognize his, Maija had begun to knit three stripes on every cuff, the top one red with two thin black stripes below it.

In the logging camps, men took their time in determining what socks went with what feet, but in the recruits' morning bedlam, the rush was too great. Every day someone discovered that his socks were missing. Sometimes there was nothing to replace them. Now, although Kauko even squatted to look under the radiator, there was no help there either.

Kauko ran to the first of the bunks. He did not see the familiar cuffs on the legs of the boys pulling on their pants there. Like a sheep strayed from the flock, he began to run up and down between the rows of bunks. The familiar stripes did not appear. Not there...nor there either. The faster men were pulling on their boots. A few stamped the floor with their lower bodies fully dressed. Then Kauko's eye lit on a leg sticking straight out, onto which a calfskin boot was being drawn. Only the familiar cuff was still visible. The other foot was pressed against the floor, encased in a calfskin boot.

"Goddamned pig! Whose socks have you got there?" Kauko roared.

"Just worry about your own," said the recruit, stamping his foot on the floor.

Only now did Kauko recognize the recruit. Rage swelled up in him.

"I asked you whose socks you're putting on."

"They're on and they'll stay on."

"And I tell you they won't, goddamn it."

Kauko did not think to keep his voice down. Bending forward he grabbed Sumala by the ankle and gave a yank. The young man fell backward, banging his head on the floor. His boot was left in Kauko's hand. Kauko tossed it aside and grabbed the other boot, jerking it so violently that Sumala slid some distance along the floor. Tearing the socks off the other man's feet, Kauko slapped Sumala across the face with them as the other struggled to rise.

"Goddamned thief!"

Only now did Kauko realize that the other recruits had formed a ring around him. He was trembling in every limb, grinding his teeth between clenched jaws. Sumala clambered to his feet. His eyes were bloodshot when he spoke:

"We might run into each other some dark night. You better believe it, you goddamned stutterer."

"You can bring on a whole gang of your kind..."

Kauko's rage had been subsiding but now it flared up again. He gripped Sumala's neck with one hand and drew the weaker lad's face closer to his own. At the same time he dangled the socks before the other's eyes and said:

"Now remember to keep your mitts off this kind of sock from now on. Do you happen to see the stripes on the cuff?"

"What the hell kind of ruckus is going on here? Is it a fight?"

The duty non-com broke through the ring of recruits and his eyes fell on Kauko.

"Is it Sammalsuo who's causing this row?"

"Ask that man, corporal, sir," said Kauko, shoving Sumala toward the duty corporal by the neck. The corporal looked at both of them first, and said:

"Recruit Sumala?"

Rubbing the back of his head, Sumala said:

"Corporal, sir, that Sammalsuo started shouting at me."

"Why? For no reason at all?"

"He claimed I took his socks. It was by mistake. In a hurry."

"I don't claim. I know. Look, all of you. Here's another pair of my socks. Aren't they the same kind? Stripes on the cuff, and even my initials. That damned bum filched them and put them on."

"Recruit Sammalsuo, this is not a logging camp. Keep it down. Is that what happened?" said the corporal, raising his voice.

"Yes it was, corporal, sir," said Kieppi.

Other men also nodded. The duty non-com shouted:

"Every man get dressed. You've got two minutes."

Kauko was the last man dressed. He rushed out at the tail end of the group for the morning run. It took a jog of nearly a kilometer in the cold morning air to calm him down, but his hands still trembled during the morning tea.

✧ ✧ ✧

The company of recruits was lined up four deep. Off to one side was the schoolhouse, its roof covered by a thick layer of snow. The eyes of the men followed the figure of a woman in auxiliary uniform walking toward them from the village. She passed underneath the yard lights and disappeared inside.

"Those *kitchen-pigs* have all the fun. All they do is play around with the women," hissed a recruit standing near Kauko.

"I think their Mother Hen is strict enough to stop any fanny-patting," Kauko whispered in reply.

"At least they don't have to shrivel up in the cold," whispered Kauko's neighbor.

"They do get out of that."

Kauko shifted his gaze. In the dim light of the morning, he could see trees coated with rime. Frost cracked somewhere in the direction of the buildings. How were they getting along at home? It was God's miracle that the Russians had been forced to retreat from Alasalmi. Even Suomussalmi was in Finnish hands. It was said to have been burned, but at least their home region once more belonged to them. Raate was said to be a hot spot now, and the Russians were on a rampage at Kuhmo too. It was good that mother had gotten such a fine place to stay and that she and the Olkivaaras were together. He must write to her this evening.

Kauko felt a warm glow as he thought of Elma. Would the day ever come that he would be alone with her? He would no longer be shy. It was good that their relationship had remained innocent. He had nothing to be ashamed of, even when he was face-to-face with Nestor and Mari.

Fading stars flickered in the sky as dawn peered out from beyond the woods. A train puffed into motion at the station. Pillars of smoke rose up from chimneys in the church village.

When the corporal presented the company to the top sergeant, the latter paced back and forth in front of them. The men were afraid of him. He had had tough military training in Germany. Kauko knew that he had belonged to the famed infantry battalions of the civil war and his thoughts left his home area when the sergeant stopped pacing.

"Companeee, 'tenshun!"

The recruits' heels snapped together and their rifles wobbled alongside their calves.

"Just like a bunch of cattle. You're young men, but you move like molasses in January. Rest!"

The sergeant stepped back a couple of paces and rocked onto the tips of his toes. The recruits were already familiar with this maneuver. The seconds dragged by. All of them got ready to snap to attention.

"Companeee, 'tenshun!"

The clack of heels came as one sound. The sergeant's eyes scanned the company from end to end, then he walked to the front end of the formation and looked off toward the school building. He turned to face the men.

"Rest!"

Pacing along the first rank of the men, the sergeant paused only to look at the squad leaders. Then he stopped before a tall youth, whose face was bluish and whose teeth were chattering. His thin summer trousers ended at low-cut shoes of gleaming leather. The brim of a black felt hat was tilted down in front, where a cockade shone on it. This, and an army belt that pinched in his suit coat, were the only equipment supplied by the army. The rifle too was the property of the state.

"Is the recruit a city man?" asked the sergeant.

"Yes I am, sergeant, sir."

"I could tell without asking. Goddamn it, some men start out for the army as if they were going to a Midsummer bonfire."

"I was a student, sergeant, sir."

"How far did you get in your studies?"

"I was admitted to the university, sergeant, sir. I didn't need any other kind of clothes. I lived only a couple of blocks from the high school."

"Didn't the gentleman student ever stop to think that in a war he might have to step into a snow bank?"

"Sergeant, sir. I came...I left home for my country."

"So much the worse. In that gear, you'll freeze like a cockroach in some border wilderness."

The recruit's face darkened. He wet his slips with his tongue and said:

"Sergeant, sir. I thought the army would equip me. I don't think it's right to get personal about it."

"The situation right now is that the gentleman student is a recruit in a company of which I am the mother, or the top sergeant. I am your superior. If things go according to form, in a year I may be standing at attention before you and saying, 'Lieutenant, sir.' Things can change that quickly in a war."

The sergeant's smile was strained. He went on to the next man and looked first at his ski boots. Then his eyes traveled up the legs of ski pants and stopped at the belt that constricted the waist of a ski jacket made of some light fabric. Finally his eyes stopped on a cap with a visor to the tip of which a cockade had been fastened.

"Well, now this is a sight too. How well educated is this recruit, model January, 1940?"

"I'm a student at a technical school, sergeant, sir."

"Well, there's some hope for you. But do you expect the army to issue skis with bindings?"

"I brought my own skis, sergeant, sir."

"Ahem."

The sergeant looked toward the schoolhouse again and dug

out a watch from under his coat. He tilted it in his palm and finally made out the hands.

"It's already five minutes after," he muttered.

The sergeant went on toward the rear of the company. The cockade and belt were the only equipment the army had been able to provide the recruits standing there. Most of them were volunteers from all parts of Finland. Whenever the sergeant passed a man who wore a short woolen or fur coat, he growled:

"That's more like it."

The sergeant reached the spot where Kauko stood. Piercing eyes glared at him from under scowling brows. Was his hat on straight, since the man was staring so? He'd had no chance to check it earlier. The cockade was probably off to one side. Then the sergeant's mouth opened.

"What is the recruit's name?"

"Kauko...correction, Recruit Sammalsuo, sergeant, sir."

"What is your civilian occupation?"

"I'm a w-woodsman, sergeant, sir."

"Recruit Sammalsuo!"

Kauko had been standing at attention the entire time. He tried to puff himself up even further.

"Six paces forward, march!"

Kauko froze. His heart seemed to be pounding at the pit of his stomach.

"Didn't you hear me? Recruit Sammalsuo, six paces forward, march!"

Kauko felt as if his knees would give way. He took the steps like a sleepwalker, not even sure of their number. From behind him, he heard the command:

"Left about face!"

Left? His mind repeated the command. One could do an about-face to the left. He turned. Facing the entire company made his knees knock.

"Company, attention! Eyes front!"

What kind of outfit is this army anyway? Kauko thought frantically. Why am I always the center of attention? I always try to do as I'm told. I even volunteer.

The sergeant's words interrupted his seething thoughts:

"Look at the model for a Finnish man going into the service. If you can't see it, I'll list Recruit Sammalsuo's equipment for you.

A fur hat with ear flaps. A woolen shirt with a high collar. A heavy coat. Heavy woolen trousers. Lapland boots with turned-up toes to top it all. How many pairs of socks do you have on?"

"T-two, sergeant, sir."

"I'm sure they're hand knit?"

"They are. Mother knit them by hand."

"You can go back into the ranks now."

There was no need to repeat the command. Kauko forgot even his military bearing as he trotted back into the ranks.

"Rest! I know that all of you don't have a place to get such practical gear. If you have anything like it at home, my good men, write and have it sent to you. What little equipment the army has, has been given to the men at the front. You'll get it very slowly, if at all."

The sergeant turned and looked toward the school once more, where the officers were marching. He dug out his watch, stretching it as far out from his belly as his arm could reach.

"Ten after..."

Then he took a step backward and eyed the company:

"Company...attention!"

Then after a short pause, the command:

"Dress right, dress! Now now—watch the intervals. Ready..."

Then sharp commands rang out in the frosty air:

"Eyes front! Right shoulder, arms!"

"Eyes left!"

The experienced soldier ran one last calm gaze over the company. Then he marched up to the company commander who was now standing there.

"Lieutenant, sir! B Company reporting for duty. Company strength..."

Both the lieutenant's and the sergeant's hands rose to their caps and then dropped to their sides. The company commander, a reserve lieutenant and a schoolteacher in civilian life, turned toward the ranks of the recruits.

"Good morning, company!"

"Good morning, lieutenant, sir!"

"Eyes front! Order arms!"

"Platoon leaders..."

3

The young second lieutenant had been born and raised in Häme. In the bright moonlight, the landscape of northern Kainu looked somehow familiar, but the moonlight itself was different. Its brightness seemed actually frightening to the patrol leader. And the successive extended patches of open swampland were also strange to him.

The men sank deep into the snow as they skied along. The track of the man plodding away in the lead was almost filled in with powdery snow before the next man skied it. The patrol was reduced to wading through snow halfway up to their calves. It piled up between the soles of the lieutenant's boots and the rubber foot pads of his skis. His toes were freezing. The rifle barrel jutting up from the shoulders of the man ahead of him swayed in a steady rhythm. The line of men was skiing through a patch of bog pines that grew on the edge of a large marsh. A high hill rose on the side from which the moon was shining. Traveling in its shade made the lieutenant feel safe.

"Boys, let's stop to listen for awhile," said the lieutenant, who was second in line.

The trail-breaker stopped and twisted his head around. His voice came through icicles that clung to his mustache.

"Did you say we should listen for awhile?"

"Yes. It looks like we'll have to ski across that swamp. The woods keep curving to the right."

The six men skiing directly behind the two of them closed up to the lieutenant. Those further back slogged up alongside. The trail-breaker leaned his armpits onto his ski poles, looked ahead for a long time, and then said:

"You can hardly call that kink in the edge of the swamp a curve. We're at the tip of one helluva long point."

No one said anything to this. When the patrol had left the village that evening, the roar of artillery and mortar fire had sounded obliquely in front of them. As they skied onward, the sounds had kept shifting more and more to the left. Now they could be heard from slightly in back of them. Bursts of small-arms fire as well broke the natural silence of the wilderness.

"They're spitting out machine-gun fire. A man's life isn't worth much out there right now."

Long hours of skiing had begun to tire the lieutenant's legs, and his mind, which had been quite alert when they set out, had been dulled by the monotonous trek through the wilderness. Now a smile tugged at the corners of his mouth. Their guide, an old native of the area, struck him as a most unlikely soldier.

"Looks that way. In a war, they shoot people," said the lieutenant.

"The sound of those guns is so far to our left rear that we must be quite a bit east of Alasalmi."

The lieutenant slid a map case from underneath his arm onto the holster at his belt and opened its straps.

"Let's look at the papers and see where we are. I just need to get some light first."

They were near the edge of the shadow cast over the marsh by the dark bulk of the hill. The lieutenant skied a few strides further out. Now his own long shadow stretched out over the gleaming snow on the marsh.

"Don't freeze your paws for nothing. The best thing to do with those maps in these woods is to wipe your ass on them."

"Now don't you — what was your name now? I forgot."

"Officially Nestor Malinen, but mostly they call me Olkivaara. I'm telling you, you'll get lost for good out here if you try to follow maps and prints. Listen to an older man, boy."

"This map is a little unclear, but one has to depend on it in a strange place. Damn, I can't see the print."

"A strange place? In my young years, I've come to learn that it's exactly in strange places that maps are good for nothing. Just tell me what point of what cape are we standing on now?"

The lieutenant studied the map closely, his nose almost touching it. The patrol route they had planned jointly at battalion headquarters showed up as a faint line running across swamps and lakes. Back there on the shore of a long, narrow lake, they had gnawed at their dry victuals, after which they had kept plodding through woods and over piney heaths.

"It's hard to say right off what our location is. I would say it's one of these swamps."

"Well now! That's the kind of blindman's buff you get when you lay out a route on a map. But I know that right now we're on Cape Ahma on Big Swamp."

The lieutenant folded the map into its case and skied back to the men.

"You see, I used to log in these parts."

As he spoke, Nestor surveyed the swamp. Then he raised a ski pole.

"Past the swamp, at a bit of an angle, you can see a small hilltop. The logging camp was at its foot. There's a pool of clear water there."

The mention of water made the lieutenant swallow. He uncovered his left wrist and raised it to his eyes.

"What time do your watch hands point to?"

"It just turned midnight," said the lieutenant.

"Damn this cold," said one of the men from the south.

"Did Malinen say there's a spring on the other side of the swamp?"

"No, a pool, and it's got absolutely pure water."

The lieutenant turned to his men:

"What do you say, boys, if we stop at this pool Malinen knows about? We'll make a fire and heat water for tea and have a decent meal."

"Now you're talking. I'll break trail. You just follow me."

The responsibility for his men weighed heavily on the lieutenant. This was his first action in a real war. At the officers' training school and on Guard maneuvers, he had only played at war. And the image of the Finnish soldier he had built up there was soon shattered. The man appointed as their guide was dressed in civilian clothing. Icicles hanging from his mustache, his speech a thick brogue, the man seemed to have just come out of the woods. He poked along on his skis at his own pace, legs spread wide apart. And stubborn too, this local logger was. But wonder of wonders, he had found the way to their first objective. When the lieutenant had set an azimuth with a compass, the man had started to curse. And did he really have to start addressing him so informally right from the start? Although one didn't expect formality in the woods, did he really have to call his superior officer *boy*?

But by nightfall, the lieutenant had begun to feel that the pace of the man breaking trail was fast enough. His speech and behavior too were beginning to seem exactly right for the terrain and for their task.

The swamp was a broad one. They passed a few dwarf pines that had withered where they stood. Devoid of bark or needles, they stuck up like skeletons.

"Who could have known when I was logging here that some day I'd be skiing this place with a gun on my back? That's where a side road crossed the swamp. A few of the road markers are still standing. This is a place where old Laukki really had to lean into the hames..."

"How far is the nearest house?" said one of the men.

"You can hike a good ten kilometers in any direction before you smell a manure pile," said Nestor.

The open area of the swamp was completely blanketed with snow. Only the ski-tracks of the patrol stretched out across its surface like twin bands of soot. Eight dark, crouching shadows stretched far out across the plain of snow.

Nestor Malinen's thoughts turned to his wife and children. Would the government see to it that they were fed? And where was Toivo hunkered down now? They said you didn't get much peace from the Russians on the Isthmus. The papers said they just kept coming at you.

Nestor raised his eyes. The camp clearing should be just about here. That hogback is a pretty high one. Eyes fixed on the sky beyond the hill, Nestor said:

"A falling star just took off over there."

The men behind him said nothing, but looked in the direction where the falling star had disappeared.

"Old people say that every time a star falls, a person dies. There's probably nothing in that saying. If there were, stars would be flying like sparks from a bonfire."

The band of men now stood in a circle in a dense spruce woods. The trees were heavily laden with snow. The setting moon had now dropped to the tree tops, which it lighted with its glow. Further ahead could be heard bursts of machine-gun fire, along with single rifle shots.

"Malinen, are you sure the road is at the foot of that hill?" the lieutenant asked in a whisper.

"Well how the devil many times do I have to tell you it is?"

"I'm not asking without good reason. We're on such an important mission that we have to make sure of everything," the lieutenant whispered.

"Well I'm sure — the gravel highway runs between Alasalmi and Kijanta, that I'm sure of. And if you don't trust me, why did you take me to guide you? You've got all those maps and compasses and things."

"Shh, don't make so much noise," said the lieutenant.

"When I put my hand to something, it turns out OK. And I know these woods like I know my tobacco pouch, so I'm getting tired of these useless questions."

The lieutenant said no more to Nestor. He and the men froze to listen. Human voices came from the direction of the road, along with the sound of motor vehicles. Finally the lieutenant turned to his men:

"Is that machine pistol of yours ready to go, Saarinen?"

"She'll spit if she has to," said a youngish buck-sergeant.

"The rest of you check to see that your rifle bolts aren't frozen."

The men unslung their rifles, worked the bolts, and wiped the barrels. Nestor Malinen jiggled his bolt open. His hands looked clumsy on the rifle.

"You mean I should let fly a round just to test her out?" he said.

"Hell no, don't do that!" cried the Lieutenant with panic in his voice.

"Ha, ha, ha!" Nestor roared with laughter. "Do you think I'm so damned stupid? I was just talking."

Nestor's laugh eased the tension in the air, and smiles spread across tired faces.

"Now, Nieminen, those hand grenades," said the lieutenant. "Two to each man."

A husky corporal from Häme obeyed the command, handing out the grenades from his pack. Nestor looked at his and said:

"These look like potato mashers. Do I pull that knob sticking out of the handle? There was some talk when we were looking at these things yesterday at Pyhäkylä that after you give it a yank, you have to start counting. You can't let it fly before you do. I don't know if I can count that far. I've always had a bad head for figures."

"But you must be able to count to three," said a corporal.

"Let's move up to the road. You all know that you mustn't make a sound now. Let's see what kind of stuff is going down that road. Remember, do nothing until I give the order. If anything happens, Sergeant Salonen will take my place."

✧ ✧ ✧

The setting moon lighted up the plowed road. The eight men lay a scant ten meters from it. Vehicles moved along it, small, angular motorized contraptions, and long lines of horse-drawn rigs. Foot soldiers hurried by at a half-trot. Angry shouts could be heard, mingled with screams of terror and pain. A chill ran down the sweaty backs of the men on patrol, and pity blended with their fear.

"What does it mean?" said Nestor in a low voice. "They're all heading east. They're in a big hurry to get to Kijanta."

The lieutenant, who was lying next to him, glanced his way and said:

"It looks like the Russians are retreating."

"That's what I figured. The Tampere boys must have given them what's for."

"There go some of the wounded," said a man on the other side of Nestor.

"And lots of them. They must be in some pain, the way they're groaning and screaming. Looks like the Russians are in one helluva hurry to get out of Alasalmi."

"They seem to be in full retreat," said the lieutenant.

"That old boy is sure in a hurry. He's really moving. He's left his gun and other gear behind. Look at that parade. Two men pulling a third on some kind of litter. He must be all shot up, the way he's groaning. It's a mean business all around."

A steady stream of limping, hobbling men flowed past the Finnish patrol. There were horses drawing sleds packed with men. Screams drowned out the sounds of firing. Then a horseman came charging down the road. Shouting loudly, the rider approached the spot where the patrol lay, his frost-covered horse galloping with long bounds. A little further on, the rider forced the horse to turn sideways, blocking the road. There he began raging more loudly than before. Foot soldiers and horse-drawn sleds began to pile up before the bellowing man. The crush from the rear turned the plowed furrow into a solid mass. The rider jerked at his horse's bridle, and the animal reared up on its hind legs.

"What the hell kind of big boss does that geezer think he is?"

said Nestor.

"He looks like an officer. He's trying to stop the retreating men," said the lieutenant.

"That warlord is on one bad mood," Nestor decided.

"They'll soon jam up and notice us," said one of the men. "A few of them are already climbing up the banks."

"Luckily they're going by on the other side of the road," said the lieutenant. "We'll just stay put."

But the efforts of the officer shouting in the saddle were in vain. His rearing horse split the oncoming horde in two, like a rock in the middle of a rapids.

"Why is that stinker reaming out those freezing wounded men? I don't like his game one little bit," said Nestor.

The men of the Finnish patrol could speak quite freely now. The uproar from the road drowned out all other sounds.

"We have a chance to do a lot of damage here," said Sergeant Salonen.

"Sounds like motor vehicles coming," said the lieutenant, pointing toward the west. "We'll throw our hand grenades and fire a few bursts from the machine pistol."

"I'm not going to hurt men in that condition. They're people too."

Nestor broke off. A tongue of flame leaped from the Russian officer's pistol. He snapped off a second and then a third shot. Two men in bulky clothes who were crawling up the bank fell back onto the road.

"That was the last dirty trick you'll play."

The men lying in ambush were shocked by the officer's deed. Before the shock could change to rage, a rifle next to the lieutenant fired. The horse on the road bounded up as if on springs, and the Russian officer on its back toppled off. The men of the patrol looked to one side. Nestor Olkivaara was just lowering the rifle butt from his shoulder.

"Looks like I still know how it's done."

"Hell, Malinen, now you've done it. You've ruined everything," hissed the lieutenant. Two men from the patrol stood up and started to draw back. "Don't go! We all stay here!" their leader barked at them.

The men glanced at him, but their eyes were mainly on the road.

"That brainless fool gave us away," said one of them.

"I did, and I would do it again. Let me see you try to do that to a helpless man just once, lieutenant. And they were his own men, too."

The men who had tried to leave got off their skis.

"That's not the question," the lieutenant said. "But you can get us all into trouble with that kind of stupidity. I'm the one who says what to do and when."

"Well, I won't make a court case of it. But when a man sets out to do something, he doesn't need bosses or fools on his ass."

Nestor was standing when he spoke. Then he darted with long strides toward the road. The deep snow did not seem to slow him down.

"Malinen!"

The lieutenant's shout was lost in the noise from the Russians. The packed mass of men and horses began again to stream toward Suomussalmi with the riderless horse galloping off ahead of them. Nestor plunged into the mass.

"Godalmighty, what a pig-headed old man!" said the lieutenant. "Damn, damn, damn it!"

"He'll get himself killed yet," said a sergeant by the name of Salonen.

"Yeah, or taken prisoner. There are some able-bodied men in that outfit. If they try to take him, open fire so that he'll have some chance of getting away," said the lieutenant.

"Try shooting into that mess. He's scrambling around with one of their horses like crazy," growled a corporal named Rajamäki.

Nestor realized what he had done only when he leaped in among the Russians. His eyes had lighted on a big horse that was pulling a load of Russians. The mob, numb with hunger and cold, pushed on ahead. Few of them realized where the shot that felled their officer had come from. Only one thought was hammering in their minds. Keep going. Keep going. Away from the grip of hunger and cold. If only I can save myself...

"Give me those reins!"

The sled was shaped like a boat with the bow and stern sawed off. It was jam-packed with men, some of whom were hanging over the sides. Nestor's shout only made the driver turn his head.

"Didn't you hear me? Give me those reins!"

The driver of the sled had the reins in one hand. With the other, he began to dig out his rifle from under his buttocks. It was a clumsy attempt. Nestor felt as if his every limb had become a steel spring. He grabbed the driver by the neck and dumped him into the road. Now the reins were in Nestor's hands. He jerked at them and shouted.

"This is no greenhorn at the reins. Get a move on!"

A sharp jerk on one of the reins turned the horse's head into the bank at the spot where Nestor had leaped onto the road. When the horse's breast collided with the high bank, the animal began to dance in place. The men, wailing loudly, began to climb off the sled. Then Nestor let out a bellow that could be heard even by his patrol comrades.

"Come on! Just get going right now!"

The horse merely tossed his head on high. Then rage boiled up in Nestor. With all his might, he lashed the animal across the back with the ends of the reins. The big bay reared up on its hind legs and lunged into the harness. The sled leaped up from the road and stood almost on end against the bank. Arms and legs flashed in one tangled mass as a cluster of men rolled down to the road. Now the horse was galloping through the deep snow. Nestor's legs got tangled and he slid along over the snow like a Lapland sled. But he did not let go of the reins. The sled banged into small spruce trees, knocking the snow loose from their limbs. Through the flying snow, Nestor could be heard shouting:

"Whoa! Now don't leave your driver behind. Whoa!"

At last the horse stopped and Nestor got to his feet. Two men sat in the bottom of the sled. Their heads were whirling. Both raised their hands.

"*Tovarisch, tovarisch!*" they kept repeating in a tearful voice.

"I don't usually dump my buddies, but it's time to lighten the load."

Nestor took hold of one man's quilted coat and rolled him off the sled into the snow.

"Start walking. Toward the road. Hop to it now. Why the devil are you standing there gawking with your paws pointed at the sky? Go! That way!"

Nestor waved an arm toward the road. Since the man still

stood there with his hands up, Nestor rapped him across the shoulder with the reins.

"Can't you get it into your head. Barrel off now with your buddy! Argh!"

Nestor roared out the last word. The man began to wade back along his tracks. He sidled off, sometimes falling, but never taking his eyes off Nestor, who continued to wave him away. By that time the rest of the patrol had come up to the horse. One of the men raised the stock of a rifle to his cheek and took aim at the fleeing man.

"Don't you point that at him. I gave him my word he wouldn't be hurt and could go back to his own side. If you pull that trigger, it means trouble between us from now on."

"Let him go," said the lieutenant.

"Hey, look lieutenant. I made a fast deal at the market. Would you believe I got a brute of a work horse here. The logs will come flying out of the woods behind him some day."

Nestor waded around to the horse's head. Although the animal tossed his head high, he opened his mouth to the manipulations of Nestor's practiced fingers.

"It's so dark I can't really see his teeth. When daylight comes, I'll tell you my new horse's age to within a year."

"There are your skis and rifle. You're some weird soldier when you go after a bunch of *Ivans* with your bare hands," said the corporal.

"We'll say no more about your behavior this time, Malinen," said the lieutenant. "But remember, this is the last time you act on your own."

"Is that the kind of thanks I get? The battalion commander at Pyhäkylä said a prisoner would be a good prize. Take a look, boy, at what's squatting in the bottom of the sled."

"*Tovarisch!*" said the prisoner, when Nestor pointed at him.

"I'll be damned if you still think I fouled things up. They could have killed me first if they had wanted to. They didn't seem to have any grudge against me. So let's both of us feel good about it, lieutenant. You got a prisoner and I got a good horse."

"Well, that does seem to be so. We don't have time now to go into the right and wrong of what you did. Some of our neighbor's ski troops may be on their way here. Start driving back the way we came, Malinen. We'll leave right now."

"You can't drive through this deep snow with a sled. Who the devil will open a track for this boat? It'll wear the horse out too."

"You mean we won't take the sled?" said the lieutenant.

"I wouldn't take a half-assed boat like that anyway. I'm no carpenter, but whatever Russian made that did a pretty poor job. Phooey!"

Nestor's tone of voice was nearly plaintive. His knife flashed and the shafts fell to the ground. Then he gestured to the prisoner sitting in the bottom of the sled.

"Here, here!"

The prisoner seemed unable to rise under his own power. The men helped him up.

"Check his pockets just in case," said the lieutenant.

They obeyed his command. However, the prisoner's pockets contained nothing warlike. Nestor and his companions helped the man up onto the horse.

"As long as you sit here, at least your balls won't freeze. Throw the blanket from the bottom of the sled over the old guy's back, Salonen. Otherwise he'll freeze."

Rifle slung over his shoulder, reins in one hand, and ski poles in the other, Nestor set off leading the horse.

"Salonen and Rajamäki will stay to make sure they don't come after us," said the lieutenant.

"Do they have any ski troops? If they're on foot, we'll soon leave them behind," said Nestor.

"We can't be sure of anything," said the lieutenant.

"When you start to question this prisoner, I'll be one of the gang," said Nestor. "Now you hammerhead, don't tramp on my skis."

"We'll see then," said the lieutenant, "but I'm convinced that the Russians have pulled back from the line at Alasalmi."

The patrol started the return trek. The horse was young and well fed. With its long legs, it waded through the snow like a moose. Their first objective was a long, narrow lake a short ten kilometers to their rear. The moon disappeared and the early morning hours grew darker, but still they could clearly make out the track they had come along. It had hardened and skiing was easier. There was no hint of harassment and no sound of big guns firing at the front.

The feeder stream of the lake appeared before them. The lieutenant turned around at its bank and said:

"It'll be safer to cross the lake now."

"Chow would taste good right now, but anyway let's cross it. There's something else to draw us there. Do any of my buddies see anything different on the far shore?"

"Just an old wreck of a barn," said one of the men.

"That shows you come from the city. That barn means a lot to me and more to this horse."

"Ahah! Is there hay in it?" said one of the men.

"Seems to be. Let's push on across the lake so we can get to eat," said Nestor.

As they climbed up the bank from the lake, the horse raised its head, let out a long whinny, and rushed past Nestor to the barn.

"The animal is hungry...but aren't we all?"

The horse thrust its muzzle through the poles closing off the door of the hay barn and began to munch on the fragrant wild hay. Nestor looked at it and said:

"I wonder if that rider is frozen stiff. Hell, it makes me laugh to look at him. He's sitting like a woman in a church sled with her shawl wrapped around her ears."

There was dry wood near the walls of the barn. In a few minutes, a fire was blazing. Mess kits were heating up over the flames. Hay was spread out on the snow. The most tired among the men threw themselves down on it, and the prisoner too was helped to a bed there.

Slowly the day grew lighter. The sudden appearance of two men across the lake startled them, but their apprehensions were soon relieved. The arrivals, Sergeant Salonen and Corporal Rajamäki, skied toward to the barn.

"Make yourselves at home. No one even tried to follow us," shouted Salonen from the ice.

"Now we'll have a good meal and rest," said the lieutenant. "No one can surprise us here, at least not by daylight."

When the tea was ready, Nestor said to the prisoner, who was warming his hands at the fire.

"Come and share my pack! You have to eat and eat hearty, otherwise you won't make it the rest of the way."

The man understood Nestor's gestures and moved over to him. At the same time he grinned so broadly that his white teeth flashed. He too attacked the food eagerly.

"That's the way. Forget to laugh and sorrow fills the heart. And you have nothing to cry about, since you're my prisoner. Cut a thick slice of that smoked reindeer meat, and throw plenty of sugar into your tea."

CHAPTER V

1

Even in peacetime, the main room at Naavala had seldom been empty, but after the Russian army's advance to Alasalmi, there was constant traffic along the road from that town, a road which ran by Naavala. Every horse-drawn column, and sometimes even columns of motor vehicles going by made a stop at Naavala. The visitors ate and drank coffee, and the more weary ones sometimes napped on benches or on the floor. The ordinary routine of the house began to seem like a distant memory. The mistress of the house had been evacuated along with her oldest daughter and the children. Aleksi Naavala himself now lived in the church village. Organizing the evacuations and other responsibilities kept him tied down there.

On this occasion, Hilja sat in the main room reading a copy of a newsmagazine. Her sister Elsa was doing the barn chores. The men of a horse-drawn column, who had stopped during the early morning hours for a nap, had left at dawn for Suomussalmi.

To Hilja, the room seemed abnormally empty. Her mind wandered from the pages of the magazine. How were her mother and the children doing? Where were Kauko and Toivo? Sometimes when the commotion was at its worst, she tired of the perpetual coming and going and longed be alone again. Now when a rare moment of solitude had come, it too made her restless.

Hilja's shift as air warden ended early in the morning. After that she would work in the kitchen for hours. Now, she thought, she really should get a few hours' sleep. Her turn on watch would begin again near midnight and last until morning. However, she knew that she would sleep like the dead if she lay down. When a moment of solitude like this came along, it was nice to let one's thoughts run free.

All the women and children from Järvenkylä were now near the coast. The men were gone, the old men evacuated and the young men at the front or at training camps. Kauko was learning the trade of war. How many letters had he written to Elma by now? Kauko's letters were nice to read. Toivo had written to her twice. He wasn't very good at writing. There was not a single word in the letters about what went on in his mind there at the front.

Although Toivo's letters said little about feelings, they still gave her a sense of warmth. When his first letter arrived, she understood why he had behaved so oddly last summer. When they were together, his eyes were on her much of the time, and although he was not exactly shy, he would lower them when she looked directly at him. Now, thinking back on it more carefully, she recalled that he had done very little cursing in her presence. After his return from Russia, he had used less profanity than usual. And last summer he had stopped in evenings at Naavala to sit and chat more often than before.

Amid all these memories, Hilja thought now and then of Kauko. Would he soon be at the front? They had been at confirmation school together. She recalled a pleasant meeting late one evening near the big pine tree. She had been out looking for the cows as Kauko came striding home from the pulp woods, pack on his back. Although it was already midnight, he was just returning from work. Everyone said that he, the oldest of the Sammalsuo boys, was a hard worker. Her father often did so. Toivo was a hard worker too. After his return from Russia, the fields of his home at Olkivaara began to expand, but through no effort of Father Nestor's. Like the Sammalsuo boys, Toivo was opening up new fields with a hoe.

Hilja went back to turning the pages. There were pictures from the front. One showed men in white uniforms around a tank. The caption read that the Finns had damaged the tank and captured it. She tried to read, but nothing came of it. When they had met at the pine tree, Kauko had had a gash on his arm from a jagged tree limb. Suddenly the wound looked just awful. Bark, dust, and other woods debris were mixed with the dried blood on it. Even now a chill ran down her spine. She had cleaned the wound, and what a job that had been. Since there was no water, she'd had to spit into a handkerchief and clear away the dirt with it. And then bandage the gash. She still blushed as she recalled it. She had ordered Kauko to turn and take a safety pin from his underwear. His tanned cheeks turned red and he could not meet her eyes. Hilja recalled that she had taken a long time to bandage the gash. She could have done it much more quickly.

A few days later, Kauko had met Hilja in the porch.at Naavala and said shyly:

"Here is that handkerchief of yours. Thank you."

It had been laundered and ironed into folds. Aili told her she had often teased Kauko about the incident. "Kauko pretended to be angry at the teasing, but he was secretly pleased," she said, and added: "You're likely to become a daughter-in-law in our house, Hilja."

Hilja stopped thinking about the meeting by the pine tree and wondered if she should go to bed. Elma would be coming soon for her turn on the evening watch. At the thought of Elma, Kauko came more sharply into her mind again. Although the eldest of the Olkivaara girls was a good friend of hers, it upset her to think of Kauko and Elma together. What was wrong in that? Elma was Toivo's sister and a spirited and straightforward girl. She was good-looking too, fair and high-breasted. There had been talk in the community last summer, and even earlier, that Elma and Kauko were sweethearts. Elma did not deny that she liked Kauko. She always had good things to say about him and was unaware that this always made Hilja sad. Once last summer the two of them had been together in Hilja's summer bedroom. It was almost midnight but Elma was not ready to start rowing for home yet. The two girls had talked about everything under the sun. It was Elma who brought up a new subject:

"Last Saturday night Kauko and I were out trolling."

Hilja could not say a word.

"Actually we were out the whole night."

Now Hilja tossed the magazine aside. She looked at the clock ticking on the wall and forced herself to think that she must go to sleep. That didn't help. Again she thought of that summer night, and her heart began to beat faster. Not as fast, though, as it had in that summer bedroom. Then she'd had to swallow a few times before she could speak clearly:

"Did you get any fish?"

"A few little pike and a couple of big perch. They weren't feeding. It was fun to go ashore early in the morning."

They were sitting side by side on Hilja's bed. Luckily it was so dark that Elma could not see her face. But her heart was beating so fast that she moved away from Elma. Then she said:

"Where did you land?"

"At Ylisaari Point. Where the big chokecherry trees are."

This time Hilja was ashamed at how quickly she spoke:

"What did you do there?"

"First we built a fire on the sand and then we fried fish. We had other food with us too."

Hilja could feel the tears in the corners of her eyes. She decided to go on asking questions, even though Elma might wonder about it or hear the agitation in her voice.

"Did you shine fish until morning?"

"Yes, we did. We built a campfire from pulpwood left on shore by loggers. It was nice there."

Hilja looked away. There was laughter in Elma's voice. It must have been nice there. A solid wall of chokecherry trees grew on the shore, thick enough to screen them from anyone on the lake or in the village. Why didn't Elma stop babbling and leave? She could go by way of the Sammalsuos'. Kauko was sleeping in his summer bedroom. Maybe they had planned a rendezvous. Maybe Kauko was waiting on the other side of the bridge. Then they would walk off together. Hilja took out her handkerchief and blew her nose hard, quickly dabbing the corners of her eyes with it as she returned it to her pocket.

"Kauko and I meant to row right off after eating and drinking our coffee, but Toivo, wonder of wonders, said that once we'd started out on a pleasure trip, there was no need to hurry."

"Was Toivo there too?"

"Why do you ask? Is there something wrong in that."

"N-no." Hilja giggled.

"Oh, didn't I say so already? Kauko did the rowing while Toivo steered in the stern."

Hilja's mood brightened. She had always been a little shy with Toivo Olkivaara. Now he seemed like a good friend.

"Kauko and Toivo slept like logs. I kept my back warm at the fire. I sat and looked at the lake through the chokecherry trees. It was calm and the birds were singing. I kept thinking how nice our lake was in the summer. I slept only a few hours in the early morning."

"It would be fun to go night-fishing sometime. We could take lunch and a coffee pot with us."

"Let's go sometime," said Elma. "Toivo won't go unless Kauko comes along. Listen, let's the four of us go and shine fish this fall. I like to do that. The pine blocks burning in the grate on the boat smell so good."

The mobilization had interfered with their plans. Hilja and Elma became closer friends. Even Toivo began to seem nice. He was so manly.

Hilja's thoughts were interrupted when she heard the roar of engines outside. She rose and went to the kitchen where she dried her eyes on her apron. There was a war on now. Only six months separated this day from the time she had been thinking about. Had she been dreaming? Lately everything seemed like a bad dream.

She heard the outer door open and then there was a knock on the kitchen door. To Hilja, that was an indication that it was not a local person, and she called out:

"Yes?"

A young sergeant had already entered the kitchen. He smiled and raised a hand to the brim of his garrison cap.

"Good morning, Miss Naavala. How did the night watch go? Did you hear any bolshie planes? May I sit here in the women's quarters and chat with you?"

"I didn't hear a thing. Go ahead and sit down."

"And the phone worked perfectly well?" said the man, seating himself.

"I just called Aili at the windmill and I could hear her clearly."

"Is it Miss Malinen's turn on watch?"

"No, it's Aili Sammalsuo's. The younger one."

"I get them mixed up. Are you home all alone now?"

"My sister is taking care of the cows. She'll be here soon."

"Come and sit near me, miss. It's so nice to talk to you. The corpswomen in the church village are such old nuns. They wear their hair in a bun and have no sense of humor."

"I'm just like them. I can't talk to people."

"That's not true, ha, ha. I won't eat you alive even if you do sit here. Right here, on this warm spot that I'm patting."

In Hilja's opinion, the sergeant talked too much. He was careful in his use of words. His speech sounded like the language one read in newspapers and books. The young man, a communications sergeant from the south, had first appeared in the area at the end of the year when called in to repair a faulty telephone. His services were not needed again until another malfunction occurred after the New Year. On that occasion, Hilja and Elma happened to be in the Naavala kitchen together. Hilja invited him for coffee. The sergeant kept the conversation going continually until Elma, whose turn on watch had just ended, rose and said:

"I won't get the work done at home by sitting here."

"Where do you live, Miss Malinen?" asked the sergeant.

"Across the lake with the spooks," Elma giggled. "See you."

"If you'll permit me, I'll come along to scare them off. I'd like to learn my way around this place."

The man followed Elma out. Nevertheless she stepped into her skis and set off with long strides on the trail leading to the lake, calling back over her shoulder:

"So far I've been able to handle the spooks and the devil too."

The man was left on the shore in frustration. But then he said:

"Let her go...this time."

After that the sergeant stopped in now and then at Naavala, once even at night, without being sent for. That time he climbed up into the windmill when Hilja was on duty. He was even more talkative then, and went so far as to put his arms around her. The windmill was so far from the house she would have had to shout at the top of her lungs to be heard there. Hilja kept evading the man's advances, and luckily Aili arrived a half hour early for her watch. When the clock pointed to the hour for the change of watch, Hilja nudged Aili in the ribs, and so the girl was not surprised when Hilja stayed on after the change. At last the sergeant left. When Hilja reached home, he was nowhere in sight, having left for the church village.

Now she tried again to evade him:

"I don't really have the time. I have to get some sleep." Hilja gave an exaggerated yawn.

"Well you must be tired, the way you're yawning. I'll be glad to come and pull the covers over you."

"I can pull the covers up myself. I'm not that tired."

"Then I'll help you light the fire."

Hilja had stooped down to light the fire. The man moved over to her and caught her by the wrist. He took the piece of wood from her hand and shoved it through the door of the stove into the fire.

"You can go..."

Hilja's cheeks flamed red. She was not angry, but indignant.

"As far away as possible, is that it?"

"I don't care where you go, but keep your hands off me."

Footsteps sounded in the entry. As the handle of the kitchen door turned downward, the man darted over to the window.

"You seem to have a boy friend, Hilja," said Elsa, who had come in.

"A would-be boy friend, but he doesn't rate," said Hilja.

Elsa could see by Hilja's look that she was upset.

"Have the corpswomen wrecked the phone again?" she asked.

"I just came to take a look as a precautionary measure," said the man, looking out the window toward the bridge. "Who's on guard at the bridge?"

"The Malinen cousins, Tuomas and Vante," said Hilja.

"Are they Miss Malinen's relatives?"

"Vante is her brother and Tuomas is her cousin. Pour some coffee for me and the telephone man, cooksie," said Elsa, sitting down at the table.

Hilja obeyed her older sister's command. While she drank the coffee, Elsa said to the sergeant, who was looking thoughtful.

"It probably wasn't necessary to move the cattle from here to the coast. What are the higher-ups in the church village saying about the war?"

"That the Russians have been driven out of Suomussalmi too, but that the Finns are being hard pressed on the Isthmus. There is little reason to be afraid here."

The sergeant's remarks sounded absent-minded. Finally he said:

"Who takes care of the animals at the Malinen's?"

"Elma herself. There's no one else at home there. Do you know about cattle?"

"Not really. I've earned my bread as an electrician. Is Miss Malinen home all alone?"

"When the boys are on guard at the bridge."

"She's a brave girl. Many thanks for the coffee."

The sergeant rose and went to the door leading to the main room. At that moment, a number of trucks drove up to the yard.

Men from the vehicles came clumping into the main room as the sergeant elbowed his way out the door. He walked along the plowed road to the bridge and stopped beside the boys standing there together. They recognized the newcomer.

"How's it going?" he asked.

"Not too bad," said Svante, who stood with his rifle on his shoulder.

"Have you seen any suspicious-looking men around?"

"Svante and I haven't had to shoot anyone yet."

"The Russians have started dropping saboteurs by parachute. Be careful, especially at night. Even if men in Finnish army uniform, who speak Finnish, come up and talk to you, you mustn't let them fool around the bridge."

"No one has tried to, and if they did, we'd put holes in them," said Svante.

"Did you boys come here on skis?"

"We did. Who the devil could plow through that snow?" said Tuomas.

"I'd like to borrow a pair and see what the other side of the lake is like. I need to know this countryside because of my job. Is that trail to the right the one you came along?"

"Yah, it goes to our home cottage first, and then if you ski through the yard, you come to the Ylikylä farm. It's easy to find, but if you get mixed up in our yard, my sister Elma will show you the way. Those are my skis leaning against the plowed bank there," said Svante.

✧ ✧ ✧

Hilja Naavala watched from the window as the sergeant set off on skis along the trail that led to Olkivaara. The truck drivers were eating their lunch and drinking the milk supplied to them by Elsa in the main room. As her sister stepped into the kitchen, Hilja turned to her and said:

"Elsa, come here."

Her sister came to her side. Hilja pointed to the snow-covered field with a knitting needle and said:

"Is that the sergeant skiing out there?"

"It looks like him. Where did he get skis from so quickly?"

"He must have gotten them from the boys," said Hilja. "Elma will soon have a visitor."

"Is that where he's going?"

"Where else do you think? I'm going to sleep for awhile."

Hilja went through the kitchen to the bedroom. It was where her mother and father usually slept, but during these evacuation days, the sisters napped there. Hilja halfway undressed and then burrowed under the covers. Night and day had lost their accustomed rhythm. One had to nap whenever she had the opportunity. Now I must sleep, thought Hilda.

But though she was tired, sleep would not come. She wondered what Elma might be saying right now. That telephone gentleman might have to beat a hasty retreat...although who could tell...They were alone in the house. The sergeant was not bad looking. Not in the least. He was just too bold and forward for her. But Elma was different — she wasn't shy. She might even be attracted to him.

I have to sleep now. My eyes and ears have to be sharp tonight. Men at the front are risking their lives. It's not right to be mulling over everyone's romances now. Kauko had written Elma that he might soon wind up at the front. He had said in the letter that he wondered what it would be like to try to kill a man he bore no grudge, a man he didn't even know.

It's a little different with Toivo. He hates the Russians because they treated him so badly when he was there. I saw from the last letter that he had been made a corporal. He must have fought hard. The men say that they give stripes to the ones who are the most aggressive in battle. Toivo said nothing about it. I just saw the word *Corporal* on the return address. *Res. Corporal Toivo Malinen.*

Toivo is on the Isthmus. Will Kauko have to go there? On the verge of sleep, Hilja was still thinking of Kauko. He said when I was bandaging his hand that I would make a good nurse. That sergeant is a handsome man. Elma might very well start keeping company with him. She's a couple of years older than Kauko too. Why do some people have to have more than others? Elma once said that Kauko was shy with me because we own a big farm. I would be glad if Elma found a nice boy friend. She's always wanted to go and live in a bigger city. She would have a chance if the sergeant married her. Anyway, I'll send Kauko a card. There's nothing wrong in that.

2

When Auku returned from watch at the bridge that morning, he gulped down the milk gruel Aili had prepared for him before leaving for her turn as air sentry. The kerosene lamp burned dimly on the table. Auku went to the cupboard and took their mother's last letter from it. It had arrived yesterday, but Auku had only glanced at it in Aili's presence. Now that he was home alone, he could concentrate on it in peace.

In evacuation 17 Jan. 1940

Dear Children

Now I'll write you a letter. I'm always thinking about how you're getting along. We had good luck and got into a good house as evacuees. The people are nice and tell us to make ourselves at home, but how can I when I'm always thinking of you, Auku and Aili. I miss the cows, and wonder how Aili will be able to take care of them. We are all well, thank God, and we have been able to stay in the same house with Mari Olkivaara and her children. We're not supposed to write a word about where we are, but I'll go so far as to say we are in Finland. Take care of the fire and when Red-Ear is due to calf, get Elsa Naavala or Elma Olkivaara to help you. Will God still have mercy enough to end the war and to bring us home? Kauko writes pretty often and it sounds as if he'll have to go to the front soon. Try not to act up too much, Auku, and you mustn't fight with Aili. Liisa and Väinö are very homesick. They always talk about how you are getting along. In the evening they cry when they miss home and Auku and Aili. Write more often so we'll know what's new because my writing is so poor. God bless you. Now we'll know what mercy is if we can only get home again. This is written by your own mother.

Tears rolled down Auku's cheeks. He looked around the room and gritted his teeth. He missed little Liisu the most of all. His hands shook as he thrust the letter back into the envelope.

"Goddamn. A big man doesn't cry."

Auku went over to the bed and lay down on his belly. His shoulders shook with sobbing for a long time. Finally he sat up, poured cold water into a basin, and washed his face.

"The whole world is gone to hell."

The deserted room made him feel depressed. The marks left on the logs from the machine-gun fire gave him a chill. He put on his jacket and walked over the snowbank to the barn, stooping to enter the low doorway. The cows jerked at their chains as they turned their heads to look at the newcomer, and the lambs thumped against the walls of their pen. Auku lighted the barn lamp. The cat was sitting beside the big iron heating pot. He took it into his arms.

"How is Auku's kitty? Did they give you any milk? Does Oscar Portimo miss Mother and Liisu?"

Auku sat on the side of the iron pot, holding the cat in his lap and stroking its back. The usually timid animal was not afraid now. It purred loudly as it sat in Auku's lap.

"Has Aili been feeding you well?"

The boy looked into the cows' stalls and the lambs' pen. The animals seemed to have food left to eat, but more would not hurt. Auku went to the loft, took an armful of hay, and divided it among the cows. Then he tossed a bunch of leafy twigs into the lambs' pen.

"Chew on that now. Mother will come to feed you some day."

When Auku returned to the house, he decided to go and check his snares. He really should have slept, but he had not seen to his wildfowl snares for many days. There had been a raging blizzard a couple of days ago. It might have sprung some of them.

✧ ✧ ✧

The storm had filled in the track to Auku's snares. When the day grew lighter, the old track shone through from underneath the new snow. Hat bobbing from one side to the other, shotgun slung over his shoulder, Auku skied toward Murhajärvi. Last summer he had traveled this route with Väinö. In earlier years, Kauko had been his companion. With his older brother, there was always the likelihood of an argument. It was because Kauko liked to read, thought Auku, as he skied along. He had been a strange companion on these snaring expeditions. Sometimes he stood gaping at the ugliness of the landscape and sometimes at its beauty. He was always babbling about how beautiful the woods over there were when the sun lighted up the frost on the trees. Such nonsense always made Auku angry. Now somehow he could have put up with it.

The sun rose into view as Auku approached the shore of Murhajärvi. He could see the dilapidated shanties on the opposite shore of the lake. There was the abandoned Nuusala place. What had once been the Kotaniemi farm was now only a point overrun with juniper trees. Near this desolate lake, Auku had lived the most stirring moments of his life. From here he had carried home sizable numbers of wood grouse strangled by the snares he had set in willow thickets. Here he had caught rabbits, even an occasional ermine. Kauko had been drawn to the place by the abandoned shanties as well as the snaring. He poked about their walls and crawled around above their ceilings. Once he had been badly frightened by a horned owl in the attic at Nuusala.

Auku cut across the lake. In the shallows along the shore, dried reeds poked through the surface of the snow. The hills in back of the lake were frost-covered. Everything was completely still. An ermine had been frisking over the snow. Auku's eyes followed its tracks to the middle of the lake. He stopped and shaded his eyes from the glare of the sun.

"What the heck sled has been traveling out there?"

For a long time Auku gazed at the strange furrows in the snow. It looked as if a sled with broad runners had dropped from the sky and been pulled along the surface of the lake.

"It must have been an airplane."

A chill ran down his spine. He scanned the whole surface of the lake. What airplane could have landed there? Something was very wrong here. It took Auku a long time to calm down. His glance swept over the entire shore, but he could see only snowy woods and the smooth expanse of snow.

"Well, those tracks won't eat me alive. I have to take a closer look at them."

Auku skied on. The runners had first grazed the snow, then the plane had skipped a fairly long distance before plowing a continuous track along the surface. Auku followed the direction taken by the furrows. They turned in a slow arc toward the longest bay on the lake. Snow was blown far off to either side of the tracks. Auku concentrated so intently on studying them that he forgot his recent fear. But then he felt another chill.

"Men jumped into the snow here. They trampled the snow around the runners like a reindeer herd around a hay stack."

Auku's head began to swivel in all directions. Wasn't that a man standing on the shore at Nuusala? Or two of them? Then his brain told him that they were juniper bushes sticking up out of the snow.

"The ski tracks go toward Murhaniemi," he said aloud to calm himself.

He looked at the tracks carved into the surface of the snow. Not even a good gun could shoot all the way here from Murhaniemi. This was where the two men had put on their skis. He could tell by the marks left in the snow by their ski poles. Then the track of the plane continued.

"The snow was really blown around here when the propeller started sucking air."

The plane tracks continued for a long time. Only quite near the shore had the plane taken off from the snow, at a point where a long swamp joined the lake. The plane had gone buzzing off in that direction. Auku took off a mitten and felt the track and the marks of a ski pole with his bare fingers.

"They aren't very fresh. The snow has had time to set. I wonder if it was last night that they put on their skis here."

Auku's eyes followed the retreating tracks. Near the Murhaniemi shore, they turned to one side. Could they have thought the shanty there was inhabited?

"I didn't get to check my snares."

Auku turned his skis around and went kicking back along the trail over which he had come. From time to time he glanced aside. Who could tell from which spit of land they might be watching with their guns? Sweat began to trickle down his face, but he still felt a chill down his back. Snow flew up from his ski poles and his bindings. Only when he reached the woods on shore did he calm down. His breathing grew steadier and he mopped his brow on his sleeve.

"Spies would have laughed if they saw me just now. Some guard, running away with a shotgun on my back."

"I'm not going to leave it at that. I have to find out more about them."

Auku wriggled out of the shotgun sling, broke open its breech, and checked that it was loaded. Holding the gun squeezed under his armpit, and gripping his ski poles in one hand, he turned his skis around and skied through the woods along the shore. It would be surprising if he ran into the men. Even if they had seen him just now, they would think he was still running away.

Auku knew every bay and point of Murhajärvi. He skied through the thickest woods, coming close to the shore at times. From the thickets there, he looked toward Murhaniemi. Soon he was quite near the abandoned hut. If he were to throw as hard as he could four or five times, he could land a stone on the birchbark roof.

The boy moved his skis even more carefully now, skulking from one snow-covered tree to the next. Fear again tugged at his heart. It would be safest to go back, to ski all-out to Naavala. If he could only speak aloud, he would not be so damned scared. Auku gritted his teeth and muttered softly:

"I am going to find out if they are still here."

Thick growths of willow left only narrow lanes open between former drainage ditches. Auku came to one of these openings. From here he could see a frost-covered gray log wall and a snow-covered birchbark roof. Were the spies there? His heart was pounding so hard that the blood roared in his ears. A new scare almost drove him to his knees. Only after a long time did he realize that it was a wood grouse thrashing around in the snow near a row of willows close to the building. The bird was on its last legs. For a long time it would beat its wings with its tail to the sky, and then collapse into the snow with its wings spread wide. Relieved, Auku skied toward the snare. If this had happened on an ordinary round of the snares, he would have been flying toward the bird.

'Wood grouse don't run around when there are people nearby," Auku muttered.

He did not go directly to the bird, but skied carefully around a corner. Ski tracks led into the yard of the abandoned dwelling. The skiers had gone into the shanty on foot, and then left another ski trail that led into the woods. Auku could tell that they had been here and left shortly.

He went back to the creature struggling in the snare and snatched it up. The white bird's heart beat wildly as it sought to escape.

"Stop flapping so I can get this loop open."

It was not easy to release the cotton cord pulled tight into the bird's neck-feathers. Auku grunted and groaned for a long time before the loop came free. Then he loosed his bare fingers from the warm feathers of the bird. The white wings began to beat the air. A short distance away stood a large birch tree, its branches looking as if they were swathed in a white veil. The bird flew toward it, but it was still so dazed that it slid down the ends of the branches into the snow when it tried to alight on them. Then it rose into flight and headed out across the lake, leaving a dark line down the frosty branches on one side of the tree.

Auku turned on his skis, went back to the yard, and entered the low doorway. In the middle of a rotted floor covered with reindeer droppings was a place where the prowlers had eaten. From among the reindeer droppings, Auku picked up shreds of newspaper.

"I knew it. This is foreign print."

Behind the ruins of a fireplace, Auku found an empty tin can. He could not read the words printed on its side. He went back outside, put on his skis, and followed the tracks leading to the woods with his shotgun under his arm. Soon he came upon a small swamp; the tracks led directly across it.

"They seem to have gone straight toward Olkivaara," Auku said to himself.

He turned off the track and began to ski directly toward the Naavala bridge. He no longer dared to follow his earlier trail. Who could tell if they had come across it and were watching it. Elma was home alone, since Vante and Tuomas were on bridge watch at the same time. We have to get this straightened out somehow, Auku decided. Then he started to ski as fast as his legs could kick out.

3

Elma was on her way out of the house, but stopped in the main room when.she heard the thump of footsteps outside on the porch. Who could be coming now? She was not easily rattled, but now she felt oddly apprehensive. A couple of steps took her to a refuge behind the big bake oven. There was knock on the door. Had Auku Sammalsuo come to visit, and was he now playing a prank on her?

"Walk right in," she said. "The door isn't locked."

"One gets good instruction here. Hello."

Elma stepped into view, her cheeks flushing.

"Hello. So that's who it is. I thought our neighbor Auku was playing tricks on me."

"Were you expecting him?" asked the sergeant, who had stepped into the room.

"Well, not exactly. He sometimes drops in."

The young sergeant stood in the middle of the floor and looked around him. Mostly his eyes rested on Elma, who was leaning one hand against the oven.

"You have a homey cottage. It's neat, and there are even flowers in the window."

"When was this old wreck of a place ever neat? But I like it. Visitors are allowed to sit down here."

"Thank you. May I try this rocker?"

"That's what it's there for."

"It's a good rocker. It won't tip over, will it?"

"Some of the brats, I mean my brothers and sisters, have managed to topple it."

Elma walked over to the table where she sat down and took up her knitting. The needles began to click. Although she kept her eyes on her work, she sensed that the man was staring at her constantly.

"Are you home all alone?" he said after a long pause.

"The cat and a couple of cows are here too. Even a lamb..."

"Aren't you afraid to be home alone at a time like this?"

Elma looked at the man. Her blushing cheeks rounded into a slight smile as she said:

"I've never done any great harm to anybody. Who should I be afraid of?"

"What if saboteurs should come?"

"They have better things to do than hang around lonely old shacks."

"Look at how brightly the sun is shining into my eyes through that window. I have to move my chair to get away from it. I'll move right next to you. It's nice to watch how well you click those needles. What lucky man will get those mittens?"

"These happen to be socks."

"Ha, ha, I was really off-base. Who is going to get that good strong pair of socks?"

Elma raised a knitting needle, stuck it crosswise in her mouth, and stretched the knitting out across her knees. The movements of her fingers were slow and gentle as she stared at the work.

"They're for father. I wonder if I decreased the calf enough."

"Where is your father? Has he been evacuated?"

"He was on the front at Suomussalmi first. They say he's been taken to Kuhmo now."

The man had shifted his chair and was now rocking directly in front of Elma. Leaning his head against the back rest, he looked up at the ceiling. Then he took out a pack of cigarettes, opened it, and extended it to her:

"Help yourself..."

"Thank you, but they're too mild. Women here smoke pipes."

The sergeant laughed. "You have a sense of humor."

"There isn't too much of that around these days. And what makes you think I'm joking?"

"Well, old ladies may smoke pipes around here, but I'm sure you don't. May I smoke?"

"Puff away. We've seen and smelled smoke here before this."

The man sat and blew smoke rings at the ceiling. Then he said:

"My mouth waters when I sit here and look at that bread pole. Those thin loaves of rye must be delicious."

Elma raised her head and glanced up at the bread pole.

"If you're hungry, I'll get you something to eat."

"I had only tea this morning. If you would be so kind..."

"No great kindness in that. These days a person has to eat whenever he can."

Elma went into the kitchen and returned with a clean, folded table cloth over her arm.

"This food of mine is nothing special, but maybe it will take the edge off your hunger."

"You're too particular."

Milk, fresh and clabbered, butter, and smoked reindeer meat appeared on the table. Elma took a stool and moved it over to the bread pole. She had to rise on tiptoe in order to reach the bread. Although dark-gray hand-knit stockings showed above her Lapland boots, they did not make her slender calves look ungraceful. The hem of her skirt rose above her knees and her reaching arms thrust her breasts out higher than usual. The rocker stopped and the man in it was forced to swallow hard. Although Elma was not long in getting the bread down, the man must have seen something to excite him. As she stepped to the floor with the bread, Elma giggled and said:

"If it makes your mouth water, then we'll take it straight from the pole."

"Do you know, Miss Malinen, why I came here?"

"I haven't the faintest idea. There's no telephone to fix here."

"I came to see you."

"Me! What the heck is there to see in me?"

The man rocked himself up out of the chair and stood beside Elma, who was setting a bread basket down on the table. He put one elbow down on her shoulder.

"It's true. I'm young and lonely and among strangers."

The man broke off when Elma jerked her shoulders to one side. He was forced to take a quick sidestep to keep his balance.

"Go tell your tale to the women in the church village. There is the food. Have some."

"This is no tale I'm telling. Haven't you noticed how often I come to your lookout? I always just happen to come when you're there. Don't go."

Elma stepped back and avoided the man's grasping hands.

'Stop talking nonsense. You, a full-grown man. Aren't you hungry any more?"

"Elma, listen. I have a big farm in southern Finland. When the war is over I'll take you there. Everything is modern and..."

The man caught Elma by the wrist. Then he suddenly put his other arm around her and crushed her breasts against him with all his strength. Along the wall was a convertible wooden sofa in which Svante and Tuomas slept. Elma had closed it as she usually did in the morning and covered it with a homespun bedspread. Now the tall and agile man carried her toward it. Only the kicking heels of the girl grazed the floor.

"Are you crazy. You're going too far when you start using force."

The calves of her legs hit the side board of the sofa and she staggered backwards. There was a crash as the full weight of two people slammed down on the sofa at the same instant. Elma was pinned underneath. The man's hand groped at her skirt.

"Don't, Elma. I'll make you the mistress of a big house."

"I've never run into such a damned ram in all my life. Get off me and be quick about it. Agh...hell! Now do you believe me?"

"Ooww! What a place to hit me with your fist!"

The man leaped up from the sofa and pressed both hands into his crotch as he danced about the floor.

"So you came here to bellow! Well, go ahead. I'll tame an even bigger stud than you."

Elma's face was pale. Her body trembled with rage and exhaustion. She smoothed down her raised skirt.

"You women are awful. You should be careful about what you go hitting with your fists."

"Yeah, and such an innocent too. Now will you believe that you can't take us by force or wear us down."

"You misunderstand. I said I would make you my wife. I beg your pardon."

"I'm not cut out to be your lady of the manor. These backwoodsmen are good enough for me, even if they don't know how to woo in such a refined way."

"Now you're mocking me. I did ask for your pardon. Will you give it to me?"

"I'm no absolver of sins. Will you eat or shall I put the food away?"

"You wouldn't be so cruel if you knew how much it hurts."

"You can believe that I'm not about to blow on it to make it stop. Are you going to eat?"

The young man glared and his nostrils distended. He took up his mittens from the bench, slammed his hat on his head, and went to the door.

"Keep your cunt and your food. Goodbye and good luck."

"The same to you. A man with your gumption should be sent to the front."

The door could have been closed with a much gentler push. The window panes rattled. There was the clunking of skis against one end of the house. Elma moved over to the window. The man was kicking along the ski track with long strides. Then he hit a steep downhill slope and was lost from sight for a moment. When he reappeared on the ice of the lake, his skis left the tracks, and a cloud of light, cold snow swirled into the air. Elma could not help laughing as the man struggled to his feet. He looked back and brushed most of the snow from his clothing, then set off skiing across the lake.

"Pfft — you do meet all kinds. Darn it anyway!"

Elma began to gather up the food from the table. Not all men were made from the same mold. There was Kauko, for instance. He was a decent boy. She had sometimes been annoyed at his timidity and backwardness. They had once sat at this very table blowing soap bubbles. She was suddenly very lonesome. They had sat side by side looking at a book and then had taken straws...

Now she was sitting in exactly the same spot. She raised her elbows to the table and buried her hands in her face. Another of her soap bubbles had burst. How many more of them would before her days were over?

Then she took up her knitting and a new thought flashed into her mind. She would send these socks to Kauko. There were other pairs she had knitted earlier to send to her father and to Toivo. Her needles began to click again. When I send these to Kauko , I'll put sweet grass from the drawer in with them. The scent will remind him of his home lake and of me. Why hadn't he written for a couple of weeks? The thought kept rattling around in her mind, like the continual clicking of her needles.

4

"There are your skis, boy."

The sergeant, who had returned to the end of the bridge, kicked off Svante's skis. There was a sour look on his face.

"How did they glide?" asked Svante.

"You've never even seen a real pair of skis. What the hell are you standing together for? One of you should be at the other end of the bridge."

Svante and Tuomas looked inquiringly at each other and then at the sergeant.

"Did you hear me? Move it now, fast."

Tuomas began to walk across the bridge. As he reached the ramp on the other side, he turned to look back. The sergeant stepped up to Svante with a scowl on his face. He reached out a hand and said:

"Let me see if your gun is well oiled."

Svante stepped back a few paces and jerked the rifle free of the shoulder it dangled from. Then he nestled his cheek into the stock and took aim at the sergeant:

"Don't touch it. One step this way and I'll blow a goddamned hole in you."

"Oh-oh, young man. That's pretty tough talk. But I'm your superior officer."

"That makes no difference...just take one step this way."

Only now did Svante notice that the rifle was uncocked. He slapped the bolt open with the heel of his hand, drew it back, and snapped it shut. The barrel pointed steadily at the sergeant.

"Who told you to act like this?"

"Sheriff Pulkkila. When he gave me this rifle, he said: 'Nobody takes this away from you when you're on guard, no matter who he is.'"

The sergeant gave an exasperated laugh.

"He gave you the right orders," he said.

A column of trucks came into view from the direction of Suomussalmi. The sergeant signaled for them to stop. The first truck braked and its cab door opened. An army cap thrust out.

"What's the problem, sergeant?"

"I'm carrying a message. Can I get a lift to the church village?"

"Hop in."

When the column disappeared from sight, Tuomas walked back to Svante.

"What was the sergeant griping about? You were pointing your rifle at him."

"He was nosy about my rifle oil."

"What did you tell him?"

"He wasn't the man to check it out."

"He was in a bad temper. I've never seen him so nasty before."

'I don't think Elma kissed the floor for him."

"Maybe so," Tuomas laughed.

✧ ✧ ✧

Less than an hour later, a lone skier came charging up from the direction of Vaarakylä. The oncomer kept up a long, steady stride along the highway. The barrel of a gun on his back swayed with every stroke of his poles. Svante and Tuomas stood watching him approach, their fingers gripping the slings of their rifles.

"That traveler is in one big hurry. What fool could be in such a rush?" said Tuomas.

"I know who it is now. I didn't recognize him at first."

At that moment the skier was clattering down the slope to the deck of the bridge.

"What's chasing you, Auku?" shouted Svante.

Auku had reached the spot where they stood. He angled his skis into a snowplow and stopped. Mopping his brow on the sleeve of his jacket, he said:

"Nothing really. Keep your eyes open now. Watch the Vaarakylä end of the bridge especially."

"Why? Are there prowlers on the loose? Have you been checking your snares?"

Svante's questions came in rapid succession. He took the rifle off his shoulder.

"I was. But there's no time to talk now. I have to hurry."

Simultaneously Auku took off again. He sprinted up the road to the Naavala yard and rushed into the house. A few soldiers who had stopped to feed their horses were sitting in the main room.

"What's the panic, Auku? How come you're rushing into the house with your shotgun on your back and your eyes popping out?" asked Elsa, laughing.

Only now did Auku notice the shotgun. He took it from his back and hung it on the wall.

"How do you use that telephone, Elsa?"

"Who do you have to call?"

"The sheriff. And I'm in such a hurry that I don't have time to call a cat anything but a long-tailed feline scalawag, ha, ha."

Auku's attempt to laugh was a dry one. His lips were trembling. Elsa saw that the quick-tongued Sammalsuo boy was under a strain. She cranked the telephone and when she got the sheriff on the line, she handed the receiver to Auku:

"This is the sheriff. Speak your piece."

Auku was holding a telephone for the first time in his life. His hand was shaking and the pounding of his heart made hearing difficult.

"The sheriff speaking."

"Sheriff, there are saboteurs on the loose," Auku almost shouted into the phone. "I went to check my snares at Murhajärvi and an airplane had landed on the lake. The devils dropped off a couple of men on skis. They skied over to Murhaniemi and had their lunch in the abandoned cottage there. They had a newspaper with cockeyed print and I couldn't make anything of the print on their meat cans. They were in..."

A question from the sheriff cut short Auku's torrent of words:

"Who is this?"

"Didn't I tell you? This is me, Sammalsuo's second oldest boy, Auku. One of the bridge watch, from near Naavala."

"Ah, from Järvenkylä. So you think that saboteurs have been dropped from a plane on Murhajärvi, young man?"

"Well, I'm sure of it. There's no doubt at all. The tracks of two skiers start out from the marks of plane runners on the lake. They seem to be heading toward Järvenkylä. They must be up to some mischief."

"Good. Some officers will be there soon. Is the bridge watch in place?"

"Of course. Svante Olkivaara and Tuomas Malinen are on guard there now. I told them to be as sharp now as if they were in a fox's den. I'm calling from Naavala now. Goodbye."

"Stay there at Naavala. You can go with the men as a guide."

When Auku hung up the receiver on the wall box, his tension broke, and he sat down. Beads of sweat rolled down his brow and his hands and knees trembled. He found it hard to talk to Elsa and answered the horse drivers' questions unwillingly.

"It's not healthy to go driving your horses toward Vaarakylä. Bullets might start flying from behind any tree," said Auku.

5

In just a short time a truck stopped in the yard at Naavala. Soldiers in white uniforms leaped down from its platform. A corporal and sergeant stepped out of the cab along with the driver. As soon as the truck came to a halt, Auku was already buzzing around it.

"Where is the young man who's been babbling nonsense about saboteurs to the sheriff?"

"Here I am. And it's no nonsense."

"You seem to be sure about it. Just get your skis on and show us the way. Throw down our skis, boys. And the rest of our stuff, weapons included. Or can we get closer with the truck?"

"Not really. My ski trail starts right on the other side of the bridge."

"You can show us the way at first. The boy is carrying a big gun too."

All the soldiers looked at the shotgun on Auku's shoulder.

"Is it loaded with curds too?" laughed one of them.

Auku scowled as he looked at the laugher. He spat far out into the yard and said:

"Judge the man and not his tools."

"That's telling him. Let's get a move on," said the sergeant. "Did the rope get taken along?"

"I've got it on my shoulder," said one of the men.

Auku started down the Naavala slope. The six men in snow uniforms who had been sent from the church village trailed after him, with the sergeant clattering on his heels. Unable to say a word, Tuomas and Svante watched in wonder as the line of men crossed the bridge. Auku glanced at his friends with a distant expression on his face.

✧ ✧ ✧

"We'll soon see the shack where they ate," said Auku, who was now skiing second in line. The corporal gliding along ahead of him raised his ski pole, pointed down the lane between willows, and said:

"You mean that gray wreck there?"

"That's it. That's where they heated their lunch and ate it."

"Let's spread out just to be on the safe side," said the

sergeant. "They might have backtracked. You three circle to the left. We'll go around this side."

The men began to ski tracks in the snow that resembled the tines of a huge pitchfork. They approached the yard at Murhaniemi with their weapons in their hands. Auku, on the other hand, skied over his earlier track with his shotgun under his arm. When he reached the yard, he shouted:

"I don't see anything."

The men came into the yard. The sergeant looked at the ski tracks coming from the lake between the lane of willows and said:

"Is that the saboteurs' ski trail?"

"They seem to have come that way," said Auku.

"Tyni and I will see if the tracks start from the plane," said the sergeant. "Meanwhile check out what traces they left in that shack."

"Do you think there's nothing in what I say? I'm sure the skiers started out from the plane."

"Don't get yourself in an uproar, my boy. We don't doubt you, but there are other reasons for checking the landing site," said the sergeant.

Auku's angry expression softened. He ducked under the low doorway. The men followed him in. One of them shoved at the black pellets coating the floor with the sole of his shoe and said:

"Who the heck's been strewing roasted coffee beans around in here?"

Auku looked at the man and saw the innocent expression on his face.

"It's reindeer shit, in case you didn't know," he said. Then he pointed at the floor and went on, "Isn't that left-handed printing?"

The men gathered up the pieces of paper and studied them.

"Seems to be written in Russian," said one of them.

"And the meat in this can was packed east of the border," declared another.

When the sergeant returned from the lake, he said:

"The boy is right. A plane landed on the lake and skiers took off from it."

The sergeant looked at the can, shoved pieces of the paper into his pocket, and said:

"Now boys, out into the yard and let's start the hunt."

The men mounted their skis. One of them pointed his ski pole at a nearby willow thicket and said:

"What the heck kind of hocus-pocus have those spies been up to there? There's a row of branches set up in the snow."

"You mean that thing there?" asked Auku.

"Yah, and there's another one like it further on. But the frost hasn't been shaken off the branches on that one."

"Haven't you ever seen snares?" Auku laughed. "I set them. There was a wood grouse in this one and it shook the frost off it. I was checking them when I saw the tracks."

"They still use last century's hunting tricks here? And aren't snares illegal?" said the sergeant.

Auku remembered his call to the sheriff. Heck, he must have said he was checking his snares. His face hardened and he said:

"How legal is what's going on this winter?"

The men looked at Auku as they put on their skis. The warming rays of the sun, which had touched the edge of the woods, gilded the frost-pictures on the boughs. The trees and limbs cast long, black shadows over the snow.

"Let's go then," said the sergeant. "Did the tracks go that way? Mononen, you take the lead."

"That's the way they went," said Auku. "If only they haven't gotten to Olkivaara yet."

The soldier Mononen set off at the head of the line. The ski track was firm enough to bear their weight. They soon reached the place where Auku had turned off that morning. The sergeant, who was skiing behind Mononen and Auku, said:

"Is this where you turned off?"

"This is where I cut across to the Naavala bridge."

"What is the land like up ahead?" asked the sergeant.

"First there's a good-sized pine heath, where some mighty big trees grow. That opens up into a boggy swamp meadow — the Vaarakylä farmers cut the swamp hay from it. There are dozens of hay barns and any number of stacks in it."

"Can you tell us how far it is to the swamp meadow?"

"If I can't, who can? I run around these woods every fall with my shotgun and I have snare circuits...umh, it's a full kilometer from here to the swamp and the same distance across it. From there to Olkivaara, it's a short three kilometers."

"And to the highway?" asked the sergeant.

"From here it's only four kilometers if we go straight."

"Now we have to ski carefully. I'll take the lead. The rest of you follow, keeping me in sight."

The rest of the line moved forward when its leader had gone about forty or fifty meters. They soon reached the pine woods Auku had mentioned. It was a level heath, without undergrowth. It wasn't long before the sergeant's raised arm brought his followers to a halt. He looked back and made slow arcing motions with his arm.

"He's signalling us to come ahead," hissed the corporal. "Don't make a sound."

Every man of them moved as if he were skiing on tiptoe. They were carrying their weapons under their arms now. When they were gathered around their leader, he gestured toward the swamp.

"There's smoke rising up ahead," said Auku. "They've got a fire on Ristiys Point."

"Shh..Does the point where the smoke is rising jut out into the swamp?" whispered the sergeant.

"That it does. There are some pines growing on it. It looks like they've used them to make a fire."

"You can smell the smoke up to here," said one of the men, sniffing the air.

"I'll take a look at the map. Don't anyone move, especially the boy, since he's wearing dark clothes."

The sergeant dug out a map from its case and spread it out. The corporal moved to his side. The sergeant ran a finger over the map, muttering to himself:

"There's Murhajärvi, where the plane landed. This is where we have skied. We should be about here. Is this called Risusuo?"

"That's as good a name for it as any."

"Well now...The smoke is rising from that point. What we'll do is to circle the swamp to the left. It's the shortest and easiest way to the foot of the point. The road runs that way too. If they are on the move, we'll have to hit their trail. They really built the fire in a strange place."

"At least they have a good view of their back trail," said the corporal.

"They seem to have stopped in that hay barn," said Auku.

"So they have. They must have gotten cold and started off again," said the sergeant.

The faint indentations of the ski tracks could be plainly seen out on the surface of the swamp. The tracks went off to a hay barn and then continued, disappearing into the woods at the point where the column of smoke was rising.

"If I were the boss of this crew, I would ski around the swamp to the left, " said Auku.

"Well then my plan is approved."

"The sergeant forced a smile as he folded the map. Everyone else's expression remained serious. The sergeant stowed the map into its case. Then he felt the pistol hanging in a holster on his belt and said:

"You all know that you have to have your guns ready now. The boy will take the lead, since he knows the country."

Auku unslung his shotgun, broke its breech, and felt the shell in the chamber with his thumb. Then he patted both pockets of his jacket. Their fullness and the slight clinking sound they gave off showed what was in them. Then he clamped the shotgun under one arm, and holding his ski poles in the other, he began to ski along the edge of the swamp. The sergeant, who had set off on his heels, said:

"Be sure you don't ski so that you can be seen from the swamp."

"This isn't the first time I've skied this bog."

✧ ✧ ✧

What the devil is making my heart pound like that, thought Auku. Thank God for those soldiers plowing along behind me. The world is in a bad way when we have to stalk people in our own home woods to kill them. It sends a chill down my spine. It would be better if we could take the men who have come to do us harm alive. One of the soldiers has a rope like a reindeer lasso over his shoulder. We could just tie his hands with that. It's brutal to kill a man. Even those who have secretly killed a reindeer are only taken to prison. They say Nestor Olkivaara once committed that crime. It troubled him for twenty years, even though he killed that animal of Sääskilampi's in a rage. Why the devil did it have to go eating Nestor's hay stack?

"Boy!"

The whisper from behind him jarred Auku's thoughts back to the present. He stopped and turned to look back. The sergeant went on whispering:

"If we happen to run into the Russians, then throw yourself down into the snow. Lie there, and don't lift up your head. We'll take care of things."

"Well I'm not so stupid as to stand there gawking."

Auku's recent pity for the saboteurs turned to anger. He would know well enough what to do if they started shooting at him. Soon they would reach the base of the point. Auku's nostrils scented the air. Then he stopped and whispered:

"We're getting very close. I can smell the smoke."

The whole line halted. Nostrils sniffed at the air.

"How far do you think it is to the fire?" asked the sergeant.

"Not a bit more than half a kilometer."

"Then, boys, we form a skirmish line. You take the right flank, Lahtela. We'll try to take them alive. If nothing else works, then...Be careful! It's picked men they send as saboteurs."

The seven skiers began to fan out.

"Stay within eyesight. If we are able to surprise them, I'll do the talking. The boy will ski next to me."

Auku's knees were trembling. It didn't help to clench his jaws. Why should people be afflicted with the shakes? It happened when they were really afraid. Or when they were really cold. Loggers said it even happened to card players. In freezing weather it keeps coming back over and over. Auku took off one of his mittens and felt his forehead with the back of his hand. Then he thrust a finger under his collar. When he looked at the hand and the finger, they were both wet.

He looked from side to side. The men were creeping forward on their skis. The corporal held his machine pistol under his arm. Next to him stalked the soldier with the coil of rope over his shoulder. Just like Jussi Ylikylä when he came to get the bull that had strayed in among the Sammalsuo cattle. The other men had rifles under their arms. The sergeant drew his pistol from its holster. At their last stop, some of the men had stuffed hand grenades into their belts.

They came to a small ridge which crossed their line of march. The smell of smoke was strong in their nostrils and they could already see it in the air. The spies were bound to come into sight over that ridge. They would spot me at once, thought Auku. The others have snow-colored clothing, but mine is as dark as can be. What if I drop back? The sergeant is staring straight ahead. His cheekbones stand out when he clenches his jaws like that. Snow is piling up on the rubber foot pad of one of my skis. It's hard to ski uphill with it. I should chip it off. Now we're just approaching the crest. I went along this ridge with Väinö last fall checking snares. The corporal is right near the spruce where we caught a big old wood grouse.

Auku stopped. His whole body was trembling now. Dear God, pump anger into my mind so that they won't see me trembling. Men always laugh at a person who is afraid. Even if a man comes at you with a knife, you're not supposed to run away. Auku bent over and began to knock the chunk of snow from his foot pad with the point of his ski pole.

"Damn it, boy!"

Auku straightened up. The sergeant, who had been herring-boning up the hill, was glaring at him angrily from a couple of meters away. He was waving the hand that held the pistol. His whisper was as angry as the spitting of a cat. All the other men were scowling at Auku.

"Now what did you start banging on?"

Auku's eyes fell before the angry stare, and he whispered back:

"My ski pad...snow was packed on it. My foot was slipping off."

"You'll give the whole bunch of us away. You just can't be so careless."

Auku was ashamed. He moved closer to the sergeant and his fear vanished.

"I didn't think," he mumbled.

"Forget it. What is the ground like over the ridge?" asked the sergeant.

"It's level. Some thin pines grow there."

The sergeant turned aside and signaled to the men, who began to ascend the slope through the deep snow. Auku skied beside the sergeant. He had crested the rise and could see over it. Everyone stopped. Almost at the foot of the slope, a fire was burning. Fir boughs were piled up around it. Two men in white uniforms sat with their backs to the ridge.

Auku glanced aside. The men were raising their weapons into firing position. The sergeant pointed his pistol at the fire thirty meters away. A chill seized Auku again, but he forced himself to raise the stock of the shotgun to his cheek. The barrel was shaking. Gritting his teeth, he tried to calm himself down. Again he looked aside. The sergeant was gesturing toward the ground with his free hand and emphasizing his meaning by nodding his head. Auku let his shotgun barrel drop toward the snow. He lip-read, rather than heard, the sergeant's next words:

"Keep your head down, boy."

The man's shoulders were now over the top of the snow-covered ridge. Auku crouched down. He could see the fire. At that instant, the sergeant shouted at the top of his lungs.

"*Rukih ver*!"

The seated men leaped to their feet. One grabbed at his side, whipped out a pistol, and aimed it at the ridge. Snow spurted up at the crest of the ridge between Auku and the sergeant. The other man raised his arms in the air as his comrade's weapon fired.

"Boys, don't shoot the one who is surrendering."

Immediately following the sergeant's words, a burst from the machine-pistol chattered in the frozen woods. A couple of rifle shots rang out. The saboteur who had opened fire dropped to the fir boughs and lay there, sprawled out on his back. The sergeant leaped to his skis and shouted a command:

"Get to the fire! You stay here, Mononen, and fire a burst if the man makes a move."

The sergeant and three men skied off toward the fire. Auku rushed to his skis too. His fear had changed to excitement. So this was what war was like. The other saboteur would soon be tied up.

When the sergeant, who was in the lead, was nearing the fire, the man who had been standing with his hands up suddenly threw himself down onto his stomach. At the same instant, the machine pistol on the ridge rattled off a burst. Ashes and snow swirled into the air around the fire. From the rear came a shout.

"Watch out! Don't go near the wire!"

The sergeant's skis rustled on the fir boughs. He sprang from them and threw himself on the prone man. Auku's skis went flying past the fire.

"Quick! You with the rope! This one is alive."

The sergeant pinioned the man's hands to his sides. But the enemy was strong and agile. His elbow jerked sideways as if he were starting an outboard motor. The sergeant screamed:

"Watch out! Hit the ground!"

At that instant, a blast of air swept the men off their feet. A tremendous explosion deafened their ears. It took Auku a while to realize that he was lying on his side in the snow. Fir twigs, embers, snow, ashes, and shreds of clothing were settling from the air. A human hand fell right before Auku's face. It lay in the snow, and the black fingers sticking up from it still seemed to be trembling. Auku pressed his head into the snow. Everywhere stars danced wildly before his eyes. His ears were ringing. Nearby someone was cursing and moaning and he heard a voice say:

"What about the boy? What happened to him?"

Auku raised his head. Ski tips came thrusting toward him. A man leaped from the skis and landed in snow up to his crotch. Auku recognized Mononen.

"Did anything hit you?"

"No, I don't feel anything."

"There's blood on your face. Let me see."

Auku rubbed his face with his hand. It felt numb. Mononen pressed his hand against it.

"It's just a scratch. Do you hurt anywhere?"

"No. My ears are just ringing."

Auku clambered to his feet. He saw a man who had been bending over near him straighten up. The man said:

"Liukki has had it."

The coat of the man lying before the speaker was in shreds. Blood poured from his neck. There was a black hole next to the fire. The lower halves of two bodies were sprawled off to one side. The frost had been blown off the trees over a wide area. Shreds of clothing and guts hung from pine boughs. A shapeless bundle of clothing lay alongside the hole by the fire. One could guess that it had been a human being. Its face was black and the blood dripping from it was red. Auku staggered as if he were drunk. One of the men looked white-faced at the hole near the fire and said:

"No hand grenade did that."

"The man under the sergeant exploded a satchel charge. He pulled the detonator, like this, when his elbow jerked outward."

The man carrying the rope was sitting bareheaded in the snow. Eyes staring, he clawed at his hair. Mononen went over and gripped him by the shoulder.

"Do you know me?" he said.

"Huh?"

"Do you know me?" Mononen raised his voice.

"I know you...the sergeant is gone," said the man.

"Liukki too. What happened to you? Are you wounded?"

"I don't think so. There's a roaring in my head and my ears are ringing."

Auku turned his back to the hole gouged in the snow beside the fire. He pressed his eyelids shut, but he could still see stars flashing. His body seemed to be swaying back and forth. He heard the men speaking in hoarse voices. Mononen was cursing harshly and bitterly. Auku opened his eyes. There between two pine trees was a reindeer trail, where he and Väinö had set a trap under the snow. It was illegal to trap wildfowl. The other fall the men cruising timber had dismantled it. The forester had been very persistent in asking at Naavala who was after birds with such an illegal device.

He heard Mononen say:

"They didn't come here empty-handed. Look at this pack! Field glasses, all kinds of maps, satchel charges, and food. Hey, look. There's a red *X* with a circle around it at the Naavala bridge, and a penciled line from Murhajärvi to Naavala."

CHAPTER VI

1

"Aren't you getting tired of having the whole gang of us here?" said Maija.

"No-o, it's a small thing to put up with during a war."

It was late evening, nearly night already. Maija Sammalsuo, Mari Olkivaara, and Tyyne, the woman of the house in which they were lodged, were sitting at the kitchen table. The steady snoring of the man of the house could be heard from the adjoining bedroom.

"It was by God's grace that we got to live here," said Mari.

"I just had the feeling when I heard that evacuees — I mean, people who had to leave their homes — were coming that I ought to offer them a place to stay. We all have to help one another now."

Maija smiled. She raised her eyes from the knitting and looked at their hostess.

"Just come right out and say it — *evacuee*. It doesn't hurt so much any more."

"One gets used to everything," said Mari.

Three sets of knitting needles went on clicking. Cardboard blackout shields covered the kitchen window. Knitting in the evening had become a habit with the women. It was cozy to sit here together when the pressure of the day's work was over for the woman of the house. Her husband went to bed early, and the smaller children had been sent off to sleep. Only Taimi Olkivaara still sat up, reading a weekly newspaper. Mari looked up at the glowing electric light on the ceiling.

"It's easy to do hand-work in the evening when there's enough light."

"At home we could only fumble around in the light from an oil lamp."

The mention of home shattered the cozy mood. Maija and Mari's thoughts left the coast of Bothnia for the eastern wilderness of Finland. They could not bear to look at each other. Although Taimi seemed not to have heard, to be absorbed in her paper, she nonetheless raised her head, wondering if the two would start crying again.

"I wonder how things are at Järvenkylä."

"You're starting that same old song again, mother. What trouble can they be having?" Taimi bowed her head over the paper again, and although she had to swallow hard, she was able to hide it from the others.

"Exactly," said Tyyne. There was nearly always a smile on her plump face, but now her cheerful expression was forced. "The enemy has been driven away from there. That's what the papers say."

"Home is always home. One can't forget it," said Mari.

"I wonder how Aili managed with the calving. It was due last week. Where was it that the spies almost killed Auku. Aili's letter about it was so mixed up."

"I'm not worried about the household. I just keep thinking about Nestor. It's strange that I'm not worried about Toivo's dying. But Nestor..."

"Shall we go and visit your husband's brother tomorrow?" said the woman of the house, glancing at Mari.

"It would be nice to talk to Kaija and Santeri again," said Mari, who added after a short pause. "If Nestor hadn't pulled that fool trick and enlisted, he would be here with us now. I wonder how Tuomas and Svante are doing on bridge guard. Elma doesn't say a thing about them in her letters."

"I worry the most about Auku. He's so reckless."

The door to the main room opened and a boy came shuffling in, holding up his underpants with one hand, his blond hair standing on end.

"Why are you sneaking out now, Väinö? You're supposed to be asleep."

Väinö stuffed his nightshirt into his pants and said:

"I'm thirsty."

"There's the water bucket. Take your own cup from the cupboard," said his mother.

Väinö went and gulped down water from the cup. Then he came back to Maija and stood pressing closely against her side.

"Well, what is it? Is there something else?"

"I was wondering what front they sent Kauko to. He wrote that they would soon be taking him..."

"Is that what's worrying you? Will you have a cookie if auntie gives you one?"

Tyyne ran her hand over Väinö's tousled hair. The boy looked down at the floor and rubbed his bare feet against each other.

"Is my pet girl asleep?" she asked.

"Liisu is still awake. So are the others," said Väinö.

"They've got the bedclothes all piled up in a heap," said Taimi, folding up the paper. With it in her hand, she left the kitchen, and they could hear her low-voiced, but sharp commands from the main room. At the same moment Tyyne went to the cupboard and said:

"Come here Väinö. You can take these to all the children."

"Väinö keeps pestering you all the time," said Maija.

With a little bow, Väinö left the kitchen. There was the sound of giggling from the main room, which was quelled by Taimi's brisk voice. The women sat where they had before, but the original cozy atmosphere no longer held sway. Thoughts of Järvenkylä and vague pictures of the front lines flitted through Maija's and Mari's minds. Tyyne had a brother at the front as well. Finally Maija said:

"How will they manage now at Latvasuo?"

"It's hard to understand," said Mari.

"Was the one who got killed a reindeer man or something like that?"

"Janne Latvasuo was the herdmaster. Why did the Lord leave him unprotected? And with a bunch of children at the age where they need the most care," said Maija.

"They live far away from anyone, and the oldest girl must be about confirmation age," recalled Mari.

"So many men from home have already been lost. It's awful to think of what it will be like if this goes on for a long time."

No one responded to Maija's words, which ended in a sigh. From the main room came repeated bursts of childish laughter, sometimes even stifled shrieks. The sounds made Maija and Mari uneasy.

"I think we should go to bed now," said Maija. "They'll wake up your husband with this noise."

"He won't even turn over for hours. But maybe it's best to go to sleep. When we finish the barn work in the morning, we'll hitch up the horse and drive like a bunch of gypsies to visit Mari's relatives."

"Maybe we should. They may even have heard something new

from home," said Mari.

Maija and Mari stepped outside. Even at night the surrounding landscape seemed strange. The woods were far away. The flatness of the land and the damp tang of the sea air were foreign to them. As they smoothed down the skirts they had raised to squat, Maija said:

"No matter how good a person has things, she misses her home."

"If I shut my eyes now, I can plainly see the heights of Lapinvaara," said Mari.

"It's lucky that there's no moon. They say the Russians can't fly on these dark nights."

"And they can hardly see to shoot at the front," said Mari.

When the two neighbors returned to the main room, everything was topsy-turvy in the bed made up on the floor. Taimi had undressed and was tossing a sheepskin quilt over her younger brother.

"Go and get a switch, Ma. It's the only way to make these little devils behave."

"Mother, Taimi curses at night," said the youngest of the Olkivaara offspring.

"Quiet everyone," said Maija, but there was no anger in her voice. "Does Liisu have to pee?"

"No," said the girl.

The Olkivaara and the Sammalsuo mattresses had been laid side by side on the floor, forming a broad bed. Turning out the lights, the two women lighted up their pipes. Then they lay down, each one at the opposite side of the row of beds. One after another, the children began to breathe evenly. After a long silence, Maija said:

"Mari?"

"What?"

"How can we ever repay Tyyne for this kindness?"

"I don't know. It may have to be left in God's hands."

Mari's and Maija's pipes went on gurgling for a long time. Although Maija closed her eyes and imagined herself lying in bed at home, she could not recapture its atmosphere. There was an odd odor here. Did it come from the many plants in the house? The impatiens and the shrub-like begonias standing in the window at home had left an unforgettable fragrance in her nostrils. In addition, the power lines outside this house kept making a humming noise.

"We were lucky to get into such a comfortable house," said Mari.

"Yes, and we got to stay here together. We were already talking about that in the yard at Naavala when we left."

"They say there's not much to cheer about in some of the houses where people from Järvenkylä are staying. Their owners put up with them for a few weeks, but soon let them know they are a nuisance," said Mari.

"Johanna Myllytörmä was crying when I saw her yesterday. The people she is staying with say she's a burden on them and even grumble that she's lazy."

2

"Mother, can you get up? I think it's beginning."

Petti Sääskilampi woke with a start. She sat up and said:

"Are you having contractions?"

"It can't be anything else."

"Have you been walking for a long time? I didn't hear you get up."

"It must be about an hour. I thought at first it was some other kind of pang. I guess we have to turn on the light."

"Does it hurt a lot?" said Irja's father, sitting bolt upright.

"Stay in bed. You're no help in these things," said his wife. "We have to wake up the lady of the house."

Irja Mäkinen went on pacing the floor. Her mother swept her hair into a bun at the nape of her neck and began to dress. The Sääskilampis had been given a big bedroom in the house to live in. They all slept in it, but spent most of the day in the main room of the house. There were actually extra rooms in the place, and although the owners had a bedroom to themselves, they kept still another room heated.

Petti Sääskilampi disappeared from the room but returned shortly and said:

"She's coming soon. Are the contractions closer together?"

"They are. This happened sooner than I expected."

The woman of the house, fully dressed, entered the room.

"How pale your face is," she said. "Didn't you notice anything last night. I see now that the baby has dropped."

"I didn't think it would come so soon. What time is it?"

Irja's mother turned the alarm clock ticking on the table toward the light.

"It's almost two thirty."

"The only thing to do now is order a car to take you to the Oulu Maternity Center."

"No, I'm not going there. Both of my boys were born at home. I had a midwife for one and my mother-in-law for the other. I can stay here, can't I, Laina, with mother and the boys near me? Everything will go well this time too."

"Of course! You know best. Your mother will light a fire in the stove and put water heating. I'll go and get the midwife."

Laina left the room. More beads of sweat trickled down Irja's brow. From time to time she had to grip the edge of the table for support.

"I wonder where Kosti is tonight. It's good that he isn't worrying about this. He has other troubles...Oww!"

Ivar Sääskilampi rose to his feet and mopped his brow.

"Wouldn't it be better to hire a car and go to Oulu?"

"No, I'll stay here."

The woman of the house returned with her outer garments on. She looked at the bed where Ilmari and Pentti were sleeping and said:

"The bed in the guest room is ready. Your mother will take the bedclothes in and you can follow her. The midwife will be here soon."

There was gratitude in Irja's pain-racked eyes when she said:

"I woke you up too."

"Nonsense. We women know all about this disease. Just hang on for awhile and you'll be able to tell the father there's been a new addition to the family. That's how it goes. Don't look so doubtful. Goodbye now."

Irja's mother moved with the speed of her younger years. She carried her own mattress and bedclothes into the guest room. Silently praying, she made up her daughter's childbed. Dear God, let things go well. When the bed was made up, she returned to their common bedroom and said:

"Let's go into the other room now."

Although movement was difficult, Irja bent over the sleeping boys and stroked their faces with her sweaty hand. Dear God, let me bring up my children... Tears in her eyes, she followed her mother out of the room. The guest room was fresh and cool. In the light from the electric lamp, it looked large and homey. Ivar Sääskilampi stood gazing after his daughter, holding up his now loose underpants with one hand and sighing heavily:

"It's a good thing that Kosti hasn't had a chance to worry..."

"Just think of yourself and the child. Everything will go well then."

"If only it would. It's coming before its time."

"Calm down. I can hear them talking out in the entry already," said Irja's mother.

"Did Laina get back so quickly? But we'll need the midwife soon enough."

✧ ✧ ✧

The following morning, Ivar Sääskilampi walked with slow footsteps toward the guest bedroom. He had been in it only a few times previously. The boys scurried busily around him. He opened the door and saw his daughter's pale face among the sheets. He stopped in the doorway and looked at a wicker basket on a chair by the bedside with a lace frill around the edge.

The boys reached over the side of the bed to put their arms around their mother's neck. Both tried to hug her at the same time. Ivar walked slowly over to the basket on the chair, then stopped and said:

"Don't crush your mother, boys. She's not well now."

"Then he looked into his daughter's eyes and said:

"You look so pale, but then you've never been very ruddy. Was it very hard?"

"Easier than with the boys. She only weighs about seven pounds."

From under the netting came a whimper that changed to the piping cry of an infant. Ivar Sääskilampi looked back and forth from his daughter to the rising and falling mesh that covered the basket.

"What do we have here?" he said, half to the boys.

"Pull the netting aside. You'll see what she looks like."

Cautiously the man lifted the mesh from over the baby's face, which could be seen clearly in the light from the lamp. Her mouth, which had been contorted as she cried, was now puckered and her eyelids blinked. For a long time the old man looked at the child's dark, wrinkled face. Finally he said:

"No need to ask whose child this is."

"Who do you think she looks like?" Irja asked quickly.

"She has her father's mouth and cheekbones. Her hair is just like yours."

Irja had a sense of relief. Her father was looking healthy and contented again. Although she had never in her life said a joking word to him, she was now bold enough to do so:

"The little miss doesn't have as thick a braid yet."

Irja moved her own braid onto the pillowcase next to her face. The father looked at his daughter and smiled as he spoke:

"But her hair will grow, if her father doesn't let her cut it in bangs."

The baby's mouth twisted and its face flushed. It began to cry in a weak but demanding voice. Father looked at daughter again: "Now boys, she's pulled a strange trick. What should we do?"

"Get grandma, quick," said Irja.

"Right. Hop into the main room, Ilmari, and tell grandma."

The boys ran out of the bedroom one after the other. The father went over to his daughter's bed. He pressed his hand to her forehead and said:

"Do you feel bad?"

"No...good..." A sob escaped Irja.

"I didn't mean to upset you. Don't. We have to write Kosti tomorrow and tell him that the boys have a sister. We'll write..."

Petti Sääskilampi entered the bedroom and stopped at her daughter's bed. She looked inquiringly at her husband, her daughter, and even the baby.

"Which one of you needs me? All three of you seem to be crying," she said.

"Well, the baby of course! Is grandma an idiot?" said Ilmari.

Irja's mother took the child expertly into her arms, felt its small bottom, and said:

"No wonder she's crying. Sweetie-pants, you're soaking wet. Grandma will change your diapers."

Ivar Sääskilampi watched the procedure in silence. Then he said softly:

"The girl should have seen the light of day at Sääskilampi." He sighed heavily, turned toward the door, and said almost in a whisper as he left: "Although the boys weren't born there either."

"Father isn't going to be around much longer," said Irja.

"Don't. Why do you say such things?"

"I don't know. He's become so kind. It makes me cry."

"It's old age and illness. And your father has always been fond of children. Has he really been so mean at heart?"

"Maybe not, but sometimes he seemed to be."

3

From early dawn, the Olkivaara and Sammalsuo children had been restless, particularly the Olkivaaras. They kept on asking:

"When are we going to visit Uncle Santeri?"

"Stop yapping," said Mari.

"But yesterday Tyyne said we were going there today," said Taimi.

"And that we were going with a horse," said Väinö Sammalsuo.

"It's the horse that Väinö's interested in," laughed Maija.

"What if I get to do the driving," giggled Taimi.

"No man will trust a woman with his horse," said Väinö, blinking.

"Don't you kids quarrel about who will do the driving. We haven't even heard if the horse can be spared for the trip," said Mari.

Leevi, the man of the house was sprawled on a bench in the main room taking his morning nap. He was not snoring now, and Maija and Mari kept glancing at him. He was a taciturn man, who kept very much to himself. When the children began to chatter loudly again, Maija said:

"Stop yelling now. Let the man sleep."

The woman of the house smiled at the children's travel fever, and said:

"They're only kids. Let them fuss."

Her husband sat up, yawned heavily, and said:

"I should clean out the lamb pen and put in new bedding."

"Listen, father. I promised the whole bunch a visit to the farm where Santeri Malinen is staying. You won't be using the horse, will you?"

The woman spoke loudly. The man watched her lip movements and said:

"Me and what Santeri? Huh?"

"Mari's brother-in-law. Come along and drive us. Is there such a big rush to clean out the lamb pen?" said his wife.

"I don't have time. The rest of you can go. What did you say about a horse?"

"That we can go with it because it's not being used."

"Why not? It hasn't been out of the barn for weeks and the exercise will do it good. Are you leaving soon?"

"Pretty soon. I left food ready. Heat it when you get hungry."

"Come along Väinö and we'll hitch up the horse."

Väinö did not need a second invitation. His eyes shining, he put on his hat and jacket and charged out after the man. His wife said:

"Let's start dressing the children to go. I like Santeri's wife. When she starts talking about bear-hunting and the life in your woods, I listen with my mouth wide open. It's so different there."

"What else would Kaija have to talk about? All her life she's lived right on the eastern border. Taimi, start putting on the other kids' clothing. I have a little pain in my chest. And I had such a strange dream last night too. Something bad is going to happen."

"There you go with your dreams again. I'd like to hear the riot act Elma would read if she heard you," said Taimi.

✧ ✧ ✧

"You sit in the driver's seat, boy. Watch that the horse doesn't bolt. He's been standing in his stall so long that he may be wild. Drive way over to one side of the road," Leevi instructed Väinö.

"That's already too many directions," said his wife.

"Huh, what corrections?"

"No, *di*-rections," his wife repeated loudly.

"He needs them. A high-strung horse and such a young boy."

"Väinö has been hauling hay and wood for a long time. He doesn't need all this talk," said Tyyne in a normal tone of voice as she wriggled herself down between Maija and Mari in the back of the sleigh. Her husband could not hear the words.

Väinö sat in the driver's seat and watched as the others tried to find places for themselves.

"Aren't we a load of gypsies?" Maija shouted to the owner of the house.

"There are quite a few of you in that sleigh. Well now, start him off nicely so he won't run away."

Väinö smacked his lips and the large bay horse ambled off down the road.

"Put a blanket over him and hay in front of him," the man shouted after them.

Väinö turned around in the driver's seat to answer the man, who was standing near the porch. His mouth was already open to answer when the woman said:

"It's no use to yell, He won't hear you anyway."

"Drive nicely, Väinö, so the horse doesn't get wild and go too fast," said Mari, who was holding little Liisu in her lap.

"Where would a twenty-year-old nag go?" said Tyyne. "Those are just father's notions."

Maija's uneasiness abated. The rising sun lighted up the frosty bushes and cast long shadows from them. On the right were endless plains of snow. Far off to the left were gently rising wooded hills. But they were insignificant compared to those in Maija's home landscape.

"Drive at a trot, Väinö, so that we'll get there sooner," said their hostess.

Väinö slapped the horse on the haunches with the end of the reins. The animal merely switched its tail and plodded on at the same pace.

"You see how he runs away, just as my husband said he would," laughed the wife.

✧ ✧ ✧

Santeri Malinen was whittling the frame of a buck saw in the main room of his evacuation home. Above the stove could be seen ax handles, bucket staves, and even half-finished harness hames he had been carving. He peeled off long wooden shavings with skillful strokes of his knife. Seldom did he join in the women's chatter, although from the flow of talk among the three women visitors, his wife, and the woman of the house, the quiet backwoodsman heard the things that interested him. But it was nice to have relatives and friends come to visit and chat. They were treated well in their present lodgings; there were electric lights, warm rooms, and good shelter for the livestock. Nevertheless, they dwelt among constant mental images of their Varanga landscape. Thoughts of the difficult times in their home woods gnawed at their minds constantly. That was the subject of the women's conversation.

"Are you sure that Näätätaipale, your home, was burned?" asked Mari.

"That's what they say."

"Elma wrote about it too," said Maija.

"That was terrible," said Tyyne. "But now the Finns have the area back, which is a good thing."

Liisu was playing with the Malinen children and their cousins. The sole child of the house they were visiting was a girl of confirmation age with whom Taimi was chatting.

Väinö sat on a bench with his eyes mainly on Santeri's whittling. At length, Santeri rose, walked over to the hearth, spat into it, then returned to his whittling. Then he said:

"Those cabins in the woods don't build themselves. All the work put into them up to now has been wasted. And what can old men do?"

The women's talk ceased. Santeri ground the wad of tobacco in his jaws as if he were sucking spiritual strength from it. After a long pause, Maija said:

"Rebuilding the cabins will be up to the young."

"If any of them come back. Two of our boys are lying in the hospital now," said Kaija Malinen.

"How are they doing?" asked Maija.

"Reeti has lost his right hand. They smashed up his elbow with one of those rapid-fire guns — what do you call them? The doctor cut off what was left of it," said Santeri.

"It was a machine pistol," said Väinö.

"And what about Janne? He was wounded on the Isthmus," said Maija.

"He was shot in the leg there. A rifle bullet went right through his calf," said Santeri.

"One of his friends in the hospital wrote to us about it. Poor Janne can't write a word himself. There were no schools in the backwoods when the older children were growing up. Reeti wanted badly to learn, and he writes a fairly good hand. Janne just didn't want to learn," said Kaija Malinen.

"And the war isn't over yet. Even if the Russians are gone from Kijanta, how are things going on the other fronts?" said Santeri.

"If we could only get our children back and return to our own home, we would even put up a tepee in our own yard," said Kaija.

Santeri looked at his wife and saw her wiping tears away with the corner of her apron. He rose, brushed the shavings off his pants with an angry motion, and snapped:

"I've told you that tears are no help at the fair. Come along, Väinö, and let's feed the horses."

When they had driven up to the house, Väinö had been allowed to put the horse in the stable. It stood there now munching on hay with the horses belonging to Santeri and the farm. The two of them stood there and watched the animals eat.

"I knew that the horses had enough to eat. I just can't stand to listen to those women whining. How are the boys getting along as bridge guards? And Tuomas too?"

"Aili wrote not long ago..."

Väinö went on to explain what Aili had written. Santeri Malinen bit off a chew from his plug of tobacco and pondered the matter:

"So the Russian plane brought spies right into Järvenkylä. They're up to pure devilment these days. If your brother didn't happen to go out to check his snares, the Naavala bridge could have been blown sky-high. What would have happened to Tuomas and Vante then?"

✧ ✧ ✧

Twilight was coming on when Väinö prepared to drive the visitors back home. Santeri came out to help him hitch up the horse. Väinö did not like that and fumed at the idea of not being able to hitch it himself. He felt a little better when he was able to close the breast strap before Santeri got around to it. Then Santeri said:

"Horses here on the coast don't have a decent collar bow."

"Our landlord's horse has a pretty strong one."

"N-no. If you tried to close my breast strap, you couldn't do it with both hands."

"You come and visit us too. It's your turn now," said Tyyne as they were leaving.

Santeri himself covered up the people in the sleigh. Although he said little, his expression showed that the visit had stimulated him, too.

"Maybe I'll hitch up the horse some day and haul the bunch over there. We could at least talk about things at home," said Santeri.

The trip was a total of some five kilometers. The horse trudged homeward willingly, even trotting at a twitch on the reins. The first stars were appearing in the blue of space when the sleigh turned off the highway and headed for the house.

"Get the horse moving at a good trot. Let father know his gelding's legs are limbered up," said Tyyne.

"Right. Let's drive into the yard like the governor-general," said Maija.

Väinö slapped the reins smartly across the haunches of the horse a couple of times. They left dark streaks on the animal's frosted coat. The big gelding began to bound forward over the last one hundred meters like a moose.

"Whee!" yelled the woman of the house, delighted with their speed.

Now the horse broke into a gallop.

"Whoa, whoa," called Väinö, pulling back on the reins with all his strength. The horse merely speeded up.

"Stop him! Stop him!" cried Maija.

They were nearing the yard. Väinö sawed on the reins for all he was worth and cried out:

"This damned crowbait just keeps going. Whoa!"

The horse was like a calf let out in the spring. It went bounding along in great leaps. Chunks of snow flew up from its hoofs, landing in the sleigh and behind it. Väinö was in a panic. They were now entering the yard. The owner of the house was standing on the porch, arms raised in the shape of a letter *Y*.

"Väinö, my God!" screamed Maija.

The horse galloped toward the wall of the cow barn. Panic gave Väinö added strength. He pulled on one rein, and the horse suddenly began to gallop in an arc. The sleigh slid off to one side.

"Ooh!"

"God save us!"

The cries were cut off when one runner of the sleigh struck something and the load spilled out to one side. Women and children went tumbling onto the ground. Only Taimi landed on her feet. Väinö was dragged by the reins a couple of times around the yard. Then the horse stopped in front of the stable. Its owner trotted up to grab it by the bridle. His face contorted, he shouted at Väinö:

"What the hell are you trying to do, boy? Wreck everything?"

"I didn't...it went crazy." Väinö blubbered as he spoke.

"I told you not to spook him. Goddamn, it's not enough for some of you if we give you a house to live in but you have to have a horse to go visiting with too. Whoa, Jekku, whoa there."

"Father, it wasn't the boy's fault. Is anyone hurt?"

Väinö looked toward the yard. As if in a blurry movie, he saw that all were now on their feet and standing still. Liisu was clutching at mother's skirts. Väinö burst into tears.

"Take it easy now, Jekku. They've driven the animal into a sweat."

Väinö looked at the man shouting at the horse. Now and then he wiped his eyes with the back of his hand. Tyyne watched her husband storming around. She tried to say something, but he began shouting again:

"And one of the shafts is broken too! My God, they even smash up your gear. I knew it would happen when I had to go and give them my horse."

Maija's heart was palpitating like the tail of a lamb, first with fear and then with anger. She saw that the shaft was bent at a sharp angle and was held together only by a few ligaments of wood. She walked over to Leevi and spoke to him loudly but calmly:

"This was no great disaster, and nobody was hurt. I don't know what could have made the horse go wild."

"There's always someone around to break things, but who's to fix them? Easy Jekku, you can go into the stable now, and I'll be goddamned if I'll let you go on any more visits."

The man unhitched the horse with abrupt, angry motions, casting dour looks at the women skulking in the yard, and especially at Väinö. When he disappeared into the stable leading the horse, his wife said:

"Don't worry about it. He's always had a temper. His loss of hearing bothers him too."

"But he took it all out on us," said Mari, her hand on her heart.

"Let's find another place to stay," sobbed Taimi.

The man came out of the barn. He jerked at the end of the shaft and a two-meter length of wood came loose in his hand.

"Who is to fix this now? It makes me so mad I'd like to beat that lousy driver with it."

He glowered at Väinö and drew back the piece of wood. His wife grabbed it and said:

"Leevi, get hold of yourself. You'll shame yourself and frighten the children."

The man shoved her aside and roared:

"What the devil are you butting in for! You were running me down again. I could see your lips moving. You've said things about me before this. You're always talking behind my back. Do you think I can't hear? Why are those evacuees laughing so nastily? I'll teach that monkey of a boy..."

Maija leaped up to the man and snatched the broken shaft from his hand.

"Just lay a hand on the boy!" she shouted. "Making a fuss like that about a stick of wood. Just try to take this away from me, old man."

Maija threw the piece of shaft far off in the direction of the woodshed. The man gritted his teeth, slammed his mittens down on the ground, and howled out:

"But I have to have a new shaft tonight!"

Maija stepped directly in front of him and shouted into his face:

"You'll get one, no matter what it takes. You will get it."

Leevi went into the stable. The children kept milling around the steps in a group. Väinö stood stock still, glaring angrily. Tyyne began to cry and said:

"Leevi is so poor at making things. He even has others make his ax handles. He's always brooding and fretting about it. Just be patient and he'll calm down."

"It's not your fault, Väinö. Taimi, you take the children into the house. Liisu and Väinö too."

"Goddamn if I'll go. I will not go," Väinö repeated, sobbing.

"Then come with me. Mari, you take care of Liisu."

"Where are you going now?" asked Tyyne in a voice that shook.

"I'm going to get a shaft for your husband's sleigh so that he won't have a fit."

"No, don't. Leevi doesn't stay angry for long."

"I promised to get one and I will. Let's start walking, Väinö."

✧ ✧ ✧

Maija, Santeri, and Väinö crossed the yard in the moonlight. Santeri carried a shaft over his shoulder like a log driver's pike. In Väinö's hands were an ax and saw. Santeri said:

"That dumb ox won't try to beat you, will he?"

"Just let him try. I'll fetch him a rap on the skull with an ax that'll make his tail fins quiver," said Väinö.

"Keep your mouth shut, Väinö. There'll be no fighting," said Maija.

"Is that the sleigh over there?" asked Santeri.

The three of them walked over to the sleigh rack, which was resting on its side. The base of the broken shaft hung from a hook on the runner. Santeri said:

"This won't take long. Give me that saw, Väinö."

Santeri went to work. He worked bare-handed and his movements were rapid. Although his brother Nestor was all thumbs, Santeri's hands were gifted. He soon had the shaft coupling free. He looked at the remains of the shaft, scratched his head, and said:

"Humph, no wonder it broke. They must have been driving with this shaft while they were still using withe couplings. This birch is rotted all the way through. Väinö and I will put the coupling on the new shaft and it will be fine. You can go in out of the cold, Maija."

"I'll go in when I can tell the man the damage is repaired."

"Well, it won't be long till this is better than it was before."

Santeri fitted the coupling to the shaft and hammered nails through its side holes with the butt of his ax. He laid the piece he had made alongside the old shaft.

"Now when I cut a pecker's length off this one and nail on a leather strip to make it look like a pecker-head, the man can drive with it for the rest of his life. I guess you don't like this men's talk too much, Maija."

"Talk won't make today's world any worse than it is, but where will you get a shaft for yourself?"

"From the same place as this — from the woods."

Santeri had soon worked the shaft coupling into the hook on the runner. Then he said:

"It's finished now. Tell the man to come and talk to me if he needs some carpentry done. I'm going right back to Kaija and the children."

"I don't really dare ask you in for coffee," said Maija.

"I'll stop in at Järvenkylä some time on the way to the church village."

"I can't thank you enough. If we ever do get home..."

"We're not going to rot here. Goodbye now."

✧ ✧ ✧

Maija entered the main room of their lodgings once more with Väinö trailing behind her. The master of the house was seated at the table and glared at them as they walked in. Maija forced herself to swallow her anger. She walked up to Leevi and said loudly.

"Now you have a new shaft and it's better than the old one."

"You don't have to shout. I can hear you."

"Good, but you have the shaft. I kept my promise."

Even on that night, the women did some hand-work. Until then, only homesickness had troubled them. Now a new and depressing factor had entered their relationship. Leevi had gone to bed, but in place of the usual snoring they could hear the harsh creaking of bedsprings.

"Shall we talk to the evacuation officials?" asked Maija.

"Because of this shaft business?" asked their hostess, wide-eyed.

"If your husband starts taking it out on you, that makes it hard for us to live here," said Maija.

"They can probably find room for us somewhere else," said Mari.

"If you could just try...My own life isn't always easy. Now with guests, my husband has been able to keep his imaginings in check. We have no children and we would both like so much..."

The woman's voice was muted. Her chin sagged to her breast and she poked at the knitting with her needles. Maija and Mari could see the tears falling onto her apron.

"If you can put up with us, we have it good here," said Mari.

"You're a good person, and we're not afraid of your husband. Now that we know how things are, we'll be as still as moulting birds. The men have to put up with much worse at the front," said Maija.

"Let's forget the whole thing. I'll put this helmet liner into a package for an unknown soldier. Does the neck come down low enough?" said the woman, lifting up her knitting for Maija and Mari to see.

"I think so," said Maija.

When Mari and Maija lay down on the bed on the floor late that night, Väinö turned over and said:

"When we get to go home, I'm going to smash that old man in the face."

"And I'll moon him," said Taimi.

"You mustn't be like that," said Maija. "The man has been nice to us up to now, and think of his wife."

When Maija thought they were all asleep, Väinö turned over and said:

"I won't help that old man any more even if he gets down on his knees and begs me to. And I won't touch that nag's reins, not ever. That hammerhead never trotted one step before no matter how you tried to chase him. Now he took off like a sea bird."

"Say your prayers and go to sleep now. We have to control our tempers no matter what it feels like. Think of the poor men at the front."

Väinö said no more, although Maija heard him turning over and sighing deeply. She herself felt that their evacuation days would pass more slowly now. Earlier, the taciturnity of their host had kept them on tenterhooks; now they were apprehensive about keeping the children under restraint. After she had lain awake for a long time, a picture in her mind began to warm her heart. It was a sunny and slightly cool day in autumn. The smell of burning moss hung in the air around the willow thickets at home. The boys were burning piles of brush, and the moss in a newly cleared area was smoldering. A small patch of field had been added to their tillage, and the boys were planting rye. How would it last out such a hard winter? Kauko too must remember and worry about it. Almighty God, let us see our home again.

CHAPTER VII

1

Lieutenant Kosti Mäkinen, Sergeant Bert Sääskilampi, and Private Simo Mutka stood in the ruins of the burned church village. Bearded soldiers moved around them, blinking eyes that were red-lidded from the lack of sleep. Their snow uniforms were filthy and their walk resembled the staggering of drunken men — even those who were standing still were swaying. A man fell to his knees and clambered up cursing. Fires still smoldered in some of the ruins. Around them were slumped men who slept sitting down. Others snored loudly, curled up like dogs sleeping outdoors.

The trees surrounding the village were blackened, their trunks and limbs splintered. Shell holes were everywhere. The snow was sooty and splattered with soil. There were foxholes and dugouts on every side. Bodies of enemy soldiers, scraps of clothing littered the ground. Bert Sääskilampi's head had sagged to his chest. He took a few stumbling steps, jerked his head up, and said:

"It's true. I thought I was dreaming again."

"It's all too true. There is no Kijanta Church any more," said Simo Mutka.

"Nor a Suomussalmi church village," said Kosti Mäkinen.

"They say that war is hell and the cavalry rough...they sure are right," said Simo Mutka.

"I have many more dead men to answer for after today," said Kosti Mäkinen.

"We were lucky," Bert said in response to his brother-in law's words.

"Those Russian boys were tough at sticking to their holes. They wouldn't come out of them alive. There are too many bodies around here." Simo Mutka looked up at his platoon leader's bearded face: "You seem to have strength to spare. Are you ever afraid?"

"Let's not lay it on like that. I'm always afraid when they're shooting at me. I wonder if I should go and get in touch with the higher-ups since Mikkola seems to have been held up."

"Let's stay here. He won't find us at all if we go wandering around," said Bert.

"I have to tell you that when you caved in that warehouse corner with a pole and the Russians were shooting like crazy from behind it, and I knew that you needed help, I was afraid to come out of my hole. I'm ashamed of myself, and that's the truth," said Simo Mutka.

"I was behind a pile of earth thrown up by a bomb, and it was safe for me to move around there. And you picked them off one after another when I broke open their shelter."

Lieutenant Mäkinen's platoon had survived the carnage at Alasalmi with few casualties. The one that hurt most was the loss of Janne Latvasuo, who had really been a suicide. But in the effort to take Suomussalmi, the platoon's losses had been heavy, at least ten wounded and four dead. Now after many attempts to take the town, its ruins were in Finnish hands. The fate of his men weighed heavily on Kosti Mäkinen's mind. He asked:

"Where did we lose Riekki? Did you see him after last night, Bert?"

"No, nobody knows. He was so damned scared too."

"Did you ask the men in the other platoons?" said Kosti.

"I asked almost everyone who came from that direction, but no one knew anything. He was still in the skirmish line at the edge of the woods."

"He must have taken a direct hit. The shells were coming in heavy then," said Simo Mutka.

They stood there in silence. Simo Mutka's head nodded. His eyeballs showed white between reddened lids.

"Don't fall asleep. Have a smoke. It'll wake you up," said Kosti.

"Yeah, take poison to stay awake," cackled Mutka, taking a cigarette from the package the lieutenant proffered him. He did not light the cigarette but stuffed the tobacco into his mouth and began to chew on it. Tobacco juice dribbled from the corners of his mouth as he spoke:

"The only time I was ever this sleepy was on log floats. We had to put in long shifts there too."

"That messenger is taking a long time," said Kosti Mäkinen.

"Things are pretty well fouled up around here, but at least the Russians aren't on our necks. It cost us plenty though..."

At that instant, there was a rattle of machine-pistol fire followed by a few scattered rifle shots. Bert Sääskilampi took up where Mutka had left off:

"Don't be too sure it's over. Did you hear that shooting?"

"Are some of them still hiding in the ruins?" asked Mutka.

"There comes Mikkola, at last," said Bert.

The three men turned a look of inquiry on the smallish man walking toward them.

"There you are," said Kosti Mäkinen. "Did you see the company commander?"

"I finally found him, but I had to run around the whole village — or what's left of it. It's an ugly sight."

"What did he have to say?"

"He said to tell you that the platoons can rest wherever they can find a place to lie down. He wants to talk to you. The battalion command tent is over that way." The messenger pointed beyond the ruins. "The other officers have been summoned too. They say that Valtanen, the leader of the second platoon, was killed."

"Valtanen!" Kosti Mäkinen almost shouted.

"So they say. Someone hiding in the ruins shot him."

Mäkinen's head sagged to his chest. Lieutenant Valtanen was a wood technician from up north, a quiet man of action. From him Mäkinen had learned how to use the Kainu wilderness to help him in combat. The two platoon leaders got along very well with their men. The backwoodsmen — migrant loggers, small farmers, and reindeer men — were fond of their superiors. When the Russians began to withdraw from Alasalmi, Valtanen's and Mäkinen's platoons were assigned the task of cutting them off. Valtanen had led the two platoons through the woods almost by instinct. They had come out on the highway in back of the retreating Russians and skied right up to the bridge that was their objective.

"It's your turn now, Kosti," Valtanen said. "I don't know a thing about explosives."

Mäkinen, Valtanen, and two non-coms crawled out under the bridge in the middle of the night. Kosti Mäkinen gave whispered instructions and he himself placed the first four charges on the bridge deck and supports. The job was soon completed, and they crawled back to their waiting platoons, the detonation fuse trailing along behind them. The men were eager, each wanting to be the one to set off the charges, but Mäkinen gripped the handle of the detonator in his own big fist. A number of trucks drove onto the bridge, and then a mass of infantrymen swarmed onto it. Kosti Mäkinen's hand spun quickly. Their ears began to ring, and pieces of trucks, poles, rags, and even human limbs began to rain from the air.

"It's an ugly job, but it has to be done," said Lieutenant Mäkinen.

Mäkinen could clearly remember a number of recent events involving Valtanen. On such and such a day, Jaska Valtanen had done this, had said that. Now there was no longer a Jaska Valtanen. How far off is the day when I will be no more, thought Kosti Mäkinen. His tired mind became even more depressed.

"Let's try to find a hole and get some sleep. Get the boys together and let's go," he said.

Three of the men started up. Some were still squatting among the ruins, while others lay asleep on their packs.

"Hey boys, let's go and get some sleep," Mäkinen urged them.

Some of the men had to be shaken hard. A few of them emitted short bursts of laughter, but most of them fell into line with apathetic faces. Some staggered along with their eyes wide-open. They were asleep on their feet, exhausted from many nights without rest, from wallowing in the snow, and from tension, but their legs responded limply to a strong effort of will. Now when the danger seemed to be over, numbness overpowered their minds.

A dirty, bearded officer came walking toward them. He was the commander of the third company of the same battalion. Brushing the brim of his Guard cap in a token salute, he stopped before Kosti Mäkinen and said:

"You've managed to get part of your platoon together."

"Most of them. They just can't stay awake."

"It's the same with us. I've tried to round up my men, but they're sleeping all over the place. I'm afraid some of them might freeze. We've seen some hard days, men, but Suomussalmi is ours."

His last comment was directed at the men.

"The ruins of it are," said Kosti. "But at least there's some good in that. Do I need to go to the command post?"

"No, I was there, and they promised to set up a watch. The commanding officer said to let the boys rest. He promised that the officers could rest too. There's no way the Russians can surprise us now. Take your men to rest. I'll do the same. We'll see you."

"Mutka, you take the lead. You're supposed to know this place. It must be familiar to you too, Bert."

"Everyone seems to know this *painted town*," said one of the men.

"Suppose we head for what used to be a travelers' inn," said Mutka.

They started off. Everywhere they passed bodies of enemy soldiers and of horses. Their own dead had been picked up. A weakening stench of smoke still hung over the ruins. Shattered sleighs and trucks, clothing dragged out of shops, parts of field packs, harnesses, shoe soles and top leather, and Russian-language leaflets littered the place.

"I never would have guessed when I came to a county fair here two years ago that I would now be staggering through these ruins. There were tall, painted buildings here then. They were showing lambs with heavy coats of wool, pure-bred rams, thick-necked bulls, and cows with huge milk-bags. Everything was going on. There was bootleg whiskey to be had. The Guard Armory was being dedicated. I went there too. Ilmari Kianto read some of those what-you-call poems of his. If I remember right, he warned us about some big bull that would break through the fence and knock the house over. We laughed at all the nonsense, and at Kianto's babble too. But the goddamn thing did come and wreck things."

Simo Mutka's weariness had brought on an attack of verbal diarrhea. Some of the men tried to laugh, but another one of them barked out:

"What are you blithering about? Just find us a place to sleep if you know this town so well."

"Stop beating your gums. I'll find a place if anyone can. That used to be a travelers' inn over there. They had a table where for ten *markkas* you could eat as much as your belly would hold. Once we came through here on the way back from a log drive. We had hiked a long stretch of woods with nothing to eat. We marched right in and started to circle that table with our plates.

After the heavy food, we heaped them with sausage and sliced cheese. The serving help didn't exactly laugh at the jokes we were telling. I'm pretty sure they didn't get rich off us. We ate so much..."

"Shut your mouth. Our bellies are growling and you have to torture us with stories like that," one of the men snapped.

"It's nice to remember a time when there was food to eat. Look boys, there's a building still standing."

They all turned to look where Mutka was pointing.

"We'll go in and find a place to lie down there, no matter what," said Kosti.

It was a wonder that the house had survived as well as it had. They could already hear thunderous snores in the entry. Bert grasped the handle of the door.

"It'll have to be jam-packed to keep us out."

It was beginning to grow dark. The fact that some of the windows were stuffed with rags made it even darker inside. The floor was one mass of men. As they walked in, one of them cursed and another struck out with a fist at the frozen footwear that had trampled on him. The newcomers lighted matches and tried by their light to set their feet down between the sleeping bodies. From the floor further back, someone bellowed out:

"What the hell night fishermen are barging in here now?"

"It stinks in here. What have they been eating?" said Mutka, sniffing the air.

"The school health nurse wouldn't approve this ventilation," said a young soldier.

'Come hell or high water, I'm flopping down right here," said Mutka.

There was grunting and cursing in the darkened room as the men who had found a place earlier awakened and raised an uproar. One had his face stepped on, another had his hand trampled. The newcomers flopped down on the common bed. Some found a space on the floor; others merely piled onto their sleeping comrades. At least it was warm in here, and fresh air filtered in from a hole in one wall.

Kosti Mäkinen managed to thrust in between the men on the floor. How were Irja and the boys, he wondered At least they were warm and could sleep in peace at night. How many years ago was it that he had spent a night in this town? Times had been tough then too. He had been in a strange town without a cent to his name. The future had seemed to be an endless road going on under a frozen sky. Was it three or four days that he had walked on from here before coming to the Sääskilampi house late at night? Had it ever really happened? Had he ever passed this way? Who could tell? Was there a war and was there a Kosti Mäkinen, a man with a family?

✧ ✧ ✧

Over and over, Kosti Mäkinen half-awakened with a feeling that the floorboards beneath him were vibrating as if someone were pounding on them. But sleep always overcame him.

"What the hell is that banging down there?"

Kosti sat up with a start. A long-bearded, oldish man who had been sleeping next to him was blinking and clawing at his hair. He repeated in astonishment:

"Who could have gone to sleep down there?"

"Is that where the sound is coming from?" said Kosti, now fully awake.

There was more thumping on the floorboards. The man examined the floor closely and said:

"We're sleeping right on top of a trapdoor."

Kosti too began to study the floor, which was made of wide planking.

"There is a break in the boards here. Is there a basement down there?"

"It's just a potato cellar. Tired men will crawl into any hole. Shall we let them out. It may be hard for them to breathe down there."

The men stood up. Although it was daylight outside, Kosti Mäkinen felt as if he had just fallen asleep. Then the floorboards were again hammered from below. Kosti's tired brain was angered:

"What the hell is your hurry?"

Kosti thrust his fingers through a stout ring that he guessed would open the trapdoor. By jerking angrily, he was able to raise it, revealing a black, rectangular opening in the floor.

"Out of there! Come on, move it. What idiots would go into a place like that?"

A head thrust up from the darkness, followed by another and

then a third. Sleep vanished from Kosti's eyes. The men wore pomponed watch caps.

"Godalmighty boys, Russians!" shouted the man standing by Kosti.

The rumble of snoring ceased. Some of the sleeping men leaped to their feet as if cold water had been thrown on them, trampling on others. Others groped for their weapons. A sergeant leaped to the trapdoor with his pistol aimed. Kosti Mäkinen seized his wrist:

"Stop it man! No shooting."

The men who had just been lying on the floor were all up and stirring. No one was yawning and all eyes were grim. Some twenty Russians crawled up out of the dark hole. When they stopped coming, Bert leaned over the trapdoor and yelled:

"Are there any more down there? Every last man out!"

A shot rang out in the darkness of the cellar. Bert leaped up from his knees.

"Are you hit?" someone shouted.

"No, at least I don't feel anything."

"Out, all of you!" roared Kosti Mäkinen, his face red.

No one appeared, and there was no sound of movement. The Russians who had come up shook their heads. One of them held up one finger, and then pointed downward.

"Does anyone here know Russian?" asked Kosti.

The throng parted in the rear. A corporal stepped forward and said:

"I slipped across the border and spent some time there. I can butcher it pretty well."

"Ask him if there are any more of them left."

The corporal did as he was told. The Russian soldiers broke into smiles and began to babble away, pointing and laughing. The corporal turned to Kosti and said:

"Only their political officer was left."

Kosti dug a flashlight from his pocket and handed it to a prisoner.

"Tell him to see if the boss did away with himself."

The corporal translated the words. The prisoner knelt beside the opening and directed the light into the cellar. Soon he stood up and spoke, waving his arms broadly.

"He says the whip is dead."

The prisoner handed the flashlight back and lifted a hand in salute. Then he started speaking excitedly to the interpreter, who turned at last to Kosti and said:

"This non-com says they forced the *politruk* to stay here. He says they've been in the cellar for three days. They have a good pile of hand grenades, but they've disarmed them. They left only a Nagant pistol behind."

The corporal scowled and his face turned sour. After a long pause, he said:

"He says they're very hungry and thirsty."

The prisoner appeared to have understood the interpreter's comment. He smiled broadly, scooped handfuls of air into his mouth and raised a make-believe glass to his lips, repeating over and over:

"*Liebushka, liebushka...*"

The corporal's cheeks flushed and his eyes glittered. Before anyone could move, he struck the prisoner in the face with his fist. The blow knocked the man down. He screamed miserably as he fell.

"Goddamn your *liebushka*! All you're going to get is a bullet in your hide."

"You bastard! Hitting an unarmed prisoner!" yelled Simo Mutka, and struck the corporal across the face with his boot.

The corporal was a big man and he moved quickly. He shook his fist at Simo and his group.

"I was a helpless prisoner too when they tortured me with hunger and cold. And there was no war then either. Every *Ivan* should get a bullet in his skull."

Kosti grabbed the front of the corporal's jacket and threw the man to the floor. Pinning down his chest with his knees, he said:

"Getting even won't help matters now. And we take prisoners to others for interrogation. Are you ready to listen to me now?"

"OK, I'll listen. Don't break my ribs, you goddamned hulk."

Kosti let the man up. An officer with the collar insignia of a Civil Guard lieutenant had been among those sleeping on the floor. Kosti said to him:

"I'll have my second in command take these men to headquarters. Do you approve?"

"I do. It's a good idea."

"Bert, get your squad and take these men to battalion headquarters. Tell them I'll follow with this officer."

2

Not too far away, in another church village and its environs, new soldiers for Finland's small army were being trained. As the winter days passed, bringing news of the successful counterattacks at Suomussalmi and Raate, the morale of the recruits rose. There was encouraging news from other fronts as well, but things did not seem to be going well on the Isthmus. The name of Summa was soon engraved in all minds. The same was true of the Kollaa river. After the success at Raate, frightening rumors about Kuhmo began to be heard. News of Finnish losses were released guardedly, but there were recruits in the company who followed the progress of each battle on the maps, from which it was evident that time and time again the Finns had been forced to abandon another slice of their home woods to the enemy. New names began to appear in the headlines: Rasti, Kiekinkoski, Rajavaara, Kälkäinen, and above all, Löytövaara.

When winter was at its worst, the recruits completed their basic training. To Kauko, the taking of the service oath was a solemn affair. The companies of recruits were drawn up into a square. A spirit of bold camaraderie filled the mind of the Järvenkylä boy. We are one large logging crew, responsible for all we do or leave undone. It was the same feeling Kauko had had when he first drew a man's full pay on a spring log drive. When these companies were spread out on line, they would plug up a good-sized gap in the eastern border.

After taking the oath, they awaited shipment to the front. Some were partly fearful about having to go, while others breathed fire. Most felt that since others had to go, they too would do their part. Men were needed for this logging job. Rumors circulated freely: one claimed certain knowledge that they were on the way to the Isthmus, and another had heard from a company clerk that they were going to the front at Salla. Another rumor had them on a fully-loaded troop train headed for Rovaniemi, from where they would go by truck toward Petsamo.

Intensive training continued. There was less of close-order

drill and more of tramping through the woods. They spread out to form skirmish lines, advanced in single file, set up defense perimeters. They banged away with wooden bullets, attacked and withdrew, rushed to air-raid shelters, learned to throw hand grenades.

Even their equipment improved. Combat jackets appeared here and there. Overcoats were issued to everyone. Those who had worn their cockades on hat-bands or cap visors were issued fur caps. Lapland boots and ski boots began to appear on recruits who had entered the service wearing thin leather shoes.

Kauko's squad leader and the other corporals from the September induction were promoted to buck sergeant. In January, officer candidates appeared to replace the lieutenants who had been sent to the front. In a few days, brass insignia of rank appeared on their collars too. By now, the soldiers who had entered the service in December and January had lost most of their rookie timidity.

3

On Saturday afternoon, the company was carrying out a thorough clean-up. To the men of Kauko's age group, the duty was as distasteful as it has always been to every serviceman. Mops were being dragged reluctantly through dust, and brushes moved lazily. The only halfway tolerable activity was airing the bedding out of doors.

Without a specific order, Kauko took a pan of warm water, a mop, and a brush, went into the latrine, and began to clean it. Soon two other men from his company joined him.

"I would damn that sergeant to the hottest hell if my mother wasn't religious," said one of them.

"My uncle is a clergyman, but still I say goddamn this work," stormed the other.

Both men dropped their pans. One lighted a cigarette and the other cleared his throat and spat into a urinal. Then he said:

"It's not in my nature to paddle around in this shit."

"Well, you push out your share of it every day," said Kauko.

"Yeah, but I don't have to stir it afterwards."

"We're always short of it at home," laughed Kauko. "The crops would grow better if we had this plant food to spread on the fields."

Kauko's squad leader stepped in through the door. Kauko went on with his mopping and the other two began to fuss with their pans.

"Come on, men. Get a move on so we can get this place ship-shape."

As Kauko brushed the wooden ring of a toilet seat, he could sense that the sergeant's eyes were watching his movements. After his initial clumsiness in training, Kauko had gotten his nerves under control. He seldom blundered or misunderstood now. Why is he watching me, Kauko wondered. Getting another stripe has probably given him a swelled head.

"Private Sammalsuo!"

Kauko turned. He had time for the sarcastic thought that he could no longer be called Recruit Sammalsuo.

"Sergeant, sir!"

"Pick up your cleaning equipment and follow me."

Now what's on his mind, thought Kauko. Am I not even good enough to shine up the john?"

The sergeant walked toward the door as he spoke. He held it open for Kauko, who was carrying the pan. Once through it, he spoke:

"Take those things to the laundry room and then you can go to town."

Kauko stood with the pan in his hands, heels together, and mouth half open in bewilderment.

"Sergeant, sir! What shall I do in town?"

"You might even look at the girls," the sergeant laughed. "Do whatever you please."

Kauko's eyes opened wide and his jaw dropped even further.

"You're a hard worker. I've noticed that whenever volunteers are needed, you're ready to pitch in. I've seen you cleaning up on your own initiative. Now when the others have to do it, you can enjoy yourself."

"I didn't do it because..."

"This is our company platoon leaders' idea."

Kauko looked at the dirty surface of the water in the pan he was carrying. It was quivering, and the brush in it was floating slowly around its outer edge. He swallowed, looked up, and met the sergeant's eyes.

"I'm used to working. And then I sometimes work without being told to because I'm homesick. My home was evacuated..."

"Put those things away and go to town. Come back in time for evening chow."

Kauko clicked his heels together. He put the cleaning utensils away and took his coat down from the rack. To the questions of his buddies, he gave only evasive answers. Kauko had seldom been outside the schoolhouse fence except on training exercises and had only a sketchy knowledge of the village. As he walked the frost-bitten roads, he felt completely at ease for the first time since leaving home. He had been given the first sign of recognition in this new job. Maybe I'm not as hopeless as I thought. And that sergeant isn't so bad either. I screwed up everything so hopelessly when I was a rookie.

Kauko stopped in at a coffee shop that he had visited before. A few other uniforms were visible in the haze of tobacco smoke. For safety's sake, he clicked his heels together in the doorway, walked to a table, and ordered a bottle of soda.

The juke box kept playing as people fed one coin after another into it. Now and then men's voices could be heard when the blaring of the juke box diminished. A youngish soldier seemed to have been enjoying his liquor. One hand dangled from his neck in a gauze sling.

"Where did you get hit in the hand?" asked a civilian at one of the tables.

"I got it at Summa."

"Right in Summa?"

"No, but near there."

Kauko took a turn going to the juke box and slipping coins into it. He had to celebrate his freedom at least to that extent, he thought. He listened at his table, face propped up on one hand, to a man's voice singing:

When I was a little child my mother dear this song did sing.
Life is dismal, love is fleeting, and it has a bitter sting.
But I did not listen to her, wandered through the world in vain,
left my mother far behind me, came to know both grief and pain.

Kauko felt both good and bad. He could see his home woods

in his mind, and mother, Liisu, Väinö, Auku, and Aili. Then he thought of Elma's face. And of Hilja Naavala too.

4

Immediately after the evening meal, the duty officer entered the room and said:

"No one is to leave the company area."

The announcement caused the men to look at each other. No one spoke, although everyone knew that his training was now over. The platoon leaders appeared in the classroom, young lieutenants who walked with one thumb hooked under the shoulder straps of their shiny new Sam Browne belts.

"I don't think we'll see another morning here," said Jalo Kieppi.

The duty officer appeared in the doorway again to shout:

"Everybody roll field packs. Turn in sheets and pillowcases to the supply room. You can report defective equipment there."

A commotion erupted in the classroom. Pillows were stripped, blankets rolled, and sheets pulled from beds.

"Equipment to be turned in will be cleaned outside," shouted the duty officer.

"Make it snappy, Kauko, so we can be first in line at the rag boutique," said Jalo Kieppi.

"I'll try to make it quick," said Kauko.

Dashing across the yard, Kieppi and Kauko shook out the bedding they were turning in, in the frosty air. When they arrived at the supply room, they saw that many of their comrades had been faster than they.

"Slowpokes to the end of the line," the men shouted at them.

"Quit sounding off."

An unheated warehouse served as a makeshift supply room for the training center. Behind a counter of rough lumber that ran across it, a supply sergeant was fussing and fuming. One of the men from Kauko's and Kieppi's induction group was helping him.

"Don't knock the counter over," growled the sergeant.

"Hey, hey, gimme a new combat jacket. My old one is torn."

"Who's the hey-hey out there?" bellowed the sergeant.

"Me, Private Sumala. This one is only good for carpet rags."

"It's good enough for a hey-hey like you. No dice! Next!"

Pillowcases and sheets were being hurled over the counter.

"Name, name! The name of every man who turns something in. Otherwise you pay for every damned rag," the sergeant growled.

"My backpack is a wreck."

"My shoes are crummy. Too small and full of holes."

"My coat is too small."

"My socks are dirty and full of holes."

"I can't get along at the front with this excuse for a hat."

"Who said you're going to the front, huh? Now where have those damned platoon leaders gone to? Don't knock the counter over. You can exchange your socks."

The uproar abated every time the sergeant raised his voice, but it soon swelled again, louder than ever. The floor boards rocked. Shoes were pulled off and dirty socks flung up on the counter. New backs kept shoving in continually in front of Kauko and Kieppi.

"We'll never get anything here," said Kauko. "Let's leave."

Kieppi wriggled his way forward between even the broadest of backs. Soon his hands were gripping the countertop. Kauko thrust in behind him.

"Sergeant, sir! Private Kieppi would not turn down a new combat jacket."

"Now who could get mad at that?" someone quipped.

The sergeant looked at Kieppi. "So you want a new combat jacket? What's your old one like?"

"It's a rag. And so big I can button it in back."

"It seems to be quite a frock. Take it off and empty the pockets. What size fits you?"

"In civilian clothes, I take a forty-two."

"Find a jacket for the boy, Jaakonaho," said the sergeant.

As the helper was digging through a pile of jackets, Kieppi added:

"This buddy of mine needs a jacket too. The one he has is too small."

"Which buddy?" asked the sergeant.

Jalo Kieppi nodded toward Kauko and said:

"This one here."

"Why doesn't your buddy take care of himself? Can't he talk?"

The sergeant looked at Kauko, who cleared his throat. But Kieppi went on blithely:

"He can hardly get into this one. He takes a big size."

"What size jacket does your buddy take?"

"Forty eight in civilian clothes," said Kauko.

"Is your jacket in poor condition?"

"It isn't great, sergeant, sir."

To prove what he said, Kauko showed him the shoulders and elbows of the jacket.

"I've stitched them up to hold them together."

"It doesn't look too good. Give this soldier a jacket too."

Kieppi checked the jacket he had been given and said:

"I'll take one of those with the infantry collar insignia."

"Get out of here. Why not ask for one with stars? What do you think this is?"

"They tell me faint heart never won fair lady, sergeant. You could give me one with a green patch so the Russians will know it's an infantryman that's coming at them."

The sergeant pursed his lips, walked over to one of the shelves, and tossed a jacket onto the counter.

"Here's one last peacetime jacket. It's your size too."

Kieppi dangled the jacket by its collar and said:

"Thank you sergeant. Now the company has one good-looking man in it."

"But there are no insignia for your buddy. Now be off with you, and quickly."

So it was that Kauko got a jacket too. Out in the schoolyard, Kieppi said:

"You have to learn to fend for yourself."

There was pandemonium in the classrooms. The platoon leaders were standing amid the soldiers and squad leaders, among them Lieutenant Salmi, the leader of Kauko and Kieppi's platoon. He was said to be a machinist in civilian life. When the two of them joined the group, he called out:

"Is the whole platoon here now?"

Sergeant Mäki looked around.

"At least my squad is, sir."

The other squad leaders reported the same. Lieutenant Salmi surveyed the entire platoon and said:

"We leave this classroom, that is, we leave the whole village tonight. The quartermaster sergeant will issue three days' rations to every man, and the munitions sergeant will distribute the ammunition. Squad leaders will check all their men."

The lieutenant tugged back the sleeve of his combat jacket and glanced at the watch on his wrist:

"We have two hours' time. At twenty-one hundred hours, the company will form up at the edge of the drill field with full field packs and other equipment. Squad leaders, take charge!"

"Right, lieutenant, sir!"

The lively chatter ceased. The men filed by the quartermaster and munitions sergeant in silence, all awed by the clips of live ammunition they were being handed. Kauko, Kieppi, and Jonas Niemi went to sit on the edge of Kauko's bed. Only a flattened mattress bag and a pillow cover with straw poking through it remained on it. Kauko said in a subdued voice:

"We may not be lying on a bed for some time."

"It won't be the first night me and Kauko will be spending in the woods. Do you know what that's like, Niemi?"

"I'm used to sleeping in a bed at home. We'll see what it's like when the time comes," said Niemi, watching his friends' faces.

"You'll learn to live in the woods. And when we stuff those live rounds into our rifles, there won't be time to think about beds."

"If we only knew where they're taking us," said Kauko.

"That's one thing they won't tell us."

5

Some time after midnight, they loaded the troop train. Sleighs, horses, skis, and tents were crammed into railway cars. The commands of officers and squad sergeants rang out sharply. The soldiers grunted and sometimes muttered curses under their breath. Their faces were stung by a bitter wind that drove clouds across the sky and sent the snow swirling from rooftops and nearby trees.

Aboard a cattle car, Kauko, Kieppi, and Niemi hoisted themselves onto the upper bunk. The barrel stove that burned in the car heated the upper air nicely, although gusts of wind sometimes blew puffs of smoke back down the stovepipe and into the car. Picking out places had produced a real melee. No one was willing to be left near the door. Once settled, the men waited anxiously to see what direction the train would take. When it began to puff steadily toward the south, Kieppi said:

"We're going south for the winter."

For some time, everyone stayed in the place he had managed to claim in the hubbub of leaving. Men conversed in small groups. Eventually the tension of departure and the shock of being issued live ammunition began to dissipate. Now they were soldiers of the Finnish army. Their time as recruits, the long hours of extra drill that went with it — these were a thing of the past. But they were a bit leery at the thought of the dark snowy wilderness out of which at any moment a bullet or a burst of fire from a machine pistol might be directed at them.

The wheels clattered and the car lurched and swayed. The wind whined at the corners of the closed coach, but the stove kept them warm. First one and then another adjusted his pack as a pillow. Blanket rolls were undone.

"Let's put our blankets under us and use our coats as covers, Jalo."

"We'll bunk together, since we're in the same platoon."

"Then I'll make my own bed," said Jonas Niemi from in back of Kauko.

The officers had a coach of their own, but the sergeants traveled in the cattle cars with the men. From the start of the journey, first one man and then another had shoved wood into the barrel stove. When the men began to lie down, one of the sergeants said:

"Which corner starts the fire watch? Each man will watch an hour."

"If it's OK," said Kauko, "I'll be first."

"That's fine," said the sergeant. "We'll go around counter-clockwise. First the men in the upper tier and then those on the floor. We'll skip the non-coms."

Kauko climbed down from the upper bunk and sat down beside the stove. For some time his comrades chattered away on all sides. The storm lantern which hung on a loop of haywire swung back and forth, causing shadows to dance on the walls and roof of the car. Now and then Kauko put into the stove a stick or two of wood from the pile that had been loaded on at the station. Sometimes the train whistled and sometimes it braked so sharply that men sleeping on their sides rolled over onto their bellies or even onto their backs. Sometimes the train careened sideways. Kauko looked at his watch. It was well into the morning hours.

One after another, the soldiers began to snore. Someone rose and crept to the door of the car, setting his feet down between the sleeping men. Opening the sliding door a crack, he undid the buttons of his fly. Points of light flashed by the narrow opening. Someone roared out from the floor:

"Who the devil opened that door?"

The urinater closed the door and went back to his place. Kauko sat and stared at the coals that were visible through the door of the stove. He tried to imagine that he was tending the fire at a logging camp. But he could not recapture its atmosphere. The swaying of a railroad car and the shrieking of its whistle did not fit the mood of a lumberjack's dwelling.

Once the train stopped for a long time. Men outside shouted, and the cars jolted as trains were coupled. The line of cars was pushed backward for a long time and there was another jolt of cars colliding. Finally the wheels began to clatter steadily in the same direction. At that point, Kauko realized that the minute hand on his watch had made a full circle. He squeezed Jonas Niemi's woolen-stockinged toes, kept on shaking them for a long time, and said:

"Did you sleep, buddy?"

"I guess I did. Is it my turn on watch?"

"The first hour is up," said Kauko, and climbed onto the bunk beside Jalo Kieppi.

✧ ✧ ✧

In his sleep Kauko was conscious now and then of the train's jolting and swaying. When he woke up fully, the train had stopped. The door had been shoved open and some of the soldiers were looking out. One of them said:

"There's a huge blizzard raging out there."

"What station is this?" asked one of the men lying on a bunk.

"Kontiomäki."

"If it weren't for the storm, boys, we would be running for shelter from air raids every so often. The bombers are grounded now," said a sergeant who was looking out of the door.

Kauko dozed off again. He awoke only toward evening. The

fire watch was still going from man to man along the upper bunks. He hopped down to the floor and had to open the door a little bit to empty his bladder. A snowy landscape was gliding past the car. A gloomy wilderness. The wind was no longer howling, but it was snowing heavily. Kauko asked the man from another squad who was sitting by the stove:

"Which way did we turn at Kontiomäki?"

"I'm not sure. Someone claimed he knew we were heading southeast."

"Then we should be seeing the Kuhmo landscape soon," said Kauko.

He had gotten hungry while he slept and dug out bread and what was left of the butter from his pack and ate. As dessert, he chewed on the bread cheese sent him by Aili and Elma. It was dry and chewy, almost hard, but it crunched between his teeth in a familiar way. Aili and Elma were taking turns sending packages. He wondered what that meant. Aili wrote that she had sent a food package to Toivo on the Isthmus, and that Elma had sent her own bread cheese to him. It was a delicacy among his home folk and now it tasted better than ever to Kauko. Elma's own hands had made it, had squeezed the whey from the curdled milk. Then she had baked it in the oven. She must surely have thought of him as she did it.

✧ ✧ ✧

For once Kauko, as well as the others riding in the cattle car, had gotten enough sleep. When the next day dawned, everyone was awake. Some still insisted on reclining at ease against their packs, but most were sitting up, and a few were standing. There was a crowd in front of the slightly open door. The storm was over. Along the tracks stretched the Kainu wilderness, its trees heavily laden with snow and its open lakes and swamps decked with an unbroken cover of white. The railway cars were nestled in the hollow between the snow banks that lined the tracks. An occasional deserted-looking cabin huddled among the snowdrifts.

"We're going to get a real freeze after a fresh snowfall like that," said Jalo Kieppi, who was among the men looking out through the door. Almost all of Kieppi's weight rested on the shoulders of Kauko, who was seated near the opening. Still others were pushing against Kieppi's back. A bitterly cold wind blew into Kauko's legs through the door. He said:

"Don't flatten me out completely, darn it. Someone else can take my place and carry the whole gang of you."

"You've got broad shoulders. Just sit there and prop us up."

But Kauko stood up. He went to the center of the car and stood by the stove. At that point, Kieppi shouted:

"Hey buddies, we're stopping!"

The train whistle confirmed the northern boy's words. The locomotive braked and the men standing on the floor strove to maintain their balance. Soon the wheels jolted to a stop. The men who were lying on the floor clambered up. One of them said:

"Shove the door wide open so that we can see where we are."

"There's not much to see. A station of sorts and a platform."

"Not even rooms that say *Men* and *Women*?"

"Not even that."

"Jump out now so we can get to walk outside."

A squad sergeant elbowed his way into the rubbernecking group and said:

"Every man stay in the car until the order to get out is given."

The injunction did not trouble the men for long. A man was approaching alongside the train. At first they could not make out what he was shouting, but from a couple of cars away, Kauko could hear his words:

"Empty out the cars. Bring your packs. Get your skis from the freight cars and start unloading."

Soon the man was shouting the command they had already heard into the car that held Lieutenant Salmi's platoon. One soldier said in a mock bellow:

"We're not deaf in this car."

"I'm glad you've washed your ears," said the man with a laugh, and went on to shout into the next car.

"Empty out the cars..."

"It's the same sergeant," said Kauko to himself.

"What are you mumbling about?" asked Kieppi.

"The sergeant giving the orders. He's the man we rode with from Oulu to the training center. I wonder where he's been hiding out. We haven't seen him in all this time," said Kauko.

"Who's got the time to go poking around in all those schools?"

Controversies were breaking out around the freight cars. The skis they had tied together when they left were being sorted out.

"Godalmighty you knucklehead. Don't you know your own skis?" someone was fuming.

"What's the difference? They all belong to the government. Who can be expected to find his own?"

"Take a look at what it says on this tag."

The soldier who had been fretting about getting his own skis back grabbed one of the pairs that were tied together, jerked them to himself, and said:

"Shit, they grab things right out of your hands."

Drivers were unloading their horses from the cars. Ears pricked forward, the animals eyed the ramps laid from the cars to the platform.

"You must have had a nice trip, buddies. You could have played billiards all the way," shouted Sumala, who stood watching with his pack on his back and his skis over one shoulder.

One of the drivers snatched up a ball of dung from the floor and hurled it at Sumala, who was grinning broadly. It struck him on the forehead, and some of it splattered on his face. He turned a furious red.

"We're not stingy. Here's a ball for you. Would you like some more?"

"You stinking horse flunky!" yelled Sumala.

Another ball missed him. Sumala scrubbed at his face with his coat sleeve. Then he dropped his skis to the platform and lunged toward the car with his fists up.

"We'll see who the real horse-shit eater is now," he said.

A soldier was just leading his horse from the car. As Sumala leaped toward it, a whole shovelful of steaming dung was hurled out at him. It caught him in the chest and face. Sumala lost control completely. Letting out a bellow, he rushed at the door, brushing the side of the horse as he went by. The animal shied and reared up on its hind legs.

"Whoa, whoa!"

The driver holding the horse's head was lifted into the air. As the animal danced on its hind legs, one of its hoofs missed the ramp. The horse fell between the train and the platform. Only its hoofs could be seen, pawing at the air.

"Help, quick, the horse will be hurt!" cried the driver, who sounded on the verge of tears.

"What the hell kind of mess is this?" shouted the company commander, who was hurrying to the spot. "What kind of driver are you, soldier?"

The driver almost wept as he calmed the kicking horse. Sumala slipped between the cars to the rear of the train. The Lieutenant's usually calm face looked black. He called out:

"Squad leaders, here. Take over!"

It was no easy task to approach the rearing horse in such close quarters. Kauko was the first to leap down between the car and the platform. One of the front hoofs that was pawing at the air knocked him flat on his rear.

"God help Sumala when I get my hands on him," the driver threatened.

"Grown men and you're fussing like children," said one of the squad leaders. "Do something."

"Who the devil is going to go down there and get himself kicked?" said a soldier.

For a long time the men struggled to help the horse. Only when the animal's legs were bound were they able to hoist it to the platform. There it rose to its feet. It seemed to have survived the mishap uninjured. The irate company commander kept hurrying the men who were unloading the cars. Sleighs, a field kitchen, and other heavy equipment were being brought out. In the midst of the work, a shout came from the direction of the second company's cars:

"Air alert! Planes coming from the east!"

Heads turned and all eyes scanned the clear, bright sky. Someone caught sight of small dots in the air. The roar of motors carried to the now silent station.

"Take the horses to that gravel pit. Spread out as far as you can, and take cover," shouted the company commander, who continued to walk calmly along the train.

Feet began to pound the earth heavily. Kauko ran toward a spruce grove behind the tracks. Kieppi and Jonas Niemi were racing ahead of him. He caught up with the two soldiers who had become his best friends.

"So this is where the rough stuff starts," Kauko said.

"Let's see if they bomb us. We'll stay here and watch."

"Let's run into the woods. They say they always bomb the

tracks. They can see the train and lots of soldiers now," said Jonas Niemi.

"There's no reason to run," said Kauko. "They say you can't run away from death."

Jonas Niemi's usually steady face was twitching. His cheeks were absolutely white and he kept wetting his lips with the tip of his tongue. The three of them stopped some distance in back of the tracks. Soldiers and even some of the squad leaders were running into the woods. Kieppi looked up at the planes, which were now clearly visible, and said:

"We won't run any further. I don't care if they drop knives, as long as they land handle down. Look at our buddies run," laughed Kieppi.

Kauko managed a laugh too. "They say that out here you have to wear your funeral shirt every day."

"Don't laugh. Let's just go into the woods, buddies," pleaded Niemi.

Kieppi acted as if he had not heard the words. He pointed at the sky and said:

"The Russian seems to have sent out a dozen planes."

"Hit the ground! Don't move," shouted an officer from near the train.

"Let's run into the woods." Niemi was almost begging.

"Not a step."

Kieppi stood looking up at the planes.

"Let's you and I go, Kauko."

"Mother says you can't dodge fate."

Kauko could hear the quaver in his own voice. The planes that had come into sight seemed to have passed by, but now they turned at the tracks and came toward the station with their motors roaring. Jonas Niemi bolted toward the woods.

"Don't move!" roared the voice from near the train.

"Goddamn, they're bombing! Did you see that black lump fall from the bottom of the plane? And there come more. Now it's raining them. Get down!"

Kauko threw himself into the snow, and so did Kieppi. Then a whine of increasing intensity pierced their ears. Kieppi said:

"They're on the way. They're coming toward us."

Kauko's hands dug furiously at the snow underneath his face and chest. Why didn't I go into the woods with Jonas? They'll land right on my neck. Is this the end of my war? It smashed right into my back. Help..."

The station yard shook and a blast of air blocked his ears. They had been advised to keep their mouths open, Kauko remembered. His hands kept digging at the snow. The whole station yard seemed to be leaping. There was a clanging of metal, human shouts of pain and misery. Bombs exploded in front, in back, and on both sides. Chunks of sand and frozen earth rained from the air. Kauko felt a blow on his back. "Help, help!" he heard his own voice cry out.

Soon the bombs were falling farther off, fewer of them now, and then none at all. The roar of the planes grew fainter. Is this what it's like to die? It isn't so awful. Why wasn't he losing consciousness? Kauko's shoulder throbbed. A moonlit night in his home woods flashed into his mind. The quiet nodding of grain heads in a field of rye. His home cottage and the people in it.

"Those Russians were in a sour mood..."

A familiar voice sounded in Kauko's ears. He almost wished that his consciousness would finally come to an end. Blood must be running from his shoulders, they felt so hot. Now he heard voices from every direction: words, calls, and screams of pain.

"Someone is in bad shape out there. Let's go and see, Kauko."

When Kauko began to rise, he was afraid that he would finally lose consciousness, but he was able to get to his feet. Jalo Kieppi was standing and looking past the tracks. He was calm, but his face was absolutely white. Near him Sumala sat up to his armpits in the snow. Kauko wondered when he had gotten there. Sumala said:

"Those were some bombs. The frozen ground didn't stop them at all. Chunks the size of horses went flying through the air. Iron was whizzing around too. The sides of the cars burst open like cardboard. I wonder if a single cattle car is left in one piece. What'll they use to haul more soldiers with," Sumala giggled.

That Sumala is a hard case. He only laughs, thought Kauko. Moving his arms, Kauko could feel the motion of his shoulder blades. So he wasn't going to die yet. Had anyone seen how scared he had been? Near the place where he had lain, Kauko saw a fist-sized chunk of sand. Was that what had hit him so hard? Then Sumala stood up and looked at Kauko.

"Were you hiding a bone? It made me laugh."

"What was there to laugh about?" said Kieppi.

"When Sammalsuo was digging the snow from under his belly. Even a dog doesn't dig like that. And then he burrowed his head into the snow."

"How do you know?" said Kauko.

"Well, I have eyes. I was sitting in the snow and watching."

"Medic! Medic! Over here!"

The shout startled Kauko and the others. A group of men was gathered around a churned-up area at the edge of the woods. Others were running toward the spot. Kauko joined them. Before them was a deep bomb crater. Some of the men who had reached the rim of it turned away. Others covered their eyes with their hands.

Kauko stood on the rim of the pit. His heart was pounding and he felt nauseous. Huge, meter-square segments of earth stood tilted on their sides. Some of them had been blown through the air. A man's body with the legs missing lay on the side of the pit. Another motionless heap lay not far off. From it a stream of blood trickled through shredded clothing and into the sand. A corporal carrying a medic's kit ran up to the place. He leaned over the legless one and said:

"This one doesn't need bandaging any more."

"Here's another," said someone.

The corporal moved to the man sprawled on the side of the crater. He turned him over by the arm and raised an eyelid with one thumb.

"Dead."

There were sergeant's stripes on the shoulders of the legless body. The blackened face began to seem familiar to Kauko. A lieutenant from the second company arrived on the scene. He looked down into the crater and said:

"Sergeant Haipus."

The lieutenant bit his lip. Kauko's company commander came up and asked:

"Do you know the sergeant?"

"He's from our company. Second in command of the third platoon. He was wounded at the start of the war but insisted on coming back before he was fully recovered."

"It's the end of the line for him," said the lieutenant.

Kauko's knees felt weak. There lay the torso of the man with whom he had come to the training center, the man who had spoken the first words of encouragement to him in his soldierly career.

"The bodies have to be picked up. The corporal and Sergeant Mattila will take care of the detail with their squads," said the lieutenant.

Jonas Niemi came up to Kauko. There was a look of horror on his face and his voice still shook as he said softly:

"It was horrible..."

"I was afraid too. I didn't know what bombing was like," said Kauko.

"First company, fall in!" came a shout.

"We have to get going," said Kieppi to Kauko and Niemi.

There were shouts for the other companies to assemble. Horses that had broken loose were galloping around the station. A few of them raced towards the woods, their tails streaming. Some of the men were shouting, others cursing. Someone moaned wretchedly. The rest of the train was detached from the shattered cars and went puffing onward. The wounded were being carried in through the door of the station. It all seemed a nightmare to Kauko. What could it be like at the front, he wondered.

CHAPTER VIII

1

The wind blew through the Kainu wilderness, driving scattered low clouds before it and roaring in the trees. Sometimes the moon's round face showed through the clouds, and when it did, the company on skis could see their bulky shadows bobbing along behind them. The older civilian skiing fourth in line said in a low voice:

"A little more to the left."

"Turn left," a sergeant relayed the information to the trailbreaker.

"That's about enough. Now just follow your nose."

"Straight ahead now," the sergeant repeated the instructions to the leader.

The company was traversing woods behind the enemy lines. A civilian guide was setting their course by sighting on familiar landmarks. Behind him was the company commander, with Lieutenant Salmi, the leader of Kauko's platoon on his heels.

"You do know this area?" said the lieutenant.

"You won't get lost if you follow me."

"Shouldn't we look at the map now and then?" asked the lieutenant.

"I have the map of these woods in my head. Have the trailbreaker bear a little to the right now."

"Turn a little to the right," the sergeant advised the lead man.

"Let's have someone else break trail now," said the sergeant.

The point man stopped and the skier in back of the lieutenant slogged by the others. In a short time the company began to move into a swamp behind a fresh leader. A cloud glided away from the face of the moon and the landscape was suddenly bright. Pointing to the land beyond the swamp with a ski pole, the civilian said:

"That line of ridges across the swamp is where the Russians first broke into this country."

"Should we form a skirmish line now?" asked the lieutenant.

"I don't know anything about this war business, but I'm pretty sure you won't see any strangers moving around here until you cross that ridge. They won't be wading around on foot in a swamp like this."

"Nobody has been through here since the last storm," said the lieutenant.

"And no one is likely to be," said the civilian.

A cloud went sailing across the moon. In spite of the guide's confident words, a mild depression insinuated itself into the minds of the men.

✧ ✧ ✧

"What do you think of this business?" asked Kauko.

Jalo Kieppi, who was skiing ahead of him looked back over his shoulder, his rifle and pack on his back swinging sideways as he turned.

"So far it's not all that bad."

"Sometimes I close my eyes and imagine we're skiing to a winter logging job," said Kauko.

"It's a good thing we've been in the woods before."

"Don't think this is only a logging trek, boys. It's a sure thing you'll be hugging the snow yet."

Two platoons of the company had been made part of a flanking unit. The rest of the men were reserves who had been in many a tight spot at Suomussalmi, Raate, and Kuhmo. At the moment, Kauko was the last skier in his platoon. The squad behind him was led by a sergeant from Pudasjärvi, a few of whose men Kauko knew from peace-time log drives. With others, he had been housed in the same winter logging camps. Although he felt close to all Finns, the men from the neighboring parish were like family.

"Isn't it better not to be afraid ahead of time?" said Kauko to the man behind him.

"Of course. Is this the first patrol for you boys?"

"The first," said Kauko. "The bombing yesterday was hard to take."

"Bombings and artillery concentrations are the worst things to put up with," said the sergeant.

They skied in silence. From time to time the landscape was brightly lighted. The ridge line that ran before them loomed higher as they approached. The sergeant said:

"They remind me a little of the woods back home."

"Except that the higher hills like Iso Syöte and Koston Pyhitys are missing."

"Have you seen Iso Syöte?" asked the sergeant.

"I have, and from up close too. We watched the logs run by right at its foot."

"My home is right near it."

A sense of security filled Kauko. He and the man behind him had peeled pulpwood at the same site to earn their bread. Looked at the same hills from close up. Toiled long days in the woods. Watched day and night on log drives. Cursed life's hardships. Now memories of the same woods warmed his heart. The sergeant skiing behind him must be thinking the same thoughts. Now they were defending the same woods. With their lives and their blood. The woods belonged mainly to them, to the loggers and small farmers.

Suddenly it was clear to Kauko. The patriotism taught them in school, which had been a feeling of pride in a child's mind, was just this. To march at midnight through woods that belong to us against an enemy who is trying to take them from us. For all of us on this side of the eastern border — woods-owners, ditch-diggers, lumberjacks, small farmers, landowners, reindeer men, and migrant workers — this is our native land.

"If we come under fire from those titcaps, remember to hit the snow. In this business, you mustn't be ashamed to do that."

Kauko turned around in response to the sergeant's comment:

"If you happen to be near me, tell me what to do."

"There isn't always time. Keep your eyes and ears open. Move like a flash when you have to move, but don't let a muscle so much as twitch when you have to be still."

"Stop and keep quiet," came a whisper from up ahead.

The halt came as a surprise. Men skied up onto each others' heels. All other thoughts were forgotten.

"Strange tracks ahead," the whisper went back down the line.

2

It was one of that winter's rare stormy days. The slender pine trees that human hands had previously spared stood ravaged amid the gusting snow. Their trunks, clipped off at all heights, and their fallen crowns formed a tangle difficult to traverse.

The men on lookout peered across a narrow river channel. Between themselves and the river was a strip of marshy ground, on which stood stunted pine trees that had dried out over the centuries. Before the storm, bodies had been visible among the holes and heaps of muck left by bursting shells. Most of the bodies were of Russians who had attacked across the river, but some were of Finns who had been killed in a counterattack. Now there was enough snow to cover the war's most gruesome sights.

Further back, where the woods had been partially spared from shredding by the shells, a few tents were huddled. Smoke oozed from their pyramidal tops, to be snatched away by the storm. There was no need to fear that the smoke would attract airplanes now, or that it would draw artillery fire from across the river.

The weary Finns knew that although they did not need to fear the fire of more devastating weapons, there were men across the river keeping watch as they were. Only now and then were they able to see across the river, and then not clearly, but they could at least ascertain that no larger enemy units were approaching. This partial release of tension permitted their weariness to gain control. They had to make an effort to keep from sitting in the snow. They were even tempted to lie down in it.

Simo Mutka, the last man on the company's sector of the line, stood looking out across the river channel. The snow frozen into the one-inch growth of beard that covered his entire face gave him a wild appearance. His sluggish senses sharpened when he heard a rustling sound behind him. He spun around and flipped the machine pistol from his shoulder into firing position under his arm.

"Keep your shirt on. I'm one of the same dirty-necked crew as you are," said the newcomer.

"Did you have to come sneaking up like that?" snarled Mutka.

"You must have been asleep on your feet. I could have hit you with my fist."

"Kiss my whatever-you-can-reach. If I hadn't known you for the company messenger, you'd be as dead as this buddy here, and that's for sure." Simo Mutka bent down, grabbed a hand sticking up from the snow, and dragged a frozen body into sight. The messenger scowled, his ice-laden eyebrows almost touching his cheekbones, as he said:

"Leave the dead alone — even the Russians."

"No reason to be afraid of the dead here. There are plenty of them around."

Simo Mutka waved his arm in a broad arc. Although the soft blanket of snow kept falling, felt boots, horses' hoofs, protruding hands, and upright human shoulders still thrust into view. The company messenger looked around and said:

"Are all these from last night's attack?"

"Most of them. The bodies from other nights have been buried."

The messenger was from Simo's neighboring parish. He was no longer a young man. He stared out across the river for a long time, then took a pack of cigarettes from his pocket and opened it for Simo.

"Have a smoke," he said.

"Now you're talking like a man. I'll dig out a light."

The men smoked for awhile. The messenger kept heaving great sighs. From time to time he glanced at the yellow, contorted face of the enemy soldier who had been pulled up from the snow.

"Will any of us come out of this alive?" he said.

"Old folks say that not everyone dies in a war, but that no civilian can escape becoming a corpse," Mutka laughed.

"Are you so hardened you can laugh and crack jokes with dead men around you?"

"You'll go crazy here if you cry about everything."

"A man can always put up with things somehow, but when he thinks of his family...They've been evacuated to the coast, and if the man doesn't get back..."

Simo looked out over the area he was watching. With his back to his comrade, he said:

"I have a boy whose legs are paralyzed. My wife writes that they got a cold reception on the coast. Poor Lassi can't stand up for himself. The strong ones always...I've started to think here in the war that my boy's paralysis is my fault. It weighs so goddamned much on my mind..."

Although the messenger behind Simo heard what he was saying, he did not say anything. Simo puffed at the cigarette so heavily that his shoulders rose and fell. Finally he went on:

"My wife was carrying Lassi. It was Michaelmas in the church village. I had been drinking there for days. Then I played cards and lost my last *markka*. Toward morning I went stumbling home flat broke and good and drunk. I was in an ugly temper and yelled out from the door of the house. My wife jumped up. She was crying and shaking. I thought she would go all haywire. Lassi was never able to walk a step."

Simo turned around suddenly, looked at the messenger, and said:

"What the devil did you come around here blabbering for? Are you just crawling around for nothing?"

"I'm looking for the company commander. They want him at battalion headquarters."

"He's not here. Go to the tent you can see in back of that big rock. A little more carefully than you came here. They'll put a hole in your gut fast enough."

"And don't you fall asleep so easily."

"Asleep? Let's find out who's asleep here, goddamn."

Simo Mutka tucked his machine pistol under the arm of the dead body on the ground, threw down his mittens, and took a stride toward his comrade. His frozen beard trembled and his red-lidded eyes glittered wildly.

"Come at me now!"

Stop fooling around. We have enough fighting partners over there." The man nodded toward the other side of the river and took a couple of steps backward.

"Then don't come farting around here."

"You were the one who started that talk."

After the man had left, Simo Mutka gazed at the line of trees across the valley. Tears gathered at the corners of his eyes and froze there. Lassi always held on to his neck so tightly when he was picked up. He would sit on the floor on winter days and play with the wooden horses and reindeer his father carved for him. He would sit alone, not asking his brothers and sisters to play with him. He was used to watching while the others raced around the house playing tag. When the others ran out, he would start talking to his play animals.

Two rifle shots cut short his thoughts. They came from the next company's sector. No further shots were fired.

"Probably some replacement panicked," Mutka declared.

✧ ✧ ✧

Crawling into the tent, the messenger said:

"Where is the company commander?"

"Snoring away behind the stove," said the man on fire watch. "What about it?"

"He's wanted at battalion. Man, it's hot in here."

"That's why I keep shoving wood into this stove."

The men lay asleep like so many fish in a barrel. A mighty rumble of snoring filled the tent. Ski boots and Lapland boots were hung up to dry. The messenger sat close to the tent fly, which flapped in the gusts of wind, as the fire watch stood scowling at him.

"Wake up the boss so I can do my job."

"I suppose they'll throw us into another counterattack," said the one man in the tent who was awake.

"I don't know anything. I'm just carrying out the captain's orders."

"We've been fighting for three days straight. The Russians seem to have plenty of men and ammo to waste. They got mixed up with our men last night," said the watch.

"It's the same everywhere. The captain himself had to take his place with the men."

"Our company has taken their worst attacks. Most of what's left of it is in this tent. A few of the men from one squad are in the next tent. The other half are on watch."

As he spoke, the fire watch shook the sleeping man by the ankle.

"They can't get along without you. They came to get you."

The big man sat up on the bed of fir boughs. His eyes slits, he looked toward the tent fly and dug out a pack of cigarettes. When he got one lighted, he said:

"What's the panic at battalion now?"

"The captain's orders are for the lieutenant to report to the command tent."

"Right now?"

"He said so."

"Are others coming?"

"Only this company's commander."

"I knew it. We're getting the shaft again."

Lieutenant Mäkinen reached for his Lapland boots, smoothed them out with his hands, and said:

"It's the first time in a long time that I got to dry my boots. I probably slept for an hour."

"More. Almost four hours," said the fire watch.

"Well, that was a rich man's rest. I mean, I thought I just fell asleep."

Gritting his teeth, Mäkinen pulled on his boots. He rose and said:

"If anything happens, Lieutenant Suomela will take over."

✧ ✧ ✧

The battalion tent was not far away. Lieutenant Kosti Mäkinen had to stoop low to pass through the tent fly. The messenger crawled in after him. The battalion commander, a youngish man with a calm face, sat at the rear of the tent. A sergeant and a couple of soldiers were using pieces of plywood resting on their knees as desks to write on. Three reserve officers sat near the captain. One was a first lieutenant and the other a fellow officer of Kosti Mäkinen. Mäkinen flicked a hand to his forehead in salute and said:

"You sent for me...but hello anyway."

"Hello, hello. A man as tall as you doesn't need an invitation to sit down in this hotel."

Kosti Mäkinen was fond of his superior officer. Although the man's cheeks were sunken, his beard of many days' growth, and his uniform smeared with soot and mud, the familiar spark of humor from more peaceful days still gleamed in his eyes. He glanced to one side and said:

"Yaah, but we've got a new officer too. This less dirty fellow officer of yours is...is...you get so mixed up here you don't even remember names. It's better if you two gentleman introduce yourselves."

Kosti Mäkinen reached out a dirty hand from one knee. Only now did his eyes, adjusting to the light in the tent, make out the face of a smallish second lieutenant who had leaped to his feet. The newcomer's hand was swallowed up by his bear-like paw.

"Backman," said the newcomer.

"Mäkinen...Communist Mäkinen's son from Pispala in Tampere."

The battalion commander looked at both lieutenants' faces and his jaw dropped in astonishment. The clerks' pens stopped scratching. It was not only Lieutenant Mäkinen's word, but his tone of voice that made the tent fall silent. The face of the officer who had just joined the battalion turned pale. Kosti Mäkinen felt the man's fingers tremble in his grasp. He was overcome by weariness and the bitter memories that thronged suddenly into his mind. The man tried to withdraw his hand, but Kosti Mäkinen's grip was like a steel vise. He stared unblinking at his fellow officer's clean-shaven face. The man met his gaze for a moment but then dropped his eyes to the fir boughs on the floor.

"Long time no see." Kosti Mäkinen let out a roar of mirthless laughter.

The man's hand went limp in his own. His nerveless fingers crunched as they were squeezed together. Finally Mäkinen let go of the hand and said:

"Welcome to the Kuusi River wilderness. Has the lieutenant come here direct from civilian life?"

"I was wounded near Salla, but only slightly. I spent a month in the hospital. Have you been here long, lieutenant, sir?"

The battalion commander and the first lieutenant looked at each other and then at the two men facing each other. Finally the captain said:

"We don't pay much attention to formality here. At least not among the officers."

"I have reason to make an exception in this case," said Kosti Mäkinen.

Mäkinen's voice was harsh and the look he turned on his commanding officer was bleak. He and Lieutenant Backman sat down. An oppressive silence lingered in the room. Finally Kosti Mäkinen turned to the captain.

"You sent for me?"

The captain was staring at Mäkinen in wonder. He seemed to be puzzling over what to say. The lieutenant kept looking expectantly at him. The captain cleared his throat:

"You have to go and put up some barriers with your platoon. They have to be well mined, with enough explosives to keep tanks from coming through. A reconnaissance patrol reports that reinforcements are pouring in from across the border. Hundreds of trucks and tanks."

"I'm not an engineer," said Mäkinen quickly.

"But your civilian occupation was close to it...and this isn't your first job of this sort. Even at Alasalmi..."

"Besides, there's little more than a platoon left of my company."

"It can't be helped. There aren't enough engineers to go around."

Kosti Mäkinen sat with his knees sticking up, staring at the fir boughs on the floor. Events from more than six years ago were seething in his mind. A dark, rainy autumn evening. An unfinished bridge. Rapidly rising flood waters and an ice jam piled up behind a boom stuck between two of the piers, threatening to sweep the bridge away. That incident had driven him to a distant corner of the backwoods. It had gnawed at his mind with increasing bitterness. There were days when all he could do was brood upon his revenge, days when he thought he would never emerge from his depressed state of mind. The episode had faded from his memory over the years, especially after he and Irja had begun to have children. Sometimes he was pleased at being forced downward on the social ladder. Had that fateful night not occurred, he would never have met his wife. And now, when every day might be his last, the episode had been thrown into his face again.

"Will you have a cigarette? Help yourself."

Kosti Mäkinen was startled out of his reverie. He lighted a cigarette and said in a deep growl:

"There's a man in this tent who's better able to do the job."

"Who do you mean?"

"Lieutenant Backman."

"He's new to this sector and doesn't know the situation or the terrain. You'll do the job and that's all there is to it."

"Once this gentleman knew exactly how to handle a tough situation."

The captain began to unfold a map. As he did so, he looked at the sergeant and the soldiers in the tent. Then he said:

"I would like all but the officers to leave for awhile."

Soon the tent fly dropped from the shoulders of the last man to exit. Snow had swirled in from the opening onto the fir boughs in front of it. The wind howled and the dried pine tree from the woods of Kainu burned crackling in the stove.

✧ ✧ ✧

The man watching the fire was sleepy. He looked at the time and said to himself:

"A full quarter-hour yet."

His words did not disturb the snorers in the tent. Early that morning, a daring member of the kitchen crew had driven his horses right up to the river bank although there were still Russians fighting on its west side. Containers of pea soup were emptied, packages of hardtack ground up in the mouths of tired and hungry soldiers. Now gases were forming in the bowels of sleeping men, and escaping, sometimes with a thin wheeze and sometimes with a soft explosion. At each such sound, the weary fire watch would grunt sourly:

"Another balloon burst."

Recent massive artillery barrages, repeated Russian attacks across the river, and endless sleeplessness had strained the men's nerves to the limit. One single thought kept hammering in their minds: "I have to hold out because my comrades can. We're all in this logging job together." Now with the easing of tension, the man on watch by the fire began to feel as if his own comrades were to blame. They just lay there snoring while he had to force himself to stay awake. The hour dragged by slowly.

"Whose balloon burst now? Yaah, it's time to wake Bert up."

The man spoke the words loudly. He rose and shoved the toe of his boot into a sleeping man who wore sergeant's stripes.

"Get a move on."

Bert Sääskilampi was sleeping like one of the dead. A grin stretched the lips of the man waking him up. He remembered how the fire watch on a logging drive would wake up a logger whose feet were getting too close to the fire. Bert Sääskilampi had thrust his stockinged feet almost into the side of the barrel stove. The fire watch picked up a fir branch and muttered:

"Let's see if the trick works here."

Bert's sock was stuck to the heel and toe of his foot, but stretched free of the skin at the arch. The man jabbed the butt of the branch into that spot. Bert's foot snapped back and he sat up with a jerk. Wide-eyed, inch-long growth of beard waggling, he roared:

"Goddamn, it's burning!"

At the same time he pulled the sock from his foot, rubbed his arch, and grunted. The watchman dropped the branch, squatted down, and gazed at the stove.

"What's the matter with you? You're thrashing around like a hooked salmon."

"A fire watch could at least see to it that a man doesn't shove his feet into the stove."

"Well at least your sock wasn't smoking. And it did wake you up."

Bert rose. He looked at the sleeping men and said:

"What happened to Mäkinen?"

"They sent for him from battalion."

"That's the end of our sleep then. Take my word for it, they'll soon be dragging us off somewhere."

"I hardly had time to close my eyes. This is some logging job, ugh...!"

"I'll go and check our buddies on the line," said Bert.

The scene outside the tent was completely different from that morning's. Snow covered the worst signs of the war. It seemed strange not to hear a rumble from either near or far. Bert crouched down and clambered through a heap of fallen trees toward the company's farthest lookout point. He saw that his arrival had been spotted. Once there, he said:

"What do you see, Simo?"

"A storm and some tall stumps. Are you making your snooper's rounds?"

"There's nothing to spy out here. It's just the army's way."

"Simo Mutka yawned. "If I could only get some sleep."

Bert did not mention that Kosti had gone to the battalion. If Simo knew about it, he would only start cursing and railing.

"No sign of life across the river?" he said.

"No. Once in awhile my eyes try to trick me into seeing them coming, but not a single tit-cap has showed up there."

Bert looked across the river. This war is strange, he thought. Last night and many nights before that they had come on like madmen. Near that rock he had fought hand-to-hand with a big Russian officer. He could still see the man's face close to his own as he pressed him down into the snow on his back. But he had been strong, had wrapped his arms around Bert, and turned him over onto his own back. Bert could still remember the glitter in the man's eyes, the face contorted with strain but still confident of victory. The man pointed a Nagant at his head. The barrel jerked once but Bert spun his head back just as the pistol spat fire. It wasn't his day to die yet. Just then his own hand worked his sheath-knife free and his arm flashed in a vicious arc through the air. The blade crunched through cartilage into the shoulders of the man above him, who screamed as blood spurted from his mouth. Bert rolled the man off of him. He had gurgled a couple of times, then curled up on his side and lain still.

"Now that things are slow I started to think of something that happened in civilian life. Those splintered trees reminded me," said Mutka.

"I was thinking of a wrestling match near that big rock."

"It happened once when we were gathering twigs for the lambs. I was thinking about it when you came up."

"Gathering twigs has nothing to do with this."

"Yaah, but let's see if we can make a connection."

Bert said nothing, but looked askance at Simo Mutka.

"I had a forestry permit to cut birch firewood. Right after Midsummer. It was for cutting in a national forest, and I went there with the wife and older kids. I chopped down some birches and they started to break off the twigs. Toward evening I started to make a base for a stack, the kind reindeer and cows can't get at. When the forester and a watchman had gone into the woods with me, the forester painted a red mark on a few of the largest birches at the height of a man's head. He told me I mustn't cut or damage those trees in any way.

"When I started to make the stack, I couldn't find a good pole to support one end. I didn't exactly look too hard, but used one of the marked trees as a brace for the bottom poles. My wife said, you can't touch a tree with paint on it. I said, if that red ring bothers you. I can get rid of it. I made a cut in the bark at that point and peeled it off, red paint and all. Then I made the stack, made another the next day, and now there were enough birch logs down and drying for the winter's firewood.

"A couple of days later the forester and the watchman came barging into my house. I saw right away by the look on the woods boss's mug that all was not right. He looked pretty well steamed up, and barked out as soon as he got himself sat down on the bench by the door.

"'What right had you to cut up a seed-tree?'

"'What seed-tree are you talking about? I'd never do any harm to this country's woods,' I said, though I guessed what was up.

"'Don't try to give us the run-around. You pulled the bark off a seed-tree.'

"Oh, yaah, I guess I did. Was it a seed-tree? Then it was a real *poglom* I went and did.

"'That birch will cost you dearly, Mutka. You've committed a premeditated crime and destroyed a choice birch tree. And now you try to weasel out of it.'

"The forester's face was red. I've always had a bad habit of laughing at the wrong time, and I did it now too. That really burned him up. He jumped up from the bench like a flea and shouted:

"'So you think this is a laughing matter, Mutka? You'll find out that laws are for backwoodsmen too. You live out here the way they did during the *Great Wrath.* You destroy the woods, shoot waterfowl during the summer, and hunt wood grouse in mating season.'

"I couldn't keep my mouth shut while he ranted, but had to say:

"Well that's a helluva ruckus over one measly birch tree. I've been a party to your doings when whole stands of fine birch have been chopped down and left to rot. Now it looks as if the forest service will go broke because of one goddamned birch tree.

"The forester stepped up to me, stamped his feet on the floor, and slammed his fist on the table. He roared so loud that the kids started to cry, and poor Lassi tried to drag himself toward me along the floor like a worm.

"'Those are conservation measures that you know nothing about.'

"'That's true. I don't understand them at all,' I said.

"'Shut up when I'm talking,' he shouted, and slammed the table with his fist again.

"Then my mind went blank. My wife told me afterward that I jumped up and let out an ugly roar. Then I grabbed up an ax from under the bench. Goddamn, but that forester lit out in a hurry. He shot out the door like a weasel and I ran after him, ax raised over my head. He was a dry, long-legged man, and he galloped like an elk over the small fields. He jumped the gate of the outer fence at full speed. I had to jerk out a couple of poles to get over it. By that time I could only hear feet pounding along down the road. That was the end of the chase. I started to feel like laughing — he must have been covering a mile at a stride. When I got back, the watchman was cowering behind a corner. I told him I didn't care to stain my ax in the blood of such a little twerp. He was someone I knew well."

"Were you fined for it?" asked Bert.

"I haven't heard a thing, at least not yet. Maybe the forester told the sheriff about it, but the old man might have winked at such a crime. He has other things to do, like keeping things peaceful at home and..."

As he spoke these last words, Simo Mutka's arm described a broad arc over the shell-torn woods and said:

"That forester would be mighty hard on those Russians now."

"Those big guns tear a place up when they keep firing them."

"And they say this is a model national forest," said Simo.

✧ ✧ ✧

Bert and Simo were among the few men left from the original company that had been transferred from Alasalmi. Most of them were dead and many had been wounded. Kosti Mäkinen was the one original officer still with the company. A couple of weeks ago he had become its commanding officer and Bert had been promoted to platoon leader.

Lieutenant Mäkinen's company had suffered the heaviest casualties on the Kuusi river line, where Mutka and Sergeant Sääskilampi now stood amid the mutilated forest on its banks. Old men had been brought in as replacements, their training outdated and in part forgotten. They were completely unfit to cope with the storm of artillery unleashed on the Kuusi River line. In addition, they had wives and children to worry about. Most of them placed their trust in God, but during these weeks, the Creator seemed to have forgotten that sector of the front. Many large families were left fatherless. Other replacements were brought in from training centers, even men recruited as late as January. Some of the inadequately trained youngsters broke down mentally. Others, perhaps a majority, overcame their fear, but in the wild excitement of youth, they forgot to be careful. Many got themselves killed when their zeal made them go too far.

"If this lull holds, we'll get some rest," said the sergeant, gazing out over the river.

"Tomorrow will just be that much worse. They'll scrounge up

more planes for the Uhtua airfields."

"It's a sure thing Uncle Bolshie's men are sneaking around us somewhere."

"Where the devil did they rush in those ski troops from? Up to now we did what we pleased in the woods because they had to stick to the roads. Now we can't hunt them down that way any longer. They're said to be good skiers."

"The looey said they were Dolin's ski brigade," said Bert.

"I hear lots of them have already been killed, but who knows how long a line is charging in here — maybe one string of men skiing all the way from Russian Kemi," said Simo.

"Well, yaah. Nothing special to see from your lookout. I'll make the rounds of the platoon and then go and make something hot to drink."

Sergeant Sääskilampi looked at his watch and added:

"You still have a half hour."

"Have any replacements come?" asked Simo.

"I haven't seen any."

"And you won't. Ugh, this is some logging job we got into."

"It's no fun, but we'll try to stick it out."

"I won't quit. I'm used to having the bosses fire me when I'm no longer needed. It would be fine if one could walk out now and ask to be paid off, but it's the mark of a man to stay on a job until it's done. I've always been kind of lazy, and the first in line on pay-day, but...Now what the hell is that? You take a look!"

Simo Mutka's eyes were fixed on the river. He and Bert were standing in a shell hole with only their heads showing over the ridge in front of them. Simo pointed a finger in the direction where he was looking.

"Isn't that somebody crawling on his belly in the snow?" said Bert.

"Not just somebody. Look further to the left."

The storm let up for a moment, and the visibility improved.

"They didn't take a snow day off after all," said Bert. "They are coming."

Simo Mutka raised his machine pistol to his cheek and said:

"And here come some more corpses, ha, ha."

Bert looked at Simo. The sound of his laugh and the glitter in his eyes were frightful.

"Don't shoot yet. They can't surprise us now. I'll run and let the others know what's going on. If they don't come any faster, don't start firing until I reach the other end of the line."

Bert Sääskilampi rushed off toward the other wing of his platoon. Having often followed the reindeer in the wilderness, he was able to wind his way swiftly through the tangle. To the man on line next to Simo, he said:

"Hey, Alapertti, the Russians are crawling across the river."

"Don't talk shit! Well, they are coming. Crawling along out there..."

The man raised his rifle to his cheek and started to cock it.

"Don't shoot yet. Wait till I get to the other end of the platoon."

Bert kept on running and passing the news on to the men. He had to order each one not to fire. He stopped to look out from one of the men's holes. There they were, creeping up, their faces dark circles in their snow uniforms. Their rifles too, which they dragged along with them, showed up as dark objects.

Bert did not get even close to the last lookout before a machine pistol began to chatter. He could hear an answering rattle from Simo Mutka's weapon at the left end of the line. He threw himself down beside one of the men and began to fire himself.

"Was Bert flying, he got there so fast," Simo Mutka said aloud as he squeezed the trigger again. Two more crawling figures fell limp into the snow.

"You won't come here to wrestle now," said Simo.

When the firing commenced, the attackers began to advance in short rushes. It was heavy going in the deep snow. There was at least a company of them. From the deep river bed, there was no chance of their reaching the Finnish positions. Only a small number made it across the river, and the very last of them were left lying on the rise of the bank on the near side. A few of the living happened to stop in back of rocks, and they crouched there to wait for nightfall.

As if to revenge the unsuccessful attack, a hail of artillery began to fall on the ravaged area. It lasted for only a short time. When Bert got back to the tent, the men who had been taking their turn at sleeping were pulling on their footgear. Other men were already milling around outside.

"He didn't send too many rounds this time," said Bert. "Let's go into the tent."

"It was a cold shift," said one of the men.

"Hasn't Kosti come back yet?"

"He doesn't seem to have."

✧ ✧ ✧

The captain broke the silence in the battalion tent by saying:

"What's gotten into you now, Mäkinen?"

"Nothing's gotten into me now. It's been there for years."

"If I've got it right, there's a grudge between you two."

"Ask the master engineer. He can testify that I'm not fit to handle a demanding job."

The battalion commander turned toward Lieutenant Backman.

"I don't understand Lieutenant Mäkinen's behavior. This is not appropriate conduct for officers. I have nothing negative to say..."

Kosti Mäkinen bounced up onto his knees from where he had been sitting, placing himself next to his fellow officer. He moved swiftly. The other lieutenants who had been in the battalion tent earlier shifted their buttocks further over. Lieutenant Mäkinen's eyes were bloodshot and his hands were shaking.

"Come right out and say that I'm not fit to take on responsibilities."

Backman looked into Mäkinen's eyes, but then dropped his own.

"Do you refuse to?"

"I don't want to bring up old issues. It was a misunderstanding."

"Now we're two equal dirty-necks in the Finnish army. Repeat the words you said to me on that bridge job and I swear you'll feel it from my fists."

"Well, this is a strange front line. Fellow officers with their fists raised. Isn't even a commanding officer able to maintain discipline?"

Kosti Mäkinen's hand gripped the shoulder strap of Backman's Sam Browne belt. His strong arm gave it a jerk, and Lieutenant Backman flew face first into the boughs.

"Damn it, Mäkinen," said the battalion commander.

"I'm not finished yet. Are you going to say what I told you to?"

Backman sat up slowly. With trembling fingers, he tried to fasten the loose end of his shoulder strap. The man was crazy...His eyes are those of a madman. He'll kill me if I don't talk.

"I was a young engineer in charge of a bridge site. Mäkinen was the supervising builder. He handled the work well..."

"Tell the truth," shouted Mäkinen from on his knees.

"Let me finish. One fall night, the waters rose suddenly because of a heavy rain. The ice broke up and began to move. The gate log of a boom came with it. I was reprimanded by my superior and I took out my anger on an innocent man. But to tell the truth, Lieutenant Mäkinen took offense too easily. He himself asked to draw his pay and insisted on leaving."

The sound of a burst from a machine pistol came from the direction of the line, quickly followed by more. Rifles banged. All the men in the tent listened.

"*Vanya* must be trying again," said the lieutenant.

"Mäkinen's boys are just warming up their weapons," said the battalion commander.

Kosti Mäkinen sat down and listened thoughtfully to the sounds from the line. When the rifle and machine-pistol fire abated, the land began to quake as a short volley of shells exploded, but the concentration landed some distance from the tent.

"Is this for real?" asked the lieutenant.

"It's only harassment," said the battalion commander.

When the sounds from the front-line ceased, Mäkinen turned to the battalion commander.

"Show me where we have to put up those barriers," he said.

"Do you have your map with you?" asked the captain.

Lieutenant Mäkinen's face was milder but his hands still shook when he dug out a map case and spread a sheet from it across his knees.

"This is the Kainu sector," he said.

"I plan a barrier at the spot marked *X*. The civilian who was with a reconnaissance patrol said the woods there are like a fort. They are heavy spruce trees. Mark the spot."

"Do we get started right away?" asked Kosti Mäkinen.

"I should think so. In a storm like this the planes won't be able to spot your unit."

"I'll do my best. But I'm afraid we'll be in for it tomorrow night. You know that I'm short of men?"

"Well at least they got a few hours' sleep."

"Only a part of them...Well, I'll be going then."

"You know where to get the explosives. Naturally you can choose the best place when you get there. Do whatever you think best."

Lieutenant Mäkinen went to the tent fly. Then the captain said:

"Wait a minute. There's a letter for you. Now where did the clerk put it? Oh, there it is, on the packing box. Here, take it. Do you know the handwriting?"

"It looks like my wife's."

Kosti felt an inward tremor as he took the letter. His wife and children. He looked at Backman and said:

"Well, so long then!"

"Good luck, and do whatever you think best," said the battalion commander.

After Mäkinen left, there was silence in the tent. The men looked mostly at the boughs on the floor. There was the sound of heavy sighs. Then Backman said:

"Would you approve a request for a transfer, sir?"

"No. There is a crying shortage of officers here."

"You gentlemen can surely see that I'm not welcome."

"This is a question of something much bigger than some disagreement in civilian life. You will take over the duties of communications officer."

"In my opinion, quarrels among officers are bad for battalion morale. Lieutenant Mäkinen behaved like the lowest of laborers in the presence of men and officers. He was downright violent."

"Mäkinen is the only original officer left in this battalion. His company has never shirked its duty. The men trust him and obey him willingly. His behavior on this occasion would be considered out of line in a peacetime officers' club. I would not have believed he would harbor such — shall I call them imprudent — tendencies. But you know that we're all dead tired. Call in the men."

The men entered the tent. The captain put his hands up to his face and rubbed his temples with his thumbs. Then he said with a heavy sigh:

"Do you have any of those headache powders left, Sergeant Määttä?"

"I have. Will you take one or two, captain?"

"I doubt that one will have much effect."

"Here are two. I'll get you some water to wash them down."

✧ ✧ ✧

Entering the tent, Kosti Mäkinen said:

"We get to go on a pleasure trip again, boys."

"No, goddamnit. Where did they break through now?"

Simo Mutka's cry came from the bottom of his heart. He and the others who had come in from their turn on the line were drinking the coffee substitute Bert had prepared.

"Well, I mean, why are you looking at me?" said Mäkinen.

"We just want to know where they're rushing us off to now," said Bert.

"It's not a counterattack this time. Is there enough in that pot for me?"

"There's always enough for the top man," said Simo Mutka. "But what the devil did you mean by what you just said?"

"Just that we have to cut off a road from Russia tomorrow night. Thanks, but I won't eat all your bread cheese."

"Take it when it's offered to you. This keeps a man's feet on the road and his bowels hard," said Mutka, dropping pieces of bread cheese into his superior officer's hand. "So that's the kind of job they've given us. On which side of Moscow do we have to put up that gate?"

"I guess it's on this side of the border," said Mäkinen.

"This country had one helluva poor fence at the border," complained Mutka. "Those people from over there keep pushing through to this side all the time. So we have to throw up a stopgap again?"

When they had finished drinking, Kosti Mäkinen fished out a letter from his map case. Opening it, he said:

"Take ten men, Bert, and go get the explosives. Twenty of us will be going on this excursion. The idea is to build a real blockbuster."

"When will you bring us word from headquarters that we *have to* go on leave, Lieutenant?" Simo Mutka washed out the dregs from his canteen cup onto the boughs and went on: "It isn't fair. Most of us are married men and we don't even get to screw after a whole six months."

No one laughed at Simo's words. One of the men asked:

"Do those of us who just came off watch have to go on this gate job?"

"Anyone who wants to take a second shift doesn't have to go."

"Skiing is fun. That's the trip for us. I'll go with Bert to get the explosives. We only need a few more volunteers," said Simo Mutka.

There was a sound of muttered complaint. Men who had come

off watch were grumbling:

"We're no dynamiters..."

"They used to train engineers at Koria in peacetime."

"Where are they sleeping now?"

"Why, we can do anything," said Simo Mutka "Soon they'll be asking us to fly airplanes."

A number of men rose from where they were lying on the boughs. Bert was already leaving with them when Kosti Mäkinen said:

"Can you guess what they wrote to me, boys?"

They all turned to look at their commanding officer, but no one said anything. Mäkinen's face, which had been gloomy, was now beaming. He looked at Bert and said:

"Your sister writes that she had a healthy girl. They suspect me of being the father," he said with a laugh.

The grumpy, disgruntled mood in the tent changed. Simo Mutka felt compelled to say:

"Well, I'll be damned. We should hoist you on our shoulders but you're such a damned big hulk and the tent is so small..."

Each man's thoughts went back to his home. How is my family doing in its evacuation home? My wife is supposed to give birth soon too. The others merely thought, but Simo Mutka knelt down by his pack that lay near the wall of the tent, quickly opened its bindings, and stood up.

"Hey men! Do you see what this is?"

They all looked at Simo Mutka's upraised hand. Adam's apples rose and fell and tongue-tips moistened chapped lips. Finally one of the men said:

"Has that bastard got a full bottle of liquor?"

"Do you think I've been carrying a water bottle?" asked Mutka.

"Where did you lift that from? Is it Ahma-Juuso's stock?"

"Goddamn — when did he ever make such clear stuff? You can't make shit clear by boiling it. Was it two weeks ago that we raided that Russian doctor's sleigh? I don't exactly remember how it happened but a bottle wound up under the waistband of my pants. I didn't feel like offering it to the big brass, but this is a celebration worth uncorking it for. You pour the fake coffee and I'll dig out the sugar for a hot toddy."

"There's plenty of it here. Just hold out your cups."

One of the men poured out the hot liquid into mugs and canteen cups. The men stirred sugar into it with wooden sticks. Simo said:

"The sugar should be melted by now. We'll split it up."

Cups were held out before Simo. Clear liquid gurgled from the bottle. The smell of the liquor mingled with the steam from the coffee substitute. Simo raised the bottle on high and gauged its contents from time to time. Then he looked from man to man. All the while he kept urging them:

"Come on, come on. We're in a hurry."

Nevertheless a good third of the men remained sitting on the fir boughs. They seemed to have no intention of complying with Simo's wishes.

"I can't hold this all day," Simo flared up.

"I'm an avowed Christian," said one of them.

"I am too."

"I've been converted too."

"In Christ's name and through his precious redeeming blood, my sins have been made white as snow by preaching, and I was a hardened drunkard..."

"Not even God is so harsh and humorless that he won't let a man drink to a child's birth. Even ministers tell us to drop in at the church and sip the communion wine," said Simo.

One of the older believers looked at his comrades and said:

"Mutka seems to be right this time. The lieutenant's daughter is a gift of the Great Creator. The others are boys, aren't they?"

Kosti looked up from perusing the letter's contents. He dropped the sheets to his knees and said:

"Boys, two of them, and now they have a sister."

"Let's take a sip, brothers, in honor of the great news."

Even the believers took their portion. Mutka thrust an enamel mug into Kosti's hand and said:

"Let's have a snort now. What is it the bigwigs say? Here's to your health but not to your habits? That slid right down — ugh. Good luck to your daughter."

"Good luck and God's blessing."

"And so says Aapeli Haapalainen too — ugh!"

Kosti Mäkinen blinked. He had more to gulp down than the toddy. One of the older believers rubbed at his eye with a finger.

"Let's go for the explosives," said Bert.

Kosti Mäkinen was still reading the end of the letter.

The boys and little Tuulikki are well. Father is better too. He keeps rocking Tuulikki all the time even though she doesn't cry. Mother and I tell him he'll spoil her. Even father says Tuulikki looks just like her father. Take care of yourself. You now have a wife and three children waiting for you at home. Mother and father talk about you as much as about Bert. Tell Bert many, many regards from all of us.

3

Unknown tracks ahead.

His shirt, wet with sweat from skiing, had been warming Kauko's shoulders a few seconds ago. Now a cold shudder ran through them. The company stood in confusion in the swamp. Kauko tried to see up ahead. Suddenly countless jets of fire flashed at them from the thick spruce woods at the edge of the swamp. At the same time his ears caught the sound of banging and an incessant chatter. Above it all rose the lieutenant's shout:

"Hit the ground. It's an ambush."

The whole line of men in front of Kauko dropped into the snow. He could sense only the rapid beating of his heart. Am I all alone? Were all the rest killed?

"Boy! Down in the snow!"

Kauko turned to look back. He could still see a few shadows moving there. Only then did he realize that the shout had come from the sergeant skiing behind him. Kauko threw himself headlong into the soft snow. He could hear the ping of bullets ricocheting past his ears.

By wriggling his body, Kauko burrowed deeper into the snow. He could see snow spurting up around him. By some incredible feat, he managed to get his rifle unslung from his shoulders. He could see muzzle flashes spitting toward the woods from the direction of the company lying prone in the snow. Now I have to shoot — I can't be afraid. I have to think. If I could only see one of the enemy. His shaking hand opened and closed the rifle bolt. "Now my rifle is cocked," Kauko panted. His confused jumble of thoughts began to settle down. Then he heard a shout behind him:

"Help, help! Help! I'm dying!"

The shout was a cry of anguish, the voice of human panic. The next wail was barely intelligible:

"I'll die...It's getting dark...Ohh!"

"Medic, crawl over here," shouted the voice of Lieutenant Salmi.

Kauko pressed his face into the snow. Bullets kept whizzing by. He was shaking. I have to shoot. I can't be afraid when the others aren't. Kauko tried to raise his head. Through the firing, he could hear the moans of the wounded man.

I have a loaded rifle in my hands. Why are my hands and my whole body trembling? There were shots on all sides. One man was groaning, another was cursing. A voice quite near to Kauko said quite calmly:

"Do you have any rags? I think it went through my shoulder blade."

"Not a stitch," said another voice.

"Push over here through the snow. Use your cap to plug it if you have to. Otherwise I'll bleed dry. I can't reach it myself."

"I'm coming. Just stay in your hole," said his comrade.

"Goddamn bushwhackers, shooting without a warning! They have plenty of powder to waste. Have a taste of that!"

Jalo Kieppi spoke aloud and fired. He lay a full ski's length away from Kauko. From time to time he turned on his side in his pit in the snow, thrust a fresh clip into his rifle, and began firing again.

My God, what a coward I am. Kieppi is firing as if this were target practice. The sergeant who had been skiing behind Kauko raised his head now and then and fired, then ducked down below the surface of the snow. "I have to...goddamn..." said Kauko, gritting his teeth. Kieppi was shouting again:

"There's one down. He stuck his head up too high, ha, ha..."

The men who had flung themselves into the snow from their skis were beginning to recover from the shock of the attack. Their machine pistols chattered and their rifles banged. Sometimes there was a scream. A head or the bulk of a shoulder thrust too high above the snow had happened to be in the path of a bullet. Kauko clamped his teeth together so hard that his jaws crunched. Sumala won't get to laugh the way he did yesterday. No, by God. The loggers had laughed too at that assistant foreman Tonkojoki who had run away the time Toivo Olkivaara pressed a barking iron to his throat. Now! I came here on my own. To fight, not to shit in my pants.

Kauko rose to his feet and set the rifle stock to his shoulder. He could see a steady stream of fire coming from the foot of a spruce tree. There! Kauko sighted along his rifle barrel toward the spot. The kick of the rifle against his shoulder dispelled his fear. He jerked the bolt to eject the spent cartridge and slam in a new one and aimed at the spot again.

"So that's where the bastard is shooting from," he said as he fired.

Now the dark shadow at the foot of the spruce lay motionless. Did I hit him or did someone else? Kauko loaded again and fired. "Always remember to take aim quickly and accurately," those who had undergone a baptism of fire taught you. The whole tangle of woods before them spat muzzle flashes. There now — was someone starting to bang away from behind that willow thicket?

"Boy, get down! We're not playing games!" the sergeant from the next parish yelled out to him. Kauko sank down into his pit.

"How did they know enough to watch for us?" he asked.

"These things happen on this job. They seem to have built a road past the swamp. Do you see the trucks on it?"

Kauko looked where the sergeant was pointing. Black bulks were actually moving along there. Motors whined. The sergeant went on:

"In weather this cold, they can soon lay even a railroad."

"Move up! We'll cut the road. Short rushes, take turns..." The company commander's orders went down the line from man to man.

"Don't stay on your feet too long," said the sergeant.

"Won't the Russians take care of that?" said Kauko.

"Hang on to your skis. And take your rifle with you."

Kauko groped for his skis and poles and tucked them under his arm. A strange calm possessed him. If others can do it, so can I.

Kauko saw a dark shadow dart along beside him. Similar shapes sped over the snow across the swamp and then disappeared into its white bosom. Kauko drew his legs up. You had to move like a flash. He sprang up. He was in snow up to his navel and the ski gear under his arm hampered his movement. His rifle too. Kauko ran, sending the snow flying.

"A little more! A few steps..."

When Kauko threw himself down face first, the soft snow sucked him into its shelter. Bullets went pinging by him, kicking up snow onto his neck. Had something grazed his shoulder? No, no...I won't die in this swamp. No, no, no! All the while he was psyching himself up, Kauko was digging new starting pits in the snow with his feet. When the stream of bullets shifted away from him, he rushed ahead once more. He heard his own voice shouting:

"Let's tell them to use blanks!"

"Boy, don't stay up so long!"

Kauko heard the sergeant's warning from behind, and then Jalo Kieppi's voice:

"I don't like men who shoot from behind bushes."

The sergeant's prohibition merely spurred Kauko on. His next rush was even longer. This was like breaking up a log jam. A tough job. When I get face to face with one of those tit-caps, God help him. He'll soon have the grin of death on his face. This is what they call a baptism of fire. Once a person's been through it, they say that war is just a job like cutting wood. That's the way those who were in the World War talked. Now I have to make another rush. The others will soon catch up with me. Now I'll show them that the community didn't give me its bread for nothing.

Then from the right came the sound of heavy firing. It seemed to come diagonally, from nearly behind them. Had some of the company's men been left back there? Strange that they risked firing from behind their own men.

"Hey men, watch out! Russians on the right," someone yelled.

"Company, move back!" shouted the commanding officer.

"We'll soon be cut off...Get back," someone yelled.

Men with skis under their arms began to dash back the way they had come. Someone screamed and toppled into the snow. Men were overcome by panic, especially those who had just come from the training center.

"In Christ's name! My time has come..."

The man who had cried out dropped to the snow. Another man near him fell, crying out:

"Help, Paukkeri. It hit my cheekbone, I feel dizzy..."

"Dig into the snow. Those in the rear, stop the flankers," shouted the sergeant.

Only now did Kauko realize that the others had outstripped him. I have to run, otherwise I'll be left here alone, he thought. He could see black lumps here and there in the swamp. Some already lay still, while others tried to keep going. Kauko ended his first rush beside a man who reached out a hand toward him.

"Don't leave me. My leg is hot. I can't stand up on it."

Men were already scurrying at the rear of the swamp. Some were swimming through the soft snow like waterfowl. No one was anywhere near the two of them.

"They're leaving me behind. Jesus, help me..."

"I won't leave you."

The promise came through Kauko's trembling lips like a cry of fear. He was forced to burrow into the snow. Bullets traced patterns in the fresh white surface. The men in the swamp were now caught in a cross-fire. Then the sound of the wilderness wind was drowned out by the roar of a cannon. On its heels came the clanking of tank treads as two of the vehicles charged into position at the edge of the swamp. For the first time in his life, Kauko saw tanks. Their cannon roared, shattering trees on the other side of the swamp. Kauko's fear returned, as strong as in the first minutes of the attack. He drew up his legs for another lunge.

"Help me, buddy! I have a big family...I can't leave them..."

Kauko turned to the man and said:

"We'll stay together, if that's the way it's meant to be."

At that moment Kauko felt a blow to the top of his head. Pressing his palm to his hat, he said:

"What rapped me on the head?"

"Stay low. They have time to take careful aim now," said the man.

Kauko pressed down into the hollow in the snow. He could feel the sweat of pain dripping down his forehead. For a moment he felt dizzy and sleepy. Then the sweat rolled into his eyes and down his cheeks.

"If you help me a little, I can get onto my skis on my belly."

Kauko started. He rolled the wounded man onto his skis, which the man had lined up beside him. Kauko dug himself deeper into the pit, for bullets kept scoring the snow around him.

"Can you stay on your skis?"

"I can and I can help pull myself along by my arms. My leg doesn't hurt. I just can't move it."

"Is it bleeding much?" asked Kauko.

"It hasn't stained the snow too much. It just feels hot."

Kauko began to burrow forward, holding his own skis and rifle under his arm and dragging the man along by the ski tips. Luckily those who had already withdrawn from the swamp had plowed an almost continuous furrow in the snow, in the shelter of which he could pull the man forward. Nevertheless he felt as if a weight were crushing his shoulders and now and then a shudder ran through them.

He was going around a fallen man when a shell burst in a dried pine tree nearby. The trunk was cut almost at its midpoint and the top fell near Kauko and the man he was dragging. Too late, Kauko sank deeper into the snow. It was some time before he raised his head and said:

"Did it hit you?"

"No. Now they're bursting in the trees beyond the swamp."

Kauko did not know how long he had been rowing through the snow before he reached the edge of the swamp. There was constant firing from the opposite side and from one flank as well. Once in the shelter of the woods, Kauko began to wade through the snow. Now it was easier to pull the wounded man.

"Someone's pulling a buddy along with him. Who is it?"

Kauko recognized the squad leader's voice. He could see other men too.

"I'm Sammalsuo..."

"We were sure you got left out there," said the squad leader, pointing to the swamp with a ski pole.

"Who did you drag in?" asked Kieppi.

"A buddy. I didn't have time to ask his name," said Kauko.

"Piri, second platoon," said the man on the skis.

"Were you hit badly?" asked one of the reservists.

"My leg is all numb. Now it's starting to ache."

Men gathered around them. One walked with a stick as a prop. Another dragged himself along with the aid of ski poles. Some had bandages on their heads.

They began checking the wounded man Kauko had brought in. Looking at his oddly dangling leg, Kauko's squad leader said:

"The war is over for you."

"If I can only get back to the human world," said the man. "Oww!"

"There's blood on the boy's face too," someone said.

Kauko mopped his forehead with his bare hand. Although the moon now shone only dimly through the trees, his hand looked black. His forehead and cheeks felt as if a thick oil had been poured over them.

"Something hit me on the head out there in the swamp," Kauko said. "I thought it was sweat dripping on my face."

It turned out that Kauko had only a flesh wound on his scalp. Kieppi parted the blood-stained hair and said:

"I'll bandage it with a handkerchief and you'll look like Döbeln at Juutas."

Gradually the firing died down. What was left of the company assembled in one area. Their spirits were low. Many familiar faces, many good friends were gone. Lieutenant Salmi said:

"The company commander was killed. We tried to outflank the attacking Russians. He took a bullet in the head. Only two of the platoon leaders are left."

"And you are the older," said the other lieutenant.

"I have to try to organize the withdrawal. We can't take our dead with us."

The men's faces were downcast. They looked at one another. Everyone knew without its being said that there were too few of them to pick up their fallen brothers-in-arms. At that moment, they heard a tired but calm voice shout from the swamp:

"Brothers, take home the news that things are well with Räisänen. My sins have been forgiven in Jesus's blood...blood and ...dearly redeemed...redeemed.....re..."

The voice died away. Even the wilderness wind seemed to be holding its breath. Then the voice sounded weakly again:

"In...precious...I'm going to heaven...the blood of the covenant...It's getting bright."

Then came the roar of motors beyond the swamp and the sound of human voices trying to rise above them. Finally Lieutenant Salmi said:

"We have to go now. We'll take turns pulling the wounded."

"Lucky the Russians don't have ski troops," someone said.

"Sergeant Korento will stay to cover us. Take two men with you."

Kauko turned his back to the men. The recent strain on his nerves and the farewell of the dying man in the swamp brought tears to his eyes.

"It was an impossible place. I thought you got left there too."

Kauko turned and looked at Jalo Kieppi who had skied up alongside him.

"The war we read about in school wasn't like this."

"That wounded man's yell was terrible. This is no fun."

"Where's Jonas Niemi? Have you seen him?" asked Kauko.

"He was wrapping someone's leg just now."

"We've had our baptism of fire now. It couldn't have been worse. I was so scared that I'm ashamed when I look back on it," said Kauko.

"I had a cold ring around my asshole too."

The men began to move out. "It's a sad trip we have ahead of us," said Lieutenant Salmi.

Kauko caught sight of Jonas Niemi among the others and skied up beside him.

"You won't believe what a coward I am..."

Jonas Niemi's words came haltingly. His voice shook, and Kauko was afraid he would burst into tears. He too was slow to speak.

"No more than I am. I was so afraid I was almost whimpering."

"At least you went along with the rest. I lay in the pit I dug for myself the whole time."

Kauko said nothing. The woods were now dark and the moon's face was no longer visible. Frequently Kauko's skis ran into limbs buried under the snow. He turned into the track behind Jonas Niemi.

"What happened to our civilian guide?" asked someone skiing behind him.

"That's right. No one saw him after they opened fire on us."

"Did he get a bullet in him? Who can tell?"

"That's true. As long as he wasn't in on the ambush..."

"You wouldn't think one of your own countrymen..."

The discussion awakened strange thoughts in Kauko's mind. There seemed to be something mysterious even in the gusting of the wind. The woods of home, the entire land aroused a sense of wonder within him. How could a person live without a country of his own?

CHAPTER IX

1

The sky above the Isthmus of Karelia was cloudless, as it had been for almost the entire winter.

"How I would have bitched if someone had told me last year that I would have to sleep in a place like this."

A big soldier with a long beard lay full length on hay spread out in one of the stalls of a stone cow barn. He spoke with his hands clasped in back of his head and his eyes fixed on the ceiling.

"Better to sack out here than in a snow bank," another said.

"I'm not complaining — damn, they're at it again."

"What's Jesus-beard cursing about now?"

"My livestock are stirring again. It always happens when it's warmer."

The bearded man thrust one hand under his waistband and began scratching at his groin, grimacing as he did so. Then he began to jerk open the buttons of his fly. A younger and much slimmer man turned over onto his side and watched his companion's actions.

"You mean to empty your bladder sitting down?" he said.

"I'm going to clean out my brush patch. Hell, I'm getting nowhere. They're sucking away at the root of every hair with their asses in the air."

The man nipped at his groin with his thick fingers. With the nails of a thumb and index finger pressed tightly together, he shoved a big paw into the other's face.

"Take a look at a real louse, northern boy."

"Get it to hell out of here. Do you think everyone has those down at the root of his sprinkler pole?" said the man, brushing away the fist.

"Well, none so well fed."

The man went on checking the patch of hair below his navel. Men were snoring in some of the stalls and others were chewing on their rations. It was astonishingly bright in the barn at midday. The sun of March was already causing flies to come alive in the window panes. Toivo Malinen, the louse-picker's companion, rose and stretched, then said in a voice that a yawn turned into a bellow:

"Maybe I'll have a bite to eat since we have the time."

He stepped off the hay in the stall but quickly leaped into the air and yelled:

"Goddamnit, I slopped up my boot. A fine barn like this and they leave the trough full of manure."

"Ha, ha, ha — your Lapland boot looks well-greased, all right."

Toivo Malinen scowled at the laughing man and started to clean his boot with a handful of hay.

"I'd sooner stand in manure than shiver outside in the cold," said a young soldier.

"I think I've done as much shivering as you. A logging camp is no bed of roses either. But at least it's not this kind of filth."

The barn door opened and a soldier with a rifle on his shoulder entered.

"You get to run for the air-raid shelter again. Do you hear the planes in the east?"

"Are they in sight yet?" asked one of the soldiers, leaping to his feet.

"Not yet, but it sounds like a lot of them."

"It's the same thing every day. Let's start running."

The men groped for their hats and coats, pulling them on as they poured out the door. Some were cursing and others grunting dejectedly. The concrete-block barn was the only building left standing on the farm. A thick layer of snow already covered the ruins of the main house. Only the chimney and a few charred pieces of timber stuck up from the snow. The wooden front portion of the barn had burned. There were bomb craters in the yard and the surrounding fields.

The men ran toward the nearby woods. Those who had already reached their shelter stood looking toward the east. Someone pointed and said:

"They're coming into sight."

"One, two, three..." one of the men began to mumble as he counted the rapidly enlarging dots. He finished his muttered count by saying:

"Uncle Bolshie seems to have sent out forty planes on this job."

"There are only thirty-nine," said another.

"One plane won't make the difference between summer and winter. They seem to be heading this way."

"If they should drop their loads now..."

"They'll skip us, and the Second Company will get plastered. But watch out if they open their bays over that river."

Not all of them men left the barn. The soldier with the open fly kept on spreading his pubic hair, his eyes glumly following the motions of his fingers. The roar of the airplanes drew nearer. Toivo Malinen sat on the hay, gnawing on a piece of hardtack. Observing his companion's actions, he said:

"Your boarders haven't started to march up the pole, have they?"

"No, they seem to be camped out at its foot."

Two more of the men sat on the opposite side of the barn. One of them looked up at the sky and said:

"That's a big flight coming. Will they lay their eggs here?"

"They're coming this way, at least," said a sergeant sitting near him.

"I'm not staying here. I'm leaving," said the man who had spoken first.

"It's too late now. Don't show yourself."

The sergeant's order was of no avail. The man leaped to his feet.

"Hell no," roared Malinen. "You'll give us all away."

His words did no good. The man raced toward the door in a panic, crying out as he ran:

"They're coming right at us."

Toivo Malinen bit down harder than necessary on the hardtack. The roar of the motors grew louder. Toivo's stomach crawled. Let them come...a man has to die some day. And this wasn't the first tight spot he'd been in this winter. Aloud he said:

"Goddamn Willberg, he left the door open."

"The planes won't come in through it," said the louse-killer.

Toivo looked at the man. He's not afraid, but I'm not whining either. Let the roof fall in...ahah, that buddy's fingers are shaking a little. They're beginning to look just like a fiddler's. He's just acting the goddamned tough guy. A nasty thought flitted through Toivo's mind.

"Show me what caliber your lice really are," he said.

The man looked at his companion and began to pluck more busily at the roots of the hairs with his nails. He could feel one the size of a kernel of rye underneath his fingertip. Why couldn't he catch the damned thing?

"You ran out of them in a hurry," Toivo said, laughing.

The laugh sounded bleak. His companion went on plucking busily. Nothing came into view, and Toivo said:

"Yaah I've got to start playing jeweler."

He dug out his watch and showed its face to his companion.

"The second hand has slipped off its shaft. It's a good time to fix it now when no one will barge in and start talking."

His companion and the sergeant on the opposite side of the barn watched as Toivo pried open the face of the watch with the point of his sheath-knife. Picking up the second hand between his thumb and the knife-point, he raised the watch up to his face.

"That second hand is such a dinky sliver of brass. Well, get into that hole now, even if there are no hairs on it."

At that moment, the barn shook. Pieces of glass tinkled to the cement floor. The sound of the explosion and the blast of air from it struck the men's ears at the same time. The long-bearded man jerked his fly shut. Toivo Malinen's hands dropped to his knees. When the next explosion shook the barn, Toivo was again holding the watch cupped in his hand up close to his face and probing at it with the knife point. The long-bearded man bent down to continue his recent activity. A cluster of exploding bombs shook the building continuously.

"They must be leaving ugly tracks in the second company's sector."

"Joe Stalin's men aren't hauling planeloads of rocks over here," Toivo said sarcastically.

"The papers say the Russians *have* run out of bombs and are dropping rocks," grinned the sergeant.

Toivo closed the watch case and lay propped up on one elbow with his back to his companions. He shifted the hay carefully and stared at the floor of the stall.

"What's are you checking now?" asked his partner.

"I'm looking at the good timothy they grow around Viipuri. A little coarse for cows to munch on. It wasn't that..."

"The second company took a lot of iron," said a man coming

back from outside.

"No, it was rocks," said Toivo, still combing through the hay.

"They were calling for medics," said another man who had come in.

✧ ✧ ✧

A small log cabin had been left untorched by the retreating Finns. Even the bombings had scarcely damaged it. One night in early March a man stood watch in its yard, while the remnants of a company that had just staggered back from the line were asleep inside it. A short distance away another human dwelling still survived. Part of it could be seen from the cabin by daylight.

A couple of days ago, the constantly withdrawing Finnish troops had managed to stabilize a line on the shore of a widening isthmus. Continuous artillery concentrations pulverized the shore. Even now the man on watch could see the muzzle flashes of the big guns. The March night was exceptionally warm, but the sounds of war carried through it clearly. Someone approached from the next house. The sentinel stepped off the trail into the shadow of a spruce tree that had already shed its burden of ice. Sliding the sling of the rifle off his shoulder and down his arm, he took aim at the figure coming toward him. Then he recognized the man's walk and stepped out into the trail. The arrival, his company commander, stopped and said:

"We have to go out again."

"Everybody?"

"Only a patrol led by a non-com. Are the men sleeping?"

"They were half asleep on the way back from the line."

The reserve lieutenant lighted a cigarette and took a few deep draws. Looking around, he said:

"There are signs of spring in the air. It's so clear and fragrant."

"But no sounds of spring. You don't even hear a cat yowling."

"That's true. Well, I have to carry out my mission."

The lieutenant opened the door. The sound of snoring carried out to the man on watch. When the door closed he could again hear the rattle and roar from the front lines.

The lieutenant struck a match. Men lay asleep packed side by side on the floor. Fitting his feet down in between them, he crossed to a table on which there was a candle-stub and lighted it. Then he cleared his throat loudly a couple of times. No one opened an eyelid.

"They want a group to go out again. Five men and a non-commissioned officer."

Although he said the words in a loud voice, only one man turned over. Then he too went on snoring.

"Men, we just have to keep plugging. We need a non-commissioned officer and five men."

A man with a tangled mat of hair sat up near one wall. He clawed at his scalp and blinked dully. There were buck sergeant's stripes on his shoulders.

"What do you say, Malinen?"

"Say to what? What the devil are you talking about?"

"We've been ordered to send out a reconnaissance patrol with five men."

"I haven't even had time to shut my eyes here. I just lay down."

"We're all tired. We just have to try to keep going."

"It's still so early too."

Toivo dug out his watch, tilted it up, and muttered:

"It's only about one o'clock. Goddamn, that second hand fell in the hay and got lost."

The words were barked out angrily, and other sleepers raised their heads. One of them sat up and said:

"What are you yelling about again, Malinen?"

"On patrol, on patrol, you hogs! Or else you'll get bed sores from sleeping and the Russians will push all the way into Helsinki," Toivo Malinen bellowed.

"Go and do it yourself. They'll get there anyway."

"You're always so anxious to go," growled another.

"To Helsinki? What the devil would I do there?" said Toivo.

"No, on patrol. You're always itching to go."

"And I'm not dodging it now either."

As Toivo Malinen began pulling on his wet Lapland boots, he unleashed a string of the purest, coarsest profanity. Teeth bared in a snarl, he grunted:

"These damned boots didn't dry out one bit. How can I get them on? Uh! Well, Moscow Tillie promised us on the radio that every Finn would get a pair of galoshes if we would just let

Uncle Joe's men come in. That wouldn't be at all bad. I've never had a pair of them to my name. Uh! Well, at last they're on."

The lieutenant looked at him angrily and said:

"I didn't order you to go."

"And you didn't order me not to. Someone has to go, and if I'm not good enough, then I'll just pull off these sopping boots and turn my ass to the side."

"Don't get excited. If you want to go, I'll be glad to have you go."

"Then stop blithering. Get your rags on buddies, and let's see what mischief we can do."

Men from Malinen's squad began to get up. One scratched his neck in an muddleheaded way and another wrapped rags around his feet. The big, bearded man stood spraddle-legged on the floor and scratched at his groin. Toivo Malinen checked over his machine pistol, then turned to the man and said:

"I think you've picked up the crabs from somewhere."

"From where. What do you mean?" the man growled.

"You're always scratching at the root of your dong."

"You'd scratch too if you had so many lice."

"Take your squad to the hill cabin. The company commander will give you detailed instructions there," said the lieutenant.

"It's always easy to give orders," said Toivo Malinen.

"It's not always as easy as you think. Besides, he has his arm in a sling and could get into the hospital if he wanted to."

The lieutenant's tone of voice was depressed, although he seemed outwardly confident. Toivo Malinen tossed his kit bag over his shoulders and clamped one arm over his machine pistol. Shoving the door open, he said:

"I didn't mean to run anyone down. It's just that I'm so damned tired."

He thrust his head back inside once more and said:

"Hey you ball-scratcher. Take the hand grenades. And the rest of you stop staring! Let's go again so we don't forget what it's like."

2

"They haven't run out of powder yet," said Kauko.

"Or of iron, even with so much of it out on this heath."

"They're turning their barrels this way again. One of the shells landed close by. Others are screaming in here — *aieee...*"

The last speaker was Jonas Niemi. The three friends were huddled close together in a trench-like excavation. A non-stop artillery barrrage was blasting the area. The shallow trench had taken many direct hits over the past days, digging deeper holes in places. Sometimes a man had disappeared so completely at one of these holes that only shreds of his clothing remained. Fallen pine trees littered the area. The snow had disappeared under layers of sand and clay, and could be seen only where footsteps had sunk deep into the surface. Blood, rags, helmets, boots, hats, and shattered weapons lay on either side of the dug-in line. Between the lines, among shattered trees, some of them merely high stumps, stood the wreckage of three tanks. Around them sprawled the bodies of dead Russians. A counter-attack had left some Finnish bodies there too. Dead horses also lay in view.

Jonas Niemi's face was pale and his eyes were rolling in his head. Shells were landing in the area, but luckily they were falling short of the line. Shell fragments whined through the air. A pine tree that had been standing till then snapped in two and its trunk crashed to the earth. Kauko and Jonas Niemi threw themselves to the bottom of the hole.

"Something tells me I'll never get back from here — *aieee!*" cried Niemi.

Although his heart was in his throat, Kauko tried not to show his fear. In recent days, he had learned to master the terror caused by an artillery barrage. I have to control my nerves, he kept repeating over and over to himself. *Not everyone dies in a war...*with this old saw he kept force-feeding his fragile courage.

"Listen, they're landing closer — *aieee...*"

Kauko could feel Jonas Niemi's body trembling against his side. *Aieee* — Niemi's cry was as helpless and pleading as the bleating of a lamb that had strayed from its mother. The sound gave voice to the panic rising from the heart of the sturdy northern farmer. If only it had been Sumala crying out in fear, that would have spurred Kauko to even greater bravado.

Shells rained down with a continuous roar. An explosion tossed a huge limb into the air from somewhere. It landed in the hole where Kauko and Jonas lay.

"I'm hit..."

Although Kauko felt as if he were choking, he managed to say:

"It's just a limb that landed on your neck. Try to hang on..."

"I can't help being scared."

Jalo Kieppi had crawled into a hole a short distance away when the present concentration began. Now he shouted:

"Kauko?"

"What?"

"Take a look at your timepiece."

"It just turned eleven," Kauko said.

Off to one side, they could hear a man shouting:

"Get it over with. Put a slug in my head. A man can't take this kind of pain."

"If I could just die and not have to suffer so much — *aieee*."

"It's a matter of luck," said Kauko. He could see the horror in Jonas Niemi's eyes. "You've heard that two shells never land in the same place. One has landed here already. If we mean to live in a free Finland, we have to hold out, no matter what."

"Those higher-ups are lying when they say..."

A shell exploded close by. Sand fell from the air. Kauko too clutched his neck and the back of his head to protect them. Then another shell exploded further off. Kauko brushed the sand from his head and shoulders.

"What did you mean about the higher-ups lying..."

"When they say the Russians are surrounded. The company commander said the Finns are tightening the noose from the other side."

"It can't be all propaganda. You can see that they're always dropping stuff from planes, so their supply roads must be cut."

The two men pricked up their ears when they heard Kieppi shouting in his hole. Kauko raised his head to look out at the ground between the lines.

"At least there are no Russians moving around out there," he said.

"Go drown yourself," Kieppi was shouting.

"Go on then if you don't believe me. Why the devil would I come out in this bedlam to tell lies?" said a second voice.

"Just get out of here. We'll die on this ridge and that's that."

Jonas Niemi's lips trembled but he made no sound.

"What's Kieppi arguing about?" said Kauko.

At that instant, a man leaped from Kieppi's hole into their own.

"Sumala! Why jump on our necks?" roared Kauko.

"Sumala — *aieee...*"

Kauko heard Kieppi shouting again: "Hit him one. I didn't get a chance to."

There was a sneer on Sumala's face. He lighted a cigarette, his eyes slits as he looked at Niemi lying in the bottom of the hole. Watching Kauko from the corner of his eye, he said to Niemi:

"Lie there and suffer for an hour more, then you can stop shivering."

"Just what are you up to?" said Kauko.

"I'm calming down a coward."

Sand spouted in the air and metal fragments pinged. The sun seemed to shine through a dirty veil. The world literally turned black before Kauko's eyes.

"You won't mouth off for long, at least not in this hole. Goddamn you!"

"Hell, now stop swinging your fists."

"Wasn't one punch enough? Here's another in the snout."

"If you hit me once more, I'll blast you with this gun."

"You'll be dead before you have time to raise it. Go straight to hell from here, or at least to another hole!"

Kauko grabbed the front of Sumala's jacket, venting his rage on the man who had tormented him as a recruit. The man wasn't afraid even at the front, he thought wildly. There was something crazy in that. I'll give him a beating he'll remember to his dying day. Kauko jerked Sumala's face up to his own and shouted into it:

"Stop picking on Niemi!"

He hurled Sumala against the side of the pit. One hand pressing into the man's throat, he hammered at his face with the other fist. Blood bubbled out of Sumala's mouth with each breath.

"Can't you ever act like a human being? Take that and that and that!"

"Stop fighting, Kauko! Leave him alone...You'll kill him!" cried Jonas Niemi. He drove his strong shoulders into Kauko's legs.in a futile effort to stop his friend.

Kauko's eyes bored through Sumala and he kept smashing his fist into the man's face and jaw. Only when fingers gripped his wrists tightly did he become aware of his surroundings. Jonas Niemi had powerful hands. He said to Kauko, who had spun around toward him:

"This is crazy."

"Well, a man goes crazy out here. That bastard won't leave us alone, even under fire."

Kauko twisted his wrists, but the grip on them did not loosen.

"You're all crazy. I hope the Russians throw a shell into every last hole. I was bringing the news that the war is over. Won't you animals believe that the firing will stop in less than an hour?"

Jonas Niemi's fingers went limp on Kauko's wrists. The tension in Kauko's body broke. HIs legs began to tremble and he dropped into a sitting position against the side of the hole. He looked at Sumala's bloody face and said:

"Y-you're not l-lying?"

Blood sprayed from Sumala's mouth as he shouted:

"Who the hell would run out into a barrage like this to tell lies? I tell you, you stutterer, you'll wind up behind bars yet."

"Let's bury the hatchet...I didn't know...You laughed and said those stinking things."

"I'll settle with you when no one's around. I hope the Russians don't run out of shells."

Sumala disappeared from the hole at a run. Kauko sat staring at the bottom of the pit. He could not even bring himself to look up at Niemi, but saw only his boots deep in the hole. Every part of his body felt slack. He heard Jonas Niemi's voice from above:

"What time is it now?"

Kauko glanced at his watch, then turned its face toward Niemi.

"Quarter to eleven," Niemi said.

The artillery fire intensified. It seemed to be coming nearer.

Kauko and Jonas pressed themselves to the bottom of the pit. Kauko began to retch and then he threw up. Another quarter hour of it to survive. Then a large chunk fell on the hole and sand slid down from it. Suddenly a black bulk cut off the light for a second. Kauko heard himself cry out. Niemi fell on top of him and screamed:

"Almighty God, have mercy!"

Only later did it dawn on Kauko that a horse which had broken loose had galloped over their hole. It was snorting through its nostrils and from below it looked like a huge spider. The animal had come from between the lines and disappeared on the Finnish side.

"Is there any truth in what Sumala said?" asked Niemi.

"He would hardly have spread such a terrible lie."

The two of them pressed more firmly into the bottom of the hole. What power on earth could stop this thunder, Kauko wondered as he dug out his watch.

"Less than ten minutes."

"Good God, does a man's life hang by so little sometimes!"

Kauko kept his watch in his hand. They tried to sink down lower with every shell-burst. From time to time, he looked at his palm.

"Five minutes," he said.

"Will these be the last minutes?"

Sand spilled onto their shoulders. The roaring intensified, but it wasn't coming toward them...not yet...not yet...

"What time — how long will it still last?"

"You look," said Kauko, opening his hand before Niemi.

"One minute."

"Men won't be able to stop this thunderstorm in a minute," said Kauko.

"I don't believe I'll ever get back from here alive."

The watch kept ticking inside the woolen glove. It seemed to burn Kauko's hand. Had Sumala just been playing a dirty trick in spreading the word, Kauko wondered. He heard Niemi panting beside him.

"I won't get back alive. I won't get back. I feel..."

"You will get back. We both will...Listen," Kauko said.

"It's just as if a thunderstorm had passed," said Jonas Niemi.

To Kauko it seemed as if a giant hood had been dropped over

the front. A few last shells fell between the lines. A feeling of emptiness dampened his joy. Could it be true? At last he stood up and Jonas Niemi rose after him. On all sides they could see men rising from tangles of trees, masses of earth, and heaps of sand. Men were also rising from the line opposite them. They beckoned, laughed, and threw their weapons down. Waving their hands, they began to shuffle toward the Finnish lines. Jalo Kieppi came over to his comrades.

"Sumala wasn't talking nonsense. We're alive."

"It's hard to believe," said Kauko.

From further off came a pain-racked cry:

"I've found eternal peace. Ohh, I'm fainting."

"Eternal peace," Jonas Niemi babbled.

A doubt stirred in Kauko's mind. Was he asleep? Was it only a dream?

3

On the same March evening, things were quiet on another sector of the line. There had been no Russian attacks for a long time and the men had had time to dig the trenches deeper. Shovels sank easily into places where shells had landed.

Early in the morning, the company commander, a man from Häme, set out to check the sector manned by his unit. The cold was not as biting on that night. A faint trace of spring was in the air. The young lieutenant arrived at the first lookout post.

"Is everything peace and love?" he said.

"Nobody seems to riled up...They're fighting at Löytövaara though," said the soldier in the trench.

Canon muzzle flashes shone in the dark night. The men at Löytövaara were under incessant artillery fire. "They'll probably call for more of my men, probably half the company," the lieutenant reflected as he walked toward the next position. Then he heard a voice from beside a hillock:

"Who are you and what's your business?"

The harshness of the voice startled the lieutenant. Furthermore, the question had not come from a regular outpost. He reached toward his holster.

"Do you understand Finnish or do I have to speak with a gun?"

The company commander's perturbation turned to anger.

"What kind of test is this supposed to be? You're not even at your post."

"I'm not far from it," said the voice from among some spruce trees.

The lieutenant walked to the position from which a watch was usually maintained on the area between the lines. It was empty.

"Uh, now I'll be light enough to fly like a sparrow," said the voice.

"Just what are you grunting about, Malinen?"

"I'm lightening my load."

"What is that supposed to mean?"

"If that's not clear, I'll say it in plain Finnish. I went to take a shit. Don't sniff too close around here. It really stinks."

The lieutenant smiled. Malinen was still the same backwoodsman. After a few more heavy grunts, the spruce branches were brushed aside and Nestor came into view, buttoning his pants. His rifle dangled from its sling around his neck.

"Do you know, Malinen, what the regulations say about a man's leaving his guard post?"

"I was in training so long ago that I can't remember all that garbage."

"What would you have said if the Russians had just crept across that swamp?"

"I don't think I would have said anything. I would just have shot the hell out of them. You don't think I would have gone out to shake hands, do you?"

"But you couldn't even see the area you were supposed to watch."

"Now that's a big lie. I was keeping an eye out all the time."

"Did you really have to empty your bowels on guard duty?"

"Do you think I'm such a damned fool as to bare my ass if I don't have to?"

"I mean, it's only a quarter of an hour till the shift changes."

"And I mean I've got the drizzling shits. They're as runny as water and come on whenever they feel like it. They don't ask if it's according to rules and regulations."

"Uh-huh. So then your stomach is out of order, Malinen."

"I've got a humongous case of the shits. And if you pushed a thermometer under my arm, you'd might get a high reading."

Nestor Malinen and the lieutenant stood side by side in the dugout. Snow covered the shell holes and the bodies of Russian soldiers who had earlier tried to cross the swamp. It was so quiet they could hear voices speaking Russian across the way.

"Did you hear me coming, Malinen?"

"Are you still stuck on the idea that someone could get into my hole without my knowing it?"

"I was just thinking that a skilled man could burrow across the swamp on such a dark night."

"There are no such snow moles among the Russians. I heard you talking with the other watch just now, otherwise you would have got a bullet through your belly when you came. I'm not feeling at all good."

"Malinen must be chilled."

"Well, it ain't the gamblers' shakes I've got. Did the lieutenant think I was faking it just now? Damn it to hell! I have to go again, and in a hurry."

Malinen ran into the spruce grove. Soon there was heard a gushing sound capped by a final blast. Then heavy grunting. When Nestor returned, closing his rear buttons, he said:

"The Russians are going to think there's a machine gun at this post. Oof, but I feel weak."

"Can you hold out till your shift is up?"

"No doubt about it. And I'll get to see my horse soon."

"What horse are you talking about, Malinen? There's no such animal here."

"There is too. The one I stole from the Russians at Alasalmi. I wonder if they even remembered to give him some bread."

"Your turn on watch will soon be over. You can go and see him then."

"It has to be then. I have only one watch left after this. Do you believe that, lieutenant?"

"Believe what? What do you mean?"

"I had a dream last night that the end is very near."

The lieutenant stared at the much older man. Cold chills ran down his spine. Was Malinen really so sick? He had come to the front as a volunteer and done his duty, most often as he saw fit, to be sure. One was forced to assume that he had forgotten the training he had received some twenty years ago. He could be infuriating at times. But the way he was talking now — the lieutenant had really grown to like the company's oldest and stubbornest man. He said:

"Who can tell when it's his time to go?"

"I'm not talking about myself or anyone else going. I just mean the war will be over."

"Now I really think you've got a fever."

"Hell, now you're making fun of me. It's true."

"And you believe in those dreams of yours?"

"Yes I do. My wife is the one who really knows about dreams, but I seem to have caught the disease. Just wait and see. This will end soon."

"You mean the whole war?"

The lieutenant's voice was annoyed now. He felt for a pack of cigarettes in his pocket and lipped one from it. Then he began to pat his pockets for matches.

"They said you're not supposed to light cigarettes when the Russians might see it."

"That's true," said the officer and put the cigarette back into the pack.

"I don't know if the whole war will end. I only know that in my dream the shooting suddenly stopped. The Russians came out of their dugouts and threw their rifles away. At the same time a loudspeaker somewhere bawled out that the war was over. The Russians came walking across the swamp. They looked a little drunk; they were laughing and flinging their arms wide open. The sun was shining. Lassi Nieminen seemed to be on watch with me. Lassi asked if we should start shooting them. I stopped him from doing it, told him you don't shoot unarmed men. Then they came to the edge of our hole. One of them jumped down, wrapped his arms around my neck, and stuck his whiskery face right into mine. All the while he kept on babbling *tovarisch*. I pushed him away and said up to now I hadn't rubbed faces with anyone, not even my wife. They were draped around Lassi Nieminen's neck too."

"A tired man has crazy dreams," said the lieutenant.

"An empty dream is never so clear and doesn't stick in your mind like this one."

"Well then, since you're so ill, Malinen, you'll have to go on sick call. At least you should go and talk to the medics."

"How much will you bet that the war won't end?"

"I don't make bets — and I have to make the rounds."

"Yaah, and it feels like I have to get my buttons open in a hurry."

4

"Cease fire at eleven o'clock sharp. Eleven o'clock sharp."

The battalion commander sat with his face propped in his hands. He repeated the message he had just received from the regiment as if he were trying to make the inconceivable fact penetrate his consciousness by repeating the words. There was disbelief in his voice. He was almost totally exhausted. Two other officers in the battalion tent sat silent. They had just been listening anxiously to an artillery concentration of increasing intensity. Now it was as if the tent had taken a direct hit.

The youngish captain raised his head and pressed his hands against his knees, bracing himself in an erect posture. No, he must hang on to the end. He glanced at his wrist and said:

"It's 9:40 now."

"A full hour and a half to go, if the colonel's report is true," said one of the second lieutenants in the tent.

The captain looked at him and said sharply:

"An hour and forty minutes, and the colonel does not send false reports."

"I don't doubt that — it's just such a surprise."

"The news must be sent on to the companies. Rantanen, you take it to Salmi. Backman will go to Mäkinen's company."

"Isn't it all right if I go to Salmi's company?"

"You heard my order."

Lieutenant Backman said nothing. Was it out of spite that the company commander was sending him to Mäkinen, he wondered. After their initial encounter, his path had crossed Mäkinen's only a few times, chiefly at the battalion commander's briefings. Mäkinen had seemed not to notice his one-time superior. He addressed him formally whenever speech was unavoidable.

"Mäkinen's company is the target of the heaviest artillery concentration. When you see him, tell him to send two men to pass along the word."

"The order will be carried out."

The captain glanced at Backman. The Lieutenant's words had

a sarcastic edge to them. Only now did he recall that the relations between the two men were strained. On principle, the captain did not retract his order. This was a crucial moment for the entire country, and two officers nursing a grudge from civilian life could be left to settle their own differences.

"You're almost sure to find Mäkinen right at the front."

Lieutenant Backman strode toward the lines, throwing himself down into a shell hole from time to time. The air was filled with flying iron. A country as big as Russia had plenty of it to waste, right up to the last minute. Planes were circling above the front lines. Backman still could not understand how the Russians could have so many quality planes. During his student days he had developed the fixed idea that a country isolated from the rest of the world could not keep up with the West in technology. Trucks captured and studied during the first days of the war confirmed this notion. They were clumsy machines, a full twenty years behind the American. But the planes — the Finnish engineer could not comprehend their high quality.

"They're bombing the lines again."

Lieutenant Backman threw himself into a shell hole. Here a man soon came to realize that he was not the kingpin of the universe. Bombs exploded off to one side, and artillery kept chewing up the terrain. After a long time, the lieutenant rushed forward again. As a young engineering student, he had been fairly well known as a runner. His body was still slim and agile.

Mäkinen's company should be over there.

In long rushes, he approached the edge of a heath that was pockmarked by artillery. In an area of splintered trees and soil pulverized to a brownish sand, he saw a trench of sorts. A man stood there with his back turned. A long growth of hair on his neck stuck out from between his hat and the collar of his combat jacket. The lieutenant ran toward him and the man spun around. When he saw the Finnish officer, his face relaxed.

"Where is the company commander?" asked the lieutenant.

"He just went that way along the line."

Backman wondered if he should tell the man about his message. But let Mäkinen do it himself, since he insisted on behaving so formally. Although the soldier had nodded to the right as he spoke, Backman nevertheless pointed that way and asked:

"Did you say your commander went that way?"

"Yes, that way. Did you have a message for him?"

The look on Backman's face was enough to tell the man he was in no mood to talk. The men said the communications officer was a slippery one, although Kosti praised him as a good man at stringing a wire. But he looked too high and mighty. He just needed a little scare.

"Mäkinen is pretty far away from here. And it's not too healthy to be moving around right now."

"I'll find him all right, if he stays on the line."

"You won't find our top man hanging out behind the lines."

"Just remember to keep an eye on our neighbor, soldier."

"I do that all the time. And that's not all I do."

Lieutenant Backman leaped up nimbly from the hole and ran crouching along the connecting trench. A feeling of defiance swelled within him. Mäkinen might crush a man with his strength, but was no match for him in speed of foot. And Backman was not afraid. He vowed that Mäkinen would never have the pleasure of seeing him scared.

"Have you seen the company commander?"

The next man on watch was not taken by surprise. He had seen the crouching lieutenant from a distance.

"He was here, but he went further on."

"How long ago?"

"We don't spend much time looking at our watches here, but it's not that long. You must be an athlete, lieutenant."

"Why do you say that?"

"The way you ran. You were really picking them up and putting them down along that trench."

"I did a little running. The shelling seems to be letting up."

"Not for long. The shells will soon be flying this way again."

"I have to go on, since it's letting up."

"But stay low. Those neighbors of ours don't sleep."

The sector which Kosti Mäkinen's men were holding was curved like a bow. Mäkinen was standing in Simo Mutka's dugout. A hill here sloped rather steeply away from the line. When shells fell behind the men, it made them cringe deeper into their pits, but they had little to fear from shells falling out in front between the lines. The company commander braced one leg against the side of the pit, rested an elbow on it, and leaned his chin on his mittened hand.

"What kind of mess will all this turn into when spring comes?"

"What about the smell, when all the carcasses start to rot?" said Simo.

"The sun is making the gravel on the edge of the pit damp. Look."

"Spring always comes, even after the hardest winter," said Simo.

They stopped talking. During the night Simo had stuck yew boughs up in front of his dugout. He had a good view of the front from behind them. Now he looked out at it and said:

"I wonder if they'll try to cross that clearing now since they've banging away so much with their big guns."

"If they run true to form, they'll try something before dark."

"Tell me, since you're better informed than I am, will we still be hunkered down here next summer keeping watch and fighting every now and then? We'll all die here, one after the other."

"Not in this place. Believe it or not, things aren't going well for the Russians. The spring break-up is coming, and they've already been cut off for a long time. The planes keep trying to supply them. You've seen them yourself."

"I'm still mad about the second company getting that bundle they dropped by parachute. The wind could just as well have blown it our way. They say they even got a whole bunch of bottles of vodka. Yaah, but let's see if our neighbor's watch has his eyes open."

Simo took a hat left by a fallen soldier from the side of the hole and crawled toward the next dugout. A short distance away, he set the hat on the end of a stick and raised it carefully above the edge of the trench. Then he began to crawl forward. The hat danced up and down slightly.

"Stop annoying them. That's not exactly a safe game."

"A man has to have some fun here. They don't seem too bloodthirsty now."

Simo Mutka came back and displayed the hat.

"Look at the number of holes in it."

"Quite a sight. But they might fire an explosive round."

"What's the communications boss doing out here now, running from one hole to another?" said Simo.

Kosti looked in the direction of Simo's nod. His easy mood

changed. Why was Backman rushing around out here now?

"He's still coming," said Simo, stepping up into the connecting trench. "He's signaling and it looks like he's yelling something too."

"If he has something to tell me then let him come after me."

Kosti Mäkinen disappeared into the next dugout. At the same moment, Backman leaped down into Simo's and said with a scowl:

"Didn't Lieutenant Mäkinen see me wave to him?"

"He did, and I told him you seemed to be yelling something."

"Why didn't he wait?"

"He didn't tell me. Just said that anyone who had business with him could come after him."

"Well if that isn't the very devil! Does he think...does he think..."

Without further words, the lieutenant dashed forward. He could see Mäkinen striding along ahead of him. He's doing this out of sheer deviltry. He probably thinks I don't dare follow him. Just then Backman plunged into a deep hole where a sergeant and a soldier were standing. Why were they looking at him? The sergeant was grinning openly. The Lieutenant's words were peremptory:

"Just what is your company commander running from?"

"What's this all about? He's on his regular rounds," said the sergeant.

"That's nonsense. He knows that I..."

"Down!"

The sergeant's shout came at the top of his lungs. Lieutenant Backman heard a sudden whine. Then something struck him in the back. He felt himself thrown against something hard. A huge explosion blocked his ears. The world went black and his breath was choked off. A spiral of glowing red filaments began to spin before his eyes. It was working toward his brain. A blacksmith's sledge hammered furiously in his ears.

✧ ✧ ✧

"Look lieutenant, the artillery fire is shifting direction."

The soldier, fresh from a training center two weeks ago, was staring wide-eyed. He froze against the side of a pit, and looked in the direction from which the company commander had just come.

"Get down, darn it!"

Only then did the young man understand what was happening. He threw himself on his belly at the bottom of the pit and buried his face in his hands. Kosti Mäkinen squatted down himself. He could see the youngster's shoulders shaking, not with weeping but from fear.

"For a wonder, they've shifted direction."

His superior officer's voice gave the young man courage. He rose to his knees and said:

"I'll look to see that the Russians aren't coming."

The soldier looked out at the ground between the lines.

"Don't show too much of your head. There's a lot of iron in the air."

"I don't see any movement...yet."

"I think they'll be trying soon. They've been pounding the line a long time to soften it."

The lieutenant and the young soldier crouched down in the pit. Although the youngster's courage had increased, his superior could still feel his arm trembling against his own. Kosti too felt fear. One could not get completely used to lying helpless under an artillery barrage. For a long time the ground around them continued to quake. Then the shells began to fall on the next company's sector.

"I wonder how Bert and Simonen are doing."

Kosti Mäkinen stood up and looked back in the direction he had come from. Where had Backman hidden his head? What errand had he been on anyway?

The concentration intensified mercilessly. It sounded as if more and more artillery pieces were joining in. Shells were literally raining down. The lieutenant and the soldier huddled in the bottom of the pit. When the lad spoke, his voice trembled.

"How many artillery pieces do the Russians have?"

"They fire too many rounds to keep track of them."

"Lieutenant, has there ever been such heavy fire here?"

"Not before this."

"Will anyone live through it?"

"Luckily our men are well dug in."

A shell whistled and burst near them, darkening the sky. Sand rained down on them.

"Did you get hit?" asked the lieutenant.

"No, but I'm scared, no matter how hard I grit my teeth."

"Make yourself think of something else."

"Aren't you afraid, lieutenant?"

"I'm always afraid when I have to lie here helpless. I try to think of other things. And don't call me lieutenant. We're all the same here. A shell fragment can't tell us apart."

"I feel a little better now," said the soldier after a lengthy pause.

Kosti Mäkinen was also feeling relieved. He looked at the face of the young soldier huddled beside him. The boy had grown thin and his expression had become somber. These latest replacements were very young, still beardless, with mere fuzz showing on their upper lip and chin, but they had stood up remarkably well under the strain of combat. Especially in counterattacks and in repelling onslaughts, they had performed with the eagerness of youth. Lying under an artillery barrage, however, tested them severely. But what was going on now? A subconscious prompting made him start. A strange atmosphere seemed to be settling down over the torn landscape.

"What are they up to now?" he wondered aloud.

"It feels as if a thunderstorm had suddenly ended."

"We'll soon hear the *Hurra* yells when they attack."

As if by unspoken agreement, they both looked out at the ground between the lines. There was total silence now, without even the rattle of small-arms fire. Kosti Mäkinen's ears felt as if the distant woods were sending back a muted echo of the recent barrage.

"What the heck is going on? The men of the next company are coming out of their holes."

"Mäkinen, look! The men are waving to the Russians."

"Now the world is upside down. The Russians are jumping into sight and just standing there."

"And they have no guns...I mean, rifles. They're laughing and waving."

Then on their left, a machine pistol chattered. Kosti Mäkinen glanced toward his sector, then back to the front, where unarmed men were throwing themselves to the ground. One of them cried out in anguish.

"Mäkinen!"

Kosti turned to look toward the next company's sector. The familiar figure of a lieutenant, one of the platoon leaders, came charging toward him. He was shouting and waving his arms.

"Don't let your men shoot. They're violating the cease-fire."

"Cease fire!"

The words hit Kosti Mäkinen like a ton of bricks. The lieutenant from the next company came panting up. Again the machine pistol chattered.

"What do you mean by letting them go on firing?"

"Hey, Mutka and the rest of you. Hold your fire. There's an armistice."

Kosti Mäkinen's shout carried a long way. His own men also began to rise into view. The Russians were already coming toward them, laughing and yipping.

"Why the heck didn't they let us know about the cease-fire?"

Kosti Mäkinen's voice was glum. He looked inquiringly at the lieutenant.

"They brought word to us less than an hour ago. Didn't you get the message?"

"No. It's so unbelievable."

The soldier and lieutenant gazed in surprise as Mäkinen strode off in the direction he had come from. They saw him lean over into the next dugout along the line.

✧ ✧ ✧

"Bert!"

"What's going on? Aren't the *Vanyas* shooting any more?"

"Did you get hit? Your face is all white."

"My back hurts. Something must have ripped it open."

Kosti grasped his brother-in-law by the armpits and pulled him from under a heap of sand. Bert Sääskilampi's eyes rolled oddly.

"Don't! It hurts like hell. I feel dizzy."

Kosti laid him on his back. Simo Mutka and other men from the company came rushing up.

"Is the fighting over?" Simo blurted out. "And what's wrong with Bert?"

"His back hurts. He must have been hit by some iron."

Simo and his companions began to open Bert's clothing. Kosti Mäkinen looked at the body of a man sprawled against the side of the dugout. Lieutenant Backman lay there dead, with blood oozing from his neck. The legs of a third man could be seen sticking out from under the sand. It was a horrible sight for Kosti Mäkinen to take in. He could hear the men talking about peace, but their voices sounded far away. He even found it hard to grasp when he heard men say that a shell fragment had pierced Bert's back.

"That dead communications officer must have been bringing word of the peace," said Simo Mutka.

*Word of the peace...*Kosti Mäkinen bent down and turned Lieutenant Backman over on a pile of loose sand. The war between Finland and Russia was over, but the news, incredible as it was, brought no joy to Kosti Mäkinen. The bitterness that had gnawed at his heart for years had turned to repentance. The peace between himself and Backman was one-sided. There was an expression of calm on the dead lieutenant's face. He looked almost contented.

CHAPTER X

1

Svante Olkivaara came in from outdoors and said:

"Elma, someone's come a-courtin' out there."

"What do you mean, *courtin*?"

"You can hear him yowling out near the barn," said Svante.

"You mean a cat?"

"It sounds like one. But who knows? It might be some soldier out yodeling for you to go out with him," Svante laughed.

"Stop fooling around. You and Tuomas go to bed now so I can get you up in the morning," said Elma.

"Not on your life. Now that the guard business is over with, Tuomas and I are gonna sleep like bankers. This whole winter we had to get up at any old time."

"You've been sleeping till noon for weeks. You'd think by now you'd have made up for lost sleep," said Elma.

"Soon we won't be able to sleep even at night," said Tuomas. "The wood grouse will be tilting their beaks and we'll be out hunting them. Every spring I go and shoot mating grouse with my father and brothers."

"Let's go on the first warm night," Svante too became enthusiastic. "We'll take Auku Sammalsuo with us and head for the woods."

Elma rocked herself up out of the rocking chair and said:

"I'll give that yowler such a send-off he'll remember it to his dying day."

"Don't be so jealous. Our Nöpö has to get some too."

Elma grabbed Svante's neck hair between her thumb and forefinger, gave it a jerk, and said:

"You and your getting some. A calf your age doesn't know what it means to get, much less to give."

"Hell, woman, don't pull my hair."

"Since when did you start calling me *woman*?"

Elma went outside where it was already getting dark and stood in the middle of the yard with her arms folded across her breast. At first there was complete silence except for the cows clattering in their stalls. Bunches of hay dropped in the yard over the winter, and soot from the chimney had been sucking up warmth all day, but now it was rather cold out.

"Miaow!"

"So there you are, you doggoned Romeo."

Snow that had corned up during the day now crunched crisply under Elma's feet. She snatched up a ski pole lying in the yard and said:

"Now, tomcat, it's time for you to make tracks."

Elma was approaching the door of the barn shed when two cats came streaking toward her. In the lead was Olkivaara's Nöpö, an almost black female. After her darted a mottled black tomcat. The scourge of the farm's mice leaped up onto the lane fence and sat there. The cat following her had stopped before Elma.

"Well, if it isn't Oskar Portimo."

Elma dropped the pole from her hand. She squatted down and coaxed the animal toward her with a beckoning finger.

"Kitty, kitty, kitty. Come into my lap, Oskar Portimo."

The cat waggled its tail like a fish about to dart off. For every step that Elma approached it coaxing, the cat retreated a step backward.

"Elma's not mad at the neighbor's boy. N-no."

Soon the cat allowed itself to be caught and sat purring in Elma's arms. Glancing around, she began to talk:

"That's what women are like. I'm sure Nöpö's been waiting for you although she pretends to run away. Soon Maija and Väinö and Liisu will be back from evacuation. And Kauko will come on leave this summer. He'll pet you and be good to you and..."

Elma kept on petting the Sammalsuo cat for a long time as the animal purred contentedly. Nöpö arched her back on the fence rail, and then advanced toward Elma, her tail twitching.

"So you're getting jealous? See how well I treat your sweetheart."

Elma pressed her neck into the side of the cat, then shifted her shoulders to the right and left. The warm, soft fur caressed her neck and her bare upper breast. She closed her eyes. When summer came, surely they would give leave even to those serving their regular term of military service. Toivo and her father would soon be demobilized; that's what those in the know were saying.

Nöpö growled angrily and loped toward her with long strides.

"You dratted porcupine, clawing my breasts and stomach!"

Nöpö clung to Elma's clothing, her claws gouging the skin through the thin cloth. With one hand, Elma knocked her loose. Then Oskar Portimo escaped from her arms.

"Go and dig your claws into that hussy's back now so she won't be jealous. Damn that Nöpö, scratching her own mistress..."

The cats trotted off into the darkness of the barn shed. Elma fetched an armful of wood from the pile. At the door of the main room, she said:

"Ahah, my masters! What are you up to now?"

"We're playing poker. Finding out who the pennies belong to."

The speaker was Svante. The boys sat on either side of the table, slapping down the blackened playing cards with torn corners. Dropping her armful of wood into the box in the kitchen, Elma went back to the main room.

"Put away the cards before the police come."

"The police have other things to do," said Svante.

"Kids your age shouldn't play cards," said Elma.

"It's only penny poker," said Cousin Tuomas.

"If mother saw you, she'd be calling for camphor drops," said Elma.

"But Father Nestor would sit right down and join us — or at least he'd kibitz."

The gas lamp hanging from the ceiling gave off a hissing sound. Elma stood by the table and watched the boy's actions.

"Clubs mean trouble, like in old 'Tina's days," said Tuomas.

"What? You trying to scare me with clubs? I'll top that with a king of spades, and what do you say to a whore of diamonds?" said Svante with gusto.

"Shame on you." Elma delivered a sharp fillip to Svante's head.

"Why the devil did you come here to kibitz with your ears sticking out? You know how ripe card players' language is."

"You should wash out your mouth," said Elma, going to the window and drawing the curtains.

"Did you open your yap and say something?" asked Svante.

"The ace flattens it. Now we're even. I won't..."

"The next hand takes it," said Svante.

"It seems strange not to have blackout curtains," said Elma.

"Did you drive off that lover boy?" asked Tuomas

"I didn't start chasing after the cats."

"But you smell of them," said Svante.

"Shall I tell you what you smell of?" snapped Elma.

Afraid she was blushing, Elma walked through the kitchen into her bedroom. There she lighted a lamp, sat on the edge of her bed, and picked up a mirror. Opening the top buttons of her dress, she pressed her chin to her neck and looked down at her breasts.

"She tore the skin all over. Did she have to jump up there?"

Elma was angry at her own pet for leaping up and scaring the Sammalsuo cat from her arms. Oskar Portimo's fur had felt so pleasantly warm on her skin. The cat's claws had left long scratches on her skin, and in checking them she had occasion to lift up her breasts. Touching them made her heart beat more quickly. Why had Kauko written to her only once after peace had been made? Toivo had managed to get two letters scrawled during that time. And they had even gotten a letter of sorts from the old man.

Elma closed the buttons. It was good that the war was over. For the Karelians and some of the Kuusamo people, the peace was a bitter pill to swallow. Even those not directly involved could feel the harshness of their fate. They were, after all, one Finnish people.

An odd restlessness seized Elma's mind. The hands of the alarm clock already showed eight-thirty. What if...It was quite late, but on the other hand, it would not be the first time. Elma rose, went to the main room, and said:

"Listen you card sharks. I'm going over to see Aili Sammalsuo."

"At night? And when Kauko isn't even home," laughed Svante.

"I said I was going to see Aili."

"And Auku won't care for such an old woman. He doesn't even like young women. He's just like Tuomas and me."

Svante's face wore a teasing grin. Elma put on a short coat, picked up her gloves, and drew on a woolen cap. She turned at the door to say:

"Don't wait up for me. I may spend the night with Aili."

"As long as you come home to milk the cows in the morning."

2

Never until that winter had so many strange people and vehicles been seen in the church village. During the early winter battles for Suomussalmi and Raate, it had been a thoroughfare for the troops. Even now, although the peace was several weeks old, the roads swarmed with people on foot, and motor vehicles droned through the village.

Buses brought evacuees back from the coast as the backwoods people returned to their home grounds. One evening in early spring, the bus bearing the Sammalsuo and Olkivaara evacuees was driving along the highway. The children were getting tired from the long journey, but their drowsiness vanished when Maija Sammalsuo said:

"Now children, we've crossed into our own parish."

"Mother, how far is it to home?" asked Liisu.

"It's about thirty kilometers to the church village," said her mother.

A storekeeper's son from the church village was driving the bus. He was one of the true believers, and was well known to all the backwoods people. An old man sitting near the driver began to sing in a quavery voice.

As I wander here in the wilderness,
Dark clouds gather over my homeland,
But consolation comes through Jesus' life
And all the clouds of darkness scatter.

The women in the front seats were the first to join in the singing, even though not all of them were confirmed believers. Then the low voices of old men swelled the song. Seldom had the teachings of Lars Levi Laestadius so profoundly stirred the devout hearts of the pious backwoods people.

"This is exactly like the wanderings of the children of Israel in the desert," said one of the old men.

"The Lord's ways were winding then too," said another.

The driver had been sitting at the wheel for days, and he was tired. To overcome his weariness, and because he enjoyed the singing, he said:

"Start another verse. It will keep me awake."

No further urging was necessary. Evacuees had already returned to some of the houses along the way. As they moved about outdoors at their last evening tasks, they could hear the strong strains of the hymn from the bus roaring by. Tears came to the eyes of some of the women. A man on his way to toss the evening hay to the horses had to swallow hard. People going back into their houses would say:

"Elias is driving evacuees back to the eastern districts. They are thanking the Lord by singing a hymn."

A feeling of happiness prevailed on the last leg of the journey. Home, home...

Now they were in their own woods. Soon they would be home. Maija pointed toward the windshield and said to Liisu, who was sitting in her lap:

"Now the bus is going down the hill into the church village."

Lights were visible through the windshield of the bus. It was now rolling down the familiar slope to the village center.

"Are you sure this is our own church village?" asked Liisu.

"I am. You can be sure of that," said Maija.

"It's dark...and what if we got lost," said Liisu.

Maija looked at Mari sitting behind her and said:

"Listen to the poor child. She doesn't believe we've come to our own church village."

Mari patted Liisu over Maija's shoulder and said:

"We'll soon be home."

On the seat across from them, Väinö cleared his throat and said:

"You can tell this place even at night. There's the crossroads. But the drug store seems to be wrecked. A bomb must have blasted it."

The bus turned into the storekeeper's yard. The driver tilted his cap back and mopped his brow.

"We made it. At least it will be warm enough for you tonight in the main room."

There were a few people from the church village among the evacuees. They climbed out of the bus. The evacuee families from Järvenkylä and Vaarakylä remained in their seats. The women all looked at each other, and the men turned to look toward the rear of the bus. When the driver stood up, one of the old men from Vaarakylä said:

"Brother Elias, won't you drive us all the way?"

"Since we're already so close to home," said another.

"We know you're tired, but if you could...The kids are so homesick they're just shaking," said Maija Sammalsuo.

"But I have no orders to drive further."

"Would they fine you if you did? I can't think of anything but home," one of the women burst out.

"And we'll all chip in for the fine."

"Of course we will. won't we?"

"Well, I'll take you then," laughed the large and amiable man. "I'll just go and get something to wet my throat. I think there would be something warm here for the rest of you."

"We don't want anything," said Mari Olkivaara.

"We can make it home without eating," said Maija.

"I won't be long. Isn't this little traveler thirsty?" said the driver, gently pinching the chin of a boy sitting in his mother's lap.

✧ ✧ ✧

"Would you sluts stop cackling so a man can get some sleep," said Auku from his bed.

Aili and Elma were sitting at the table. Although watching the skies from the top of a flimsy windmill tower during the winter had been a grueling experience, now in retrospect much of it seemed hilarious. From time to time the girls burst out laughing as they talked. When Auku's prohibition did not help, he spoke out angrily again.

"Isn't it way past midnight already?"

"It's just one o'clock," said Aili.

"Button your trap. Giggling all night."

"Well, if the man isn't a sourpuss," laughed Elma.

"He's mad because he can't hear what we're saying," said Aili.

"Here's one boy who doesn't care what women babble about."

"Would you be happier if I lay down beside you?" asked Elma.

"A mare your size wouldn't fit in this bed."

"Well at least you're not phoney polite about it," giggled Elma. "But even your Oskar Portimo was out prowling for a female at our house."

"Let him. Goddamned if I ever have anything to do with women."

"Then all I can do is to lie down with Aili."

"Let's go to bed. It's not worth starting for home before morning," said Aili.

"I guess the boys will get along by themselves. When I left, I said I might stay."

"And besides, I wouldn't hug my brother Kauko's sweetheart. Who can tell what kind of temper he picked up in this war business."

The girls undressed and went to bed, blowing out the lamp. Aili and Elma exchanged a few more giggles. Auku was strangely restless. That Elma has a nice body when she strips to her underthings, he thought. What would it feel like to lie down next to a woman? Elma had been mocking him just now. She was too old for him. but that Taimi, her sister, was a handsome girl, and there was no big difference in age there. But brothers don't often marry sisters. Kauko is bound to lead Elma to the altar. And no one has proclaimed in church that Taimi even likes me. I've thrown snowballs at her and played other mean tricks on her too.

✧ ✧ ✧

Elma was the first to awaken at the creaking of the outer door. She leaped up from the bed. The first thought in her sleepy mind was of saboteurs.

"God help us! Who's there?" Elma almost shouted.

"Is that Elma?" came a voice from the door.

"It is. Is it Maija? And the children too?"

"We're here. We're home again."

"Aili, your mother has come! Where's the match box?"

This time there was no need to shake Aili repeatedly to wake her up. The match box soon rustled in her hand. She lighted the lamp. Elma ran through the main room to throw her arms around Maija's neck.

"We did get to see you again. It's so nice."

Both Elma and Maija were weeping. Then Maija said:

"Look at who else is in the doorway."

"Mother. And Taimi. And my little brothers and sisters."

"Elma, my own child! Oh..."

Mari sagged onto the bench from her daughter's arms. She sat there wiping her eyes on her kerchief. Elma lifted her little sister into her arms. Liisu stood facing the doorway with her face in her hands. Taimi and Väinö Sammalsuo sat on the bench like strangers. Maija could not restrain her emotions as she sat on the bench and said:

"Joy like this seldom comes in a lifetime. To be in one's beloved home with dear friends around one."

Auku remained lying in bed. He could smell the fresh air from outside. It seemed hard to get up or say anything.

"Ho-hum, I must have been sound asleep."

Maija's powerful surge of emotion had spent itself and she said:

"Aren't you even going to get up to see us?"

"I'm tired. Those girls kept me up so late."

Auku's voice was not as indifferent as his words. It trembled. Aili turned her back on the newcomers as she lighted a fire in the stove. Tears were rolling down her cheeks. Finally Auku raised himself into a sitting position with his covers to prop his head. Taimi too was staring at him like a startled cow.

"Throw my pants up here brother," said Auku.

Väinö picked up the pants from where they lay and took them to his brother, who donned them and went to sit on the bench.

"What's the news from the coast?" he said.

"We could spend days talking about it," said his mother.

"Come and tell me about all the fool things you saw there, Liisu," said Auku.

Liisu hesitated for a long time, then sucking her thumb, she went over to her brother and sat down beside him, her eyes fixed on the toes of her shoes. Auku too was silent for a long time, but finally he said:

"Were you afraid in the bus?"

"No, I was only a little sleepy."

"Of course. How did you happen to come in so late at night?" said Elma.

Maija took off her head scarf and coat as if she were a shy guest in her own home. Then she stood in the middle of the room and looked slowly about her.

"You wouldn't believe how completely unfamiliar a home can look after only four months away from it. I still feel as if I should walk around on tiptoe. Only the smell seems the same."

"And you can bet I haven't touched a broom," said Auku.

Väinö tittered.

"Auku found his tongue," said Maija. "What were you just asking, Elma?"

"I wondered why you came so late."

"We coaxed the bus driver into driving us all the way. We just couldn't put up with spending the night in the church village. The people from Vaarakylä came on the same bus."

"And you came wading here from Naavala?" asked Auku.

"We didn't have to wade. The path was hard enough to carry us," said Väinö.

"We would have crawled this last stretch if we had to," said Maija.

The aroma of coffee spread through the room, and Elma went over to help Aili. Moving briskly, she set out the cups and chopped pieces of sugar from a sugar cone. Aili went out to the porch and returned with a package wrapped in waxed paper.

"We happen to have bread cheese too."

"And such rare visitors," said Elma with a wink.

"Elma seems to have moved in here to live," said Mari.

"Almost. I came this evening around ten."

"What about the boys, Vante and Tuomas?" asked Taimi.

"Those buggers can get along by themselves. I had such an odd feeling that I had to come and see Aili. Something must have told me you were coming."

"Let's have the coffee now," said Aili.

They drank the coffee. Väinö and Auku were already exchanging a few words, while Taimi and Aili chuckled away at their own silly chatter. Elma sat ruddy-cheeked like a lush midsummer flower between the two already age-worn backwoods women. She was telling about the winter's happenings and asking Maija chiefly about the evacuation. Never had a feeling of such warm companionship pervaded the Sammalsuo cottage. Finally Maija started and said:

"I have to see the cows yet. When I do, then I'll believe that I've come home."

She crossed the yard with the now frozen corn snow crunching under her feet. There was a golden glow in the eastern sky where the sun was rising. Her joy increased as she reflected: "The last time I left this barn, the sounds of war thundered in the east and fires lighted up the horizon. Then I did not know what lay ahead of me. I give thanks to the Lord, who brought me home again."

The familiar barn smell greeted her. Instinct guided her hand to the prop against the door. Even the creaking of the door was familiar. Feet began to patter in the lamb's pen, and the cows' chains clinked. When Maija lighted the barn lamp, the animals began to heave their hindquarters up from the floor, and then to raise themselves up on their front legs. They turned their heads back along their sides as far as their chains would reach and began to moo.

"Do you still know me? Now I can take care of you again," said Maija.

She went into the cows' stalls and patted and stroked them, speaking to them as to people she knew. The animals licked their mistress's hand.

"What a pretty-faced calf has shown up in this pen. My, my but you're beautiful. I'm your mistress."

The lambs thumped against the sides of their pen, bleating and trying to nibble at Maija's clothing.

"Now, now, my babies. Stay in your pen."

Maija's heart softened. She got an armful of hay from the loft and spread it out before the cows, then fetched a bundle of twigs for the lambs to nibble on. She spent a long time gazing at the animals. When she returned to the house, Elma asked:

"Did the animals still know their mistress?"

"They licked me and lowed, and the lambs bleated."

"And the cows are still alive, though mother doubted they would be the morning she left," said Aili.

"You've grown up already. But I didn't see Oskar Portimo. Did he run away from the war too?"

"Not at all," said Auku. "He's chasing women at Olkivaara."

"He was running after Nöpö at our place," said Elma.

There was a brief pause during which they all looked thoughtful. Then Mari said:

"Did Kauko write about where he is now that the war is over?"

"He said he was on guard near the war zone," said Auku.

"Kauko is the only one who isn't here now," said Maija. "Nestor and Toivo are sure to be home soon, since they are reservists."

Mari sighed and then immediately said:

"We have to go the rest of the way, children."

"You're not going anywhere," said Maija. "You're close enough to Olkivaara so that it will be no problem to find."

"I do feel as if I were home already," said Mari.

"Aili and Elma can get the covers and warm them up," said Maija.

While the girls were making the beds, Maija sat down beside Mari, dug out her pipe and tobacco, then said to her friend:

"Fill your pipe with this. We haven't even been able to smoke."

"That's true," said Mari. "And no one will gawk at us now if we puff on our pipes."

Väinö undressed and plumped down on the bed beside Auku. The quiet buzzing of the brothers' talk mingled with that of the women. Others in the room on the verge of sleep perked up their ears when Väinö said:

"I was so scared of that old man in the house where we stayed."

"Why? Was he all that bad?" asked Auku.

Väinö laced his hands beneath his head and stared at the ceiling in silence for a long time. Finally he said:

"He must have been crazy. He was so goddamned mad about that old nag of his. I never said a word to him after that."

"Is it right to start cursing as soon as we get home?"

"I wasn't cursing about getting home. I was cursing that old grouch."

"We happened to get a good evacuation home. The woman of the house even..."

"She was great. It's just that the old man was so weird," said Väinö.

"Let's get to sleep now. In a few hours mother and I have to milk the cows at Olkivaara. We'll talk about the trip then," said Elma.

"Vante and Tuomas don't know how close we are."

Elma could not bear to upset her mother by telling her the boys might still be playing cards. She merely said aloud:

"They'll sleep late in the morning. We'll go and give them a scare."

"Didn't Santeri Näätätaipale's family get to leave there yet?" asked Auku.

"Not yet. I imagine people from out his way are getting home now too," said Mari.

The room began to grow lighter with the rising sun. Maija clasped her hands. Her bed felt good. Its straw mattress seemed to be just what her back had ached for all winter. Eagerly, her nostrils breathed in the fragrance of firewood drying, of bread on the pole, of tobacco smoke. She could hear Väinö saying to Auku:

"You must have been scared when you were chasing those Russian bad guys the plane dropped off."

"I was almost shaking in my boots," said Auku. "But there was a war on, and it had to be done."

"Some morning when the snow is hard, we'll go and see where they got killed."

"When we get a warm enough night for the wood grouse to mate, we can take a trip there. It's an ugly sight," said Auku.

Although nothing more was said, Auku and Väinö tossed and turned for a long time. It was daylight before Maija fell asleep.

3

"Can't we fix it up, lieutenant, so I can get out now?"

"You must know, Malinen, that demobilization orders haven't come through yet."

"Well, even if I have no orders to sit down, I'll plant my butt on that stump and explain my business a little bit," Nestor said with a laugh.

"Yes, do. This tent living makes us forget our manners."

The lieutenant smiled. Although the price of peace had stunned him at first, as it had all the others, the nervous strain of the winter was beginning to subside. The company commander's tent had been pitched in a spot where pine trees had been cut at a height of about two feet, leaving stumps to serve for chairs. The table was a huge pine stump. Nestor Malinen sat down and said:

"Doesn't it say there in the lieutenant's papers that I took on this war job without having to?"

"I know that you came to the front as a volunteer."

"Well, yaah...Now I figure I'll draw my last pay."

"It's not so simple to leave the army. But I am sure you will be one of the first to leave."

"I can't hang around here any longer. It's time to start hauling the manure at home, and I should get there for the spring log drive. And I feel the need for a woman too. I've gone without one for four months now."

The clerk, a regular army corporal, turned his face to one side. The lieutenant hemmed, but the corners of his mouth twitched. The master sergeant who was in the tent looked back and forth from his superior officer to Malinen.

"I can't deny that you have pressing reasons to leave."

"I sure do. I'm not stretching it a bit, now am I?"

"There is no question that the first to be released will be the oldest age groups. I believe that in your case, it will happen before summer comes," said the lieutenant.

"And I tell you right to your face that I am not going to wait here till summer."

"It may happen even sooner. You should just be patient."

"I will not hang around here one minute longer. I came into the army without any slip of paper and I can leave without one. I'll wait for permission until tomorrow morning, but then I'm going."

His weatherbeaten face set in a determined scowl, Nestor Malinen rose from the stump. Glaring at the lieutenant, he thrust his hands into his pockets and hoisted up his sagging pants. The lieutenant tried to meet his gaze, but was soon forced to look down at the huge stump that served as a table. Drumming his fingers on its top, he said:

"I wouldn't want to say a flat *no*, but because of my position, I have to tell you that army orders apply to everyone, and that includes volunteers."

"We'll see, goddamnit."

"Private Malinen! Is that any way to speak to a superior officer?"

The big master sergeant rose from his seat as he spoke and took a step toward Malinen.

"You keep out of this. I always speak from the head, and I'm not about to start blowing it out of my ass. You just sit on that stump if you want to stay healthy."

Nestor Malinen spoke the last words with his eyes on the pack of tobacco he had dug out of his pocket. Tearing a piece of paper from one side, he creased it with a deft motion, and sprinkled grains of tobacco into it with his fingers. The lieutenant looked at the purple face of the master sergeant. With a nod and a glance, he directed the man back to his seat. After swallowing several times, he said:

"You're good at rolling cigarettes..."

"This is no cigarette, it's a butt," said Nestor in a surly voice as he wet the finished cigarette with his lips.

"Well, a butt then. But it was neatly done."

Although Nestor Malinen's fingers moved with the expertness developed by thousands of repetitions, they were trembling noticeably. He lighted the butt and took a few deep drags. Smoke poured from his nostrils as he sat back down on the stump and said:

"Us ordinary men don't have the money to carry cigars around in our pockets." He turned toward the master sergeant. "And now that the Russians didn't get to be our bosses, the bigshots are smoking Gold Medal cigars."

The lieutenant's face went red. The master sergeant took out cigarettes, fished one out, and inserted its end in a holder.

"Shouldn't we agree to stop this crude joking, Malinen?"

"I didn't start this shit. That master sergeant ought to know that if he starts jawing with a logger, he'll come off second best."

The clerk went out of the tent, but remained standing outside its flap. The master sergeant's eyes flashed, but he controlled himself at a warning glance from the company commander. The lieutenant's mind worked feverishly as the silence lengthened. He had to say something to the man sitting on the stump and staring at the toes of his boots. Nestor Malinen resolved the difficult situation by raising his eyes and saying:

"It's strange that we have to start fighting among ourselves now. Didn't we get more than enough of that sport this winter? And what fun is there in drilling an old bear like me in forming a double line and crawling on my belly like a snake? I'll never learn the right way to make those turns and about-faces at my age anyway, and I don't want to either. This winter I was able to go forward when I had to and run away when I was scared, and I wasn't the first one to run. There are younger men to stand guard. A man with a big family like me is needed more at home than he is sleeping away in a tent corner here."

Nestor Malinen's voice was low and harsh, with no hint of

bravado. The words sounded to the lieutenant like a plea for pardon, one that was wrung out with great difficulty. Therefore he said:

"I promise to do my best for you. I share your point of view completely."

"Well. I'm depending on you. You were always a man of your word last winter, the kind of man I can trust. But that permission slip has to be here by tomorrow morning, otherwise I'll just leave. You can put a hole in me then, if you think it's so important."

Nestor Malinen rose and ducked out of the tent. The sun outside was nearly blinding, and for a time he stood blinking before setting off along the hard-packed trail. The woods were dark green and the smell of pitch was fragrant in his nostrils. Now the bark would be sappy at the peeling sites, but who would have done the logging this winter? Only a few youngsters and doddering old men, evacuees most likely, had stayed out of the war. He had to get on with his peacetime work.

Nestor's foot slipped off the path into the soft snow. He entered the tent where he was lodged and tried to rest on a blanket spread over fir boughs. The tent was completely abandoned; the other men were out training. After the war ended, Nestor Malinen had become a driver, and so he was able to spend his days at the tent.

"Time just drags on now," Nestor said aloud.

He rose, left the tent, and walked over to the field kitchen. A reservist was stirring a meat stew there. The soft snow was packed smooth. Blocks of wood, pine needles, patches of soot, and bunches of hay were appearing from under the melting snow. Nestor addressed a member of the mess crew:

"Where are those plywood boxes hiding?"

"At the foot of the tree there."

Nestor went in the direction indicated. Boxes of hardtack were stacked up on fir boughs. Nestor opened one of them.

"Hey, you don't mean to start taking that bread?" said the mess hand.

"That's what I came for. This hardtack looks pretty good. I'll have to break off a good pocketful."

"No you won't," barked the mess hand.

"This isn't your property."

"No it isn't, but every man gets the same amount. Get out of that box. Everybody gets only his share."

"I broke up one piece to put in my pocket and there it stays. It's the damndest thing that we have no food now. As long as I could get fish from the Russians this winter, you had enough to eat."

"I don't set the amounts but I see to it that the food is equally divided. Shut that box cover now."

Grumbling to himself, Nestor closed the box and set off in another direction from the field kitchen.

✧ ✧ ✧

"He's a real character," said the master sergeant.

"You mean Malinen?" asked the lieutenant.

"That sad sack who was here just now. I'd like to have him under me in a peacetime garrison. One incident like this doesn't convince me that I couldn't make him shape up...ahem...shape up somehow." The sergeant moistened his lips with his tongue as he considered the matter.

"He would always be in the guardhouse," said the lieutenant.

"Why are the reservists from around here so bullheaded? They seem all ready to fight if you have to give them an order."

"They were stubborn and self-reliant during the winter too. They don't seem to trust an outsider's orders or his ability to think things out. Here in the backwoods, they've always had to manage on their own. Any involvement with higher authority has always repressed them and made life more difficult. Well, I was entrusted with a mission by Private Malinen..."

With a laugh, the lieutenant put the receiver of the field telephone to his ear and wound its crank. When he heard an answer, he said:

"Battalion commander."

When the commander responded, the lieutenant said:

"Salminen here."

"Hello, how are things going?" said the voice on the wire.

"Well enough otherwise, but when will the releases come down?"

"Soon, but I can't say exactly when."

"I have a request to make. I have an old volunteer in my company. As stubborn as sin, as you can imagine. Now he's got the notion that this logging job, as he calls it, is over for him. Negotiation time ends tomorrow morning," the lieutenant laughed.

"What's the name of the bullheaded one?"

"Private Malinen. The man who made that crazy charge at the retreating Russian column. You probably remember. The way he volunteered was extraordinary too."

"The one who took that key prisoner?"

"Yes, and he brought back a horse too."

"He's done some other wild things too."

"Actually, he did what he thought best most of the time, but he was a good soldier," said the lieutenant.

"I'm sure you promised the man he could go," the battalion commander said with a laugh.

"I promised to do my best. Malinen has a big family, and he's almost sure to give us nothing but grief from now on. It seems to me that clamping down on him now would be poor pay for his winter service. In any event, his kind will soon be discharged."

The battalion commander was slow to answer. A confused rustling and crackling traversed the line. The lieutenant was about to say more when he heard:

"I was just lighting up. Now then, I do remember the man very well. It's just not the army way, though, to let a man strip off his uniform whenever he feels like it..."

"But he started thinking of doing it now, not when the fighting was going on. I think we should put up with it this time."

"Well, I'll phone the colonel at regimental. But you won't be getting a leave yet anyway. Don't make any promises. Who knows what kind of mood the old man is in."

"No I won't, captain, sir."

"I see that combat conditions no longer prevail, lieutenant. Does Private Malinen address you as *lieutenant, sir*?"

"Not as sir, but he probably squeezed out a *lieutenant* every now and then along with the *Hey you's*, captain, sir."

"Did you have anything else on your mind?"

"No, captain sir. We'll be in touch, captain, sir."

"Goodbye then."

Lieutenant Salminen set down the receiver with a smile on his face. One of the platoon leaders, a young second lieutenant, had entered the tent during the conversation.

"You can tell that the battalion commander is starting to feel rested," the lieutenant said to him.

"Did he promise us a leave?" asked the younger lieutenant.

"Not yet, but spring is only beginning."

"Without asking leave of the guns," said the other with a laugh.

✧ ✧ ✧

The makeshift stable erected for the company's horses was in a gloomy spruce grove. The man hurrying toward it caught the familiar scent of horse manure and sweaty harnesses. Ears pricked forward, a large bay horse raised his head, then turned to look over his back. His nostrils quivered and the sound of a whinny spread through the early spring woods.

"Is it *Bolshoi Khuy* whinnying like that? Does the boy know Nestor?"

Raising his front hoofs, the horse began to thrust his muzzle into the man's chest. Then he rubbed his outstretched forehead into the man's shoulder.

"Hell, don't knock me over. Hey, hey..."

Nestor was forced to step back. The horse's nostrils began to flare and narrow as he sniffed all around the man. The other horses began to whinny also.

"Guess which pocket has bread in it for you, boy?"

The horse began to nudge Nestor's pants pocket with his muzzle.

"You've got a pretty sharp sense of smell. Here's the bread. Only the mess sergeant was so stingy that I got to break only one piece of it to put in my pocket. Look, I'll chop it up now, and you'll get to taste Finnish hardtack."

The other horses strained toward Nestor and his pet, the smell of bread making them restive. Nestor patted the horse's neck as the animal crunched one piece of hardtack after another between its teeth. Nestor kept on talking.

"Tomorrow I'm leaving for Jarvenkylä. That's where my home cottage is. My wife and kids must have gotten back there from the coast by now. I get to go home, but it looks like you'll have to live in this new country. I wonder where you galloped around when you were a colt. It might have been far away from here. That's all the bread for now. The other horses have to get a taste of it too."

Nestor went around to all the other animals, thrusting a bit of hardtack into every mouth and patting necks and flanks. But soon he returned to the side of his favorite, picked up a currycomb, and began to brush the horse's flanks and haunches, which were already gleaming. As he left, he stroked the animal's soft muzzle once more and said:

"We're good buddies now. I can't leave you here for someone else to take care of, *Bolshoi Khuy*. We've stuck things out together and we'll leave here together."

It was a restless night for Nestor Malinen. In the small hours of the morning, a stiff wind arose and at last sleet began to fall. The tent cloth flapped in the wind, and the fir boughs pressed into Nestor's sides. Some of the men had played cards almost the whole night through.

When the card sharks had gone to bed and the rest of the men still lay sleeping, Nestor was already out visiting the horses. On his return he picked up packets of tea from the field kitchen.

"Get up, you brutes, and drink your tea," he barked.

Here and there a man sat up and blinked his eyes. Someone cursed the sleet that was causing water to drip through the tent cloth.

"This is a farewell tea," said Nestor.

"Huh? What's are you up to now?" said the squad leader.

"It's just that I'll soon be gone."

The men in the tent looked at one another. Nestor Malinen was nothing, if not colorful.

When the others fell out and left for their day's duties, Nestor lay sprawled out on his overcoat. His duties were entirely self-supervised. No one doubted the old logger's ability to take care of the stable.

Nestor did not have time for a proper smoke before the company commander's messenger came crawling through the door. The young serviceman stayed on his knees on the fir boughs and said:

"Malinen has been summoned to the company commander's tent."

"I figured it was that when you shoved in through that flap."

"Well then, I've done my duty."

"Tell the big brass they won't have to wait long."

The sleet was beating down, but it felt comfortably cool on Nestor Malinen's flushed face. Throwing away the butt of his cigarette, he entered the company commander's tent.

"Hello...It's really coming down out there," said Nestor.

"Hello. Won't you have a seat, Malinen," said the company commander.

"I see the lieutenant took the hint about not asking me to sit down yesterday. Guess I will plant my butt on that stump."

Nestor Malinen noted that the battalion commander was also seated at the rear of the tent. He looked at the man's good-humored face. What was he doing here? There were too many other officers around here too. But he would not be rattled. Officers were human beings too.

"I know that you're homesick, Malinen."

The battalion commander spoke without any preliminaries.

Nestor turned a look of distrust on the captain and held it for awhile.

"That isn't what I told the lieutenant. I just asked if the old men couldn't leave this logging job now. You can get along without us."

There was a long silence. The captain's mischievous mood was sobered. "You can get along without us now," the man said. A month ago, he and a thousand others had known that they were needed, and had not defaulted. The captain dug out a pack of cigarettes and put one between his lips. Then he stood up, walked stooping in the low tent over to Malinen, and said:

"Have one. As I recall, you do smoke."

"And how. I'm a roll-your-own man, but when such a higher-up makes an offer, I guess I have to take one of those damn fool smokes."

The captain sat down on the fir boughs as Malinen lighted his cigarette. After a short pause, he said:

"You can leave now, Malinen. Your papers are ready."

"I kind of thought so. I knew all winter long that there wasn't a single rotten officer in this whole battalion."

"Now that's a real testimonial," laughed the lieutenant.

"I never talk shit about good men. My own business is settled now, but I was thinking, and I sort of promised too, that I would take *Bolshoi Khuy* with me. How can that be arranged?"

All the men in the tent looked at the others. The faces of the clerk and messenger turned beet red. The lieutenant struggled to suppress a smile. The captain turned toward Nestor. Seeing that his expression was serious, he said:

"Have I missed something? What are you talking about?"

"I'm talking about *Bolshoi Khuy*. The horse I took from the Russians between Alasalmi and Suomussalmi. The time we took the prisoner."

When a broad smile spread across the captain's face, the others dared to relax their own stiff expressions. One of the second lieutenants went so far as to titter.

"Who gave the horse a name like that?" asked the captain.

"We didn't need a priest to christen him. I started calling him that."

"Do you know what that means in Finnish?"

"I speak enough Russian to know that. When I worked on the Murmansk railroad, I learned some Russian and even a little Chinese. He's a fine horse and should have a fine name."

"Isn't that a little too...highfalutin...at least to appear on official papers?" said the captain.

"I can start calling him something else at home. But in a war, one has to have a sense of humor."

"At home? What do you mean by that?" asked the captain.

"That I'm taking him along with me. He's a strong draft horse. I'm sure he'll pull the biggest loads of logs in camp."

The captain gaped in astonishment and his cigarette dropped into the fir boughs. The messenger seated next to him rushed forward to look for it, but the captain had already picked it up. He looked at Malinen and said:

"The horse is government property. Or rather, the Army's."

"Well, hell! The government was nowhere around when I took it from the Russians. I've been carrying porridge and leftover gruel to it, and I've fed it bread from my own rations. Its coat is like silk now. If you could have seen what a shaggy brute it was when I got my hands on it, you wouldn't doubt at all that I'd take good care of it at home."

"There's no more to be said on the matter. All booty of war belongs to the army. The horse stays with the company."

Nestor Malinen's jaw quivered. He blinked and angrily blew away the smoke that was curling up before his face. Then he said:

"Do you really mean that?"

"Absolutely."

"But they took my own horse to war. They took it in the fall, and they didn't stop to ask if it could be spared. To tell the truth, he had a bad temper, and if I can take this *Bolshoi Khuy* with me, then for my part, the army can keep my old hammerhead."

"These matters go through official channels. You'll get your horse back in time, and if not, you'll be reimbursed. You will leave here without a horse."

For a long time Nestor Malinen sat swinging a leg crossed over his other knee back and forth. He blew smoke through his nostrils and looked at the wet tent wall flapping in the wind. Finally he said:

"If that's the way things are, then I have to go back on my word. It'll be hard to admit it to the horse when I already told him it was a sure thing. It's like what a fellow at home did a couple of years ago..."

Everyone in the tent waited for Malinen to go on speaking. With an angry gesture, he flung his cigarette butt toward the stove and sat there with his cheek in his hand. Finally the company commander spoke:

"What did the man do?"

Nestor looked at the lieutenant with an expression of disgust and continued:

"A city woman who sold herself for money was visiting there. The hometown man paid her in advance, the way they're supposed to. When the man had done his thing, he took the money back. Is that any way for a man to act? I promised the bay to take him with me."

"Breaking this promise is not as dishonorable," said the captain.

"I don't have the gall to show my face to the bay. Yesterday evening I told him for sure we would leave together."

The lieutenant coughed and then said:

"Give me Malinen's papers, clerk. They are all in order. Then he will have to speak to the supply sergeant."

Nestor Malinen's hand trembled when he took the papers the clerk handed him. He looked at them for a minute, thrust them into his pocket, then said as he rose:

"I must have been a pesky old man, but I tried to do what I thought needed to be done. If it's OK with the bosses, I'd like to say goodbye with a handshake."

"Well, goodbye now. You were a tough man in a battle."

"Thanks...Without men like you, Malinen, there would be no Finland now. Good health and good luck in your work at home."

"You've always been a square man, Salminen. I sometimes forget soldierly ways and all that, but when it came to the real thing, I did my best. If you ever come to Järvenkylä, you have to stop at my place. Most people there know me as Nestor Olkivaara. We'll go fishing in the Ii River."

Nestor Malinen finished saying goodbye to all the men. In the doorway he still turned to say:

"It does my heart good to know that I was out here with the younger men. You have to feed that boy *Bolshoi Khuy* plenty. He's a wise and good horse."

Nestor stooped down at the tent fly but turned once more:

"If my own horse happens to be lost in the war, I'll write to this company and ask if they are going to sell these horses. I'll be happy if the captain will write me in that case. Goodbye then."

The wet tent fly dropped from Nestor Malinen's broad shoulders and flapped a few times. Outside the soft snow crunched under his footsteps. There was a long silence in the tent. When they had all sat down, the lieutenant said:

"It wouldn't have been too much to give the horse to Malinen."

"I don't think so either. But the army is the army, and its regulations must be observed. But the horse's name will not be changed as long as it remains in this battalion."

CHAPTER XI

1

The sun of early spring warmed the clusters of houses in Ii Hamina. The ice on the Ii River was melted much further upstream than during the fiercely cold days of winter. The war was over, and the first of the evacuees were leaving town.

These were trying days for the Sääskilampi family. Soon they would be leaving for home. Father Ivar and his wife were the most eager to go, while their daughter Irja's longing for home was tempered by the fact that her daughter had been born within these walls.

For a time Ivar Sääskilampi was almost his old self. News of the war's ending had restored his will to live, but that was soon followed by the news of Bert's having been wounded. That, combined with spring fever, caused him to spend most of his time in bed. Rarely did he go out for a walk of any length.

"My husband will soon be back," said their hostess.

"You'd think they would start releasing the reservists soon," said Irja, who had carried the baby's basket into the main room and was seated beside it.

Ivar Sääskilampi lay on a bench, his cheek resting on his hand. He listened to the women's talk for a time and then said:

"They'll be slow in letting the men out. Your husband is a sergeant too, and they'll keep the men with rank longer."

"Then Irja's husband won't get out until summer," said the woman.

"People who know say that officers will have to stay in longer," said Irja. "There's a great shortage of them."

"It's even bad luck for a man to have done well in battle," said the young mistress of the house. "I saw Hilkka — you know her, Irja, the one who had the son out of wedlock — and she said her boy Eino was promoted to top sergeant. He was a buck sergeant when he went in as a reservist, and they say he fought well. Hilkka says he might have to go to officers' candidates' school."

"But isn't he the only man on their farm?" asked Irja.

"He is, and he's badly needed at home, since he lives alone with his mother. Eino was always a spirited boy. He worked hard and took care of his mother. Hilkka is getting old now, and they have a lot of land to farm. He should be there for the spring planting."

"His mother still carries herself so well," said Irja.

"She always has. You can imagine what it was like to have something like that happen to her when she was young. Some migrant who worked at log-sorting during the summer seduced her. It wasn't easy to bear such a shame in those days. She had to hold her head high out of sheer defiance. Another person would have left the community."

"Did they ever find out who the father was?" asked Petti Sääskilampi.

"Hilkka didn't go after him too much. People say the seducer wasn't an ordinary logger. The boy is proud and handsome too."

"Where are you going now, father?" asked Irja.

Ivar Sääskilampi had risen from the bench. He was overcome by a strong fit of coughing and his pipe flew from his mouth and clattered to the floor. He began to put on his woolen coat.

"Uh, darn it. The lining of that sleeve is all tangled up."

"Now don't, father. I'll straighten it out. The lining is all twisted."

"Then straighten it. I can't even bend my arms any more."

"Where are you going now?" asked the mistress of the house. "I was just about to make coffee. It's my turn to share the ration. And the Hilkka I mentioned is planning to drop in for coffee. You haven't met her yet."

"The air in here is getting too close for me. I'll breathe easier if I go out in the fresh air. Where are my mittens, Irja?"

"Do you need your mittens, and do you have to pull a fur cap down over your ears like that?" asked Petti Sääskilampi.

"No sense in freezing when I don't have to."

"But my good man, it's already a warm spring day," said his wife.

"It's not so warm when your circulation is as poor as mine. Uh, there's no need to worry if I'm gone for some time. I'll walk toward the station; I haven't been there since midwinter. I have to get out in the fresh air quickly now."

When the door closed, Irja, who was looking out the window, said:

"So many things come with age...You can see it in father. A few winters ago, he would harness a horse bare-handed in the coldest weather, and now he's tottering along wearing gloves and a fur hat pulled down on his ears."

"In thirty or at most forty years, we'll all be facing the same thing," said the mistress of the house.

"The best years are few in number," said Irja. "Now where did those noisy boys go? They could have gone with grandpa."

"Your father doesn't seem to want company," said Petti Sääskilampi.

"Why? — I was just thinking that if he has an attack..." said Irja.

"Your father has become more of a loner. It's almost as if he were afraid of people. Luckily, it's warmer already."

Petti Sääskilampi's words ended in a heavy sigh. Irja turned around, looked at her mother for a moment, and then said:

"Aren't you feeling well, mother?"

"It's just that I was thinking about everything...Bert lying in the hospital at Vaasa...and I want to go home more every day."

"There's no need to worry about Bert. Even Kosti wrote that it was only a flesh wound and would soon heal. Bert said so too in his letter."

"Look at that little thing in the basket. She's kicking up a storm and I smell something," said her mother.

Irja went to the basket on a bench near the stove. Little fists were waving so vigorously that lace cuffs were flashing in the air.

"You didn't dirty your didies, now did you?" said Irja.

She lifted the blanket and laughed.

"Well now, our miss has had an accident."

2

At midnight, the dark woods were sighing heavily. It's going to snow, thought Kauko. He was walking slowly near a number of tents huddled in a spruce grove. The sling of the rifle was pressing into his shoulder, so he flipped it to his elbow and laid it loosely over his left shoulder with the stock to the rear. In the darkness one could carry his weapon this way.

"I wonder if there's much time left," he muttered.

He stopped, rested the rifle in the crook of his elbow, and pulled out his watch. It took a long time for his eyes to adjust and make out the hands.

"It's just about one-thirty."

Kauko actually enjoyed the night-time guard duty, when he could be by himself. Sometimes a horse whinnied from the stables or an ill-tempered one gave a shrill, angry cry. Sparks rose from the tent stovepipes, and when he passed very near a tent, he could hear the sound of snoring from within. Until a few minutes ago, they had been playing cards in a third-platoon tent, but even that activity was carried on softly. The company officers did not approve of that pastime.

This was very different from the winter, when a man's life had been worth so little. To Kauko, it seemed as if the war had been over for a long time, although only two weeks ago they had been lying under a concentration of artillery fire. Now it all seemed impossible. He thought at length about the nervous strain they had been under. What more could a person ask for now — if only he could get enough to eat.

Until this moment, hunger had merely been lurking in the background of his mind, but now his mouth watered and he had to swallow continually. The stomach of a young man used to toiling in the woods demanded large helpings, and here there were taxing training exercises during the day. While the war was going on, food had not been so constantly on his mind — life was a dearer priority — and whenever the chance came, they had been able to cram their stomachs to bursting. But now the army's rations were not enough for a young man with a hearty appetite.

"Why don't they have sense enough to send packages from home?" muttered Kauko. "Aili at least has milk there to churn into butter and even to make bread cheese. During the winter they deluged me with packages all the time. Even Elma often..."

Thinking of Elma made him forget his hunger. He wondered would it be like when he got home? I should wear a combat jacket with insignia, he reflected, even if I have to borrow it from someone. The branch-of-service shoulder patches look so neat. I have a pair of whipcord breeches at home. I'll put them on and saunter over to Olkivaara. Or maybe it would be nicer to paddle a boat there. Dangle a trolling line and first pretend to scull past Olkivaara, then swing back toward it. Reel in the line and then nose into Nestor's landing. I'm almost sure Elma will come down to meet me. Nestor may come to the bank and say, "Come for coffee, soldier." "We just happen to have some bread cheese," Elma might add.

Cheese — God, but his mouth was watering. Did the army brass think a soldier could live on the Holy Spirit in peacetime? Heck, there wasn't even a canteen out here in the wilderness. He remembered Toivo Olkivaara's tales of his peacetime service.

"You won't believe how much coffee bread and pancakes we screwed the mess kitchen out of when we were on KP. Sometimes the mess sergeant even gave us cheese and sausages."

Such were the tales Toivo had told. The boys from Järvenkylä who had served in heavy weapons units told the same kind of stories. They would return from the service as fat as pigs. Kauko remembered asking Toivo if taking things without permission wasn't stealing. "Hell yes, it's not allowed. If someone gets caught, it means a trip to the guardhouse. One of our buddies even wound up in Ilmajoki Prison. You have to be slick enough not to get caught. But taking things in the army isn't really stealing. You're just screwing the army," Toivo had said.

At the time, Kauko had answered, "I thought that word had another meaning. Isn't it just plain robbery to take something without permission?"

"When did you see me take anything in civilian life?" Toivo had snapped angrily.

Kauko had laughed and said: "I've seen you cut down pine trees in a national forest and pick pine cones from them. You certainly didn't have the forester's permission."

"But that was government property, which belongs to all of us," Toivo had said.

Without intending to, Kauko began to circle a kind of tepee made of spruce trees thrust into the snow, where the company's provisions were stored. During the day one could see sacks of rye bread inside it, along with the frozen carcass of a heifer and large boxes in which the mess sergeant stored butter and sugar. He had seen all this when he got his soup ration from a kitchen hand.

In the army, taking without permission is not stealing. A man has to be slick enough not to get caught. Kauko walked right up to the fir tepee. Of course a man on guard duty was allowed to look. The smell of fresh bread flooded his nostrils. It seemed as desirable and as unattainable as had the community's bread a few years ago.

No, no...Kauko turned away and began to tramp the guard path at a faster pace. But his hunger would not go away. With an unpleasant shudder, he recalled having to get a flour slip from Ivar Sääskilampi. That goddamned bigshot. Hanging on tooth and nail to the community flour. Where was that old hypocrite in the storm of iron at Löytövaara? I was there. Community and country. Weren't they nearly the same?

At intervals, Kauko looked at his watch. A quarter to two. He had to act now if he intended to. He walked to the spruce shelter with slow steps. As if on order, a heavy, wet snow began to fall. There would be no tracks now. Kauko stood and listened. No sound, nothing but the throb of blood vessels in his temples. Now — he needed only to be so slick that no one would ever know.

Kauko moved a spruce tree enough to get through and stepped inside the shelter. What if someone should come? Who would come at this time? There stood a sack filled with long rectangular loaves of rye bread, tastier than any Kauko had ever eaten as a civilian. If only he could get enough to eat. He slipped one loaf into the pocket of his cloak. Then another. Did he hear someone moving? No, it was merely the beating of his heart and the throbbing of his temples. There hung the nearly intact carcass of a heifer. The meat would be a tasty snack when roasted in the barrel stove. Kauko's trembling fingers snatched the sheath-knife from under his cloak. Agh, the meat was frozen solid. But he hacked off a piece the size of one hand, and that too he shoved into his pocket.

Setting the spruce tree back in place, Kauko began to pace his guard round like a caged lion. The loaves of rye bread in his pockets seemed huge. They seemed to burn his thighs. If only no one came along. Did his pocket flaps cover the rye bread? What time could it be?

"A-ha! It's two on the dot."

Kauko walked to his tent. He would leave the bread outside in a snow drift. The piece of meat could stay in his pocket. Kauko ducked into the tent. There was no fire watch; the men on guard put more wood into the stove at each change of the guard. Kauko shook his smaller companion by the foot.

"Hey, Jalo, get going. It's your turn on guard."

His friend sat up with a jerk and blinked.

"Again?"

"You've slept for five hours already. Don't look so befuddled. Just go and protect the company," said Kauko.

"Goddamnit to hell, I just can't keep my eyes open."

Grunting, Jalo Kieppi pulled on his clothes, took his rifle from near the door, and said:

"Is it snowing out there?"

"It started just in time for your watch," said Kauko.

"Wouldn't you goddamn well know it."

Jalo Kieppi disappeared into the darkness. Kauko stripped off his cloak. Everyone in the tent was asleep. He stepped out, brought the rye bread back inside beneath his cloak, and hid it under the packs along the tent wall. Then he put more wood into the stove and took the piece of meat from his pocket. He had a jar of salt under his pillow, and he sprinkled salt from it onto thin slices of the meat to flavor them. They were soon sizzling on a stick in the flames of the barrel stove.

Kauko kept a sharp ear out, but no one woke up, nor even so much as turned over. Soon the meat was browned, except for a shriveled black portion. The smell was irresistible.

Kauko went to sit down near the place where he slept. He took out one of the loaves of rye and cut a five-inch slice from it. The roasted meat nearly burned his mouth. What if someone happened to wake up and smell it? His comrades were just as hungry as he was. Jonas Niemi was sleeping nearby, most likely dreaming of a proper meal. Now when there was such a to-do about transporting the evacuees, packages were being held up. Not even Jonas had been lucky enough to get one of late, although they had once come in a steady stream, especially to the training center.

Kauko wolfed down the meat and the piece of bread. His stomach was full, but he felt depressed. What if they found out that he had stolen food from the common supply? Now the others' rations would be short those two loaves of rye.

Although he lay down on his blankets, Kauko could not fall asleep. Why the devil is it that I always have so much trouble getting my daily bread, he wondered. For a few years now, we've managed at home without the community's bread. We even had enough to eat our bellies full. I thought that for the rest of my life, I would not have to go short of food. Isn't it the very devil? Now I've had to steal, something I've never done before. *Screw the army?* God, what a fool trick to pull! What if I were to take back the bread, the way I once did a migrant worker's wallet? At least my conscience was clear after that.

Damn it! Are two loaves of rye bread and a piece of meat enough to make a man toss and turn like this? Haven't I committed much greater sins this past winter? This declaration, spoken aloud between gritted teeth, helped ease Kauko's mind. These were army supplies; more were to be had at the supply depot. The soldiers, and especially the officers, would see that they got their share.

The warmth of the tent made him weary. He could feel the large lumps under his head. He moved the loaves of rye to the wall of the tent, covered them with fir boughs, and soon dropped off to sleep.

✧ ✧ ✧

"The mess sergeant was just wild..."

"What's the sarge so mad about now?"

Through his sleep, Kauko could hear the words of the platoon member assigned to fetch the morning tea rations, and the squad leader's response. As he spoke, the man dropped the packets of tea near the stove. Once asleep, Kauko had slept so soundly that he had been only dimly conscious of the wake-up call, and had not heard the man leave. Now the words struck him with the force of a hammer-blow. *The mess sergeant was just wild...*

Kauko was wide awake now. Although his limbs were trembling, he kept his eyes pressed tightly shut. A clear day had dawned, and one could see in the tent without a light. Kauko opened his eyes a slit. The man who had gone for the tea took his time in answering the sergeant's question. He merely said:

"Grab that stack of tea packets before they fall over."

"Well, what was the mess sergeant so wild about?"

"Thieves got into the food supplies last night."

Kauko felt as if his heart would crack his ribs. God what a wretch he was. He heard Sergeant Mäki say in chagrin:

"And our squad was on guard duty."

"Your men aren't worth much," said another squad sergeant.

"How could they have been so careless? Now we're in for it. Goddamn, the guard was sloppy. They must have been napping somewhere while someone did the pilfering. I wonder what will come of this," said Sergeant Mäki.

"I've never seen the food-boss so angry."

"What was missing?" asked Sergeant Mäki.

"Some bread, at least. He was checking to see what else had been stolen. He said he would talk to the company commander."

Oh my God, thought Kauko in panic. Let the earth swallow me up right now. I must do something, quickly. It was stupid to leave my rifle near the door. What if I jump up and grab it? Run out and shoot myself in the temple. That would be certain death. But the bullets are in my coat pocket. They'll see me and take the rifle away. Then they'll take me to the officer of the guard. And my knife is in its sheath under my pack. No one is talking about screwing the army now. *Thieves got into...they stole...*

Kauko gritted his teeth. Luckily he had been sleeping on his side. At least they won't see my face right away. They're looking at me now. I can feel it. That's why they're all so quiet. They're looking at me, and perhaps at Jonas and Jalo, who are innocent. Somewhere I've heard that even the young die of a heart attack when really scared. Has anyone ever been so afraid and so ashamed?

"We have to wake up the men who were on guard," said Sergeant Mäki.

"The company commander will send for them soon enough to talk to them," said one of the squad leaders in the tent.

"We have to start making spot checks from now on," said Sergeant Mäki. "It's hell when you can't trust your own men. It's not the guards alone who will be punished."

Greenish spots danced before Kauko's eyes. He sat up.

"I'm the thief," he almost shouted.

They stared at him. He could see looks of amazement and the angry glare of the squad leader. Kauko did not lower his eyes.

"I stole two loaves of rye. And I stole a piece of meat too. It's the plain truth, and there's no use in trying to cover it up. I'm going to jail anyway."

Sergeant Mäki stared at the fir boughs on the floor, a stunned expression on his face. The other sergeant's eyes stabbed into Kauko like knives as he said:

"Let the group give him a thrashing and a goddamned sound one."

"He needs to be taught a lesson," said Private Sumala,rising to his knees.

"You're one man who won't hit me, Sumala! No, goddamnit. Kill me if you like, but I won't be the only one to go."

Kauko sprang to all fours like a cat. This time he was afraid of no one. If they killed him...if only they would kill him...

"Let's have no more stupid tricks," said Sergeant Mäki, and he too rose to his knees. He could see the savage gleam in Kauko's eyes, which had turned toward the rifle rack.

Jonas Niemi and Jalo Kieppi sat up on either side of Kauko.

"Damn it to hell, don't start fighting. Sammalsuo isn't the only thief. I took a loaf of bread too, and a little butter."

Kauko's taut muscles went limp. He stared at Jalo Kieppi as if he were seeing an apparition. All eyes in the tent turned to the new culprit. One of the squad leaders said:

"Hey listen, Mäki. You seem to have some gang there. Too bad."

Jonas Niemi coughed so heavily that the tent walls seemed to shake. Then he said:

"I'm the same kind of guard. I took a loaf of bread and a handful of sugar. I ate some marmalade straight from the jar."

"Wheew," a whistle escaped Sergeant Mäki's lips.

"You've got a real squad of heroes there. What a helluva bunch," laughed the other squad leader.

The earlier homicidal mood in the tent had changed. There were muttered curses, glances of malice and compassion. Sergeant Mäki sighed heavily, looked at Kauko, and said:

"And I thought Sammalsuo and Niemi were model men. I trusted Kieppi more than my own self."

Kauko pressed his face into his hands. His mind was in turmoil. His defiance had melted like snow in springtime. His body felt completely limp.

The feeling lasted only a short time. Then Kauko raised his head and spoke:

"If we're still in this squad, Mäki, you won't need to be

ashamed of us. We won't steal again."

Kauko turned on his knees, shifted his pack, and drew the loaves of rye into view. With them in his hands, he stood up and said:

"We have a tough trail to walk now, buddies. We have to go and tell them."

"Let's go. It can't make matters worse."

"Let's go. A thief is a thief," said Jonas Niemi.

✧ ✧ ✧

Mess-sergeant Käsmä was one of the few reservists in the company. At that moment he was still checking the paper sacks. Early in the morning, he had flown into a rage when he had noticed the missing loaves. The morning tea distribution now over, he could study the thieves' trail himself. He kept muttering:

"Three or four. I don't remember exactly how many loaves there were in the sack, but I'm pretty sure three or four of them are gone."

In his fit of rage that morning, it had seemed a simple matter to report the theft to the company commander. Now he felt compelled to think it over. He felt no pity for the thieves, but the guards would also be punished. If only his release had come through, he would have been spared this grief. Oh well, it couldn't be helped. Would the company commander be awake yet? The theft should be investigated while it was still fresh.

The sergeant stepped out of the shelter and closed it after him. It was easy to steal from such a storehouse if one wanted to. But on the other hand, storehouses at home were not even locked, and nothing ever vanished from them. The thieves should be caught. Perhaps punishment would eradicate the wickedness in them.

Looking up, the sergeant saw three soldiers approaching. The first carried two loaves of rye in the crook of his arm as if they were firewood. The man was of a husky build. He looked like a soldier by the name of Sammalsuo. What was he doing here?

The men were now quite near. The old sergeant saw that their steps were heavy and their faces almost gray. Private Sammalsuo stopped a couple of meters away, stood at attention with the loaves of bread on his arm, and said:

"Here are your last night's thieves, sergeant, sir."

The sergeant did not so much as blink an eye. Sammalsuo's companions stepped to his side. Two big, strapping soldiers stood there with their heels pressed firmly together. Between them was a smaller soldier with a slighter build who said:

"We're all thieves."

"I'm the third guilty one," said the largest of the group.

The sergeant had a bad heart. He pressed the hand that had been mangled by a bear to the left side of his breast, and his voice trembled when he spoke:

"Weren't you on guard duty last night, Sammalsuo?"

"I was. I stole this bread during my turn on watch. Then I took a piece of meat the size of my hand, and roasted and ate it last night. And I had time to cut a piece this size from one of the rye breads..."

"Good God! On guard duty!" Sergeant Käsmä burst out.

"All three of us were."

Having said this, Kieppi presented a loaf of rye, at least a fourth of which was missing. Then he dug a small paper wrapping from his pocket, which he opened to disclose a tablespoon's worth of butter.

"I took some butter too. It didn't grow any, as you can see."

A half a loaf of rye bread also rested in Jonas Niemi's large palm. He dug a small glass jar containing cubed sugar from his pocket.

"This is what's left of the bread I stole. I took thirty-one lumps of sugar. I ate nine of them on guard duty. And like a sorry wretch, I gobbled down some marmalade from a jar."

Sergeant Käsmä looked at the three men standing there. My own boy is out on the Isthmus somewhere, he thought. Maybe he's hungry too. I have no other heritage to leave him, but I've tried to teach him honesty. There stand three soldiers of my son's age. From their faces, it's plain that they are no hardened criminals. Sammalsuo and that big lad whose name I don't recall have always been humble and model soldiers. I still remember Sammalsuo's zeal for volunteer duty during those days at the training center. Three pairs of eyes looking at me so steadily that I have to turn away.

"Why did you do something so wrong?"

"I can't explain it," said Kauko.

"It was a battle between hunger and good sense," said Kieppi. "Hunger won."

"I was hungry. That's my only defense," said Niemi.

As always when he was nervous or startled, Sergeant Käsmä felt a stab of pain in his chest. He was forced to turn aside and press his hand firmly to his heart.

"I know these rations are small for men of your age, but there's nothing I can do about it. I've done my best to get more."

A kitchen helper had approached, and stood watching with a malicious look on his face. To him, the three men standing before the sergeant with loaves of bread in their hands were a laughable sight. He looked at the mess sergeant's expression. Käsmä turned toward him.

"Go back to your kitchen," he said.

The soldier obeyed. The usually calm Käsmä's voice had been angry. Now he stood looking at the ground.

Kauko's fear and initial defiance had turned to shame. He saw the hand that had been mutilated by the bear pressing against the man's heart. If only he would curse them out. Give them a tongue-lashing, an earful — that would make it easier. Why is he dragging it out, he wondered. The whole company will soon be standing here gawking. We'll wind up in Ilmajoki, with a vengeance. This will be a blow to mother.

The sergeant, who had been staring at the morning's fresh snowfall, raised his eyes and met three inquiring gazes. He cleared his throat with a cough and said:

"I'm a religious man. Since you've behaved so manfully, I won't report this to the company commander. I can see that you are not born thieves. I also know that it isn't easy to confess to a crime. I believe what has happened will teach you more than a trip to jail would."

The eyelids of all three men reddened and they looked down. Sergeant Käsmä could see them swallowing hard.

"I myself have borne a heavy load of sin. It was not easy to shed. For years now, my soul has been at peace. I'll soon get to go home, but you will have to stay on here. Be men. Now hand over the bread quickly and go back to your tent. The day's exercises will begin soon."

Only Jalo Kieppi was able to speak. He gave the remains of his loaf to the sergeant and said:

"We're so ashamed."
"Let's forget about it now."

3

"Our home shanty is none too neat, but this is pukey," said Simo Mutka.

He and a group of men fulfilling their service obligation were cleaning up the winter battlefields. Almost without exception, their own dead had been picked up during the winter's action; those left between the lines had been cleared away as soon as peace was made.

During the spring thaw, the ghastly smell of rotting human flesh had spread over the ravaged battlefields. Now when the snow had melted, the stench nearly made one retch. During the morning, Simo Mutka and his companions had grubbed out a long trench in the earth, into which they dragged the burned brown and crumbling bodies of the enemy.

"Until now I would not have believed that human life could be so cheap," said one of the men with a look of distress on his face.

"Who can tell what a high-and-mighty VIP this once was? Hey, he's got a wallet in his pocket. Give it to me; I'll put the rubles away," said another soldier, a big, hard-faced man.

"Hell, don't do that," said Simo Mutka. "You'll catch some kind of plague."

"I'm not afraid of dying."

The soldier fished out a wallet from the dead man's pocket, opened it, and said:

"What did I tell you? There are rubles here, a wad as thick as an almanac."

Taking the bills out, the man looked into the wallet and said:

"And photos too. Let's see if the man had a good-looking *matyushka*."

There were two photos. He looked at them for a long time. Hands reached out toward him.

"Let me see them too."

"Show them to me."

Finally the soldier handed over the photos. As they were passed from man to man, curious faces turned sober. Soon all the men in the squad were looking at them. Finally Simo Mutka said:

"That must be his mother's picture."

"I wonder who that little girl is."

"She has such long, pretty braids."

The man holding the wallet said:

"Give me the pictures."

He stuffed the money and pictures into the wallet and shoved it back into the dead man's pocket.

"Let them go into the same grave."

"I wonder where he was born," said the man who had commented on the worthlessness of human life.

"His stamping grounds could have been far away," said Simo Mutka.

"And he had to come to die out here in the cold. And now he'll be buried in a pit in foreign soil."

"Yaah, but come on men. We have to get moving. There's no shortage of bodies."

It was the squad leader who was speaking. He looked around and continued:

"There comes a lieutenant. Let's get busy."

"It's Mäkinen splashing out this way," said Simo Mutka. "And there are felt boots and pants legs showing at the bottom of that hole."

Lieutenant Mäkinen came up to the burial detail. He too swallowed hard. The sight was not an uplifting one.

With the coming of spring, some degree of soldierly demeanor had been instilled in the soldiers. The squad leader brought his heels together with a snap and touched his fingers to his cap. The company commander waved a hand and said:

"Apple-polishing is silly here. Are there enough bodies to bury?"

"Enough and to spare, but I'd gladly quit this business."

"It's over for you, Mutka."

"Did my papers come through? You mean it?"

"Just go to the office and you'll soon be Simo Mutka, lumberman."

"Log driver, you mean," said Simo Mutka. "Hey, I'm on my way to the log float."

"That's right. You and a couple of reservists will get your

releases."

"Hey boys! *The old folks are leaving*, as the song goes. What about you?"

"There's no word yet," said Kosti Mäkinen gloomily.

"That's too bad. Besides the log drives, you would have construction work...So this hill didn't turn out to be the end of Simo Mutka. Let's go, as death said to the old man."

Simo Mutka left the place quickly with the lieutenant walking beside him. The others gazed wistfully at their receding backs. Every face was sober. One of the men said:

"We won't get out till fall. Our turn won't come till Santa Claus is due."

✧ ✧ ✧

A day in May was drawing to a close. The sun touched the tips of the Kainu hills as the air cooled down. The heat absorbed during the day still lingered on the high heathland, but mists were gathering in the woods and swamps. Four men stood beside the highway, looking toward the east, their ears straining to catch any sound.

"Won't that damned wreck ever come?" said the shortest of the men.

"It's sure to get here. They called from battalion that the truck would be in the church village before midnight. Just be patient, Mutka."

The speaker was Lieutenant Mäkinen. Two other reservists who had been released were pacing a small circle on the roadside. When one cigarette was gone, they lighted another. Their eyes kept forever turning to the straight stretch of road leading east.

"It's taking a long time," said one of them.

"A long time. Give me a stronger cigarette. These seem to have no taste," said the other.

"Just be patient, men. It's only a question of an hour, at most. Things were a lot worse during the winter," said Kosti Mäkinen.

"That's true. But a person is just in a hurry, even if there's no need to be."

As Simo Mutka spoke, the long-awaited roar of the motor came to the men's ears. They all turned in the same direction. A truck came rumbling down the pothole-pocked road. It drove slowly, rocking like a boat in the waves. The men snatched up their packs from beside the ditch. Simo Mutka thrust out a paw to his company commander.

"It's time to go now. We'll see you. Whenever you get to the church village, let me know. We'll have a long talk then."

"We'll see you. I want to thank you. I wouldn't have believed you'd turn out to be such a tough man. Be sure to take the package to my wife at Sääskilampi. Give her my best regards, if you can."

"I will. I'm not ashamed to carry a buddy's greetings, even if that's usually a thing for women and choir members. And the package will get there. Well, so long again. I'm glad I was able to do this job."

Simo Mutka climbed onto the platform of the truck. Lieutenant Mäkinen took leave of the other men too. Although there was little outward display of affection, the handclasps and the parting looks told of a deep mutual fondness.

"So we part again. There aren't many of us now who left Oulu together for the front. But that's enough talk. I saw what you could do — and what I couldn't." Mäkinen gave a short laugh. "We'll see you."

The men found room on the truck platform where other reservists were sitting. All their faces were beaming with satisfaction. There was some slight sadness at parting from their comrades of those trying days. Home, wife, children, small fields, log drives, and pulpwood cutting — these were what going home meant. A lieutenant peered out from the truck cab, a man who like Kosti Mäkinen had survived the winter's battles. His second rosette also gleamed more brightly than the first. Mäkinen said to him:

"Did you get a leave?"

"Just orders to Kajaani for a couple of days."

"Our leaves seem hard to come by," said Kosti.

The truck driver stepped on the gas, and the white-painted truck lurched forward. Kosti Mäkinen was left standing by the roadside. A few of the men sitting on the truck platform touched their hands to their caps. The lieutenant did the same. Then the truck dipped into a hollow and soon the whine of a motor climbing a hill could be heard.

"There went the last of my buddies," said Kosti Mäkinen.

He stepped across the ditch, sat on a stump sticking up beside it, and began to smoke in peace. The sun was no longer in sight. Only a red glow like the flame of a far-off fire could be seen beyond the hilly terrain. The rising mists rolled uphill toward the higher ground. From the direction the truck had taken, a sergeant of the regular army came pedaling a bicycle. He gave a real start when he noticed the lieutenant underneath the trees, and his hand flew to his cap in a flawless salute. The lieutenant responded with a mere wave of his hand, and the sergeant kept on pedaling. When the rattling of the bicycle was beyond earshot, all was silence.

Are these the lands for which we spent sleepless nights and staggered in our weariness? Peace for this land was dearly bought. Human life, impossible effort, suffering...If we had feared those trials, we would not be a free people in a free country. There goes Simo on the way to his cottage home. The man didn't ask for much, and none of it was frivolous. To go on a log drive. To spend sleepless nights huddled in the cold with his feet soaking wet.

The lieutenant rose and tossed his cigarette butt onto the gravel road. It was tough to stay when his men were leaving. Homesickness raged within him. I have a daughter and I haven't even seen her, he thought. But now his spirits rose. I'm one of the leaders in this army...they call me an officer. There was substance in Mannerheim's Order of the Day, although the saccharine praise of reserve officers had seemed like so much desk soldiers' babble. Many of our men fell. Who had been there to lead them and hold them together? Most of them, at least those from this area, knew what they had to do and did it. I have to hang on and see it through. Probably they'll start to release us soon.

As Kosti Mäkinen walked back to the bivouac area, the smell of pitch came to his nostrils. On higher ground the air still breathed out warmth, while in the hollows, a chilly mist drifted against his face. From one side, he heard the call of mating heath grouse. The sound of the late birds resembled the gurgling of brooks in the springtime. Kosti Mäkinen stood still and inhaled the woods' fragrance. Although his hand went into a pocket, he thrust back the pack of cigarettes it grasped. He would not now pollute the fragrance of the woods, of his own home country's woods, with the smell of tobacco smoke. The first time I walked these woods, I was freezing cold, he reflected. I was angry at everything: at the city, the wilderness, the cold, and the people, especially people who were well off. Now I have a wife and children. Summer lies ahead, and I am content that I was able to be there where men were needed. Now to the tent and to bed.

CHAPTER XII

1

The train chugged northward, the cattle cars rocking along the rails. The trip had lasted for nearly twenty-four hours. At first the men on board would open the sliding doors a crack and gaze out at the landscape, as someone announced the names of the stations they were passing. Once the train was held up at a backwoods stop for hours. Evening turned into night, and the soldiers began to yawn.

Although Kauko could hear the clanking of wheels on rails in his sleep, it was still sweet to rest. He realized that he had slept for a long time when he was startled into waking by these words:

"Damn it all, they stopped at Oulu for such a short time."

"What? Have we passed Oulu already?" asked Kauko, sitting up.

"A long time ago. We'll be in Kuivaniemi soon."

"And you didn't wake me up at the Oulu Station?" said Kauko.

"Why should I bother a sleeping man?" said Jalo Kieppi.

"Some buddy you are," said Kauko. "You know it's just like home to me."

The company to which Kauko belonged had suddenly received orders to move from the border wilderness to the nearest railway station. No one regretted the move. The last of the reservists had been released and almost all the remaining men were filling out their obligatory term of military service. It was pleasant to leave the now all-too-familiar spruce woods. Who could tell, they might be taken to an urban area, the young men kept repeating enthusiastically. One of the non-coms responded to that talk by saying:

"Life isn't a ball there either. They crack down on discipline."

"At least you can get evening passes and be with girls."

"Who stopped you from getting evening passes here?" said the same sergeant.

"Where was there to go? The same woods on all sides."

Neither the men nor the non-commissioned officers knew

where they were going, not even what direction they were taking. At the station, they saw that another company had already been loaded onto the train. When the equipment was aboard and the men were stowed into the cattle cars, the train headed west.

"At least we're heading in the right direction," someone said.

Only when they reached Ylivieska did the train begin to chug north. Many were disappointed, but a number were pleased.

When Kauko clambered up and went over to the door, he saw that the sun was shining brightly. Solitary houses flashed by. From where he sat at the door opening, Jalo Kieppi spoke:

"We may wind up in Rovaniemi, boys. It's only a short hop home from there."

"Do you even have a good-looking sister?" said a boy from the south of Finland. "Most likely they're all withered crabs like you."

"I have many sisters. But not one that could stand to look at a face as ugly as yours."

Kauko stood looking out the door. There were still patches of snow on the hillsides, but the weather was beautiful and warm. It was a shame he had slept through Oulu. He might have seen someone he knew at the station there.

✧ ✧ ✧

Early in the morning, the train pulled into the Rovaniemi station. Everyone looked fresh and curious. Jalo Kieppi and a few others who had grown up near the Arctic Circle were enthusiastic.

"Didn't I tell you boys? Spell out what's printed on that station wall."

"Rovaniemi. They always said at home when we climbed up on the big stone bake oven that we were in Rovaniemi," said Kauko.

"We are high up now," laughed Jalo Kieppi.

Immediately on arrival, the train was unloaded. Kauko's company was billeted in the firehouse. That same day the soldiers transported from the border wilderness were free to walk the streets of the town. Some even had money saved up, especially those who did not smoke. Soldiers and civilians moved through the streets, among them men whose occupation was a familiar one to Kauko. Loggers in pitch-stained trousers, rubber-bottomed boots, and caps worn askew tramped the sidewalks.

The company commander had given a speech that evening, promising passes to almost the entire company. Only the men actually on guard duty would stay to keep an eye on the equipment and the lodging area.

"We've had to live in the woods almost continually. You came straight to the front with only the most limited basic training in the art of war. I have been satisfied with you. In the war and afterwards, you have shown yourselves to be men. Keep on doing so this evening and during the days to follow."

When as usual Kauko, Jalo Kieppi, and Jonas Niemi had laid out their packs side by side in the meeting room of the firehouse, Kauko said:

"It feels good to know that we could take it last winter. Even the lieutenant could see that."

"We don't exactly want to foul up now either, since he put it so well," said Jonas Niemi.

"Let's go and look over the girls," said Jalo Kieppi.

"The Rovaniemi girls have probably had more than enough of ogling by now," said Kauko.

"Well, I at least am going to see a girl. She's from my hometown and works in a store here. She sent me a package at the front."

"Then Jonas and I can wander the streets. I hope we don't get lost," said Kauko.

"We are buddies, but I've got only one girl. She's sure to be an easy lay."

When Jalo Kieppi touched his visor in parting, leaving Kauko and Jonas Niemi standing there, he said:

"When we meet again tonight, one of us will have been laid, so don't you two go without trying."

Jalo walked off swiftly with such an air of confidence that neither Kauko nor Jonas doubted that he had a clear objective in mind. They were left standing on the street corner like orphans. After they saw Jalo disappear through a gateway, Kauko said:

"I guess we'll take a walk around and go back to camp."

"Let's see what this gateway to Lapland looks like."

Fresh from the woods, the boys felt clumsy and shy. Most of the men walking the streets were soldiers. There were many officers too. Kauko and Jonas scarcely had time to look at anything else, they were so busy watching in all directions for the next wearer of a Sam Browne belt to appear. Staying in step with each other was an effort. In the Kuhmo wilderness, they seemed to have forgotten what they had learned at the training center. One or the other of them was always skipping to get in step with his partner.

"Shouldn't we go and have a bottle of beer?" Jonas Niemi said at last.

"We should have just one to give us courage. They say that too many go to your head. There's a bar," said Kauko.

He grasped the door handle boldly. A mighty roar of talk and a thick cloud of tobacco smoke spewed out at them when he opened it. Inside, a phonograph howled. The tables were packed. A wall of men in line blocked their further view of the interior of the room.

"Is it worth standing in line for a bottle of beer?" said Kauko.

"I've changed my mind too. Let's go."

The evening sun shone warmly. The hump of Ounasvaara stood out against the blue sky. There were drunks in the streets and on rare occasions a young man in civilian clothing. But sometimes they even ran into girls, whom their eyes would follow after they had passed by. Suddenly they both stopped and Jonas Niemi said:

"Those were Lapland girls going by. Was that some kind of folk dress they were wearing?"

"That's what they look like in pictures I've seen. I've never seen a real one before either," said Kauko.

They stood looking at the backs of three mottled red costumes. The girls' step was light, and Lapland bonnets bobbed on heads held proudly erect.

"They are beautiful girls," said Jonas Niemi.

"You can tell by the way they hold their heads that they wouldn't care for our company," said Kauko.

"What are you soldiers gawking at? Don't you recognize your superior officers?"

Kauko and Jonas took their eyes off the Lapland girls and snapped to attention. A lieutenant and captain stood before them. The lieutenant wore gilded rosettes and the captain brass buttons. It was the lieutenant who had spoken. Both were obviously drunk, the captain actually staggering.

"We didn't notice, lieutenant, sir," said Jonas Niemi.

"What's your name and your unit?" said the lieutenant.

"Kauko cleared his throat as Jonas Niemi said:

"Private Raudassuo, lieutenant, sir."

The lieutenant took out a pen and a pack of cigarettes, and scribbled on its wrapper. The captain pursed his lips and tried to whistle as he struggled to keep his balance. The lieutenant looked at Jonas and said:

"What's your outfit?"

"Let the boys go," said the captain, looking at Kauko. "Were you at the front?"

"I had just a taste of it," said Kauko. "For a little while."

The lieutenant put the pen and cigarettes back in his pocket. Peering at the captain through sagging eyelids, he said:

"I want to prove what I just said, captain, sir."

"Wha'? Wha'd you say?" asked the captain.

"That I'm a champion finger-wrestler. Why, once last winter, when they wouldn't believe me at battalion headquarters...You there, you big soldier, hook your finger into this vise. Rest, both of you."

The lieutenant extended his right hand toward Jonas Niemi. Both soldiers looked askance at him, as did the captain. Then the captain said:

"Let's put an end to this man's fantasies. He beat a couple of soldiers we met, but you're a strong man."

It took Jonas Niemi awhile to catch on, but then he hooked his middle finger onto the big lieutenant's. Leaning back, the lieutenant braced his feet firmly and said:

"Now, soldier. Don't let my being a lieutenant bother you."

Jonas Niemi felt a bony finger clamp onto his own like the talon of a hawk. He planted his army boot alongside the gleaming calfskin boot of the lieutenant. Passers-by stopped and newcomers rushed up. A civilian cried out:

"Show him what strength is, soldier!"

"Now, spindleshanks, you put your mitt in a trap that'll leave you only four fingers to count on," cried another.

"Well soldier, are you ready?"

"I'm no star at this sport, but let's give it a try."

"With the fist on that soldier, the looey won't offer his finger a second time," laughed an old civilian.

Kauko's recent scare vanished, and he stepped to his companion's side. Jonas Niemi was gritting his teeth, his sturdy frame leaning back at a sharp angle The lieutenant bent lower and his left hand groped for added leverage on the surface of the sidewalk. Both men's faces were strained.

"Pull! When do we start?" the lieutenant grunted.

"Pull! Straighten out the lieutenant's finger," a man urged Jonas.

"Pull it out, root and all, and stick it in your pocket," someone laughed.

"Is this a fight? Is that a lieutenant and a private with their claws hooked? Hurray for the officers!" yelped a second lieutenant who had arrived on the scene.

Then Jonas Niemi's finger straightened with a jerk. The lieutenant leaped to keep his balance, but his garrison cap flew from his head.

"Do you believe, Lauri, that my fingers are made of steel?" he said to his walking companion.

The captain lighted a cigarette and said:

"The soldier let you win just to please you. Put your cap on the right way."

"Did you do that, private? Let's try again," said the lieutenant, turning his cap.

"No, lieutenant sir. If that's not an order, then I refuse," said Jonas Niemi.

"It isn't," said the captain. "What do you do in civilian life?"

"I'm a farmer, captain, sir."

"Who wants to be next? I heard someone making dirty cracks."

The lieutenant stood swaying slightly, his middle finger sticking out like the tail of a lamb. He swept his arm around the entire circle of spectators.

"Nobody wants to try? Do you believe that this spindleshanks is the champion finger-wrestler of Rovaniemi?"

"Goddamned if you are!" said a big man, and stepped to the center of the growing ring of people. He wore a northern logger's outfit, and had an empty-looking pack dangling from his back. A huge wad of tobacco was tucked tightly into one corner of his mouth. "Can an ex-soldier have a go at it?"

"Gladly," said the lieutenant.

"Jouko, shouldn't we be going?" said the captain.

"Don't run away," grunted the civilian.

"I'm not in the habit of running," said the lieutenant. "Do you think I am?"

As he spoke, the civilian pulled his cap down over his ears. Then he put his boot alongside the lieutenant's. The men hooked fingers and the civilian said:

"You can get your horse to help if you like."

"Let's try without it. Are you ready?"

"Raring to go." The civilian's pipe jiggled in his teeth as he spoke.

The civilians in the ring of people exchanged mocking looks and shouted coarse encouragement to their companion. The soldiers gathered around backed the lieutenant with their cries. Even Jonas Niemi called out:

"Pull, lieutenant, pull as hard as you did just now!"

The civilian's backpack was nearly dragging the ground. He exhaled a stale smell of liquor along with the smoke from his pipe.

"Goddamnit!" he grunted from the corner of his mouth.

No more was said. The civilian's body began to straighten up. First he was drawn upright, then into a forward lean, and soon his finger straightened with a jerk.

"Goddamnit, the man has strong fingers," he said.

"Anyone want another try? I'm ready," said the lieutenant.

"No takers, at least not me, but I'll stand the drinks, if they're good enough for you," said the logger.

Two policemen came up and shoved their way through the circle of bystanders. The larger representative of authority spoke:

"What's this crowd of people here?"

"It's nothing. Just finger-wrestling."

"Break it up. You can't block traffic."

"Let's go," Kauko hissed to Jonas Niemi.

With that, they left the place, and the others too began to scatter. The civilian slapped the lieutenant on the shoulder and kept repeating:

"You've got talons like an osprey, talons like an osprey..."

✧ ✧ ✧

The setting sun cast a reddish glow over a pine grove at the edge of Rovaniemi. Kauko and Jonas Niemi had made their way from the restless streets to this refuge of nature. After the finger-wrestling, they had witnessed a couple of fights. First they had seen two migrants flailing away at each other. The police had taken them into custody. Then they saw fists flying in a gateway, where two civilians were battling a lieutenant and two soldiers. One of the soldiers used his fists to such good effect that the civilians had to take to their heels.

"This is like the Klondike during the *Gold Rush*," said Jonas Niemi.

"We're not having much luck," said Kauko.

"Let's look around a little more," said Jonas Niemi. "It's so quiet in these woods."

The partners were walking along a trail in the woods. From the center of town they could hear the chugging of a locomotive and the roar of vehicle engines. An occasional yell carried to their ears. There was still snow in the hollows. The cool of the approaching night and the fragrance of the fir trees made Kauko think of home. If I were a civilian, I would be a pikeman sitting on the bank of a float river. Auku is big enough to be there too. Poverty would no longer torment us. But I will be a civilian next spring. My period of service will be over. It will be good to talk about this last winter when life hung by a thread and we were at war in the wilderness of Kuhmo. Almost all the men from around home were there. A few, like Toivo Olkivaara, wound up on the Isthmus. Could Toivo be a civilian yet?

"I was just thinking that they're working the fields at home," said Jonas Niemi.

"I was thinking about the log drive. If I were in civilian clothes, I would be on the bank of some river with my younger brother."

"I wonder how my brother is doing with the tractor."

"You have such a big place that you really use machines to farm?" said Kauko.

"Thirty hectares. I'm worried about how they're getting along. I always drive the tractor."

"They'll manage all right. And next summer you'll be sitting in the driver's seat again."

"No, damn it. I have a feeling that I won't make it back from the service."

"Stop talking nonsense! What the devil can kill us now that we stayed alive through the war?" snapped Kauko.

"Something just tells me. I can't explain it myself. I've always had a serious bent, but ever since I left home, I've had this extra weight on my mind."

"It's because you're homesick. Just breathe in this pine smell deeply and you'll forget about the war. It makes me think of home and a float river. And we have to do our hitch in the service sometime anyway."

"That's true, but we came as volunteers and shouldn't mind it so much," sighed Jonas Niemi.

"Things could be worse. We still live in a free country. When we turn in this gear, we can go where we please," said Kauko. "Would you look at those buddies. They're feeling no pain."

Two men came down the path toward them. Kauko could see at first glance that they were lumberjacks. They were walking abreast and were now only about four meters away. One of them was singing at the top of his lungs.

In the Hennala barracks they were playing a song.
Over and over to comfort their woes
lifelong prisoners were playing the song...

Kauko and Jonas Niemi stepped off the path. The men's expression showed that they were in no mood to brook opposition. When they reached the spot where Kauko and Niemi were standing, the men stopped. Sheath knives hung at their sides. Suddenly the singer shouted:

"Attention!"

Kauko started. Jonas Niemi's neck twitched.

"Didn't you hear me, soldiers? Attention! Goddamn.."

"We do that for officers," said Kauko with a smile.

"Do you think I'm not an officer, blubberface?"

The man was shouting almost directly into Kauko's face. Then the other civilian bellowed:

"This buddy of mine is a top sergeant. Hands at your sides!"

Kauko glanced sideways at Jonas Niemi and saw that his lips

were tightly compressed.

"We don't knuckle down to everyone," said Jonas.

"I don't know what kind of big-shot civilians you were, but I'm giving the orders now," said the singer. "Hit the ground!"

"Cut it out," said Kauko. "We're no big shots. I'm a pulp cutter and my buddy is a farmer."

"Don't try to weasel out of it. A blubberpuss like you couldn't cut down one spruce tree. Your buddy looks like the minister in my home parish. Just as big and with the start of a fat belly."

"Do what he tells you to, buddies. This partner of mine killed ten Russians single-handed near Salla this winter. I'm not bragging, but I got two stripes myself," said the singer's companion.

"Was there a head between the stripes, or which shoulder were they on?"

"I won't put up with a couple of snots like you making fun of my orders. We put holes in bigger bags of garbage than you at Salla. Just pull your chin back..."

The singer grabbed Kauko's nose between his fingers and doubled up his fist. Kauko jerked his head back and got his nose loose. He did not notice his hat fly off. Flecks of red danced before his eyes. He seized the man by the shoulders and hurled him back with the full force of his rage. The man tried to step backward, but failed, and landed so hard on his back that the heath resounded. Kauko hissed through his teeth:

"I'm sure as hell not going to let a crud like you massage my nose."

"You Korvatunturi devil, you're a dead man now."

The man sprang to his feet and his right hand flashed to his left hip. Kauko's every limb was like a nerveless spring. He leaped at the man. He found the knife sheath, tore it loose, and flung it far off into the woods, knife and all. Again he hurled the man away from him. This time the man had no chance to backpedal, but was thrown into a nearby pine tree. His head slammed into the trunk, and he slid to the foot of the tree as limp as a mass of dough. Blood dribbled from his mouth.

"Now someone's going to die! Goddamn, you can't do that to my buddy..."

The other man drew his knife and lunged at Kauko with the weapon held high over his head.

"Not quite yet...Here's for a starter."

Jonas Niemi's long arm swung and his clenched fist caught the man on the jaw. Kauko heard a nasty, crunching sound. He had never believed that the blow of a fist could lift a man off his feet, but now he saw the man fly some three meters to one side and land on his face. The knife went spinning over the moss, its blade reflecting the last rays of the sun.

"Has everyone gone crazy now?" said Jonas Niemi.

"Didn't they get enough of fighting last winter?" Kauko said in wonder.

"Damn, everyone from officers to civilians wants to fight," said Jonas Niemi.

"Are they dead? The one you hit isn't moving at all," said Kauko. "What should we do now?"

"Maybe we should turn tail and run," said Jonas Niemi.

"That's probably best. Let's go."

"Get your hat," said Niemi to Kauko, who had already started running.

Kauko returned and picked up his hat from the moss. The man at the foot of the pine tree made a gurgling sound, groped with one hand, and turned over on his side. Kauko gulped and said:

"There'll be the devil to pay if we get caught."

"Let's go. We'll cut through the woods," said Jonas.

They trotted off through the pine grove and soon reached a graveyard of junked vehicles. They could see a barracks off among the trees. Jonas Niemi said:

"Now we walk as if we were coming from church. There's a bunch of card players."

Kauko followed Jonas's pointing finger. A ring of men was seated there. He thought of the pine grove in the church village at home. He had sat in on a game there a couple of years ago. Now the event seemed insipid. He turned to Jonas:

"Are you a boxer too?"

"I've done a little. Last year I was the club junior champion."

"But you never talked about it."

"It's no big deal...You should wipe your nose."

Kauko took out his handkerchief. When he blew into one of its folds, spots of blood appeared.

"Let's not tell anyone we were here," said Jonas.

"No. We'll head straight for camp and avoid everyone...even

women," said Kauko.

"We've had enough brawling for one night."

✧ ✧ ✧

Kauko and Jonas turned in their passes to the man on duty. The company's men were arriving constantly, but only a few were lolling on the floor on their blankets. When the two of them went over to their packs, they saw Jalo Kieppi lying near the wall with his hands under his head. They could see that his eyes were open. Kauko began to spread out his blanket near his wry companion and said with a laugh:

"Let me smell your fingers."

"Go to hell!"

"Well is that any way to talk to a buddy?" said Kauko.

"I'm not in the mood for jokes."

"Are you all worn out from doing it?" Kauko asked.

"Just hit the hay and leave me alone."

Jalo Kieppi sat up and glared at Kauko as if he were an enemy. He even glowered at Jonas Niemi. Then he sat staring at the floor, scratching the back of his head furiously from time to time.

"Rovaniemi seems to be a strange place," said Jonas. "Nothing here but angry people. Now we've even lost our buddy, Kauko."

Jonas plopped down on his cloak as he was speaking and sighed heavily. Then he took a box of candy from his pocket and said:

"Sweeten up your mouth and temper with this, Jalo."

"Nothing will melt in my mouth now. I don't want any."

"Well at least they'll melt in Kauko's mouth. Have some."

Kauko lay down too and sucked on the candy Jonas had handed him. Men of the company kept streaming into the room, which was growing only slightly dark. A few had obviously been drinking, and the man on duty had to order them to stop making noise. Jalo Kieppi just sat there, resting his chin in his palms and giving an angry grunt now and then.

Not having been in a real room for a long time, Kauko found it home-like to lie there. The heat was even, and although there was only his coat to cushion the floor, there were at least no stubs and roots poking into his back. Jalo Kieppi's strange behavior was slightly disturbing and every time he thought of the loggers left in the woods, shivers ran down his spine. What if they died? Or someone might rob them, and then he and Jonas would be in trouble. How could they prove who had started the fight?

"Are you asleep, Kauko?"

"Not yet."

"Who broke your nose?"

Kauko felt his nose.

"What do you care about my nose."

"Don't be sore at me. I'm having a hard time."

"Do you think I'm having fun?" mumbled Kauko.

"Did someone punch you in the snoot?"

"I'm not going to start explaining."

Jalo Kieppi went on staring at the floor. Finally he turned to Kauko and said:

"She made such a fool of me."

Kauko knew that Jalo was expecting him to be curious, but he said nothing. He and Jonas were not to blame.

"I went to the girl Saima's house. I'd been there before, the last time before I went into the army. I knocked on the door. I could hear a woman's voice inside so I pressed down on the handle. The door wasn't locked. Oh, goddamn, why didn't I have a knife with me."

Jalo Kieppi opened his collar button, then he sighed.

"Give me a piece of that candy now, Jonas."

"It wasn't good enough for you earlier. But I don't hold a grudge."

"You can hear how I made out too."

Jalo Kieppi's hand shook when he put a piece of candy into his mouth.

"I stood there in the doorway. She let out a screech and pulled the covers up over her. I had time to see that she was bare naked. A man jumped up from the bed. He had only an undershirt on. He yelled out: "Get the hell out of here, soldier."

"So early, and they were in bed already?" said Jonas Niemi.

"What did you say then?" asked Kauko.

"I gaped at them for a minute. Goddamn, but I was boiling mad. Then I gave a big laugh and said: 'What an awful accident. You spilled your churn.' He started toward me. I said: 'Don't come too close or I'll grab your tail and pull it out by the roots.' He started looking for his pants. Then I saw a lieutenant's coat hanging on the back of a chair. The covers over Saima were shaking. I didn't know if I should laugh or cry. I said to the lieutenant, 'Don't put your pants on for nothing. Take your plunger to bed and go back to your churning.' Then I shut the door."

For a long time the companions listened to the din made by the returning men. Finally Jalo Kieppi lay down. Kauko said:

"It's not worth spoiling a night over a woman like that."

"I don't think so either. It's just that Saima and I used to talk about stringing our bread on the same pole. We even babbled about having little kids. You haven't known anything like this yet."

Kauko thought of Elma. She would never do anything like that. When would the leaves start coming through? Elma was so nice to talk to, he thought. We should start making plans. We might even talk to the minister early in the spring. Many men have married even younger than I. Elma and I could even live rent-free at Olkivaara for a few years while I look around for a place. That abandoned farm can't cost so much that I couldn't afford it. I'm sure Kosti will advise me about the buildings to put up. He could even draw the plans...

"Our night was a flop too," said Kauko finally.

He peered over at Jonas Niemi, who was lying on the other side of Jalo, and said:

"Shall we tell Jalo what a rotten night we had?"

"Yes, but let's keep it among the three of us."

The rays of the sun were already shining from the Lapland wilderness to the northeast when the three comrades ended their hushed conversation. Already half asleep, Kauko said:

"I never would have believed Jonas could lie as quickly as he did when he gave a false name to that finger-wrestler."

"And the lieutenant would have spent a long time leafing through papers before finding the number of the company I was ready to give him."

"Lucky the captain took a hand in the matter," said Kauko.

2

The cows were late in coming home. It was almost midnight before Maija had finished milking them and running the milk through the separator. Liisu and Väinö were already asleep and Maija was opening her own bed when Aili entered the house.

"I wonder that you didn't spend the night," said Maija.

"Elma sort of wanted me to, but I thought you would be waiting up for nothing then."

"There would have been work to do. Does it look good to leave the yard all spring without cleaning?"

"It has been cleaned. Is there butter on the shelf? I could do with a little snack," said Aili.

"I tried to do some churning with Väinö and Liisu, but it doesn't come to much without help. Has Toivo showed up yet?"

"Not yet. Mari isn't feeling well again...Where's the butter dish?"

"Don't you know where things are? So she's not well. Is her heart acting up again?"

"That's what she was complaining about. And she's getting so muddled."

"It's no wonder when she's tried for years to run the house in such ill health."

"She no longer has to. She should let Elma and Taimi do the work and take it easy herself...On the way back I passed by the swamp. You should see the cloudberry blossoms. It was all white with them."

"With the right weather, we'll have a good year for berries. We could really use them to buy things during the summer. We seem to be running out of everything."

Aili ate a piece of bread and butter and picked bones from a salt fish to go along with it. Maija undressed and lay down. Where is Kauko, she wondered. Mari's poor health is really a problem. She would have to go and talk to her tomorrow. To Aili she said:

"The first logs of the float have reached the river mouth. I heard the log-drivers yelling out there this evening."

"I saw the side of the float in back of that point. The winch boat was lying alongside the boom," said Aili.

"Is Auku with the lead group or is he with the tail crew?"

"He could just as well be a pikeman along the river, just lying there and watching the current carry the logs by," Aili said to her mother.

"You come to bed now too so you'll be able to get up in the morning."

"Don't give me that same nonsense every night. Change your tune already."

"Is that a nice way to talk to your mother?"

"I didn't mean to be nasty, but I get tired of the same old song."

"Everything is so nice at home. A person understands that only when she's been at the mercy of the world. You were spared that."

Aili looked at her mother. Her words were almost tearful again. What use was there in crying?

"It hasn't been all fun and games here either. Standing watch in that rickety windmill and doing the work at home in between times. Going without sleep a lot. And cold as the devil, but crying didn't help."

"That's how it was but it's over now. Let's be satisfied that we can live at home. Even Kauko came through the war unscathed."

"The lake is so calm now. Only the fish breaking the surface."

Aili began to undress. Flies buzzed in the window. She opened the louver board.

"Get the heck out of there with your buzzing. Shoo...all of you."

When the flies were driven out, Aili stood by the window for awhile.

"The winchmen seem to be singing a catch."

"You can hear it all the way from there," said her mother.

✧ ✧ ✧

Not within the memory of man had so few logs been floated down the Ii River as in the spring of 1940. That winter, the best loggers had been fulfilling a contract on the country's eastern border. Most of the men from the region had been in the forests of Suomussalmi, Raate, and Kuhmo, and many of them did not return. The names of places where people had once eaten pine-bark bread were now known throughout Finland and even in the world at large. Only old men and spavined nags had been left to drag scattered handfuls of logs to the banks of streams. In addition there were assorted piles left over from the previous winter and these too floated in the Ii River, dryer and blacker than the rest.

"Now boys, we'll take the end of the tow rope to that spruce on the Sammalsuo shore."

Nestor Malinen stood in the stern of a large log drivers' boat steering it with a big oar. The prow of the boat leaped forward, propelled by a team of oarsmen. One of them looked toward the middle of the boat and said:

"What does the man of the house say to that?"

The young man resting a foot on the winch handle looked ahead, drew smoke in through a cigarette holder, and said:

"It's not the first time a tow rope has been tied around its trunk."

"So that's how Auku feels about it," laughed Nestor.

The sun had risen above the treetops, but still the lake remained calm. Somewhere from the direction of Lapinhieta came the cry of a loon.

"That damned squawker is going to call down a rain," said Nestor.

The boat neared the shore. Auku picked up the rope and made ready to wrap it around the spruce tree.

"That was good rowing," Nestor said.

Months had passed since Auku had left for the log float at the headwaters of the Ii River. It felt good to step on the rocky shore of home after such a long time. Crows had taken wing before they landed, and were now perched on the roofs of the sauna and barn. Auku tied the rope in a logger's slipknot. Then he picked at his trouser buttons and said:

"At least they seem to have caught some fish. The crows are keeping a sharp eye out."

"That's right. They seem to be sitting there and planning to feast on the guts...Now if all of us take a leak here we won't have to spill it into the lake."

Nestor and the others followed Auku's example. One of the oarsmen said:

"The boy has a nice home. The grass is already poking up through the withered hay."

"It's a good place to eat our bread if we don't have to get it from others," said Auku.

"You won't have to do that for long. These boys have a monstrous good start for a rye field. It started out with a few grainheads, and now they'll be getting enough to thresh. How is the winter rye coming along, Auku?"

"I haven't checked. When I left, it was still under the snow. But at least the reindeer didn't get at it last fall."

The men got back into the boat and rowed to the containing boom of the log raft. Auku wound the tow rope through the ring of the boom. The men sat opposite each other at the handles of the winch and began to turn it. There was the same type of handle on either side of the winch. The clank of the stopper when it dropped into place at each gear tooth carried far across the calm lake. The raft was also moving naturally with the current. The tow rope between the winch and the shore kept rising from the water, breaking the surface with a straight line of bubbles each time it rose.

"Shouldn't we yodel a song?" said Nestor.

"If you say so, chief," said one of the rowers.

"I mean, shouldn't we have a little wake-up concert?"

"It's not up to us," said Auku. "Just sing out."

"Well, yaah, I'll start it out. This is the way we used to sound off when we were turning a winch handle."

Home came Pappa in the evening, home he came and home he came
Banged his dong upon the table, Mamma on her back in bed,
On her back, on her back, Mamma on her back in bed,
asked what all the racket was...

Life began stirring around the shores of the calm lake. Cowbells began to clank in the barns, and the rooster at Naavala began to crow as if he were afraid he had overslept. A duck flew whirring over the lake, and dogs began barking at a couple of houses.

The third of the older men in the boat was from somewhere in the south. He seldom spoke and now he had not joined in the song. While the woods on shore still resounded with its power, he asked:

"Does that Malinen have a screw loose in his head?"

"Well, I'll be god...so what do you think is the matter?"

Nestor's cry came straight from the heart. His eyes bored into those of his sullen companion like the tines of a pitchfork.

"Singing like that. And all that stupid running around in the war."

"Just what the hell do you mean? The cantor picks his own hymns. And I won't stand for any cracks about the war."

"Hadn't you had enough of mucking around in the woods for poor wages? The bosses almost made you kiss their asses. And then to charge in and ask to fight on their side. They say you were a real cock-of-the-walk there too. Goddamnit!" The man spat.

Although the spit broke the surface of the water far off to the side, it had spewed from his mouth with such force that Nestor, who sat opposite him turning the handle, had to wipe some droplets from his face. Then he said:

"Do you think you could stop turning a winch if you changed masters? You and I have to keep on working like this, that's all there's to it. And I tell you, if a man isn't satisfied with the wages they've been paying the last few years, I don't know what to make of it. And if that's all you have to say, then just keep your mouth shut."

The man grunted and went on turning the handle. Nestor's eyes remained fixed on him. He's a loudmouth, but let it go, the man thought.

"And if you don't like this business, I for one am not forcing you to do it. And isn't there a hole in that border big enough for you to slip through?"

"I hear your boy didn't stay there," said the man.

"No, he didn't. Why don't you go and try it."

From then on, the only sound was the clunk of the stopper in the gear. A small gust of wind caught the surface of the open lake and moved toward the north shore.

"A south wind is rising," said Nestor.

"It looks that way," said Auku.

"Shouldn't we sing that song again, since my buddy seems to like it so much?" said Nestor.

Auku lighted a cigarette and joined in the song with Nestor and the other men. Nestor seemed to be working off his anger in the force he put into the singing. The winch boat was nearing the Sammalsuo shore. Nestor was sitting with his back to the spruce, which drew slower nearer with each pull on the winch. Auku looked at the walls of his home, which glowed red in the morning sun. The tow rope was so taut and so high out of the water that a high-wire performer could have run to shore along it.

The stern of the boat was close to the landing rock. The last refrains of the song were echoing across the lake when Auku saw the window of the house open. He stopped singing and instinctively snatched the cigarette from his mouth, cupping it in his palm, but then he cut the motion short and put the cigarette squarely back into his mouth. Nestor could tell from his expression that something had startled Auku. He too stopped singing and looked back over his shoulder. Maija Sammalsuo's head and shoulders had appeared in the open window. At the same time Auku was aware of smoke rising from her pipe.

"Is that Nestor singing those ugly songs?" came a voice from the window.

"Is that Maija there? You shouldn't have listened. Anyway, the song was not all that bad."

"The words were awful. And with a half-grown boy listening besides," scolded Maija.

"Yaah, but there was nothing wrong with the music. It's a pretty tune."

Maija went on looking out of the window. Auku wondered if he should toss his cigarette away. But his mother had seen it anyway, and the men would laugh at him if he did.

Soon Maija appeared on shore. She was fully dressed already. She walked over the rocks onto which the boat was just gliding. Nestor rose from the winching seat, straightened his back, and said:

"Greetings from the grindstone seat."

"Thanks. Even the years don't make you any wiser," said Maija.

"Everybody's down on me," laughed Nestor. "My partner was just giving me a hard time and now my neighbor starts right in."

"I heard the most awful noise in my sleep and got up to look out the window. And there was Nestor, sounding off again."

Auku leaped ashore, cigarette in his mouth, and walked over to free the tow rope. Maija looked at her son and swallowed, but said nothing. Then she turned to Nestor and said:

"I have to give you coffee even if I didn't like the song. Come in, all of you. The pot will soon be boiling."

"Listen men, to what a good woman this neighbor of ours is. Did you really say coffee? It's not easy to come by these days."

"I happen to have a little put away," said Maija.

As the men ascended the shore, Nestor said:

"Where is Kauko lately?"

"We don't know. A lot of lines in his last letter were blacked out. But I think he's somewhere in the north."

"Everything's so secret nowadays. Is it only a little after three?"

When the others had gone in, Auku walked over to a thicket and stood looking at the rye field. His recent tension vanished. Kauko and I planted that last fall, he mused. I have to start hoeing a new clearing as soon as the log drive is over. Since Kauko won't be here this summer.

When Auku went in, he said:

"That's a monster rye field out there, Nestor."

"We'll have to look at it as soon as we have coffee."

One of the men extended a pack of cigarettes to Auku and said:

"Have one of mine this time."

Auku looked at his mother, but took the cigarette. As he lighted it, she said:

"Don't you think you look like a man unless you're smoking?"

Auku looked out the window at the lake and said:

"The raft is moving along all by itself."

3

Late at night, a lieutenant with brass buttons on his uniform stepped from an army vehicle that had driven from Oulu to the church-village store. A group of men there stared at him for some time, and then a slightly built civilian broke off from the others, walked over to the newcomer, and held out his hand.

"Hello, hello. So they let you out now?"

"Hello and greetings from the woods of Kuhmo. My pass is in my pocket."

"It's good that they finally let you go."

"They did. What have you been up to?"

"I just came off a log drive. I should start hiking home."

Simo Mutka's face wore a cheerful look. The visored cap and woolen shirt he wore looked strange to Kosti Mäkinen. Mutka's face was burned almost black and his hands were chapped.

"Do you know if I can hire a car here?"

"They're probably hard to get, but let's ask the storekeeper's son. I'll go wake him up right now."

Before Kosti Mäkinen could say a word, Mutka went tripping up to a building that seemed to be silent. Soon he returned and said:

"We have to see that our boss gets a ride. Here he comes now. I left him pulling on his pants."

None of the men with Simo Mutka were well known to Kosti Mäkinen, although he remembered having seen a few of them. Simo Mutka stood before Kosti and cocked his head to look up at his commander of the previous winter. Then he drew a pack of cigarettes from his pocket and said with a laugh:

"Here's a welcome-to-civilian-life cigarette."

"Thanks. Can a smoker still get cigarettes here?"

"Loggers get them. Others grumble a little bit about shortages."

"Have you already got the feel of civilian life?" asked Kosti.

"Yaah, I worked peeling pulp early in the spring and then went on the log drive."

"How...I mean, how did your family do when they were evacuated?"

"They were fine. It couldn't have turned out better."

Simo Mutka nearly turned his back to Kosti. He drew a deep breath. Looking up into the night sky, he said:

"Summer seems to be going by. It's just about time to start gathering twigs...I delivered your package as soon as I got to the church village."

"Irja wrote me about it. Thanks for your trouble."

"No need to thank me. I just learned this summer that it feels good to be alive. I even sat in jail once...I told you about that. But coming back from the war was even better than getting out of jail."

"I'm walking on air myself. I'll see my family again."

Simo Mutka turned and looked directly at Kosti. Then he said:

"I couldn't say it just now, but this was my best homecoming because Lassi — you remember the crippled boy — can get around a little on his own. When I left for the log drive, he could walk if he held on to something."

Although Simo Mutka's voice shook, he managed to finish what he was saying without stopping. His eyes were red as he sucked on his cigarette. His chapped and bearded face quivered.

"Well that is good news...I mean, I'm happy about it too."

"You see, Lassi got this fever and his mother took him to the hospital. A young doctor took him on as a special patient. He gave him shots and massaged and kneaded his legs."

One of the men in the group Mutka had parted from came over and asked:

"Are you coming or not, Simo? We won't wait around for long."

"I'm not going. You go ahead. I'm too tired."

"If you change your mind, we'll be on Koninhauta Hill."

The group of men moved off into the shelter of the outbuildings. One of them laughed and another cursed. Soon they were lost from sight. Simo said:

"They're going to play cards. They were asking me just before you came if I would sit in on a few hands. They say Ahma-Juuso is set up in the woods nearby. He's bound to have a good supply of booze. But I'm not going. Once you're on your way, I'll be trudging off for home. We'll see how well Lassi can walk."

A large number of soldiers were billeted in the village and entire units were stationed in the vicinity. Young men serving their compulsory time in the army walked the streets and occasionally some wandered into the yard of the store. A broad grin spread over Simo Mutka's face as he said:

"Isn't an officer supposed to return a salute?"

Kosti whirled to one side, where three soldiers had snapped sharply to attention. He touched his hand to his cap and said:

"Evening boys. My mind was so full of civilian thoughts that I didn't notice. How do you like this village?"

"Fine, lieutenant, sir."

At that moment the driver came out of the door. He had gotten to know the Sääskilampi son-in-law the previous autumn, and now he said:

"Good evening and welcome to the home parish."

"Greetings from Löytövaara. I just can't wait until tomorrow to get home."

"I guess we can get you to Vaarakylä," said the driver.

An automobile was soon backing out of its garage. Kosti Mäkinen clasped Simo Mutka's hand and said:

"We'll see you. It was an autumn night when we left the Guard Armory for Oulu."

"We'll see you. And the right time for a man to see his family again is on a summer night like this. I'll be seeing mine too."

✧ ✧ ✧

A mean and elusive fly had been annoying Irja for the whole evening. She rose from her bed a couple of times and tried to catch it, but it flew back and forth between the room's two windows as if mocking her efforts. Occasionally it alighted on the wallpaper and then flew on to the children's faces or bare feet. Irja could have crushed it as it bounced against the window panes, but she tried to pick it up gently and flick it outside. The fly would always find some hiding place and stay there until Irja went back to bed.

She was just falling asleep when she again felt the tickling on her check. She slapped at her face and heard the taunting buzz. She badly wanted to sleep — she had washed and ironed throughout the whole hot day and the baby had whimpered for a long time before falling asleep. Irja sat up with a jerk, stepped onto the floor, and said:

"It's your own fault, fly..."

Her tormenter was butting its head into a window pane. Irja went to the window and swept her hand across it, but when she closed the hand with a snap, she did not feel the expected crunch.

"Did it get away again? Now where will it start to buzz?"

Irja turned to the other window. When she reached it her hand flew to her breast and her voice rang out in the still room.

"My God, can I believe it!"

An automobile had stopped in the yard. It was dark enough

at midnight so that her eyes could not make out the interior of the car, but a premonition told her who it was. Her knees trembled, and she seized the window sill. As in a dream she saw the dog come out of its house and leap on its hind legs at the end of its chain. It's joyful whine could be heard in the house.

"Kosti...It's Kosti."

An army cap emerged from the car, followed by a pair of broad shoulders crossed by the diagonal strap of a Sam Browne belt. Then a tall, slim body stood erect. The automobile roared and made a sharp turn around the yard. Suitcase in hand, the man stood in the middle of the yard and looked all around it. Then he turned his eyes toward the window.

Irja drew the curtain aside, waved a hand, and went to the door. She ran across the porch, pushed the outside door open, and rushed toward her husband.

"Kosti, you've come!"

"I'm home, Irja."

Irja pressed her cheek into her husband's chest. She felt a heavy hand crushing her shoulders. The other hand was stroking her hair slowly and caressingly from the top of her head down her neck. The dog pawed at the grass with his front feet, its belly almost scraping the ground. Then it crawled into its house, and watched the man and woman standing face to face.

"You're cold," said Kosti.

"No, I'm warm. I feel so good. That's why I'm trembling."

"Let's go and see the children. I'll carry you. The grass is all wet."

"No don't. I didn't even say, 'Welcome home.'"

"Words don't mean much now. I'll set you down on the railing. Look, you can see my tracks on the wood."

The porch was quite dark at night. Kosti had to feel his way along with his feet until he followed his wife into the bedroom. Without even taking off his cap, he bent over the two brothers asleep in the same bed, and gazed for a long time at the two brown faces side by side. Then he touched both boys' foreheads carefully one after the other. He could feel his wife's side against his own.

"Those rascals have really grown," he said at last.

"Come and see what's sleeping in this basket."

Kosti went over to a basket decorated with lace that lay across two chairs. His wife carefully drew aside its lacy covering.

"Why, she's a big girl already. Oh my, her mouth is all puckered up. Does she have a very bad temper?" Kosti said softly, with a laugh.

"What kind of temper do you think you have? She looks and acts just like you."

"As long as she doesn't grow up to be as big as I am."

When they had looked at the children for a long time, Kosti stood up. He took hold of Irja's hair where it fell down to her shoulders, tilted her head back slightly, and said:

"Now let me look at you."

"Do I look very much like an old married woman?"

"No, you look as if you had just come of age."

"No mother of three big lunks can look like a girl. Don't take your hat off yet. I've never seen you in uniform."

"No you haven't. We had to leave in such a hurry last fall. Well, how do I look?"

"Just too handsome. Is lieutenant a very high rank?"

"Simo Mutka used to call me the great warlord."

"You must be pretty important then. When Mutka brought that package here, he praised you to the sky. I actually was afraid of you when people talked like that."

"And now you're not?" said Kosti, drawing his wife nearer.

"Not when you talk so sweetly about your children."

Kosti Mäkinen took off his army jacket, hung his hat on a peg, and sat down near his daughter. The baby lay sleeping, small beads of sweat on her upper lip. He turned and said with a laugh:

"You did win out."

At first, Irja looked askance at her husband and then she too laughed.

"So I did. I turned the head of a one-time prizefighter — or how would you put it?"

"You have a baby that big, but the Kuikkala school is still not finished. Did you remember what I said that autumn night?"

"I remembered it every evening and even during the day. Even when I missed you and was afraid for you while we were evacuated, I could still feel your arm holding me."

Suddenly Irja burst into tears. She knelt beside Kosti and

pressed her face into his knees. Her shoulders shook with sobs. Kosti Mäkinen felt his cheek twitch and he made no effort to check the tears that poured from his eyes. For a long time, neither of them said a word. Although Irja's emotional outburst had spent itself by now, she did not feel like rising. Kosti's heavy hand felt warm on her shoulder. Finally she struggled up and said:

"What a stupid wife! I don't even feed my husband."

"If you do it this minute, I'll forgive you."

"I'll try. What will the master builder have to eat?"

"Just a second. My mouth is watering."

Squinting one eye, Kosti Mäkinen looked at his wife and said:

"Fresh-baked barley bread and butter from your churn, buttermilk, sun-cured reindeer meat, and...that's the end of my culinary requests."

"Bread you get, but rye, not barley. All the rest can be had."

"Don't you remember? I mean, y'see, I'm a Tampere boy, brought up on fresh-baked barley bread."

Irja was soon back in the room with a bread basket and butter dish in her hands.

"Well, you're not in Tampere now, and you can learn to live with the local rye. I'll fix up the food in the bedroom so that father can sleep in peace."

"How is your father?" asked Kosti thoughtfully.

"He gets muddled sometimes. The evacuation had a bad effect on his health."

✧ ✧ ✧

The mistress of Sääskilampi had gone out with the hired girl to do the milking while Irja stayed in the kitchen to make breakfast. Kosti slept so soundly that he did not know when his wife rose from beside him on the bed.

Irja tried to move without making a sound. The sun grew stronger outside. Irja paused from time to time in her morning chores to open the bedroom door a crack and peep in. The children slept without stirring. Kosti lay snoring away next to the wall on the broad, home-made bed. A smile played on Irja's lips as she looked at her husband's sun-browned face. That soldier had a real crop of long, black stubble. Irja closed the door and went back to the kitchen, where she walked straight to the mirror.

"I knew it. A kitten's been scratching my face."

Irja stroked her cheeks for a minute, then she pulled down the neck of her dress and rubbed the upper part of her breasts. She smiled happily.

"Irja! Are you there?"

"What is it, father?"

Irja lifted the neck of her dress closer to her chin than usual and went through the door into the bedroom.

"What is it, father?"

"Was it cold last night?"

"No. It's midsummer now."

"Yaah, are the log drivers heading for Kijanta?"

"Log drivers don't work during the summer. Shall I bring you some coffee, father?"

"I heard some men talking last night. Were they reindeer men?"

Tears came to Irja's eyes and she swallowed a few times.

"Father, Kosti came home...from the army."

"What Kosti? What about Bert?"

"Kosti, my husband. Ilmari and Pentti and Tuulikki's father."

Ivar Sääskilampi rose from the bed. He walked almost as he had two years ago. He looked at his daughter and said:

"He wasn't angry then...Has he left already?"

"He's still sleeping. And he wasn't angry."

"He's not going to take the children away, is he? Don't give him the boys or Tuulikki."

"Kosti came to be with us and the children."

"That's good. I'm going to nap a little longer."

Irja closed the door and went back into the kitchen. The milk gruel was boiling over onto the stove and sending fumes into the room. Irja opened a window. Birds were singing outside. A neighbor who had been out checking his nets was sculling toward the shore. The hills of the neighboring parish could be seen far off through the misty air. It was her mother's home parish. It was good for people to have a home, a family, relatives, a region and a country of their own to live in, thought Irja. Her father's illness and her husband's return kept her thoughts shuttling back and forth between tears and laughter.

✧ ✧ ✧

Kosti is the boys' father. Tuulikki is sprung from his loins too. Tuulikki...Tuulikki looks just like her father. Irja is my dear daughter. She takes good care of this old bull...How old is our farm bull now? Is it ten years ago that it was a calf? No, it must be only a couple of years.

Ivar Sääskilampi rolled over in his bed and lighted his pipe. His thoughts continued to hop around. *That Hilkka's boy is handsome and proud...His father wasn't an ordinary logger. Some migrant log-sorter seduced Hilkka.*

"And what about that tall, black-haired bum. He didn't look like any hunchback either when he came out of Hilkka's window."

The bedroom door opened. Irja looked in and said:

"Did you say something, father?"

"Nothing important. Just lighting my pipe."

"You won't drop any burning ash onto the bed?"

"I know how to handle a pipe."

Irja closed the door and left.

Why didn't I stop in to visit Hilkka? She might have had a picture of the boy at home. I could have seen what he looked like. Did the woman there call him Eino? Hilkka must have had an enlarged army snapshot on the wall. We have one of Bert in the attic bedroom. It would have showed if the boy looks like me or that black-haired bum. But who knows if he belongs to either of us. There were many log sorters at the mouth of the Ii River in those days.

Hilkka has grown older too. She's still erect, but her face has changed. I saw her a couple of times on the road. It was good that I wore that cap with the big ear flaps. Hilkka didn't guess that a man she knew was passing by.

"Why didn't I visit her after all? This misery would be over then."

He spoke in a whisper and looked at the door. There was no sign of Irja. Dishes clattered in the kitchen.

I would have gone there, but we had to leave so suddenly. They told us in the morning we would get on a bus that evening.

It was because of the rush. Who would go and visit a neighbor at a time like that?

Eino...Do I have two sons, Bert and Eino? I'm getting so sleepy now. Petti keeps this room so hot, but now it's freezing cold. That's an icy winter sky out there...Strange that there's no frost on the window.

✧ ✧ ✧

Irja took the kettle off the flame. At that moment, she heard the sound of uncontrolled weeping from the bedroom. There was a patter of feet and the bedroom door burst open. Irja almost dropped the kettle.

"Mother, mother!" yelled Ilmari through his tears.

"What's the matter? A big man bawling like that."

"Waah...there's an ugly hobo in mommy's bed," wailed Pentti.

The boys dashed over to their mother's skirts. Irja could not remember ever having laughed so hard.

"Now stop it boys. Father has come home."

Just then Kosti came stooping through the door, his eyes still puffy with sleep. He saw the quivering shoulders of the boys who were pushing their faces into their mother's skirts and Irja's whole body shaking with laughter.

"Look, boys, the hobo came into the kitchen."

"Why are you calling me that?" laughed Kosti.

"The boys were afraid some hobo was in their mother's bed."

Kosti leaned over and looked into the mirror. Then he said:

"It's no wonder they were afraid. But anyway come over here. Men mustn't be scared over nothing. Father has come home."

For a long time the boys looked from the shelter of their mother's skirts at the man sitting by the table. Irja Mäkinen kept assuring them that it really was their father.

"Come here to father's knee, Pentti. Don't you remember seeing a man who looks like this?"

"I remember...father. We have a picture too."

"Well then...! You come too, Ilmari, onto the other knee. Pentti is already sitting here."

Finally Ilmari too climbed onto his father's knee. Both boys laughed as he jiggled them up and down. Cowbells clanked from the direction of the barn as the servant drove the animals down the lane to the pasture. Then the sound of harsh coughing came from the bedroom, followed by the words:

"Who's bothering the boys in there?"

The boys slid down from their father's knee and raced to the door of their grandparents' bedroom. They were already shouting as they opened it:

"Grandpa! Father came back from the war!"

"Did he? Pentti, give me that package of tobacco from the table."

Kosti looked at his wife, who returned the look and glanced toward the room where they could hear the boys chattering with their grandfather. Irja nodded and Kosti went to the door the boys had entered. He stood in the doorway. He had last stood there on a winter night.

The man lying on the bed first raised his head and then sat up slowly. Kosti Mäkinen was shocked by what he saw. Was this the same man he had last left sitting in a rocker?

"Morning, and greetings from the woods of Kuhmo."

"Morning..."

"Did the boys wake up their grandpa?" said Kosti.

"I've been awake many times. The boys always come to see me."

Kosti Mäkinen walked slowly across the room. He did not look directly at his wife's father, but gazed out at the yard. He could feel the man's eyes on him.

"I mean, it's a nice summer morning," said Kosti.

"A nice morning...yaah, it's summer out."

Kosti looked at Irja's father. The boys came over and hugged his legs.

"I've been a little sick. You seem to have come through the war in one piece."

"I was lucky."

"Do you know where Bert got shot?"

"We were in the same outfit. It happened to Bert in the last hours of the war."

Kosti knew that it was not the custom in the area to invite people to sit down, so he moved back a chair and sat facing the man, who was filling his pipe. Ivar's hands shook and pouches of flesh hung loose on his face, which looked as if it was scattered about in a skin that was too loose. His eyes were staring.

"Are you taking your family away right now?"

The question came suddenly in an angry tone of voice. Kosti hesitated.

"No one's going to...I mean, I thought I could help with the hay-making. Irja can at least help around the house."

"Don't take the boys and Tuulikki. You can make yourself right at home here. Irja is my own daughter and..."

Tears rolled down the old man's cheeks. Kosti had to turn away and look out the window. The air in the room was stale with tobacco smoke. Barn swallows twittered under the eaves.

"Have they buried Bert already? They haven't told me..."

"He's not going to be buried. The wound isn't even serious."

"I got Bert mixed up with Janne Latvasuo. They're both reindeer men."

The sound of women's voices could be heard in the kitchen. The door opened and Petti Sääskilampi entered the room. The boys darted over to meet her.

"Father! Our father came!" they shouted.

Kosti rose from the chair and clasped the woman's hand.

"Greetings."

"Welcome home. Thank God you came back safe and sound to your family."

Tears came to Petti Sääskilampi's eyes and she turned away to dry them. Ivar rose too and held out his hand.

"I haven't greeted this visitor yet. What's new? We came from Ii Hamina."

Kosti squeezed the proffered hand. The man's eyes stared unblinking. His wife turned and said:

"Don't you know Kosti, father? He's Irja's husband and the father of those little ones."

"Of course I know my son-in-law. How long ago did you come from Tampere?"

Irja spoke from the doorway:

"Everybody come and eat now. Can you come to the kitchen, father?"

"I can still eat a good breakfast."

4

"Go on now, you broomtails so you'll get to decent pasture sooner and I can get home," said Hilja Naavala as she drove the cows along the road. The lead cow, her bell clanking vigorously, chewed at the grass on the roadside. The others followed their leader's example. On either side of the road, cones fallen from pine trees lay on the gleaming white moss. The cattle, now let out to feed, were trying to gorge themselves on the grass growing between the gravel road and the ditches. Although Hilja was swinging a sizable birch rod in her hand, she contented herself with swishing away the horseflies and other insects attacking the animals.

"If you don't get moving, I'll whack you one."

The cows ambled along for awhile and then began to crop the grass again.

"Well go on now. Just keep moving."

Suddenly the bell cow raised her head and sniffed the air. The other animals followed suit. They all stood still, only their tails moving as they switched at the flies. Hilja looked in the same direction as they did. Her heart began to pound. A man in uniform was sitting by the ditch, puffing on a cigarette. In spite of her rapidly beating heart, Hilja said to the animals:

"What are you gawking at? Get moving."

A light whack of the rod on the bell cow's haunches gave emphasis to her words. The animals began to plod slowly along one side of the road. The man stood up and Hilja recognized him.

"What the devil made those cows stare like that? I wasn't going to twist their tails."

"Is it you, Toivo? Where did you come from?"

"From the church village, just now. From Lappeenranta before that."

One by one, the cows filed past the man, who had crossed to the other side of the ditch. Hilja swatted the last one with the stick and said:

"You can find your way to the pasture from here."

Hilja stood beside the road stirring the gravel with her stick and raising little puffs of dry sand. The man stepped back over the ditch and remained standing on the other side of the road.

Neither one of them looked at the other. Finally the man spoke:

"Looks like it will be a pretty hot day."

Hilja looked at the blue sky and said:

"It feels warm already and it's so early in the morning."

"I broke a sweat walking this king's highway."

"How far have you walked?" asked Hilja.

"I just told you. From the church village."

"You walked the whole way?"

"Well, I wouldn't have got out of a car halfway."

"Of course not. I was being stupid. I was a little scared."

"It wasn't stupid to be scared when a damn gorilla like me was sitting by the ditch."

"I didn't mean that. It was just a surprise to see you there so suddenly."

For awhile neither could find anything to say. Toivo Malinen dropped his cigarette to the gravel and ground it out. Finally he spoke:

"Well, it's over now, and things went badly for us, to tell the plain truth. No use to cover it up. But they didn't kill me, though they tried hard."

"You weren't even wounded?"

"There are no extra holes in my hide."

Hilja blushed. She was almost afraid of this somber-faced man. His expression was not new to her. The older Malinen boy never smiled. She raised her eyes and met his. They were different now; they were shy, and avoided her gaze. Toivo traced a triangle on the road with the side of his boot and said:

"Do you know why I walked from the church village?"

"I can't say. Army vehicles do use this road."

"I'm not too short of money to hire a car. I walked so that I could run into you. I remembered that you always drive the cattle to the pasture early in the morning, so I hoisted my pack on early and paced myself so I'd be sitting here in time. I got hot as the devil, though."

Hilja turned a little to one side. Toivo looked troubled. He had a manly face, she thought, but he seemed to think that the whole world was against him. The trip to Russia had made him even more somber. She should speak to him, but what could she say?

"It was nice of you to send those packages," Toivo said. "I'm not one for writing letters and I couldn't thank you properly. And I've always felt bad about cursing like the devil when you brought the reserve call-up orders to the Sammalsuo place."

Hilja crossed the road to stand beside him.

"I wasn't any too happy to have to bring the news. I knew you weren't cursing at me."

"I didn't mean it for you at all. But now that's all over and it's good that it is. When I was walking from the church village, I kept thinking all the way how good it is that a person can go where he pleases. That's really true."

Hilja's heart was warmed. Toivo was not one to tell little white lies. He had walked all that way for her sake.

"You must be hungry," she said.

"I ate some bread and sausage along the way. I'm just thirsty."

"Let's go to our place for coffee. I'm sure father will be glad to talk to you."

"I have to go through your yard to get over the bridge...I hear that some fool men squeeze women and even rub faces with them. I think that's all rot. But will you believe me when I say I think of you all the time?"

"I do believe it. Aren't you coming along with me?"

"I'll follow you. There'll be needless talk if we walk together."

"Will you be ashamed to hear that kind of talk?"

"I won't, but we're from such different families. It doesn't matter to you, and maybe not even to your family, but you go on by yourself. I'll come through the yard in my own good time."

"I'm not going alone. Come and walk beside me. We were all in the same boat last winter."

"If you're not afraid of gossip, I can stand it too."

As they neared the Naavala yard, Hilja said:

"Don't walk in on your mother suddenly."

"Is she worse? There was nothing about it in the letters."

"She wasn't well when I was there on Sunday."

"Is her heart acting up?"

"It's been bad for a long time. A sudden joy may be bad for her. Mari missed you a lot."

"Has Kauko gotten a leave yet?"

"I haven't seen him. He must be up north somewhere. Let's go into the kitchen now for coffee," Hilda said with a laugh.

"Welcome to Järvenkylä."

"Well...if you say so."

Toivo stopped in the yard, and Hilda stood by his side. He looked all around the lake. His cigarette went out. Squinting his eyes against the sun's glare, he said:

"It's high summer here now. It's about time to start wrestling with the hay in the swamp meadow. That's one helluva job. As long as the old man's strength holds out, he can cut the fodder there on his own. I'll start turning over the Olkivaara bottomland with a hoe."

"What was it like in the east?" asked Hilja.

"What do you mean?" said Toivo, scowling at her.

"I mean the vegetation and the land."

"The land there really pushes up plants. Even the woods are so thick you can hardly get through them. Goddamn, if we only had the same kind of soil here."

Hilja looked out at the lake. She could think of nothing more to say and didn't know what Toivo might want to talk about. After awhile he said:

"While I was sitting and waiting by the ditch, I started to feel that the growth in the east is too rich for our eyes. Reindeer moss and barren heath are so familiar to me. Even my nose is damned glad to sniff them on a hot day like this. Well, let's drink that coffee."

CHAPTER XIII

1

The company had been in Rovaniemi for three days now, days spent in marching and close-order drill. The activities were of little interest to men fresh from the wilderness, a fact which made them welcome evening passes with great enthusiasm. Jalo Kieppi was cheered up by a 24-hour Sunday pass. He now had a chance to visit his home after almost a six-months' absence. Kauko and Jonas Niemi received evening passes. Without any spoken agreement, they went to walk in the pine grove on the edge of town. The sky was cloudy, but it was not raining. They stopped at the auto repair place and watched others who were strolling there.

"Shouldn't we go and see if the men recovered?" Kauko said.

"Well of course they did. The dead man they found — the one the papers wrote about — was killed at the foot of Ounasvaara," said Niemi.

"There are stories about fights in the papers every day. I hope we don't meet the same men. They might recognize us."

"Let them. If they start a fight, they'll run into a fist again."

Tight-lipped, the quiet Jonas started out along the fateful path, with Kauko at his heels. They soon came to the spot where they had gotten into a fight on their earlier evening out. Kauko bent over to check the base of the pine tree and said:

"Nothing but spots of clotted blood. Let's see if they took that sheath knife."

The boys circled the mossy heath, searching.

"Here it is," laughed Kauko.

"It flew all that way. It looks like the tail-fin of a perch on that moss — aha, the tip of the sheath is carved in the shape of a tail-fin. It will make a nice toy for someone to carry on his hip. Shall we draw straws?"

"Leave the damn thing there. It's on my mind enough as it is."

"It's too fine a sheath to leave in the woods, but since that's what you want..." said Jonas Niemi, reluctantly dropping the sheath to the ground.

"Someone is sure to pick it up," said Kauko. "And now, where shall we go to spend the evening?"

"We're always planning on a bottle of beer."

"Let's go and have one this evening. Or what do you say to a bottle with the lion-seal from a bootlegger."

"I've seldom had liquor, but they're making men of us in other ways too," laughed Jonas.

They began to walk along one of the paths that crossed the heath. The air felt heavy, as it does before a summer thunderstorm. The moss sank beneath their feet like the deep pile of a carpet and they could not smell the usual odors of the woods. Suddenly Jonas pointed ahead of them and said:

"Look, there are two girls out for an evening stroll."

"So it seems. One of them has a nice shape."

"She really has. Tall and trim. What do you think?"

Kauko looked at his friend's questioning eyes. Then he said:

"If we have the nerve to try. We're both such mama's boys."

"They won't eat us alive. Let's grit our teeth and have a go at it."

"You go first, Jonas. I've lived in the woods all my life."

"Will you be sure to come with me."

"No question. Do you have a mirror so I can see how my cap looks?"

"Take a look, but there's nothing wrong with your cap."

"Well, let's do it, no matter what happens. Hey, they're looking back at us."

Jonas Niemi lengthened his stride. At the same time, he smoothed down the sleeves of his summer blouse. Kauko did the same and also straightened the back of his blouse. A wrinkled uniform looks ugly on a soldier, he thought.

"Good evening, ladies. This is a lovely pine woods," said Jonas.

The tall girl glanced sideways at Jonas, who had reached her side. She smiled and said:

"Good evening to you. There's no shortage of pine trees in Lapland."

Her companion, a small, short-legged girl, linked arms with her and looked back over her shoulder at Kauko, who stayed behind her. Then she leaned forward and her shoulders shook in a fit of giggling. Kauko's face flushed hotly. Just what was she laughing at? In a panic, his fingers leaped to the buttons on his fly. No, they at least were closed. Was his cap at the proper angle? It was, and his collar insignia were straight as well. The buckle of his belt seemed to be right at his navel. What the devil was that stinking girl cackling about?

"My buddy and I are complete strangers to Rovaniemi. If it's okay with you girls, we would like to get to know your beautiful city. With such attractive guides, it would go...I mean, it would be a pleasure."

"It's no fun to walk the streets of the city and have to squeeze by all those soldiers and officers. We're from the country ourselves," said the tall girl.

"So much the better. Shall we have a look around the countryside? My friend and I are both country boys too. You don't mind?"

Jonas Niemi slid his arm underneath the girl's. She looked at the tall soldier walking beside her and said nothing, but she did not withdraw her arm. Niemi looked at Kauko walking behind him. Although his face wore a nervous flush, he gave a significant wink and nodded toward the other girl.

Kauko kept walking in back of them, his heart racing faster with every step. Godalmighty, that Jonas has a nerve, he thought. I'm getting nowhere, trudging along behind them, while Jonas is leading the girl by the arm. Now the smaller one is looking this way and pressing close to her companion's side.

"Hee, hee, hee," giggled the shorter girl.

Jonas looked back over his shoulder again. He was frowning and seemed to be mouthing words. Kauko saw the tall girl lean into him and heard her say:

"You're such a nice-looking boy. Why should I mind?"

"But I'm no playboy, and neither is my buddy," Jonas said.

Either I have to run away now, or move up to that girl's side. Jonas, who is so quiet, is leading that girl as if there were nothing to it. Kauko closed his eyes. There are no stumps or pits in the ground here. I won't stumble even if I close my eyes. Now! Kauko could feel himself walking up alongside the girl. He was shaking in every limb. The girl was looking at his cheeks. They must be as red as a rooster's wattles. What an ass he was. Kauko gritted his teeth and tried to thrust his hand under the girl's arm, but she held it tightly against her side.

"Tee-hee, it tickles," said the girl, and moved so as to thwart his efforts.

Kauko dropped his arm. That's the last trick I'll ever try, he vowed to himself. He walked beside the girl with his eyes averted. His temples throbbed. He started only when his face hit a low pine branch.

"Look, tee-hee, he ran right into a tree. It didn't poke your eye, did it?"

"N-no. I didn't even notice. I was looking at the pine trees and..."

That's all I needed, Kauko fumed. A pine needle had scraped his eye hard enough so that it began to water. Now she'll think I've started to cry on top of everything else, he raged inwardly, as he took out his handkerchief and dried his eye.

Jonas Niemi seemed oblivious to everything except himself and the tall girl. The two were talking and laughing, and the girl was leaning heavily into his side.

"Just call me Alli," she said with a laugh.

"That's good. I'm...I mean, Esko. Let's just use our first names."

Kauko looked at Jonas and began to feel a little bolder. The girl walking beside him had let go of her companion's arm. She looked at Kauko with her head cocked to one side.

"Tee-hee-hee..."

"Why are you laughing so much, Selma?" said the tall girl.

"The soldier walked into a tree, tee-hee. Now his eye is as red as a roach's."

"Don't laugh at another person's accident. You look ahead, Esko, so the same thing won't happen to you."

"I'll put my head under your hat for protection," said Jonas Niemi, and Kauko saw him thrust his puckered lips behind the girl's ear.

The pine woods became denser, but the path widened. In sandy places, they could see human footprints mingled with the split-hoofed tracks of reindeer. Niemi stopped and said:

"This path is used a lot. Shouldn't we go a little way off it?"

The girls looked at each other and Kauko looked at Jonas. The latter winked at him in reply. That Jonas seems to be a real womanizer. He talks so smoothly it makes me feel like puking, thought Kauko.

"Let's go, but not too far," said Alli.

"Just so we don't stay too long," said the other girl, looking at

Kauko.

They moved off the trail. A short distance away stood a large boulder. It's at least as large as our porch, was the thought that flashed through Kauko's mind. Jonas and the tall girl stopped. The smaller woman walked right up to the rock. Kauko hesitated, but then he too walked up to it. Jonas and Alli were standing face to face. "As long as they don't start slobbering each other with kisses," said Kauko to himself. They were saying something in low voices. Then Jonas turned to Kauko and said:

"You stay here. Alli and I are going to look around."

"As if that Esko wants to see the woods. Isn't he silly?"

"We'll stay by this rock. As long as you don't stay too long, hee, hee, hee."

Brushing aside pine branches, Jonas and Alli disappeared from sight. Jonas's hand was resting on the girl's hip. Slowly Kauko turned his head. The girl was standing close to the rock, scratching at the moss that grew on its side. When she looked at him, Kauko dropped his eyes.

I should say something to her, Kauko thought. Is there any sense in standing so far away? Then the girl said:

"It might be nice to sit up on that rock."

"It sure would. It's quite a boulder."

"I would climb up on it, but it's too smooth and my foot slips."

"I can help," said Kauko, and walked over to the rock.

Kauko grasped the girl tightly under the arms, and with boyish enthusiasm, hoisted her high into the air alongside the rock.

"Oh my God, not like that!" screeched the girl.

Kauko was so stupefied that he dropped the girl. She straightened her skirts and said:

"Not like that. You could see everything on me."

Although there was a smile on the girl's face, she was not giggling this time. That gave Kauko the courage to say:

"How then?"

"You can climb up first and give me a hand."

On the back of the rock, Kauko found some protrusions by means of which he clambered up. Kneeling, he reached out a hand to the girl. She was small, and came up easily.

"That's the way," said the girl. "You're a strong man."

Kauko could say nothing. The girl sat on the smooth surface of the rock and gazed at the woods. Kauko hesitated and finally sat down, leaving space enough between them to seat two people. The girl seemed thoughtful and looked at him a couple of times. Finally Kauko said:

"It might rain."

"I don't know if it will. The air seems heavy, though."

Kauko looked at the girl. She wasn't much to look at. Elma, the girl next door, was different. The image of the oldest Olkivaara girl came suddenly into his mind. What would she say if she saw this? It was anything but manly to be sitting here with a strange woman. But last winter had been so terrible that perhaps he had earned the right to stray a little. He could even tell Elma about it some day. The girl is older than I am, he thought. What did she think of it when I tried to grab her arm right away? Should I tell her I wasn't getting any wrong ideas?

"Sure enough, it's going to rain. A few drops are coming down already."

Kauko looked up at the sky. A few large drops came splashing down. He said:

"I think that's the end of the hot weather too."

"The air has really turned cold. My shoulders are chilly," said the girl with a shudder.

So she's cold. It's almost as if she wants me near her. If I hadn't tried to take her arm a minute ago, I would move closer now.

"I don't happen to have a coat with me, or I would give it to you."

The girl looked at him, her lips parted in a smile, and he went on:

"I didn't mean anything wrong when I tried to take your arm. I somehow...I thought maybe like Jonas...he was holding the other girl's hand..."

"I wasn't all that scared by it. Men are just like that. And it felt so ticklish."

"If you'll just forget about it, you won't have to worry that it'll happen again."

"I'll forget it."

"Can I see you again?"

"Why not? But I've been warned about soldiers..."

Kauko's heart leaped. She's looking at me warmly. He opened a front button on his blouse and took out a small notebook and the stub of a grease pencil.

"Would you be willing to write your name and address here?"

"Why?"

"Because I don't know when we'll be moved, or where. I'll write to you then. May I?"

"Of course. It would be nice to get a letter from a soldier. I write such a bad hand, but I can scribble it somehow."

The girl wrote with the notebook on her knee. The raindrops were already splashing down quite heavily. She handed the book back to Kauko, and he read:

Selma Luusuanhauta, Rovaniemi, Viirinkylä.

"There it is, if you can make it out."

"Very clearly. Many thanks."

Kauko put the notebook back into his pocket. He could see Selma looking toward the place where Jonas and Alli had disappeared. They were staying away a long time.

"How far did those two go?" said Kauko.

"They're not far. Hee, hee, they'll be back soon. The rock is wet and I really can't lie down on it to rest."

"Why the devil didn't I bring my coat," said Kauko.

Selma did not seem to hear him. She turned her head to search through the woods and then she said:

"So there you are."

"My goodness, how high up you've climbed," said Alli.

Kauko saw a slightly sated expression on Jonas Niemi's face. The knees of his pants were so thoroughly soaked that they looked like black cups over his kneecaps.

"It started to rain, darn it! My back must look like I've been swimming. The branches of the trees are dripping wet."

"Shouldn't we take the girls back to town, buddy?"

"Yes, children, come down from the rock," said Alli.

It was now raining hard. Jonas and Alli walked ahead arm in arm. Kauko and Selma followed, walking side by side, but without touching each other. Jonas and Alli kept on whispering, but Kauko could find almost nothing to say to Selma. At the center of town, the two couples separated, and Jonas took Alli to a doorway that was out of the rain. Kauko and Selma stood against the wall of the same building.

"Oh dear, I'm getting all wet," said Selma, with a shiver.

"It is pouring. Would you like to go for a walk with me

tomorrow evening?"

"I might, if you want to."

"That would be nice. We might even go to a movie," said Kauko.

"They have such miserable pictures. But there are other ways to spend an evening."

"Of course. Where shall we meet?"

Selma looked around, then nodded to one side, and said:

"We could even meet right over there in front of the Lapinmaa Restaurant."

"At what time?" asked Kauko.

"About six-thirty. Is that okay?"

"We should be off duty by then. You won't leave if I'm a little late?"

'I'll be sure to wait awhile."

Jonas and Alli came up to them. Alli took Selma's arm and said:

"We're going now. So long, Esko."

"So long, Alli."

"See you, soldier boy," said Selma.

"See you, see you," said Kauko.

"Let's head for camp," said Jonas.

2

The order to leave came as a surprise in the middle of the night. The duty man yelled out the wake-up call. As the last of the men were returning from their evening passes, the trucks were already being loaded.

"Move, shake a leg," yelled the duty man.

"Where are we going in such a hurry?" one of the men asked.

"You don't ask questions in the army. Just climb on the trucks," said a sergeant.

The company commander walked around among the trucks. The field-kitchen stovepipe stood out against the sky, and the rifle barrels held between the knees of the men sitting on the truck platforms also pointed upwards.

"Is everyone on board?" asked the company commander.

They all looked at each other. Then Sergeant Mäki stood up on one of the trucks and said:

"Lieutenant, sir. Private Kieppi is missing from my squad."

"Damn it, I had to go and give him a Sunday pass. Well, he can report to Headquarters Company. Top sergeant!"

"Lieutenant, sir!"

"Leave a notice in our quarters telling Kieppi where to report."

"Got it, lieutenant, sir."

The lieutenant strode to the cab of the lead truck and the engines roared into life immediately. The column began to rumble through the streets of Rovaniemi. Everyone waited tensely to see which way the lead truck turned. When they drove over the Kemi River Bridge, Jonas Niemi said to Kauko:

"We're heading north."

"Looks that way."

"Don't be eager, boys. When you've been sitting for a few hundred miles, you'll be glad to start walking," said one of the squad leaders.

The Arctic sky began to clear and the dusk of midnight grew lighter as the trucks carried them northward. Kauko whispered to Jonas:

"It looks like tomorrow's date will be broken."

Jonas glanced at his wrist watch and said:

"More like today's, but things have really gotten screwed up."

"And Selma will be waiting for nothing. Who could have known?" said Kauko.

✧ ✧ ✧

In the spring of 1940, the highway from Rovaniemi to Liinahamari was undergoing a crash repair program. Land mines were being disarmed, rotting carcasses of humans and horses picked up, and potholes filled in. Gravel and other fill were being hauled to mucky stretches along the highway. The road was Finland's only link to the great world, for it was the ships that sailed the Arctic Ocean which brought the necessities of life to a country devastated by war. In addition, soldiers were needed to clean up the city of Petsamo after the war.

"They're really moving stuff here now," said Kauko.

"The trucks keep coming in a steady stream," said Jonas Niemi.

"And they're all new Fargoes. Finland's credit must still be good," said another of the men squatting on the same truck.

"Look, they gave a brand-new truck to a poor driver," said Kauko in astonishment. "It's lying upside-down in that gully."

"The rolls of barbed wire really went flying."

"There's truck after truck rolled over off the road with the front end smashed in."

"I wonder how much farther they'll take us."

"Another twenty-four hours of sitting and we'll come to the Arctic Ocean."

"Do you have any cookies left, Jonas?" asked Kauko

"No, but I have some other civilian left-overs. Here are some sandwiches," said Jonas, opening his pack.

Hands reached out toward Jonas. The truck lurched, and the platform pitched and tossed.

"We're close to Norway. There are high mountains on the other side of that river," someone said.

"You can't make a living by farming in that landscape," said Jonas Niemi. "Did anyone miss out on the food?"

"Here, if you still have some," cried a voice from the rear of the platform.

Kauko looked at the river along which the column of trucks was driving. Only that big, swiftly flowing stream separates me from the country where Hamsun, Gulbrandtsen, and Sigrid Undset once lived, he thought. It was that landscape which had kindled their imagination.

✧ ✧ ✧

The company had pitched its tents on the north bank of a mountain brook that seethed in a deep channel under the highway. The men had finished their work for that day. It was taking entire days to fill in soupy stretches of the highway with the boughs of dwarf birch trees, which promptly sank into the gravel and mucky clay. An unending stream of trucks kept roaring toward Rovaniemi while as many drove on toward Liinahamari.

"Godalmighty — and that bottom will be mush again tomorrow," said one of the soldiers wrestling with the branches.

"Isn't this the damndest place? You can't even get fir boughs for a base," added another.

"But the landscape is awesome. And the nights!" said Jonas Niemi.

"It sure is different from anything around Raahe," declared

one of the soldiers.

"Who cares about mountains? I sure hated having to follow you out of Rovaniemi."

"You could have gone AWOL if you're afraid of mountains," said the boy from the plains area to Kieppi.

"Stop jabbering. We have mountains to roll around on every day."

"Cut out the wrangling and let's play cards," someone said.

"Right. Who has the deck? Let's have a game of poker."

Kauko nudged Jonas Niemi's side and said:

"Let's go and have a look around the place."

"Let's all three of us go. I'll come along too."

When he, Jonas, and Kieppi came out of the tent onto the roadside, Kauko said:

"Let's go and visit the Upper Monastery. It must be a fine sight."

"Let's go," said Jonas Niemi. "It must be a mysterious place."

"I'll come too, although it's probably nothing to see."

✧ ✧ ✧

It was a walk of several kilometers. There was a thin cloud cover in the sky. Soldiers were strolling here and there. The environs of Petsamo had always been thinly populated, and even the many army units now there did not appear to make it much livelier. The broad wilderness seemed to swallow up people. Only the roadsides were teeming with life. The turn-off to the monastery was enough to send Kauko's imagination soaring. I may have grown up in the wilderness, but this is the true North, he thought.

"You can see the monastery over there," said Jonas Niemi.

"It's quite a building."

Two army engineers came walking toward them from the monastery grounds. They were of the same conscription class as Kauko and his companions.

"Do you infantrymen know what that mound of earth is?" asked one of them.

"It must be some of your work, since you're a shovel man," said Jalo Kieppi.

"Let's not start any bickering among branches of the service," Kauko said. "What's so special about that pile of earth?"

"One monk carried it in a sack from the area around here," said the other engineer.

"He had to haul a few sacks to make that pile," said Kauko.

"What put that crazy idea into his skull?" asked Kieppi.

"They say he was punishing himself for his sins," said the engineer.

"What kind of sin did he commit?" asked Jonas Niemi.

"They say he led a Lapland girl into sin," laughed one of the engineers.

"Only once!" exclaimed Kieppi.

"They didn't know. They say the old guy carried sackfuls of sand for forty years."

"Well isn't that something! It's hard to believe the penance for sin could be so heavy," said Jonas Niemi in a near-whisper.

"If there's nothing else to see, I'm leaving," Kieppi said.

The engineers walked away and Kauko and his friends entered the monastery grounds. Under the spell of an excitement tinged with fear, Kauko and Jonas wandered through the deserted rooms of the monastery. Jalo Kieppi sat stubbornly smoking outside, laughing at his peripatetic companions. Finally he shouted:

"Watch out you don't set off a mine by sticking your noses into everything."

At last Kauko and his friend returned to the grounds outside, where they stood gazing at a mountain that rose in back of the Petsamo River. Kauko said:

"Juha Vesainen once destroyed this monastery. It's said they threw the monks who fled to that mountain for refuge down from its top."

Kauko forgot his homesickness. He was treading the same ground walked by people who had secluded themselves from the world hundreds of years ago in order to serve God. Mighty hymns had resounded outside these walls, had echoed over the serenely gliding Petsamo River, and among the mountains beyond. I have to write home about this marvelous feeling — and to Elma too. But the first thing this evening, I must write to Selma in Rovaniemi. I'm late in doing it, and I'm so ashamed. When I didn't show up at the Lapinmaa Restaurant, she must have thought me a liar. Now when I write and describe this visit, she's sure to get over her anger. Then when I get a leave, I'll spend a few days with Selma.

"You can stand there gawking till morning if you like, but I'm leaving."

Kauko awakened from his thoughts, and Jonas Niemi's abstracted expression returned to normal.

"What's the big hurry, Jalo?" asked Jonas.

Jalo was already walking away with his hands in his pockets. Kauko and Jonas caught up with him as he stood in the *Community of Penitents* area. There he spat profusely between long drags at his cigarette, and said:

"He sure paid a price for that goddamned piece."

He strode off again. When Kauko and Jonas caught up with him this time, he said:

"I'm sure the lieutenant I found in Saima's saddle hasn't carried one handful of sand."

✧ ✧ ✧

The indirect rays of the sun had been lighting the mountains in the background dimly. By the time its beams shone directly across the Petsamo river, Kauko was sitting on the slope of the mountain with a writing pad on his knee. Smoke from the tents, and mist from the brook running into the Petsamo River were rising into the air. Trucks roared in both directions along the road, and the spire of the monastery church was clearly visible in the distance.

Kauko looked around him for awhile and then again read through a letter many pages long. Selma was sure to fall under the spell of Petsamo when she read it.

I thought about you so much on the grounds of the Upper Monastery at Petsamo. It was a memorable visit, and I repeat what I told you at the beginning of the letter, that I didn't stay away from the Lapinmaa Restaurant of my own free will. What could I do when we had to leave at night? I'm sure you think all soldiers are the same. It must have annoyed you if you waited in vain for hours. You can be sure, my Lapland girl, that I'll come to see you whenever I get a leave. Maybe we'll get to be good friends then. The Petsamo sun is rising now, and I'll stop this scribbling. The landscape is ruggedly beautiful, even at night like this. I'm going to sleep for a little while, because I hear we have to unload ships in the morning.

Heartfelt greetings from Private Kauko Sammalsuo.

"Now just the Army Post Office address, and Selma will get a letter," Kauko muttered half aloud. "If only she isn't angry over having to wait so long."

"What verses have you been composing now?" asked the man on guard when Kauko returned to the tent with his pad in hand.

"Just scribbling a letter."

"To a girl friend, of course."

Kauko looked at the rising sun and replied:

"Well, sort of."

3

"The Germans have occupied Norway."

Although the development was no longer a completely new one, it still seemed shocking. Kauko and Jonas Niemi were discussing it as they sat beside a ditch at the roadside.

"What will happen to Finland now?" said Kauko. "We're so close to the Norway."

"The world seems so small. It looks as if one man will soon rule all of it," said Jonas Niemi.

"We belong to an age that will see the birth of a new world order. That Hitler seems to be all-powerful."

"We've both done some reading, but nothing seems to make sense now," said Jonas Niemi.

"The war last winter shocked me, and now comes this German invasion. It seems that when a man goes to bed these days he doesn't know who his master will be when he wakes up. Luckily Germany is a cultured country. If we can't live as a separate nation, I'm less afraid of living under the Germans than under last winter's attackers. An ordinary man's life won't get any worse under them."

"I think so too. They would leave me alone to farm my land."

"If only we don't get into a war again," said Kauko.

"I don't think we will. Who would we be fighting? Germany

couldn't get Finland into a war even if she wanted to, and the Russians will hardly dare tangle with a small country again," said Jonas.

"I trust that a country won't get into another war as soon as the first one is over. I think last winter was enough for Finland."

"I should think so," said Jonas Niemi. Then he stared for a long time at a far-off mountain ridge, sighed, and said, "But damn it, I still feel somehow that I'm not coming out of this alive."

"Are you still harping on that? What is there to kill us when even the mines are being disarmed by the engineers?" Kauko said with a scowl.

"They can't be sure to get all of them. One of our men was killed by one just the other day."

"Don't talk like that. Look at that mountainside. Don't the patches of snow look like sheets spread out to dry?"

"This spring has been an experience for me. All my life, I've seen nothing but flatlands. Sometimes I crave the smell of earth, but when I look around I feel a sense of awe. It was a stroke of luck that our company was sent here."

"Although I've lived all my life with the scent of pitch in my nostrils, I don't mind spending a spring, maybe even a summer, in these surroundings."

"What are you sitting there for? Come and drink my brew," they heard Jalo Kieppi say.

"Have you made the fake coffee?" said Niemi.

"It's ready, if you'll just bring the sugar and coffee bread."

"It's such a nice night that I really don't feel like crawling around in a tent," said Kauko.

"I'm not one for tramping the woods. Let's go in and drink so that I can get into the card game."

✧ ✧ ✧

The sun shone on high, and waves ruffled the surface of the Bay of Petsamo. Kauko looked around from time to time and wiped the sweat from his brow with one sleeve. They had just finished loading a truck and it had begun to crawl away from the ship. Soon the load went roaring off toward Rovaniemi. A new Fargo drove into its place. The side of the ship loomed high above the dock. Kauko's partners craned their necks over the side to look, as Kauko leaped onto the platform of the truck.

"Let's go buddies! Heave on another load."

"Stop croaking like a raven. Let's take a little rest," said Jalo Kieppi.

"We'll get to look around the port that much sooner," said Kauko.

"Yeah, you old Laplander. Just pitch those reels of barbed wire onto the truck."

"You're the one who's an old coot. And with all this barbed wire, it's a cinch no cows will trample any hay fields this summer. I tell you, with this much barbed wire, you could fence in a whole province."

"Where the heck are they taking all of this?" said Jonas Niemi. "At home, this would be enough for years."

Kauko had suddenly been given a corporal's stripes. At first he was surprised but gradually he got used to them. On many days he and his squad were ordered to the harbor at Liinahamari on loading detail. The work was arduous, but it had its own special interest. Of his crew, only Jonas Niemi had seen an ocean-going ship before.

When the hot day's work was over, Kauko said:

"Let's go to chow then."

"It's a wonder you didn't make us do an extra load."

Kauko's blouse was dark with sweat, and the barbed wire had torn a long gash on the loose skin between his thumb and forefinger. Sucking the blood from it, he said:

"I haven't exactly been standing here like a lord and master."

"That's just it. You kill us weaker men who try to keep up while you're busting a gut as our leader."

The ship's cook had become a good friend of the boys — not this ship's cook alone, but those of the other ships being unloaded in the harbor. The soldiers climbed down the steep hatchway. They were greeted by a very black man whose white teeth gleamed in a smile as he pointed a finger at a table.

"Hey, Finnish soldiers!"

"What shall we say to that chief cook?"

"We won't say a word — we'll just eat."

The black cook brought a roast to the table. Adam's apples rose and fell as the men feasted after a hard day's work. White bread vanished into mouths accustomed to scanty rations of rye bread. Butter was loaded onto plates like gruel. The smell of roast beef tantalized the nostrils of the men.

"I wouldn't like to be left alone with that cook," said one of the men.

'Me neither, but he sure can cook," said Jalo Kieppi.

As he ate, Kauko gazed out through a porthole on the side of the ship. Waves splashed against the glass, and the rough surface of the water reflected the sun's rays. The hermit of Ahmaluoma had once ridden these same waters, gaffed up codfish from them, and ridden out their savage storms.

Hölkkä-Simo's picture came clearly to Kauko's mind now. What kind of memories were stirring in his thoughts as he brooded in his camp on the shores of Ahmaluoma. It was a small lake, with waters as clear as those of a spring, and with not the slightest tang of salt. Was the smoke-begrimed picture of Signe Knudsen still sitting on the hermit's shelf? The picture of a girl from Oslo, out in the distant wilderness? Only now did Kauko realize how limited was the world-view of those who dwelt in the backwoods.

It was a good long time before the men began to belch with satisfaction. The black man kept on smiling and gesturing toward the cooking pots and then toward his mouth, urging them to eat more. Jalo Kieppi opened the belt of his uniform and said:

"Here's one man who's letting out his belt a notch."

✧ ✧ ✧

When the men returned to the camp area on trucks that evening, two letters had arrived for Kauko in the field mail. The handwriting on one of them was familiar, but the address on the other made Kauko's heart leap. He did an impatient slapdash job of washing at the brook and returned to the tent. Tucking the letters into his bosom, he ducked outside.

"Don't be in such a hurry. I'll come along too."

"I'm not going far and I'll be right back," Kauko said.

"Well, I'm not taking any long trip either," said Jalo Kieppi.

Annoyed, Kauko strode off into a grove of dwarf birch trees which were now in full leaf. Jalo thrust out from under the tent fly and shouted:

"Now what's the fire in your pants?"

"Nothing. I'm just going for a little walk."

"It's those letters you're sneaking around with. I'm not trying to stick my nose in and read them. You're a grown man, but you should be wearing a kid's pants."

"Have I ever tried to pry into your letters?" asked Kauko, shoving birch limbs out of his way. Then he muttered to himself: "At least Jonas is a little more sensitive as a friend."

Sitting on a moss-covered rock, Kauko looked at the letters. Mail does get here, he thought. These were the first letters to arrive at the Upper Monastery area. Kauko took out his notebook and looked around. No one was there to hear him or see his facial expressions.

"It must be from Selma. My name and address are in her handwriting. *Private Kauko Sammalsuo...*"

As he spoke these words, Kauko pressed his chin into his shoulder to look at his corporal's stripes. His mood grew brighter. Selma would surely see it was no ordinary cub she was keeping company with, since he had been made a corporal so soon. Kauko looked back and forth from the envelope to the name and address in his notebook. Some of the writing in grease pencil had turned into broad purple splotches. It had started to rain on that day...If only Selma were with him now..."

Slowly Kauko opened the letter. He wanted to torture himself as long as possible and then swallow his joy in one gulp. Finally, with trembling fingers, he thrust the tip of his knife into one corner of the envelope and slit the top edge. Was that logger's knife still in the woods at Rovaniemi?

"This doesn't seem to be very long," Kauko said to himself.

And now his eyes remained fixed on the narrow sheet of stationery.

> *Soldier*
>
> *I can tell you the letter came. It was long and kind of childish. I wondered as I read it what soldier could have wrote it. Then it hit me like a ton of bricks that it must be from the boy I sat roosting on that big rock with in the rain. I laughed myself sick when you wrote that I got left waiting for nothing in front of the lapinmaa restaurant. I never got there. I happened to meet this sergeant coming along right in front of where I live. He*

> *had roving hands, but otherwise he was very nice. He even promised to make me his Wife. I don't mind if you write but don't write so much. It takes so long to read. Alli and I read it together. She laughed too, and said to give her regards to Esko. Alli has a man with the rank of Lieutenant for a boy friend now. Many greetings. Selma Luusuanhauta. My address is the same.*

"Well of all the...of all the..." Kauko spluttered, tearing at his hair. "Of all the...!"

His heart burned and he ground his teeth as he skimmed over the difficult-to-read curlicues of the handwriting:

"I happened to meet this sergeant...promised to make me his wife...he had roving hands..."

Kauko kept grinding his teeth. There was a tearing sound as he ripped the paper into two and then into four parts. They fell to Kauko's feet like the first snow of winter. He leaped up pale-faced, stamped the paper into shreds, and plucked moss with his fingers to cover them over. Lastly, he packed the earth firmly over them.

"Of all the goddamned letters for a man to wait for!"

On first reading, Kauko could not make sense of Aili's letter. Only after he had spelled it out many times, did he get its meaning:

> *Toivo got out of the reserves. They say Kosti Mäkinen has come to Sääskilampi too. Auku was on the log drive with Nestor Malinen's crew, but he's home already. We've started to gather twigs. Your rye field has grown a lot. Nestor says it will yield lots of grain. Elma was with us one day gathering twigs. We slept in the store-house and babbled away for half the night. Elma says many regards and wonders why you haven't written for so long. You could write to her now that it's easy. She sent you many packages at the front. Mother keeps saying that you should watch out for mines and other things. Mari Olkivaara's health is getting worse.*

"I won't ever write a letter to a woman again. At most, I'll write home, and then either to Auku or Väinö."

With a determined stride, Kauko returned to the tent. His eyes sought out Jonas Niemi, but he was not to be found. Only a circle of card players and their kibitzers sat at the rear of the tent.

"Which way did Jonas go?" asked Kauko.

"Must have gone to read some letters," snapped Jalo Kieppi without turning his head.

"Cut out the crap," said Kauko.

"Our fluke corporal is in a bad mood," said one of the men.

"You can say that again...Here's five on the nose. Niemi went off toward the brook."

Kauko left the tent and headed toward the brook. Its springtime roar had changed to a murmur. There was only enough water left to wind its way among the stones. Kauko looked up and down the stream bed. Upstream someone was trying to work a fishing lure among the stones. It was no fun to watch him, and Kauko started downstream, walking carefully over the slippery stones. Birds fluttered into the air and branches in full leaf stretched out over the stream like hands raised in blessing. Kauko stopped. He could see Jonas Niemi standing spraddle-legged. All the front buttons of his pants were open and his hands were pawing at his crotch. His neck was bent at at angle and his face was close to his probing fingers. Kauko coughed. Jonas Niemi straightened up with a start and jerked his fly shut.

"Are you picking lice?" said Kauko.

"Something of the sort," said Jonas Niemi, his face averted.

"I got rid of mine. The Kuhmo delousing sauna shook them off."

Kauko walked up to Jonas, He felt better now with a good friend at his side, and he said without any preliminaries:

"Greetings from Alli."

"What the hell Alli?" Jonas's expression was gloomy.

"What are you scowling about? From Alli to Esko," laughed Kauko.

"I don't like being nasty to a buddy, but shut your mouth."

"Don't get mad, but I got a nice warm letter from Selma."

"What did it say about me?"

"Selma sent regards to Esko, but Alli has a lieutenant for a boy friend now. *Lieutenant* was written with a capital letter," Kauko laughed.

Kauko's recent rage had changed to a kind of gallows humor. Jonas Niemi's face stayed sour. Kauko's fit of good humor faded and he said:

"Don't take Alli's behavior so hard. She was a good-looking girl, but if she's chasing after a lieutenant already, then..."

"I don't give a damn about that!" Jonas Niemi shouted the words.

"Don't look at me as if I'd committed murder. I only said what was in the letter. It's not my fault if..."

"I got the crabs from that goddamned slut!"

Kauko's jaw dropped. He looked at his friend as if he were afraid.

"They...don't you catch them from a woman's lower hairs?" Kauko said.

"Well, you don't get them from the hair on her head."

"Did you lay her?"

"Twice. Damn, did I get a case of them. They go wild when you sweat. I had a rough day at the harbor. I was just putting on the gray salve."

Kauko gulped as he watched his companion's hand constantly scratching at his crotch.

"Does that salve get rid of them?"

"So the old hands say. I've just shaved the hair off. I'm like a less-than-ten-year-old now."

"We must be real mama's boys, as they say back home. And I was so lonesome for that rotten Selma."

"How much lower will we sink? It's a good thing mother doesn't know about it," said Jonas Niemi, turning his back.

"Why did you give Crab-Alli a false name?"

"I didn't plan to at all. I have some kind of instinct for secrecy that puts words into my mouth in such cases. You remember that bread-stealing episode. Besides, Jonas is such a Biblical name. Godalmighty, how it itches!"

Kauko watched his companion scratching and a shiver ran down his spine. It could have happened to me if I hadn't been playing the gentleman. Elma and the woods of home. When will I get back there?

"Shouldn't we climb up this mountain? I don't think there's a more beautiful sight than the flowing Petsamo River," said Kauko.

"Let's go, even if it stirs up the crabs again."

CHAPTER XIV

1

"Why, it's Bert!"

Irja's cry caused a stir in the main room at Sääskilampi. The hired man and woman rushed to the window. Irja called out:

"Boys — Ilmari, Pentti — go tell your father that Bert is out in the yard."

The boys pattered across the room to the door of the kitchen and yelled through it.

"Father, Uncle Bert is in the yard."

Kosti Mäkinen was just finishing his evening coffee. He had been out mowing in the barley field longer than the rest. The mistress of the house was also in the room. She rose, passing her hand over her breast, and said to the children:

"You're not just fooling, are you?"

"It is Uncle Bert. Mother told us to tell you."

By that time the door to the porch had opened. A man in uniform strode directly across to the kitchen. Outside in the yard, an automobile spluttered into motion.

"Greetings from Vaasa," said the newcomer, reaching out a hand to his mother. Then he grasped his brother-in-law's huge paw, squeezed it hard, and said:

"This trip is almost over for me now."

"Did it hurt much?" asked his mother.

"There was some pain at first, but after that it was like being in a rest home. Ah, there comes my sister too! Hello, hello!"

Bert moved about the kitchen. Everything about it was completely familiar to him and yet somehow strange. His sister Irja was more buxom than he could ever have imagined her to be. Kosti was wearing a flannel shirt and his suspenders were dangling to one side. He looked like a well-to-do farmer.

"Uncle, come and see what's crawling on the floor in here."

Irja went through the kitchen door with Bert in tow. His walk was still a bit awkward. He's not completely healed, thought his mother as she looked at her son from behind.

"So this is what your daughter looks like."

Little Tuulikki lay kicking on her belly on a sheepskin spread out on the floor. The boys dropped to their knees beside their sister.

"Look, uncle came home," said Ilmari.

"And he's not wounded any more," said Pentti.

The baby shrieked and kneaded the soft wool of the sheepskin with her fingers. Bert watched her delighted antics and said:

""Uncle would pick you up but he's gotten so old on this trip that he can't bend over so far."

Kosti followed Bert into the main room, grasped his daughter under her arms, and handed her to his brother-in-law.

"Look at the kind of man you have for an uncle."

"Well, what do you think of this man? You sure look like your mother. Kitchy-coo..."

Irja looked at Kosti and said:

"Did you hear what a beautiful wife you have?"

"Didn't Bert say it's Tuulikki who is pretty?" said Kosti.

"But he's the first to say she looks like her mother. All the others say she's a pretty girl and..."

"And praise her for looking like her father, I mean."

The August sun shone into the room. Outside in the yard, the mountain ash trees swayed in the breeze. The familiar smell of the room was in Bert Sääskilampi's nostrils. There was the rack made of reindeer antlers nailed to the wall, with the lasso and reindeer rifle hung on it. Was it scarcely a year since they had been on his shoulders? On his return from Viipuri, these same objects had been the first to catch his eye. Then the room had seemed much barer. Irja's boys had been missing, and there had been no baby playing on the floor. Now his brother-in-law was standing there too. It felt homey and truly peaceful in the Sääskilampi household. Earlier only his father and a hired hand had been there to lend a subdued life to the room.

Bert handed Tuulikki to his sister and said:

"And how is father?"

Kosti and Irja also looked at the mistress of the house, waiting for an answer. Petti Sääskilampi cleared her throat and said:

"He's sitting in the bedroom."

"Is he able to go out?"

"Sometimes Kosti leads him to the edge of the field and sits him down there. He watches the others at work. But he keeps saying crazy things."

"I have to go in and see him. But for heaven's sake, if there is one slice of dried reindeer meat in the house, get it for me."

Bert started off toward the kitchen. Irja thrust the baby into Kosti's arms and said:

"We're some hosts when we don't even offer food to uncle."

✧ ✧ ✧

At the end of that August, Petti Sääskilampi's brother died. It was a heavy blow for her. Her brother's children were no longer close to her, and now the one remaining link to her home parish was broken. Wearing a black dress of Merino wool, she bustled back and forth between the kitchen and main room preparing to leave. Her brother was to be buried in the graveyard of the neighboring parish. Petti's eyes were red and she sighed heavily from time to time. Bert too was dressed in mourning.

"Take care of father," he said to Irja and Kosti.

"We will...don't worry," said Kosti.

Bert, who was still convalescing, was going to the funeral with his mother. He was already pacing restlessly back and forth between the yard and kitchen. The hired automobile was due to arrive at any minute.

"What is father doing in there?" Bert asked.

"Probably fooling around with the boys," said Irja.

Bert went into the main room and looked at his father, who was sitting in the middle of the floor with the boys crawling around him. Ivar Sääskilampi held a small brass bell in his hand. He would ring it in either boy's ear and say:

"That's the way the reindeer canter."

"How does the bell ring when the reindeer gallop?" asked Pentti.

Grandpa Ivar shook the bell furiously.

"That's the way the bell jingles," he said.

Bert remained standing near his father and the boys. Although his father was facing him, he did not seem to notice his son. When Ivar finished shaking the bell, he began to turn it over in his hands. Then he scratched at one side of it with the nail of his index finger, raised it to his face, and said as if to himself:

"This is Bert's reindeer bell. He's just as little as you are. Here are the letters *I* and *S*. This is Hookhorn's bell. Grandpa put it on Hookhorn's neck with Bert. Then a Nestor Olkivaara killed Hookhorns. They sent him to jail, but the sheriff from the church village brought the bell here. Now we'll put it on Hookhorn's neck again. Bert is just as little as you are. He's going to be a tough reindeer man. I did not forgive that reindeer thief. Has the sheriff put him in irons yet? He smashed it in the head with an ax. Listen to grandpa when he really rings this bell."

Bert Sääskilampi wiped at his eyes and looked around. There was no one else in the room but his father and the boys.

"Shouldn't you go and rest, father?" he said.

"Huh? Yaah, rest. Are you going out to look after the reindeer?"

"Mother and I are going to a funeral."

"Who died now? Was it Ryti-Veeti?"

"If you get up now, you can go and lie down in the bedroom."

Bert helped his father to his feet although his own back was still sore. His father weighed very little now, he thought, as he led him through the kitchen, where Petti Sääskilampi was putting on a black head-scarf.

"Lie down there. Shall I take your boots off?"

"No, my feet will freeze in this cold."

"Well then, father. Rest now, so you'll be able to drive the hay in the fall," said Bert as he went through the door into the kitchen.

The automobile drove into the yard. Now fully dressed, Petti went in to see her husband and said:

"You don't feel bad that Bert and I are leaving?"

"Why should I? You have to go to Oulu sometime."

"Father dear, we're not going to Oulu. Just to my brother's funeral."

"Hilkka wasn't very old yet. Younger than I. Is she being buried at the Ii cemetery?"

"Let me feel your forehead. Your cheeks are flushed — who knows, you might have a fever."

The wife pressed her palm into her husband's forehead. It did not feel hot. Petti Sääskilampi's lips began to move, but it was difficult for her to get the words out. Finally she spoke, still pressing her hand into the man's forehead:

"It would have been better to have talked things out with

Hilkka while we were evacuees. It's preying on your mind now."

Ivar Sääskilampi's wandering gaze focused sharply on his wife's eyes. He held his breath for a time and finally said, his jaw trembling:

"You knew about Hilkka?"

"It hit me like a bolt from the blue. I went to visit her with the woman we were staying with and saw her son's picture."

A sob cut off her words. She saw her husband's eyes open wide.

"Was it? What did the boy look like?"

"He's Bert's brother."

"God help me!" Ivar Sääskilampi gasped.

"Rest now. When Bert and I get back, we can talk about it. We're old now. It's best to set our souls at peace."

"And you took this without saying a word?"

"It happened before you were my husband. And I wasn't pure when I stood at your side before the minister."

"Forgive me."

"As far as I'm concerned, it's all forgiven."

"Mother, the car is waiting," said Bert from the doorway.

"I'm coming. Play with the boys and don't trouble your head over nothing. God's peace..."

"God's peace. Give your brother my regards."

As Petti left the kitchen, she said to Irja:

"See to it that your father gets his medications on time."

2

"Do you need anything, father?" asked Irja.

"Is there skim milk in that mug?"

"There is. Shall I put it on the chair near you?"

"Do, so I don't have to get up at night."

Irja set the mug on the chair at the head of the bed. Ivar Sääskilampi was smoking his pipe as he lay on his side facing his daughter. A package of tobacco and a box of matches stood on the chair. The father looked long and searchingly at his daughter. She was a handsome woman, better looking than her mother in her prime.

Her father's stare troubled Irja. She glanced down along her body and smoothed out her apron with a tug. Her father's mustache began to stir as he spoke, and Irja's tension eased.

"Would you give me the reindeer bell from that table?"

"Reindeer bell? The brass one?"

"That's it. It's the only one there."

Irja put the bell on the seat of the chair. Its clapper struck the side of the bell, and a brassy tinkle trilled through the air of the bedroom.

"What do you want with this?" asked Irja.

"I'll look at it and if I want anything during the night, I'll ring it."

"Of course. Then either Kosti or I will come at once. One of us could really sleep here."

"There's no need. Just stay with the children."

"Be careful with the pipe and tobacco."

"Don't worry. You go to sleep too. You've been on the go all day."

"If you need anything, father, just ring that bell."

"I will for sure. Tell the boys grandpa is sleeping."

"They're asleep already, but I'll tell them in the morning."

✧ ✧ ✧

The sun was just going down. Ivar Sääskilampi picked up the bell from the chair and turned it over in his hands. "*I* and *S*," he muttered aloud. "*I* and *S* — Hilkka and Eino are in the town of *Ii*." His mind began to revolve around the subject. "Hilkka and my son are in *Ii*. Petti, my wife, knows it too."

With a thumbnail, he scratched along the grooves in the brass surface. *I* and *S* — it sounded almost like the word *Isä* (father). The boy was sure to be back from the war now. He would be able to see him in the flesh. Was he as handsome as Bert?

Ivar filled his pipe. He lighted a match but held it for so long between thumb and forefinger that it burned him and he dropped it into the ash tray. I must go to Ii and see my son. I'll tell Hilkka to come and see us here. I'll give the boy a reindeer brand and some reindeer to start a herd with. What am I waiting for? Cars drive there, and I have the money. Army vehicles don't charge much for taking you to Oulu. The trip won't come to cost much. The only problem is, they won't let me go alone.

Ivar Sääskilampi's thoughts were cut off when the door

opened quietly and Kosti looked in.

"You're still awake," he said.

Ivar set the bell down and answered:

"I'm smoking an evening pipe."

"I just looked in to see if you need anything."

"I have everything I need. Sleep in peace, and cover up the boys so they won't get cold."

"Good night."

"The same to you."

It began to get dark. Soon it will be night, thought the old man. Night, night...It'll soon be my last night. It was night that time I went to see Hilkka, when that dark good-for-nothing was there. Is he in Hilkka's bedroom now? The boy is sure to drive him away. No, maybe he's still there. What would Hilkka say if I were standing at her door? She's sure to drive that dark one away and leap into my arms. She's sure to do it. I have to go there now. My wife isn't here to stop me. It's dark out already. Now I have to go. I have to go quietly so that Kosti and Irja won't hear me. Or Bert either, or Hilkka. Are they asleep already?

Ivar Sääskilampi rose and sat on the edge of the bed. Many a person has sat here, he mused. Preachers. My wife and I late at night. The boys slept on their own side against the wall when Irja had her last...

Now just to get my pants on. I don't need shoes. They would just clump on my feet. These woolen pants are warm. I'll put on a woolen blouse too. Do I have a wallet with me? I seem to have. A man needs money wherever he goes. But I don't dare go through that door. Irja and Kosti may wake up. Petti sleeps lightly too. They and Bert might run into me in the porch. I'll go out through that window. When I was young, I would slip out of it when I was playing with Bert. It's hard to get up onto the window sill, but I can make it from that chair. It would be nice to have a watch with me. I could tell from it where I'm going. And there's a big book. I can read Scripture on my way there. It tells about the Prodigal Son too.

Soon Ivar Sääskilampi was standing outside underneath the window. The dew is really heavy. It cools the feet so nicely. Now down to the shore. This is where the water starts its course toward the mouth of the River Ii.

The dog came out of its house and wagged its tail but did not bark. The path to the shore was familiar to his feet even in the darkness. The moon was just rising and it cast only a dim light. A mist hung over the river. Soon the man was setting the heavy Bible from under his arm down on the bottom of the boat. Leave the watch in my pocket. Now into the water with the boat. The drain plug has to be shut tight.

It took little effort to slide the boat into the water. Now I have to move softly so they won't hear me. You can hear a rattle easily over the water. Suppose I paddle as far as to the outlet? The oars might creak, and Petti would be on the shore at once shouting. She might start after me in the other boat.

The light boat began to glide toward the bank of mist. Was that a nude woman on the sandy shore? Who was she? She was lying down, but now another woman with a white body was standing upright. She was so tall! Let's see if she calls out after me. No, she said nothing. Now she had disappeared behind a thicket on shore.

The mist swallowed up the rower, but he could see land on either side. The lake grew progressively narrower as it approached the outlet into the river. Soon I'll hear the sound of flowing water and it will carry me toward Ii. Even if I sleep at times, I will always be traveling toward Hilkka and the boy. Will I get there before morning? If not tonight, then certainly I'll get there some night. The water will be free of ice for months yet, and the rapids never freeze. Now then, this is where the river begins. The boat is moving swiftly. The trees on shore are rushing by. Here's a little rapids. There's only one bad rock in it, on the north bank of the channel. It flashed by already. I made it through this rapids by memory.

A series of rapids began immediately below the lake. Ivar shot a few of them by steering at the rear of the boat. Then he began to feel unbelievably weary. Should I head in toward the bank? It doesn't pay; I wouldn't get to Hilkka tonight. I'll stretch out on the bottom of the boat. It will go by itself. Oh! What a pain in my chest. I have to rest a little now.

Ivar Sääskilampi dropped to his knees at the bottom of the boat. An oar slid into the water and was left floating alongside the craft. That big book is a good pillow. It's like a small bolster. It must be hard, but it feels warm against my cheek.

"Where did you come from, Petti?"

Petti Sääskilampi sat in the stern of the boat. She had simply appeared there and was steering with the rudder oar under her arm. Where had she gotten such a gleaming white dress to put on? She had been wearing black this morning. Petti didn't even have a white dress like that.

"Petti?"

The only answer was an echo from the steep banks of the river. He could hear a roaring up ahead. Välja Rapids is seething up there. But I have nothing to worry about. Petti has shot the rapids many times. The bank is really flying by. Water is even splashing over the side. I have to protect the Bible, keep the Sacred Word from getting wet.

The man curled his arm around his pillow. The boat is rocking nicely, just the way mother rocked the cradle when I was a little boy. I can barely remember it. Petti just keeps on steering. She's not afraid. A person doesn't laugh when she's afraid.

"Steer down the center of the channel, wife. There are bad hidden rocks near the banks. Say something! Tell me if you'll come with me to see Hilkka in Ii Hamina. Then we'll talk the thing over and it will stop preying on my mind."

Ivar Sääskilampi saw a constant smile on his wife's face. The skirts of her white dress billowed far behind the boat. The tops of pine trees over on the ridge are beginning to glow red. The sun is rising. Petti's cheeks look as if firelight were shining on them. They are wrinkled, but her lips are fixed in a pretty smile.

"Now what! This is such a soft bed, like a reindeer hide and..."

The boat, which had been running sideways, caught on a bottom stone and instantly turned over. When it came right side up again and continued its course down the boiling rapids, it was filled with water to the gunnels. The man was no longer to be seen as the boat swept on with one oar dangling from an oarlock. There was a momentary break in the voice of the rapids, but soon it resumed its former steady roar. By then the craft was gliding along in the gentle current of calmer waters.

3

A boat had almost reached the shore at Sammalsuo when those in the house noticed it. Aili, who had happened to glance out of the window, said:

"There's a boat coming."

"Who is it?" asked her mother.

"Hilja Naavala seems to be steering. A soldier is rowing."

"It's some soldier coming to ask for milk," said Maija.

Now Auku's curiosity was also aroused. There were army units stationed near Järvenkylä, and men came to bargain for milk even as far out as the Sammalsuo farm. Auku had come to know a few of them, and he went over to the window to identify the arrival.

"The one rowing is a broad-shouldered type," said Aili.

"It's not the first time he's handled a pair of oars," added Auku.

Maija too came over to the window, a knitting needle held crosswise in her mouth. It fell clinking to the floor as Maija grasped at her heart.

"It's Kauko!"

"Kauko?" said Aili.

The boat was nearly on shore. The rower leaped to his feet and turned to look toward the cottage.

"Goddamn! It is my brother Kauko."

Even Maija did not hear Auku's resounding curse. The door flew open and the whole group spilled out into the yard. Liisu and Väinö ran down to the shore. Their mother toddled along as fast as her legs could carry her, and Auku and Aili brought up the rear, walking with proper decorum. The boat nudged into the landing rock.

"Greetings from Petsamo," said Kauko, touching his cap in salute.

"Good heavens, you came without writing a word to us," said Maija.

For the first time in his life, Kauko squeezed his mother's hand. He did the same with his brothers and sisters. Lifting little Liisu high into the air, he said:

"You're a big lunk of a woman already."

From the stern of the boat, Hilja watched the joyful reunion of the Sammalsuo family. A light breeze was blowing across the lake, sending waves splashing into the side of the boat. The stones on the lake bottom seemed to sway when viewed through the water. Hilja strained into the oar, trying to free the boat from the shore. Maija noticed and said:

"You aren't in such a hurry that you can't stop in?"

"I'm in a bit of a rush and you can be alone with your soldier on leave."

Kauko turned to look at Hilja and said:

"Come in for awhile."

"I'll come and look at the rye field. Father says it's growing well," said Hilja, walking forward from the stern of the boat.

Kauko caught hold of the prow and raised the boat far up on shore with a jerk of one hand. Although she made an effort to help, Hilja was too late. Looking up at Kauko, she said:

"You pulled it so far up on shore that I won't be able to push it back into the water by myself."

"Well, I think the puller can do the pushing too," laughed Maija.

The whole group walked up the pathway from the shore. The hay had been made long since. Kauko looked around and said:

"Auku didn't do such a great job of mowing."

"Don't start off by complaining. And Väinö did it, not me."

"Don't criticize your brothers. They've been working very hard. We got up before four every morning during hay-making," said their mother.

"Well, are you happy now, you wilderness bum. You were most likely turning over in your sleep then, if you weren't getting back to your tent after a night with some Lapland *matyushka*," said Auku.

Kauko looked at his brother, and then his eyes caught a glimpse of Hilja. She was looking down at her feet and blushing. Darn that Auku, he thought, but he merely said:

"Let's go right out and look at that rye field."

The whole group walked toward the rye field over stubble, through which new growth was already thrusting its way. Oskar Portimo came trotting up to join the group, his tail erect, and began rubbing his side against Kauko's boot. Kauko bent down and caught the cat up in his arms.

"So you came through the winter alive," said Kauko.

"And in good shape too. Why not, when he was lapping up as much milk as his belly could hold. And in the fall, he got to hump all the neighbors' she-cats. He's got scads of offspring at Olkivaara and other places too."

They stopped at the very edge of the rye field. Maija and the other women in the group tried to ignore Auku's talk, but he would not let up. Going over to Kauko, he began to pet the cat that was purring in Kauko's arms and said:

"Oh, you poor old thing, if you had to support the products of all your fun last March, there wouldn't be a mouse left alive on this whole point. That's the way it is, Oskar."

"Don't you have anything else to talk about?" said Maija.

"A person has to talk about such things. They're the truth too," said Auku.

Kauko dropped the cat and said:

"There are loads of shocks here. When was this grain cut?"

"We finished it the other night. Damn, if we had only known you were coming, we would have left it for you to hack at," said Auku.

"That's why I didn't write," said Kauko, with a wink at his mother.

Hilja stood with her arms crossed, looking at the rye. The flush was fading from her face as she said:

"You're sure to fill many sacks of rye from this."

"The grain heads are huge," said Kauko, lifting up a handful of sagging kernels.

"A lot has happened in these wood since that grain was sown," said Maija. "Has there ever been a winter like the last? The evacuation, and the war coming so close to us. And now it looks as if everything will soon be rationed."

"There was no guarantee of safety in those days either, when Russian raiders came sweeping down the Ii river. They say they plowed the men's wives and broke the arrows of their cross-bows," tittered Auku.

"Let's go and make coffee, girls. No one can stand to listen to that smutty Auku," said Maija, although the corners of her mouth were twitching.

The brothers remained standing at the edge of the field. Oskar Portimo went stalking, belly to the ground, among the shocks of rye. Every now and then a little bird burst into flight, almost always to the accompaniment of a frustrated yowl from the cat. Auku looked at Kauko, scowling first at his boots and then raising his eyes to his older brother's face.

"What did they mean by giving you those corporal's stripes?"

"They make all kinds of mistakes — even the higher-ups."

"Well, those stripes will do, but where the hell did you get such ugly boots?"

Kauko looked down at his footwear, shifting slowly from one foot to the other as he gazed at them. He said:

"What's wrong with them? They're polished enough to go between a woman's legs."

"You could never use them for a mirror — and they're such huge gunboats."

"I have big feet...You and Väinö turned over a lot of ground. When did you do it?"

"I started swinging a hoe with Väinö as soon as I came back from the log drive. Toivo Olkivaara came and plowed it, after Väinö and I cleared out the roots and brush," said Auku.

"Yeah, and there were big stumps too," added Väinö.

"We have to get this rye threshed quickly so that we can finish the sowing before my leave ends," said Kauko.

"We can pack the drying barn tomorrow," said Auku.

"How long is your leave?" asked Väinö.

"Ten days. And this is already the second."

"Come for coffee, you farmers," shouted Aili from the porch door.

"That porch is turning gray," said Kauko, as they walked toward the house. "We should put a coat of red ocher on the walls next summer."

"You don't have many months to go...or reveilles, as the soldiers say," said Auku.

"Two hundred," said Kauko.

Auku opened the door, banged his heels together, and said with a titter:

"Corporal, sir, step right in."

"Stop clowning."

✧ ✧ ✧

After the coffee was drunk, Hilja sat on the bench for awhile. It bothered her to sit with her hands idly clasped. She had not even brought any handwork with her. That Kauko is a good boy, she thought. One can see that he cares for his mother, brothers, and sisters. He had saved his soldier's pay and brought homecoming gifts for them. He was completely different from Toivo. Auku was nice too, but sometimes he said such nasty things.

The littler ones were messing with Kauko's traveling bag. From it, Kauko took out a small package tied with a thin ribbon. He went over to Hilja and said:

"You can have this if...if you want it."

Hilja's heart beat faster. The package was so small that two of its size could have fit into a match box.

"Thank you...For me...You didn't...for me."

"It's for you, but you mustn't look at it until you get home."

"It can't be an engagement ring," said Auku.

Kauko looked angrily at his brother and then stood gazing out the window. The saplings swayed in the breeze, and the hay barns were as gray as ever.

"That's a mighty mysterious looking package," said Aili. "Show me what's in it sometime, Hilja."

"It's no military secret. What the devil business is it of yours? I found it at Parkkina, where the Russians were last winter."

"What is Parkkina?" asked Hilja.

"It's the same as Petsamo."

Clutching the package in her hand, Hilja said:

"I have to go home now. Come and visit us too."

"I'll always find time for that. I'll come and push the boat into the water," said Kauko.

"And I'll go along to see that nothing improper is said."

Auku was grinning as he spoke, and he actually did disappear in the wake of Kauko and Hilja, although Maija said to him:

"Your talk makes others ashamed. Kauko and Hilja can get the boat into the water by themselves."

Kauko held on to the prow of the boat while Hilda walked to the stern, striving to keep her balance. Looking out at the lake, he said:

"There's quite a breeze blowing. Can you make it across by sculling?"

"It's mainly a favoring wind."

"Thank you for bringing me when you were so busy. I could have crossed over the bridge and come by land," said Kauko.

"Wasn't it nice to row on your home lake after being away so long?"

"It was...and otherwise too."

Kauko glanced at Auku, who was carefully raising the edge of a flat rock lying in the shallows. He scooped at the water with his cupped hands, and then burst out angrily:

"There was a fishing worm there, but the damn thing scooted away."

"Well then, I'll shove the boat off," said Kauko. "I'll come and visit when I get a little settled. Are you always at home?"

"Where else would I be?"

"Don't make too many dates, Kauko. You have to go and talk to Toivo and Nestor this evening. And then there's the best of all," Auku tittered. "All those soldiers from everywhere have been chasing after Elma in vain. I don't know exactly who she's waiting for."

"Goldarn it boy, stop that nonsense," barked Kauko.

Hilja stirred the water with the oar more vigorously than usual. Then she no longer needed to look toward the shore. The Sammalsuo boys were behind her now. As she sculled some distance away, Kauko said:

"If you weren't my brother, I'd throw you into the water clothes and all."

"The water isn't very cold yet."

✧ ✧ ✧

Hilja stopped in at the kitchen, then went on to the outbuilding where she slept during the summer. Her hands trembled a bit as she opened the small package. Her mood was hardly joyful, although she was a little excited about what was wrapped up in the paper. She dallied in opening it, but finally straightened out the last fold.

"A brooch!"

She moved to the door to check her gift. It was in the shape of a leafy branch which had a small hammer and sickle at the base where the pin closed.

"Could this be silver? At least, there are small inlays in it."

Hilja tried the brooch on her breast. It was pretty even on an everyday dress. But Hilja did not feel the joy of one who has received a gift. It should have gone to Elma Olkivaara. Why did Kauko give it to me, she wondered. It must have been as payment for taking him home. *"And then there's the best of all..."* Hilja dug out her handkerchief. For the first time in her life she was disgusted with Auku Sammalsuo. He said such ugly things and was always wisecracking. Kauko had turned beet red, had even said something in an angry voice when she was some distance away.

Hilja looked around the storehouse and then only did she give free rein to the thoughts that came thronging into her mind. Kauko belongs to Elma — why should I be thinking about them? If Toivo would only look at me warmly sometimes. He couldn't bring himself to say anything tender even if he were coached. He is nice in other ways. And there's nothing wrong with his looks. It's just that he has such a gloomy view of the world.

4

"Men come back from across the sea, but never from under the ground."

Nestor squeezed Kauko's hand hard. Kauko would already have withdrawn his own, but his neighbor prolonged the handshake.

"You had to wait a long time for your leave, but you finally got it," Nestor exclaimed as he released Kauko's hand. "They didn't mean to let me go last spring, but the battalion commander was a good man and he fixed it up. I made it in time for the log drive. Auku was in my crew. He's got the makings of a tough man. Mari, come and see the soldier."

Kauko stood in the room feeling a little forlorn. The neighbor's place was familiar and somehow strange at the same time. Mari came in from the kitchen. She certainly did look bad, thought Kauko.

"Welcome, welcome...You're here Kauko. When did you come?"

"I got home today," said Kauko.

"The young look better and better and the old decay," said Mari with a sigh.

Kauko could say nothing. Mother had told the truth when she said that Mari was doing poorly. The younger children entered the room. Svante came in to blurt out his greetings, and Taimi as well. Taimi had grown so much that Kauko scarcely knew her. He had had time to sit down before she entered and he stood up a little embarrassed to shake hands with her.

"You...you're a grown-up woman," said Kauko.

"They treated me like a child during the evacuation. Welcome."

Nestor talked a blue streak. He told Kauko about the battles of

Suomussalmi, Raate, and Kuhmo. Although he was interested in them, Kauko's eyes kept roving around the the room and his ears were pricked up to catch Mari's and Taimi's talk in the kitchen.

"I was there in it with the younger men too. It was no big problem for me except for that business about military courtesy. No way I was going to go stretching my spine in front of even the biggest brass. And I put up a real public protest about flipping my fingers to my cap. I would never do that. I didn't like that business at all. But things really went bad for those Russians. It turned out to be such a cold winter and they started out in such skimpy clothes. They killed a lot of us, but they lost their looeys down to the last man."

"I saw a little bit of fighting at Kuhmo too," said Kauko.

"I heard about it, but we never ran into each other. Toivo fought himself into a sergeant's rank on the Isthmus."

Nestor's flow of words halted for a moment, and Kauko said:

"Isn't Toivo at home?"

"He is, and he's turned into a full-blown farmer now, always clearing more land. There'll soon be plenty of room to fling around the rye seed at Olkivaara (*Straw Hill*). I've told the boys we should change the name to Jyvävaara (*Grain Hill*)," Nestor laughed.

"Father has as many words as a penniless cow buyer," said Taimi. She looked at Kauko and added, "Elma and Toivo are packing the drying barn."

"That's right. Someone should go and tell them we have visitors."

"No, don't," said Kauko. "I'll go and see them myself."

"Well, we made it back to our home, though we had it pretty tough out there last winter. And is the peace a sound one yet? To me it's a bad sign that the woods are full of soldiers digging machine-gun nests and all kinds of holes. If there wasn't something strange going on, why are they digging those war pits?"

Thoughts of Elma and Toivo vanished from Kauko's mind at this point.

"There's something false about this peace," he began. "I was supposed to get a leave at the beginning of August, but it was withdrawn. Then one of my good buddies, Jonas Niemi, got a leave to harvest grain. He has a big farm near Raahe. The leave was cancelled a couple of days after Jonas got home. Many other leaves were cut short and the men called back."

"That's just what I was saying. So you're stationed near Petsamo?"

"I've been spending the summer there. The scenery is nice."

Kauko could hear Mari rattling the coffee cups in the kitchen. He rose from the bench and said:

"I'll pop in on Toivo."

"Don't be long. The wife seems to be making coffee," said Nestor. As Kauko was on his way to the door, Nestor grumbled at his younger offspring: "You don't have to follow Kauko. Grown-ups have their own things to talk about. Why the hell do you have to chase after a visitor like a fox after a ram's balls?"

Kauko suppressed a smile. Nestor seldom spoke so roughly to his children. As he walked toward the drying barn at the edge of the woods, Kauko's nostrils picked up its scent. Barley had been threshed there. The black-browed door was open and from inside came the sound of thumping against the rafters, and of voices. Over the door, where the log walls were completely blackened with soot, was a palm-sized piece cut from a bright paper. Toivo had adjusted his gun sights there, thought Kauko. The paper was well riddled with bullets, which had left black spots that looked like flies sitting on the paper.

They hadn't seen him coming.

On purpose, Kauko turned aside from the straight route to the door. The mown field was thrusting out new shoots, and its fragrance was wafted to his nostrils. He felt the coolness of the coming night on his hands and face. He could hear Toivo saying:

"Doggone that old man. He wouldn't let us borrow the Naavalas' thresher."

"It's strange he was so dead set against it."

"But next year we're going to borrow it. I'm sure Akseli Naavala will lend it to us. Don't stick the top of that sheaf into your eyes."

Kauko stepped to the door. Toivo, who was standing up on the rafters, saw him at once. Elma noticed only that the barn grew darker. She turned.

"Is it you? Where did you pop up from?"

Elma's white teeth gleamed and her eyes shone in her sooty face. She dropped the sheaf and took a few steps toward the door. Without conscious thought, her arms twined themselves around Kauko's neck and she pressed her face into his shoulder.

"I did get to see you again...Kauko...Kauko..."

Kauko put his arms around her shoulders.

"They gave me a leave," was all he could say.

The two of them stood there in the same position for awhile. The high, sooty threshold of the drying barn was between them. Elma's upper body was leaning heavily into Kauko. She could not say a word. Toivo, to the contrary, began cursing angrily:

"Now those goddamned sheaves are coming down! What made them start falling now? Every last straw will soon be on the floor again. Everything's going to hell!"

It was some time before the harsh invective penetrated Kauko's ears. At first it frightened him. Now what was Toivo so angry about? Elma turned to look at her brother, who was struggling with the sheaves with his back turned toward them. Tears were pouring from her eyes and tracing paths down her sooty cheeks, but she giggled as she spoke:

"You can stop yelling, my good man. I'm not hanging onto Kauko's neck any longer."

Toivo turned slowly and looked at Kauko standing in the doorway. At last Kauko said:

"Greetings from the Arctic mountains."

"When did you come?" said Toivo.

"Today."

"Elma and I just got the rafters packed again. Did you see the old man?"

"We've already had a long talk."

Elma tossed the few remaining sheaves to Toivo, who came down from the rafters and walked out of the barn. Blowing his nose heavily, he said:

"You breathe in a lot of dust on this job."

Elma too came out. She looked down at her feet. Toivo turned to look at Kauko and laughed uproariously.

"You should see your mug. Now that is a sight! That stupid Elma has gone and rubbed her snoot into it."

Even Elma laughed. She scrubbed at her wet cheek with the palm of her hand. Her face was so sooty it was hard to believe that her skin was white. She was wearing an old and too-tight dress that ended above her knees. The top half of it threatened to burst a seam with every breath she took. In between spasms of laughter, she said:

"Don't I look like a real wilderness rose?"

"Get the hell in and change your clothes! You got Kauko's neck and the collar of his shirt all sooty. With your brains, you can't have too many headaches."

"I'm not worried about Kauko. You've seen me in my threshing rags before, haven't you? And best of all, I'm seeing you alive again."

"Water is the cure for dirt," said Kauko.

"And I'll start the.cure. Let's go to the sauna shore. There's warm water there. I'll wash your shirt too, since Toivo's grumbling so much about it."

"It wasn't all that clean," said Kauko. "But I can rinse off my neck."

As they walked toward the Olkivaara yard, Toivo said:

"You're rye is coming in like crazy."

"It seems to have grown plenty. Are you all through threshing yours?"

"We have to pack the barn three more times," said Toivo.

"You can go to the sauna with the men, Kauko. It's warmed for the threshers," said Elma.

"Maybe there isn't enough steam for a soldier too," said Kauko.

"There's bound to be. Come and wash your face," said Elma, running toward the shore.

Kauko and Toivo walked after her. She was already on her way out of the sauna, balancing a pan of water in her hands.

"Here's warm water. There's soap on the shore rock and rinse water in the lake," she said with a laugh.

5

"It was nice that Elma had bread cheese baked," said Mari.

The entire Olkivaara family was seated around the kitchen table. Kauko's shirt was soaking in a pan of water on the sauna shore. Soot was no longer visible on his face or that of the threshers. Elma was sitting near the stove seeing to it that the coffee was poured.

"Break up plenty of that bread cheese into your coffee," said Nestor.

"I had some already. It's really good," said Kauko.

"Did your mother think to make bread cheese?" asked Mari.

"No, I couldn't let them know I was coming."

Toivo looked out at the darkening evening and said:

"It's going to be a cold night. Otherwise Kauko and I would go out shining. Fish won't come near the shore when there's a mist on the water."

"Now don't start coaxing Kauko into your night-time doings. Let's sit and chat, since the Lord has let us come together again," said Mari.

"I've already said it was no weather for shining fish," said Toivo.

"Kauko is probably tired," said Mari.

"Damn it, a man that age doesn't sleep nights," Nestor burst out. "A young man has to be up and doing. Will Elma have the sauna ready soon?"

Elma rose and left the room without saying a word. Kauko tried to question Toivo about the winter's events, but all he got was a mumbled response.

"He doesn't talk about the war," said Mari.

"What good does that do?" said Toivo. "There are other things to talk about than how people were butchered."

Elma returned to the kitchen and said:

"The sauna is ready. The men can go."

✧ ✧ ✧

After sauna, the family crept off to bed one by one. The last thing the younger children did was to eat bread and butter at the kitchen table. Nestor too went silently off to his bedroom after Mari. Toivo and Svante slept in the stable loft during the summer, and Taimi and Elma in the storehouse on the shore. Taimi too went out, and Kauko and Elma were left alone in the kitchen.

"Let's go into the main room," Elma said.

The room was almost dark. Kauko seated himself at the head of the table. Elma sat down beside him and said:

"I was really watching to see if you would sit here."

"Why did you expect me to?"

"Ever since you were a little boy, you've always sat there. I remembered it again when you were away in the army."

"I probably did...now I remember."

A long silence followed. What can I say, Kauko thought. He could smell the calming fragrance of the birch whisks from Elma's body. Finally he said:

"We did get to sit together once more."

"Once more...Were you waiting for it?"

Kauko groped for Elma's hand and squeezed it hard. Selma and her letter came into his mind.

"It goes without saying," whispered Elma.

It felt good to sit here like this. A feeling of well-being filled Kauko's heart. What more could a person ask? Jonas and Jalo could have no idea how good he felt.

"Should I leave?"

"Why?" Elma's question sounded frightened.

"I don't know myself. It's good to be here, but I'm embarrassed about your family."

"About Nestor too?" asked Elma. "You weren't asked to leave."

"I know that. They must have thought you would tell me to go when you were tired of me."

"Do you think I am? Your shirt is drying too. Do you intend to go home in your undershirt?"

"I hear that Taimi sleeps with you in the storehouse."

"What does she matter to us?"

He was not shy with Elma now that he could not see her face and her fingers were squeezing his own. Her shoulder was leaning against his arm. He did not even have to clear his throat in order to say:

"Where will we sleep?"

"We could even sleep in this room. I'll get a mattress and a bolster. That's all a soldier needs for a bed."

"A coat would be nice to pull up to our ears," Kauko said.

"We'll get father's fur coat," Elma laughed. "But seriously, let's go into my bedroom. The bed is all made up in there."

At that moment the outside door to the kitchen opened. Kauko tried to move away from Elma, but she said:

"It's only Taimi."

Taimi peered in from the kitchen and said:

"So that's where the lovebirds are perched."

"What are you peeping at? Are you jealous?"

"And Auku isn't even around," Taimi laughed gaily, and then she said: "The storehouse is empty. I'll sleep in Elma's bedroom."

Taimi disappeared into the kitchen, and Kauko said:

"How time flies. Taimi is a big girl already."

"She is, and now she insists on wearing the few rags I own. She's growing, and now you can't get clothes anywhere. But shouldn't we do as my sister said?"

"Let's go."

✧ ✧ ✧

The small oil lamp was familiar to Kauko, as were the log walls it lighted up. Right now the other boys are stumbling around the tent, he thought. If only my leave doesn't get cancelled. Kauko was sitting on the edge of the bed and Elma near a table of sorts. Suddenly an odd notion struck Kauko so strongly that he had to say it:

"What do you say, Elma, if we go and bathe?"

Elma looked at him in surprise, and then her lips lengthened into a smile as she said:

"Together?"

"Yes. We have so little time together. Why should we waste it?"

"That's true. We won't light the sauna lamp," said Elma.

"Are you afraid to be with me in the lamplight?"

"I'm not afraid, but what about you?"

"We can manage by just feeling our way around. Shall we go right now?"

"Let's go before the steam is all gone."

"This extra bath seems like a sham," said Kauko.

"Are you starting to play, *Well I don't know*?" said Elma.

"Not really, but since we've already bathed..."

"A person could bathe many times a day during the threshing season. Your skin is always itching. Have you given up bathing in the army?"

"Not at all. In the spring, when we went to Petsamo, we used juniper and pine whisks to beat ourselves with."

"Well then...kersplash! The lamp is out now. Shall we leave our clothes here?"

There was a soft rustling sound from Elma's direction. She's pulling her slip up over her head, thought Kauko. He dropped his own suspenders from his shoulders. Soon the storehouse door creaked and the dim figure of a nude person could be seen against the mountain ash tree in the yard.

"I'll go and get the water ready."

6

Kauko walked slowly from Olkivaara toward Sammalsuo. It was another hot day, although the breeze was actually from the north. The hillocks beside the road were red with lingonberries. Mixed in among them were leafless blueberry plants from which hung huge blueberries. But they were already frost-bitten.

Kauko stripped off lingonberries to stuff into his mouth. On the one hand, he was eager to get home, but on the other hand, he felt like a criminal returning from the scene of a crime. Godalmighty, he had a weird mind, as brother Auku used to say. Was it such a heinous sin for a soldier on leave to stay the night with a woman and not come back before morning? Wasn't it viewed as manly behavior? During the ruckus at Lõytõvaara last winter, this would hardly have upset him. After all, he and Elma were both adults.

Kauko glanced at his watch, which showed almost eleven. A reindeer trail began here, along which he and Auku had always set snares. Kauko could actually remember when he had made his first snares with his deceased father. That had been a hot day too, with the coolness of autumn breathing from the woods. Auku had been very little, and his own head hadn't reached too high either. Had Auku set the snares out by now?

He set off along the path of soft evergreen needles. The first snare was at the foot of a large spruce tree. Auku had once caught a cock wood-grouse there, and many smaller woodfowl. The spruce was a couple of meters from the trail. Kauko bent down beneath its low-hanging branches.

"Auku seems to have put up a new fence of twigs here," he muttered.

The noose made of fishing line seemed to have come loose from one of its supports. With experienced fingers, Kauko picked up an old pine needle, caught the snare line in its fork, and anchored it to a twig alongside the snare gate. As he did so, the toes of his boots caught his eye, and the words Elma had spoken, which had kept flitting through his mind all that morning, came back with a rush. *"Almost every night there are soldiers tramping around here. You see track upon track outside the storehouse, and people think they are carrying on inside it too."*

Fear and panic assailed his mind. Elma will never be able to wait for me, with all these soldiers here, each one flashier than the next.

They swarm around young women like flies around a cow's rear. And Elma's conscience couldn't have been too clear. She was sighing so heavily this morning. She didn't seem to care much for the gift I brought her. And she was so willing to go to the sauna. Who knows what she's already been up to with soldiers? All women must be the same. That stinker in Rovaniemi too. Small, and not much to look at, but she had the nerve to write: "*...it must be from the boy I sat roosting with on that big rock in the rain...*"

Kauko strode along the path beaten by reindeer hoofs. Out of a sense of duty, he glanced at some of the snares. A number of them were already sprung.

"To hell with them," said Kauko when he noticed it.

He turned toward home long before completing the circuit. Not even familiar points on the landscape interested him. As he stepped onto his home ground through the gate of the outer fence, he gritted his teeth and said:

"And I had to go and spend the night with her. And that trip to the sauna. Now I'm really in a mess. There was a reason they were all so nice to me. The whole thing was a set-up."

Gloomily Kauko walked through a plot of hoed land. The smell of freshly turned virgin soil made his nostrils tingle. Auku was out there now, tilling new fields. As he flipped over the turf with a hoe, he said with a laugh:

"So you got away..."

"Just what are you driving at?" Kauko nearly bellowed.

"Stop shouting. I was just afraid you got stuck with Elma. They say such things have happened."

"That someone got stuck with Elma?"

"No — somewhere else. That's what the grown-ups say. Why are you gawking at me?"

Kauko went over to Auku, snatched the hoe from his hands, and began to turn over the soil in a frenzy. Auku watched his brother's furious efforts for awhile and said:

"Even a bigger stallion than you will soon tire at that rate."

"I've always told you to turn the ground over properly," panted Kauko.

"Then Väinö and I have been trying to hoe this patch of ground for nothing."

"Why? I didn't say that."

"Well, it sounds like we did a poor job of it."

"It's good enough...Where is Väinö loafing?"

"Over there in that university," said Auku, pointing in the direction of the public school. "You're mucking up your boots for nothing."

"Boys, come for coffee," called Maija, who had come out onto the porch.

For an unnecessarily long time, Kauko wiped his feet on the grass in the yard. When his mother saw the angry look on his face, she said nothing for a long time. Had he and Elma quarreled about something, she wondered. They were still children...Had it been necessary for him to dally there for so long? As he was drinking his coffee, she said:

"It's strange that after eleven months a man can't spend one night at home."

Kauko looked at his mother. She did not seem very angry.

"I've gotten used to being away. Now I have to break in my bed at home gradually. At least I was in my home community."

"Have you had breakfast?"

"They don't send a guest away without food."

"What did Mari say when you fooled away half the day there?"

"How do you know that I didn't spend the night in hell?"

Kauko jerked his boots off heatedly, hung his shirt over a nail, and said:

"Where are my clothes so I can put them on? I'm going to carry rye to the drying barn with Auku."

His mother brought an often-patched pair of pants to Kauko and said:

"If you can stand to put these on, you won't have to worry about them in the drying barn. Was your summer shirt so clean yesterday?"

His mother looked suspiciously at the shirt and stroked the smoothly pressed insignia on its collar. Then she said:

"These stripes were almost black. This has been washed."

"I came by way of the snare circuit on the way back," said Kauko.

Maija sighed and thought: Am I no longer good enough to wash his shirt?

✧ ✧ ✧

Kauko and Auku carried the sheaves of grain to the drying

barn and began to pack them on the rafters. Mother came to light a fire in the fire pit of the barn. While the boys hoed more of the field, she kept going out to add more wood to the fire. Väinö and Liisu came rowing home from school. While she was still in the doorway, Liisu said:

"The master of Sääskilampi drowned."

"Drowned? What kind of nonsense are you talking, Liisu?"

Maija's eyes turned to Väinö.

"It's no nonsense. They say the boss man of Sääskilampi drowned."

"You can't mean it. God help us! Where would a sick man go and get drowned?"

Kauko and Auku were drinking their evening coffee. They too pricked up their ears.

"They say he ran away from home last night. He took a boat from the shore. They found the boat overturned in the calm waters below Väljä Rapids. It must have run into a rock. There was a heavy mist last night. The lady of the house and Bert had gone to Kijanta to her brother's funeral. That's how he was able to slip out."

Maija's body trembled. The boys too looked grave.

"Didn't they find the body?" asked Maija.

"Not yet. They found his Bible on a reef in the rapids."

"Did he have his Bible with him?" asked Maija.

"They say he took it along," said Väinö.

"Well, we wretched human beings leave the world in all kinds of ways," sighed Maija. "They say the master of Sääskilampi has not been of sound mind for a long time."

Bitter thoughts intruded into Kauko's mind. He was about to say that the devil takes his own in due time, but the tears in his mother's eyes made him swallow his words.

"Lots of soldiers are out looking for him," said Väinö. "They're dragging the calmer waters to find him."

"He'll soon be at the mouth of the Ii River," said Kauko. "A body that fat can't even sink to the bottom."

"It's horrible to talk about the dead like that. As if a dog had drowned. And poor Ivar was no longer fat. They say that only skin and bones were left."

"Where I was last winter, they taught us not to fear death or bodies either. And that old man always treated us like dogs. If he weren't Irja's father and Kosti's father-in-law, I wouldn't bat an eyelid. Come along, Väinö, and we'll go and get the field in shape for planting. It has to be sown before my leave is up."

7

The sauna at Olkivaara was right next to the storehouse. As soon as Elma had vanished into the darkness, Kauko too went out and walked naked to the sauna shore. The wet sand felt cold, but nevertheless he waded into the water up to his knees and splashed water over his arms and chest. Darkness and mist hung in harmony over the water.

As Kauko ducked in through the sauna door, he heard the hiss of steam on the rocks and the voice of Elma from back on the benches:

"Come up on the bench. There's water ready for you too."

Kauko groped around in the dark. Although he knew every corner of the Olkivaara sauna, he climbed up onto the benches with his arms extended to feel his way.

"Ooh! Darn it, you've got such clammy hands."

"Don't scream, they'll hear you at the house," Kauko said, startled.

"Well, darn it, sticking your cold hands into a person's breasts," giggled Elma.

"I went wading in the lake," said Kauko.

"You get the craziest ideas. Brrr, you're cold all over."

"I'll sit further away so you won't get cold."

"I'll throw on more steam to warm you up."

The stones sizzled and the odor of the smoke sauna filled their nostrils. Elma swished a bath whisk around in the water and extended it to Kauko:

"Hey, here's a whisk for you. Start beating away...How far did you go, anyway?"

"Far enough so you won't get cold or scared. I'm not going to bathe."

"Are you taking more steam?"

"No."

"Why did you go all the way back in that corner?"

"Just because."

"Well, I'm going to bathe anyway."

Kauko said nothing. Elma began to beat herself with the whisk, and a draft of hot, damp air rushed into Kauko's corner. His earlier tension had turned almost to rage at Elma's shriek. Just when his hand touched her breast, she had had to go and squawk like that. Those were just women's wiles. Well, I'm not going to beg for anything, he told himself. I won't lay a finger on her. Did one have to be a sergeant or something to rate with women, as with Selma from Rovaniemi? Elma kept throwing water on the rocks repeatedly. Does she want to drive me down from here? She's beating herself with that whisk like the very devil. I have to duck down.

"Do you have a good sauna in the army?" asked Elma when she had finished with the whisk.

"It's not so great."

Elma stepped down to the floor and said:

"Shall I throw on more steam?"

"No need to."

"I'll open the door for awhile then. Shall I?"

"It's okay with me."

Elma pushed the door open. Kauko could see her squatting by it and looking out. She did have a slender waist... She spent some time cooling herself. Then she closed the door and said:

"If you want me to, I'll wash your back."

The thought of Elma's hands stroking his bare back, of her breast accidentally grazing his shoulder, flashed through Kauko's mind. Needing to calm himself enough so that his voice would not quaver, he was slow to answer.

"Your mother told us that she washed your back and hair almost until you went into the army," Elma giggled.

"That's a lie. It was many years ago. No woman has to scrub my back."

"Well, I won't then. You sound as if I had done something bad to you."

"I didn't say that."

Water splashed in Elma's wash pan. He heard her pouring the water over herself. Then she darted out without saying a word. The door creaked more irately than usual when it was slammed shut.

"What made her flare up like that?" Kauko muttered.

Kauko did no more than rinse off his face and pour the water prepared by Elma over his head. If I hadn't left my clothes in the storehouse, he thought, I would trot straight home. I don't care for these women's tricks.

Elma was already dressed and lying on the bed when Kauko re-entered the storehouse. He put on his clothes and took out a box of matches. Shaking it, he said:

"Can I light the lamp?"

"It's okay with me."

Kauko struck a match. He could see Elma curled up on one side with her face to the wall. Her neck and part of her shoulders were visible above the fleecy edge of a sheepskin quilt.

Kauko stood looking at her for a long time and then he said:

"What is this lying with your back turned supposed to mean?"

Elma's shoulders seemed to be quivering and she was pressing her face into her hands. There was no answer.

"I didn't come here to quarrel with you. If you can't force yourself to look at me, then you don't have to. I can make it home in the dark."

Elma turned over. She looked at him with teary eyes, and said:

"You were so nasty in the sauna. It was enough to make anyone feel bad."

"You started it by screeching. You screamed so loud it scared me."

"Your cold hands gave me such a shock. Heck, when someone clamps a pair of cold duck's webfeet on your breasts — how else can I say it — and women are so touchy about them..."

"You would have squawked just as loudly if I'd dipped my hands in hot water before coming into the sauna."

"I would not...if I knew they were your hands."

Kauko looked at Elma and said:

"If you sit up I'll show you something."

Elma reached out a hand to Kauko and said:

"If you pull...see if you can get a mare like this to sit up."

Elma was smiling happily by now. Kauko caught her by the wrist and pulled her into a sitting position at the edge of the bed. He sat down beside her and began to search though his pockets. Elma watched him and said:

"I'm dying of curiosity. You're not going to show me something ugly, are you?"

Kauko brought out a small case carved of wood. He thrust it into Elma's hand and said:

"Do you want this?"

Elma looked at the bright wooden case. Etched on it with a hot iron in decorative script was the legend: PETSAMO 1940.

"What's inside it?"

"You can open it yourself."

Elma's hands trembled. She opened the cover of the case and drew out a thin chain between her middle and index fingers. A heavier object at the end of it dropped out of the box and hung down from the chain in Elma's hand.

"A cross!" she almost shrieked.

Elma's frightened expression and her cry put an end to Kauko's good mood. His eyes followed the shadow of the cross as it swung back and forth across the log wall. Elma too was looking at it. The shadow loomed large on the wall. Elma dropped the the chain into her lap. After a long pause, she said, fingering the cross:

"Where did you buy this?"

"I didn't buy it. I found it on the ground near the Upper Monastery. Only a little piece of the chain was showing from under the soil and moss."

"And this box. It's pretty."

"I whittled it myself. The wood is from the same monastery."

Elma picked up the cross carefully, leaned closer to the lamp, and said:

"Is this silver?"

"It seems to be."

✧ ✧ ✧

When Kauko lay down beside Elma, it was well into the morning hours. She ought to be pleased with the gift, he thought, but she seemed almost afraid of it. She was breathing heavily on the wall side of the bed. How many years is it since they had slept in the same bed? They had been shining fish that night, and had caught a huge pike.

"You didn't seem to like the gift?"

"It's nice otherwise, but a cross is so morbid."

"I gave Hilja Naavala a sort of brooch..."

Elma started. He's given Hilja a brooch, she thought. No wonder he's been acting so odd all evening. A brooch...that's a suitable gift for a girl friend. Why not? Hilja is a fit girl friend for Kauko. They're the same age too. I'm practically an old woman, and Kauko most likely thinks of me as a mother...or an aunt at best. A cross is the symbol of death. Of a dead affection.

Kauko turned over onto his back, clasped his hands beneath his head, and said:

"The Russians had dropped that brooch of Hilja's. I found it in their lodgings. It was well made."

Elma turned toward the wall and said:

"And a fine girl got it too."

Kauko could tell from the tone of Elma's voice that she was being sarcastic. Let her stew for awhile, he thought, and then I'll tell her the brooch was in return for Hilja's taking me across the lake. Why is Elma acting up about it? She should know that someone of my standing wouldn't aim as high as the Naavala girl — nor would I want to. I'll rest a little first, and then it'll be nice to take Elma in my arms and caress her.

At that moment, another thought occurred to Kauko, and he said:

"They say there are lots of soldiers around here."

Elma was slow to answer. When she did her tone of voice was harsh:

"Almost every night, there are soldiers tramping around here. You see plenty of tracks around this storehouse. And people think they are prancing around inside it too."

"Shouldn't we sleep a little?" Kauko said with a yawn.

"You couldn't have slept much last night."

"I dozed a little on the train."

Kauko awakened reluctantly to the sound of someone hammering on the door of the storehouse. It was a long time before he recognized Taimi's voice.

"You darned lovebirds, you're sleeping the day away. Get up now, Elma, and come to the house."

In his sleep, Kauko had put one arm across Elma's shoulders. Suddenly she threw her arms around his neck and pressed her head into his chest.

"Kauko..."

Then she leaped up and said through the door:

"Do we have any visitors?"
"Not a blessed soul. Come in quickly for coffee."
"I don't think I should," said Kauko.
"It's too late to run away now. And I'll iron that blouse."

8

The days of Kauko's leave went by too quickly. He threshed the grain with Auku and they planted the new rye. Early one morning, he went to get the horse from Nestor while Aili and Auku rowed the harrow and manure cart across the lake. Kauko and Elma exchanged only a few words. Each was waiting for the other to say something more personal.

When the rye field was harrowed, Maija came out to the edge of it and said:

"Next fall you'll be out of the army. You won't have to hurry and finish before your leave ends."

"That line of woods has been pushed back quite a bit during these years."

Kauko looked out across the rye field and then he added:

"If we could just get a horse for next summer."

"The two of you can work at logging over the winter," said Maija.

Maija watched as Auku unhitched the horse and then said:

"Are you taking the horse to Olkivaara before we eat supper, or shall I get the food ready right now?"

"Neither before nor after. Auku can take it."

"Well..." said Maija, looking at Kauko.

"I feel tired. I think it's better if I go to bed."

"Well, I just thought you should pay Nestor for the use of the horse."

"And better still, pay Nestor's daughter," said Auku.

"Well, if you won't take the nag, let Aili do it then, or even Väinö. And you, boy, don't open your mouth so much."

Auku looked at his brother. Now what was making him so bad-tempered? He was in no mood for joking. He had been in a foul mood the whole time he'd been home.

"We won't send women there. I'll ride the horse to Olkivaara," said Auku.

✧ ✧ ✧

The following day Kauko made a quick visit to Naavala and exchanged a few casual words with Hilja. The master of the house was away, and Kauko was shy in the presence of women. He walked both ways, and both coming and going, he stopped on the bridge to gaze at the landscape, chiefly toward the east. The horizon beyond the lake was blue-gold and the woods a deep green. Soon the colors of autumn would arrive.

Last winter I was walking here on guard duty, he reflected. There's where a captain tried to shoot me and Auku. We could hear artillery and mortars thundering in the direction of Alasalmi. People were being evacuated. Live soldiers were being trucked east, and dead bodies were being trucked back. Was that only eight months ago?

On the way back, Kauko made a swing through the woods. The wild meadows and swamps of his childhood seemed very small now. The whole wilderness no longer seemed as large or as mysterious as it once had.

✧ ✧ ✧

On Kauko's last evening at home, there was a beautiful moon out. It was already casting shadows in the dewy stubble as he walked around the yard at home. He sat down on a stone in the middle of the yard. The setting moon was reflected in the water across the lake. His mother came out. She too looked at the moon and said, with her back to him:

"Aren't you planning to go and say goodbye to the Olkivaaras?"

"Well, I'm not going off to be killed," said Kauko.

"They're sure to think that I've been causing trouble between us when..."

"Why should they? I haven't had time to visit other places either."

"You'll be going by way of Naavala tomorrow, but you could have gone to Olkivaara."

"They'll be asleep already."

"Elma won't be, at least, and I hardly think Toivo would either."

Kauko said nothing. For a long time he sat chin in hand, and then he rose and started out for Olkivaara. Maija gazed after him. What was wrong between him and Elma, she wondered. Elma is such a good girl. Had Kauko's nerves been affected by the war? Mari too complained that Toivo was impossibly irritable. There must be some sort of trouble between Kauko and Elma. She was not a girl to sustain a quarrel. She says right out what she has to say, but in the next breath, she is laughing. Kauko is the one who is sulking. He's been irritable at home too. Maija set out to visit the barn once more, saying to herself:

"They're sure to make up."

✧ ✧ ✧

Kauko did not approach Olkivaara along the usual path. Before reaching the yard, he turned off into the shelter of a grove on shore. Although he had walked the last stretch in no great hurry, his heart was beating quickly...I have to sit here in the shelter of the aspens to catch my breath. I have to be very good to Elma, ask her pardon for being so cross and not visiting her. This time I'll hold her close, the way a grown man does a woman. I can't even imagine myself with anyone but Elma. I wonder how she feels toward me. At any rate, I'm going to say, no, whisper in her ear, that we're going to be man and wife.

"What the heck boat is that?"

Kauko saw a boat coming across the lake. The rower was inexperienced, for the boat swerved with almost every stroke of the oars. For Pete's sake, pull with the other oar now, Kauko thought. Who was that bumbler anyway? Now he was looking over his shoulder. He hadn't pulled hard enough on the oar. The boat had swung crosswise again.

I'll have to see where he's going. I don't dare go to Elma's storehouse now that he's so close. Let's see what kind of wanderer he is. Although the boat is swerving around the lake, it's slowly getting closer. He must be heading for the Olkivaara landing. Well, let him come. Now he's standing up. Kauko saw that the man was wearing an army cap, and a chill ran down his back.

The newcomer ran the boat up on shore, and looked around. Kauko's fists clenched and unclenched. Now he's walking to the door of the storehouse. He's standing there, gawking. Now he's reaching toward the door. Kauko heard a light rapping of knuckles. Should I go and punch him in the mouth? Kauko gritted his teeth. He heard a woman's voice say something. It was Elma's voice, he was sure of it. The moon shone on the wall, and Kauko saw the door open wide and swallow up the soldier.

"Well, good riddance."

Kauko hissed out the words and began to run away. Wet branches slapped against his face and clothing. In the yard, Olkivaara's dog began to bark. Kauko thought he heard a woman's voice cry out. That's right, keep the dog quiet so it won't wake up the house, Kauko raged to himself. When he was well on his way along the trail home, he gave vent to his inner torment:

"They're all the same kind of whores! Goddamn the goddamn! She was all ready to meet him there. And I was stupid enough to spend the first night with her.

"Elma fed me a good line, all right, but she was in too much of a hurry to let that stud into the storehouse while I was still on leave. The only good thing about it was that I didn't get there in time to knock on the door. They would be laughing themselves sick at me tomorrow. After this, I won't write a word to any girl at home. And very little to the others either. What the hell brush has been left here in the road?"

As Kauko leaped up in his rage, his foot caught in the top of a spruce tree left lying across the road and he fell crashing into its branches. This is the end of my chasing over to Olkivaara, he vowed. There are others of her kind to be had elsewhere.

✧ ✧ ✧

"Won't he even come tonight?" Elma asked herself.

She sat at the table for a long time. The lamp flickered as she turned the pages of a newspaper but her eyes formed no clear image of the lines she scanned.

Elma felt as if she were on tenterhooks. Why hadn't she gone to Sammalsuo this evening, she wondered. Mari had even suggested it. What was Kauko so miffed about? His leave was to end tomorrow. Should she go and visit their neighbor? It would be embarrassing at this late hour. Everyone would know why she had come.

Even father snapped at me, asking what I had done to make Kauko angry. Did he take it so badly when I needled him about

Hilja's brooch? I didn't have to say that. But it annoyed me when he brought me that symbol of death and gave Hilja a brooch, as if she were his sweetheart. But it was wrong of me to speak so sharply. Kauko at least is honest. It's his own affair if he's been to see Hilja.

During all of Kauko's leave, Taimi had slept in the bedroom. Every evening Elma had waited for a knock on the door. She had waited in vain. Now she arose and blew out the lamp. She would leave the door open. What if Kauko had come some night and she had not awakened? Was that what had upset him?

Elma lay down on the bed and drew the warm quilt over herself. Her heart beat so that she could hear it in her ears. Do come and love me, Kauko. Her thoughts ranged all the way to the Sammalsuo cottage.

Now what? She heard the creaking of oars. Raising her head from the pillow, she heard them plainly, scraping and chunking in the oarlocks. The sounds came nearer. The rower is coming here. It must be Kauko, coming in a boat. Toivo or Svante hadn't left in one, had they? No, both of the boats had been on the rollers when she had come to the storehouse.

A wave of warmth surged through her heart. Kauko had not really been angry. I'll squeeze the life out of that lunk now. I'll treat him in a way that he'll remember in Petsamo. Kauko is so shy. We could just as well be engaged. Elma smiled at her own silly notions and said softly:

"I'm quite the vamp. Kauko will propose some day when he's out of the army, if he really cares for me."

The boat crunched onto the shore. Now feet were trampling the wet vegetation. There was a rustling sound as the boat was drawn ashore. Now he's walking toward the door. Why is he standing there? Elma's heart was thudding. Surely he's listening to see if I'm alone or if Taimi is with me. Now he's right at the door and his knuckles are rapping at it. I should really keep him in suspense for a little while, but I can't bear to tease him.

"I'm alone and the door isn't locked."

Elma turned her back to the door and drew the quilt almost up to her ears. It will be nice to have Kauko come and draw back the quilt. Now the door creaked. He has his army boots on, he stepped so heavily over the threshold. Now he closed the door. The patch of moonlight it cast on the rear wall disappeared. Now it was completely dark.

Elma felt almost like laughing. Why is he standing so still? Soon his hand will be reaching for my shoulder.

"Miss?"

Elma felt as if she had suddenly been plunged into cold water. She leaped to her feet, rushed to the door, flung it open, and plunged through it.

"Who the hell are you?" she cried.

The dog began to bark. She heard a throat being cleared and then an army boot thrust out the door, followed by the entire man.

"Who are you?" she shouted.

"Sergeant Heinämaa," came the soft reply.

"Why in the hell are you barging into people's storehouses?"

"You let me...You even said you were alone."

"I was talking to someone else. Now if you'll jump right into that boat, I won't wake up my mother and the men of the house. But make it fast!"

"The women around here sure are freaky."

"We are, and you won't get what you're after in this storehouse."

The man muttered to himself, but went back to the boat and rowed off. The dog stopped barking and Elma returned to the storehouse. Closing the door, she threw herself down on the bed. "This is what the cross meant..." she cried, bursting into tears. The sound of her weeping could be heard outside the building.

CHAPTER XV

1

Winter was advancing rapidly on the shores of the Arctic Ocean when the company received orders to move. The same road from Rovaniemi to Liinahamari they had taken north during the bright days and translucent nights of summer, they now followed south, in the midst of sleet and darkness. At Rovaniemi, as they were being loaded onto railroad cars, a train came puffing up from the south. When it stopped, soldiers began to peer out of the windows and doors of coaches.

"Those are strange-looking soldiers," Jalo Kieppi said to Kauko.

"At least they didn't have to stick cockades into their hat brims," said Kauko.

"They're Germans," said someone.

"Well I knew they weren't Chinese."

"I wonder what they're doing here?" said Kauko.

"Are they some of those supermen?" asked Jalo Kieppi.

Kauko had a vague feeling of admiration, mingled with a slight tinge of fear. He looked at Jonas Niemi, who stood next to him, and said:

"They don't exactly look like Prussian statues to me. The one in the helmet on the steps would look funny if he had our uniform on."

"Jonas, you speak German. Go and talk to them."

"That's right. You interpreted for the German seamen at Liinahamari. Go and ask them what they know."

"My German is bits and snatches," said Jonas hesitantly.

"Go and talk to Adolph's soldiers," said Kieppi.

The Finnish troop train was nearly loaded and there was time to gawk at the train which stood a couple of tracks away. Reluctantly Jonas walked over to one of the German coaches. Packs of cigarettes were thrust at him from the steps and men gestured to him to come nearer, but he merely shook his head. Then Jalo Kieppi leaped down from the door of the cattle car and said:

"You can't turn down a visitor's offerings."

Others followed in Jalo Kieppi's wake. Soon soldiers from

both sides were crossing the tracks along the entire length of the train. Salutes were exchanged, even handshakes, but not for long. A stiff-backed German officer stepped down from the train and shouted out words that few of the Finnish soldiers could understood. But the Germans soldiers did, and they quickly disappeared into the coaches. The doors were slammed shut. Only a few helmets appeared at the windows.

The Finns too moved away from the German train and began to congregate in groups on the tracks. Packs of cigarettes a few had managed to get were examined. But soon the Finnish soldiers stopped congregating between the trains. One of the platoon leaders got out and did exactly as the German had done, although his commands did not ring out as angrily. Nevertheless the tracks emptied of soldiers.

"Goddamned spindleshanks had to come here squawking," said Kieppi.

"Give me a cigarette so I can see what kind of smokes that Hitler gives his men," said someone.

"I'm not passing them around. I was only able to get one pack."

"You're sure a tight-fisted buddy," said the one doing the begging with a scowl.

"You should learn to hang on to what you have. Jonas and I got some."

"Will you smoke, Kauko, if I give you one?" said Niemi.

"If you do, then I will," Kauko assented.

"It's okay with me. Let's see what a Juno tastes like. The rest of you too, all who can hear me," said Jonas.

The cigarettes soon hung from the corners of men's mouths, and Jonas and Kauko found themselves standing and looking at the empty pack. Kauko said:

"*Juno* — what a strange name for cigarettes. Did you find out what they're doing on Finnish railroads?"

"They didn't have time to talk much. They said they were on their way to Norway," Jonas said.

"Isn't there a more direct route than this?" said Kauko.

"They didn't have time to say. They say they're going to northern Norway."

"This German cigarette is no taste delight either," said Kauko. "If anyone here wants to, he can puff on the rest of it."

"Give it to me," said one of the men in Kauko's squad. "It looks like a straw in a pig's snout when you try to smoke it. And Jonas is just about as clumsy with his."

The German troop transport train soon started off. Immediately afterward, the wheels of the Finnish train clanked into motion, but the locomotive pointed south. Jalo Kieppi said to his friends:

"Those Germans seemed to have their ears open."

"They looked like sharp boys," someone said.

Rovaniemi began to fade behind them. The daytime sleet changed into clear, cold weather. Jonas and Kauko looked back at Ounasvaara receding in the distance. Both of them were thoughtful. Kauko said softly to Jonas:

"We didn't have time to drop in on Selma and Alli."

Jonas looked suspiciously at his companion. Although Kauko was grinning, he muttered:

"Alli can keep her friend with his lieutenant's rank. Do you plan to write Selma a letter when we get to our new station?"

"Stop assing around. I'm not writing anywhere but home."

"Quit crying over spilt milk, buddies. Who knows — they may send us to Helsinki. There'll be skirts enough even for us there," said Jalo Kieppi.

"Doesn't it feel bad to be getting farther away from home with every clank of the wheels?" said Kauko to Jalo.

"It isn't often that a man like me gets to travel."

The door was pushed shut. One after another, the men in the car stretched out to sleep. Being jolted on truck platforms during a journey of 500 kilometers had beaten their minds into a state of weariness.

Why don't you write to Elma? Or at least to Toivo? The people at Olkivaara will think you're mad at them about something. Nestor is asking what part of Finland they might be sending you to. Elma once told me that Hilja Naavala was a better pen pal for you, but her eyes were red when she said it. Hilja Naavala once asked if you went to Olkivaara every night. It was hard for her to ask, but she did it. The rye came up beautifully in the field. Toivo Olkivaara came with the horse for a couple of days, and he and Auku turned over a good-sized plot of new land. He took only fifty markkas *for the work. Did I tell you in my last letter that they found Ivar Sääskilampi's body? It was caught in a huge old spruce tree that had sunk below Väljä Rapids ages ago. Community officials found it. Soldiers were out searching too. They had a fine funeral at Sääskilampi and a revival meeting too. Irja was converted and so were many others. But Bert and Irja's husband weren't among them. Mother was at the funeral too. Auku has been snaring birds and cutting pulpwood. Mari Olkivaara is sicker than before. Greetings from all of us and from all your friends. Your sister Aili is writing this.*

Kauko folded up the letter after reading it. It had arrived just before their departure from the Upper Monastery. He swallowed hard. *Why don't you write to Elma?* Couldn't that clumsy boatman write to her? He was probably still in Järvenkylä. What sense was there in writing then? I'm not about to scribble letters for everyone to laugh at. I could write to Hilja, but she thinks I've been chasing after Elma. Besides, I have to remember that the daughter of a storekeeper whose home is one of the largest in the parish is not for the likes of me. The people at Naavala are not proud, but it's not so many years ago that I hauled charity flour home from there on a sled. The world does turn in strange ways. Ivar Sääskilampi, the man I had to beg a flour slip from with my heart in my throat, is in the grave now. I'm being jolted over the rails in a cattle car not knowing where I'm bound. And here I'm as good a man as any, perhaps one of the top men in the company. Only two of us were made corporals. It's a good thing I joined the army last December. I managed to get through the war somehow, and I feel almost as if I were propping up some corner of Finland.

"Come and sack out, Kauko. There's room between Jonas and me."

"I guess I should," said Kauko.

2

The old are leaving, the rookies can sing
this song in their grief
A civilian moon is rising in the sky.

"Shut your damned trap," growled Jalo Kieppi.

"We didn't make the law," said Jonas Niemi.

"You should have joined the army when we old men did."

Kauko's laugh annoyed Jalo Kieppi even more. He took a long drink from his canteen cup, blew through his snarling lips, and said:

"That's really a shit-eating law they passed. How much earlier than me did the two of you stick a cockade in your caps last winter? Tell me, Kauko."

"Almost three weeks. And I, at least, put the cockade on the band of a fur hat," laughed Kauko.

"Don't laugh, or the cork stays shut," snapped Kieppi.

"Hey boys, let's sing that song again," said Jonas. He took the canteen cup from which Jalo had just drunk and handed it to Kauko. "Have some. *The old are leaving, the rookies can sing...*"

Kauko took a drink, then thrust the cup toward Jonas.

"Honestly, that Jalo is a fine man. He brought his buddies the liquor for his mustering-out celebration when he came back from leave."

"We get along well. The *Coffee Substitute Brigade* is going on its second year without disbanding," said Jonas.

"We're buddies, all right, but damn the men who made those laws."

Jonas Niemi was irresistibly drawn to sing the song that had been sung hundreds of thousands of times in the Finnish army, in the lowest of spirits or bursting with joy. He began to hum again:

The old are leaving, the rookies can sing
this song in their grief...

Jalo Kieppi leaped up, his face almost white. He snatched up the half-empty bottle with the lion seal on it and roared:

"If you start that verse once more, I'm taking this liquor."

Jonas Niemi seized him by the shoulders and forced him to sit down.

"Don't go crazy now, Jalo. We're your buddies."

But Jalo Kieppi leaped up and slammed the bottle into the side of the upper bunk. Swaying and holding the broken bottleneck in his fist, he yelled:

"Are you calling me a rookie? Didn't we all lie shaking just as long in that ruckus at Löytövaara? What extra hero's work have you two done, just tell me that."

Jalo glared angrily at Kauko and Jonas. Kauko too rose and said:

"Stop this damned fooling around. You spilled the last of that liquor all over the floor. Get that bottleneck out of your fist right now. You'll cut your hand yet."

"I'm not afraid. When have you ever seen me turn tail?"

"It's not a question of being afraid. What you need now is a sense of humor. Jonas already said that we didn't make this law. We've all had enough of the army. Right at the start, we had those training exercises in the woods of Kuhmo to make an impression on us. What other age groups in the Finnish army have had that kind of initiation?"

"None," said Jonas Niemi.

Jalo Kieppi was the drunkest of the three. He threw the bottle-neck under the bed and sat down with his face in his hands.

"Why the shit did they go and pass a law like that?"

"We don't know. First they lengthened the term of service for all of us by half a year. And now those who came in in 1939 get out in a year and a half, while those who came in in 1940 serve for a full two years. That's just the way it is, Jalo. Kauko and I leave for home in a couple of days."

"And I have to drag out another whole half a year in this wilderness."

"Six months is a short time in a young man's life," said Kauko.

"I'd say so too if I were getting out. But damn it all, three days can mean a lot sometimes."

"Don't be such a sorehead. Just dig out another bottle," said Kauko.

"I just don't know, goddamn."

"Summer will pass quickly in these woods for someone who made it through the miserable winter here," said Jonas Niemi.

Jalo Kieppi lifted his suitcase from the floor and took out a bottle from it. The three men were sitting in the non-coms' room of the training-center barracks. Its other occupant was on duty as sergeant of the guard. Jonas Niemi and Kauko Sammalsuo, whose shoulders had borne two stripes since midwinter, were drinking to Jalo Kieppi's return from leave. The day's duty was over. Soldiers stationed in the wilderness military district were wandering around at random. Most of them were bathing in the June heat along the shores of wilderness ponds and streams. The men who were soon to leave for civilian life were in high spirits on that beautiful Midsummer's Eve of June 1941, but all those inducted from January of 1940 on wore sullen faces. Separation from their good friends and the news of six months more of service were no laughing matter. Jalo Kieppi twisted off the seal of the bottle and said:

"What's the good of sitting here together sulking? Pour in some of that substitute from the canteen as a mixer, Kauko."

"And I'll go and get that package from home. There's roast meat and plenty of butter in it."

Jonas Niemi staggered slightly as he rose. He looked out of the window at one end of the barracks and hummed:

"When your country doth into peril run, home chores are left undone..."

Then he gripped the door handle and said:

"I'll soon be making hay, buddies. It'll be nice to hear the clack of the mowing machine. Yup...*grain grows high in the plowman's field...*"

"Next winter I'll be skiing after the reindeer — whew, that was a fierce snort."

"I was thinking my brother and I might cut pulp before hay-making. The trees will come crashing down and the money will come rolling in," laughed Kauko. "Give me a bite of something salty before I starve!"

At that moment the door opened in front of Niemi and the corporal on duty for the day came in.

"Here you are, drinking, and not a worry in the world," he said.

"What do you expect to get by hanging around here?" snapped Jalo Kieppi.

"I sure wouldn't drink any of that rotten liquor — and on duty too, ahem."

A nasty grin appeared on the corporal's face. Jalo Kieppi said:

"You couldn't take this liquor."

"Cut out the racket and save your rot-gut for medicine. I came to order Sammalsuo to report to the office. The company commander wants to talk to all the squad leaders."

"Go to Russia! What the hell kind of time is this to be talking?" said Kauko.

The duty man was already on his way out the door. He said from the entry:

"That was an order, not a request."

Kauko buttoned his summer blouse, ran a comb through his hair a few times, and said:

"Could the lieutenant have smelled that bottle?"

"Tell him to come here if he's envious. We'll fix up a good boss like him with a drink."

"What the heck business does he have to thrash out now?"

"Have another drink to settle your innards."

Kauko took a sip from the canteen cup Jalo handed him and went out the door. Jonas Niemi turned toward the enlisted men's barracks with the package from home in his hands and said:

"Come back soon for your share. Jalo and I will wait."

✧ ✧ ✧

During the winter of 1940-41, the bulk of the Finnish army lived in the woods. Units were housed in barracks and partly in tents. The company to which Corporal Kauko Sammalsuo, Jonas Niemi, and Jalo Kieppi belonged spent the dark winter on the shores of a wilderness lake about ten kilometers from a large church village. Summer found their reinforced training battalion still in the same barracks. The winter's cold and storms changed to summer airs that caressed their nostrils with the fragrance of heather. The snow which had crunched beneath their boots melted, and dry moss now rustled beneath their feet.

All winter they had been working on fortifications during breaks from training. The same work was still going on, but digging was easier now. The spring rains had thawed out the frozen earth of winter, and picks and iron bars were no longer needed. The mere pressure of a foot drove a shovel into the sandy soil

Kauko walked slowly along the path that led from the barracks to the company commander's office, which was in a building on the shore. It too was a foreshortened barracks building covered with camouflage paint. The lake was completely calm. Out on it soldiers were rowing in boats of their own making. They were shouting to one another, and one was hoisting a lunker of a perch into a boat. Soon I'll be paddling on the bay at Järvenkylä trolling a line behind me, thought Kauko. Maybe I'll go to Alajoki with Auku for salmon and grayling. I might even go with Elma...

Although Kauko stopped the flight of his thoughts at this point, he could not keep his mind off civilian pursuits. Only two more reveilles and I'll be as free as a bird. It would be nice to visit Jonas's home for a few days. I could stop in Raahe on the same trip and maybe even in Oulu. The only bad thing about it is that Jalo can't be with us. Well, we'll remember him and our other buddies. It wouldn't be a huge trip for me to make if I came to visit the boys here during the summer. No, I won't do it before the fall weather sets in. Then the days are long for them.

Kauko's brother non-coms walked toward the office building buttoning their blouses. The leader of the third platoon, who was from Kauko's neighboring parish, stood there waiting.

"Now what nonsense do they have to talk about?" he said.

"I don't know. Luckily we have only a few more orders to listen to," said Kauko.

"Yes, you're one of the lucky ones. Are you drunk?"

"How so?"

"You smell like it and you look it too."

"Kieppi came back from leave today. He brought a few homecoming bottles with him. Does it smell? We only started on the second bottle."

"I don't guess the big brass will notice it."

The last of the squad leaders emerged from the barracks, which had been set up in the shelter of trees and painted with camouflage paint. The heather exuded a fragrance and the dry moss felt slippery underfoot. Kauko's spirits rose. He had tasted liquor only a few times in his life. There was nothing wrong with it, as long as one didn't make a habit of it. He felt so good. He should really sing a little. But let it go — the office door was right before him.

✧ ✧ ✧

Several of the squad leaders were already in the office when Kauko and his companions entered. Their heels banged together at the same instant, and their hands rose to their visors as if turned by the same crank. The platoon leaders were sitting on chairs around the office, and the company commander was in back of his desk, a grave expression on his face. His fingers kept turning the pen stand on his desk, first lengthwise and then crosswise. He responded to the greetings of those who entered with an absent-minded nod. After a long time, he raised his eyes toward the men standing at the door and said:

"Are all the squad leaders present?"

The soldierly top sergeant sitting across the desk leaped to his feet and slammed his heels together. Hands rigidly pressed to his thighs, he said:

"All present, lieutenant, sir."

The company commander stood up, paced a few times around the office floor, then looked out the window. He took note of the men who were fishing and of the air, which shimmered over the lake. The mountains rising in the distance were screened by a light haze. Summer had come early this year. Its fragrance was already that of a season well advanced. Fragrance...scattered thoughts piled up in the lieutenant's mind. He sniffed the air a few times and then turned around and surveyed the faces of all the non-commissioned officers standing there.

"One of you has been drinking," he said.

The platoon leaders stared at the door as the squad leaders turned slowly to look at each other.

"Do I have to start smelling the breath of grown men?"

Kauko's carefree mood vanished. The lieutenant seemed to be eyeing a big corporal standing on the other side of the group. Without further thought, Kauko stepped forward, stood at attention, and said:

"There's no need to, lieutenant, sir. I...Corporal Sammalsuo, am the guilty one."

The lieutenant began to pace in a circle again. Kauko was troubled by the officer's look. It was at once disturbed and accusing. The lieutenant stopped before Kauko, looked him in the eye, and said:

"Where did Sammalsuo get liquor in this wilderness?"

"From civilians, lieutenant, sir."

"I wouldn't have imagined that Corporal Sammalsuo would take liquor. You've been a model soldier in every way."

"I'm no drunk, lieutenant, sir. I started sipping too early to celebrate my discharge. I won't try to cover it up."

"At least that was spoken like a man," said the lieutenant.

Kauko was not overly scared. He knew he had no duties to perform until the morning, but he was a little upset for the sake of the lieutenant.

"Rest, Sammalsuo," said the officer, glancing out of the window once more. Finally he turned to the squad leaders, cleared his throat, and said:

"The platoon leaders already know about this matter, but now I have to inform the squad leaders and the supply non-coms. The company will have to leave the training center this evening. All leaves and releases of non-commissioned officers and enlisted men are temporarily deferred. This is not pleasant news, but as soldiers, we must obey orders. Even these barracks, which have begun to feel like home, must be left for the use of others. But at least you belong to an age group that has not spent all its time at one barracks and drill field."

Kauko listened to the lieutenant's low-voiced and somewhat halting speech as in a dream. His knees trembled. His release deferred...no chance of getting home. What on earth was going on now? The heart-warming visions of the day when he could turn in his army gear were shattered. His term of service was being extended for the third time with no inkling of how long his return to civilian life was being postponed.

"...supply and weapons non-coms? Transport corporal too!"

"The company will fall out immediately. The supply sergeant will issue rations and the weapons man live ammunition. The transport corporal will see to it that everything is loaded and ready to move. If there are no questions, you may leave."

Sober-faced, the men left the office barracks. A single thought hammered in Kauko's brain: his dreams of civilian life were buried again. No more were there only two reveilles, but an endless string of gloomy days. Would there even be many of those? Timid rumors of a new war that had been quickly brushed aside now seemed to be croaking like ravens over the peaceful landscape. Whispers about the intentions of the Germans, labeled untrustworthy, and ignored, now became a fear that clouded all thinking. The other fall, an age group that had just been put on reserve was called back into service, and a war had ensued. Now I understand why Toivo cursed so wildly, thought Kauko, as he opened the door to the non-coms' room.

"Give me a drink, and quickly!" he bellowed.

Wide-eyed, Jonas Niemi handed him a canteen cup. Afterwards Kauko remembered nothing of their leaving the barracks, although no one noticed that he had been especially drunk.

3

As they passed through the church village, they could already see German baggage trains and soldiers. Jalo Kieppi said to his companions who sat with him on the truck platform.

"German Adolph doesn't seem to have sent his men off without weapons."

"They have everything. Even small bogs can't stop them. They have strips of corduroy roadway wrapped up on their trucks," someone marveled.

"They look well fed," said another man on the truck.

Kauko's drunkenness was passing. He felt nauseated and annoyed. Why the devil had he been such a fool on this particular evening? Jonas Niemi too sat on the truck with his rifle sticking up between his knees.

"They're laughing away even though they are far from home. You can tell they've been brought up to be soldiers."

"Go and talk to them so we can find out where they're going. You talked to the same hardhats last year at Rovaniemi."

"I don't feel like it. It doesn't matter where they're going," said Jonas Niemi.

"Our discharge was put off because of those bastards."

"Sammalsuo's in a bad mood. What's your hurry to get out? We're on a logging job."

Kauko gazed at Kieppi. He doesn't even have a hangover, he thought. Just then the company's officers who had entered the Civil Guard building the minute the trucks stopped, approached the column. No one else had been allowed off the trucks. The vehicles, which had arrived at the company barracks in the evening, had, according to the drivers, left Oulu that day. They had been rounded up in the middle of deliveries, and been sent off toward the eastern border.

"No one has left the trucks, have they?" asked the platoon leader.

Kauko heard the question, but delayed answering it. He was tired as well as annoyed. His back was resting comfortably against the front of the truck platform, and he kept his eyes shut. Jalo Kieppi nudged him with a fist and said:

"Hey, they're asking you."

"Why the devil are you shoving me? What's up now?"

"They're asking if anyone has skipped from the trucks."

"No one but the platoon leader," snapped Kauko. "He went charging off to town. When they find him, everyone will be here."

The second lieutenant swallowed hard, but said nothing. He climbed into the truck cab and the vehicle joined the column heading east.

✧ ✧ ✧

During the last days of June, the company was bivouacked on the shores of a fairly large lake that spread out near the border. There were other outfits around the lake as well, Finnish reservist companies and German units. There were fish in the lake and the men circled its bays and islands in pursuit of them. The boats belonging to the farms on its shores were in constant use. Some of the men even floated out on rafts. One lucky man caught a salmon, and that, plus the stories of large catches of highly prized fish, inspired the soldiers to try their luck.

Kauko was like a cat on a hot tin roof. Jalo Kieppi and Jonas Niemi became enthusiastic about the fishing, but Kauko took no pleasure in it. Disappointment kept hammering away in his mind. If this had not happened, I would be home already. I would be felling spruce trees in the pulp woods. It would be night work now; the days would be too hot and the mosquitoes too pesky.

One day Kauko met a tall lieutenant on the new highway

leading to a village nearby. He raised a reluctant hand in greeting, when he recognized the oncomer.

"Lieutenant Mäkinen," Kauko said.

The lieutenant stopped and stared at Kauko for a second. Then a broad grin spread over his face. He held out a hand and said:

"It's Corporal Sammalsuo, I mean. Hello, hello, how are things?"

"So-so, but this gets me down. How about you?"

"It's no fun, I have to admit," said Kosti, letting go of Kauko's hand.

"How long have you been in again?" asked Kauko.

"A week. I had to leave the job on the Kuikkala school again."

"Isn't it finished yet?" asked Kauko.

"Actually it is. I mean, they're putting on a few last touches."

"Was your family at Kuikkala?"

"No...we, I mean, things have happened at my wife's house. Grandpa drowned, as you may know. Irja has to take care of the house with her mother. I spent only Sundays at Sääskilampi last winter and this spring. Now Bert and I are in uniform again. Like all able-bodied men."

"You must be a company commander."

"Something like that. My company is from the home parish again. Come and stop by sometime. Our tents are in back of that long point. You see..."

Kosti Mäkinen pointed across the lake. Kauko said:

"Maybe I'll come by this evening."

"Have you been in the army all this time?"

"I had two reveilles to go when this ruckus came up...goddamn it."

"It must be hard to take. How many times have you been on leave?"

"Only one time in late summer. Just when old Sääskilampi drowned."

Lieutenant Mäkinen took out a pack of cigarettes and offered one to Kauko.

"Have you learned to smoke yet?"

"No, but thanks anyway."

Kosti Mäkinen inhaled deeply. After a long time, he said:

"I have a daughter now too."

"Your boys must be big already," Kauko said.

"They've thrown rocks through a number of window panes at Sääskilampi. It was hard to leave them. I mean, just when Irja was expecting."

"They're well off, on a large farm with plenty of food," said Kauko.

"That's not a problem. Irja...my wife, if only she can keep up her spirits. Her father's death still troubles her."

"Maybe this won't go any further," said Kauko.

The lieutenant went on smoking his cigarette with a thoughtful look on his face. Kauko watched him as if he offered the last hope in the world. Officers always knew more than the enlisted men. Kosti's expression was sober...There was something serious behind all this.

"Well...I mean, let's hope so. Come and chat this evening."

"I'll try to come. I'll see you, lieutenant, sir," said Kauko with a laugh.

A more cheerful expression crossed Kosti Mäkinen's face as he said:

"I'll be glad to see you, Corporal Kauko."

4

Kauko did not have time to visit the men of his home parish that evening. By then, his company was already on the move. The supply and transport men were left behind. As the sun rose on the following day, they crossed the national boundary where it had been drawn on what had been Finnish territory before the Winter War. There was not the slightest bit of resistance in their sector. Only to the north was there a brief flurry of heavy firing.

"Someone overran an advanced Russian outpost," said the company commander.

"Will it be this easy to take back the land we lost in the Winter War?" said one of the soldiers.

"I hope so," said the company commander.

With no danger to life, the company advanced to the edge of a small lake. Green fields stood on its shores, where other units were already moving about. An older reservist stopped to talk to Kauko and Jonas. He looked at some smokestacks standing in a field, and said:

"We used to play cards around those chimneys."

Kauko and Jonas too turned to look at the ruins.

"After the Winter War, the border was shifted so far this way that the ruins of that house were left on the other side. For years it was on the route of Russian and Karelian travelers. Often the owner emptied their pockets of money. 'Cards didn't stick to that man's hands,' they used to say. He had large mirrors hung all over the walls. There was no point in the Finns' burning it when the Winter War began, since it's back on our side now."

"The Russians don't seem to care much for the whole place. They seem glad to pull back," said Kauko.

"What the devil would they do with this wilderness?" said the reservist.

"They probably had enough woods before," said Kauko.

"I wonder why the hell they came storming in here the other winter."

As he spoke, Jonas Niemi gazed at a high hill that rose beyond the lake. Low waves splashed on the surface of the water, and the sun's rays turned it into a shimmering network of light.

"Ordinary men like us don't know," said the reservist.

"Uncle Joe has other problems this time," said Kauko. "The Germans are smashing toward the Ukraine."

"Which explains why there are no Russians here," said Jonas.

"It was like drinking tar to leave home again," said the reservist. "I had just built a new cottage. They burned the old one in the Winter War. And now we're involved in this business. But it feels different this time. We're not alone, and we're going east."

"Those Germans are frisky boys," said Kauko.

"They are that. They say the Finns don't have to fight now except maybe for fun. All they need to do is come along and move the boundary markers. And they say we can move them pretty far east this time."

The reservist's face relaxed into a near-smile. Kauko said:

"My buddy and I did a lot of cursing when this new jaunt started. We had only two reveilles left to go."

"You've had a damned long hitch in the service too. How about a smoke?"

"My buddy and I are sort of Sunday smokers. What do you say, Jonas, if we light one up in honor of this logging job? It seems to have started out well. We've been gone from home now for a year and a half."

"Let's take a few drags," Jonas said.

Soon the three men stood side by side. The older man's cigarette dangled from his lips as if he had learned the knack in the cradle. Smoke poured from his nostrils as he gazed at the woods that stretched to the east. The two younger men sucked in the smoke with hollowed cheeks, the cigarettes jutting out from the middles of their mouths. All three had sprouted whiskers nearly a centimeter in length. After a long silence, the reservist said:

"War is no business for human beings, but we all have to stick it out. I was born and brought up right on this eastern border, but maybe after this my cottage will be well inside the country."

"It's sure to be," said Kauko. "We've got the backers with us to guarantee it now."

"I think so too," said the reservist.

"It looks that way. But remember Napoleon's fate. And history tells us what happens to overreachers," said Jonas Niemi.

"Napoleon didn't have planes and tanks," said Kauko.

"I think things will go badly for Joe Stalin too. The Germans seem to be smashing them the way they did the French last year. And Belgium and Holland and Denmark and wherever else they happened to go," said the reservist.

Smoke was rising from the company field kitchen in a grove of willows right on the shore. Jonas Niemi looked toward it and said:

"The boys seem to be gathering around the kitchen."

"Looks as if they're crowding around the soup kettles. We should head over there with our mess kits," said Kauko.

"They're eating at my company too. We won't have the strength to move those markers unless we eat," laughed the reservist.

5

The call-up of the reservists had taken the up-country men by surprise. Some were on log drives, some planting their small fields. Others were fetched from pulp-cutting and from digging drainage ditches in the woods. What now? said the believers. Oh, my God, said their panicky wives, clutching at their hearts. Well I'll be a son of a bitch! What goddamned logging job are they cooking up now? cursed the unbelievers.

But the log drives went on, and after the initial consternation, pikes were left in the hands of boys and old men. Women and children completed the potato planting. The men who had been summoned arrived at the pine grove bordering the church village. Their step was heavy and their minds in shock. Vivid memories from the Winter War a year and a half ago weighed heavily upon them.

Their equipment was better than in the fall of '39, but the men donned their uniforms reluctantly. Slowly the company formed up into ranks of four. The parish was short of officers, and their reservist replacements, who had been rushed in from the coast, stood looking doubtfully at the sullen faces of the men. A big and obviously aging regular army captain had also appeared. He watched impatiently as the company dragged itself into formation. The men were milling around like tired lambs. Who was that sour-faced man standing around with his hands in his pockets and giving no indication that he planned to take his place in the ranks? And the tall lieutenant who was moving so oafishly? What — now he was striking up a conversation with the man, who looked like a perch. Damn it all! They had set out for the Winter War more smartly than this. True, those stiff-necks had been just as stubborn at the front, where their stubbornness had been all to the good. But nothing would come of this if each man had to be coaxed individually at the very start. Should war come, there would be time enough to adopt a more comradely attitude. And what would the Germans say? Every man in their units understood the significance of discipline. It did an old infantryman's heart good to see such soldiership. It was even more perfect than he had seen and experienced in Germany during World War I.

The infantry captain was seething internally. Memories of his own military training flashed through his mind and made his cheeks twitch. In addition, the swiftly changing situation of recent days and the still unclear objectives of the mobilization had stressed out his tired mind. The captain stepped up briskly to the soldier slouching there talking to the lieutenant.

"Why isn't the private obeying orders?" he shouted.

The soldier glared from under lowered brows.

"I'm no private," he said.

"What are you then? Name and rank?"

"Toivo Malinen, sergeant."

"A non-commissioned officer, and that's the example you set! Your hands in your pockets, and smelling of liquor too? Shame on you!"

"There's a big difference between liquor and bootleg booze. A man of your age should know that."

Toivo Malinen's glance did not waver. The captain's eyes slid down to the fists clenching and unclenching in the man's pockets.

"Why don't you fall in?"

✧ ✧ ✧

Toivo and his father had rushed through the spring work in the fields. It cost them little sweat to get the seeds sown and harrowed into the soil, although the fields had grown by a half in the last three or four years' time. When the work was finished, Toivo said:

"You stay and plant the potatoes with the women, old man. Svante and I will take off for the log drive."

"Time drags when I'm working in the fields. I'm so used to mucking around on the river banks every spring."

"Well, you'll have to stay here for now. When the potatoes are planted, then you can go to the Ii River as a pikeman," said Toivo.

"Well, I guess it has to be that way," Nestor conceded.

"It won't take long with Elma and Taimi to help."

Nestor bent over to rub his calves between the palms of his hands and said:

"These legs of mine don't really feel like wallowing on the river banks any longer. They started to get rheumatism out in the woods of Kuhmo."

"You can get on as a boatman on the Ii River," said Toivo.

✧ ✧ ✧

"It's not often a pikeman gets this good a spot."

Toivo was sitting in front of a tepee of sorts on a river bank as he spoke these words to his brother. It was midnight. The water moved swiftly between the steep banks of the river and a solid raft of logs ran by under the eyes of the brothers. Occasionally the logs would run into each other, sending up a spray of water and a muffled boom that reached the pikemen's ears. Further down, the river plunged into a steep rapids where the logs continually pounded into the rocks and one another.

"This is real easy money," said Svante.

"Isn't it a week that we've been here now?"

"A little more than that," said Svante, "and we haven't had to pick up a pike."

"Put the coffee on the fire," said Toivo.

The younger brother went down to the river with a blackened pot in his hand, swished aside the bark debris on the surface a couple of times, plunged the pot into the water, and brought it up full. While Svante watched the pot dangling from the end of a cooking pole, Toivo kept an eye on the floating logs. The campfire warmed his back, and his thoughts wandered back to the events of the winter before last. The thunder of the logs in the Ala Rapids forcibly reminded him of an artillery barrage. It was always the same happenings on the Summa front that came to mind, try as he might to think of other things.

"That was one goddamned..."

"What are you cursing about?"

"Nothing. One log just crashed into another."

When they had drunk the coffee, Toivo said:

"I'm going to take my turn at sleeping now. Wake me up about six if nothing happens. If there's a jam, wake me up at once. You mustn't try to free it by yourself."

Toivo had not yet fallen asleep when the crew chief came up to the tepee.

"Is your brother asleep?" he said to Svante.

"He just crawled onto the boughs."

"We have to wake him up. I have something to tell him."

The flames of the campfire were toasting Toivo's feet and his woolen coat kept his shoulders comfortably warm. He was just on the verge of sleep when someone tugged at his ankles. Throwing off his woolen coat, he said:

"Who the devil is clawing at my hoofs?"

"It's me — Manninen. You have to get up."

"What's the problem, The logs are running free and it's my turn to sleep."

Toivo crawled out from the tepee and stood there in his stockinged feet on the fir boughs, his hair standing on end. He looked at the already wrinkled face of the crew chief.

"The world is such a mess that you have go back in the army."

"What nonsense are you babbling?"

"It's no nonsense. You have to go to the church village immediately. To join the reservists."

"Go and tell it to the devil," said Toivo. He flopped back onto the boughs where had had been and pulled the coat up over his ears.

"Well, that's telling the world. But it's a fact that you've been called up."

"I'll be goddamned if I'll go before I've had my sleep. You can be sure of that."

"I can't do anything about that, but what I'm telling you is the truth. The cashier is figuring wages due so fast that his pencil is smoking. Most of the men on this job are of reservist age. Well, I've delivered the message they told me to."

The crew chief went on to the next pair of pikemen. Toivo could not fall asleep, but lay there until the men from downstream who had received the order began arriving. He was no longer cursing when he joined them. His brother Svante was left standing by the campfire leaning on a pike. Toivo turned and said:

"Don't go out dancing on those logs."

On their way to the church village, the log drivers went by way of Ahma-Juuso's and demanded moonshine. Once he got started, the slippery, dark-complected bootlegger literally thrust his product upon them. Toivo Malinen rarely touched liquor, but now he drank without restraint. However, by the time he and the other log drivers who had received orders reached the church village, the effects of the drink had mostly worn off. The *painted town* was swarming with men, some of them already in uniform. A German motorized column stopped on the outskirts of the village but soon went on its way. His face gloomy, Toivo Malinen walked into the Civil Guard building.

"They're in such a goddamned hurry that a man can't even

stop in at home," he cursed.

Outside the building, he ran into a familiar figure in uniform. Toivo started and said:

"Did they drag you out here too, old man?"

"I had to come. And I was just hired for the drive."

"Did the potatoes get planted?"

"They're in the ground," said Nestor.

"What did mother say?"

"I left her sniveling."

✧ ✧ ✧

Toivo Malinen clenched his fists in his pockets. What was that pig of a captain bellowing about? Goddamn, I should grab him by the head and throw him into that thicket. If I hit an old wreck like that just one punch...

"I'm asking you again: Why don't you get into the ranks?"

The captain's eyes were blazing again. Try to make me look down at my shoes, old man. He got nowhere with that. Now he's looking at my fists in my pockets again. He's just shaking. Why doesn't that son-in-law of Sääskilampi say something? But what's the use of fighting the reins? They'll take me anyway.

These thoughts flashed through Toivo Malinen's mind as he stood there. He was aware that the men of the company, who were already in formation, were staring at him. He had to say something.

"Because I'm standing here gawking."

"Do you refuse to take your place in the ranks?"

The captain now spoke in a measured tone, without a hint of shouting. His eyes were questioning.

"I didn't say I wouldn't go."

"Then why did you stand here when you were ordered to fall in? What did you say to your company commander?"

"I told him I'm goddamned pissed off about going to war."

"Who told you you were going to war?"

"I have eyes in my head like all the rest of us. Why else are Adolph's men buzzing around here, huh?"

"I don't understand. What are you hinting at?"

"Don't talk shit. A man of your age and rank knows Adolph Hitler better than any of us. His men are going east so fast their hobnails are screeching. They're not going to Norway by that route."

"Lieutenant! Is this man a sergeant?"

"I've heard that he was raised to the rank of sergeant during the Winter War, captain, sir."

"Were you promoted for this kind of behavior?"

"At least I wasn't afraid, and I didn't hide in dugouts like some higher-ups I know. Goddamn, I've faced the storm before, and I won't back down now, no matter..."

"Malinen, get into the ranks, I mean, so that we can get organized," said Kosti Mäkinen firmly.

"Toivo," came a shout from the ranks. "Come into the same squad with me."

"Well, I'll go then so the others won't have to stand here because of me."

Toivo Malinen turned. He had already taken a few steps toward the rear of the company, but then he stopped, looked at the captain again, and said:

"Lieutenant Mäkinen is a man. The old man who yelled out from the ranks is my father, and I can't be less of a man than he is. Let's see what comes of this logging job. But there's one thing I'm sure of. I'm not afraid of anyone."

Toivo Malinen was the last man to step into the company's ranks. Immediately afterwards, Kosti Mäkinen called the unit to attention and gave the command to dress right. Then he reported the company as present to the captain.

6

A guerrilla battalion and a few other advance units were approaching Kiestinki. With astonishing speed, the troops following behind them had opened up a road of sorts for trucks to jounce along as far as the village of Kiimasvaara. The first leg of the journey from the border was now open to travel by vehicles. Extending the road beyond that point would have been easier, but now other hindrances arose. Russian resistance, hitherto non-existent, began to make itself felt. Big guns began to hammer away from the direction of Suvanto and Kananaiset, but in spite of them, large detachments of Finnish troops occupied the area around Kiimasvaara.

A man with nothing to mark him as a soldier except for an army cap pulled low over his ears sat on a hillock struggling with a can of field rations and muttering to himself:

"Some damned people in this world must have nothing to do but..."

He was unaware of a tall sergeant standing there watching his efforts. Pausing from time to time to mop the sweat from his brow on the sleeve of his flannel shirt, he bent nearly double over his task again.

"Just what are you doing, soldier?" asked the sergeant, stepping forward.

"I would open this can of fish if I could."

The shirt-sleeved man scowled at his questioner. The blade of his knife had already opened a short slit at the edge of the can's cover, and he went back to his task, teeth bared and talking to himself.

"Is it worth it for a few damned fish packed into this sheet-iron container? Without an ax and a good chopping block, a man is sure to die of hunger. I'm getting nowhere, and I'm going to cut my hand yet."

"It was easier to go and get a whitefish from the storehouse at Olkivaara," said the sergeant.

"Olkivaara!"

The word was a near-shout. The man raised his eyes toward the sergeant standing before him and then he said:

"You know Olkivaara?"

For a moment, the sergeant looked incredulous, and then he answered:

"Well hell, I should know my own neighbor."

"What do you know! If it isn't Kauko Sammalsuo. Hello, hello."

The man rose as he spoke and grasped Kauko's hand like a bear.

"I already recognized you from the road. I thought for awhile that maybe you didn't want to know me."

"What made you think that? It's great to run into you. I thought your voice was familiar, but you've grown that excuse for a beard. You look like a calf's rear end that's been freshly licked," laughed Nestor. "Let's go and boil up a pot of that fake coffee right now. Toivo is in this company too."

"I heard...I mean they wrote from home about it," said Kauko.

"Funny I didn't know you. Of all the places to meet a neighbor."

As he walked beside Nestor, Kauko felt an urge to ask about Elma. And I wonder how Hilja is doing. Loneliness tore at his mind. I can't even get a leave. Maybe I would rate now that the army units are gone...or are they still there, he wondered.

"There's Kosti's tent, and this cloth house is where I live," said Nestor. "Let's go on in."

✧ ✧ ✧

"There's not much new around here," said Nestor.

"That's right, you've been here before," said Kauko.

"We skied through here on our way to build that Murmansk railroad," said Nestor. "The same shacks were sitting there at Kiimasvaara, but they were newer then. They seem to have cut a few more logs and built quarters for the border guards."

The pot from Nestor's mess kit filled with coffee substitute stood close to the campfire. Toivo, Kauko, Nestor, and a couple of other men from home were sitting around it. The road from the border ran right by the spot. It was thronged with troops moving east. Trucks went roaring by, and horse-drawn wagons teetered along its surface. A German column passed them, its odd-looking vehicles rocking easily along. Glancing at the traffic on the road as he poured the brew into canteen cups, Nestor said:

"I'll be damned if we don't soon see Kannanlahti and the Murmansk railroad."

Toivo looked at his father and said:

"It hasn't been printed or announced in church yet."

"It'll be funny if they can't clear the way with all those men. I've been watching the loads on those German wagons and trucks. They won't run out of stuff soon."

"Yaah, and they've got this invention so they don't even have to haul gas with them. They have this powder and they just mix it with water," said one of their Järvenkylä acquaintances.

"It isn't a powder. They say it's a kind of round plug they mix with the water," said Kauko.

"Bullshit. I don't believe that crap," said Toivo.

"Don't say that. One day I saw this German motorcycle stop by a pond. The rider opened the gas tank and dumped water into it from his canteen. When it was full, he took a plug about as long as your index finger from his coat pocket, unwrapped it, and slipped it into the gas tank. Then he looked around and shook the bike a little so that the water sloshed around. Then he lighted up a Juno, kicked the starter, and took off, leaving a trail of fine smoke behind him," one of Nestor's visitors asserted.

"So there! Now do you believe it?" said Nestor. "I've heard the Germans say there'll be no shortage of gas as long as there is water in Finland."

"And there's plenty of water," said Kauko. "Look at the map. Why, Pää and Tuoppa Lakes are like seas."

"They are seas. Will you have more?" said Nestor.

"Gladly, if there's enough."

Nestor's face was content. He blew on his coffee substitute to cool it and said:

"We won't grow old in this war. The man from Posio who predicted the end of the Winter War to the very day says we'll be home from this job in time to make hay."

"In what summer? Is there any rye water left in your pot, old man?"

Nestor looked at his son, poured out the last of the rye water, and said:

"This summer, of course. At first the man was willing to bet his cow, but no one would take him up on it. Now they say he's willing to bet his house."

"Goddamn, if you let me do it, I'll go and bet Olkivaara with the man. It would be nice to come out of this alive and owning two shacks," said Toivo.

"Nestor and I really believe we'll get out in time to harvest the grain," said Kauko. "The Germans are driving full speed into the Ukraine."

"I don't doubt it one bit," said Nestor.

"And I don't either, not one little bit," chimed in the man who had seen the German fill his motorcycle tank.

Kauko sat with his neighbors for a long time. The weather was pleasant and so was his mood. The units passing by constantly reinforced his belief that the war would end soon. Even having to stay away from home no longer seemed as painful. It was good to be with the men on this last jaunt. Then it would be nice to return to his home and his community. I'll write to Elma any day now, he concluded. Finally he rose and said:

"Well, I'm going to stop in and talk to the company commander. Will there be many other officers there?"

"Not likely. Only those from this company," said Nestor.

CHAPTER XVI

1

"Don't try it, damn it!" hissed the soldier to the sergeant.

"I won't leave a job half done."

The sergeant's words came in a whisper as he grasped the lower branches of a sturdy spruce tree and began to creep upward.

"They'll shoot you down from there like a wood grouse," said the soldier.

The climber was already two meters up the tree. Panting, heart pounding, he mopped the sweat from his brow, although it was not especially warm in the middle of the night. Then he hissed:

"When I climbed trees to pick pine cones as a boy, I never thought the same skill would be needed in war."

"And neither did you know, or I for that matter, that there would be a war."

"No, we didn't. Now I'm going higher. Fix the distances in your mind, if I'm able to give them to you."

"You're crazy, Kauko, but there's no use trying to stop you."

"Jonas," came a whisper from some five or six meters up.

"What?"

"I can see the upper part of the bank."

"Do you see any movement there?"

"Joe's men aren't sleeping either."

"Climb carefully. Use your head, and stay close to the trunk. Stop! Stop it! The branches are starting to shake. Climb more slowly."

"There was such a damned thick clump of branches I could hardly get through it."

The Sohjana River between Pää and Tuoppi Lakes was a broad, swiftly flowing stream. From further upstream came the roar of a rapids. Although the night was still, there was enough noise to force Kauko and Jonas to whisper quite loudly. Kauko tried to pretend nonchalance, but sweat was pouring from him. Climbing a tree with such stout limbs would not have made him sweat if it were not for the fear. The company commander had given him the task of checking what could be seen across the

Sohjana River. He was permitted to choose his own partner. Although Jalo Kieppi had been eager to go, he chose the more placid Jonas Niemi. The assignment did not call for a detailed investigation, but when they were able to reach the shelter of a clump of trees near the river bank with little difficulty, Kauko took a notion to climb into a big, thick spruce tree. The opposite shore beyond the trees looked completely deserted, but it was not. It was known that the regiment was up against a difficult obstacle for the first time.

Kauko stepped onto a sturdy branch. Why the hell was he trembling in every limb? It was not effort that was making him sweat. There was no reason to panic. There lay the Sohjana River, its water absolutely clear. I've seen clear water before, Kauko reflected, but nothing like this. Those sunken trees must lie pretty deep. Water grasses are swaying over the bottom rocks. Some large fish are staying in one spot in the current by wiggling their fins slightly. I ought to pretend that I'm somewhere at a smooth stretch along the Ii River, watching for salmon swimming upstream. I can actually hear the hum of motors. Nowadays they drive between Järvenkylä and the church village. A clump of reeds is tossing in the current there. How impressive Nature is in the middle of a night like this.

"Kauko?"

Sitting on the branch, Kauko gave a start, and his hands and legs began trembling again.

"What?"

"Do you see anything?"

Now I have to look across the river, Kauko told himself. I have to climb up a few meters higher so I'll get a better view. Goddamn, but I'm scared. The sound of one's voice is a good antidote against fear.

"I see something. Goddamn, I'm going to go higher even if Joseph Stalin himself comes walking down that bank."

"Don't talk so damned loud," hissed Jonas Niemi.

"You can't hear small noises over the roar of those rapids."

Kauko reacted to the spirited tone of his own voice in the usual way: his fear evaporated. He climbed higher. The muscles in his arms were like steel bands and the weakness in his knees had vanished. The branches were now suitably spaced for him to climb between them.

"Hey buddy. Are your pencil and pad ready?"

"I already had them out."

"Right across from here there are three machine-gun nests. About thirty or forty meters apart, and about twenty meters back from the water's edge. Then mark down two more nests close to one another, to our right, about a hundred meters from the other three. Close to the same distance from the river. Further back are some mortar sites. Mark them with a circle, say."

Kauko was standing quite close to the trunk of the tree on two branches. He could see the glow of the sun beyond the wilderness. Swathes of trees had been felled on the hills across the river; the leafy ones were burned brown, but the firs were still a sickly green. Russians were moving around at their camp sites. There were log fortifications, camouflaged mortar emplacements, and further back, even the covered barrels of artillery pieces. By now Kauko felt completely natural as he reported his findings to Niemi at the base of the tree. From time to time, Jonas would whisper:

"Not so fast. I haven't had time to mark them down."

Am I really the same Kauko Sammalsuo who once ate the community's bread, Kauko wondered. Now I'm filling a man's shoes in my second war. The bitterness I suffered during my growing years turned out to be a necessary spur. I'm not worthless, not at all. No one is living high these days, but when the war is over, life may still have much to offer to an enterprising man. Now I'll climb a little higher to get a better view of the machine-gun nests along the river to the left. The sun is already starting to shine over the woods there.

"Goddamn!"

A thin bough bent under his weight and snapped in two. As he cursed, Kauko was already hugging the trunk of the tree and trying to find new support for his feet. Then a rattling sound came from a mound on the other side of the river. Kauko only sensed the muzzle flashes as splinters flew from the trunk of the spruce tree.

"Kauko! Kauko! Come down, quick!"

Kauko felt fir boughs slapping against his face and slipping through his hands. After a long slide, he felt as if his ribs had slammed into springs that were pulled taut. Then Jonas lay beside him, his face twisted.

"Were you hit? Do you know me?"

"I don't know. At least my brain is still working."

As luck would have it, there was a small rise between the spruce tree and the river bank. Kauko could see the moss spurting up from its crest. A number of machine guns were now firing. Is there a hole in me? It seems hard to breathe. Why is Jonas opening my shirt?

"What are you looking for?"

"I'm trying to see if you're hit."

"Do you see blood anywhere?"

"Not yet. Your face is as white as a sheet."

Kauko's breathing had eased. In the end they found no damage except for hands cut by branches and an elbow that was rapidly turning black. The firing across the river ceased. A little bird hopped on the limb of a birch tree near his face and began to twitter.

"If you hadn't landed on that willow thicket, you'd be a gone goose," said Jonas.

"That was a real stroke of luck," said Kauko. After his pounding heart had settled down, he crawled into a sitting position and said:

"Let's go back to the company. Are the notes you made safe?"

"I put them in my pocket. They seem to be here."

"I guess we have to crawl the first part of the way."

"We don't dare raise our heads until we get over that ridge.

2

Forty-eight hours later, they were again creeping toward the west bank of the Sohjana River, careful not to make a sound or cause a branch to stir. No one knew how many of their own troops were hidden in the woods along the bank. The most significant piece of news circulated as a rumor:

"The Germans are attacking. Stukas are coming in to bomb."

"There's the big spruce Kauko fell from."

Jonas Niemi's whisper caused the men in Kauko's squad to turn their eyes to the right. The tension afflicting them was eased slightly. Jalo Kieppi rose to his knees, looked at the tree, and said:

"Did that crazy son of a bitch climb up into a place like that?"

One of the men unconsciously shoved a filter cigarette into his mouth as he looked at the tree, and rattled a box of matches in his hand.

"No smoking now!" said Kauko.

"I guess it's best not to," said the soldier and put the cigarette back into the pack.

"What time is it?" someone asked.

"Five to twelve," said Kauko, after digging out his watch.

"It'll be a wonder if anyone makes it across the river alive."

The doubter was a member of Kauko's squad. He lay behind a hillock, his eyes blinking and his hands shaking. His breath was coming in gasps.

"We'll make it all right," said Kauko. "This time we've got the supermen with us."

"That's right, and the Russians just won't have the goddamn time to shoot every man."

"Well, we'll see when the ruckus starts. It won't be any too easy for the men on the other side either," said Kauko.

"They're buzzing in now! Listen hard!"

They all held their breath. Every ear caught the roaring sound approaching from the west.

"The Stukas are coming," said Jonas Niemi.

"Be ready to move fast when the time comes. And stay low — shrapnel can fly in any direction," said Kauko.

"Here they come. Goddamn, they're turning toward us."

As Jalo Kieppi spoke, the planes began their dive. The roaring sound changed to a frightening howl. Anti-aircraft guns across the river opened fire. Kauko had resolved to endure it all without being afraid. He saw his men pressing their faces into the earth and he felt as if something were grating along his spine. Now the planes were coming right at them. Had they turned toward the wrong side of the river, Kauko wondered. Then the earth began to shake, and when he raised his face from the moss, he could see only smoke and clouds of dust on the opposite bank. Rocks and stumps spun through the air and fell splashing into the river.

"Kauko, I've got the shakes again."

Kauko's spine tingled as he watched the planes dive. It was their howl especially that made his heart contract. He looked aside. The sound of a human voice helped to dispel fear. He said:

"It won't last, Jonas. It's a passing thing."

Jonas Niemi's eyes stopped rolling wildly. He looked at Kauko and said:

"That first bombing...when we were on the way to the front and they bombed us at that station. I thought of it again."

"We were the ones they were bombing then in the Winter War. Now you can see that the other side is having a rough time across the river. Our mortars are opening up too. Do you hear them?"

"I hear them. I just have the feeling that I won't make it back from here."

"Don't say that. We're all as scared as the devil."

"The dive bombers have left now," said Jonas.

"They have, but there's no shortage of shrapnel on the other bank," said Kauko. "Now the artillery is firing too. Get ready, boys."

The platoon leader ran crouching from squad to squad.

"As soon as the smoke lifts enough, we'll start crossing."

Men were already crossing the river on their right. The roar of shells, the rattle of small-arms fire, and even the yells of men had turned the calm summer night into bedlam. A messenger came running up to the platoon leader and said:

"The company commander has gone with the right wing. You are ordered to cross as soon as the boats get here."

"Good. Sammalsuo will cross first with his squad. I'll come along with you."

The second lieutenant went over to each squad leader one more time. When he returned, a boat ran into the bank. Kauko leaped up and said:

"Now into the boat, men!"

The squad dashed across the river bank. Kauko's fear vanished. His body was like a coiled spring. Not everyone dies in a war...not everyone gets hit, Kauko repeated to himself. He stood beside the boat and said:

"Into the boat, into the boat. Don't keep the ferryman waiting. Sit nicely so you don't tip the boat, as mother always used to say when I was little. Into the boat, ha, ha."

"What's all that goddamned crap? We've been in a boat

before," said Jalo Kieppi.

"Damn it, Jonas. Don't lie down. Make room for the others," barked Kauko, pulling his friend up into a sitting position.

"We won't get back alive. They'll shoot every one of us," Jonas Niemi kept repeating.

"Jump in, quick! I've shoved a boat off before," said Kauko to the platoon leader.

"Shove off then, fast!" shouted the engineer who was piloting the boat.

When Kauko pushed the boat off the shore with all the strength of his youth, most of the company were already boarding their own craft A pall of smoke swallowed them up. It took only a short time to cross the river, and the men leaped up on shore, impelled by the momentum of the boat. Kauko shouted:

"Follow me, boys!"

"Shove the boat back into the water. What is that sergeant making such a fuss about? We have to get the rest of the men over to this side of the river," roared the big engineer.

The engineer's angry words seemed to Kauko to come from another world, but he turned and said to the men:

"Right, shove the boat back into the water."

The boat quickly disappeared into the smoke on its way to fetch another load. Craft filled with men kept crunching into the shore as wedge-shaped waves splashed into the stones along the bank.

"Take your squad and wipe out the three machine-gun nests you know about. I'll follow with the other men," said the lieutenant.

"Follow me along this slanting gully. They can't fire on us directly here. I could see that plainly from the tree," said Kauko.

"Do you expect us to stand here scratching our balls, the way you keep rushing us. Goddamn, if only a man could see what's up ahead."

"Hey boys, they're firing short rounds. Watch out, one just went off there."

Jonas Niemi's voice was hard and calm. Kauko was blind to all else but moving ahead. Now a second and third round from their own mortars burst quite near them. Everyone threw himself down into the shelter of a hillock. Fortunately the range was corrected before anyone in the squad was wounded. The advance continued.

"Kieppi, stay in the bottom of the gully. We can get right up to the machine-gun nest along it," said Kauko.

Kieppi, who had crept up the bank of the gully, descended to its bottom again.

"How will we know when to get up and when not to?" he asked.

"You weren't listening when I tried to explain it on the other side of the river," said Kauko.

"These things are easier said than done. Goddamn that branch."

Jonas Niemi did not have to lie face down for long. The rest of the men hurried up. Soon the whole platoon was closing in on them. The lieutenant came to Kauko's side and said:

"You take your squad and try to silence the nest on the right."

"The ones on your side are a little farther along. You can go almost to the end of the gully," said Kauko. "Hey, Kieppi and company. Up on that bank now."

The machine gun was firing steadily. A couple of shells burst near it. Kauko Sammalsuo and his squad lay like a string of swimming waterfowl at the lip of the gully.

"If I don't smash that machine gun, then my name isn't Jalo Kieppi."

Kieppi swung his arm, but his hand grenade landed short of the nest and exploded there.

"No, goddamnit, it's too far."

"You just haven't got the arm," said Kauko. "Here she flies!"

"You didn't get any closer."

"Yeah, and now he's peppering us," said one of the men.

The burst of fire kicked up moss and dirt as bullets whined through the air. Everyone huddled down behind the bank. The biggest assault of the drive toward Kiestinki was now under way. The number of men on the east side of the river grew steadily larger. The resistance of the defenders began to weaken. The pulverizing of earth and human beings begun by the dive bombers continued. The broad and near-desolate banks of the Sohjana River had never witnessed such a man-made commotion. Only during summer thunderstorms had the region roared and blazed in such fashion.

"It's lucky the Russians don't have curved machine-gun barrels or they'd salt us into this slope," said Jalo Kieppi.

"Damn, but that nest is far away," said Kauko.

The machine gun was now firing elsewhere. The lieutenant came running up the gully and said:

"The two guns firing from over there have been silenced."

"We can't do a thing with this one," said Kauko in frustration. "You can't even get to it by crawling."

Jonas Niemi got up all on fours. He pulled the pin of an egg grenade and stood up. His large upper body described an arc through the air. Everyone watched the flight of the grenade. For a second it disappeared into a thin veil of dust, and then a pillar of earth erupted into the air. Pieces of wood flew skyward.

"That was a knockout," said the lieutenant.

"Looks like that gun has had it."

"It flew into the air like an old mitten."

"Goddamn, but one of their men is in a hurry. Look at him scramble," said Kieppi.

"The Germans are already charging the line of machine-gun nests," said Kauko.

"They went across that opening like wild men," said Jonas Niemi, wiping the sand from his rifle bolt.

"Someone ran into a mine. Godalmighty, that was a bad one," said the lieutenant.

"But those German boys just keep moving ahead," said someone.

"We'll move up too. Form a skirmish line and watch out for mines."

They obeyed the lieutenant's order. He said to Kauko and the two squad leaders nearest to him:

"I talked to the Germans on the other side of the river. They tell me some of them were in the war in Poland. Well then, now we have to see this Sohjana ruckus through."

✧ ✧ ✧

Then it's the devil said Rannanjärvi
if there's a man I'm afraid of.
Hit him in the snout with a heavy pine club
and slit him up the back with a dagger.

The aging top sergeant shuttled back and forth across the Sohjana River, singing out in his powerful voice. His boat ran up onto the west bank and he stopped singing.

"Next boat load. Fare fifty cents a head for officers and half that for enlisted men. *Then it's the devil said Rannanjärvi, tralalalalalalala...*"

"You think we're afraid, Grandpa? And we're not paying a penny."

A young soldier grabbed the prow of the boat. Others leaped up onto the rocky shore behind him. The man holding the boat continued:

"Down on the boat bottom. Goddamn the man who moves!"

"That's the way, young man," said the sergeant with a broad grin.

"Goddamn, you don't have to tell me. I don't need any orders."

"Now, now, simmer down. Just grab an oar and we'll take the boat over."

"And stop singing that crappy ballad. An old man like you and not a scrap of shame. Which oar should I grab? Give me that lousy slab."

"Well there's a grouch for you. This tub has made many trips across the river. So just sit in the bottom of the boat and calm down. There's a war on."

"First of all, we only take orders from our company officers. And secondly, this is no goddamned tub but a boat. And a lousy one at that. Try to haul this across the river in a hurry and the Russians will sink us by throwing stones. Push, old man, so we can get loose from the bottom."

"Let's not go this trip, Malinen," said one of the men.

Toivo Malinen stood up on the front seat of the boat. Gritting his teeth, he tried to push the loaded boat off by thrusting against the bottom with an oar. His hands were held high, like those of a man poling through rapids. Glancing back over his shoulder, he said:

"Just plant your ass calmly on the boat bottom, and don't butt into mine and the sergeant's business. This thing is stuck so tight..."

The boat lurched free, and the long-bearded man in the prow struggled to keep his balance. The sergeant began to turn the boat, saying:

"Scoop with your oar on that side. As if you were paddling a canoe."

"You better believe this isn't the first time I've rowed the priest to church. I've ridden the Ii Rapids since I was a kid and I know how to ride in a boat."

"Let's not argue. There are buddies the other side of the river you can take it out on. *Then it's the devil*...ah, but this buddy doesn't like music," said the sergeant.

Toivo Malinen did not seem to hear the man's words over the din. He was digging his oar into the water with all the strength of his shoulders. The heavy boat began to glide toward the opposite shore. The west bank was lost from view behind a curtain of smoke. Ahead there was only a gray blanket to be seen, but sounds rang out sharply. The water near the boat seemed suddenly to be boiling. One of the men threw himself face down on the bottom.

"Machine gun bursts! They're firing at us."

Water splashed against the side of the boat. The man in the prow turned and said:

"What are you going to do when you get to the other side?"

The spray kicked up by the bullets moved off. From ahead came the sound of explosions. When the man he had asked the question did not answer, Toivo said:

"They always shoot at you in a war. And don't turn the boat straight across the stream, sergeant. Keep it at a little angle to the current, and it'll ride across almost by itself. That's how we used to do it on the Ii River."

The top sergeant smiled. He himself came from a region of quiet waters. The memory of a winter battle on the Aa River flashed into his mind, but now it was summer and the battle was on the Sohjana River. The clear water of the river flowed swiftly. He realized that the man in the prow knew what he was doing, and he stroked the oar along the side of the boat, turning it at a slight oblique to the current. He was oppressed by a faint sense of dread. Singing helped drive it away, but the young man didn't like the singing.

The sergeant did what I told him, thought the man in the prow. Does he feel that I'm really angry? I'll have to say a few words to him when we get to the other shore. He's a tough old guy. He's already taken many boatloads across, and he just sings away. A lieutenant just told me he volunteered to row the boat. The lieutenant said something about some Hades ferryman, and then he laughed. I wonder what kind of boatman that could have been. I'll tell the old topkick when we land that I've crossed this river before, the time I ran off to that workers' paradise with Hemmi and Hugo from Ii. I'll tell him that's why I'm in such a lousy mood. Things will be hot as hell when we get to that other bank. I might even come face-to-face with one of the whips from the days when I defected. I should pin these sergeant's stripes to my shoulders. Why do I feel like hanging back now? Since we're in this, every man has to pitch in to get the job done. I wonder if Kiestinki still looks the same. Now I can see the other shore. Things are really a mess here. Now I can say a few words to the sergeant.

"That's the way to make a quick and easy crossing," said Toivo Malinen. "That bank looks pretty steep, but it will shield us. Soon..."

The words were cut off. The oar dropped from Toivo Malinen's hand and he fell in a heap on the seat. A couple of the men sitting in the prow groaned. A row of thin fountains began to spurt up through the bottom of the boat. The sergeant kept paddling toward the shore, but this time he wasn't singing.

3

One could see far through the aperture in the windmill. The distant hills had a bluish tint and a mist hung over the waters. The far-off hill barely visible to the eye was Iivaara. Beyond it the Finns were driving toward the east. It was awful that so many men from this parish had been lost near Uhtua.

The last thought cast a cloud of melancholy over Elma's bright mood. Two of the Uhtua dead were related to the Olkivaaras, one of them a cousin.

The guard duty was easy now. The other winter she had had to huddle here in a sheepskin coat. No Russian planes were flying west now. Toward the end of the Winter War they had come droning over nearly every day. Now the Russians had their hands full with the Germans.

"What can Naavala have on his mind?" Elma wondered aloud

as she watched the storekeeper nearing the path to the mill. Perhaps he wanted to look at the view. Many people from the village had already done so.

"Oh darn it, I'm almost naked!"

Hastily Elma began putting on her Women's Auxiliary uniform. It had been so warm when she came on duty that afternoon that she had taken it off, along with her cap and shoes. Now she was wearing only a filmy slip with thin shoulder straps. She had to hurry. Naavala was already thumping on the lower rungs of the ladder leading to the mill.

"There's a good view from here," he said, looking toward the east after he had reached the loft.

"You can't see as much on a hot day like this."

Elma was still fastening her Auxiliary pin to her collar. I must have turned beet red, she thought. A person shouldn't take off her clothes like that. It's probably against the rules when on watch. I had to rush to get back into my uniform. The man can probably see that I pulled on whatever I had time for. That's why he's standing with his back to me. He's acting almost afraid too.

"You haven't seen any planes?" said Naavala, still looking away.

"No. Last night some German dive bombers flew over toward Kiestinki."

Akseli Naavala started. He glanced at Elma's face. She was a good-looking, high-spirited girl. A person was so full of life at that age.

"The men won't make it home in time for hay-making," he said.

"That's what they say. Father said so too when he wrote."

"How is your mother?"

Why was he asking, Elma wondered. He didn't usually.

"She's not doing too well," said Elma hesitantly.

"She hasn't been to see us since she returned from evacuation."

"Mother isn't really strong enough to go out visiting."

"She's a good friend of Maija Sammalsuo's. Don't they visit each other?"

Elma looked directly at Naavala. What could have happened?

"Mother does go there. And Maija comes to see us often."

Naavala turned and looked directly into her eyes. She could

see that he was troubled as he spoke:

"Hilja will soon be here to take her turn. You will have to go and talk to Maija Sammalsuo and tell her..."

"Oh, my God! Is...is Kauko dead?"

Elma looked into the older man's eyes as if pleading for help. Her glowing cheeks had turned dead white and sweat stood out on her brow. Akseli Naavala's lips drew into a thin line.

"Just tell me. I know what's coming."

"It's even worse. It's a terrible thing to have to say."

"Is it Toivo? Or father?"

Elma's voice trembled but her eyes stayed dry. Her knees felt shaky. Naavala cleared his throat and said:

"Your brother."

"Mother knew it already. She had a dream."

Although tears were pouring from Elma's eyes, she did not sob. Akseli Naavala turned his back and said, after a long pause:

"It would be wiser for you to go home with Maija Sammalsuo. This...when the news came, Hilja happened to answer the phone. They had...she and Toivo had been writing to each other during the Winter War. Hilja ran into her bedroom and her mother went after her...I guess they'll manage to cope with it somehow."

Akseli Naavala knew the tale of this windmill's origin, knew why it had been built on this particular hill. Here the winds had an unobstructed path from far to the east. From beyond misty Iivaara, they could sweep in with nothing to bar their way. Good news had come from that direction, but now the news was sorrowful. Although he had often looked out from this same hatch, had sometimes climbed up on the birch roof of the structure as a boy, he felt that only now was he really seeing his home wilderness. Their ancient forebears had really chosen a beautiful place to live.

Elma's shoulders were shaking. Her chin had sunk to her breast, and she was drying her eyes with the back of her hand. Toivo, Toivo, my brother. Oh my God, what kind of person am I. I weep for my brother's death, but isn't it partly for joy that Kauko is alive? This will be a terrible blow for mother. I wonder how father will take it.

"Toivo was a real man's man."

Drying her eyes on the sleeve of her Auxiliary uniform, Elma turned and looked at Hilja's father as if waiting for him to say more. He cleared his throat a couple of times:

"The vicar wrote that your brother was in the prow of a boat, rowing his squad across the Sohjana River. He fell onto the seat."

"Didn't the Germans dive-bomb the banks of that the same river?" asked Elma.

"They did. And they say the Finns and Germans are far past the Sohjana now."

Naavala looked sideways at the road that ran from the mill to his house and then said:

"I guess Hilja didn't get over this so quickly either. You go by way of Sammalsuo now and take Maija home with you. My wife had the same idea. I'll stay here while you're gone."

"No, I'll stay till my time is up. This is my job."

Akseli Naavala put a hand on Elma's shoulder.

"You must go now, Elma. The situation demands it."

"I can finish my stint. The worst is over now. I have to endure."

"You always do. It's different with your mother. Some visitor might even go and blurt out the news to her. You go with Maija."

Elma had always kept a respectful distance from the elderly storekeeper of Naavala, and now the touch of his hand warmed her. Truly we are all in this together, she thought.

"I'll go, and I'll come back to finish my watch."

"I'm not much good when it comes to dealing with women. But tell your mother that this was your turn to suffer a blow. The vicar sent many of those — how do the believers put it — God's greetings. Your father will get a leave too."

✧ ✧ ✧

"We can't go to your mother looking like this from crying," said Maija.

"I haven't really cried since I left the Naavala windmill."

"Yes, but your eyes are as red as a roach's. Let's wash our faces."

The two women were standing near the gate of the outer fence at Olkivaara. The footpath here ran right next to a swamp. Maija looked toward it and said:

"I think we should be able to find water in a hollow here."

"There's a pit off to the side that has water in it even during dry spells. Toivo hauled mud from it to the fields."

"And Toivo is dead!" Maija wailed out the words. She pressed her face into her hands, and her shoulders shook with weeping. Elma too burst into tears. The mosquitoes feasted, swelling themselves with blood sucked from the two weeping women. They flew off heavy laden, some so full that they burst as they took flight. Neither woman felt the thin, hollow stings pierce their pores.

"Stop now, Maija," Elma said at last.

"It's awful to have to go and see Mari now," said Maija.

"You have to be able to calm mother down or she'll just die. Let's go and wash our faces."

They walked over dry moss that crunched underfoot until they reached the mud pit, where they both rinsed their faces in the brownish swamp water at its bottom. Maija dried her face on her apron, which she had forgotten to take off, while Elma turned up the hem of her uniform and dried her face on her slip.

"Can you still tell from my eyes that I've been crying?"

"You can't really. And mine?"

"They're not bad. Light up your pipe and that will help to cover it up."

As she began to smoke, Maija said:

"These are heavy steps to tread. God help us, Toivo was such a good boy. As a little boy, he skipped along this trail to visit us. He was like a son. And now I have to bring this news to my best friend, who..."

"Take it easy, Maija. We'll soon be crying again. Let's go."

Elma slid open the gate poles and they walked along the footpath between fields of barley. Toivo will never walk this path again, thought Elma. Before he left for the log drive, her dead brother had planted these and other fields. He had not been able to come home after the drive. Before the two women entered the house, Elma realized that all the children were out in the hay fields. In some ways, that made things easier, in other ways, more difficult.

Mari was standing at the window when Elma and Maija stepped over the threshold of the open door. She turned to look at them. Her eyes were deeply sunken and looked pained. Good Lord, mother is always pressing her hand to her heart. Seeing it makes me feel ill too, thought Elma.

"God's peace...greetings," said Maija.

"God's greetings," said Mari. The hand she extended was shaking. "I was watching you from the window," she added.

"We came together to visit...to see you."

Maija dug at her pipe with a matchstick in pretended annoyance, muttering softly:

"Is it so full of oil that it won't draw?"

"Why have you come in the middle of the day, Elma?" asked her mother.

"I switched hours with Hilja because..."

Mari sat on the edge of the bed where Toivo slept in the winter. She began rubbing her temples with her thumbs, and then she lay down.

"Just tell me outright what happened," she said.

Elma and Maija looked toward the bed. The calmness in Mari's voice sent a shiver down their spines. Then they looked at each other, and Elma said:

"What do you mean?"

"I knew that this blow was coming. Did Toivo suffer, or was it a painless death?"

Elma rose from the bench and ran with her shoulders hunched forward into the kitchen. Tears rolled down Maija's cheeks as she said:

"He didn't suffer. He fell onto the seat of a boat without a sound."

Mari said nothing, but merely clasped her hands over her breast. After a long time, Elma returned from the kitchen carrying a cup in her hands. She went to her mother's side, lifted her head, and poured the contents of the cup into her mouth. The pungent smell of camphor spread throughout the room.

"Toivo did come back from his first trip to Russia. At least I got to know that much happiness."

"You must endure this too, Mari. God tests all of us."

Maija herself realized how empty her words sounded. Mari rose and said:

"One's child is always one's child. Toivo did not accept God."

"Perhaps God will be merciful to the dead for the sake of

those at home."

"You and I know, Maija, that a person must be converted. Toivo wouldn't even talk about it. Put the coffee substitute on, Elma. I'll lie down now for a little while."

In the kitchen, the clink of the dipper against the water bucket could be heard. Elma's voice said:

"It's already on the fire. Rest now."

Elma could hear her mother's voice from the main room.

"Nestor and Kauko are still there. They will come back alive."

Although Elma had often been angry at her mother's tendency to prophesy, she hoped that these words would come true, and that Kauko too would return.

4

When the last of the men, tired but content, had crossed the Sohjana River, Nestor heard a man some distance off say:

"That Malinen boy was a hard man..."

"Did he die there in the prow of the boat then?" said another.

"That's where he got it. He had just told the top sergeant to angle the boat into the current. If he hadn't done that, either we'd all be goners, or no one would have taken a single bullet. The burst hit the front end when the boat was turned almost directly downstream. That Toivo was all man."

Nestor Malinen rose and walked away from the rest of the men in the company. Only when he was all alone did he dig out a plug of tobacco. Never, even when he had rolled his first cigarette on the sly as a small boy, had he made one so clumsily. Finally he gave up, threw away the paper, and shoved the tobacco into his mouth. Then he looked around and said:

"Try to roll a butt when your fingers shake like a man's with a fever."

Nestor slid down from the hillock he had been sitting on and wormed himself into the deepest hollow next to it. Then he leaned his back into the mound and clasped his hands behind his neck. The sun shone on high, and he pulled the visor of his cap down over his eyes. His body felt numb, but his thoughts were seething.

Toivo was gone. Why did my son have to be in the way of a burst from a machine gun? Few Finns fell in this scuffle...Toivo had ordered the boat to be turned at an angle...

"Didn't that top sergeant know that a boat should be steered at an angle in a swift current? It just shoots across a river then, and you don't have all that fuss with the oars."

Nestor took off his cap. He arched his neck and looked around, then sank back into the moss and covered his face again with the sweaty cap. From underneath it came a sound of muttering:

"Toivo knew how to do that too. Toivo knew how...My boy knew how."

From the time he was little, Toivo was different from the other kids. He almost never tried to get into my lap. As soon as he could say a few words, he wanted to go logging with me. I often had to sneak off from home to go out and earn money. When he was three or four years old, he would come from the wood pile dragging a big ax or cross-cut saw with him and repeating, "wogging, wogging wif father..."

With *father*...That's what Toivo had called him then. When had he started to call him *old man*? It had felt good. He was big enough now to call his father *old man*. How old would he have been then? Six, at most. And not much older when he began to smoke my tobacco. It warmed my heart to see how well he rolled a cigarette. The women were appalled at it. Even Mari didn't like it.

Mari — how will she take this? Good God! If only they don't break the news to her suddenly. You wouldn't think they'd be so stupid. Our parish minister is a fine man. They can phone Naavala and take her the news from there. They can break it to her gently. Elma wrote that she's on air watch again. She might be on duty. I can take this...I have to, but Mari...Damn it, my eyes are stinging. It's no wonder, when I haven't slept a wink for two nights. On the log drives too my eyes would smart and turn red after going sleepless for a long time.

"Agh, they're stinging. I have to wipe them on my sleeve.

"I have to think of something else now. Nothing will change this. I'll lie down again and keep my eyes shut so the lids will stop throbbing. Toivo always faced things as they were. Did he ever really play, even as a little boy?" Strain his memory as he might, Nestor could not think of a single instance when Toivo had played like other children.

✧ ✧ ✧

"So this is where Nestor is dozing?"

Nestor Malinen sat up with a start. His cap rolled off to one side.

"What? What now? Oh, it's Bert standing there gawking."

Nestor Malinen's wildly roving eyes settled down. He fumbled for his cap and replaced it, then took out a plug of tobacco.

"I must have scared you," said the sergeant, who was sitting on a hillock nearby.

"No, I must have fallen asleep. I only meant to sit down for awhile."

Bert Sääskilampi swung his bulging knapsack around to the front and said:

"Shouldn't we have a bite to eat, Nestor? I'm getting so hungry."

Nestor moistened the edge of a cigarette paper with his tongue and said:

"I'm not so very hungry, but if you've got food to spare, then let's eat. I won't light this butt, but let it dry on that mound."

"I got a package from home. There's cured reindeer meat in it, and a birch-bark dish the women have packed full of butter. And a roasted piece of dead pig. The flat bread and fish pie were hairy with mold. I had to throw them into the garbage pit."

Bert Sääskilampi took the food from his pack. Of all the things a man lets slip from his tongue, he'd had to go and mention a dead pig. Poor Nestor's face flushed and he looked almost afraid. And those eyelids aren't red because he's tired.

"Why, there's no end of food here."

"Start carving. You can borrow my knife," said Bert.

Nestor Malinen picked up a reindeer haunch. A large notch had already been carved out of it. An event from the distant past flashed into his mind. The reindeer haunch was suddenly heavy in his hand, almost as heavy as an anvil.

"Damn paws are as shaky as a thief's..."

"Every one of us is so tired that we're shaking," said Bert. "Take a good slice of that dried meat."

Nestor Malinen's jaws worked as he looked around at the sighing woods. It must be blowing pretty hard to shake the pine boughs like that. The sun seemed to be on its downward course.

What point was there in brooding over things? It wouldn't change them.

"You must have heard that when I was a young man I killed your pet reindeer."

Bert Sääskilampi glanced quickly at Nestor and said:

"Father said something about during his spells."

"And I was low enough to steal the meat too. My wife cooked a stew from it, and never knew where it came from."

"We won't talk about such things any more. And it wasn't robbery. Anyone would lose his temper if his haystack was trampled and eaten. It's all nonsense and we don't have to bother our heads about it. We have more important things on our hands now. Have some biscuits and butter."

"The thing has always troubled me. It was pretty well settled otherwise, but it bothers me to think that Ivar might have held a grudge against me to his dying day."

"You know that my father drowned and had his own misdeeds to worry about. Oh, but once he said, not long before he died, that Nestor was an honest man who settled his debts."

Nestor Malinen's expression softened. He looked inquiringly at Bert, but the latter was sawing so furiously at the meat that his face was hidden, muttering as he did so:

"That damned animal's tendon is so tough."

"He was talking about me?" said Nestor.

"Well sure...of course. You don't doubt it, do you?"

"Then at least that's one load off my shoulders."

A vein in Bert Sääskilampi's temple was throbbing. He remembered his father shaking the same reindeer's bell for Irja's boys in the last days before his death and repeating: "A reindeer thief returned this bell. A Nestor Olkivaara from Järvenkylä. Grandpa never forgave that reindeer thief. The sheriff took him to jail. Listen to Grandpa ring this bell..." The look on Nestor Olkivaara's face now seemed to wipe out the sin in the lie. What was he about to say now, his lips were trembling so?

"Did you see my boy's body?"

"Listen, have some more of this pork. It has kept well, even in this hot weather...I did see Toivo."

"Where did the bullet go in?"

"It was a burst. At a slight angle, through his chest."

"Then the boy didn't have to suffer. That's the one good thing about it."

"He didn't have time to feel anything."

"Not that Toivo ever complained much anyway. That man didn't cry or whimper over nothings. If only his mother can bear it."

"Aren't you going to eat any more?"

"I'm not hungry. The food is good, but..." A wail of grief escaped Nestor.

Bert shoved the food back into his pack and looked down at his hands. The skin underneath his eyes was itching. Nestor turned his back and wiped his face a few times with his hand.

"We have to go and talk to Kosti. The truth is, he sent me to get you. You'll get a leave now."

"Let's go then," said Nestor, and stood up;.

"Take your smoke from that mound."

"Right. Did we lose other men from the company?"

"Four altogether. Some five were wounded. Simo Mutka from the church village got a bullet in the thigh."

"So Simo took a shot in the leg," said Nestor Malinen. "Will we be in Kiestinki soon?"

"There shouldn't be any more bad rivers to cross," said Bert.

"And German Adolph's men work on contract. And they won't run out of stuff too soon."

Near the company commander's tent, Nestor said:

"I can't stand to look at Toivo's body. My system won't take it."

5

"When did Toivo last visit us?"

Maija Sammalsuo looked disapprovingly at Aili, who had asked the question, and said hastily:

"Put the water on the stove, Aili. We're going to make a pot of real coffee. I've been saving it like diamonds in a small jar."

"He came in the spring to haul the manure," said Mari.

"That's right. Toivo was such fun to talk to then. We were all laughing so much. You remember, mother and Auku," said Aili. "You asked too why Toivo was in such a good mood, didn't you?"

"Light a fire in that stove and stop babbling," said Maija.

"Toivo was like a different man all spring," said Elma.

"He was waiting for the snow to melt so he could get back to work in the fields. Then when we got to planting, he couldn't stand to sleep except for a little in the middle of the night," said Nestor.

"Toivo was always so quiet. After he ran off to Russia, you had to pry the words out of him. This spring, he even whistled many times. They say that often people before they die..."

"Come and look out this window, Mari, and see what a good-looking rye field these boys have. If a field that size heads up well, then the Social Welfare people will have broad grins on their faces when they come here to visit. Come on Mari," Nestor urged, interrupting his wife's comment.

Mari looked at Maija with tears in her eyes, then walked over to her husband. She was wearing a black head scarf. Nestor's uniform looked odd to Maija, especially the cap pulled far down over his ears, which made her neighbor look like a stranger even from behind. It was rare too to see him call his wife to his side. Nestor's finger was thrust almost into the window pane when he spoke:

"Look how far back the edge of the woods has been moved. Has Auku cleared more land there this summer?"

Nestor turned his head and met the eyes of Auku, who was sitting on a bench.

"When it's time to plant the new rye, feel free to come and get our horse," he said.

On the way back from the churchyard, Maija had asked the neighbors to stop at Sammalsuo. Both cottages had been empty during the funeral. They had all been at Toivo's burial. Many other Järvenkylä people had been there to escort the oldest Olkivaara boy to a hero's grave. In all, five of the community's young men had been laid to rest under the pine trees that swayed in the summer breeze, near the end of the church that stood on a high hill.

"I just remembered that Kauko sent some money home," exclaimed Nestor. He fished out a wallet from his back pocket and took out a wad of money.

"Take it Maija. There should be about six hundred *markkas* in it. Here..."

Maija's hands shook and her heart felt a pang as she took the money. Kauko had handled these notes. Even out there he remembered his home and saved his money.

"How could he have saved so much? Doesn't he need the money for himself? Has he sent it all home again? He's always thinking of us."

"Now don't start crying. The food is on the house out there. What the hell would a man who doesn't smoke do with his money? Why do they mess up these wallets nowadays? There's no way you can close these snaps. They didn't used to have them."

Finally Nestor got the wallet into his pocket. Maija cranked the coffee grinder, which she held squeezed tightly between her knees, crunching the coffee beans in its gears. The aroma of roasted coffee filled the whole room. It brought an odd sensation to minds accustomed to the smell of their coffee substitute. Aili and Elma were talking to each other, while Svante and Auku listened to Nestor's tales of his latest adventures. There had seldom been so many people in the main room at Sammalsuo. Only Kauko and Toivo were missing; otherwise all members of both families were present. As they were drinking the coffee, Mari said:

"Now Toivo is listening to the roar of his home rapids. And those other men too. That's what the minister said in his sermon."

Mari's eyes were dry but her voice seemed to come from far away.

"How many will be buried in that churchyard before the war is over?" said Maija.

"There's no need to worry about running out of burial ground. The way the war is going, it won't last long. I doubt if I'll get back to my company before they reach the Murmansk railroad," said Nestor.

"It would be good if that happens," sighed Maija.

"It will. We'll be back in time to dig potatoes at the latest."

"Will the young men get out then too? Kauko and..."

Elma's question was timid and shy, as if another person were asking it.

"Of course. Kauko is already in the reserves," said Nestor.

Maija and Mari exchanged a glance. They had already been making plans in quiet whispers on the return trip from the graveyard. Mari blinked her reddened eyes and nodded encouragement to Maija, who hemmed a couple of times and said:

"What do you say, Nestor, if we hold a memorial service for Toivo?"

"Where and when?"

Nestor's eyes widened, but his face did not turn grim. Maija continued:

"You have the room. A big main room and a kitchen. And even bedrooms."

"There's no lack of space, and memorial sermons have been given for lesser men..."

Maija's and Mari's eyes sparkled. Maija said:

"I've always said you had a soft heart at bottom. It will be easier for Mari to bear her grief with her brothers and sisters in the faith to console her."

"I didn't get when the services will be held."

"What about day after tomorrow?"

"That won't do at all."

Nestor's face darkened. He rose from the bench and walked to the window facing the lake. Although the weather was calm and the birch trees and willows on the shore were green, he was oblivious to them now. A memorial service for Toivo...

"It can wait until my leave is over," said Nestor, turning from the window. "Shouldn't we start rowing home now? The cows will be coming back from pasture soon."

"Will you take a package to Kauko if I bring it to you?"

"I'll see that it gets to him. And come and visit us. Come to the shore, Mari and you kids. I'll go and bail out the boat."

✧ ✧ ✧

Hilja Naavala stood beside her father as the coffin was lowered into the grave. The vicar picked up a small shovel. "Dust thou art..." The sand made a hollow thump on the coffin lid and the sound could be heard over the roar of the rapids. Elma said Toivo had liked the sound. He was always on the river. Once the three of them had gone fishing for grayling, Toivo in the stern and Elma at the oars when rowing was needed. She herself had sat in the center of the boat. They had gone ashore at the head of Saari Rapids. Toivo had said:

"You and Elma make the coffee. I'm going to sit on the shore."

When the coffee was ready, they brought out the lunch. There were rapids on either side of the island they were on.

"What happened to Toivo?" Elma said. "Go and call him."

Hilja found Toivo on the shore rocks, sitting with his chin in his hands. He became aware of her only when she stepped onto the slippery rocks in front of him. Then he started up and snatched her by the wrist.

"Keep off those wet rocks. They're as slippery as a fish's back."

"Are they?" asked Hilja.

"Well, of course. One slip on them, and you're gone."

Toivo did not let go of her wrist, but said:

"Sit on that stone. It's smooth, but not slippery."

He kept his hold on her wrist when she sat down, gripping her so roughly that it hurt, but he did not seem to notice. He looked at the rolling waters and said, or rather, shouted above their roar:

"Russian raiders sometimes landed here on their forays to the Ii River. They say that one of their boats filled with treasure from the coast capsized here. Jussi Ylikylä says the treasure is still among the rocks at the bottom of the rapids. Maybe it's all nonsense, but I like it when the rapids are really roaring."

Hilja did not remember ever having seen such gentleness in Toivo's eyes. Although the pressure hurt her wrist, she did not move the hand that rested in his lap. She was really angry when Elma came and cried out:

"So here's where the lovers are!"

"What the hell loving is this? Get back to the fire, and be quick about it!"

Toivo was scowling now. He literally thrust the hand away from his own.

Now Hilja clasped her hands beneath her breasts and then rubbed the wrist with the fingers of her other hand. She could still feel the grasp; it had hurt, but it had warmed her. The rays of the sun shone on the vicar's glasses. He had confirmed both her and Toivo, and he was speaking warmly of the dead man. Mari Olkivaara stood in back of the grave with Elma on one side, an arm linked through hers. Nestor stood on the other side, holding his army cap at waist level. The cap was crushed out of shape in his huge hands. Maija Sammalsuo stood close by with her children. Only Auku Sammalsuo stood further off.

The grave was closed up with shovels. The pines and the hay drying on hurdles below the church hill gave off a fresh odor. The stench from the coffins was buried under the sand. Toivo is there now, thought Hilja. Mari was literally hanging between Elma and Nestor, her legs limp. When Hilja had laid the wreath down with her father, she walked away from the grave to a mixed grove of trees on the other side of the churchyard. The aspen leaves quivered. Hilja took out a handkerchief from the pocket of her Auxiliary uniform. She could hear how powerfully the hymn rang out from the other side of the church.

6

"Now we're like a herd of reindeer driven into a corral," said Jalo Kieppi.

"That we are," said Kauko. "Now we know what it's like to be cut off."

"Are you ready to believe that we won't get back from here alive?"

Jonas Niemi's voice was as crushed as the visor of his cap, from which the water was dripping down. A thin drizzle was coming down and night was fast falling. The three of them were sitting under a big spruce tree, their turn on watch over. Their ragged clothing was dripping wet. The wind soughed heavily in the spruce grove. Off to one side a machine gun began to chatter and a mortar coughed a few times.

"Are the *Vassilies* trying to break through again?" said Kauko.

"Why should they bother? All they have to do is tighten the ring and grind us to mincemeat."

"Don't make such gloomy predictions, Jalo," said Kauko.

"That's the way things go in a real war," sighed Jonas Niemi.

"We're on the gallows now, but we won't start to cry yet. In the logging camps, they used to say there's no use to cry on life's highway. If things get tough, a logger just whinnies and wades on," said Kauko.

"Well I for one don't feel much like a stallion now."

"What was the point in spreading the regiment so thin? They should have known that without a continuous front line, the Russians would eventually break through and cut off communications with the rear."

Jonas Niemi began to dig into his food pack. Kauko and Jalo followed suit. Kieppi said:

"The Russians are kicking up a big fuss for nothing. They should have let us march in triumph all the way to Louhki and then loaded the whole regiment on a train for Leningrad. Then even the officers would have learned that Joe Stalin's men didn't want us to guard the Murmansk railway."

"Do you have any biscuits left?" asked Kauko.

"Not a bite," said Kieppi.

"Me neither. I still have some butter and pork," said Niemi.

"How come you ran out of bread? I have enough left even to feed the horses," said Kauko, trying to laugh.

"We have a model squad leader. Where the hell did you rustle up the bread from? Give me some butter and meat, Jonas."

"I happened to walk past a supply kitchen," said Kauko.

Only Kieppi and Niemi were left of Kauko's original squad. Two men had been lost in the bombing of Kiestinki. Others had fallen during the advance from Kiestinki to Louhki. Many more lay along the railway spur from the Murmansk line to Kiestinki. War had begun to feel like war again. The Pudasjärvi guerrilla battalion had taken especially heavy casualties in taking the rails built high up on railroad ties. The Louhki station had seemed almost within reach when the Russian resistance became a stone wall. Soon, when the spearhead of the attack had been repulsed, the Russians had cut the spur line. It had indeed been reopened, but only temporarily. Now the regiment's only connection to Kiestinki, and to the west in general, was a winding by-pass through the swamps, unuseable by vehicles.

Soon after the regiment was cut off, the unusually warm and beautiful summer changed to a rainy autumn. Pits dug into the swampy ground turned into mudholes. Heaps of dead lay piled up near the aid station. Only the slightly wounded could be dragged out of the trap through the mire of the by-pass. Food and ammunition had to be used sparingly, yet the physically fit stayed in their positions. There were not tents enough to go around, and so the three-man group crouched beneath a spruce tree as they shared their meager rations.

"Goddamn, it's hard for even the mail to get through. Otherwise Kauko and I could live on Jonas's gifts from home."

"We won't have time to starve here. We'll die some other way."

"I'm the world's greatest pessimist, but I have to start bucking you up. We aren't completely cut off, as Jalo says. We are in direct contact with Kiestinki. Start making the tea, Jalo. I have some sugar and some real tea leaves."

"So you think we'll get out of here yet? But are you sure?"

There was more question in Jonas Niemi's face than in his voice. His eyes waited for an answer. Kauko watched Kieppi making the fire, and said:

"I went over to visit the company that comes from my home parish. That tall lieutenant — you've seen him — said the regiment might be moved back at any minute. The commanders won't give up these advanced positions willingly. Lieutenant Mäkinen said that help is on the way. The Germans are sending more troops here."

"They should. They're poor soldiers out in this wilderness...This damned fire does nothing but smoke."

"Don't start making a mosquito smudge-pot now. Get some better wood," said Kauko.

"Get it yourself. Every piece is as wet as if it had been fished out of a lake."

Kauko did not answer Kieppi's outburst. He pulled off his wet boots and with gritted teeth, began to wring the water out of his foot wrappings. Then he said:

"To tell the truth, it's because of those hobnailed Germans that we're here. If they had been able to move up along the highway, Joe's men could not have surrounded us. The soles of my feet are starting to rot. Hey boys, you under the ass-end of that spruce, come and put some water on the fire for tea. I've got some of the real thing."

The other men of the squad came over to the campfire. When the tea was ready and they had begun to drink it, the rattle of machine-gun fire began anew on the right wing. It was joined by the chatter of a machine pistol. The twilight was turning to darkness. The tiny fire did little to warm the soaking-wet men, who tried to sip the hot tea through chattering teeth. The din on the right kept increasing in volume. It was nothing new. Although everyone was inwardly tense, none wanted to speak the truth aloud. Perhaps it would be over soon. One of the squad's replacements said:

"Where did Sammalsuo manage to filch real tea and sugar?"

"Yes, and biscuits too?" another added.

"I dropped in on my home parish company. They always try to take care of their own. They had gotten some..."

"Hey!" came a yell from the dark woods nearby.

"Hey, hey yourself! What the devil *hey-hey* is that out there?"

"Is Sergeant Sammalsuo's squad here?"

"Don't say anything. It's the platoon leader's messenger."

The men obeyed Kauko's whispered command. Everyone sat silent. Soon a little corporal had entered the circle of firelight.

"What is this? A deaf-mute tea party? Aha, some good pork and some butter to spread on my biscuits."

"Hands off!" shouted Kauko. "Jonas, hide the stuff!"

The messenger was already wiping his sheath knife on his pants leg and cutting himself a slice of pork. He pulled a piece of hardtack from the hands of Kieppi, who was scooping it up into a pile. Kieppi doubled up over the butter container and the squares of biscuits to shield them and grunted:

"That Jonas moves like a wooden horse. If I wasn't here to save the day, this would all be up the corporal's ass by now."

"Don't be a hog. Give me some butter," said the messenger.

"Lard is what I'll give you. You're bringing us lousy news anyway. Drink some tea from my mug, and don't grab everything."

Water dripped from every spruce tree, and now a heavy rain began to fall out of the dark night sky. Firearms rattled on the right, and mortars began their hollow barking. Muzzle flashes blazed in the darkness. The messenger's jaws ground on. He blew greedily on the hot tea Kieppi handed him, and said between breaths:

"It's so hot it burns your nostrils."

"We should have sent you the mug of tea before you found us," said Kauko. "Spit out your message now. What is it?"

"To arms, to arms...Don't those sounds mean anything to you?" The corporal nodded in the direction of the firing.

"It would have been a wonder if we got to rest our eyes a little," said Kauko. "You can't rest anything else when you're shivering cold and wet."

"We won't even look that way until we drink our tea."

"The Russians are really trying to break through," said the messenger.

"Drink up so we can get going," said Kauko, pulling on his boots.

"Are you starting to believe that we won't get out of here?" said Jonas Niemi.

"We're not laying bets," said Jalo Kieppi. "Just follow Kauko."

Sergeant Kauko Sammalsuo stamped out the small campfire, kicking the embers out of the the blackened pit to die hissing on the wet moss. He said angrily:

"Goddamn the Russians for not doing what Stalin told them to do."

"What did he tell them?" asked Jonas.

"In that Finnish language pamphlet we saw in Suvanto, it said they had to roll up the railroad tracks. You read it yourself. Don't you remember?"

"And it said to burn everything that might be left to the enemy," said Jonas.

"If Uncle Bolshie's soldiers had done that, we would never have gotten this far. Where did the corporal go?"

"Just follow me," said a voice from the darkness.

7

The shrunken and exhausted remnants of the regiment circled westward through the woods. Men and horses wallowed through swamps softened by incessant autumn rains. Those who had died in the encirclement had only a thin layer of turf to cover their mass grave. The withdrawal was a journey of torture for the seriously wounded. Many closed their eyes for the last time on dismal Archangel swamps, where gray dwarf pines seemed to nod a lazy farewell before the final darkness.

The men were forced to leave their heavy equipment to the wilderness. Luckily the Russians seemed to have other things to do than harass the slowly plodding units. Only small nuisance patrols reminded the regiment that its withdrawal had not gone unnoticed.

The fall rains had turned the rails of the spur leading to the Murmansk line red with rust. The blood that had drained into the gullies along the tracks seeped more deeply into the soil of Karelia. The lighter mood of the summer had turned black many weeks ago. Everyone now understood that unless winter produced a miracle, no Finnish soldier, or any of Hitler's men either, would ever catch sight of the White Sea, except for the pilots. Leading by the bridle a horse that wallowed up to its flanks in the swamp, Nestor Malinen turned to Kosti Mäkinen and said:

"Why the hell didn't the Germans come to help us?"

"Ordinary men like us don't know."

"I guess they're not the great warriors they seemed to be when we crossed the Sohjana. Come on, you poor animal, try to crawl through."

CHAPTER XVII

1

"When did Elma leave for Karhumäki?" asked Kauko.

He was sitting with his mother in the main room at Sammalsuo. Maija, who was knitting a stocking foot, glanced up at her son. Rubbing her eyes, she said:

"A person's best years don't last long. I really need a pair of glasses. I can't see to knit, and anything in print is a blur."

Kauko rose from the bench, took his combat jacket down from a peg on the wall, and began to empty its pockets. Maija's knitting needles began clicking again as she spoke:

"Were you asking when Elma left?"

"It's not that important — Goddamn, look at the mush in the bottom of this pocket."

Kauko went over to the stove with his jacket, turned the pockets inside out, and brushed the dirt from their seams. As she knitted, Maija looked at her son, who was standing with his back toward her. His shoulders were already broader than his father's had been, and he didn't seem to have lost much weight. Only now did she notice that he had the same cowlick as his father on the back of his head. Funny she hadn't noticed it earlier.

"Hasn't Elma written to you?" Maija asked.

"Goddamn, this collar is dirty. It's shiny with all this shit. Ugh!"

"Do you have to curse so much? A person would think that eternal life would be more on your mind during a war."

"If you start thinking about such things, you go crazy there. Elma did write a few times, but I didn't get around to answering."

"What happened between you and Elma the other summer?"

"What other summer? Who said anything happened?"

"Elma was crying about it to Aili. She said that no matter what she wrote, you didn't answer. She said she got a couple of letters, but you were just awful in them. You know that Elma doesn't cry easily."

"What the devil business is it of yours and Aili's?"

"None at all, but it's just that Elma says she's done nothing to offend you. She is the deceased Toivo's sister, and you've known each other since childhood."

Kauko went on checking his jacket and cursing. Maija could tell that he was brimming over with defiance. The look of pleasure that had been on his face when he walked through the door of his home that morning had vanished.

"And you won't stay a bachelor if this war should end."

Kauko turned and looked at his mother. Then he said:

"Just what are you getting at?"

"Every mother wants a good life's companion for her son. There's no better woman for you than Elma."

"What's wrong with Hilja Naavala? Tell me that."

Maija's eyes dropped to her knitting. She pretended to be counting the stitches. For a long time, her lips moved silently, and then she said:

"Nothing. It's just that Elma is more one of us."

"What the devil kind of caste system is there in this civilian life? At the front, we're all the same, I mean, the enlisted men, the non-commissioned officers, and even some of the officers. Here's that jacket. Put it soaking."

His mother picked up the jacket he had tossed to the floor, looked at it, and said:

"You have so many stripes on your shoulders. What kind of officer has three?"

"With a head in between," smiled Kauko. "A sergeant."

"It says *corporal* on your letters."

"The third stripe is only a couple of weeks old."

"Why did they give them to you?"

"For the life of me, I don't know. But not for going to school, anyway."

"Nestor said, at Toivo's funeral, that you were hard-headed and did your job well."

"Here's a woolen shirt. It wouldn't hurt to heat it a little in the sauna."

"What? Good God, there aren't lice on it, are there?"

Maija snatched the shirt from her lap and held it out at arm's length. Then she rose and went to the door, saying:

"I'll at least put it outside in the cold until I have time to warm the sauna."

Kauko looked out of the window at the lake. The panes were

frosted over, and only along the edges were there thawed strips. He could hear his mother's footsteps crunching outside on the crisp snow. Was it a year and a half since he had last been home? It was all of that. It had been nearly fall, that other summer, the night when the soldier disappeared into Elma's summer bedroom...His thoughts were interrupted by his mother's return.

"Brr! It's cold out there. How do you manage to stay warm at the front?"

"You have to. The officers don't send you home if you complain and say you want to be inside where it's warm."

"What will Liisu say when she comes home from school?"

"She probably won't know me. Even Aili looked at me for a long time when I stopped at the windmill to see her," said Kauko.

"Her turn on watch will soon be over," said his mother. "Should I make some coffee substitute?"

"I don't feel like having any. I just ate so much. How long will Auku and Väinö be in the woods?"

"They keep on plugging away until dark. It's nice that they can stay at home while they are logging."

"And Svante Olkivaara is driving for them?" said Kauko.

"He is. Why is there such a long time between leaves in this war business?"

"There wasn't time to come before this. The married men got leaves first, after things had settled down."

Kauko was silent for a time. He went from window to window, looking mainly at the frost flowers on the panes. The same smell he had known as a child was still present in the room. Home, this is the home I so often longed for, he thought. Home is what Jonas and I talked about; Jalo didn't really talk about such matters. How are my buddies getting along in that dugout now...? Elma is at Karhumäki...Although he had known that she was there when his leave came through, Kauko had hoped she might happen to get a leave at the same time as he did. Why wasn't being at home what he had imagined it to be? He no longer felt the contentment and peace of mind that had been his when he had come home on a Sunday from his job as a logger or hired hand.

His mother rose and began to light a fire in the stove.

Abruptly Kauko said:

"At the front, the officers said they couldn't stand to see the men walking around with a perpetual hard on. That's why they were the first to get a leave. They were afraid the wives would send a delegation after them."

Maija was just lighting a match. It was left burning between her fingertips as she stared at her son. The back of his flannel shirt was black, and his suspenders looked as if they had not been washed since leaving the store.

"You deserve to have your mouth washed out with soap," she said.

"It's not your mouth that gets dirty there," Kauko laughed. The match began to burn Maija's fingertips. She flicked it quickly onto a curl of birch bark and blew on her fingertips to cool them.

"To judge by your talk, it does. You weren't so foul-mouthed before."

"There wasn't a war on then. I've known for at least fifteen years that husbands screw their wives, but before this I haven't..."

"Good God, the way you talk. Just don't bawl out such things when the children come home. You should be ashamed to do it in front of your mother."

Had he gone too far? Kauko turned to look at his mother. She didn't look angry. She had gotten older too. Actual wrinkles showed on her face as she blew on the fire to get it started.

"I didn't mean anything bad by it. Only it's hard to be a mama's boy at the front. And it isn't easy to kill men, especially when I can't make myself hate those on the other side."

"Do you have to be just as brutal at home? Are you ashamed to have a mother?"

Maija stood up and wiped her eyes. Kauko said:

"I didn't say I was ashamed of you. Even you don't understand me. We're no longer living in the days when we whined to get slips for sacks of flour and cried together. That was long ago. Even before the war, things were starting to go well for us. Our needs were no longer so urgent. Now when all would be well, this war came along. A person can feel that he's as good as the next man. Those childhood days are gone forever. But no one knows how this will turn out. It seems so hopeless when you can't even get out of these army rags. I'm on my second war already. It's hard to take."

"But you volunteered."

"I did, and I won't come back before the others do. Get some rags for me to put on and I'll go and work at the woodpile for awhile."

"You might rest for at least the first day of your leave."

"I'll go and spit those blocks and then bring in the bucksaw and sharpen it. That Auku is a strange one — he won't learn how to file a saw. I looked at it just now, and the teeth are worn down to a bedbug's ass."

2

The frost was popping in the trees. Fir boughs stuck into the snow as a shelter around the field kitchen did little to keep in the warmth. The mess helper dipped in his ladle at regular intervals and said:

"If you don't live till tomorrow, it's no fault of mine..."

The line filing by the man moved more slowly than usual tonight. Although the smell of pea soup from the cooking drum was wafted to the server's nose, another odor drifted in along with it. Sometimes the dipper would forget his now famous quip, and growl:

"You're looking mean enough now, with that liquor fuming around in your brain."

"Are you jealous?" said the man who had just been served.

"We'll talk about it tomorrow when you come here moaning with a hangover. Raise your dish higher. What are you gawking at? Get back to your dugout."

"Damn, but that soup-dipper is slow..."

Nestor Malinen had come out to the soup line with only a woolen shirt on. The full moon cast black shadows of the trees on the snow. The other men in the line kept their hands in their pockets. Some were blowing on their fingers to warm them.

"The line does seem to be moving slowly," said Bert, who was in front of Nestor.

"Joe's men don't seem to be asleep either," said Nestor, looking toward the front.

"You can hear them talking," Bert agreed.

"Keep still, men, so we can hear what our neighbors are up to."

Nestor's command stilled the buzz of talk among the men. The lines were so close to each other that especially on a cold night, ordinary speech could be heard from the Russian side. The zeal for battle seemed to have ended on both sides. For a long time, few shots had been fired by either. Nestor drew in a deep breath of cold air and shouted:

"Hey, Stalin's men! Come and get into the soup line!"

The echo rang through the snow-laden woods for a long time. Then an answering shout was heard:

"You come here! We have thick rye bread and meat in our cabbage stew!"

"We have better food. Plenty of hardtack and pea soup. Pork enough to feed to the livestock!"

This time the answer was slower in coming. All other chatter had stopped and the soup line had slowed down. Then a shout in perfect Finnish rang out through the woods:

"Come here! We have women too!"

"We're not coming. If you can't handle those tarts, send them over to us. We have large-bore skin cannon, ha, ha!"

"On every one of us," yipped a man who had just received his liquor ration.

"You can't do much with a woman on the rations those butchers feed you."

"Send over a few *matyushkas* and I'll bang away hard enough to drive a hole through even a sound skin, ha, ha!"

"Stop bragging, you Kijanta crud! Just come on over and you won't have to gnaw on rock-hard bread and lick at frozen potatoes."

Nestor stepped out of the line, dropping his mess-kit bottom into the snow.

"How the hell did you know enough to curse me out for a Kijanta type?" he bawled out.

The answer was slow in coming. There was the sound of confused and heated talk.

"Bring those mess kits here. Why the devil are you yelling at those titcaps?"

"Well, hell, they insult a man to his face."

The stench of the liquor Nestor had just drunk was expelled

along with his words. He picked up his mess kit from the ground and blew onto his fingertips. Then another shout came:

"When I spoke that dialect myself, my belly was growling with hunger."

"Tell me your name. We might have known each other."

"Don't yell any more. The officers don't like it," said Bert.

"You tell me yours," came the shout.

The line was coming to its end. Many of those who had already been served stayed huddled around the field kitchen listening to the exchange. Then a young second lieutenant came bustling up from the direction of the lines and hissed:

"Who the devil is doing all this yelling here?"

"I did a little bit to warm myself up," said Nestor.

"Oh, so it's Malinen again. Isn't it about time you learned that you don't shout across the front lines? A sergeant standing here too, and he doesn't order a bonehead like you to stop."

Nestor squeezed the mess kit under his arm, blew on his hands, and said:

"Tell me more exactly what kind of man has a bonehead. I always thought this extension on the end of my neck was an ordinary head. And what's the harm in yelling a little bit about women over the lines?"

At that moment a shout came from a rise in back of the Russian lines:

"Did the bosses shut your mouth already? Tell me, how many of you were moved here to Uhtua from Kiestinki?"

"Does Malinen realize now that this kind of shouting can reveal far-reaching military secrets?" said the lieutenant.

Nestor had not shaved in weeks, and his mouth was a black hole in his bearded face when he opened it to bellow in the direction of the lines:

"Look down along your prick since you don't even dare mention your name."

"My God, Malinen..." the lieutenant began, but Nestor interrupted him.

"I didn't reveal any great military secrets that time at least."

"Don't say another word," said the lieutenant.

"I don't plan to. Scrape the bottom of the pot," said Nestor as he held out his mess kit.

✧ ✧ ✧

When Kosti Mäkinen's company was shifted from Kiestinki to the Uhtua sector late in the fall, neither he nor his men were sorry. Incessant alarms and patrol activity ended. The company was assigned to a short sector of the line which seemed to be occupied by a particularly peace-loving detachment of Russians. The days they had spent huddled in their encircled position during the fall rains now seemed only a bad dream.

As soon as the unit arrived at its new position, Kosti Mäkinen's civilian occupation began to produce results. With his men, he built dugouts that even a division commander stopped in to admire. The small farmers, loggers, reindeer men, and even some migrant laborers who had strayed into the company became enthusiastic about the work, which reminded them of their civilian occupations. The company commander himself drew sketches of the men's quarters on the sides of bread boxes. His master builder's trade now dominated his thoughts. It was a relief from the mental stress of the autumn combat.

A telephone in the command dugout shrilled. The top sergeant sitting near it, who was taking the place of a sergeant major in the company, answered it, but soon handed the receiver over to Mäkinen and said:

"They want the company commander."

"Mäkinen speaking."

"Siltanen here. How are you?"

Kosti Mäkinen responded to the greeting, then listened as the young second lieutenant on the other end of the line spoke. The longer he listened, the broader the grin that spread over his face.

"You're of the opinion that I should punish Malinen?"

"There is good reason to," replied the voice on the phone.

"If that's all he shouted, then it's no big deal. The men need something to laugh about."

"Who knows what he might have said if I hadn't run to the spot? Your non-commissioned officers could use a little discipline too. The sergeant standing in line ahead of him just laughed. And they're raising a real ruckus in the dugouts right now."

"The boys are sharing the liquor ration. And the sergeant

happens to be my wife's brother. I'll administer any punishment you suggest with a real brotherly hand," laughed Mäkinen.

There was a gulp at the other end of the line, and then the words:

"I wouldn't have called, but the commander is annoyed at such behavior."

"You were right to do it. I've told Malinen about it myself, but he's such a talker he can't seem to keep his mouth shut."

"He should be told again."

"It won't stop with just telling. Malinen will be sent to hell out of this company and Sergeant Sääskilampi will be given extra duty here at the office."

"In my opinion, the punishment is unreasonably severe, but you are the company commander. But for goodness sake, don't send the old man out of the company. He's a good soldier otherwise."

"I will show no mercy. I'm very angry now. We'll be hearing from each other."

When the lieutenant had hung up the phone, the sergeant and the two platoon leaders looked askance at him.

"Who was calling?" one of them said finally.

"Siltanen, from the next company," said Mäkinen.

"Has Malinen been doing as he pleases again?" asked the sergeant.

"I hear he's been talking across the lines. I'm going over to talk to him and Bert right now."

"Aren't you going to have a drink? We haven't touched our liquor ration yet," said the lieutenant who had previously spoken.

"Not now. Maybe when I get back."

"Don't be too rough on anyone. You look so angry," said the sergeant.

Kosti Mäkinen put on his combat jacket. His scowl disappeared as he slipped the strap of his Sam Browne belt underneath his epaulets.

"We haven't had a fight here for a long time," he said.

✧ ✧ ✧

Why the heck is that button-head Siltanen sticking his nose into another company's affairs? thought Kosti Mäkinen as he stood outside the dugout. The man just got his lieutenant's bars so he shouldn't be going around giving instruction to others. He has to learn to understand men older than he is.

Mäkinen lifted his face toward the cold night sky. The moon was at its fullest now. One would scarcely believe they were so near the front. There were no detonations except for the cracking of trees at the hands of the frost. There was a good deal of noise in the dugout, but luckily it sounded muffled, as if it were underground. In the next company's area, someone was singing a rollicking song. Should he call Siltanen and tell him to discipline his men?

Siltanen — Silta (*Bridge*) and a word-ending that once denoted membership in a noble family. Malinen's name had the same ending. Kosti Mäkinen's thoughts became restless. He looked up at the sky again. The moon was as bright as this when I first stopped at Irja's home. *Siltanen*. It was a bridge that started me on this journey. What would my life have been if it were not for that bridge catastrophe? Would I be trailing along somewhere in a company of boys from Tampere? I would probably have built many kilometers of roads across the Häme landscape. And seen a few bridges through to the end. Hopefully without the bad luck which led to the break between me and the late Backman.

The late Backman. He thought of the lieutenant again. Not so much because of the bridge — that seemed of little consequence now. But it was the bridge that literally drove me into the wilderness, where I met Irja, he reflected. Without it there would be no Ilmari, Pentti, or Tuulikki, at least not as Irja's children. It was unmanly behavior to run off from Lieutenant Backman out of sheer spite. I didn't know, of course, that he was bringing the news of peace. I didn't act at all like an officer. I had already heard and seen at the front that Backman was no coward. I know I could have flattened him at any time, but that wasn't enough to feed my revenge. I was furious that he dared to come where I was, and I reveled in the thought of seeing him trembling at the bottom of a hole. It would have tickled my vanity even more to see him run away from the line.

Kosti Mäkinen looked down at the smooth-packed snow. The shadows of trees on it looked as if they were tarred. Bridges too were tarred. The scent of tar seemed to be in his nostrils. They were tarring the steps outside the Kuikkala school when the reserve call-up arrived. I was watching the work, thinking I would be able to join my family over Sunday. It was a hot day and it smelled of tar. The landlord came and brought me word that they had called, that I must go to the church village.

I barely had time to stop in at home. Irja was crying. There was panic in the boys' eyes too. They hugged my knees. "Daddy, daddy, don't stay long," they kept repeating.

Only now did it dawn on Kosti Mäkinen: they were not here as individual men. The road of fate for all of them, for the entire country, was being built through an unexplored and tangled wilderness. Everyone had to pitch in, to suppress his own feelings. Lieutenant Siltanen was right too. Damn it, what a racket they were making. Now someone had charged out of Bert's dugout and left the door wide open. Quite a party was going on there. The glow of light from the open door was clearly visible. Now if a Russian reconnaissance plane happened to be flying over...He had to go right in.

"That was a rousing song. Let's hear it again."

"Right on! Nestor has a great voice. Let 'er rip."

The men sitting around a table built of pine planks were swaying back and forth, with their hair hanging over their eyes. Nestor sat with one arm draped loosely over a younger man's neck. His long-bearded jaw waggled and the song he roared out at full volume boomed off the walls of the dugout.

Far behind me is the life
I lived on the ice of Lake Eldanka

"What the heck is all this howling going on here?"

The song stopped short. Mouths sagged open as the drunken men at the table turned around to look. Nestor said:

"What the hell! Is that the head man himself standing there?"

"It is. You should be ashamed to act like that. Men with full beards bawling their heads off."

"Hey, he looks so mad I'm almost scared."

"I am mad."

No one but Nestor could face the scrutiny of their commanding officer. Nestor turned on his seat to face him and said:

"What are you so mad about? We didn't yell *attention* but we don't usually. Hey, Riekki, you the religious one, why didn't you yell it out? You were sitting right at the door."

As he spoke these words, Nestor looked accusingly at Corporal Riekki, who like many others, had not touched the liquor ration. Lieutenant Mäkinen stood there, tall and stern-looking.

"I don't give a damn about calling men to attention. You did enough shouting in the soup line."

"Well, is that what started this war? So that eager-beaver lieutenant came and reported it. I was just sounding off for the fun of it."

"There are orders against it," said Mäkinen.

"So there are, but I didn't think we were so finicky on this logging job. We can be tight-lipped when we have to."

"We'll settle this in the command dugout, but I'm telling you this is your last night in this company. Where is Sääskilampi?"

"He must have gone to the next dugout," said Nestor, but he looked around to make sure and then added, "I don't see him."

"You come along with me. Malinen. Riekki will go to get Sääskilampi and send him in to talk to me. And I think you can drink these few drops of liquor with less noise. Let's go, Malinen."

As Lieutenant Mäkinen leaned forward to go out of the door, one of Nestor's companions who was seated at the table shouted:

"Attention!"

They all leaped to their feet. After awhile, someone said:

"I've never seen Mäkinen so angry."

"This would make even a good man lose his temper. First you guzzle down the share of those who don't drink and then you carry on like that. You could start to think a little about eternal life."

"There's no getting around this one," said one of the drunks. He clawed at his hair and goggled at the log wall of the dugout. "I wonder how tough the lieutenant will be on Nestor."

✧ ✧ ✧

"Just stop whistling and spit out what my punishment is."

"Well, examine your conscience for awhile. It'll sober you up," said Kosti Mäkinen.

"I'm cold sober now, I got so damned scared."

The lieutenant drummed his fingertips on the pine table he had made himself and blew through pursed lips. The other officers and the sergeant sat in silence, as did the clerk. Nestor Malinen could not seem to find a comfortable spot for his buttocks but sat squirming on a block of pine.

"If that other sinner would get here, we could hand out the sentence to both of you."

"Who? Bert?" exclaimed Nestor.

"Yes. Sergeant Sääskilampi."

"What has Bert done wrong? He's your relative."

"That's beside the point. I mean, he didn't order you not to shout."

"Who the hell told you that lie?"

Nestor took a pack of cigarettes from his pocket, thrust one of them into his mouth, and went on:

"Bert told me to stop, but I couldn't keep my mouth shut. Punish him and you're punishing the wrong man. That's the plain, honest truth."

Lieutenant Mäkinen drew a sheaf of papers toward himself from one corner of the table without answering Nestor.

"You wouldn't really send an old man to a disciplinary company, would you? I can keep my mouth shut if it comes to that."

"Who said anything about a disciplinary company?"

"You yourself said in the dugout that I would be shipped out of the company."

The door of the dugout opened. Bert Sääskilampi entered, brushed at his cap by way of a salute, and said:

"I was told to come."

"So you were, so you were. Sit down and hear your sentence. You, I mean, the second culprit, are to suffer pangs of conscience."

Bert stared in wonder at Kosti and the other occupants of the dugout. Then he sat on the end of a massive bench and said:

"What kind of court is this?"

Mäkinen cleared his throat and scowled at the visitors, although he looked mainly at Nestor Malinen, whose eyes were brightly inquisitive. The slender cigarette looked hopelessly insignificant in his bearded face. A roll-your-own is really best suited to his face and character, thought Kosti Mäkinen. He coughed once more and said:

"We have to straighten out this business of yelling on the chow line..."

He stopped talking and looked at Nestor, who turned toward Bert and started to say loudly:

"That damned..." He checked himself, and looked at the two lieutenants present. Then he went on more softly "...is supposed to have turned in a report to this company about it. I already said you told me to stop..."

"Explanations won't help," said Kosti Mäkinen. "Private Malinen is hereby sentenced to be expelled from the army into civilian life."

Nestor's jaw dropped and the butt of the cigarette fell from his lips. He tried to catch it in his fingertips at waist height, but had to pick it up from the floor.

"What's that supposed to mean? I don't get it at all."

"An order has come down to send the oldest age groups home. Your papers are ready on the table."

"Well damn it all to hell! You should be ashamed to scare a friend that way. I'm not sure that I didn't let a little go into my pants."

"You had to be punished somehow for being so hard of hearing," said Mäkinen with a grin.

"My ears get to be plugged up when people are bossing me around, but there's no wax in them now."

"That's good. Tomorrow you can bawl out your farewells to the ice on the Eldanka and the shores of Röhö," Mäkinen laughed. "The rest of us will stay on watch here."

"Damn, but I was scared. I never had you figured for a joker. So I'm going to be a civilian."

Kosti turned to Bert and said:

"I got some fresh reindeer meat in a package from your sister. You can start roasting it. I mean, you do a better job of it."

3

"You really have to scrub before the wood shows through."

"What would you say if I took off my jacket and rolled up my sleeves?"

"Why would you do that?"

The young and ruddy-cheeked woman hitched up the skirt of

her Auxiliary uniform and squatted down on the canteen floor. She took a brush made of roots from a water bucket and scrubbed vigorously at the layer of black mud coating the boards. Then her arms, on which the sleeves were rolled up nearly to the shoulders, dived into the bucket again and came up with a rag mop. Soon a patch of bare, unpainted boards showed in the middle of the grimy floor.

A young artillery lieutenant sat smoking on a bench nailed to the wall of the canteen. His eyes followed the woman's vigorous, but feminine movements. It wasn't the first time she had wielded a mop, he thought. The Auxiliary uniform looked as if it had been designed expressly for her. It was clear from her answer that she had understood his meaning, but was not taking it seriously. After a moment, he said:

"I mean, what would you say if I rolled up my sleeves and helped you?"

"I would wrap this wet mop around your ears."

"That's a direct answer, but I think you're joking."

"You'd better not try it. How the devil do they track in so much dirt in the middle of the winter?"

"Have you figured out how many feet have tramped on that floor in the course of one day?" asked the lieutenant.

"I have better things to do."

"I'm sure you have. Are you very tired?"

"I don't exactly feel like dancing. Lift up your clodhoppers so I can wipe under that bench."

"Of course. I'm sorry, I didn't notice. I could really help you with this mopping."

"Go chase yourself. Don't you officers even have the enlisted men shine your boots?"

"Sometimes in peacetime garrison life. Very seldom during a war."

"Then why are you so eager to crawl around on this shitty floor?"

"I would be helping you. You could get to sleep sooner."

"It won't take me forever to finish it myself."

"I can see that by the way you move. May I be so curious as to ask where you were born? I know it's nosy, but since we're here alone..."

"Not at all. The miracle took place up north in the land of

hunger. A wolf trotted over the mossy heath and farted into a pine stump. Lightning brought it to life. That's how the old man told me it happened."

The lieutenant swallowed hard. The girl's blond curls were bobbing very close to him. The brush scraped over the floor and at intervals, the mop sloshed across it. The girl was smiling.

"That was a clever answer. Can I wait until you're all through cleaning up?"

"You can as far as I'm concerned, but if the officer in charge shows up, you may have to leave in a hurry."

"I'll run the risk and wait for you."

"I can work without being watched. This will soon be mopped. I did tell you when you stayed that the canteen was closed for the day and that there was nothing more you could get."

"Would you be very much against my walking you to your quarters?"

"I don't need anyone to lead me."

"I would just walk alongside you."

"Not even if you walked behind me. Darn, this floor is so full of splinters. I just caught the point of a big one under my fingernail."

The woman swished her hands to dry them and then walked over to stand under the gas lamp and look at her fingers.

"Darn it, there it is. Now why did that have to happen."

"Let me get it out."

The lieutenant walked over to her. He took her hand into his own, looked at it, and said:

"Oh my, it's almost a centimeter long. Luckily the end is showing. Will it hurt if I pull it out?"

"No, just give it a yank. It's worse to leave it in."

"There, it's out now. I'll keep this as a souvenir."

"Thank you. You did that well."

The lieutenant dropped the reddened splinter into the pocket of his combat jacket. He was still holding the girl's hand. He looked directly at her, then down at her hand and said:

"You have beautiful hands and an even more beautiful face."

The girl's cheeks turned even redder. She raised one hand up in front of her breast and said:

"These aren't worth praising. They're as red and wet as a duck's webbed feet."

"We need hands like that now. Our country's future lies in hands that know how to work. Polished nails and powdered cheeks are of no help."

The girl did not withdraw her hand. The man looked sincere. The pressure of his hand was firm but gentle.

"Do you have dear ones at the front?"

"My father...the only one now..."

"It was hard for you to say those last words. I didn't hear them."

"My brother was killed right at the start of this war."

"So that was it. It's very sad to hear. On what front?"

"Near Kiestinki. Now I have to finish this mopping."

"That could be risky. Dirty water could get into the skin puncture."

"No it won't. That's not the first cut I've had."

"There's always a risk. Really, can't I see you home?"

"I already said no."

"Is that absolutely final?"

The lieutenant looked into her eyes. She tried to meet his gaze, but had to lower her own. Then she said:

"It is. At least for tonight."

"I won't bother you further. Good night until next time."

The girl finished the mopping soon after the lieutenant had left. As she was leaving, the woman in command of the Auxiliary entered.

"You really have the place clean, Malinen."

"It took a long time. I hope it's not as stormy tomorrow."

"The floor doesn't get this filthy in cold weather," said the elderly woman. She watched the actions of the younger one and said:

"Was the lieutenant here long?"

"He just left," said Elma Malinen.

You know that wearing the uniform obligates a person to observe a high moral standard. But there are other reasons to turn a deaf ear to a man's words and propositions."

"I didn't ask the lieutenant to stay," said Elma.

"I know that. I've always admired the firm way you deal with men. As a matter of fact, this lieutenant — his name is Salonen — is a vicar's son. He's a nice young man. But still the uniform obligates one..."

"I don't care if he's a bishop's son. I'll shove a cup of substitute coffee into a lieutenant's or a dirty-necked soldier's hand in exactly the same way. Rank means nothing to me."

The elderly woman looked at the younger one again. Then she said:

"You might have put it more delicately, but the sentiment is absolutely right. Let's go to sleep now. Good night."

4

A young major entered the tent. His eyebrows and even the hair that curled out from under his fur cap were coated with frost and icicles. He stopped to warm his hands at the barrel stove. German enlisted men, non-commissioned officers, and even some officers sat huddled along the walls of the tent, a look of misery on their faces. One had a hand, another a foot, some of them both hands and feet bare. A Finnish doctor who was a captain in the medical corps and a couple of corpsmen were attending to the frozen limbs. There were deep pouches under the doctor's eyes. The tent fly opened again, and the heads of Germans wearing watch caps thrust into the tent. He turned to the door and said in German:

"No, not one man more can come in."

"We're cold...We're freezing."

The words came like an animal howl from the mouth of a German soldier. His lips were frozen stiff, and his eyes, like those of the other men peering into the tent, were prayerful.

"We'll all freeze to death. Save us...have mercy on us, Captain."

"Hell, I can't change myself into a tent. If no more will fit in here, there's nothing to be done," the captain said in Finnish.

Then he turned to a German officer, both of whose feet were bandaged and said the same thing in German, without the profanity. The officer dropped on all fours to crawl toward the door and shout:

"Get out, damn it!"

The tent flap fell back into place. From outside came the sound of unrestrained weeping, accompanied by another noise like the bleating of a calf when its throat has been slashed. The major's eyes circled the tent. It was indeed full.

"Are there many more out there?" asked the captain.

"Dozens, at least. And they're bringing in more of them from their positions," said the major.

"This is the height of misery," said the doctor. "We had it bad enough when we were surrounded, but that was nothing compared to this. This man's toes are frozen and his face is full of frozen patches."

The sun, which had traveled a low arc in the sky, was setting in back of the frozen woods. The sky was a dark blue. Frost snapped in the trees, and sunlight filtered through the woven cloth of the tent. The major straightened up beside the stove, rubbed his hands together, and called out:

"Laurila."

One of the medical corpsmen rose. His sleeves were rolled up to his elbows and he held a roll of gauze bandaging in his hand.

"Major, sir," he said.

"Go and take a look at the thermometer. I forgot to, even though I walked right by it. But roll down your sleeves and put on a hat. I don't know what will happen if we lose you."

The corpsman left the tent. From outside came the sound of words in German that registered varying degrees of misery. Laurila's answer could be heard inside.

"Soon, soon, you'll get in soon when the others are taken away."

When Laurila re-entered the tent, he said:

"Thirty-five and a half below."

"Thanks. At night it'll drop to forty," said the major.

Going back to his own corner of the tent, the major asked the communications corporal to contact the regiment. He himself took a piece of hardtack from a package on top of a crate, spread it with butter, and began to eat, staring at the peak of the tent roof. After repeated attempts, the corporal handed the receiver to him.

"The adjutant is on the line, major, sir," he said.

It took a while to get the colonel to the phone. When he heard the major's voice, he said:

"Well then, what's happened since we last talked?"

"Nothing good. The Russians keep pouring in reinforcements."

"I'm a little surprised that your advance was halted at the

very beginning. The reconnaissance reports were accurate."

"They were. We just needed more men," said the major.

"Well, damn it! You had a reinforced company of our men and eight hundred Germans. You had a clear edge in manpower, damn it!"

"All I ever had was one Finnish company!"

The major's voice had become sharp. He looked at the Germans in the tent as he listened to the colonel's astonished response.

"Can't you get it through your heads in the command sector that the Germans are just a burden on us? Haven't we sent enough frozen Germans back to you these last three nights?"

The calm and even-tempered colonel could be heard to swallow at the end of the line, and his breathing quickened. Then he said:

"Surely not all the Germans have frozen?"

"Will they stop compounding this misery only when the last of them is frozen? It's my profession to command men in battle, but I can't even put on the mask of an officer when I'm faced with something like this. Goddamn, the whole tent is full of your *guarantors* right now. You can hear them crying outside all the time because they can't get in. And they keep leading and carrying in more of them. My adjutant — a name like that is a mockery under these hellish conditions — is taking horses away from the supply train to transport these pitiful wrecks out of here. You can come and see for yourself, and ask the General to come along too, when the frozen start coming in by the wagonload at night. Damn it to hell — sending poor human beings into this kind of weather in summer gear..."

The major's voice trailed off. He shoved his cap back off his forehead and chewed at the hardtack as he listened to the colonel's words.

"Why are you using your own horses and men for this kind of transport? Aren't our own forces badly needed there?"

"I'm doing it because the Germans can't and it's not in my nature to leave them here to freeze."

"Well, so that's how things stand," came the voice over the wire.

"We need more of our own men here, and we need them at once."

"Where can we spare them from? It was agreed that this would be a joint operation with the Germans."

"We have to get men from somewhere and they have to be Finns."

"I'm sure you can carry out this mission. You've done wonders before."

"Flattery is no help in this situation. I can't do it alone, with almost no men. Are more coming or not?"

"How many do you need then?"

"Two companies. Free the rest of the battalion and send them here."

The colonel could be heard discussing the situation with the men near him. The words came to the major's ears as an unintelligible murmur. Then he heard:

"Attention!"

"Yes, let's hear it."

"You will have the rest of the battalion as soon as possible."

"Thanks, colonel, sir. When you promise a thing as soon as possible, I can start believing again."

"Thanks. It's more important to believe in yourself."

"I hope you'll contact the Germans and tell them to get winter equipment before they start an operation like this. We'll be in touch."

✧ ✧ ✧

"That rumbling is a bad sign. They'll be coming with tanks tonight," said Jalo Kieppi.

"It sounds that way," said Kauko.

Jalo Kieppi was kicking the toes of his boots together and flailing his arms across his chest to keep warm. His face was almost black. Kauko pressed his lowered ear flaps into his cheeks. His teeth were chattering. He took off his mittens, squeezed them under his arms, and thrust his hands into the waistband of his trousers.

"Goddamn, but it's cold!"

"Are you squeezing your balls now?" said Jalo Kieppi.

"My paws won't stay warm otherwise. Godalmighty, my fingers are like ice," laughed Kauko.

The snow around the large boulder behind which Kauko and Kieppi were huddled was packed smooth. The eyelids of both men were red. Although they were loaded down with an excess of clothing, they were constantly cold. Sometimes they laughed at nothing, while at other times they quarreled for no reason. The other Finnish men involved in the flanking movement were at the same pitch of tension. For three days now, they had been huddling in the hollows of the same area. At first they had seen the watch caps of German troops in the spearhead, and heard the crunching of their hobnailed boots, but this morning not a single one of them was to be seen. The men of the Finnish company knew that the severity of the winter had come as a total shock to the Germans in their summer gear.

"Jonas was lucky he got to go and haul those *guarantors* of ours back," said Jalo Kieppi.

"We"ll see how this trip turns out," said Kauko.

"We won't live to see another day. Tonight at the latest, the *Vassilies* will start pushing through and then woe to us boys."

"Well, the major said when he was here just now that we have to hold."

"But he didn't say how," said Jalo. "How can we, when we have to cart the Germans around too. Hey, are the Russians coming now?"

Kauko snatched up his machine pistol from against the rock, as did Kieppi his rifle. On the left, they caught the flash of snow uniforms in the darkening evening. There was a mutter of voices too. Kauko and Kieppi were no longer cold.

"Shall we let fly?" said Kieppi.

"Let's wait a bit," said Kauko. Then after a pause: "No need to panic. They're our men."

"But why are they ganging up like that?"

"Hey buddies, come along," said a sergeant who was walking at the head of the troop of men.

"Where?" said Kauko, looking at his comrades gathering around them.

"To hell, maybe, but at least out of here."

"Has the order been given?" asked Kauko, in amazement.

"We're not waiting for orders now," said the sergeant who had just spoken. "Can't you hear what a hell of mass of men and machines the Russians are piling up here? You'll see the results tomorrow."

"Those goddamn Germans, they're nothing but trouble."

"You freeze out here, even in winter clothes."

"And not a smell of warm food."

"Let's just go and talk to the major."

"Is everyone with you? Do they all feel the same way?" asked Kauko.

"The officers stayed. There's only the company commander and one platoon leader left. The others were wounded the other night."

"Do you think we didn't see that?" said Kieppi. "We were in the same ruckus."

"There's not going to be any argument about this. The wilderness warriors have had it up to here."

The sergeant walked at the end of the now long line of soldiers and the others followed him. There were almost a hundred men, angry and shivering with cold. One of the group yelled back:

"Of all the goddamned things they force people into. Come on."

The group of men moved off. Kauko's mind was in a turmoil.

"Shall we join them?" said Kieppi.

"It's insubordination," said Kauko.

"But what can a few of us do here?"

"If it weren't for our commanding officer, I would join the others."

"I don't like to do this to the major either."

Kauko and Kieppi stood there. They could tell by the rumble of voices that most of the company was already marching toward the command post. Soon the voices faded. Kauko raised his ear flaps. Moans of misery came from the direction of the command tent. They were the complaints of the German soldiers. The merciless cold was tormenting the thinly-clad men from the south beyond endurance. Suddenly the sound of clanking treads and the roar of motors rose above the bark of mortars firing. Instinctively Kauko and Kieppi threw themselves to the ground. Shells burst in the area between them and the Russians. Fragments dusted the frost from the trees. They could hear the sound of new rounds being fired.

"Let's get out of here," shouted Jalo Kieppi.

"Let's go. What can a few men do?"

They began running the shortest route to the command post.

✧ ✧ ✧

There was a lighted lamp in the tent. Its walls still bulged with the crowd of frozen men. There was even a Finn here and there in the group. Outside the temperature was close to forty below. The freezing Germans were hugging one another to keep warm. The tent flap flew open.

"No more can fit in here," barked the doctor, who was working with his back turned to the door.

"That's a goddamned lie. We're coming in, even if it's over dead bodies. Is the major here?"

The captain from the medical corps turned around. He wanted to relieve his pent-up weariness by shouting, but he checked himself. A long-bearded sergeant crawled in through the door. Others thrust in behind him. The major dropped the map he had just been checking from his hand and said:

"Here I am."

The sergeant stood up. There were black splotches on his uniform and his eyes were staring wildly. In the warm tent, the ice on his face began to melt immediately. The major rose to face him. He was tall, and stood straight and dignified. His eyes met those of the sergeant and held them. His instincts told him that the endurance of this man and the others fitting their feet in among the frozen men on the floor had run into a wall of weariness and cold. For a long time, he and the sergeant looked at each other. Then the sergeant said:

"We came to say good morning."

The major lifted one foot onto a block that served as a stool. Then he leaned an elbow on his knee and rested his chin in his palm. For a long time he was silent, and then he said:

"Is that so?"

More men in snow uniforms shoved into the tent. Others peered in under the flap. Grumbling and cursing could be heard. The sergeant searched furiously through his pockets. The major could see how violently his hands were shaking. The man had been promoted from corporal to sergeant. He was one of the battalion's best squad leaders, phenomenal at finding his way on patrol, although he knew no more about a compass than its name. He was said to be a itinerant laborer in civilian life. It was unlikely that the knife scar which slanted across his lip had come while eating.

"If this brand will do, then have one."

The major extended an opened pack of cigarettes to the sergeant, who looked gloomily at the profferer. Nevertheless he took the cigarette, pressed the tip of it into the red-hot stove, and began puffing on it.

"Things have reached a point where we've had enough of this job," said the sergeant.

The major too lighted a cigarette. There was nothing he could say. There was not a shadow of doubt in the eyes of any man who had shoved his way into the tent.

"The whole company is here. Only the officers stayed. We're heading back to Kiestinki. They can send us to jail from there if they want to."

"I won't try to stop you. Just say hello to the men at Kiestinki and tell them the major stayed here."

The young major sat down at the table and rested his chin in his hands. His cigarette lay smoking in an empty tin can. There was silence in the tent. Outside one man cursed and another moaned. The sergeant turned and tried to catch his comrades' eyes. They were all looking at the floor. From time to time they would steal a glance at the major.

"Well goddamnit, we won't go either," shouted the sergeant. "We won't leave our buddies behind. Let the Germans have their turn at hauling our bodies back to Kiestinki."

"The Russians are starting to shell us now," said a soldier in back of the sergeant.

"Let's go back to where we came from," said the sergeant, turning around.

At the door, he turned from his departing comrades and said:

"Is it okay with the major if we settle this man to man, or will it get into the hands of the legal beagles?"

The major, who had left cadet school only two years ago, swallowed hard. It took him awhile to answer. When he was sure his voice was under control, he said:

"We've always settled things man to man up to now. And the rest of our battalion is on its way here."

"That'll do it. Now we have to get back to our positions in a helluva hurry, before the titcaps get moving."

The tent flap fell and the sergeant's voice could be heard from outside:

"Get back to your positions, fast. Our buddies are on their way...I mean, our battalion is."

5

"You'll let me in this evening, won't you?" said the lieutenant.

"It's night already," said Elma Malinen.

"You're just teasing me," said the lieutenant. "I've tried all winter to win your trust."

"I didn't lead you on. You could have believed me the time you stayed to watch me mop up the canteen floor," Elma said with a giggle.

The yard, slushy during the day, was now frozen crisp, and crunched underfoot. The quarters of the Women's Auxiliary was in an old three-room cottage in the war zone. The lieutenant raised his head suddenly, caught Elma by the hand, and said:

"I can tell by your face that you're only teasing. Elma, sweet..."

"What kind of teasing is this? It was nice when we we took walks and talked about everything. I don't..."

"What are you trying to say. I think you're afraid of me."

"I'm not the kind to be afraid."

"But you're afraid of me, since you won't even let me into your room."

"It's not fear."

"What is it then?" said the man, and squeezed her hand more tightly.

"You know yourself what they say about officers and Auxiliary women. That's why..."

"Why listen to that kind of talk. The enlisted men and the non-coms are just envious. But you are afraid of me, aren't you?"

"I've run into pigs before this. One was a traveler who tried to mess with me in our sauna, and the other a corporal who came to the house. He thought he had it made, but he left howling."

The spring night was dark enough to conceal the flush that spread over the lieutenant's face. For some time he kicked at the ridges of snow with his boot toes, and then he said:

"I wouldn't like to be included in that group."

"What group?"

"The one that's connected with — how shall I put it — swine culture."

"Oh, pigs. I didn't mean you," Elma giggled. "Now you know how unromantic us wilderness roses are."

"You're just talking. You don't mean it from the heart."

"Ha, ha to you. But since you ask so nicely, come on in. My roommate is on leave. Do you know how to play poker?"

"I've learned a few things in the army. You know that parsonage children are not given cards to play with."

✧ ✧ ✧

Elma tossed the cards onto the table and said:

"You have to go now. Look at the time."

"It's only a little after two," said the lieutenant.

"Maybe, but I have a lot of running to do behind the canteen counter tomorrow."

"I'll smoke one more cigarette. You have one too, please."

"Not tonight, or rather, this morning. My tongue is parched from the others."

The man had taken off his combat jacket and was sitting beside Elma on the bed. He watched her gather up the cards, arrange them deftly in a pack, and put them up on a shelf.

She had to rise on tiptoe to do so, and the lieutenant's heart beat faster as he looked at her silhouette from the side. Elma sat next to him again, so close that her arm pressed against his side.

"You should have gone," she said.

"Don't send me away yet. Look at me."

The man took Elma's face gently between his fingers and turned it toward him.

"You're not angry with me. I can tell by your eyes."

"I didn't say I was. It's because I'll be so tired tomorrow, and because of the gossip, and because of one more thing that I'm telling you to go."

"We'll face the gossip together. Oh what lovely hair you have."

"Stop flattering me. All that talk is just hot air."

The man put his arm around Elma. He did not squeeze her hard, but let his arm rest lightly around her. It gave her a warm, pleasant feeling inside. She reached out a hand for an envelope that lay on a picture magazine at one end of the table in the room, tilted it on its side, then turned it over in her fingers for a moment, deep in thought. The lieutenant turned his eyes to it as well, and said after a pause:

"From: Sergeant Kauko Sammalsuo."

"A neighbor. I grew up with him," Elma said.

"Is it because of him?" asked the lieutenant, nodding toward the envelope.

A feeling of bitterness clashed with the sense of well-being in Elma's mind. The letter from Kauko had arrived in midwinter already. There had been no answer to the reply she had written, although she had waited for almost three months. She had read the letter again last night. The first time she read it, she had wept. Who on earth was the man he had written about, some boarder in the Olkivaara storehouse? And that was not the first mention — he had hinted at the same thing last winter already. During his leave he had acted so strangely and then gone sneaking off like a thief.

Suddenly Elma tossed the letter back on the table and leaned over to unlace her shoes. Then she slumped to one side on the bed.

"Not because of him or anyone," she said.

The lieutenant was confused. He stood up and swung Elma's feet over onto the bed, then stood uncertainly beside the simple wooden bunk. Elma lay with her eyes closed, her breasts rising and falling rapidly and irregularly. The lieutenant sat down on the edge of the bed.

"I'll stay with you," he said.

Elma said nothing. She felt a warm hand stroking her temples. The caress soothed the bitterness she was feeling. To hell with it all — I won't listen to any more of his crazy accusations. The man's hand shifted to stroking her neck. His warm voice said:

"Can I stay with you?"

"Take your boots off, at least."

Elma heard the man undressing.

"Shall I put out the light?"

"I won't need it."

✧ ✧ ✧

"I wonder what time it is," said Elma.

The man scratched a match, raised his head from the pillow, and said:

"It's almost five. I guess I have to get back to the battery."

"That's plain to see."

"Why are you being sarcastic?"

"Just because. Are you happy now?"

"What happened to all your sweetness?"

"This spoiled it."

"Was it so awful, darling?"

"Don't you dare try to sweet-talk me."

"Why...now you're the same as before," said the man.

"Hardly. Now that I've lost my only virtue."

The man lighted a cigarette. He could see the irregular rise and fall of the woman's breasts, and wondered if she would begin to cry. His satisfaction was incomplete. He knew that he had had only her body. Why had she practically offered herself to him? All this winter's preparations seemed so pointless. He felt as if he had besieged a fort with the strength of an entire battery of artillery, laid plots to overthrow it, fired barrages at intervals, tried to sneak over the walls. Then one night after all this trouble, the gates of the fort had opened, and an unarmed soldier had stepped out and said: "Lieutenant, sir. Please march right in. I'm the only one who's been here the whole time and I have no weapons."

"Was it so terrible to lose your virtue to me?"

"I'm an adult, so it's no earth-shaking event. In these days, it's no big deal."

"I'm glad you're not bitter."

"Well, at least you were honest. You didn't promise to marry me or to make me at least the dean's wife before you had me," Elma said with a snicker.

"Now you're being nasty. I have to go, but I'll see you soon."

"And I have to go and soak cowberry leaves to make tea for the soldier boys."

"Can I pick you up at the canteen tomorrow evening?"

"If you're still interested. I don't plan on becoming a common mattress for officers. Go now, so you won't run into our top sergeant in the entry. I hear them stirring on the other side of the wall."

"I'll see you soon. You are being nasty."

"I've been called that before."

✧ ✧ ✧

During the worst of the spring break-up, a letter for Elma arrived in the field mail. She recognized her sister's handwriting on the envelope. Usually she waited until evening to read her mail, but this time she went into the canteen storeroom and opened the letter. White-faced, she staggered into the commander's office.

"Good Lord, Elma! What happened?"

"Mother died. My sister wrote."

"Sit down, Elma."

"I don't have time. There's a long line of soldiers waiting."

The elderly woman came over to Elma and put a hand on her shoulder. She looked at her bowed head, and said:

"The girls can manage. There's never such a rush that a person can't observe a few moments of silence for her own mother's death. Sit down."

Elma sat down, put her arms on the table, and pressed her face into them. She felt a gentle hand pat her shoulders a few times. Then the older woman walked softly to the door and said:

"Just take it easy here. I'll go and see to the girls."

Elma's breast ached, but no relieving outpouring of grief would come. Mother. Mother was gone. When did I last see her? It was the first day of December. She was standing in the yard. Her head scarf was tied in a firm knot under her chin. A cold wind was blowing. Tears froze on her cheeks. Her bare hands were clasped over her heart. She was wearing father's old work jacket, and her skirts were billowing in the wind. "It will be strange when you're gone," she said. "Taimi will be here. You'll get along," I answered. Mother pressed a finger to her eyes to dry them and brushed the frozen moisture from her cheeks. "You could have stayed on air watch at the windmill," she said. "So many people come there." "This is a good chance for me to see more of the world," I said. "The world...Yes, people should see more of it. I got to see a little during the evacuation. I've spent my whole life on this lake. This shore and this house are so familiar to me," mother said. "I never did get to go to Oulu," I said. "Now I get a free ride. Everything is paid for, and I get to serve the Woman's Auxiliary."

My brother Svante was logging in the woods. Taimi and the younger children were inside. I took down my skis from against the corner of the house. I hesitated about whether to say goodbye with a handshake, but decided against it. It isn't the way of backwoods families. I got onto my skis. I was wearing my Auxiliary uniform and overcoat. "Well, mother, don't worry about me," I said.

"Goodbye my child," she said. "Be a good girl out there in the world."

Then the tears came. I kicked off on my skis and flew down the slope to the lake. There I turned to look back. Mother had walked to the end of the house and was standing there. Her hands were clasped in the same position over her heart. Her skirt was billowing in the wind. Even the sleeves and tails of father's big work shirt were fluttering. She didn't wave, nor did I. That's not our way. Then I skied off toward Naavala.

"Elma," said the Auxiliary commander, who had re-entered the room.

"What is it?"

Elma raised her head, dabbing at her eyes. She could see that the eyes of the older woman were misting over. She was said to be a stern, hard person.

"You have to get home for a visit now."

"I have to get out of the service altogether. Can you arrange it? They can't get along without me at home."

"It will be a loss to me and to all of us. You've been the best of us in all our duties. And you've withstood all temptations."

"Not all of them. But I've tried to do my job."

✧ ✧ ✧

Artillery Lieutenant Salonen was on leave when Elma departed. It was evening when she gathered up her belongings. She put his picture into her pocketbook. From her travel locker, she took out a small object, took it over to the window, and stood looking at it with her head bowed. Her roommate came up behind her and said:

"What are you looking at so prayerfully?"

Elma said nothing, but extended her hand, palm up. The young woman leaned over to look and said:

"A cross...at the end of a silver chain."

"It is a cross. I wonder if it was given to me for this."

"Who did you get it from?"

"From a person I've known for a long time. He found it at the Petsamo monastery."

"How romantic! Give it to me so I can look at it more closely."

But Elma dropped the keepsake into her pocketbook.

CHAPTER XVIII

1

“For once God was on the farmer’s side,” said Auku.

“Don’t think we got this good weather for your sake,” said Aili from atop the haystack. “It’s only because I came along with you.”

Haystacks stood in every quarter of the Paarma swamp meadow. They looked like giant eggs standing on end. The Sammalsuo haymakers were finishing off one of the stacks: Auku was wielding a pitchfork, Väinö was raking up the last armfuls, and Aili was atop the stack, tramping down the hay around the center pole. Auku speared a bunch with the fork and tossed it up onto the stack.

“Now the haying is done,” said Väinö.

“If this war would only end and we could clear enough of the woods around home, we wouldn’t have to go gathering hay in these crane pastures.”

Auku’s face was thoughtful as he spoke. His mind was on the war front:

“If Kauko could have come home,” he continued, “we’d really have something to see. But now it looks as if I’ll have to go myself and put an end to this war.”

“Stop blithering and help me down,” said Aili.

“Why should I? You’re in a good place to spot airplanes.”

In spite of his words, Auku reached up alongside the haystack with the long-handled pitchfork and said:

“Climb down now and grab hold of the tines.”

Holding on to the center pole, Aili slid her feet down along the narrow stack. Moving her body down and shifting her grip from pole to pitchfork demanded skill and precise movement. The maneuver was a familiar one to Aili. Auku held on to the end of the fork handle and said:

“That isn’t a tear in your pants, is it?”

“Stop fooling around or you’ll make me fall.”

Soon Aili was down with her brothers. Auku patted the stack in order to compact and shape it. Finally he tossed a triple-pronged wind-weight over it and said:

“Now to the sauna, and then off we march to Järvenkylä.”

The late July sun was setting. Mosquitoes and horse flies were disappearing from the swamp. The Sammalsuo haying crew had spent their nights sleeping on hay in a smoke sauna and preparing their coffee substitute and scanty food on a campfire before it. In early summer, Aili had put in extra time on air watch, and now for the better part of a week, she had been raking for her brothers.

The scythes and rakes were bundled and the food packs ready to go in front of the sauna. Auku was still poking around in the windowless building, but Aili and Väinö were already shouldering their loads.

"Come on so we can get going," Aili said.

Auku came out of the low doorway, shotgun in hand.

"How about sleeping the night here and leaving in the morning?" he said.

"I'm not going to toss around on that floor one more night with my heart in my throat," said Aili.

"What were you afraid of — lizards or snakes?" asked Auku.

"You know very well what there is to be afraid of," Aili said with a snort.

Auku gave his sister a questioning look, but there was a gleam of mockery in his eyes.

"Why did you have that shotgun with you? It isn't hunting season," said Aili.

"In case we ran into a bear. It's not so many summers ago that one showed up in Nestor Olkivaara's meadow."

"Is that why you and Väinö took an ax and scythes into that shack every night? Because you were afraid of bears?"

The brothers exchanged glances. Then Väinö said:

"A bear — that's what we were afraid of."

"Those Russian partisans must look pretty much like bears too. What did the spies who carried off a whole haying crew in the next parish look like?"

The sun was already getting low in the sky. Aili's eyes searched every corner of the meadow. The boys too looked in every direction, but more slowly.

"Let's go, for God's sake." Aili's voice was panicky. "I don't see anything yet."

"Let's go then, before this heroic member of the Women's Auxiliary starts to cry."

Auku set a prop against the sauna door. Aili and Väinö were already striding toward a gloomy spruce woods at the other side of the swamp.

Auku broke open the shotgun and muttered to himself:

"It is loaded. At least one Russian will be safely put away if any of them try to come sneaking in."

Auku picked up the bunch of rakes and the milk jug from the ground. Shotgun under his arm, he set off after his brother and sister. He felt safer when he caught up with them, but still he said:

"These are some times. You have to take a gun with you even when you go to take a shit."

"Stop scaring me. I've had enough of shivering," said Aili.

Väinö stopped and said:

"You go ahead, Auku. You know the way better."

"A blind man could follow this trail," said Auku, but nevertheless he stepped ahead of his brother and sister.

✧ ✧ ✧

When the Sammalsuo haymaking crew reached the road that ran from Järvenkylä to the church village, only the red glow of the sunset was still visible. But the weight that had oppressed them in the woods dropped from their shoulders as they strode along the highway. When the first truck caught up to and passed them, the last trace of fear vanished. While dust raised by the vehicle still hovered in the air, Väinö said:

"That must have been a German truck."

"You can tell by the model that it was," said Auku, hooking the sling of the shotgun over his shoulder.

"We don't have to be afraid of Russians if there are Germans around," said Aili, and then she added: "They're such handsome men."

"They're nothing special," said Auku.

German motor vehicles went by now and then. The fear that had gnawed at them in the swamp meadow now seemed completely laughable. It was already past midnight when they approached the Naavala's land. Suddenly Auku stopped.

"Now what are you gawking at?" said Aili, as she and Väinö stopped too.

"Look over there, across the road," said Auku.

The two of them looked in the direction where Auku was pointing.

"How come Big Piney Woods looks so low?" said Väinö.

"Aha, now I see something odd," said Aili.

The high point of summer was over, and now a dim twilight covered the wilderness. The Sammalsuo children stood there and stared.

"Something is wrong," said Auku.

"What a racket they're making," said Aili.

"Something is cockeyed, but let's go and see what it is," said Auku.

They walked forward carefully. The rasp of gravel underfoot sounded ear-splitting to them, so without any arrangement, they all walked at the very edge of the ditch, where the growth of moss and hay cushioned their steps. No more vehicles passed them either.

"What the devil! They've cut down the whole woods. Not a tree has been left standing."

Auku's pronouncement made his brother and sister stop short. The two stood there helplessly, looking at Auku's face.

"Has the goddamned war come all the way here now?" said Auku.

"We were in the woods for only four nights," said Aili.

"Is that what war is like?" Väinö's eyes looked askance at the cleared area.

"The whole heath is covered with trucks and wagons," said Auku. "There are horses over there. You can see them switching their tails."

"Who are those men walking around with rifles?"

"They're guards. Don't you know that much about war, Aili?" said Auku.

"There are many buildings here already. What are they, and how did they build them so fast?" wondered Väinö.

"They're only barracks," said Auku.

"Who are they? Have the Russians come?" asked Väinö.

"They seem to have German caps and uniforms."

"Aili is right this time," said Auku. He picked up the bundle of rakes he had set down and went on: "How could they cut down the woods so fast? And I've never seen a whole village spring up so quickly."

"Do we dare to walk past it along the road?" asked Aili.

"How the devil do I know? Maybe we should circle through the woods to Naavala."

Auku stepped over the ditch, and Aili and Väinö leaped after him. They bypassed the site by walking through the woods. Odd sensations ran through their minds. Had the war come here? Only at the front were there large numbers of men. Why hadn't mother come to tell them, Auku wondered. He unslung the shotgun and walked through the dim night with the weapon under his arm.

"If Naavala is the same as usual, we'll head for the windmill."

Aili's words sounded extremely loud. Auku said:

"Don't talk so loud. We'll go all the way to Naavala through the woods."

Only when they came in sight of Naavala did they turn back onto the road. Everything seemed calm there. Cowbells clanked in the barn and the blackout curtains were drawn over the windows. Aili said:

"Shall we go to the windmill together?"

"Let's go and see who's looking east there now," said Auku.

Cautiously they approached the windmill. The observation port looked dark. The broken blade of the mill stood out against the sky. A duck quacked on the shore.

"Do we dare go there?" asked Aili.

"I wonder whose turn it is? Do you remember?" said Auku.

Aili raised both hands to breast level and mouthed the numbers as she counted on her fingers. Finally she said:

"If they haven't changed the schedule, it should be Elma's turn. But I'm afraid to call out."

"Come hell or high water, I'm going to let out a yell," said Auku.

"Let's at least stay hidden in this brush," said Väinö.

"I'm going to yell now. E-elma-aa!"

Although Auku did not shout at full volume, an echo resounded from across the lake. A Women's Auxiliary cap appeared in the observation port and turned in all directions.

"Good Lord, who's bellowing out there?" said a frightened voice.

"Elma, it's so damned good that you're here," said Auku.

"Is it Auku out there scaring the wits out of me?" said Elma.

"And heck, there are Aili and Väinö too. What are you all doing here? You really scared me."

"We're on our way back from hay-making," said Aili, walking toward the mill.

"Is this place still in Finnish hands?" said Auku.

"What do you mean?" said Elma, peering down from above. "Come up here, all of you. You don't need those rakes and scythes."

"And the jug?" said Auku.

"Not if it's empty."

The Sammalsuos climbed up into the mill. After exchanging some words, they all crowded up to the observation port. Leaning their elbows on its bottom log, they all turned out of long habit to look out over the woods that stretched eastward. The first stars of late summer sparkled in outer space. Then they turned to look north. From the Big Piney Woods area, several smokestacks rose into the air. A tall woods had stood there, but now the area resembled a hollow.

"The Germans moved in there on Monday," said Elma.

"Why the devil did they cut down all the trees?" said Auku.

"It was all done so quickly. The power saws kept buzzing and the trees kept crashing down."

"What are they doing there?" asked Auku.

"No one knows for sure. Some claim to know that they're building a railroad here from Kontiomäki."

"A railroad? How come the Germans are building it? That's for the Finns to do. This is Finland," said Auku.

"No one knows. They are nice men. All kinds of people from Järvenkylä have visited them. They say they give chocolate to the children. Some of the men have gotten cognac too."

"I have to go there. I'm sure they're civilized and know how to act," said Aili.

"Don't get carried away. They're no supermen. Kauko and others who were on the Kiestinki front said they froze like cockroaches when we had that bitter cold spell last winter," said Auku.

"Many of them have visited with people here too. They laugh so nicely and they know how to be polite. But most of them are prisoners. Did you see the barbed-wire fence they built around that clearing?"

The Sammalsuo children looked at each other. Then Auku said:

"Have they brought Russian prisoners here?"

"No, they're German prisoners. Akseli Naavala says they're the kind of Germans who don't like Hitler."

"Have you been to see them? Oh boy, it's great to have men from so far away out here in the wilderness."

"I haven't and I don't plan to go soon. They come here and talk a lot, but I don't know the language," said Elma.

Weariness and fear were soon forgotten. A lively buzz of conversation filled the upper story of the windmill. Now and then Elma looked out from the port and said:

"I'm almost forgetting my job here. But at least I don't see any Russian planes."

"Wait till they find out there are Germans here, and the bombs will start falling," said Auku.

"It's all hard to believe," said Elma. "A few years ago, this wilderness was nothing but a hungry, sleepy place, and now there are Germans here, and the whole world's trucks and war machines keep passing through all the time."

"And the Russian soldiers got almost to this parish," said Auku.

"Yes, and here comes Hilja now to take her turn on watch."

The figure of a woman in Auxiliary uniform had appeared at the edge of the clearing. Hilja Naavala climbed up to the watch site, and Elma left, along with Auku, Aili, and Väinö. Aili said:

"Tomorrow I'll climb up here and take my turn. Come and spend the night with us. There's not much left of it anyway. We'll sleep in the storehouse."

"I have to go home. Taimi isn't much of a hand at taking care of the cows without mother to advise her."

As Elma and the children were rowing across the lake, a machine pistol chattered in the direction of the camp and echoed from the slopes of Lapinvaara. Watchdogs began to bark and somewhere on a bay, a loon cried out.

"What can they be shooting at night?" Elma said.

"I don't know," said Auku.

Two boats traveling in opposite directions plowed wedges in the calm surface of the lake. The fragrance of hay drying on hurdles hung over the waters.

2

It was January of the year 1943. There was a storm blowing, an exceptionally severe blizzard. Snow fell from the sky, and the north wind tossed it about violently. Nestor Malinen had driven his horse home from the logging woods. After drinking his coffee substitute, he said:

"Hell, that cold really gets to my shoulders."

As soon as he had entered the door, Elma had seen the pain in his face. A slight pang of conscience stopped nagging her. It was a good time, she decided, to tell him what had been weighing on her mind this winter.

"My shoulders were freezing in camp already. I'm so damned cold now that if I had false teeth they would fall out. You don't have any fever powders, do you?"

"I don't happen to."

"Would they have any at Naavala? I don't suppose Maija Sammalsuo would...she never gets sick. I'm the only one who does."

Elma rose from her chair and went toward her bedroom.

"But I've got another medicine," she said.

There was a look of suffering on Nestor's face. He gazed at the door through which Elma had just disappeared. If only I don't get pneumonia, he thought. I nearly did on the Murmansk railway. That was quite a time. Chinese, Kirghiz, Finns, Russians, maybe an Englishman or two playing cards in the same barracks. They stuck a knife in a Russian who tried to cheat. Just kicked the body under a bench and kept on playing. I'm never sure if I dreamt that or if it's the truth. But I didn't die then, even if I shook with cold and spat up blood.

"Will you take some of this medicine, father?"

Nestor awakened from his reverie. Elma stood before him with a bottle in her hand.

"What is it?"

"Cognac. German cognac," Elma said, looking down at the floor.

"Well, hell. Liquor is the best medicine for the chills. Where did you get it?"

"I got it from Hans. Shall I mix it with the coffee substitute or will you take it straight?"

"I wonder how strong it is. And who is this Hans?"

"It's pretty strong. Maybe I'll get some coffee substitute to mix with it."

Nestor watched as she poured the substitute into a glass and dropped in some sugar. A pleased expression came over his face.

"Where did you get that sugar? Everyone else is using saccharine."

"Hans gave it to me. They have everything."

"Who is this Hans? Hell, don't fill up the glass if it's the right stuff."

The right stuff. The words sank into Elma's mind. *The right stuff.* Why didn't her father at least look at her in disapproval. The wilderness, Järvenkylä, the entire region — they were not what they had been a few years ago. Everything had been ravaged. It was no longer their own wilderness. Such were the thoughts that flashed through Elma's mind.

"He's a German first lieutenant," she said. "He's one of the higher-ups at the prison camp back of Naavala."

Nestor Malinen sipped from the glass, smacked his lips, and said:

"Say what they like, they make good cognac in that Aatu Hitler's distilleries. It's starting to warm my insides already. Did you buy this or how did you get it?"

"Hans was here just last night. He's a nice man."

"So Hansi came to visit? I hope you served him some coffee substitute?"

"I did. He said he would like to meet you."

"Pour me another glass. Feel free to have Hans come any time. Man oh man, is that Hitler's drink warming my belly."

✧ ✧ ✧

That night Svante had to feed and care for the horse. Nestor had not been as cheerful since Mari's death. He sat at the kitchen table, and Elma prepared several glasses for him.

"Now I got rid of that chill. A man doesn't get sick when he's got the proper medicine. Is there any left in the bottle?"

"There is, but you'll soon be sick in another way," said Elma.

"No, I just keep feeling better all the time. Pour me another glass."

"Take it then, but you have to go to bed soon," said Elma.

"Soon, I'll go to sleep soon. I'll just sing a little first. Ah!"

Nestor wiped his mustache. Then his boot began to tap the floor as he trolled:

Tilly's road is muddy, it starts in Röhö town
And winds along to Uhtua...la la

From time to time, he would start the same song over again.

We tramped the muddy road, we conquered
all the land,
set off mines and drank our liquor ration.
Oh, war is tough, but we can take the guff...

At this point he would always begin to repeat himself. In the main room, Svante listened to the raucous singing with his brothers and sisters. His face was sour. Finally he yelled into the kitchen.

"Elma, come here!"

"What is it?" she asked, stepping into the main room.

"Why the devil did you get that old man drunk. No one can stand his bellowing. Put him to bed."

"He was sick. The medicine is good for his chills," said Elma.

Svante walked across the room, took a half-finished ax handle down from above the fireplace, and started to whittle on it. At the same time, he looked at Elma with a scowl on his face. She turned aside and fingered her apron as she listened to her father's braying. Svante said:

"I know very well why you're pouring that cognac into him."

"What business is it of yours? Are you jealous 'cause you can't get any?"

"I could get it all right if I wanted to. How long do you think it would take me to hunt a few skinny rabbit and wood-grouse carcasses? You can get all the cognac you want for them. In a pinch, the Germans will even trade it for a skinned cat. I was so ashamed when you started getting cozy with those hobnails. People are talking about it. Now you're trying to buy father off."

"Have I spent any time hanging around their camp?" asked Elma.

"Well, why is a certain iron-hat always hanging around here?"

"Hans doesn't *hang* around. I just wish you stood as straight and moved as fast as he does."

"They're fast, all right, at least when they're chasing after women."

Elma drew the half-curtains shut. Her hair swung sharply as she did so. Svante noticed it, and said as he shaved a curl from the ax handle:

"What are you tossing your head for? I thought you would at least give a damn about yourself. Everyone knows what those yobboes from the other end of the world want out of women."

"Go and tell Aili Sammalsuo about it. And the other women in this place. They come all the way from the church village to visit the German barracks," Elma said hotly.

"The boys and I will play a trick on them yet."

"What harm have they done to you?"

"Nothing to me. But it's the devil when the men of the village are laying down their lives at the front and you are just laying for the Germans here."

"Shame on you, talking like that in front of the children. Take that!"

Elma snatched up a ball of carpet rags from the bench and flung it at Svante, but it missed and disappeared somewhere in back of the fireplace. Svante said:

"I guess the stick hit the right dog that time. You should be ashamed, at least for Kauko's sake."

"What do I owe him? He went to Oulu on his last leave and stopped here only one day."

"I know very well how hard it was for him to take when he heard how you were carrying on with our *guarantors*."

"Don't exaggerate. I'm seeing only one."

"Elma! Do you have any cognac left?"

"Goddamn that old man," said Svante, getting up. Then he strode into the kitchen and said:

"Go to bed now and not another word."

"Don't get mad about a little fun, Svante. I'm taking care of my fever a little."

"You should be ashamed of yourself. I can stand just about any sight, but the younger kids don't even have a mother..."

Those younger children sat bunched up on the end of a bed in the main room. They had been sitting there all evening staring at their father's increasingly noisy antics. Now the youngest burst into tears, and that set the others to sobbing out of nervous tension. Svante swallowed hard when he heard the children crying and went on:

"This life is all gone to hell. Are you satisfied now?"

He went into the main room. Nestor staggered after him and dropped into a sitting position on the bed. He tried to pick up the youngest child, but the girl ran into the kitchen after Elma. The others followed her.

"Don't. Father won't hurt you. Father was just sick."

Soon Nestor toppled over on the bed. Svante pulled off his boots and opened the dirty collar of his logging shirt.

"You left too soon, Mari...the children have no mother, Mari," Nestor bawled out.

✧ ✧ ✧

At midnight, the wind was still roaring around the walls and howling in the chimney. Elma had not slept a wink. Taimi had not come home until late at night. Elma wondered if she had managed to stay away from the German barracks.

Elma rose, lighted the oil lamp, and then lit up a cigarette. The room had gotten cold and she felt a chilly draft on her legs.

"I wonder if the children are cold," she said.

She went through the kitchen into her parents' room. By the light of a match, she began to draw the covers up over the children. Then she went to stand by the side of the two youngest, who slept in her mother's bed. Now I have to be a mother to these little brothers and sisters, she thought. How well have I done? Well enough, until last winter. Then Hans came along. I didn't set any traps for him, or for any of the new men here. Other girls from the village were soon visiting the German barracks. Not all, but many. Hans often came to the windmill, always when I was on duty. Lieutenant Reino Salonen wrote just one letter. I was overjoyed when I wrote back to him. Even my grief at mother's death was eased. There was no answer to that letter, nor to the second one I wrote, no matter how long I waited. Hans kept on visiting the mill. At last I let him hold my hand. Then he stroked my hair. On one visit he held me close and kissed me. No one is as gentle in caressing a woman as Hans.

Taimi slept in this bedroom after mother's death. When father was home, he too slept here. When he wasn't home, it was up to Taimi to put the children to bed. She sometimes got so carried away in romping with them that I had to intervene. On those nights when I was on air watch, my own bedroom was empty. From early winter on, Hans Böhmer began staying in it till early morning.

Taimi had kicked off her covers so that her bare leg was exposed. Elma had to scratch many matches before all the covers were straight. Finally she pulled a heavy fur quilt over Taimi's legs and said:

"What a nursemaid! She can't even keep herself warm."

Elma stopped to listen at the door of the main room. She could hear the heavy snoring of her father and the lighter rasp of Svante and Jaska in their bed on the floor. She went back to her bedroom where she sat on her bed and smoked a cigarette to the end. As she did, she looked at three framed pictures on her table. In one of them, a keen-eyed Hans looked out at her. He wore an army cap and jacket. In the other, a young man was standing under a blossoming mountain-ash tree. His floppy army cap came down over his ears. Why did Toivo look so angry in the picture? He really never laughed. From the third picture, a bareheaded, but jacketed sergeant looked out. Elma reached for that picture and picked it up. Kauko seemed to be looking directly into her eyes. It was nice of Aili to have given her the picture. Kauko had had it taken in Oulu on his leave last fall. Elma looked at the picture for a long time, then wiped the glass in the frame with the sleeve of her uniform blouse that hung on a chair. Where could Kauko be tonight, she wondered.

3

"Maijaa!"

"My God," cried Maija Sammalsuo, and dropped the armload of wood she had just picked up onto the chips at the woodpile.

"Maija, nicht scared."

"Well, it's Josef. How you scared me."

A man in a ragged army uniform leaned out from behind a corner of the barn and stared at Maija. His cheekbones stood out sharply in his narrow face. He looked around and excitedly whispered something to Maija, which she could not understand, but from his expression, his gestures, and a few of the words, she could make out his meaning.

"Nix, nix officers. There are no officers here," she said.

"German soldat?" the man's entire face waited for an answer.

"No German soldiers either. Nix soldiers," said Maija.

She stooped down near the woodpile and began to gather up the armload of wood she had dropped. As she did, she smiled at the man who had stepped out from behind the corner of the barn.

"Come along into the house, Josef," said Maija.

The man trotted over to her and snatched from her hands the blocks she had managed to pick up. He smiled broadly and spoke at length, but Maija did not understand his words. He finished stacking onto his arm all the wood she had dropped, and began adding more from the pile.

"Well let's both carry in wood then."

As she spoke, Maija was already loading the wood onto her arm. Soon they walked into the house, Maija in the lead, and the German prisoner after her. Aili, who was doing the dishes from the noon meal, cried out when she saw the man following her mother:

"Josef!"

"It's Josef Leber, Aili."

The man's weathered face glowed with joy as he looked around the room. Liisu was in school, and Väinö and Auku were in the woods debarking pulp wood. Maija and Josef dropped their armloads of wood into the dark corner behind the oven. Dropping to one knee, Josef began to stack the wood, looking inquiringly at Maija after aligning the first few sticks.

"That's the way, just like before," said Maija.

"Where did he come from?" asked Aili.

"He peeked out from behind the barn and called my name. He gave me such a scare," said Maija.

"How did he get away from the guards?"

"He must have sneaked off from the work on the railroad. I wonder where Herman is."

The prisoner turned a glance of inquiry toward Maija. His face wore an expression of fear. By now Aili had learned enough German to relay her mother's question to the man. Tears welled up in his eyes and he looked down at the floor. Then he thrust a finger into his breast, and said, looking at Maija:

"Bang, bang!"

"They shot him," said Aili.

"We thought so," said Maija. "God, what will this come to?"

Aili was able to pry out the reason Herman had been shot. He and Josef had left the work site. The guards had caught up with Herman at Ylikylä. They had found bread and butter in his pockets and claimed he had stolen them, although Jussi Ylikylä told the men he had given the food to Herman. Josef had been at another farm, and managed to slip off when he saw the search party coming.

Josef finished stacking the wood and sat down near the window, glancing out from time to time. Occasionally he looked at Aili as she washed the dishes, and his Adam's apple bobbed up and down in his long, skinny neck. The he took two dirty, crumpled packages of tobacco from his pocket, and walked over to Maija.

"Tabak, Maija."

Maija shook her head, but the man thrust the packages into her lap.

"Maija, tabak. Nicht Josef tabak."

"Take them. He doesn't smoke himself," said Aili.

"I couldn't bear to take them from a prisoner, even though I wanted to," said Maija. Nevertheless, she put the packages into her pocket and thanked the man for them.

Aili finished the dishes, explaining to Josef what her mother had said. The prisoner bent down and pulled up a pants leg to expose a knitted sock with a red stripe above his worn combat boot. Then he opened his combat jacket, under which he wore a homespun woolen shirt.

"Maija give..." he said.

Maija was speechless. The prisoner dug a small package wrapped in paper from his pocket and said:

"Nicht Liisa...?"

"Liisa is in school," said Maija, pointing outside. Josef handed her the package and kept repeating:

"Liisa. Liisa..."

"The poor man has dug up some chocolate from somewhere," said Maija.

"He's thinner than he was last time," said Aili.

"Go and get some bread and butter for Josef. He eats salt fish too, and he's very fond of buttermilk."

The prisoner's eyes focused on Maija immediately when he heard his name mentioned, and his eyes roved past the door to the window. Aili went out to the entry to get the food, telling him that no one was coming.

When the man sat down to eat, it was easy to see the effort it cost him to keep from wolfing the food down. He stowed away huge quantities of bread and salt roach, along with buttermilk. From time to time, he looked askance at Maija and Aili.

"Eat, Josef, eat. Tell him to fill his stomach, Aili."

Aili interpreted for her mother. Josef ate heartily, but only picked at the butter, of which there was only a little on the table. Noticing that, Maija said:

"Get me Liisu's potato dish from the oven. She can eat something else when she gets home."

Aili brought out the dish and set it before the man. The potatoes were left over from the noon meal. At the bottom was liquid in which the potatoes had been cooked, with flecks of melted butter floating on its surface. The man looked inquiringly at mother and daughter and said:

"This Liisa...nicht."

"Lie to him, Aili. Tell him it's not for Liisu," said Maija.

Aili did as she was told. The man looked doubtful, but began to empty the dish. Maija began to pedal the spinning wheel. As it hummed and she spun the carded wool into yarn, she pondered the recent course of events. The changes that had taken place in the peaceful village seemed almost beyond comprehension. First there had been the Winter War. The evacuation. The interim of peace, with Finnish soldiers there. Then another war. The Finnish soldiers had left, except for some in the church village. Then the Germans had come and built a barbed-wire enclosure in which they penned up their own countrymen like worthless animals. Over a hundred dead prisoners were said to lie buried here and there around the prison camp. Life was horrible. How could human beings treat their own countrymen with such brutality? The German had always been praised as a cultured people.

Although civilians were forbidden to allow the prisoners into their homes, the people of Järvenkylä ignored the order. Early that winter, Josef Leber and Herman Schmidt had begun to visit the Sammalsuos. Others stopped in sometimes, but these two prisoners, already middle-aged, became friends of the family. Now Herman's visits had ended. Where had they dug a pit for his body, Maija wondered, and a bitter lump rose in her throat. Would his family ever know where he had been buried?

"How many children does Josef have? Ask him, Aili," Maija said.

"Four," said Aili, after an exchange of words with the man.

"How old is the youngest? We talked about it, but I forgot. Herman had a six-year-old."

As Aili struggled with her German, Josef Leber began to blink. When he answered, he kept his eyes on the floor.

"Josef says he has a seven-year-old girl. He hasn't seen her since she was less than a year old. He's been a prisoner since before the war."

The prisoner covered his face with his hands. Tears dropped onto the board floor. Maija's spinning wheel hummed. Through misty eyes she looked at the way the man's ragged clothes hung from his stooped torso. Should she be tormenting the man, she wondered. Perhaps it helped, even though it brought back painful memories of loved ones. She said to Aili:

"Ask him his daughter's name, and his wife's."

Footsteps sounded in the entry. The man leaped up, his eyes rolling wildly in all directions. Aili cried out:

"It's Liisu. She's coming home from school."

Liisu's wind-burned cheeks appeared in the doorway. Color returned to Josef Leber's face. Liisu recognized the man and smiled. He dropped to his knees before the girl and clutched her to his breast, repeating:

"Liisu...Liisu...Gertrud..."

At first Liisu looked at him in astonishment, and then with her school bag still on her back she flung her arms around the man's neck, but only for a few seconds. Then she ran to the end of the bed and hung her head in shame.

Maija shoved the spinning wheel aside and turned her face away. Aili turned to stare out of the window at the lake. Josef Leber sat down on the bench, looking in all directions out of the window from time to time. Finally Maija rose, walked to the door, and said:

"Keep your eyes open, Aili, to see that no one comes sneaking up."

When the man walked past the woodpile and disappeared in back of the barn, he was carrying pieces of bread in his pocket, along with two packages, one containing a small birch-bark butter dish and the other a sizable bunch of salt roach wrapped in paper.

Maija and the girls went out to watch as Josef Leber waded through the soft snow to the woods, his clothing billowing on his skeletal frame. At the outer gate, he turned to wave a bare hand. Maija and the girls waved back and Aili called out:

"Come again some time."

"What did Josef answer?" Maija asked.

"That he would come as soon as the snow melts."

"Do you remember, Aili, when the people who went to Russia passed through that same gate?"

"They had a little girl with them too. It was like a bad dream," said Aili.

"Was the girl my age?" asked Liisu.

"She was the same age as your dead sister Anni. I wonder where those people are now. Did they get caught by the war too?" said Maija.

4

It was still dark in the room when Auku's eyes opened. He blinked once or twice, and when the film of sleep had dissolved, he could see the gray sky through the window. He still felt like sleeping, but he remembered the trip he had told his mother and sister about before going to bed.

He lay there for awhile with his hands clasped beneath his head. Where would he be sleeping in a couple of months? He would be in uniform then. They said it was tough on a rookie. He would be going in with Svante Olkivaara. Would they get into the same outfit? Actually, it would be good to stay at home, especially during a war like this. Even time passed by quickly now, especially since the Germans had come, he thought. They treated us well, were even very polite. But they were devils to the prisoners. Strange that they treated their own countrymen with such brutality. No way I would ever shoot a Finn, not even my worst enemy, he thought. In a war, you have to shoot men. Kauko says that if you don't, you get a bullet in you. Well, it's time to get up now.

Auku rose from his bed on the floor. His mother stirred too and began to strike a match. It burst into flame and she lighted the lamp.

"Shall I make you some rye water?" she asked.

"I'm not staying to suck on it," Auku answered.

"It's still all dark outside," she said, looking at the alarm clock. "It's only three-thirty."

"It's just the right time. It will be daylight before I get to the neck of Murhajärvi. Where did you put the shirt you were patching last night?"

"It's on the nail by the door."

Auku put on his clothes. Maija too began to dress.

"Are you getting up so early too?" asked Auku.

"I'll start weaving. I'm not sleepy anyway."

Auku took the shotgun down from the wall and fastened his cartridge belt.

"Aren't you taking any lunch with you?"

"I'll eat more when I get home. I'm not hungry."

"You could have taken Väinö along. He wants so badly to go."

"What can he do there when we have only one gun?" said Auku.

"He'll be angry when he wakes up and finds you gone."

"I won't be here for long any more. Then he can tramp around with the gun as much as he wants to. When he wakes up, send him right out to the wood pile."

"Don't you be long either. Remember, don't go out on thin ice no matter what."

"Don't be silly, mother. There are much worse dangers in the world today...This braid of yours is shrinking to the size of a lamb's tail."

Auku drew the braid that hung down his mother's back through his fingers as he walked by her. Then he picked up the shotgun and went to the door.

"This life will make anyone lose her hair," said Maija. "Come home in time to be here when Aili gets back from her turn on air watch."

"Yeah, yeah. 'Let's go,'" as Vattu-Paavo said to his lamb.

✧ ✧ ✧

There was a film of water over the swamp pond but the ice beneath it was still strong enough to bear Auku's weight as he cut straight across marshes that were impassable in warm weather toward the neck of Murhajärvi. It's three years since the Russians dropped those saboteurs on the lake, he thought. Although day was already dawning, he felt compelled to look in every direction. Who could tell what spies might be lurking around? Next summer people would have to fear them again. They would leave no tracks then, and it would be warm enough for them to hide in the woods. The swamp, dead in the winter, was now teeming with life. Sandpipers cried out, and heath grouse called from beyond the swamp. The honking of geese caused Auku to stop.

"There they go, flying over the woods south of here," he said.

This spring Auku had shot a number of waterfowl in the melt at the neck of Murhajärvi, where he had a blind made of spruce trees stuck up in front of a mossy mound. The boughs he had heaped on the mound rustled dryly as he sat down on them.

"The thaw line has already moved far out into the lake," Auku muttered to himself. "If the birds land far from shore, they'll be out of good shooting range."

Mating heath grouse were fluttering around far out on the lake close to Murhaniemi. Their whistles and cries of alarm carried easily to Auku's ears. Cranes too called out from far beyond the lake, but the melted area remained empty, and Auku said:

"Now isn't that strange. Not a bird has landed."

He heard the whirr of wings, but could see that the birds were headed across the lake.

"Where's their hurry?" he growled.

The sun shot its rays over the lake. Spawning pike splashed in the shallows. The cries of the heath grouse intensified. Auku wondered if he should go along the shore to the point. It would be easy to shoot heath grouse there. If I were feeling ambitious, he thought, I could soon be there, but the distance was so great that he decided to wait longer. He thought of the time when he had waited for waterfowl in almost the same spot with a crossbow. Then the birds had come and landed in the melted area almost as if they were mocking him. It hadn't been as late in the spring then, Auku thought. I came on skis. And fired away with my crossbow.

"That was some attempt," he laughed.

He had forgotten about having to go to school. Mother had come to get him, and he had gotten a sound whipping. That was probably his last. She must really have gotten worried as the time went by. We were poorer than poor in those days...hunting waterfowl with a crossbow. Now when I leave, Väinö will get this shotgun. He won't need to...

"Godalmighty!"

The words came in an excited whisper, and Auku's body tensed. A swell passed over the calm, gleaming surface of the water as a large white bird settled down on it.

"A swan," Auku whispered to himself.

There it sat floating. It was the first time Auku had seen a swan so close up. He had seldom even seen them on the wing. Now, now! His hand must not shake. He mustn't panic. Auku thrust the shotgun barrel through the branches. The swan was gliding along as though pulled by an invisible cord. Now it had turned almost toward him. What a long neck it had. Its body loomed huge as it floated on the surface of the water. I mustn't panic now. The officers at the prison camp will give almost anything for that. Chocolate, preserves, jellies, even real coffee for mother. Now!

The recoil of the shotgun drove Auku's shoulder back. Was the bird hit? It was! When the smoke cleared, he saw the swan thrashing in the water. It was beating its wings, and its long neck was writhing. Then, flapping its wings, it rose into the air, but soon it fell back into the water.

"It's not badly hurt. It's going to get away!" said Auku frantically.

His fingers trembling, he broke open the barrel and ejected the spent shell. Now the bird was thrashing through the water heading away from the shore. Soon the shot would not kill it. In his panic, Auku could see the red staining the bird's long neck. Now I'll load with this charge. It has smokeless powder and coarser shot. This will do the trick if anything will.

The bird was drawing further away. It kept trying to fly, but always fell back on its side into the water. Now its head was as low as a rooster's. It's badly hit in the neck. It's bleeding so much. Now I have to take careful aim. If it swims under the ice in a daze, it will be left there. I'll have to shoot lying down.

Auku threw himself down on the boughs and rested the gun on the crest of the mound. Why is the barrel wavering so much, Auku thought. Now the bird was thrashing again, and then it settled down to swim. Now he had it lined up. He had to aim a little high. Now, before it began thrashing again.

Auku pulled the trigger. There was a flash before his eyes. He felt something strike his head, and then there was darkness.

The swan floated on its side, feebly paddling with its large webbed feet. Near the edge of the ice it stopped and lay floating like a large feather pillow. Auku's cap and a piece of bone from his forehead had been blown into the dirty slush nearby. His face was black, and something like thick curds of milk dripped from his temple along with the blood. The stock and chamber of the gun were shattered. Auku's left hand was still tightly gripping the burst barrel of the piece.

5

One day the Finns and the group of Germans who had wintered near Kiestinki received a shock. In the middle of the worst spring thaw, they suddenly came under heavy fire from a position right along their supply road. The still sleep-befuddled troops were dumfounded.

"Who the devil is shooting from there?"

"The Russians will soon be at our soup kettles."

Their winter sleep was over. Everyone moved as if his life were in the balance. Soon the resting troop was in action. Surprise turned into fury. The Finns poured out a hot fire and even hand-to-hand fighting broke out.

"How the devil did they get here through that mush?"

"They came right up to our tents."

"Did they fall from the sky?"

There was an answer to the mystery, revealed only after many days of fighting. By then, the Finns were advancing along a corduroy road built by the Russians. They had been able to cut off the road in segments. As the spring thaw progressed, the last of the flanking Russian troops surrendered. In truth there were only a few. Most of them preferred to die by their own weapons.

The grisly smell of rotting bodies drowned out the scent of heather as a part of Kauko Sammalsuo's squad sat at the edge of a swamp and looked at the men and horses that had died on the road. The men had just come to the place and dropped in their tracks out of weariness. Cranes were flying over the swamp and Kauko, deep in thought, was watching them when Jalo Kieppi said:

"Look at that, boys. There's a man sitting against that spruce tree."

"He was gnawing on the raw calf-bone of a horse when he died. Ugh!" said Jonas Niemi.

Kauko heard the talk as if it were part of a nightmare. He turned to look toward where Kieppi was pointing. Slowly his brain registered the fact that the already smelly body was clutching a hairy bone in its hands.

"Is that what they bring people up for?" he said.

"At least you'll be out of here soon. You'll get a funeral leave now," said one of the men in the squad.

"I should think so," sighed Kauko.

The surprise attack of the Russians had begun just at the moment when the news of his brother's death arrived. Since then, Kauko had acted in a state of total numbness. It didn't seem to matter if he lived or died. Just when I should have gotten out of the army, he thought, this war began. Now when I was hit with the news of my brother's death, this ruckus broke out.

Kauko looked dully at the geese flying heavily over the swamp. He could hear the sound of honking. Was it the voice of the geese? Hardly. It was more like the croaking of ravens on their feast day.

Kauko's leave was a brief one, so he was able to spend only a couple of days at Järvenkylä. Traveling during the spring breakup took most of his time. The road from Kiestinki to the old Finnish border was in the worst possible condition.

✧ ✧ ✧

"Show us, Kauko, what kind of old bag she really is."

"That's no way to talk about a woman. I'm surprised at you, Jonas."

"Jonas and I have been coming in a poor second with the women ever since Kauko started going to Oulu on leave."

"Well, which one of us is flashing an engagement ring on his finger?" said Kauko in mock wonder.

Jonas Niemi looked down at his left hand, on which a brand new engagement ring sparkled. During his leave for hay-making, he had become engaged to a girl from Raahe. It came as a surprise to everyone in the company, especially to the other two members of the close-knit trio.

In the latter part of August, warm weather had returned to their quiet sector of the front. It was late at night now as Kauko, Jonas, and Jalo sat outside their dugout. A single cloud mass covered the sky, but not a drop of rain was falling. Kauko had just finished reading a letter that had come in the field mail. A picture had been enclosed, and Jalo and Jonas were trying to get a look at it. Jalo reached out a hand and said:

"Let us have a look, Kauko. Why the devil are you hiding it?"

"I won't show it to you, but if Jonas still dares to look at another woman, then here's a model for him to check out."

"Jonas is already gaping at it with his tongue hanging out. Give me a look."

Jonas was already gazing at the picture, cupping it in his palm like a card-player at a crucial point in a game. Jalo tried to stretch out his skinny neck, but Jonas kept drawing back. Kauko said:

"Don't show it to Jalo. He knows my girl friend and will look her up when he gets to Oulu. I don't trust even my closest buddies where women are concerned."

"You can keep your chippy. Now that girl of mine in Kemi is a real knockout."

"Okay, show it to Jalo then, since it's putting his nose out of joint." Kauko stopped teasing. "But only if he goes and makes the coffee substitute right afterwards."

"It's your turn to make it now."

"All right then. In that case, give me the picture, Jonas."

Kauko grinned, as did Jonas, who handed the picture back to him. Jalo Kieppi glowered at his comrades and spat far off. Kauko handed him the picture and said:

"Well, look at it then, but by God, keep your hands off her if you go through Oulu."

As Kieppi looked at the picture, his half-feigned irritation vanished.

"She looks just like a human being. And she's really got a come-hither look." Kieppi turned over the picture and read from the back of it: "To Kauko from Helga."

"Stop, stop! Who told you to look at that. Give it to me, right now!"

"Hey, big deal. The guy has a wallet stuffed with pictures and has the gall to be stingy with them."

During the long winter, Kauko had begun to write to unknown girls, a practice which had developed into an unexpectedly voluminous correspondence that brightened the dark nights in the dugout. In addition to his zeal for reading, Kauko had always found it easy to write letters, but he had been so thoroughly devastated by the letter from Selma at Petsamo that he had not put pen to paper in nearly three years, except for the letters home and to Elma. One of his best pen pals was just this Helga from Oulu. Earlier Kauko had received a long-awaited snapshot from her, and today's letter had contained a print of a studio portrait.

Kauko put the picture into his wallet and said:

"It's Kieppi who looks like a skirt-chaser, but it's Jonas who took that city girl's ring."

"I wonder about that too...a future farmer like him..."

"What are you going to do with her? A city girl won't even be able to milk a cow. It'll be expensive to support her for just one thing."

Jonas Niemi took off the ring and looked at the engraving on it.

"I'm sure Kyllikki will learn to do farm work. She's a carpenter's daughter, and used to working in the kitchen, at least."

"But she'll never be able to do barn work," said Jalo.

"A person can learn just about anything," said Jonas. "Look what we've been doing for almost three years."

"I know, but it's different to teach a miss from the city," said Jalo.

Kauko looked up at the treetops and laughed aloud.

"Kauko is showing signs of shell-shock," said Jonas Niemi. "What are you laughing about?"

"You'll get mad if I tell you."

"If we lose our sense of humor, then we're all goners," said Jalo Kieppi.

"It's so nice to loll around here that it won't be easy to make me mad," said Jonas Niemi.

"Well, they say a Helsinki family was evacuated to a farm. The woman of the house came in one day and said the cow was in heat, but she didn't have time to let the bull loose to it. Then the city girl, who was almost twenty, blushed shyly and said, 'Your bull looks so gentle that I can help you.' 'Oh, that would be very nice,' said the woman. 'He isn't at all mean. You can let him loose without a worry.'"

Jalo Kieppi was starting to grin. Kauko looked at him and said:

"Go and make the coffee substitute."

"Finish the story first."

"I can't tell dirty stories to a little man like you. Go, go on, put the pot on the fire. Or what do your say, Jonas — Shall we let Jalo hear the end of the story?"

"Just this once, but we won't make a habit of it," laughed Jonas, sitting up on the hillock.

"The girl went into the barn. After a long, long time, missy came back all sweaty and puffing. 'Well, how did it go?' asked the woman of the house. 'I got the bull loose fine, but that darned cow won't lie down on its back no matter what.'"

"Ha, ha, that's how it will go with the girl from Raahe."

Jonas Niemi smiled his usual weak smile.

"Mother takes care of those things at home. Go and make our drink, Jalo. I have some toast and maybe even some ginger-snaps."

"Well then, I have to get on the ball. It's great to be in the same unit with a big landowner."

Jalo Kieppi lighted a fire on a sandy patch off to one side, while Jonas and Kauko sat where they were. The company had been pulled back for a rest, and the men were sitting around in groups. There were even a couple of poker games going, from which loud exclamations could be heard after each round of play. It was almost completely quiet in the direction of the front. The only sound was the firing of Finnish mortars, and they were far off to one side. The sound was so infrequent and lulling that it nearly made the listeners yawn.

Jonas Niemi sat stripping a pine cone to its core with his fingers. He had been made a corporal in the spring, and his stripes were smudged and wrinkled. While they were looking at Kauko's picture, he had been in a rare cheerful mood, but now he looked gloomily at Kauko and said:

"A person can't really make plans to marry...I always have the feeling that I won't get back from here alive."

"Hey soldiers. Come and drink up!"

"Let's go," said Kauko, leaping up quickly.

✧ ✧ ✧

"Well, we got through the summer," said Kauko.

"Things are quiet now, but it's all so depressing. I wonder if they've gotten around to threshing the grain at home."

Jonas Niemi stared into the small campfire which they had kept going after finishing the coffee substitute. Jalo Kieppi threw some dry sticks onto the coals. The fire blazed up, lighting the faces of the men and throwing their eye sockets and the hollows on their faces into shadows. All three stared into the flames. A soft breeze had risen gradually and now rustled in the treetops. The remnants of Jonas Niemi's package from home lay on the wrapping paper near the fire. After a long pause, Kauko said:

"Nothing will come of the rye at home — the field I started from scratch with Auku. I told you about it."

"You still have one brother at home," said Kieppi.

"How much planting and clearing can a kid do?" said Kauko.

"We'll see where we are next summer," said Jonas.

"We'll be at Uhtua. Where else?" said Kauko.

"We won't be here. Things will start happening. The disaster at Stalingrad and the German retreat are bad signs," said Jonas Niemi. "Pooh — rubber-band tactics. That's what Hitler called them."

"That Jonas reads every stupid book in the world. All I study is a deck of cards, and there's plenty to learn from them," said Jalo Kieppi.

"You're right. Cry only when you have to," said Kauko.

Jonas Niemi kicked partly burned sticks onto the coals with the toes of his hobnailed boots and stared unblinking into the flames. After a short time he seemed to tear himself loose from a profound meditation.

"Well, buddies. Time will tell, but I'm going to sack out on the boughs. I'll pack up my life and go to sleep. Take the package into the dugout, Kauko."

Kauko and Jalo stood up. Jonas Niemi disappeared from the small circle of light around the campfire. A man from another squad came over and said:

"Don't put it out. I'm going to boil up some substitute."

"Go ahead. We've had plenty already, but then put out..."

Kauko's words were cut short. They heard a nasty sound whose source they all knew, but the fact of their being in a rest area behind the lines made them hesitate. Only when the first shell exploded did they hit the ground. Tree limbs and sand showered down around them. There were further screams of incoming shells and the heath shook with explosions. The barrage ended as suddenly as it had begun. Men and officers of the company ran around cursing. Even the poker game had been thrown into chaos. A man came running up from a hollow nearby, and said:

"Someone was sitting on the boughs back there! Now there's nothing but a hole."

Instinctively, Kauko and Kieppi ran in the same direction. Near the hollow, Kauko picked up a boot, held it up in the dim light, and said:

"Hobnails!"

CHAPTER XIX

1

"Can't you spend one whole leave at home any more?" asked Maija.

"Well, I've been here a week already."

The early fall day was just dawning. Kauko fastened the belt of his coat as Maija watched him. Standing before him on the floor, she had to tilt her head back in order to see the expression on her son's face. He had become a tall and broad-shouldered man. Although he had shaved that morning, his face still wore a dark shadow.

"You still have three days left of your leave," she said.

"The trip will take that long. You could have pressed this coat collar a little."

"Take the coat off. I'll heat the iron."

"There isn't time. The postal bus will soon be at Naavala."

Maija turned away. Kauko walked over to the wall and took down a small mirror. He looked at his face in it by the light of the lamp and said:

"I don't understand why the girls here are no longer satisfied with Finnish soldiers as boy friends. That's a damned good-looking home-grown warrior in that mirror — wouldn't you say so, Aili?"

Aili, who had spent the night on air watch at the windmill, was mending a tear in her Women's Auxiliary uniform. She looked at her brother and said:

"I wondered what the smell in here was, but now I know. They say that self-praise stinks. And are those digs meant for me?"

"You're too closely related for me to date."

"Then is it Elma you're grumbling about? At least you can't say that Hilja pals around with the Germans."

"Of course not. She's been on the Isthmus for two years. There aren't many *guarantors* clomping around there in their hobnailed boots."

"Have you tried to date the Järvenkylä girls?"

"No thanks. And I don't plan to." Kauko turned to his mother. "Is my pack ready?"

"It should be. All your clothes are in it, and as much food as we had."

"Then I won't die of hunger, so I'll be okay as long as Uncle Bolshie's boys don't put a hole in me."

Maija bowed her head and rubbed the back of her hand across her eyes. Kauko already had his pack on his back. He looked at his mother and swallowed.

"I don't understand what's made you so coarse. You're not at all like you used to be. You always came home on Sunday, no matter how far away you were. Even when you were a hired hand at Korkeamaa, you tramped through the dark woods in the fall to get home. Now you seem to be in a hurry to leave home. I'll soon be alone here."

"Is life what it used to be?"

Kauko waited for his mother's answer. She looked at him through her tears and said:

"Life has changed a lot, but do the relationships between children and parents have to change too? We fought against poverty together and lived on the community's bread. Now I no longer have Anni or Auku. Aili is having her fling, and you are going your own way. Since Anni died..."

"Stop crying! Everything has gone to hell...The war goes on and on. I'm wearing this uniform for the fifth year. We drove the Russian out of these woods in the Winter War, but then these goddamned hobnails had to come along..."

Kauko blew out the lamp and then looked at his watch.

"I have to go now or I'll miss the bus."

"At least write, and don't go running into danger for nothing."

His mother's words were spoken in a tearful voice. Kauko went over to Liisu, who was sitting silently on a bench. He snatched her up in his arms and said:

"You're growing so big that soon I won't be able to lift you. So long, then, Maija and you kids. Pappa's going fishing, ha ha."

2

The charcoal burner propelled the bus onward, slowly but tenaciously. On several of the seats, people were sitting on each others' laps, and the standing room was packed. Most of the travelers were soldiers. At Pudasjärvi, Kauko managed to squeeze his rump onto the edge of a seat. The window seat was overflowed by an oversized citizen. Long mustaches and a wrinkled face explained his being out of uniform.

"Where are you fighting now?" he asked.

"At Uhtua."

"Are you on your way home on leave?"

"Actually I'm on my way back."

"You must be from up country."

"From out that way," said Kauko.

"You said you're on your way back from a leave. Why are you going this way then? You can go straight to Uhtua by truck. My brother often goes that way."

"That's the way I came. I'm taking the direct circle route back."

"How will that take you back?"

The man was speaking loudly. Heads turned in their direction and people stole side glances at them. Kauko was slow to answer, and he could see the man staring curiously at him. What the heck kind of inquisitor does he think he is, Kauko thought.

"In Oulu, there's a thing called a train. I take that to Hyrynsalmi and go by truck from there."

"Will the Germans soon have trains running to Kuusamo? Aren't they laying a railway there by way of Järvenkylä?"

"They seem to be doing something of the sort," said Kauko.

"Are they really so cruel to the men behind the barbed wire? People say they make them work bare-handed and feed them only scraps even in winter. Don't they put a bullet through them for the slightest infraction?"

"I haven't been keeping watch over them. Would the lady like a seat?"

A middle-aged woman standing in the aisle before Kauko looked at him gratefully and sat down beside the fat man. The last part of the trip was over level ground and the charcoal-burning bus was able to make good time. Still it was late afternoon before they arrived in Oulu. There Kauko went up to a man standing in the bus station to ask a favor of him. The man answered:

"The store is close by. I'm always willing to help a soldier."

"Shall we step out of sight so I can give you the money?"

"I have that much on me. Do you want a full quota?"

"I do if you'll get it for me," said Kauko.

"I will. What sector are you on?"

Kauko told him where his unit was stationed. The man's face lit up.

"I was at Uhtua too. I got out a couple of years ago when they let the older men go. You'll get your bottles."

The man left. When he returned, he transferred the bottles from his pockets to Kauko's pack behind some tar warehouses. Kauko kept one of the bottles in a pocket. He took out his wallet and said:

"Now for the money. The price of the bottles and your payment for getting them."

"For that I won't take money. I don't make a living at this."

The man told him the price, and Kauko suggested:

"At least take a healthy swig." He looked around the corner in either direction and said: "There are no policemen in sight."

"I don't want that either. I have to catch a bus soon. I did this as a favor for a fellow soldier."

✧ ✧ ✧

As he wandered the streets of Oulu, the city no longer seemed as intimidating as when he had first arrived in it during the Winter War. He had already visited it twice on his way home for leaves, after getting off the train there to continue his journey up country by motor.

Although he did not see a familiar face, he was in high spirits, His conscience, guilty at leaving home, had ceased to trouble him. Several times during the evening, he ducked behind a corner to twist off the stout wooden cork of the bottle. He did not drink much, just enough to make him feel good. It felt great to be young. Just let someone come along and bad-mouth me, he thought. Shall I or shall I not salute that young second lieutenant coming toward me? I might, or I might not. His collar insignia sparkled and his breeches were sharply pressed. If he sounds off to me, I'll tell him I've killed lice with higher mucky-mucks than he is.

Kauko glanced behind him. No other soldiers were in sight, and the lieutenant, now some twenty meters away, was slightly built. He wouldn't dare say anything to me, thought Kauko. Oh well, it won't take any years off my life to salute him. It's stupid to brag about flaunting regulations. Kauko touched his fingers to his cap. The lieutenant responded with a smart salute and a smile.

"Good day, sergeant," he said.

✧ ✧ ✧

Entering a restaurant, Kauko ordered a beer. As she delivered his order, the waitress clipped off a coupon from his ration card. Loud talk resounded in the room, and thick clouds of cigarette smoke hung over the tables. Beer bottles were being emptied at a great rate. Taking a letter from his pocket, Kauko read it over.

> *...if you don't know Oulu well, here are the directions. I live on the north side. Find my street and the number; it's a private house and I live in the attic. Don't come until about seven in the evening. If you get there on the day you wrote you would come, I'll be watching for you from the window. I'll know you from the snapshot you sent. If you don't get here then, ring the first-floor doorbell, and the landlady will come and let me know. With all my love, Helga.*

Folding the letter, Kauko stowed it away in his pocket. The clock on the wall pointed to a little after six. The dream he had dreamed for many months, the dream that had relieved the drabness of life at the front, was soon to be realized. It was almost a year since he had answered a girl's greetings to the front-line soldiers printed in the *Kaleva*. That had been the start of it all. How many letters had he received by now in the field mail, sender: Helga Korte?

I have to go now, he thought. It's getting dark already and I may have trouble finding the place. On the way, Kauko ducked around a corner again. A long swig from the bottle made him gasp. Then he set off, pack on his back, to cross the Oulu bridges.

✧ ✧ ✧

"Well, I found the right street at last. But do they call this a street. It's more like a side road," Kauko muttered.

Again he read the name from a plaque on a smallish wooden

house on the corner. It was the right name. Which way did the numbers run? This was six; he had to find fifteen. The next number was eight. He was going the right way, but he had to cross the street.

There it is. This is number thirteen and there's her attic window. But the window was dark. Disappointment flooded Kauko's mind. This is going to be Rovaniemi all over again, he thought. I'll walk by as if I weren't looking for anything. I'll see if there's a lighted window on the other side. There are the steps and an entry. Light gleamed around the edges of blackout curtains on the first floor. Kauko walked on by, determined not to go and ring the landlady's doorbell.

The attic window on the other side was dark too. What a damned fool to come muddling around here in the middle of a leave. I could have stayed at home for two days yet. Things wouldn't have been any worse if I had swallowed my anger and gone to see Elma, seen how high and mighty she is now that she's keeping company with a German officer. This road is plowed so damned poorly that your feet sink into it, and the cold wind is freezing my ears.

Behind him a door creaked and he heard a voice say:

"Kauko, don't go."

Kauko felt as if his knees would give way. He hesitated for a moment and then turned around. A woman was running down the steps. Her head was bare and she was coatless. Coming up to him, she said:

"Why did you walk by? Welcome! Let's go right in."

"N-no. Hello. Greetings from Uhtua. It was all dark upstairs."

"I had put out the lights and was watching from the window. I knew you right away."

The woman was slender and of average height. As soon as they reached the attic steps, she threaded her arm through Kauko's and said with a laugh:

"I'll lead you. The steps are so narrow and steep."

It's the same old story, thought Kauko. What the heck can I say to her? She's laughing, but she doesn't seem to be making fun of me. I have to say something.

"How...um...ah...how did you know me?"

"Why are you so shy? We've been close friends now for over six months. Welcome again, and please call me Helga."

Kauko squeezed the small hand that was clinging tightly to his. Helga's eyes looked directly into his own.

"Thank you. And you call me Kauko. I didn't know if we should talk the same way we wrote to each other. One forgets how to act at the front." Kauko laughed nervously.

"Take off your things and make yourself at home. There's the coat rack and a mirror next to the door."

Kauko ran a comb through his hair. He could see in the mirror that his jacket was unwrinkled and his stripes shone brightly. His mother had washed his jacket as soon as he had arrived home on leave.

As Kauko stepped into the room in his heavy army boots, Helga switched on the light and said:

"Let's have some light so you won't be afraid. Sit down at that table."

Kauko could see that the room's occupant was both neat and feminine. The table was set with coffee cups in the war-time fashion. Helga sat down opposite him and said:

"I'll get the coffee substitute right away, but first I want to see if you look like my pen pal Kauko. How did you get to town?"

"On the postal bus. Well, do I look at all like him?"

"A lot, really. Your picture is stamped in my mind from the photos. I could already tell that you were quiet and...that's all."

"Timid and shy. They call me a mope at home."

"You're not. You write so beautifully. A brash person could never do that. I really have a better picture of the war from your letters than from the Information Service's press releases."

"They're not that good. It's just that I have the time and I like to write," said Kauko.

"Then we feel exactly the same about things..."

Helga said the last words softly. Her legs were stretched out before her and she kept touching the toes of her wooden-soled shoes into each other, watching them rise and meet, then fall to the side again. The room was warm and so was Kauko's heart. It was good that I didn't drink more, he thought. Now that his initial tension had passed, he felt a huge surge of well-being. Should I ask her to go to the movies, he wondered. Should one stay late with a lone woman. Would it be out of line to offer her a cigarette? Someone had been smoking in the room lately. I won't make that faux pas. She might not smoke. She looks like such a nice girl. I have to be honest with her. It's not easy, but I will say it.

"I write to other girls, but I can honestly say that no one's letters mean as much to me as yours do."

Helga looked at him and then she said:

"Soldiers do write letters. It's a harmless pastime."

"There's really nothing else to do. It's been so quiet for a long time, although we really don't miss the action."

"I'll go and get the pot and we'll drink our war-time coffee."

Helga soon returned from the kitchen and filled the cups. She sat down and shoved the sugar bowl toward Kauko.

"Please have some," she said.

Although Kauko heard the words, he sat as if frozen in his chair, staring wide-eyed at the woman's hand. Helga flashed her ready smile and said:

"What is it now? Are you so scared of my rings?"

"I'm sorry. I didn't know you were married."

Helga laughed. "If they scare you so much, I'll take them off."

"No, don't. I'll leave right now. I really didn't know you were married."

"Have some sugar. Am I really so terrible looking that it makes you turn pale? I was single when we started writing. We were married only two weeks ago."

Kauko thought first of Elma, and then of Selma from Rovaniemi. Were they all the same? Damn it, why had he come dragging in here and ruined his leave? He might even wind up in jail because of the fool tricks of another man's wife. Kauko looked toward the door. What kind of trap had been set for him anyway?

"Where is your husband? Or do I dare ask?"

"But Kauko dear. Don't look so sour. You won't will you, if I ask you not to? I'll throw these rings into a drawer."

"Not on my account, you won't. If your husband comes, you won't have time to put them on again."

"He won't come. He's on the Isthmus. I thought of taking the rings off in the kitchen just now, but you were so honest about your pen pals. There now, they're off and they can stay put."

The rings clinked on the bottom of a bureau drawer. Kauko's thoughts began to settle down. They drank the coffee substitute and then he asked:

"Do you smoke?"

"A lot, especially now when cigarettes are hard to get."

"Have one, if these suit you. Shall I light it?"

"You don't have to coax me. Don't you smoke?"

"Sometimes, for the fun of it. It's not a habit."

"Have one, to keep me company."

"I guess I can practice. I'll leave the pack on the table. Take one whenever you feel like it."

When they had smoked and the talk had gradually begun to flow, Kauko looked at his watch.

"Oh-oh, it's almost nine."

"Time flies. It seemed to go so slowly when I was waiting for you."

"I have to go and see the night life of this *White City of the North*," said Kauko with a smile.

"Do you find it so dull here?"

"Not at all, but a man can't stay late, at least not with a married woman."

"Stop the married woman talk. Let's agree that I'm just Helga. Besides, a friend of mine is supposed to come over tonight. She's a very nice person. She's divorced."

✧ ✧ ✧

A half hour later, the doorbell rang below. Kauko was startled.

"It can't be..."

"It isn't. You remember our agreement. I'll go down and open the door."

Kauko felt nervous and wondered if he had time to sneak a drink to give himself courage. The night was sure to turn into a sewing circle meeting now. What could he possibly say to two women? Now he clearly heard a man's voice and the sound of heavy footsteps on the stairs. Damn it, now he was trapped. He moved quickly to a chair that stood close to the door. The man's voice rumbled on in the entry, and the handle of the door turned downward. Kauko flexed his knees.

"Come right in. Oh there you are, near the door."

A plump young woman followed the hostess into the room. A large combat boot stepped over the threshold in her wake.

"Sergeant Sammalsuo, Hellin Laani," Helga introduced them.

Kauko greeted the woman. Then a big soldier stepped forward. He stared sharply into Kauko's eyes and reached out a large hand. Then he banged his iron-cleated heels together and said in a bass voice:

"Private Heikkinen, *lieukenant*, sir."

Kauko had to lower his eyes before the fierce gaze. The man's handclasp was crushing. Kauko mumbled his name, upon which the man saw fit to relax his grip. Helga said:

"Sit down, Hellin. Your friend can take this chair."

"I'll be glad to sit, *Lieukenant*, sir."

The man walked over to the chair Helga had pushed forward, and moved it next to his woman companion. Then he banged his heels together and roared:

"Thank you, *Lieukenant*, sir!"

Kauko looked incredulously at the man and remained standing. Helga too stared, as Kauko took the pack of cigarettes from the table and offered them to the two women. Then the man's thick fingers snatched a cigarette from the pack.

"Thank you, *Lieukenant*, sir!"

"My rank is much lower," said Kauko.

"Yes, *lieukenant*, sir, but I'm crazy."

Kauko sat down. He tried to keep the cigarette smoke in his mouth for a long time and to look cool. After a moment, Mrs. Laani spoke:

"We were sitting around in my place, but we ran out of drink."

Kauko had already smelled the liquor on their breaths as he greeted them, and Hellin Laani was looking gay.

"You could have saved some for your friends," said Helga.

"I told her, *lieukenant*, sir, that we would try to find a black-market bottle."

"That's a hit-or-miss proposition. But what if we all go to some place that serves drinks? What time is it?"

"It's ten already," said Helga, glancing at her watch.

"They won't be open then," said Hellin Laani.

"If my bottle will do, then we won't have to go anywhere," said Kauko.

"Do you have one?" said Helga.

"Enough to change the flavor of coffee substitute," said Kauko.

"Then let the party begin, *lieukenant*, sir," said the man.

"Get it out right now," said Helga. "And you didn't even tell me."

"You didn't ask."

"I'll go and make the coffee substitute. You come with me, Hellin."

✧ ✧ ✧

"What time is it now?" asked Hellin.

"Past midnight," said Kauko.

"Do you have any of that stuff left, *lieukenant*, sir?"

"Stop gibbering, Kunu. We drank three of Kauko's bottles already."

"Sure there's a little," said Kauko. "*...in the war we marched along,/ and listened to the bullets' song,*" he hummed as he went out to the entry.

"Half a bottle, but that's the last of it," he announced when he returned.

"Well, let's drink that and go to bed. Right, Helga?"

Hellin Laani's plump cheeks were flushed. Kauko had already taken off his jacket. Sometimes life even offers us a night of fun, he thought, as he divided the bottle equally among the four cups.

"Yes, let's," Helga answered.

"That's the last of the liquor. Drink up," said Kauko.

"But the other fun is just beginning, ha, ha! Isn't that so, *lieukenant*, sir?"

"Damn it, stop groping me in front of the others!" cried Hellin. "Wait till we're in bed and the lights are out. What are you dilly-dallying for, Kauko? Take Helga in your arms and give her a good squeeze. This *lieukenant* of mine is always at me."

Although Kauko was very drunk, he had still been hanging back. Now in answer to Hellin's bidding he got up, went over to Helga's chair, and picked her up in his arms like a little child.

"Like this?" he said.

Helga threw her arms around his neck and pressed her cheek to his. Private Heikkinen let out a roar of laughter.

"That's the way, my boy. Now you're starting to look like a man."

"Let's make up a bed on the floor," said Hellin.

"Let's, but for god's sake, *Lieukenant*, stop making so much noise. You'll soon get me thrown out of the house."

✧ ✧ ✧

"Let's go to bed now, boys. We'll step outside once more," said Hellin Laani.

Heikkinen's eyelids had dropped shut. He was sitting on the bed from which the women had just moved the mattress and the other bedclothes to the floor. Kauko watched them make up the bed there. Was he too expected to flop down on that common pad? His ears were buzzing and his heart pounded in excitement and anticipation. The liquor had really come in handy. Heikkinen, who had been silent for a moment, said:

"Do any of you know who I am?"

"You're Heikkinen," said Helga.

"A *lieukenant* babbler," said Hellin.

"Aren't you a crazy man?" said Kauko.

"Crazy as a loon," Heikkinen laughed. "I just walked out of the asylum, but I have to be back before six, or I'll get caught."

"Stop making up stories," said Helga. "You're probably only too smart."

"I'm absolutely crazy. It's true. Last fall I got a leave from my unit on the Isthmus. On the way back to it, I changed at Kouvola for a train going the opposite way. When an MP patrol questioned me, all I said was, 'Yes, *lieukenant*, sir!' I never said anything else. For a couple of weeks, I rode the country's railroads in every direction. I went to Hanko, Viipuri, Kemijärvi, Helsinki, and every place under the sun. In every corner of Finland, they would write on my leave papers: '*To be directed to his unit, because he can't find it by himself.*' Ha, ha, ha. Then I got off in Oulu and wandered around the streets. An MP patrol stopped me and I said, 'Yes, *lieukenant*, sir,' and not another word, rolling my eyes, and letting out a bellow every once in awhile. They tested me for months. The doctors just shook their heads. Now I'm officially insane, ha, ha. Whether they shout at me or treat me nicely, I still act the same. I always say, '*lieukenant*, sir' to everyone."

The women sat on either side of Heikkinen and listened to his story. When he had finished telling it, he grabbed Hellin into his arms.

"Ha, ha, Hellin, I'm not advertising, but in the morning you'll tell me: 'Well done, *lieukenant*, sir. You've got everything a man needs.'"

Kauko looked away. Now the damned idiot was kissing her. Why the hell did that loudmouth have to come barging in here?

"Stop moping, sergeant, ha, ha. Helga, take him and show him where a woman's slit is. This is the way to treat a woman."

The man pressed his thick lips against Hellin's mouth and crushed her to him like a gorilla. Kauko looked at Helga, whose laugh was more than a little forced. When the man released the woman, Helga said:

"You mustn't talk like that. You've even got Kauko blushing."

"The boy must have been raised in a monastery, ha, ha. To bed, now, quick. You can go to the toilet, but hurry back. We're not going to fool around any longer. Next stop, Toijala, standing time, five minutes, ha ha."

"For Christ's sake, stop the racket or you'll wake up the people downstairs," hissed Helga.

"We'll be ready for battle when you get back. Let's throw off our clothes, *lieukenant*, sir."

The combat boots were already flying off the man's feet. His shirt went sailing to the floor, sleeves spread wide, followed by his pants. They landed by the door, looking as if they were in mid-stride.

"I didn't get them folded exactly right, but this is a rush operation and these are unusual times we're living in."

The *lieukenant* threw himself down on the bed. His shirt was unbuttoned down to his navel. His hairy chest and belly shook with laughter as he said:

"Take a look at that tool down there, ha ha. I've got a good-sized shank hidden away in my underwear. War can be fun sometimes."

Slowly Kauko unbuttoned his shirt. It takes all kinds, he thought, including that *lieukenant*. The man had no sense of shame.

"What kind of soldier are you. fumbling and blushing like that? You can't be afraid on the home front either, boy. '*March bravely into battle, son of Finland...*' That's what we sang when things were tough in Kuopio."

Kauko's fingers were trembling as he finished taking off his shirt and began shedding his pants. Now he moved quickly —

he had to make it under the covers before the women returned to the room.

"I can see that you take this all very seriously. No, no boy. You have to relax when you're away from the front. Life is a gamble now, and you never know if a leave is going to be your last. *'Who knows if our journey's end/ will come in the tumult of battle...'"*

Kauko had managed to get under the covers by the time Helga and Hellin returned.

"Look at my beast presenting arms, Helga," giggled Hellin. "And there's even something left to drink in one of the cups."

She checked the others as well, but they were empty.

"Now it's time to strip for bed. Let's see who's the first one done."

Hellin was already tossing aside her garments. Kauko was afraid either to turn his head or to close his eyes, although the woman was undressing without a trace of modesty. Now she was taking off her undershirt.

"Look at that bashful mama's boy. He turned his back," Hellin giggled.

"That's not why I turned. The liquor is making me sick to the stomach. I won't throw up if I lie on my side," said Kauko.

"Turn onto your other side if you want to see a perfect shape." Hellin giggled again. "Shall we turn out the lights, or aren't you men enough to do the deed of darkness?"

"I think we can find the way, but stop fooling around. A-rrrrr," said the *lieukenant.*

Although he had earlier turned away, Kauko could not help watching as Hellin circled the bed and walked to the light switch. For God's sake, he thought. She's stark naked, with just a couple of pins in her hair...Elma has a nicer figure. Elma! The name flashed into his mind at the instant the lights went out and the room went black. Elma...this was really a weird situation he was in. She must never know about this...or anyone else for that matter. But what of it — the Germans were carrying on in the same way with women in Finland. What kind of games went on in the bedroom at Olkivaara? Goddamn, if I ever catch Elma and that officer in bed together. Then Hellin clambered into the bed. Kauko heard the *lieukenant* grab her immediately, and he felt cold sober. Were they really starting to do it now?

What else could it be? Hell, what a bunch I've gotten mixed up with, he thought.

Helga undressed in the dark. When she dived into bed next to him, Kauko could feel that only a thin nightgown covered her body. She put an arm around his neck and drew herself close to him. It felt so good. Why make an issue of her being married? After all, there was a war on, a good excuse for soothing a guilty conscience. And I didn't lead my neighbor's wife into this. She herself begged me to stay. And there's small chance that Elma is thinking about me. Hell, why be so fussy?

"Hellin is impossible when she's had something to drink," whispered Helga.

"Well, she's not shy anyway," Kauko hissed back.

The thrashing on the other side of the bed continued.

"Shall I take off my nightgown?" Helga whispered into his ear.

"Why be bashful, goddamnit."

✧ ✧ ✧

Kauko awoke when the lights went on in the room. At first he started violently. Where was he? A blond woman was sleeping on his arm. The *lieukenant* was standing by the light switch, wearing only a flannel army shirt. His hairy legs were bare up to his buttocks. He walked over to the bed and exclaimed:

"Godalmighty, buddies! It's almost seven. Now I'll be caught."

The man dressed as if he were a frightened recruit, cursing the pants legs and shirt sleeves that had been left inside out.

"Now I have to run like hell. I'll come to see you, Hellin, when I skip out again. We'll try to break ten next time, ha, ha. Fight bravely, sergeant, and keep the big, bad, bolshie uncle off our necks. So long, *lieukenants*, sirs."

"A goddamned AWOL like you should be caught and shipped to the front," growled Kauko.

The *lieukenant* was already crashing down the steps.

"It's good that I don't have to work till the afternoon," said Hellin. "I'm all worn out."

"No wonder," said Kauko, sitting up.

"Where's your hurry? Let's rest like the idle rich," said Helga.

"I just have to make a certain call. I'm in no hurry."

"Put out the light," said Helga, when Kauko returned.

Daylight was already sifting in around the edges of the blackout curtains. Kauko stretched out on the bed and Helga burrowed into his arms. His whole being was numb, and he forced himself to think of places other than this room. He could feel the warmth of Helga's body, and a shudder of loathing ran through him.

"Let Kauko come between us so I can smell a man too," said Hellin. "Don't hog him all to yourself."

"I'm not going to share my cute sergeant with anyone," said Helga.

Kauko fell asleep again, and so did the women. Although he woke up when Helga rose from beside him, he kept his eyes shut. He felt tired and ashamed. Helga drew aside the blackout curtains and said:

"Oh, oh, it's ten o'clock already."

"So late? I'm so tired," said Hellin. Helga began to dress. Hellin stretched her naked body under the covers and yawned, then turned on her side and drew the covers up to her ears. Helga busied herself in the kitchen for awhile and then returned.

"Listen, Hellin. I lighted a fire in the stove and put your coffee substitute on to heat. Add wood to the fire if I'm gone for long. I'm going to the store. Let Kauko sleep."

"Don't worry. I'll take care of it."

Helga went down the stairs and the outer door slammed shut. Hellin immediately moved over to Kauko, threw her arms around his neck, and said:

"Hurry up, Kauko. I know you're awake, even if you're pretending to be asleep."

"Hurry up what?" said Kauko, but nevertheless he pressed the woman close to him.

"You know. Hurry up now."

But what about the *lieukenant*...and Helga too. It would be a dirty trick."

Kauko's throat was dry. He could feel the woman's body clutching his tightly. She was writhing like a snake.

"All life is a dirty trick. My husband made me like this. He was completely faithless and did whatever he pleased. Come on now. Helga may be back soon. You don't know the world yet. Decency will get you nowhere."

"You'll tell Helga...But if you're not going to say anything, then let's do it, goddamn."

"I won't say a word, you can be sure of that. But you don't need any underclothes on. You know how to be gentle. The *lieukenant* was a brute."

✧ ✧ ✧

Helga saw Kauko off on the evening train. She stood arm in arm with him on the platform. She was wearing a fur coat, and the eyes of passing men lingered on her. Despite his weariness, Kauko had a feeling of pride and defiance. If Elma and others could just see him now, see what a fine lady friend this former ward of the community was squiring...The cleated boots of German soldiers hammered on the icy platform.

"Those damned *guarantors* are everywhere," said Kauko.

"Oulu is full of them," said Helga.

"I'll write when I get to the front," said Kauko. "Will you answer?"

"Of course I will. Do you get another leave in the spring?"

"In three months, if the situation doesn't change."

"Will you come here then?"

"If your husband isn't here at the same time. I think the train is leaving."

"I'll see you again. Be sure to come," said Helga, squeezing his hand.

"In a war like this, you always have to say *if* I see you again."

3

In the early summer of 1944, the slumber at the front ended. The Russians began a large-scale offensive on the Isthmus of Karelia. On the other fronts as well, the days no longer dragged by in their former dull fashion. It was almost three years to the day since men had been laying bets that their armed excursion would end in two weeks. Now the situation was completely reversed. Almost everywhere, the front lines were falling back toward the west.

During the spring thaw, Finnish units were shifted from Uhtua to the Isthmus. The long transit of Kosti Mäkinen's company ended only when they reached the vicinity of Siiranmäki. Spring was just becoming summer on the Isthmus: green was bursting forth on the bosom of the earth and the boughs of trees. The new terrain was different from the now familiar woods of Uhtua, nor did it resemble the heaths and woods around Kiestinki.

Siiranmäki and its environs had been quite extensively fortified. Rows of tank obstacles traversed the landscape. Concrete bunkers and emplacements were being built at a great rate. But all was not ready when the Russians began to roll forward.

✧ ✧ ✧

Russian air activity had already picked up when Kosti Mäkinen boarded a train at the Raivola station. His leave had come through at the same time as the unit was ordered transferred from Uhtua, and so he was able to leave for home soon after arriving on the Isthmus.

Spring work in the fields was already beginning in Vaarakylä. Although the work was new to him, Kosti began plowing on the day after his arrival at Sääskilampi. The sun was shining, and the lake at Vaarakylä had just swallowed up the last remnants of the winter's ice. The fields were still damp, but firm enough for the plow to turn over the ribbons of soil. Kosti wiped the sweat from his brow with a sleeve while guiding the plow with one hand.

"Now, stay close to the furrow."

The boys were running along the banks of drainage ditches at the bottoms of which yellow flowers were opening their petals. At intervals they would come running across the soft, plowed earth crying out:

"Hey father! Do you see the pretty flowers we found?"

"I see, I see. Stay off this field. You'll carry muck in on your shoes."

"You didn't look, father."

There was disappointment in the boys' looks and voices. The man, who had been completely absorbed in his work, noticed it and stopped the horse.

"Let's see then. Those flowers are bigger than the last ones, I mean."

"There are loads of them at the bottom of that ditch," said Pentti.

"Pentti didn't find them all. I gave him more."

"You're a bigger man, Ilmari. I mean, you always have to help a younger person."

"Father, why do you always say, 'I mean'?" said Ilmari.

"Why do you ask?" laughed Kosti.

"No one else here talks like that. And you say other things different too," said Ilmari.

"Come and take a rest with father, boys. We'll sit down at the edge of that ditch. The horse can take a breather too."

The three walked over to the side of the ditch. The boys each sat on one of Kosti's knees. He put a hand on their shoulders.

"So you think your father talks funny, ya' see." He said the last words with a broad grin, and Ilmari spoke up at once.

"And now you said, 'Ya' see.' Other people don't talk like that."

"It's 'cause father's been in the war so long," said Pentti.

"Father was in Tampere when he was as big as you. He grew up into a big man there. Everybody in Tampere talks that way. But now that I've been here so long, I won't talk my home-city talk any more."

"That's what mother said. Do you ever miss the place where you were a little boy?"

"You're too nosy, Ilmari," laughed Kosti. "I never miss any place but this. You're my boys, and Tuulikki and Leila are my girls. I mean, here comes your mother now."

The boys looked where their father's finger pointed. Pentti went galloping off to meet his mother, who was leading Tuulikki.

"Mother, father said 'I mean' again," he shouted.

"And he said 'Ya' see' too," added Ilmari.

Irja stopped at the ditch. Hands outstretched, Tuulikki ran toward her father crying:

"Wap, wap!"

"You want to come into my lap? Father's hands are a little dirty, but he has to pick up his girl, I mean, when he's home so seldom."

The boys began to giggle and looked at their mother. Tuulikki immediately knocked her father's cap from his head and shrieked:

"Daddy's cap fall. Daddy pick up."

Irja stood with her arms folded and watched the antics of the child in her father's arms. It was by the good fortune of God that the children had such a good father and she such a good husband. If only the war would end. The habitual expression of Kosti's face was somber, almost angry. Now it had softened, as it always did when he got to play with the children. Fear and pleasure tugged at Irja's heart strings. A leave passed so quickly, and then another three-month period of waiting began. For that whole interim, her heart was in her throat. Luckily it had been quiet at the front. The lake, which had just shed its ice, was beautiful, and the hills looked blue. The cows were spending their first days outdoors, but they had not gone far because she could hear the sound of their bells. Irja cleared her throat.

"I came, I mean, to ask the plowman in for rye water."

"Now you're all mocking me," Kosti laughed. "I'll move the horse to fresh grass and then we'll go."

With Tuulikki in his arms, Kosti led the horse to the grass. As they started back toward the buildings at Sääskilampi, Ilmari said:

"Pick me up too, father."

"Father can't carry all of you," said Irja.

"Let's try. Father will stoop down and one of you get on each shoulder."

There was no need to repeat the command. The boys draped themselves over his shoulders and wrapped their arms around his neck. He walked off toward the yard.

"Now only Leila and I aren't on father's back," said Irja.

"Don't you think I could carry you too? And Leila wouldn't really add any weight."

"You'll strangle your father, boys, hanging on to his neck like that," Irja said.

"Let the boys ride. Father is seldom at home."

✧ ✧ ✧

The following morning Kosti was busy hitching the horse to a wagon with a dump rack. He was threading the reins through their rings when Irja appeared on the steps.

"Kosti, telephone," she said.

He handed the reins to a hired girl who was standing by the wagon with a manure fork on her shoulder and said:

"You drive the horse to one of the manure piles, Helmi. Start pitching on the load. I'll be right back. Who's calling, Irja?"

"They didn't give a name, just asked for Captain Mäkinen."

Kosti Mäkinen's face was somber as he walked toward his wife on the steps. They went into the house together. The hired girl twitched the reins and said:

"Let's go, as death said to the old man."

Bert's leave had come when the spring thaw was turning the snow to slush. While at home, he had hauled large piles of manure out to those fields that were slated for planting. Now the hired girl drove the horse and wagon over to one such pile and began to toss on a load with a manure fork. When the wagon was fully loaded, she looked inquiringly toward the house, but Kosti did not appear.

"Well, I guess I can drive the load too," she said.

Grasping the reins, she drove to a far corner of the field and tipped up the rack. The load slid onto the black ribbons of earth, exuding the smell of ammonia to mix with the fragrance of the fresh earth. The hired girl was already pitching on another load when she saw the Sääskilampi son-in-law coming toward the field. He was walking slowly, looking down at his boots. His movements were usually brisk. And he never puts on airs, she thought, even though men on leave say he's a big officer in the war.

Kosti Mäkinen stopped and said: "You're going to have a tough spring, Helmi."

"How so? I've always been used to work."

"You and Irja will have to work the fields. I have to go."

"Away? Your leave just started."

"The sheriff called. I have to go back to my unit."

"Why? You need a leave now that it's sowing time."

"In a war even those things don't matter much."

"That's terrible. But the young mistress and I will scatter the seed and plant the potatoes. War is war. But will it ever end?"

"Every war up to now has ended. Try to manage here at home."

✧ ✧ ✧

Petti said goodbye to her son-in-law in the yard. She had become thin after her husband's death, and her once-erect posture had sagged. The lines in her face were deeply etched.

"Say hello to Bert for me, and tell him his mother's heart is with him every minute at the front. My only son..."

"Don't cry now, mother," said Irja.

"I can't help it. I miss my child. If only Bert had accepted religion."

"Bert isn't in danger," said Kosti. "He's quick-witted and used to getting around in the woods."

"It's the good men who are always lost in a war. What can I do except believe that God will do as he sees fit. I no longer have your father to protect me."

"But we're here, Grandma, me and Pentti and the girls," said Ilmari.

Petti looked down through tearful eyes. A smile erased the lines on her face.

"So you are. You're God's gift to me too."

"Take care of Leila, mother. Tuulikki and the boys and I will see father off."

"Go ahead," said Petti. "Tell Bert to write more often."

"I will, I will tell him, Grandma. Goodbye and stay well," said Kosti.

Kosti carried Tuulikki on his arm while the boys skipped around him. For the first time in her life, Irja took her husband's arm by daylight in the village of Vaarakylä. The morning, which had dawned clear and bright, suddenly clouded over and the wind picked up strength. A side road ran from the yard at Sääskilampi to the main highway. Its surface was pitted and poorly graveled, and it was this rough road that Captain Mäkinen and his wife and children were forced to walk.

"Why did they call for you to leave so suddenly?" asked Irja.

"That's — how should I put it — that's just the way things are with officers."

"This isn't an ordinary cancellation of leaves. Something unusual is in back of it."

"Don't worry your head now. Just take care of the children."

"We'll get along here, as long as you and Bert come through safe and sound. I wish every Finn could."

"And the field work didn't get finished. You and Helmi will have a hard time with it. Ask our old neighbor for help and advice with the planting."

They had come to the main road. Even the usually lively Tuulikki sat quietly on her father's arm, fingering his collar insignia. She was jabbing a finger at the rosettes on them, and counting half to herself:

"One, two, free."

"Can you count already, you little peanut?" said Kosti with a smile.

"Daddy got free bright buddins," said Tuulikki.

"They're not buttons, they're stars," said Ilmari.

"Why does father's belt go over his shoulder?" asked Pentti.

"It's a useless decoration," said Kosti. "They call it a bawling-out belt."

"A bawling-out belt," tittered Ilmari. "You never even scold us, father. Mother always says that you never say a bad word and grandma too tells visitors that Irja has a good man."

Kosti Mäkinen looked at his wife, who lowered her eyes. He patted both boys' heads in turn.

"What Irja is that?" he said.

The boys looked at each other, then both wrapped their arms around their mother's hips and said:

"She's our mother."

Kosti Mäkinen turned away. They were all silent. Then he turned back and said:

"The truck must be coming. I hear the motor roaring."

"I hear it. I hear the truck," said Ilmari.

The man pressed the girl to his breast, then placed her in her mother's arms and said:

"Come on boys, let's see if I can still lift you."

First Kosti hoisted Pentti up over his head.

"Whoops-a daisy," he said, then lowered him to his breast and hugged him before setting him down. He did the same with the older boy. When Ilmari's feet touched the ground, he said:

"Remember to be good boys. You will, won't you?"

"We will," said Pentti.

Ilmari began to walk away, rubbing at his eyes with his knuckles. The truck, which had a plywood shelter built on its platform, was drawing near. Kosti raised a hand; the truck turned toward the side of the road and stopped right before them. He reached out a hand to his wife and said:

"I'll see you, Irja. Don't worry about me."

"I'll see you. Like mother, I'll trust in God. Give my regards to Bert."

"'Bye now, Tuulikki. Grow big."

A young sergeant leaped down from the cab to the roadside. He touched a hand to his cap and said:

"You can ride in the cab, captain, sir."

"Thank you, but there's plenty of room in the back."

"But..." said the sergeant. But Captain Mäkinen had already mounted the platform from the rear of the cab.

"Okay, let's go," he called out.

When the truck started out, Irja grasped Tuulikki's wrist and waved her little hand. I don't care about local ways now, she thought.

"Wave your hand to father, boys," she said.

Ilmari, who was standing off to the side sniffling, turned around. Three hands are waving to me, but the thoughts of four go with me, Kosti Mäkinen reflected. He waved back. The road turned, and now he could see the well-sweep and the tops of the buildings at Sääskilampi. There Leila was kicking in her grandmother's care. Then all he could see was the receding surface of the road. In back of the ditches were stumps that had begun to rot and the trunks of felled trees. Rocks rolled aside from the roadbed were beginning to grow a coating of moss. Kosti Mäkinen was almost startled to think that he had supervised the building of this road. Homesickness and thoughts of road-building made him feel almost numb. What kind of ruckus had broken out on the Isthmus? Although the sheriff had mentioned it, he had not wanted to burden Irja's and Grandma's minds with the news. Somehow or other, the war had to end this summer.

Some twenty men were sitting in the shelter on the back of the truck. Only after a long time did Kosti Mäkinen look around him. A young lieutenant sat on the same bench as he. He greeted Mäkinen and said:

"Where are you headed for, Captain?"

"For the Isthmus."

"And your leave was cut short?"

"Yes, I had only three days."

"The same with me," said the lieutenant. "I have to go to the Isthmus too."

"Then we're headed the same way," said Mäkinen.

4

"Come on, Jalo," said Kauko.

"Let's get out of here. A man could go blind in this dugout."

"Shut off that noise box, Sumala. This minute!"

Sumala merely cranked up the phonograph further. Looking at Kauko out of the corner of his eye, he said:

"This is my private property. I'll play it when I please."

"I don't want any part of it. How can a man stand to listen to that stuff?" said Kauko, as he walked toward the door of the dugout.

"What the devil has gotten into you. You're the one who was always playing that moony stuff before," said Sumala angrily.

"That was before. In grade school too, we sang *Black Sarah* and cried our eyes out," said Kauko from the door.

From the dugout, buried in the spring snowdrifts of the Uhtua wilderness, the strains of the song drifted out:

I heard you talk of happiness.
Your lips brimmed o'er with tenderness.
It was so grand,
so lovely too,
but all was a lovely lie...

When the last measure ended and the needle began to scratch on the smooth center of the record, Sumala said:

"Exactly what is Sammalsuo grousing about?"

"He's just back from leave. Do you expect him to be going around singing already?" someone said.

"Kauko always gets bad homesickness hangovers," said a member of Kauko's squad.

"I've seen him sulk before, but he's never been so damned bad-tempered. We always had to play schmaltz like *Lamplighting Time in the Valley* for him. Let's give *The Western Lumberjack* a spin to see if that suits him better."

Sumala wound up the phonograph. Someone said:

"Aren't our German *guarantors'* boots still clumping around in Kauko's home area? You'd be sour-faced too, Sumala, if your sweetheart was parading around on a *nichtsman's* arm."

"You'll never see me moping over a woman," said Sumala.

The needle scratched on the record and the phonograph began to rasp out the strains of *The Western Logger.*

✧ ✧ ✧

"Let's go over to the stable," said Kauko.

"Why not? It's a nice day, with the sun shining like that."

"So it is," said Kauko, looking at the dirty snow.

"In civilian life, we would be on our way to peel pulpwood," said Jalo.

"The bark should be good and loose by now."

"We've seen another spring come, and we're still in these duds. It's already the fifth."

"Who's counting?"

The sun was shining brightly and the paths leading from the dugouts were turning soft. They looked like black ribbons among the trees that had shed their burden of snow. Kauko walked on ahead, and Jalo followed along behind, looking at his squad leader's broad back. Kauko's shoulders sagged and he stared down at his toes as he walked. Why wasn't he looking around, Kieppi wondered. He had always found things to investigate in the woods. He would stare up at the sky and listen to the songs of the birds. What could have ruined him so completely? Last night, after going outside, he had sat cursing to himself for a long time. Was that neighbor girl's keeping company with a German still eating away at him? Kauko had not really talked about it, merely dropped hints once when they had drunk their ration of liquor. And why did he keep wearing that holster on his belt? Earlier, he had always left it hanging on the wall of the dugout when they were back of the lines.

Kauko Sammalsuo's foot slipped off the high ridge of path left by the melting snow. He almost fell, but kept his balance with a nimble leap. Only one foot sank into the soft snow.

"Goddamned clumsy ox, falling on my face first thing!"

"You're in a foul mood. What's bugging you now?"

"This whole life..."

"You've got a worse leave-hangover than usual."

Kauko said nothing, but checked the flap of the holster on his side. He walked past the stables. Bunches of hay, cellulose panels, and raveled rolls of twine were coming into view from beneath the snow. The smell of manure was in the air, and a pair of crows took flight from the manure pile.

"Summer is coming. The migrating birds are back," said Jalo Kieppi.

Beyond the stables, the paths became furrows that had been trodden only a few times, and their feet sank at every step. Kauko stopped and looked into the gloomy woods. Jalo Kieppi took out a pack of cigarettes and offered them to Kauko.

"I don't care for one," he snapped.

"Well, an offer is as good as a gift," said Kieppi.

Although he laughed when he said it, Kieppi was frightened at the tone of Kauko's reply. Had his mind snapped under the constant strain they suffered? His wasn't the usual post-leave depression.

Suddenly Kauko turned to him and said:

"I guess this is the end of the road for me."

"I don't understand. What's your problem?"

"It's not just a problem. I'm done for."

"You look to me like a man who will live a long time."

Kauko Sammalsuo turned his back and sighed heavily. Then he said:

"Write home and tell them I died in action. Tell the company commander too, so that mother won't have to be ashamed. I've always tried to do my best, even on this job."

Jalo Kieppi's eyes opened wide. He rushed past Kauko and stopped in front of him.

"Now, goddamnit, you're going to tell me what's wrong with you. We're buddies."

Kauko's head sank. He clenched and unclenched his fists, and his cheeks bulged out as he gritted his teeth. Then he said:

"I have some kind of sex disease. Oh God!"

"That's not true! What kind?" said Kieppi.

"I'm dead sure. This damned mucking around could have ended in some other way. I laughed my fool head off at Jonas's crabs, and now I've got something a thousand times worse. Ugh!"

"What kind of disease do you think it is?"

"I can't tell. I've only heard talk about where it shows up."

"Well, let's see it. Let me take a look."

Kauko's weather-beaten face flamed red as he spoke:

"There's no way I'll show you. It'll soon get better."

Kauko's eyes were staring and he was breathing hard. Kieppi said:

"Goddamnit! Haven't we always been good buddies?"

"We have. I thought I was pretty good and I bragged..."

"Just show me your pecker!" ordered Jalo Kieppi.

"I'm ashamed to. It won't make things any better. It's that..."

"Dig it out so I can see it."

Kauko gritted his teeth and stood still for a moment. Then he jerked his fly open with both hands. A button flew off into the snow. At the same instant, he lifted his shirt tails.

"Do you believe me now?"

"Well ain't that the devil. It's draining pus like toothpaste from a tube. Does it sting when you piss?"

"Like the devil!"

"That's a real dose of the clap. Did you pick it up around home?"

"Not unless I caught it in the sauna. I messed around with some women in Oulu."

"Worse luck. I saw a case of clap on a logger in camp once. He panicked and hanged himself."

Kauko's hands shook violently as he buttoned his fly. His eyes rolled and took on a moist and savage glitter. Suddenly he dashed forward, the soft snow splattering as he ran toward a spruce grove. I will not hang myself, he thought frantically, but this nightmare must come to an end. I'm sure Jalo will lie for me when he writes home. Mother won't be shamed. Hell, was that Jalo?

Kauko fell on his face in the snow. A blow had caught him on the neck and made him see stars. As his hand reached for his holster, he felt a violent tug at his waist and heard Jalo Kieppi roar out:

"Are you crazy! There are doctors, and they go to school to learn to cure diseases."

Kauko lay prone on the snow. He no longer cared if Jalo saw him weeping. After a short time, Kieppi said:

"Get up so you won't get chilled. We're going straight to the doctor."

"How in God's name can I face going there?" said Kauko.

"We're going. I'll be your second."

On the way back, Kieppi thrust the holster into the front of his jacket and said:

"You're not the first man to catch this, nor the last."

"If they need a man for patrol duty, I'm ready to volunteer...if I'll ever be a man again."

CHAPTER XX

1

The railway embankment ran through the gloomy swamps of northern Kainu and Koillismaa. The parallel rails laid along it crossed ridges that ran east and west without exception. In the summer of 1944, the rails gleamed from the scouring of train wheels rolling over the Ii River toward Kuusamo.

Finns had nudged the track along from Kontiomäki for almost ten years before the rails reached Hyrynsalmi, but the final stretch was completed in record time. It is true that the new builders, the Germans, laid the rails closer together beyond Hyrynsalmi, but nevertheless, the speed of construction was dizzying. The inhabitants, accustomed to the leisurely pace of the backwoods, were astounded to hear the shriek of locomotives far to the north of the Ii River two years after the work began.

Although the Germans showed the backwoods dwellers what it meant to work fast, they also gave them a fearful lesson in the cheapness of human life caught up in the world's maelstrom. In the cold and the blizzards of the backwoods, hands bare and dressed in clothing fit only for summer wear, prisoners waded along the tracks. Many succumbed to hunger and cold. Hundreds were shot. Among them were Germans, Poles, Russians, Ukrainians, and men from even milder climates. Here in the cold and two-meter-deep snow of the Kainu and Koillismaa wilderness, they came to know what human misery is.

After winter came spring and summer. The benumbed wretches woke from their winter torpor. Berries grew in the swamps and woods. There were fish to be caught in the brooks and lakes. In the winter, a prisoner who slipped away from the work gang left tracks to follow in the snow. In the summer, he could hide in the woods. While the others hoodwinked the guard who carried the machine pistol, a man could make a far-ranging and fruitful pilgrimage in search of food. The sympathies of the backwoods people lay with the prisoners. Even those few women who had taken the straight-backed and fawningly courteous prison officials as lovers pitied them at heart.

◆ ◆ ◆

"You didn't work on the Murmansk railroad, did you, Akseli?"

"No, I didn't. I hauled a few loads of freight there, but that was all," said Akseli Naavala.

"That was a monster of a job. A man's life was pretty cheap there," said Nestor.

"Even during the Winter War, we would never have guessed what we would see here some day," said Akseli.

"Nothing like this would ever have entered my head. For a long time I've had the feeling that these aren't our home woods any more. Those men of Hitler's have an awful way of treating their prisoners."

Nestor Malinen was seated in the main room at Naavala. Only the master of the house was at home. It was a warm Sunday, and the smell of new-mown hay hung over Järvenkylä. Barn swallows darted after insects outdoors.

Some of the age groups that had been released from duty nearly two and a half years ago had been called back into the army. Even reservists who had remained civilians during the Winter War and up to now during the Continuation War had been called into service. Arthritis had spared Nestor Malinen. It had affected his limbs so badly that he still walked with a cane. Things had gone badly on the Isthmus that spring. Now the newspapers told of stabilized positions. The Russian avalanche had been stopped.

"How far along are you with the hay-making?" asked Akseli.

"We're not half done. I'm not good for much of anything. Elma and the other kids have been grubbing away at it. Vante didn't even get a leave for hay-making. You must be almost finished already."

"Almost. The weather has been good."

"And you have mowing machines and other good gear."

"They're a help to me now when we don't have the manpower," said Akseli.

The talk turned to the war again, and to recent life in the area. Nestor's spirited disposition had begun to sag lately. Toivo's death, and Mari's, and the arthritis he suffered from had begun to turn his hair gray at the temples. His partner in the dialogue, Akseli Naavala was a man with a broad grasp of affairs. Fears regarding the outcome of the war had long gnawed at his mind. Lately they had grown stronger, making him uneasy. He often wondered how it would all end.

"So they blew up some dynamite under that German Hitler's table?" said Nestor.

"But they failed to kill him," said Akseli Naavala with a start.

"He was lucky again," said Nestor.

After a brief silence, Nestor said:

"Shall we stop by at our *guarantors'* camp?"

"I really don't care to. I've seen enough just walking by."

"But let's go. I'll gimp along on this leg of mine. I haven't really seen the place, except when I passed by it during the winter."

"Well, we might do that, and take a look at my swamplands on the way back."

"Let's see what it looks like in the summer. I know some of the prisoners too, and I've seen this Hans at our house many times."

Akseli Naavala glanced at Nestor, but kept his thoughts to himself.

✧ ✧ ✧

Nestor's walk was labored, and although he used a cane to help himself along at every step, his companion was forced to stop at times and wait for him to catch up. At last the barbed wire enclosure of the prison camp came into view. Pine trees had been left standing between the camp and the fence. The sturdy main branches of one reached out toward the road, and up at its top, a platform had been built, on which a guard with a machine pistol stood watch day and night. On clear days, he could see far and wide over the surrounding countryside.

"Why is that prisoner digging a hole in the middle of a Sunday?"

Akseli Naavala was seething with rage. He did not answer Nestor's question. They stopped a few meters from the spot where a ragged, bearded man was slowly tossing up sand from the bottom of a deep pit. Some little boys from the community were standing further off, staring silent and wide-eyed at the man standing up to his armpits in the hole in the sand. A guard stood nearby with a machine pistol under his arm. The prisoner leaned his shovel against the side of the pit and wiped the sweat from his thin face. The guard shouted at him, so sharply that the boys broke into a run. Nestor Malinen and Akseli Naavala felt a chill run down their spines.

The prisoner ducked out of sight at the bottom of the pit. The guard shouted again, and a pair of narrow shoulders clad in an army jacket came into view. The guard stepped to the edge of the pit, and kicked the prisoner's shoulder with his hobnailed boot. Moaning wretchedly, the prisoner fell to the bottom of the pit. The sound of uncontrolled weeping rose from it.

"Goddamn, they're like wild animals," growled Nestor.

The guard shouted again. Only a moan answered him from the bottom of the pit. The guard yelled something toward the camp, and a number of riflemen came into view from that direction. The guard dropped to his knees at the side of the pit, leaned down, and groped toward its bottom. Then his husky body strained upright, dragging up the prisoner by the collar. The man pressed his chest into the side of the pit and covered his face with his hands. His shoulders shook, and he could be heard sobbing again. Now the guard kicked the back of the prisoner's hands, and the man disappeared from sight again.

"I'll hit that devil one with my cane."

Nestor's jaws were tense. He took a stride toward the pit, but his arthritic joints would not obey his enraged brain's commands, and he fell headlong on his face. Akseli Naavala leaped over to him and caught him by the shoulders.

"There's nothing we can do. Those devils will kill us too."

"I'll hit that animal yet. Now he's kicking the prisoner in the face."

Nestor tried to crawl toward the pit, but Akseli's grip held firm. He hurled his cane at the group of men who had come to the pit, but it missed them. One of the men picked it up and with a friendly smile, handed it to Nestor, who raised it in the air to strike him, but the blow came to naught. Akseli had wrapped his fingers around the cane. The man who had brought him the cane turned red in the face and stepped back a few paces. Nestor tried to limp after him, and the man pointed his rifle at Nestor.

"*Nicht, nicht.*"

"Don't get yourself killed," said Akseli.

The rifleman jabbed a finger toward the road and shouted

angrily:

"*Weg, weg!*"

Some of the guards who had come to the pit began walking toward Nestor and Akseli. Their expressions were hard and their face muscles rigid. Others pulled the prisoner up to the side of the pit, where he stood looking down into it. He was no longer crying, but his ragged clothing quivered on his thin body.

"Damn it to hell, if I could just go man-to-man with that guard," said Nestor.

"They'll never get another sip of milk from us, not if they pay us in gold," said Akseli, his eyes flashing.

"I guess we have to go. That goddamned hard case is putting a round into his barrel."

Akseli and Nestor retraced their steps. The boys who had run off into the woods gathered around them. Soon they heard a volley of rifle shots, whose slightly delayed echoes rebounded from the slopes of Lapinvaara. The group from Järvenkylä turned to look back. Men were filling in the pit with shovels and the prisoner was nowhere to be seen.

"What did the prisoner do?" asked Akseli Naavala.

"He tried to escape," said one of the boys.

Nestor Malinen's jaws were taut. He stared straight ahead.

2

The roar of the rapids sounded from upstream and down. The sand on the slope of the ridge was hot from the sun, and alders along the shore rustled gently in the breeze. The burnt-out embers of a campfire smoked nearby, and a boat was drawn completely out of the water.

"Don't Hans, not so high up. They'll see the marks under my collar."

"*Liebe* Elma. *Liebe, liebe.*"

Elma and Hans Böhmer lay naked on the sand. They had set out from Olkivaara for the river that morning in the boat. All summer long, Hans had begged her to go boating with him. Evenings they had rowed around the bays and points of the lake, with Hans trolling a lure and Elma rowing. On occasion they would pass close to the outlet into the river, and then Lieutenant Hans Böhmer's face would light up with joy. The roar of the rapids softened the hard, and in Elma's opinion even cruel, lines of his face. He hated winter in the backwoods of Finland, but he loved the summer, and he was an avid fisherman. When on weekdays, the boat glided near enough to the rapids for the first whitewater to come into view, he would say:

"When we go there, Elma?"

"Some Sunday. When the weather is nice. There's time on Sunday."

Elma had learned German much better than Hans had learned Finnish. They almost always spoke Hans's native language; they had begun to do so last winter. During the summer, the man in his well-fitting German uniform was often seen leaving the Olkivaara storehouse early in the morning. He had never learned to row and would take the footpath around the outer fence of Sammalsuo and then go to the camp by way of the bridge.

The ridge that ran parallel to the river had been eroded to a strip of sand along the shore. The sun was shining from across the river. Further up the ridge was a grove of aspen trees, whose leaves quivered in the breeze. Although Hans was stroking her body again, Elma could not help thinking that Christ's cross was made of aspen wood. That was why its leaves trembled even on a perfectly still day, her dead mother used to say. Now the legend of the aspen tree, which brought thoughts of her mother to mind, changed Elma's mood to one of depression. The man's hairy chest bore down on her, his hands stroked her. His kisses were sucking, sometimes outright bites. Suddenly she squirmed loose and sat up.

"What now?" said the man with a look of frustration.

"We have to go now. It's afternoon already."

Hans glanced up at the sun and said:

"The sun is still high. I can make love to you once more."

"That's enough for today."

Elma's voice was indifferent. She reached for her clothes and began to dress.

"No, no. I want you again."

Hans Böhmer caught Elma in his arms and pushed her back down onto the sand. She was startled at the expression in the eyes boring down into her.

"Do you want to take me by force? Hans, don't be so rough."

"No...why did you turn cold? I'll take you to Germany, to Berlin, where I live. You can walk the streets of Germany's proud capital. I'll show you..."

"Don't promise so much. I haven't asked you for anything. If you want me, I won't fight you. Then we have to start poling toward Järvenkylä."

✧ ✧ ✧

Hans had admired Elma's skill in shooting the rapids on the way down, but he marveled even more at her when she ran the boat ashore on the return trip and said:

"You go along the shore. The boat will be lighter to pole."

Hans Böhmer strode along the rocky shore. He could not help her, no matter how much he might have wanted to. Her body straining, Elma drove the prow of the boat into the boiling whitewater. Slowly, but surely, steadily, the boat moved upstream, the length of one stroke at a time. Now, fortunately, the last of the rapids lay ahead. Hans Böhmer tried to speak to her from time to time, but the roar of the rapids swallowed up his words. Elma could only see his mouth opening and closing when she glanced at the shore. All she could do was shake her head. At the head of the rapids, she ran the boat ashore on the sand.

"Hop aboard and throw out the lure," said Elma.

"You're wonderful, Elma. A real blond girl of the North."

"You can stop the empty praise. At best, I'm a backwoods plaything."

Hans sat in the rear of the boat and watched the lure flash through the water behind them. As she spoke, he turned to watch her rowing with strong strokes of the oars.

"A plaything? What? I don't understand," he said with a shake of his head.

"A woman to fool around with," Elma said with a smile.

"No, Elma love. But no."

Elma turned to look behind the boat. The lure was already wiggling along quite close to the boat, and she said:

"Let out more line!"

As they moved forward, the flow of water toward the rapids slowed down. The boat was now skirting a line of reeds and little effort was needed to propel it. On its bottom were a blackened coffee pot in which they had made coffee on the shore a number of times, and a greasy frying pan in which Elma had fried the salmon caught by Hans on the way out. In Elma's bag were a marmalade jar and a few tins of sardines Hans had taken along just in case. Elma had brought a blanket with her for the morning, but the sand had already been warm when they made camp, and they had needed no covers.

"Aha!" shouted Hans suddenly, and began to draw in the line.

"Not so fast," said Elma.

Hans Böhmer's face glowed when a pike that weighed nearly a kilo lay thrashing in the bottom of the boat. He snatched up the bailing bucket and began to hammer at the pike's head with it. The boat rocked and the bottom braces popped.

"Don't swamp the boat! You can keep a little pike like that in the boat without all that fuss. You'll tangle the line too," said Elma.

Before they reached the shore at Olkivaara, they passed through a bank of reeds. From it a duck came rushing toward the open water with a brood of young behind it, splashing wildly through the water. Hans Böhmer was used to moving fast. He dropped the lure, and before Elma knew what was happening, he rushed to the bow of the boat. The long pole used for the rapids flashed through the air, and the end of it smashed down among the swimming ducklings. He struck again, but the birds, paddling for their lives, were now out of reach. One of the ducklings, struck by the first blow, lay lifeless on the water. When Hans scooped it up, he wrung the neck of the thrush-sized tatter, gritting his teeth. Then he came crouching along the boat toward Elma, dangling the bird in front of his face.

"Elma, me good hunter," he said laughing.

"Are you satisfied now?" she said, winding in the line without looking at him.

"Are you angry? Did you see how quickly I got the bird?"

"What will you do with a little thing like that? You might at least take it to the prisoners."

"Why are you looking at me so angrily?"

"Because you and all the rest of you are like a pack of wild animals."

Hans Böhmer's face darkened. Elma had earlier accused him of the same thing. She had pleaded nicely, even spoken nastily, on behalf of the prisoners. These backwoods people seemed strange to Böhmer. No one gave orders to anyone else. Finnish soldiers were shiftless and self-willed too. The guards at the prison camp did not really dare to travel around the community by themselves. Even then, many had been beaten till they were nearly dead. For some reason, the pseudo-soldiers on leave would beat up on guards from the prison camp. They were pleasant only when they came to ask for cognac. The Germans had always tried to maintain friendly relations with the inhabitants of the area, and with the soldiers as well, but one evening, as Hans Böhmer had been crossing the Naavala bridge, a Finnish soldier came weaving toward him, jacket open and singing away. When he reached Hans, the man leaped up like a flea, yelled out, and drew his knife. Luckily for his sake, Böhmer had kept up his training as a middle-distance runner even in the army. He wondered if Elma had heard of the incident. Uncertainty on that score had spoiled many of his evenings with her.

On shore he offered her the left-overs from the lunch.

"Keep your goodies!"

Elma dropped the cans and the other wrappers to the ground at his feet. Then she threw the pike and duckling from the boat toward him and said:

"The men behind the barbed wire will eat these."

"Why are you angry? I'm a soldier and I obey our Führer's orders."

"Obey them then, but get going."

"I can come and see you? *Liebe* Elma..."

Elma did not answer. She opened the drain plug in the bottom of the boat and bent over to clean out the sand and other debris from it. Hans Böhmer walked away uncertainly.

✧ ✧ ✧

When Elma entered the main room at Olkivaara, Nestor was sitting there on a bench with his head bowed down. He scowled at Elma and sighed heavily. From time to time he inhaled the smoke from a cigarette deep into his lungs. She could see that he was in a surly mood.

"Why are you glaring like a mad bull?" she said.

"I was just looking. Did you row all the way to the rapids with that spindleshanks?"

"I did. We went all the way to Hevonperse Neck. Why do you ask?"

"I've never said a bad word to you but now I'm so mad that I have to tell you straight to your face: Stop going around with that German."

"I don't care about your orders. I'm a grown-up now."

"I don't like those men one bit. They're devils, not men. Just like wild animals..."

"You haven't complained about Hans's cognac till now. And you've even been to the sauna with him, many times," said Elma, sitting down on the bench.

"But not any more. I'll never touch a drop of a *nichtsman's* cognac again. Not if I have to walk to Oulu to get a drink."

Father and daughter were silent for a long time. Finally Nestor said:

"I can't be angry with you. You're my best child. You'll just get a bad name because of them — and other grief besides."

Elma turned and looked out of the window. A sturdy balsam plant was blooming profusely in the soil of a birch-bark planter on the window sill. She listened as her father told of what he and Naavala had seen at the prison camp. Only when his cane thumped on the floor did she come out of her daze. She rose and went into the kitchen. There she said to her sister Taimi:

"From now on we sleep together in the storehouse."

"What about Hans Böhmer?"

"Just keep your mouth shut," said Elma. "Let's go and carry the dry hay into the barn."

"On Sunday?" said Taimi.

"It may rain tomorrow."

3

The day after Finland agreed to an armistice with Russia, Hans Böhmer came striding up to Olkivaara. Elma was on her way from milking. When he appeared at the end of the house, she set down her milk pail and pulled down the skirts she had tucked up for milking. She had seen him only a few times after the outing at the rapids, and they had merely exchanged a few words. She had rejected his offers to see her home.

"What is it now, Hans?" she asked as she stood there by the milk pail.

"I came to say goodbye." Both his voice and expression were harsh.

"The war is over now. There's an armistice..."

"Traitors! All Finns are traitors, cowards, scared rabbits, and, and..."

"Is that so? Try to crap out a few more ugly names."

Model soldier Hans Böhmer grabbed his jacket collar and tore the garment open to the waist. Although the weather was cool, sweat was pouring down his face. A puff of steam rose from under his jacket.

"You're all a bunch of cows. Two-faced double-dealers. But Germany isn't on her knees yet. You can blame yourselves when the Führer's anger turns on you."

"There's no point in raving at me. I'm no military leader, not even a worthless crew chief," said Elma, picking up the milk pail.

"Don't go, Elma. Come to the barracks tonight. We'll be together for the last time."

Hans Böhmer looked at her pleadingly. Elma took a few steps toward the porch. Hans moved nearer.

"Leave everything. Come with me. I'll take care of you. I'll protect..."

He reached out his hands and walked toward her. Then a window of the main room opened.

"Nix, goddamnit!"

The shout sent a shock down Elma's spine. She set the milk pail hurriedly on the ground. Hans spun toward the window from which a double-barreled shotgun protruded. Böhmer fumbled at his holster as Elma shrieked:

"Father, don't!"

Her cry was drowned out in a roar. Hans Böhmer crouched low and dashed around the corner. Elma's face turned white. Nestor Malinen hobbled to the rear window of the main room and thrust the shotgun out through a window pane, which fell to the ground in tinkling fragments.

"Where the hell did that spindleshanks get to already?"

Seeing no one from that window, Nestor hobbled to the side of the room. At the window there, he raised the shotgun to his cheek and pulled the trigger. The charge blew a hole the size of a man's head in the window pane, but just as the shot was fired, the shoulders of a running man disappeared into a fold of land along the shore. When Elma, trembling, came into the room, Nestor was reloading the shotgun.

"God help us! Are you crazy?"

"What makes you think so? I've got new shells in it now if the others weren't enough to convince him."

"Trying to kill a person," said Elma.

"I wasn't trying to kill him. Do you think I'm such a damned poor shot that I would have missed a man his size if I aimed at him? I was just scaring him off."

Nestor went back to the window from which he had fired in the direction of the retreating figure. After watching from it for a long time, he said:

"There he goes high-tailing it onto the Sammalsuo road. Just what was he yelling at you out there? He looked to be mighty mad."

When there was no answer, Nestor turned to look at Elma, but she was not in sight, nor were the other children. A bleak draft of late autumn air blew through the room. Nestor hung the shotgun on the wall and went into the kitchen. The milk pail had been left on the table and there was not a soul in sight in this room either. A fire crackled in the stove and the kettle on it was boiling. Nestor walked over to Elma's bedroom and opened the door quietly. His oldest daughter was lying face down on the bed. He limped to the center of the room, stood there a long time, and said:

"Our whole life here has gone to pieces. But no matter what you've been into, you're my daughter, and I won't give up on my children, come hell or high water."

Nestor returned to the kitchen and entered the other bedroom. Taimi and the other children sat there frightened. Nestor said:

"Why the devil are you sitting there like a lump, Taimi? Go and separate the milk and make supper. Elma's feeling a little sick."

✧ ✧ ✧

It was all over now, she thought. Hans has left for the last time. Why didn't I break it off when I read that letter of his? It had been in early summer. Hans, and she too, had had a bit of cognac in the storehouse. He had completely relaxed there. Like the other Germans, he drank in moderation, but that night he had said: "We're alone now. I'll drink all I please. Cheers, Elma! A toast to the northern night and the blond girl of the north." He raised his glass high and almost emptied it in a single draught. Then he poured himself another. Elma drank some too, but the cognac seemed too strong to her. When she awoke early in the morning the sun was already high in the sky, filling the storehouse room with light. Hans Böhmer's jacket hung on the wall, with the flap of its front pocket open. The corner of an envelope protruded from it.

Elma glanced at the man sleeping next to her and shuddered. He had fallen asleep with his shirtsleeves rolled up and his shorts kicked into a clump of white cloth around one ankle. Elma rose, took out the letter, and began to read through it. Her unspoken doubts became certainties when she reached the last words of the letter:

> *"Helmut and Klaus send their heartfelt greetings to their father. Do you know what — one day Helmut put the Führer's picture up on the wall with a thumbtack. Dear Hans, our separation is a long one, but it's not forever. All my love. Your little wife, Gretchen. (I'm kissing the place on the letter where I wrote Helmut and Klaus's names)."*

Elma put the letter back in the pocket, picked up the covers, and threw them over the man. He sat up with a start, eyes wide and puzzled.

"You should be ashamed to be lying there in the raw," she said.

"Was I? Forgive me. Did anyone see me drunk?"

"No, but they heard you," said Elma.

"That can't be. Who was listening?" said Hans, his eyes as disturbed as the tone of his voice.

"The crows on the roof."

"Dear Elma. You're always so witty."

On that occasion, Elma melted under his caresses. Once you start going to hell, you might as well go all the way, she thought.

The whine of the separator awakened her to the present. She heard Taimi rattling the lids of the stove. Elma sat up, wiped her eyes on her apron, then looked at the table by her bedside. From it, the keen eyes of Hans Böhmer stared at her from under the visor of his cap. Another picture displayed the determined, but somehow gentle features of an army sergeant. The expression on her brother's face she could not see from this distance, but she remembered it from before. She rose, picked up Hans Böhmer's picture, looked at it for a moment, and tossed it into a bureau drawer. Then she picked up Kauko's picture. As she looked at it, tears welled up in her eyes. Opening another drawer, she hid the picture in it. Only Toivo, his cap flopping down over his ears, was left to look at his sister.

✧ ✧ ✧

After they had eaten supper, Nestor said:

"Taimi, you run over and ask Maija Sammalsuo how things look out toward the highway. Or will you go, Elma?"

"Taimi can go."

"Go and find out, but come back before dark."

"It's almost dark already," said Taimi.

"You might run along the Sammalsuo boys' snare trail. There's no knowing what the *guarantors* will be up to now."

It grew dark, but no lamps were lighted at Olkivaara. Nestor patched the windows with cardboard and then planted himself before a window with a view of the trail that led to Sammalsuo. He hung his shotgun on the nail that held the curtain cord on that same window. All the younger children sat on the same bench with their father. That evening, there was no need to stop them from squabbling. Elma did the dishes and other evening kitchen chores. Her pain and loneliness were subsiding. At least I'm a free human being, she thought. If Finland remains a country, I'll stay here in the backwoods. I'll take care of father and bring up the children. Elma felt as if her mother were sitting at the end of the table, nodding and pressing her hand to her heart. I'll always get along with father. If others hate me too much because of Hans, there are other places in the world to go to.

Elma found herself humming a tune popular during the war, which had been running through her head:

I'm nothing but a play-time wife.
Fate denies me a part in your life.
Loving you has left me forlorn,
cast aside and treated with scorn.

"There comes Taimi now," she heard her father say.

Elma went into the main room. Taimi entered breathlessly and said:

"They told me the highway is packed with Germans racing north. Aili Sammalsuo had been to Naavala. She said they're wild with rage. They're supposed to have burned the houses along the highway already."

"Hell, that can't be!"

"It's true. They even had Finnish women along with them. They were a foul-mouthed crew," said Taimi.

"Anyone knows that a woman who would go off with them has no respect for herself or her family. I was afraid of what they would do. Now that the war with Russia is over, it looks like we'll have to start fighting the Germans."

The darkening night was like a weight pressing down on them. From time to time, they looked out toward Sammalsuo. Finally Nestor said:

"What you'll do, kids, is drive the cows to Peräsuo meadow. No one will find us there. We'll take the bells off the cows. There's hay in a barn for them there. You can take food along for yourselves and wait there. We'll see what comes of this."

✧ ✧ ✧

Leading the cows, Elma, Taimi, and the other children headed for the Olkivaara swamp meadow some five kilometers away. There in the dense woods was a hay barn which outsiders would not be able to find. They were all heavily laden. Their more valuable possessions they had carried to a pile on the shore and loaded into the boat.

Nestor hobbled to the barn after the children.

"I'll row that stuff out at night and hide it along the river bank, then come back and stay in one of the outbuildings. You come here tomorrow night when it's dark, Elma, and whistle at the end of the lane. I'll answer you."

"If you'll just be careful not to fall into the hands of the Germans," said Elma.

"You don't have to worry about that. If one or even two of them show up here, they'll be a target for buckshot. I have a feeling that this place hasn't seen the last of Hans Böhmer."

A light breeze was blowing from the direction of the Naavala bridge. It brought the constant roar of motors to their ears. Nestor looked at his children, who were disappearing from the lane into the dark woods. Then he limped to the shore and shoved off in the boat. I'll have to go and tell Jussi Ylikylä so that he'll know he should hide his goods, thought Nestor as he sculled the boat. This is just like a hundred years ago. The old people say that they rowed away to hide from the Russian raiders, who were supposed to have come down this river.

The water lapped against the sides of the boat. The treetops traced a faint line against the sky. There is a thick spruce grove below the rapids, thought Nestor, with big caves in the rocky crags. The old people say that bears used to have dens in them years ago. They even claim that people took their goods and grain there to hide them from the Russian raiders.

"The world has really gone crazy," Nestor said aloud. "For almost five years now we've been at it, first with the Russians and now with the Germans. Will my eyes ever see peace in these woods again?"

4

Fear prevailed in the house at Sammalsuo. The flame of the wall lamp was turned down almost to nothing. When Taimi Olkivaara set out for home, Maija said:

"Should we go and spend the night in the woods?"

Before dark, Väinö had brought the axes in from the woodpile and leaned them against the wall of the room. His eyes and those of the other children turned toward them as he said:

"S-somebody's skull will get split if they try to come in here."

"Let's go into the woods, mother," said Liisu, her voice shaking too.

"Why go into the woods?" said Aili. "We'll freeze there. The Germans won't do us any harm."

"We'll believe that and trust in God to take care of his creatures."

There was a tapping at the window pane. Little Liisu scooted under the bed. Väinö darted behind the fireplace, but Aili went over to the wall and picked up one of the axes. Maija went to the door and stood listening. Again there was a tapping at the pane. Maija opened the door and went out into the entry.

"Who's there?" she said sharply.

Footsteps moved toward the door and heavy panting sounded through it.

"Maija...Josef."

"Is it you, Josef? Then I'll open the door," said Maija, lifting the hook.

The man came into the entry. Maija's last words had been spoken in a glad tone of voice, free of fear. Now she covered her eyes with her hands and screamed.

"My God, the condition you're in!"

Aili came out too and started to cry. Josef Leber stood leaning against the door frame. Blood was dripping from his head, and some of it had congealed around his eyes. He was wringing his hands. Although the light was faint, it shone directly on the man. Maija said:

"What have they done to you, Josef? Ask him, Aili."

In between sobs, Aili managed to get out some words in German. Josef panted and swayed as he spoke:

"I escaped. They caught me near Naavala. They beat me with their rifles. I got the rifle away from one of them. I hit him with it and shot him. The other shot at me as I was running away and hit me in the head. I feel dizzy. They're after me."

After Aili had explained it all in Finnish, Maija caught the man by the arm.

"You poor man. Come inside."

"*Nicht*," said Josef, shaking his head. "After me, searching..."

Josef sat on a box in one corner of the entry. Maija went to get a sheet, from which she tore a long strip. The bullet had grazed Josef's skull, and a blow from a rifle had torn open his cheek. Aili bound the wounds that were bleeding the most. The escaped prisoner kept talking to her the whole time.

"Josef would like a little bit of bread. Then he needs a map. Josef says he knows we won't inform on him. He's going to try to escape to the Russian side of the lines."

They found Väinö's school map on the wall shelf and Aili gave it to Josef. Maija packed him a good lunch. Then he stood up and said:

"Where are Liisu and Väinö?"

Liisu had already crawled out from under the bed. Väinö sat head down on a bench with a scowl on his face. When the two went up to Josef Leber, he squeezed their hands and said:

"I...children too. Do I see them again?"

When Josef Leber disappeared into the darkness, he was sobbing, as were the women. From out of the darkness came broken words:

"God bless you. Watch out for the Germans. They destroy everything. We'll never see each other again. I'll write if I get out alive."

✧ ✧ ✧

Soon afterward, when the darkness had swallowed up Josef Leber, Aili said:

"We're not going to sleep in the house."

"No, let's take the bedclothes and go into the woods," said Väinö.

"Who knows — his pursuers may soon be here. I'll get some water to wash our hands. We all look like butchers. It's awful what human beings have become," said Maija.

The Sammalsuos rolled up the mattresses and other bedding and abandoned the house. Maija went into the barn and stuffed the cow's bell full of hay, then let the animals loose. They snorted, nostrils flaring in surprise, but nevertheless the second cow and the calf followed the bell cow which Maija was leading. The lambs were still running free in the woods.

Maija and the children followed the cow path for a full kilometer and then she felt her way for a short distance off the path. Around them grew long-limbed spruce trees. At the base of one of them, she and Aili unrolled the mattresses. The cows bawled, but settled down when they realized their mistress was staying near them. When they were all lying on the same bed underneath the thick covers, Maija said:

"You can never tell what you'll run into in this life. All of you say your evening prayers now."

They all did, even Väinö. From the highway, they could hear the constant roar of motors. The spruce at whose base Maija and the children slept sighed heavily. Through the darkness of the night came the sound of two shots in succession. Maija felt Liisu, who was lying next to her, tremble.

"Don't be afraid, Liisu," she said.

"Are they shooting people?" whispered Liisu.

"No, I don't think so. Maybe they're just shooting for fun."

"How will Josef make it through the night?" said Aili.

"We won't talk about that. If only it doesn't rain, with the trees sighing like that," said Maija.

✧ ✧ ✧

In the morning the Sammalsuos returned home by roundabout paths. The cows they left in the woods along with the bedding. The sky had a thick cloud cover and the chill of autumn was in the wind. There was no one in sight, and everything was as they had left it the evening before, but hardly an hour had passed when a boat rowed up to the shore.

"There comes the Naavala hired hand," said Väinö.

"I wonder what he's doing here," said Maija, who was looking out the window.

The man was already up in years. He came through the door and said without further greeting:

"Gather up your clothes and put a lead rope on the cows."

"What's going on now?" said Maija, wide-eyed.

"We're being evacuated and we have to hurry. Where the devil did the Olkivaaras and Jussi Ylikylä go to? There wasn't a Christian soul at either place."

"Who are we running away from and why?" fumed Aili.

"Our *guarantors*. Those stinking bed pals of yours."

"Don't talk nonsense," said Aili.

"This is no nonsense. You have to leave at once. The Germans say they won't bother the civilians if they start walking now. Buses will be coming to Naavala, and you have to start leading your cows to the church village."

"God help us. We're starting the same journey all over again," said Maija.

"That Jesus talk won't change anything," said Juuso, the hired hand. "Just start making bundles. Where the devil did Nestor's gang go? And Jussi's place was all empty."

"Did you go there?" asked Väinö.

"How else would I know? I had to sweat the whole distance there."

"Were the boats on the shore?" said Maija.

"I didn't see any? The rollers were empty on the shore."

"Maybe they took their stuff to the church village in boats," said Aili.

"Could they have done that? The houses did look empty."

"But where did they take the cows and other animals?" said Maija.

"That's right. Didn't they go by here?"

"We didn't see them. We slept in the woods," said Maija.

"Maybe they went by then," said Aili.

"But where did they hear about the evacuation, when Juuso is just bringing word of it?" said Väinö.

"Maybe Hans came to tell them," said Aili softly.

"Of course. That nixman was Elma's bed pal. He must have come to say goodbye," laughed Juuso.

"Don't talk like that," said Maija. "My God, we have to leave home again."

"No use to cry about it. I have to go on with my rounds."

That day the cattle began flowing toward the east. The backwoods people were forced to leave their homes again. At least it was not cold this time, but the evacuees, packed into buses, were downcast. On the lake, Maija turned to look back:

"When will we see our home again?"

"When the war is over," said Väinö, who was rowing.

"Will it ever be over?" said Maija. "When peace with the Russians comes, we go to war with the Germans."

"The Germans aren't really fighting against the Finns."

"Your sweetheart didn't come to say goodbye, did he?" retorted Väinö.

"I may see Franz at Naavala," said Aili.

"Talk about something else. We've got a sad journey ahead of us. I wonder where Kauko is," sighed Maija.

5

On the following day, Nestor stopped in at home and then limped over to see his children. They were living in the hay barn. Elma milked the cows and did the cooking. Nestor slept the night with them and then went home with Taimi. It was as silent and deserted there as on the previous day. The rooms were beginning to feel cold and dank.

"Trot over and see how the Sammalsuos are doing," Nestor said to Taimi.

It was two hours before Taimi got back.

"Everyone has been evacuated," she said.

"Hell, it can't be. How do you know?"

"I walked right up to the highway and watched the German trucks and wagons going by. There were no Finns in sight. There was a lot of smoke rising in the direction of Vaarakylä. See for yourself!"

Nestor looked in the direction indicated.

"That is a huge mess of smoke rising from there. Are they burning people's houses? But how do you know everyone has been evacuated?"

"Aili Sammalsuo wrote a note on the edge of a newspaper she left on the table. She wrote that they were forced to evacuate, that Juuso from Naavala brought the bad news. But I really don't understand why she wrote that the Olkivaaras and Jussi Ylikylä went by boat to the church village," said Taimi.

"Who started that lie going around?" said Nestor angrily. "And why the devil didn't Juuso bring word to us?"

"What can we do now?" asked Taimi.

"I don't know what's best. The devil himself wouldn't head for that highway with his kids and cattle. Who can be sure the Germans won't put a bullet through us and fill their bellies on our animals? Damn it, I'm stumped."

"What about going to the church village?" said Taimi.

"Who knows what kind of war is going on there? That huge column of smoke must be coming from the houses at Vaarakylä."

Father and daughter watched the smoke rising in back of the woods with a feeling of helplessness. Only a few vehicles were still moving along the road. A heavy and unfamiliar air of desertion hung over Järvenkylä and the surrounding wilderness. Nestor coughed and said:

"What we'll do now is live in the hay barn at Peräsuo. I'll start hanging around the house here. We don't know what might happen. You go and join the others. And don't make a lot of smoke."

"Are you going to stay here, father?"

"I'm not going to keep limping back and forth on my bum leg. You and Elma can take turns bringing me food."

"What if the soldiers shoot you?"

"I'm not going to stand out in the middle of the yard and be a target."

✧ ✧ ✧

That afternoon the weather turned freezing cold. As the sun sank close to the rim of the woods, Nestor got out his sheepskin sledding coat and a fur cap with large ear flaps from the storehouse. As he gimped toward the threshing barn with his winter gear, he muttered to himself:

"In a war, you need heavy clothes when you're on watch...Now what the devil!"

He stopped and looked toward Naavala. Cold shivers ran down his back.

"Those devils are burning the whole place down. That smoke there is coming from Naavala and that to the right is from Sammalsuo."

Nestor looked around, keeping an especially sharp eye in the direction of the path toward Sammalsuo. No one was in sight yet. This was no children's game. It was good that Mari had not lived to see it. Now into the threshing barn, quickly.

His arthritic leg gave way a number of times as he hurried to the barn, but he felt no pain. Soon he was over the high threshold and into the building. His shotgun and ammunition belt hung from a wooden peg on the wall. Nestor leaned the gun against the door frame and began to put on the sheepskin coat. Then he remembered a German belief that the little boys of Järvenkylä had sometimes mischievously reinforced.

Nestor took off the coat and turned it inside out. Its lining was sewn from alternate strips of white and black sheepskin. The wool was long, and very warm in the winter. Then he went to the fire pit and fished out a dead coal, with which he blackened his bearded face. He turned his fur cap inside out too. Although he was afraid, it occurred to him that people who were lost were said to find their way back to the world of men if they turned their clothing inside out. Then he pulled his ear flaps down and climbed up onto the rafters of the threshing barn, holding the shotgun and the ammunition belt. There he opened a hatch a good two feet square. As he buckled on the belt, he said between gritted teeth:

"If Adolf's men start breaking in here now, they'll need a lot of bandaging to wrap themselves up in. I won't have any mercy. I'll aim for the gut."

✧ ✧ ✧

Nestor did not even dare to roll a butt. He stuffed pinches of tobacco against his gums and stared out of the hatch. He was a little nervous. Damn, he couldn't see to the other side of the threshing barn. What if they came sneaking up from that direction? Where would he go then? If only the children didn't wander carelessly into sight.

"Here they come now!"

Nestor, who had been sitting and watching, went down on all fours.

"Damn it, that knee is stiff and sore. How did they find the end of the lane?"

A mounted party of five came jogging down the lane. The men were talking to each other. They split into two groups in back of the cow barn, circled the building, and met again in the yard. One of the men was better dressed than the others. His posture and the marks of collar insignia told Nestor that he was the leader of the patrol. The man pointed with his riding whip, first at the house, then at the cow barn, the hay barn, the sauna, and finally the storehouse. The men dismounted. The first to reach his goal was the one who had run toward the cow barn. He jerked out a bunch of hay used to stuff cracks so that it hung down along the log wall and struck a match.

"The devils are burning the place down," muttered Nestor.

Hands shaking, he tried to thrust the shotgun out through the hatch. He cocked both hammers. The bunch of hay was already burning, the flame climbing up the wall like a squirrel.

The men had first-rate weapons. One of them was trying to pry open the porch door. Luckily he had nailed it shut. In his excitement, Nestor thrust his body further out through the hatch. He was already hanging out over the wall up to his navel, and he almost lost his balance. He waved his arms wildly to maintain it. Clumsy ox! I'll land on my head yet, he thought. Rage and fear caused him to roar out like a wild animal:

"Aargh!"

The horses tossed their heads and snorted. All the men stopped what they were doing in mid-motion. Only the man who had lighted the hay brushed out the flame with his hand. The patrol leader's whip, which he was using to gesture along with his orders, froze in position to strike. The men's eyes swept their surroundings and fixed on the creature moving above the door of the threshing barn. They saw a hairy, black-and-white-striped being squirming like a worm wriggling out of its hole. There was a black face on its hairy head. Then a thunderous bellow echoed from the walls of the buildings:

"Aargh...Nix!"

The patrol leader's whip lashed the flank of his horse.

"*Donnerwetter*... Lapland devil!"

The shout set the frozen men into motion. They leaped pell-mell onto their horses and galloped off. Their leader was already nearing the gate at the end of the path to Sammalsuo. The others spurred and whipped their mounts after him. Tails streaming out behind them, the spooked horses leaped over the gate. For a time, the heath thundered under their hoofs, and then all was silent. Nestor Malinen descended to the floor of the threshing barn and stepped outside, his stubs of teeth gleaming in his laughing face.

"He didn't even have time to put out the fire properly."

Nestor walked to the wall of the cow barn and brushed the tuft of smoking hay to the ground. Then he looked toward Sammalsuo for a moment. There was nothing to be seen or heard. Prying open the porch door, he went into the kitchen. Taking down a mirror that had been left on the wall, he stared into it for a long time. He was grinning broadly when he spoke:

"I wouldn't exactly call them yellowbellies even if they did run away."

Nestor went to spend that night with his children. In the

darkness, he and Elma woke up with a start on the hay where they were sleeping. The earth shook, and the sky was brightly lighted in the direction of Naavala. In a few seconds, there was silence. The dark night covered everything.

"What was that explosion?" asked Elma.

"I think they blew up the Naavala bridge," said Nestor.

✧ ✧ ✧

All day long the chickadees had chirped and fluttered in the spruce trees at the edge of a swamp. The bolder ones hopped in the branches of a leaning spruce that grew almost parallel with the ground. The sun was already setting. Suddenly the birds took flight. A man who had been sleeping under the tree was stirring. He was covered with moss scraped from the hillocks nearby. All day long, the chickadees had seen only his face and one hand, which sometimes twitched on the moss.

The man tried to open his eyes. One of them did open, but the other was swollen shut. Pain shot through his head and his entire body. The shivers that ran through him intensified the pain, but he could not stop them. A high fever had muddled his thoughts. Why was the sun shining from that direction? When the ground was white with frost, it looked over the rim of the woods from a completely different quarter of the sky. The cold was just as sharp now as during the dark.

I saw some high mountains just now, he thought. They rose in folds, almost to the clouds. The sky of Bavaria is blue. He was a small boy. Mother was calling him to come in. His father and brother were coming up the steep mountain trail. They were coming from work. He ran to his mother. Then he heard an odd croaking in the sky. Her mother lifted her face and looked up, then tilted it further still, to where the topmost peaks rose into the air.

"Mother, what's making that noise?"

"The cranes. Look there, where mother is pointing."

"I see them. Why are they flying like a big spear?"

"They say it's easier for them to fly long distances that way."

"How far away do they come from?" he asked, staring upward.

"From the north. From countries like Sweden, Norway, Finland, and...and..."

"Why don't you say them all, mother? What others are there?"

"A big country that mother doesn't want to talk about."

Then his father and brother entered the yard. His father said:

"Come up into my lap, Josef. We'll watch the cranes fly."

The small boy skipped to his father, who lifted him up and sat him on his strong arm.

"It's fall now and the cranes are coming from the north," he said.

"Why do they come from there in the fall?" he asked.

"Because winter is cold there. The birds would freeze," said his father.

"Now they're gone behind the mountains," said the boy. "Is the north far away, father?"

Then Josef Leber awoke. His question was left unanswered. In the delirium that his dreams had become, this one dream from his childhood stood out clearly. His mother, father, and brother were in it, exactly as they had been at home in Bavaria. Cranes flew over the mountains there in the fall.

Stiffly, shivering, the man rose to all fours. His head ached, and the images that registered on his single eye were fuzzy. The food Maija Sammalsuo had prepared for him was all gone. The fever had not been present on the first days of the flight, but had developed later when the wound became infected. He did not feel hungry. Sometimes he would lie down on his side and eat cowberries. His wounded head, swollen into an abnormal shape, could not stand his bending over. He had left the map in one of the places where he had slept. It had not actually been of much help in cloudy weather. At first he had been able to determine where he was going, using lakes and rivers as points of reference and using the sun as a compass. Then the fever had muddled his thinking. The other evening, or was it longer ago than that, he had come to the edge of a big swamp, crawled under the branches of this hanging spruce, and fallen asleep there. He had awakened shivering with cold, scraped up moss in the darkness with his hands, and buried himself in it.

"I have to go now. I wonder if I'm on the Russian side yet."

His confused thoughts clarified. It was just that he felt very weak. He crawled out from under the branches. On his knees, holding on to a small spruce, he looked out toward the swamp. It was some distance across, but it ran left and right for many kilometers in either direction. Right in front of him were high hillocks, which opened up further ahead into brown expanses dappled with gray. Beyond the swamp there was level woodland, its leaves showing yellow and red in the sunlight. The shadows of the spruce trees under which Josef Leber was standing stretched far out over pools and hillocks.

"I have to cross that swamp. The sun is in the west."

The man drew a pole which he had used as a support for many days out from under the branches. He picked a few handfuls of ripe cowberries. Grunting, he rose to his feet. Pain hammered in his temples and he felt as if his head would split. Then he shuffled forward, sinking up to his ankles in the yielding ground. Every step was an effort.

There was absolute silence in the swamp. The boughs of the trees were completely motionless. Withering swamp vegetation stuck to the soles of his boots. The swampland was more heavily dotted with pools of water. Ridges of higher ground ran lengthwise along the swamp. Between them were bogs, with tufts of swamp hay growing on their jelly-like hummocks. Josef Leber began to follow one of the ridges, which seemed to wind toward the opposite side of the swamp. His feet kept sinking, making the going difficult. Gasping, looking in all directions, the escapee continued his journey. At times he was forced to stop and rest. A low spruce tree grew on one of the hummocks, and the man lay down beside it for awhile. Then he rose and staggered forward.

He had almost reached the middle of the swamp when the winding ridge line came to an end. He trembled and felt black despair as he looked around. There was only slough ahead of him. Here and there stood a gray dwarf pine. Not back, not back, his benumbed mind kept repeating. The slough, which ran at a slight angle, was only some ten meters across. Beyond it, his eye could make out a ridge that went on.

"I have to get across to that," said Josef Leber.

His boots were already full of water. What did more of it matter? There, some tufts of hay were growing there. He had to step onto them. He tensed his muscles and stretched out one foot toward a tuft of hay turned gray by autumn. Slowly he shifted his weight to the foot. It sank, but the tuft seemed to bear his weight. Josef Leber jerked his body forward. Then the patch of hay, no more than a span in diameter, gave way. His foot sank into the oozy mud. His leaning body continued its forward course, and although he turned the pole he was carrying crosswise, it could not support the weight bearing down on it. His hands and arms went under and his face sank into the muck and water. Paddling wildly, he tried a few times to get out. For a short time he managed to keep his head above the water. Making swimming motions and turning his head to one side, he could see the woods beyond the swamp from his one eye. The sun's rays flashed on the surface of the pools of water. The cry of cranes sounded in the air. He could not see them, but he had heard them calling now for three years from the swamps near Järvenkylä. They were coming from the north and going toward the south. In a few days they would probably be flying over the mountains of Bavaria.

Josef Leber's strength gave out. He could no longer thrash with his arms, and his head and shoulders sank into the muddy water. His body twitched for a short time, and then the water began to clear. After some time, only the bottom of one foot was visible. The sun, which had reached the rim of the trees, glittered on the hobnails in the sole of his boot. Slowly the bottomless pool dragged down its victim. Josef Leber's body sank to the same depth as dwarf pines and animals which had sunk there over the course of time. This man, whose life had begun at the foot of Bavarian mountains, disappeared into a grave where he would never be found.

CHAPTER XXI

1

"Listen, Kauko," said Jalo Kieppi, turning his head.

Kauko Sammalsuo was walking with his head down. The hair on his neck curled up over the collar of his sooty, wrinkled summer shirt. His face was bearded and his machine pistol was slung over his shoulder, barrel forward. Although he was squishing along in his soaking wet boots right beside Kieppi, his face did not change expression at the words.

"Are you asleep, or what the hell are you brooding on?"

"Why are you cawing with your mouth open like a baby crow?" growled Kauko, glaring at Kieppi.

"How long is it since we left Petsamo for Rovaniemi?"

"Try to figure it out."

"Isn't it almost exactly four years?"

"Why did you need me as a yes-man when you have such a sharp head for figures? You can count all the way to four, ha, ha."

"Stop needling me. It just struck me that we'll soon be there again."

"Well, yaah, if we keep tramping at this pace and the soles of our shoes don't wear out, the devil knows we might even make it to the Upper Monastery in time for the Christmas Service. Almighty damn, that boot is rubbing my heel."

"I had the same trouble at Atshinki," said Kieppi.

"How could a boot rub a bone? The only flesh you have is in your tongue, and that's as poisonous as a snake's."

"You're no muscleman yourself. Let's see which of us lasts the longest."

"You won't have to start carrying me," said Kauko.

"Are you buddy-buddies arguing again?"

Jalo Kieppi and Kauko looked aside. The soldier who had come up beside them had a forced grin on his face. Water dripped from the visor of his cap. Jalo Kieppi said:

"We haven't asked you to settle our quarrels yet, Sumala."

"And I haven't tried to butt in either, but it's fun to hear you jawing at each other all the time."

"Then you can pay admission to the show," said Kauko, looking glumly at Sumala.

"What'll I pay with? I don't even have a cigarette to smoke," Sumala complained.

"But I do. Walk behind me with Jalo and you can smell the smoke."

Kauko drew a pack of cigarettes from his pocket, stuck one of them into a holder, and began puffing out thick clouds of smoke. Sumala moved up close to him. He and Jalo eyed the pack as Kauko put it back in his pocket. Blowing smoke through his nostrils, Kauko said:

"That old catch phrase is right. I would never have believed it."

Kauko walked with his head exaggeratedly high. Although he was looking straight ahead, he could feel his companions' eyes on him. Finally Sumala said:

"What old phrase?"

"I'd rather skip a meal than a smoke."

"Stop the teasing, Kauko, and offer us a cigarette."

"Come on, give us one. Or sell it to us, if nothing else. How much do you want for a smoke?"

Sumala began to grope in his back pocket. Kauko said:

"What happened to your cigarettes? Did you lose them?"

"Cut out the crap. My mouth is watering so much I can't swallow it all. Toss me and Sumala a smoke."

"I got my ration at the same time as you did. Do you think I pluck these things out of thin air? Or have them delivered by angels?"

"You've got a nearly full pack," said Sumala.

"You smoke a few cigarettes just to spite us when we run out. And your mouth still looks like a pig's snout with a straw stuck in it," said Kieppi.

"You don't have to look at it. And Sumala, you're whining for cigarettes now, but remember how cocky you were in basic training?"

"Are you still harping on that? I thought it was settled a long time ago."

Sumala's voice was exasperated. Kauko's weariness was apparent in his own tone of voice.

"Do you remember stealing my socks then?"

"I was beginning to think you were a man, but this summer you've turned into some freaky kind of sour-ass. Jalo, don't you think our chief went to hell in that cannon shop?"

"He did, and sometimes he acts as if it was our fault."

"What cannon shop are you talking about?" growled Kauko, whose face had turned fiery red. He looked back. There was no one close behind them, and the men up ahead were trudging along a good distance away.

"You remember very well where you went when your gun got rusty on that leave. But we won't talk about that," said Sumala.

Kauko drew in his breath so sharply that he got a lungful of smoke. He was forced to stop and cough. Kieppi and Sumala stopped beside him. Kieppi began to pound Kauko on the back as he doubled over coughing.

"You help too, Sumala, or we'll lose our squad leader."

"Go to hell...goddamn you," Kauko gasped between spasms of coughing.

"He'll recover, all right," said Kieppi. "Then we'll get to show him how to smoke a cigarette."

When Kauko caught his breath again, he took out the pack of cigarettes and said:

"There you are, but if you start bumming another before the hour is up, I'll punch you in the mouth."

"You gave in because I started to beat you," said Kieppi. "But we have to thank you anyway."

"He's not as bad as he looks. Maybe he got a little scared when I started talking about the cannon shop," said Sumala with a laugh.

"How would you like it, Sumala, if I told them how fast a certain Finnish soldier took off from the Murmansk railway when the Russians spotted him there?" said Kauko.

"We'll both keep our mouths shut. You would have gotten us all killed if I hadn't taken off."

"The patrol got back safely and we cut the rail line," said Kauko.

"Look at that, boys. The Germans have no shortage of TNT," said Sumala, pointing to a highway crossing through a swamp.

"Walk in the center of the cleared area. Mines!" came a shout from ahead.

✧ ✧ ✧

A drizzling rain shrouded the woods on the fringes of Puolanka and Pudasjärvi parishes. The partially cleared mine fields and barriers of felled trees, even the the highway embankments, were still dangerous. The Germans had spared neither labor nor explosives in their retreat to the north. No one questioned their skill in this type of endeavor.

This company and other Finnish troops pursuing the retreating Germans resembled a herd of cattle on the move. No one cared about maintaining intervals or staying in a formation of any kind. One man walked alone, deep in thought. Others trudged along in small groups. Some sought out the company of their best friends. The picked men of the company, screened in the battles of Kiestinki, Uhtua, Siiranmäki, Tali, and Vuosalmi, were sustained by one thought in their benumbed state: I have to keep going since my buddies are still trudging along here. The clay and gravel mix underfoot clung to their boots and made them slip and slide. Many kept asking themselves if this could be real. A short time ago, they had been fighting with their *guarantors* against the Russians, and now they were allied with Stalin's gang to drive Aatu Hitler's soldiers toward the Arctic Ocean.

Evening was falling when one of the company dropped back beside Kauko and Kieppi and said:

"We'll have to pick 'em up and put 'em down many times before we get to the Norwegian border."

"Godalmighty, we're not going that far," hissed Kauko.

"If we pass by my home we'll warm up the sauna," said Kieppi.

"You don't think the Krauts will spare your sauna, do you?" said Kauko.

"Your home is over toward the northeast," said the man who had dropped back. "There was a lot of smoke in that direction yesterday."

"I saw it," said Kauko. "I wonder if the civilians got away."

"I think so. The Germans are only taking their own tarts with them. There'll soon be a lot of Finnish skirts in Aatu's Reich."

"Hitler won't have a Reich for very long," growled Kauko.

✧ ✧ ✧

The next day the sun was shining. A chill wind was blowing. Their clothing dried and even the marching seemed easier. Kauko said to Jalo Kieppi:

"We've been lucky for a long time."

"So we have. We've been through two wars, and both of us are mostly sound in body."

"But I'm all messed up inside. I mean, my mind..."

"Don't start running on about that. You'll make me cry."

"No, really...If I live through this, we'll get together after the war. You and the dead Jonas have been my best buddies."

"Jonas knew from the start that he wouldn't live."

"Now I'm beginning to believe that we won't make it through this in one piece. You really don't have any ill will toward me for any reason, do you?"

"Why are you talking like that? You look so down in the mouth. What do you see on the other side of that ditch?"

"Nothing. I just have to take a crap."

"I'll come and hold your hand."

"No, just go on ahead. I'll catch up with you."

"Watch out for mines."

"I'm going to lay a slippery one myself," Kauko cackled.

Kauko's laugh was completely mirthless. He leaped over the ditch and disappeared into a dense woods. Footsteps of the men marching up from behind crunched along the gravel road, followed by the clunking of wagon wheels.

This was the place. The Germans had picked just the right spot to pause in their march. They had opened ration cans here and built a campfire. Kauko had been able to tell from the road that they had camped here. His eyes were wide open and glittering. He dug a roll of trip wire from his pocket. Fasten one end to that spruce tree. It was German wire. They would not suspect. Kauko kept looking in every direction as he fastened the wire. He unrolled it past a pine stump and fastened the other end to a projecting root. So...six inches from the ground. That was how to set a mine in a war.

Kauko's hands were shaking as he took a hand grenade from his pocket. No one knows I have this, he thought. Not even Jalo. I found it at a Finnish campsite. Kauko's jaw tensed and his heart pounded. This is the end of my war. They won't suspect. They've always thought of me as a man who didn't dodge the tightest spots. I've always volunteered. There now. The fragments won't go through that stump. Then I'll crawl toward the road. Are the troops still coming?

Over the pounding of his heart and the throbbing of blood in his temples, he could make out the sounds of marching men. They were still coming. I won't have time to die from loss of blood. They'll come when they hear the explosion. I might even cry out for help. I'll have to open the buttons on my pants. I'll say my foot caught in the wire just as I squatted down. But what if I faint? Well, men who have stepped on mines have been found in many positions. I'll just lie down next the stump and curl my leg around it. That way the fragments won't tear up my knee, they'll just chop up the toes. Which foot is more useless? Probably the right. I can use a crutch on that side better if I get to walk again.

Thoughts flashed quickly through his mind. What if I don't do it, but just head for home through the woods? I saw by the platoon leader's map this morning that it's only about sixty kilometers, and thinly populated backwoods all the way. Today already I would make it to country I know. It's only twenty kilometers to a camp where I stayed when I was logging before the war. Near home there are haying saunas and hay barns in the swamp meadows. They're full of hay, and there are plenty of cowberries. There are reindeer in the woods and the sheep are still out to pasture. I won't die of hunger. Then when the war is over, I can show up among people again...and wind up in jail and be laughed at as a deserter. They'll say the Sammalsuo boy joined up as a volunteer but wound up going over the hill. I won't be able to stay at home. When the others come back, they'll haul me off to jail.

Sweat rolled down his forehead. No, I won't be able to stand the shame. Just do it...deliberately, cold-bloodedly. I'll be taken to a hospital. My foot will be ruined forever, but I'll be able to limp around on it somehow. Kauko sat down beside the stump and began to unpack the grenade. I'll stick it behind the stump, shove my foot up close to it, and lie down on my back. It'll hurt just once. Then I'll get to a hospital where it's warm and there's food enough to live on. I'll fix the pin now. In a few seconds it will go off, and the others will go on toward the north...

The others will go on...The thought hammered in his mind. The others will go on and on. I, like a wretch, will cripple myself, while my buddies have the strength to go on — Kieppi, Sumala, Sorola, Risuvaara...They're all physically weaker than I am, and I've barely made it up to now. But even if no one ever knows what I've done, it will always eat at my mind. If I'm delirious in the hospital, my conscience will shout it out for the world to hear. And even if that doesn't happen, it will still nag at me. Disabled! There goes a poor man who lost a foot. That's how it is in a war, the best men suffer, people would say. No by God! Going there for the clap was enough. I won't run out on my buddies. Let a German mine blow me up, if it has to be.

Kauko leaped up, and rubbed his eyes with his knuckles. He stuffed the grenade into his pocket, jerked the trip-wire free, bunched it up, and tossed it into the woods. Machine pistol over his shoulder, he loped back to the road. How far had his buddies gotten by now?

✧ ✧ ✧

The moon lighted up the woods. Kauko and Jalo sat on the bank of a river, along the shore of which a thin sheet of ice was forming. The calm surface of the water gleamed in the moonlight. Further up on the bank, smoke rose from tent stoves. On either side of the river were shattered earthen bridge approaches. Shapeless heaps rising from the water were all that remained of the bridge structure itself.

The friends looked at one another. From the tents came the sound of voices. Somewhere behind them, wagon wheels bumped along the road. The sound of an ax echoed in the air as a soldier chopped wood for a stove.

"The moon just keeps on shining," said Kauko. "The Russians can't do a thing to it, or the Germans either. It shone at the front too..."

"You're getting all mushy again."

Kauko looked at the river and said:

"I almost drowned in that river when I was a boy. The boat capsized during a log drive and I fell into the rapids. The man who was rowing drowned."

Kauko told about how the boat Nestor was steering had capsized and how close he had come to drowning. Running his fingertips across his temples, he said:

"These scars came from that ruckus. My forehead and whole body were banged on the bottom rocks. The scales of life don't always weigh the same. That spring, and many a one after it, we went hungry. We were always weeping for shame at our poverty. But we weren't the only ones who were poor. The whole area was living in need. Scarcity and poverty seemed the end of the world then. Now we've learned that there are other problems as well. A second war is destroying the backwoods. I'm fairly sure our house has been burned down. Many of my childhood friends are dead."

"No point in trying to sort out things in a situation like this. My face will look like a buzzard's rear end too when we get to my home grounds."

Kauko picked up a stick from the ground and began whittling it.

"You'd never guess the crazy thing I was thinking of doing."

"You weren't planning to go over the hill?"

Heavy strokes of the knife blade cut off wood shavings of differing thickness. The task seemed to demand Kauko's concentration. After some time, he abruptly hurled the stick away. It splashed into the water. He turned to Jalo and hissed:

"I thought of that too. When I went over the ditch today, I was going to set off a grenade under my foot. I didn't need to take a crap."

Jalo Kieppi gave a silent whistle. Then he said:

"Didn't you have the guts?"

"It wasn't only that. I thought of other things."

"Do you know when I thought of pulling the same kind of stunt?"

"You mean you were that far gone once?" Kauko said quickly.

"The time that winter when we were at that outpost where the Germans were freezing like cockroaches, I meant to take off one of my socks. I could have passed myself off among the other cases of frostbite like counterfeit money."

"I would never have guessed. What stopped you?"

Jalo Kieppi lashed at the frozen moss with a willow stick. After a pause, he said:

"It would have been a dirty trick to leave my buddies in a spot like that. I was ashamed to go, if the rest of you could take it. And then, when that major said he would stay even if he was alone...Do you remember?"

"I guess everyone remembers. That dead major was a man."

The stick Kauko had thrown into the water was approaching the wreckage of the bridge. From the same direction came a distant roar. Kauko said:

"I was just thinking that a man's life is like that stick. Now it's got smooth sailing down the stream. Then it hits the rapids. When it reaches calm water, it may float into a stagnant hole along the bank and rot there. Or the rapids may toss it ashore to be buried in the sand."

"Goddamn, don't start with the sermons. Let's go into the tent."

2

The Olkivaaras had been in the hay barn at Peräsuo for a week. Nestor spent the nights with the children, sleeping in the hay at night and leaving for Olkivaara at dawn. There he mostly lay in straw spread out above the rafters of the threshing barn. No one else came within the fences around Olkivaara, at least not by day.

Elma was cooking the morning porridge in front of the barn while Nestor warmed his hands at the fire. The other children were asleep. Elma looked at her father across the fire and said:

"Holy cow, what a mess you are!"

"I was thinking I must be some kind of a sight."

"You could wash your face and shave."

"No way, " snapped Nestor.

"At least take your coat off. With it inside out like that, you're uglier than a bear."

"Leave the bears out of it. How the devil else will I scare off others if they come to burn down the house?"

"Who's going to come any more? Aren't those...those others gone for good?" asked Elma.

"Who can be sure? I'll wear this uniform until I see Finns around here."

"Finns will shoot you on the spot if they see you in that get-up."

"They're not that damned stupid."

After they had eaten breakfast, Elma said:

"I'll take a skip to the highway to see if any one is there, or if it's completely empty."

"Right, go and take a look. We haven't heard the sound of a motor from it for many days. Maybe Teuvo can go with you. Sneak up all the way to the Naavala bridge."

✧ ✧ ✧

Elma walked along ahead of her younger brother. She kept wondering if it could be a bad dream. They did not dare go onto the highway, but stopped within sight of it, and Elma headed toward the Naavala bridge. They slogged along over the soggy ground out of sight of the highway but not far from it. There was no sound on the road. Everything seemed deserted.

"Are we the only people left?" said Teuvo.

"It sounds that way, but keep your voice down anyway."

"Will this place be left empty?"

"God only knows. Darn, how that brush scratches my legs."

Elma bent down and tossed aside a dried branch that had caught on her skirt. They were already near the Naavala bridge, with only a stretch of wet land and then a bit of dry heath to cross. Elma picked some cowberries and said:

"Now we have berries when there's no one to pick them."

Her brother stripped a few handfuls into his mouth and said:

"What will we do if we're left on the Russian side?"

"What business is that of ours? Don't step on twigs or you'll make noise. We'll soon be at the bridge."

"Look Elma. They burned Naavala too."

"Only the chimney and fireplace are still standing. They blew up the windmill too. This is the end of the world!"

Her mind numb, Elma drew near the bridge approach under cover of the woods. There was no longer a bridge. Water lapped against the mounds of earth that were left of the approach. Low clouds passed by overhead. The roar of the rapids could be heard at times when it was not drowned out by gusts of wind. Is this what her dead mother had spoken of, Elma wondered. She had said it was written in the Bible that before the end of the world, people would vanish from the earth. So few would remain that they would kiss the footprints of others in the sand. Had that time come?

She and Teuvo crept down to the rocky shore. The boy stopped and pointed across the river.

"Elma, there's a tent past the willow grove at Naavala."

"There's smoke rising from it too. Who can it be?" said Elma.

"There's a Finnish soldier coming out of it," said Teuvo excitedly. "What is he shouting? Let's go closer."

✧ ✧ ✧

The soldier coming out of the tent with a mess kit in his hand was from southern Finland. The field kitchen was in back of the ruins of Naavala. He stood looking at the raging black river. Everything here seemed so forlorn. Would people ever come back here to live? He turned to look at the wreckage of the bridge and gave a start, but the instincts of a man who had been at war for years responded quickly, and he shouted:

"Hey, stay away from that bank!"

But the woman and the boy standing at the edge of the woods started walking toward him. They were already close to the water. A sergeant peered out from the tent and said:

"What's all the yelling about, Honkanen?"

"Don't move! There are mines!"

The man's shout was cut off. There was a flash of light across the river. It took a full second for the sound of the explosion to reach his ear drums. For a moment the soldiers were stunned, but soon they came pouring out of the tents. A ring of them gathered around the soldier who had shouted the warning. They all stared across the river, where a column of smoke began to slant in the direction the wind was blowing.

"Who ran into a mine?" someone asked.

"Two people were coming down the bank, a boy and a woman. I yelled, but they kept coming."

"They're laid out on the ground there now. The woman was blown into the water."

"Go and help," said a lieutenant who had come out of one of the tents. "Take your first-aid supplies along."

"It's the goddamndest thing. Killing innocent women and children," panted one of the men running toward the bank of the river.

3

The moon was shining as Ahma-Juuso stepped lightly along the forest path leading to the church village. He arrived at his destination some time after midnight. From the shelter of a pine grove, he peered out toward it. At least the church was still standing, but many of the other buildings had gone up in smoke. He could see their blackened chimneys jutting into the air. The village looked completely uninhabited, but he could hear the sound of human voices, and vehicles were moving about. Was it Finnish they were speaking? Or German? Or might it even be Russian, he wondered, as he peered out from behind the pine trees. For a long time the small, black-bearded man stood gazing at the church village and then he muttered:

"It's best to stick close to home now."

Ahma-Juuso set out on the return trip. The sun was dragging itself up out of the autumn woods when he neared his cottage. He could hear the furious barking of his dog. Frowning, he said:

"Why the devil did that woman let the dog out? He might lead anyone here."

The dog's barking grew louder. Juuso cursed inwardly. Occasionally the words came through aloud. His short legs tripped along quickly now.

"Damn it Jupe, stop — God help me!"

A bearded man had leaped out from behind a tree and was thrusting a rifle barrel into his chest. His eyes glared wildly, his gums were bared, and his teeth clenched like a dog guarding a bone. Juuso's cry was wrung from him before he had time to think. He tried to shove the sling of the hunting rifle that hung from his shoulders over his head, but the man said:

"Leave the rifle where it is or you get a hole in your chest."

"Simo, what the devil are you doing wh...wh...when..."

"What are you shaking about? Is there any booze in your pack?"

"Not a drop. What are you doing here, scaring people like that?"

"I came to stay with you."

Having recognized Simo Mutka, Ahma-Juuso calmed down, but the man's wild appearance and behavior made him wary. Did it mean he was crazy when his eyes glittered like that, he wondered.

"What do you mean, stay with me?" he asked.

"I'm going to stay in your loft. You have to bring me food and tobacco. And you won't say a word about me to anyone."

"G-go...at least point that gun barrel somewhere else. What have you done? They took you into the army last spring. You've even got a uniform on now."

"I took off when they started loading us on ships at Oulu. The others went north, and I came east."

"You came all the way on foot?"

"I didn't come by plane. I had to slog through the woods because I couldn't use the roads. Didn't they evacuate you?"

"They sent word, but I didn't go. The Germans didn't come out here."

"That's enough talking. Tonight I'll climb up into your loft and stay there."

"Do I have to...do you think I'm going to hide a deserter?"

"It won't hurt your reputation as a moonshiner."

"That's not a crime now. Go somewhere else. You can keep warm in the woods for a long time yet. There are haying saunas and..."

Simo Mutka's eyes blazed. The rifle barrel, which had been pointing at the ground, now rose to zero in on Juuso's chest. Mutka bared his teeth.

"Will you take in a boarder, or do I kill you and screw your wife? I'll burn down your shack..."

"You can come, you can come! Are your nerves shot wh-when you..."

"Try to guess," said Simo Mutka with a wild, hoarse laugh.

"I'll end up in the hands of the police over this."

4

"Brrr! This room is cold," said Heidi Pulkkila, who had stepped into the sheriff's office. "Those walls have to be chinked."

"We'll manage to keep warm in here somehow," said Sheriff Pulkkila.

"You're getting on in years and your health isn't any too good either," said his wife.

Ilmari Pulkkila blew on his hands to warm them and looked out through the window. He could see chimneys standing amid the storm. Further off were a number of houses that had survived the war. Even the church on the hill was still standing. His thoughts went back over the past years. The Winter War, the Continuation War, and then the Germans making a chaos of everything. The bitterly cold and stormy weather deepened his melancholy.

"We have to get a builder in here. At least those walls that have been riddled by bomb fragments have to be chinked," said his wife.

"We can manage well enough, but it's another story for the evacuees coming back. Their houses are ashes and they have no food or water."

"It won't make things better for the parish if you purposely freeze yourself and make yourself ill. You can be of more help as a well man."

"Yes, yes, Heidi. Go back into the kitchen."

"Are you driving me away? Did I say something wrong?"

Heidi Pulkkila 's eyes fell. The sheriff hemmed and closed the top button of his uniform.

"It was good of you to pop in. Some soldier is coming in on business."

Mrs. Pulkkila left the room. Footsteps sounded in the entry, and there was a knock at the door. A large army boot stepped over the threshold, and a hand rose in a salute.

"Good day, good day," said Sheriff Pulkkila. "I see the men are coming back."

"That journey finally ended."

The newcomer held his cap under one arm while he dug into his breast pocket and then walked to the desk.

"I guess you have to stamp this army pass."

"That's the way it's been done."

The sheriff signed his name, then blew on the seal and stamped the pass. As he did so he said:

"That takes care of this pass for my part. How far did you have to chase after the Germans, Sammalsuo?"

"They sent me back from Kittilä parish."

"That was a long walk."

"I had my fill of it," said Kauko.

"You were in for a long time. I remember you volunteered during the Winter War."

"Something like that."

Kauko Sammalsuo put the pass into his pocket. Out of habit, he buttoned down its flap. Turning up his coat collar, he said:

"I was in for just a month short of five years."

"Without a break?"

"Except for leaves to go home," said Kauko, putting on his hat. The snow on its ear flaps was beginning to melt.

Sheriff Pulkkila looked out. The storm was intensifying. He could feel a strong draft in the room. His fingers drummed on the desk top. Then he turned toward the sergeant who was walking toward the door and said:

"Welcome home, Sergeant Sammalsuo. Things are bad at Järvenkylä. I don't know..."

The sheriff swallowed hard and stood up. He walked to the window that looked out over the village. He had gazed through it a thousand times, but seldom with such disconsolate thoughts in his mind. Kauko waited for the sheriff to continue his interrupted statement, but when he heard nothing further, he said:

"Thanks. It's even worse in northern Finland."

"So they say. The young will always pull through, but we old folks...My steps are getting short...my steps are getting short..."

"We have a lot to do. I'll see you, sheriff."

Sheriff Pulkkila watched as the young man strode toward the center of the village. The wind whipped his coattails to one side, but his head was erect, his stride long and driving. The sheriff's drooping spirits revived. There walked one of the men who would begin the job of rebuilding. When a man strides along like that, his life is still ahead of him. My step is short now, my walk a mere shuffle.

Ilmari Pulkkila's eyes roved over the partially burned village. Beyond it was the pine-covered hill, obscured now and then by the drifting snow. The sand was soft under the pine trees. It would be good to sleep there, when his step had shrunk to nothing. This parish needed a young and energetic man to succeed him. He was tired and ill. The moral struggle with the Germans had worn him out. It had left him with shocking images that would not fade from his memory. But at least his orders had ended the torture and execution of prisoners in the church village. Perhaps those unburned buildings will remind people of me when I am gone, he thought. His contacts with high German officers during the worst period of destruction had had results. Out there lay his life's work. Twenty years ago he had looked out of the same window, a younger man then, longing to go to a bigger place. Heidi had been especially lonely. The church village had been smaller then. It had grown in the years following the depression. Now many of the houses were in ruins. His life's work...? There it lay before him. He had not been able to erect many visible monuments, but people had always been dear to him. And they were even dearer now. Look, now the pine grove in the cemetery was clearly visible. Heidi was no longer yearning to leave here. In the summer, the pine trees in the cemetery smelled strongly of pitch.

Ilmari Pulkkila locked the door and went into the kitchen.

"I don't feel quite right. I locked the door. I'm going to lie down for awhile."

"You don't look well," said his wife, a question in her eyes.

"I'm a little tired. I'm an old man and my boots are slippery," he chuckled.

There was no joy in his laugh. His hands were clumsy as his wife, looking worried, helped him off with his jacket. Then the old man opened the bedroom door and said:

"Don't mind if I lie down on the bedspread with my boots on."

5

Before the war, the well-sweep at Sääskilampi had been visible from as far off as the highway. Now, on a day near the end of November in 1944, it lay toppled in the snow of the yard. An explosive charge placed at its base pole by the Germans had cut it down. The ruins of the cattle barn were covered by snow in which could be seen the tracks of mice and of the weasels that stalked them. The sauna on the shore had been burned down, along with a number of hay barns, but the two-story residence was still intact, to the wonder of all the residents of Vaarakylä who had returned from evacuation. Not a single other dwelling was standing on the shore of Vaara Lake. Only chimneys rose amid the snowdrifts.

The house had not been ignored by the retreating Germans.

Flames had scorched the fireplace wall of the main room and burned large holes burnt in its floor, but there the fire had died out. The believers called it a miracle; Kosti Mäkinen and a few of the younger folk talked about a lack of oxygen.

The main room at Sääskilampi and the attic bedrooms were crammed with returned evacuees. There were as many people present in the house now as there had been at revival meetings there before the war. The village householders drove logs to the ruins of their homes during the day and otherwise got ready to put up temporary shelters, while their wives and children bustled about at Sääskilampi. At night the men returned to find a place to lie down for the night. There was no talk in the village about the spirit of brothers-in-arms. They merely said gratefully that it was lucky for them that one house had been spared.

Cattle were kept in hay barns. Bert began herding the reindeer as soon as he returned from the war. That provided them all with meat. There was no point in grieving if one of the slaughtered animals happened to be a cow or a heifer. The Germans had already done their part in decimating the herds of the Järvenkylä feeding grounds. Bert Sääskilampi had been chosen as the chief herdsman during the interim of peace, to replace Janne Latvasuo, who had fallen in the Winter War.

✧ ✧ ✧

"Kosti dear, I'm ashamed to go to the city with you."

It was getting on toward evening in the bedroom at Sääskilampi as Irja paused in her packing and spoke these words to her husband. Kosti had just finished shaving and was drying his implements preparatory to stowing them in an ammunition box where he had kept them during the war.

"Is it me you're ashamed of?" he asked.

The boys were pawing their Sunday clothing which Irja had just been folding onto a chair. She pushed them away and looked at her husband.

"No, but there are your sisters...and it's such a big city. Boys, keep away from those clothes."

"Who's going to hurt you if I'm there?"

"But you might be ashamed of a farm girl like me..."

"Well shame on you...I wonder if I should run that razor over my face again."

"What did you say?"

"I said shame on you, which means that you should stop talking nonsense, I mean."

"Are you angry with me?"

"Almost. Were you ashamed years ago when you put out food in the kitchen for a hungry wanderer?"

"No. And I didn't know then what a handsome husband I would catch."

"I think it's high time I showed my sisters in Tampere what the mother of my children looks like."

"I feel so shy. We could go in the summer."

Kosti turned to the boys and said:

"Go into the main room, boys. There are plenty of friends for you to play with there."

"They don't play; they just fool around," said Ilmari.

"Well, go and fool around then, but clear out for awhile."

"You won't leave us behind?" said Pentti.

"We're not leaving until morning," said his father.

When the boys were gone, Kosti Mäkinen sat down on the side of the bed. He put his hands on his wife's shoulders and drew her down beside him. For awhile he tapped his foot on the floor in silence and then he said:

"I've told you about the dead engineer Backman, the one who was killed at Kuhmo during the final minutes of the Winter War. He was my superior on the job that fall when the bridge under construction collapsed."

"Wasn't he killed when he was bringing word of the peace to you? Bert was wounded by the same bomb, or whatever they call it, wasn't he?"

"He was. What happened then won't give me any peace. I haven't told even you that I ran him around the trenches during a heavy barrage out of sheer spite. I felt as if I was possessed by the devil. I wanted so badly to see him afraid."

Kosti told his wife the whole story. She watched as he spoke with head bowed. When he had finished, she said:

"Did he have a wife and children too?"

"He did. The thing troubled me during the peace. But this fall when we landed at Tornio..."

Irja did not press her husband. She saw him put a hand to his forehead and wipe away the sweat. He sighed heavily before he went on:

"I was never so afraid in either war as I was then. The German bombing and the other fire was awful. The whole business seemed unnatural, you see, since we had been fighting on the same side against the Russians till autumn. I was afraid for myself, but even more afraid for you. I was sure that you and the children would be left alone just when the war was ending. I knew that it couldn't go on much longer. I prayed and I promised that if I came through it alive, I would seek out Backman's wife and children. Now I have to keep that promise. I won't be at peace unless I do."

"I mean...I'll be glad to go with you," said Irja.

Kosti turned to look at his wife. His eyes were moist when he spoke.

"Maybe life has been too good to us."

The door of the bedroom opened and the boys entered, followed by their grandmother leading little Tuulikki.

"I came to tell you that Irja has to take a lot of reindeer meat along. Kosti's sister in Tampere may be short of food. People in the cities don't have much to eat nowadays."

"We don't dare take too much. The trains are carefully patrolled," said Kosti. "Sit down, Grandma."

Tuulikki ran to her father's arms. Both girls had been shy with him when he had returned to civilian life less than two weeks ago, but now Tuulikki in particular would always run to him with her arms outstretched.

"How long will you stay?" asked Petti Sääskilampi.

"A full week, I think. I wonder how Irja and the boys will spend their time."

"Let's stay a long time," shrilled Pentti. "Is there a train there?"

"Are there lots of brick buildings?" said Ilmari, raising his voice too.

"Your father doesn't have a chance to answer when you're both yelling at the same time," said their grandmother with a smile.

"It seems I'll have to start rebuilding the Naavala bridge since the engineer asked me to," said Kosti. "That's another reason we can't stay in my home city for long. Damn those Germans, blowing up a good bridge."

Irja stood up and said:

"It's getting dark. We have to light the lamp."

As the wall lamp, which gave off kerosene fumes, lighted up the room, Irja walked over to the window and gazed out into the darkness. Drawing the half-curtains, she said:

"Won't Bert and his bride be driving up soon?"

"My goodness, yes. I'm sitting here, and there's so much to do."

Petti Sääskilampi rose and left the room. Irja smiled at Kosti and said:

"This daughter-in-law seems more welcome at Sääskilampi than a certain younger daughter's husband once was."

"There's nothing to find fault with in Bert's bride," said Kosti.

"And mother never said a bad word about you...It seems odd not to need blackout curtains," said Irja, looking at the darkening window panes.

"The war is over. Come on, boys, see if you can get your father's fist open," laughed Kosti.

The boys rushed to their father's knees and wrestled with the large fist, gritting their teeth with effort. From the main room and the attic came the hubbub of the homeless children. Irja watched the boys tussling and said:

"It was a gift from God that this one house was spared. The whole village can get through the winter this way."

"You'll see a huge number of new shanties in this village by next fall. Uh, darn you boys, you're so strong. You got your father's fist open."

The door opened again. One of the men from the village came drifting in. He sat down, fur cap solidly planted on his head, and said:

"I have to ask how many trees I have to cut down for that new place of mine."

"I can't say offhand. I have to figure it out," said Kosti.

"So maybe you'll figure it out then, since that's the kind of work you do."

When Kosti had figured out the man's quota of logs, another of the villagers entered the room. He too got straight down to business.

"You can start drawing up plans for my house too. Though I hear you can't get nails or money to put up a house."

"I won't have time till Christmas at least, but maybe I can do it by the end of the year."

"I guess you won't be short of paperwork now, but if you can get around to it then..." said the man.

When the Mäkinen family had gone to bed close to midnight, Irja said:

"Do you remember when we were living in the Kuikkala bedroom during the Winter War?"

"How could I ever forget it?" said Kosti.

"Do you forgive me for being angry at those people who kept the radio on every single night?"

"Didn't we decide that then?" laughed Kosti. "But if you want further absolution, I'll give it to you."

"How can a person be as selfish as I was?" said Irja. "All they were doing was sitting and listening to the radio, and even that annoyed me. Now we have more people buzzing around here at all hours than there used to be at the revival meetings."

"And with no major squabbles either," said Kosti.

The room was dark. The children were asleep and their things were packed for the trip. Tomorrow the whole family would go by sleigh to the church village, thought Irja. She turned onto her side. Kosti's breathing caused her hair to tickle her forehead. His large and heavy hand settled on her shoulder. On the other side of the wall, she heard Bert's laugh, and then the clear voice of a woman that barely carried to her ears. It would be good for Bert to settle down at last. His wife would see to that. After awhile, she heard Kosti say:

"Up to now, my only tie to these backwoods has been you and the children. Now I'm beginning to feel as if I'm needed here."

6

Soon after stopping at the sheriff's office, Kauko caught a ride to Järvenkylä on the back of a truck. He pressed his back against the charcoal burner as the storm swirled around him. The truck stopped in the Naavala yard. Kauko stepped down, his legs stiff with cold. He slung his almost empty pack over his shoulders, and then stood petrified. From this same yard he had set out for the army five years ago. Then red-painted buildings had stood in all parts of the yard. Now the storm blew over their ruins. Near a cluster of pine trees, a tumble-down barracks had been set up. Gusts of snow blown by the northeast wind swept away the smoke that poured from its stovepipe. Should he go and see how things were with Hilja? Surely she was home by now. No, he would start wading toward Sammalsuo now.

He set off along the shore, and near the remnants of the bridge, he began wading through the snow on the lake. At one time, the construction site for the bridge had been a big thing. So had the bridge itself. And what was left of it now? Piers that had been shattered by explosives lay almost buried in the snow. One center pier had disappeared completely. Another was a mound in the snow. The deck was completely gone.

Was this what it was like to return to civilian life? They had repeated the words for years, relished the thought in tent, dugout, foxhole, trench, and on patrol. Now this was it! Crawling through a storm with only the ruins of his home village to bid him welcome.

Kauko walked almost straight across the lake, and then followed the shoreline closely. It was a way of getting very near home without seeing the whole of it until he was there. Although he knew what had happened, it was some consolation to postpone seeing it with his own eyes.

The slope of Lapinvaara was visible through the storm. How long ago was it, Kauko wondered, since he had skied down it? He must have been a schoolboy then. That was twenty years ago. At its base was Lappi Pool, where he had romped in the water as a child. The sand had burned the bottoms of his feet, and the air had been fragrant with heather, juniper, and meadowsweet. You could see its gently-sloping bottom of light brown sand from a hundred meters away. How long was it since he and Elma had returned together from a bridge dance at Naavala? Kauko swallowed hard. It had been nine years in August.

"Why the devil keep mulling over what happened in the past? It does no good. What's over is over and that's that."

A gust of wind swallowed up his words. Kauko kept on going. He reached the willow grove near his deserted home. Now! It would only hurt once. He turned his face toward the land. Wind-driven gusts of snow played hide and seek with the chimney of the house. The chimney of the cow barn had collapsed. Where the sauna and storehouse had been, pointed ends of charred timber protruded from the snow. As he mounted the shore, he saw that the hay barn at the edge of the woods had been left unburned.

"Why the devil did the Krauts leave that? They should have burned everything. Maybe they ran out of oil."

Kauko stood beside the stone foundation of the house. The storm swept over the charred ends of the logs. Snow swirled around the fireplace and the chimney. Mother had had her bed in this corner. I slept near the fireplace with Väinö and the deceased Auku those last days. The separator was along the wall by the door and one end of the bread pole was on top of the stone oven. With tears in our eyes we would count how many loaves were left of the bread baked from the community's flour.

Kauko started when an animal leaped up out of the black maw of the fireplace. It ran to a cornerstone that stuck out from under the snow and sat there twitching its tail.

"Oskar Portimo!" said Kauko, and tenderness replaced the bitterness he was feeling. "So you didn't leave home. Here, kitty, kitty, kitty."

The old animal did not move, but merely wet a paw with its tongue and began washing its face.

"Your face does need a washing. Poor Oskar, you're all covered with soot. Come here and I'll pet you. It's been a long time."

When Kauko started toward the cat, it leaped from the stone, and looking back over its shoulder, ran toward the cow barn and disappeared into a crevice in the fallen chimney. Kauko stood for a short time looking toward the place where he and Auku had cleared land for a rye field. The line of woods had been moved back, but there was no new crop wintering under the snow. Where would they get new seed when they needed it? Kauko started toward the shore again. The snow had nearly filled in the tracks he had made in coming.

"Some reward for spending the five best years of one's life in that struggle," he muttered.

"...we got back from evacuation yesterday," Aili had written. *"We get to live at Olkivaara, since the Germans didn't burn it down."* The letter had reached Kauko at Kittilä two weeks ago.

Head down, chin buried in his coat collar, Kauko waded on.

◇ ◇ ◇

Before the porch at Olkivaara, Kauko took off his pack and wiped his feet an unnecessarily long time on the fir boughs that lay there. Then with his lips compressed into a thin line, he walked through the entry, opened the door, and stopped inside the threshold. His mother was sitting on the rear bench, knitting. She raised her glasses to her forehead and stared at her son.

"That journey is over now. Greetings from Kittilä."

Maija dropped her knitting into her lap. Her mouth worked, but she could not say a word. Her eyelids reddened, but no tears came. Nestor, who was mending a harness near the fireplace, took a knife from between his teeth and said:

"Thanks...So you came through it alive."

"They didn't kill me," said Kauko, looking around the room.

"Take off that sloppy coat before the snow melts on it," said Aili, who had come in from the kitchen.

"Yaah, take off your things and make yourself at home," said Nestor, dropping the harness to the floor. It took him many tries before he managed to get the knife into the sheath on his hip. Then with angry movements, he brushed strips of leather from his knees. Taimi came in from the kitchen and Nestor said:

"Go and boil up some rye water in one helluva hurry, Taimi, and maybe you can scrape up some of that bread cheese too."

"We have some grain too. Go and make some coffee substitute for the homecoming, Aili," said Maija.

"I know you do, but this is such a special guest that we'll put the house's pot on the fire."

Kauko sat down. He saw Nestor's hands patting his pockets, a gesture familiar to him since childhood. He took out a pack of cigarettes and walked over to Nestor with it.

"Have a ready-made one," he said.

"Spoken like a man. Here in civilian life, cigarettes are hard to come by, and other things too. Don't you smoke?"

Kauko looked at his mother and said:

"I don't dare to, with mother watching."

"Well, hell..." Nestor laughed. "At least your sense of humor didn't dry up on that trip."

Kauko tossed another package into his mother's lap and said:

"Stuff that into your pipe. But where are Väinö and Liisu? I don't see them."

"They went with the other kids to take the mail to Jussi Ylikylä. Did you stop at home on your way?"

Before Kauko could answer, Maija rose and looked out of the window. Then she bowed her head.

"I did. It was quiet there. Only Oskar Portimo came out of the fireplace to take a look at me."

"He won't stay away from there," said Aili. "We've brought him back here many times, but he always escapes."

Nestor sat leaning on his elbows exhaling smoke and staring at the breeching that had fallen to the floor. Finally Maija turned to Kauko and said:

"Aren't you going to say hello to Elma?"

A hot flush swept over Kauko's face and he felt as if an accordionist's cold fingers were running up and down his spine.

"Is Elma here?" he said.

"In the bedroom," said Aili.

Kauko stood up and ran his fingers through his hair. Crossing the kitchen, he opened the bedroom door, walked in, and stopped in the middle of the room. Elma was almost sitting up in the bed, with several pillows stacked under her back. Her face was turned toward the door. One eye and cheek were covered by a bandage that slanted across them. Crutches leaned against the foot end of the bed. Kauko's knees trembled and he could not get a word from his mouth.

"Say hello now, Kauko."

Elma's lips were smiling, but her voice trembled. Kauko's eyes fell.

"Well greetings. It's been a long journey. I-I didn't know you were home."

"I've been here for almost a week. Father came to get me from the hospital. Aili and Taimi told me you were here."

Kauko looked at Elma, who kept fingering the edge of the covers. From time to time he wet his lips.

"Don't stand when you can sit down," Elma said finally.

"May I sit on the side of the bed?"

"Of course you can."

Kauko sat on the side of the wooden bed. He looked at the window. Fans of ice were visible on the panes. The wind howled in the chimney. Turning to Elma, he said:

"Aren't you cold? I can feel a real draft in here."

"Not really."

"Does it still hurt a lot?"

"It throbs around my eye. My leg really has no feeling."

"Is Teuvo still in the hospital?"

"He's all the way in Oulu. He lost a leg as far as the knee. He stepped on the mine that tore me up."

The talk ceased. Kauko sat on the side of the bed, thinking. Elma could not get a word out. Finally Kauko forced himself to say:

"Will you smoke if I go and get cigarettes?"

"My smoking days are over."

Suddenly Kauko straightened up and turned toward Elma. Resting a hand against the head of the bed, he looked into her eyes. Then he caught sight of a of thin silver chain running down under her collar. He took one strand of it between his fingers and tried to draw it up, but it would not come. Kauko thrust his fingers under the collar and touched firm breasts and skin that felt hot and smooth. His fingers found what they were seeking, and brought a small silver cross into view. He laid it on his palm, as his thoughts went leaping back into the past, to the Upper Monastery at Petsamo, to his leave, to his giving the cross to Elma, to the Germans.

"You've still kept this?" Kauko said.

"I have...Do you want it back?"

"I gave it to you...once. I found it on a plain near the Upper Monastery. My first thought was to give it to you."

Kauko looked at the cross for a long time. His mouth was dry. Finally he pulled Elma's collar out and slid the cross back.

"That's where it was meant to be," he said.

Elma covered her eyes with her hands. Her breast rose and fell rapidly.

"And after that I was a German's baggage and an officer's mattress pad. That's what people call my kind, and I don't deny it. It's the truth."

Kauko sat staring unblinkingly at his hands. Then he reached into his pocket. A jackknife came out in one hand, and he began to clean his nails with it. Suddenly he turned to Elma and said:

"I can't exactly brag about myself either. I even got a dose of the clap when I was on leave in the spring. Goddamnit!"

Elma looked at him. Her eyes misted over.

"You're a young, strong man. You'll get on with your life."

"You're going to get better too," said Kauko, closing the knife.

"I won't die, but I don't know what I'll look like. There's a big piece of one brow missing and there will be a big scar across one cheek. Who knows if my leg will ever be the same."

Neither said a thing, until Elma sighed at last:

"But on the other hand, I deserved it."

Kauko was forced to turn away. No matter how tightly he shut his eyes, the tears squeezed through. Then he said:

"Everything is ashes and cinders. We must try to do something if we're not all going to sit down and pray to die."

There was a knock at the door and Aili peered in.

"What kind of trick is that?" said Kauko.

"What do you mean, *trick*?" said Aili.

"Since when did people start knocking on doors in Järvenkylä?"

"Well, I didn't want to surprise you," Aili giggled. "Come and have the coffee substitute. Shall I bring it in to you, Elma, or will you come into the kitchen?"

"I'll come in. Hand me the crutches, Kauko."

When Nestor came back in, he brushed the snow from his clothing, limped to the table where they were all sitting, and said:

"This is one helluva storm. If it keeps snowing like this all night, we'll have all we need by morning."

Liisu, Väinö, and the Olkivaara children were still away delivering the mail. Little was said as they drank the rye water. Kauko and Elma sat on the same short bench. Aili and Taimi kept exchanging glances. Finally Aili said:

"Bert Sääskilampi and Hilja Naavala are engaged."

Kauko felt a slight twinge at the news, but it passed quickly and was followed by a sense of relief. Bert would make Hilja a good husband. He said aloud:

"When did they have a chance to arrange that?"

"You've turned all red in the face, Kauko," said Aili.

"Good thing I didn't turn blue," said Kauko.

"Hilja was in the Women's Auxiliary on the Isthmus. They

must have started seeing each other there," Taimi put in.

Again there was silence. Kauko looked at Elma and then at his mother, who now seemed content. He cleared his throat and said:

"How about it, Nestor? Will you have us as boarders until we get a roof over our heads on Sammalsuo land?"

"No question about that. You can be right at home here. Maija and I have already talked about it."

Kauko tried to look at Elma, but could see only the bandage that covered her face. She seemed to be looking toward the door that led to the kitchen. Nestor sipped the rye water. When his saucer was empty, he said:

"Mari should have been at this table."

✧ ✧ ✧

The storm continued into the evening, but the pine logs burned steadily in the fire. Elma sat by the hearth and began knitting a woolen stocking. Her crutches were leaning against the stone oven. From time to time, she stoked up the roaring fire.

Kauko and Nestor sat side by side on the rear bench. Nestor was smoking a cigarette. Liisu stuck close to Kauko asking him a world of questions. Väinö was making kindling by the hearth, his shadow moving huge and shapeless on the log walls. Kauko could tell by the movements of Elma's lips that she was counting stitches. Whenever he looked at the crutches, he felt a constriction in his chest. Then he looked at Elma's face. The side toward the fire had a ruddy glow, while the bandaged side was in the shadows. A homey, but at the same time sad, feeling possessed him. The wind howled at the corners of the house and the sleet beat against the window panes. Taimi and Aili left in the twilight to pay a visit to Naavala. Maija came in from the kitchen and watched the movements of Elma's needles.

"Do you always carry twenty stitches on a needle?"

Elma turned with a start and said:

"Isn't that a good number for the leg of a man's sock?"

"That's what I always use for Kauko's."

Elma bent down, picked up a couple of pine blocks from the floor, and shoved them into the flames one by one. Kauko and his mother looked at each other.

"Did that other good friend of yours get back alive?"

"You mean Jalo Kieppi?"

"Yes, that boy from the north you were always talking about."

"He did. Without a scratch. But his home was burned."

Nestor sat up and said:

"You can haul logs for a new house with that nag of mine. I can't handle the reins any more. They're keeping Vante in the army, and he won't be here to help me until next fall."

"I guess the only thing to do is to start learning how to work," said Kauko.

"Well, hell yes. Who's going to build homes in these woods if you young people don't do it? About all I'm good for is filling a grave in a hurry. When that damned leg of mine went..."

"Shouldn't we hope, Nestor, that God will again turn His face toward these woods?" said Maija.

"Well, maybe He's good for something, but I don't think He'll notch many logs. Let believers trust in him, if they want to. Hitch up the horse tomorrow, Kauko. Maybe you can drive some hay to begin with."

"I can only try," said Kauko. "If this storm lets up during the night..."